THE CELLULOID CLOSET SERIES:

BROADCAST

Brennen Tammons

This story is a work of fiction. Any correlation between people, names, places, events,
or politics, are simply coincidental. Although, in this and in practically every other
story, there are elements of inspiration based on actual events. However, any exact
correlations are simply coincidental.

This story is graphic. There is strong vulgar language, criminal activity, drug use, and
strong violent content. Due to the extreme subject matter, reader should be advised.

The opinions expressed by characters in this story, may reflect the opinions of the
author, or may not. The author wishes to have a neutral stance.

CHAPTERS

To my twin brother, Berton.
To my mother, Brenda.
To my grandmother, Sharon.

To everyone else close to me, I appreciate you as well.

To God Be The Glory

CHAPTER 1:

THE DJ

In the world of entertainment, many have aspirations to succeed. But only few will actually make their dreams come true. This is a world, to where people must have ambition in order to advance. The radio world, usually and typically pertains to music, but not always. Talk radio, and podcasting is also very big in the realm of radio. One podcast which has gained much controversy and popularity is, The "DJ S. and K. Show". This show premieres on "WBCT, Broadcast Radio", in Downtown Los Angeles. It is a radio station, that plays music from the 70s, 80s, and 90s, with occasionally playing current pop music hits. The station is only transmitted through the Los Angeles area. The radio station also has talk radio shows in the morning, and at night. Many which range from politics, news, romance, and comedy podcasts. However, the "DJ S. and K. Show", is one that many tune in to listen. It is the main talk show that is the most entertaining, as opposed to the others.

The podcast is mostly a political, and conspiracy theory related talk show. It is named after the main hosts, "DJ S.", and "DJ K.". The show airs every night at Seven o'clock. It is a show that is aired on the night shift. So, the main listeners are people that work during the night, or those who stay up late at night, willing to listen to a radio show. The show airs until 11 PM. So, it is a four hour show in total. With reruns available to listen to, on streaming, through the internet. The show allows listeners to call in, and offer their input to the current topic of the night. Many listeners call into the show, wanting their opinion to be heard over the air. The show is not politically correct at all. The on-air hosts do not make it a habit to censor themselves, and they occasionally use foul language during the show. This is why the show is so controversial, due to the fact there are no holds barred. The radio station is owned by a private company, so they do not have to follow any FCC codes. The uncensored content and theme of the show, adds to the popularity. The listeners of the show, enjoy the fact the show is not filtered, and it allows more free-spirited energy. The show is neither liberal or conservative. It is a centrist show, and the hosts seem to follow suit along with this.

"DJ S", and "DJ K", are the hosts of the program. They are really close friends, and have been hosting the show for now over five years. Both of them have gone through different ventures before they began to host a radio show. Despite all of that, they both gain success from hosting the radio show, and enjoy the fans of the show, and they never miss a show. Even if one of them is ill or sick, the show continues to go on. There are times to where the hosts disagree, but it is usually over petty things. They do not hold grudges over one another, and they remain the best of friends. In order to host a radio show for as long as they have, they would have to get along with one another, or else the show would not be as successful as it is. They are not the only show that is aired on the radio station. There are a total of two more additional radio shows that air on the radio station. There is a pop culture show that airs right before the "DJ S. and K. show", called, "All Access Entertainment." It is a more lighthearted radio show, that mostly discusses celebrity gossip, and pop culture related discussions. The show comes on at 4 P.M. and ends at 7 P.M. The "DJ S. and K. Show", airs live, Tuesday, Wednesday, and Thursday. The second radio show that comes on early in the morning, after the "DJ S. and K. show", is a news politics radio show called "Politics Now", hosted by two older men. It is not as entertaining as the "DJ S. and K. show", and has a completely different theme and approach to it. There is one more talk show that comes on the radio station, and that's the morning radio show. Which is a mix of pop culture news, and current events. It is the "WBCT Morning Show", hosted by several male and female hosts. People usually listen to this show on their way to work, and when they are stuck in traffic.

The "DJ S. and K. show", features two DJ's. "DJ S.", is Stuart Bennington. He is a thirty-two-year-old, slender man with auburn short hair. He is Caucasian, of Jewish descent. Stuart was born in New York, and grew up in a large family. He is an only child, and always wanted to be an actor when he was growing up as a child. He would partake in drama classes all throughout his youth, to further gain experience for his dream passion. However, Stuart later lost interest in becoming an actor, and then turned his attention to being a radio host. His voice is that of a broadcaster, so he figured he would be perfect for radio. He realized that there are advantages to being on the radio. That he can use acting skills, but without having to stand in front of a camera. He can show up to work in his pajamas if he wanted to, yet still act in some shape or form. Stuart is a timid and quiet man. Out of the two hosts, he is the quieter one. He keeps to himself usually. He has very few friends, and doesn't associate in parties usually. After the radio show is over, he goes straight home, and he partakes in a normal and usual lifestyle. Stuart is very neutral when it comes to politics, and doesn't take a side leaning to the left or right. He listens to issues that both sides have to say, and keeps a neutral opinion or response. Stuart is not married, and doesn't have any children. Stuart is bisexual, but doesn't make a big deal about it. He lives a solitary life by himself, and despite his prolific job as a radio host, he doesn't let that define him. He wishes to live a normal life, as he possibly can, in addition to keeping his job as a radio host as well. The fact his face is not shown on the radio, it allows Stuart to keep a low profile, yet he is still able to be an entertainer. Stuart's close and best friend, is his co-host, "DJ K."

"DJ K." is Klaus Kleinberg. Klaus is a thirty-two-year-old, stocky and pudgy man. He is a balding man. Klaus has poor eyesight, so he wears eyeglasses. Klaus is more opinionated, than his co-host Stuart is. Klaus is of German, and Lebanese descent, and he is also Jewish. Klaus was born and raised in the Los Angeles area. Like Stuart,

Klaus always wanted to get into entertainment. However, unlike Stuart, he did not want to be an actor. Klaus wanted to be a movie director or television producer. Perhaps being a camera man as well. That was his main ambition. Klaus is an opinionated man, and whenever he has an idea, he wants the whole world to hear it. Unlike Stuart, Klaus has no filter to himself. If he wants to say something, he is going to say it. Even if it is offensive, and it makes someone upset or mad, he doesn't care. He will say what he wants, whenever he wants. Klaus is also more sociable out of the two. Whenever a listener calls into the show, Klaus usually offers harsh truths, and says things that everyone else is scared, or afraid to say. When he is not hosting the radio show, Klaus is remarkably more introverted. However, Klaus is always outside in public, taking pictures and shooting video blogs. He likes to meet different people, places and things. He also associates with Stuart quite often. They are best friends after all, so it would make sense for them to do so.

Klaus is not married, and has no children, likewise with Stuart. Klaus, like Stuart, is also bisexual. They both are aware of each other's sexuality, but don't discuss it in detail that much. Klaus is very centrist with his political beliefs. He can have political stances that range on the more liberal side, and he can also have many conservative ideas to himself as well. Klaus is more outspoken than Stuart is during the show. His voice overpowers Stuart usually, and it causes them to get into rifts. Klaus can be disrespectful and impolite at times, by interrupting and cutting others off when they wish to talk. This causes many to get angry and upset at Klaus. He couldn't care less though, as that's his attitude to be ruthless like that at times. If Klaus wants his point across, he is going to say it. Regardless, if he is overpowering another person that is also trying to discuss something. Nevertheless, Stuart and Klaus still manage to get along, and become close. They wouldn't be able to do the show as long as they have otherwise.

Stuart and Klaus both met, when they were attending the, "University of California, Los Angeles". They were both taking media courses, and fate seemed to be in the same direction, for the both of them to meet. They initially and immediately became the best of friends, and vowed to always stick by one another. After they both graduated, they moved in together, and Stuart got a job at an advertising company for a television studio, and Klaus got a job being a cable technician and cable installer. How they both ended up on radio, is actually a luck occurrence. Stuart and Klaus would always talk about having their own radio and podcast show, but didn't know exactly what steps to take, in order to achieve that dream that they both had. By luck and sheer chance, they started to contact several radio stations, asking if they could host their own radio show. They received many rejections, but luckily, there were a few radio stations that were interested in what Stuart and Klaus had to offer. They eventually signed a contract with "WBCT", to host a nightly radio show on a trial basis. They were originally only going to host the show for a month, but due to the ratings, and how well the reception of the show was, they were offered a longer deal to host the show. Five years later, the rest is history, as far as the success of the show goes. It was like clockwork, how Stuart and Klaus became radio hosts. Two friends that met at University, were able to do something unthinkable, out of total luck. Having a career as radio talk show hosts. Not long after they graduated, they were able to achieve a dream that they thought would not be possible, and would forever be a pipe dream. Two friends that came together, with a common goal to achieve. Now being radio hosts, all the pieces are coming together. Their friendship is strong, and their radio show is successful.

It is Thursday night, and it is almost time for the "DJ S. and K. show", to start. The show will begin in less than ten minutes. Klaus is currently at the radio station, waiting for Stuart to arrive. This is very peculiar. Stuart is always on time at the studio, before the show begins. Klaus starts to slightly worry, but still is adamant that Stuart will arrive soon. Klaus decides to pull out his phone, and call Stuart to see what is keeping him. The phone rings, but Stuart does not answer. Klaus then leaves a voicemail message.

"Hey man, I was just wondering where you were at. Is something wrong? Because I'm about to do the show without you for the first time ever, and that's going to be weird. I can't do the show without you. Anyways, please get back to me ASAP. Okay man."

Klaus puts his phone back into his pocket, and waits for Stuart to arrive. Klaus does not want to do the show without Stuart. They have been doing the show for over five years, and there hasn't been one show, not one, to where one of them was absent. Klaus is at a crossroads as to whether he should do the show, even though Stuart might not be in attendance. It is after all the "DJ S. and K. show". If "DJ S.", isn't there, then it wouldn't be the same at all. As more minute's pass by, Stuart has still not arrived. Klaus now starts to worry, especially after the fact Stuart did not respond to his voicemail message. If Stuart doesn't arrive in two minutes, Klaus would have to either cancel the show, or do the show without him in attendance. This is something Klaus still hasn't made his mind up, as to what he shall do. Part of him wants to do the show anyways, whilst the other part of him cannot do the show without Stuart. He feels that it just wouldn't be the same at all, and the show would be boring, or incomplete, without Stuart. It is now a minute before the show has to begin, and Stuart is still not there. Klaus then makes the harsh decision to do the show without Stuart. This is something he would never fathom doing, but he has to do it. It is now time for the show to begin, and Stuart is not there. Klaus then starts to speak into his microphone, starting the show.

"Ladies and Gentlemen, you are listening to 'WBCT', 'Broadcast Radio'. You already know what time it is. It's time for the 'DJ S. and K. show'. The show that offers raw and unfiltered content, and we talk about relevant issues. I'm DJ K., and let's start the show."

Even though his voice sounded jubilant and happy, Klaus couldn't be further from that. It just felt weird for the opening of the show, not to feature Stuart. Klaus begins to doubt whether he can actually continue on by himself. He manages to gain the strength to continue the show by himself, letting the listeners know that Stuart for the first time ever, will not be on the show.

"I hope you all are having a good night. I have to sadly say, that there is a first time for everything. Throughout the years we have done the show, we have a first. Stuart is not here. I don't know why he's not here. Maybe he's sick, but it's okay. He's going to be here in spirit."

Klaus then starts to pause himself. Before he continues, he realizes that he simply cannot do the show without Stuart. It wouldn't be the same, and he doesn't have the mental capacity to carry on without him. Klaus then makes the difficult decision to end the show early.

"I'm sorry, but I can't do this without Stuart. Tonight's show will be cancelled. I'm really sorry. Instead, you guys are gonna listen to some music jams. Some oldies, but goodies though. Ha Ha. I'll be back tomorrow night, hopefully with Stuart with me. Goodnight everybody."

Klaus continues to feel worried about Stuart. It is not usual for him, to not be in attendance at the studio, whenever they are doing a show. In the very least, Klaus felt that Stuart should have at least left a message or called, if something happened. Klaus starts to gather his things, and prepares to exit himself, out of the studio. Still feeling upset, and concerned over Stuart, Klaus manages to pull himself together, nevertheless. With half of his mind thinking that Stuart is fine, with the other half of his mind, thinking that something is wrong. During this time however, Klaus starts to reminisce, about the first time that he met Stuart, and the both of them would form a very long bonded friendship.

Klaus first met Stuart, when they were both attending UCLA. They were both Broadcasting majors at UCLA, and hoping to get into the world of news entertainment. Also studying telecommunications. With Klaus having giant inspirations of becoming a news cameraman, and news reporter. With Stuart having more or less, essentially the same career aspirations and goals. To break into the news business as well. Klaus and Stuart in the end, managed to have the same courses and classes. Although they would come across each other during classes, they decided to have a more cordial relationship with each other at first. Klaus didn't think much of Stuart, as Klaus was not the type to immediately be sociable, and quick to make friends. Klaus usually kept to himself, and didn't bother others. Funnily enough, Stuart was just about the same. He was introverted as well, and usually didn't circulate with others. So, the fact both Klaus and Stuart, were equally as shy, it's a miracle as to how they became lifelong friends. It wasn't until one day, late into the semester, that Stuart decided to approach Klaus. He just had a feeling that the both of them would hit it off, despite the both of them, giving off an introverted energy. As Klaus was preparing himself to exit out of class one afternoon, Stuart decides to finally introduce himself to him.

"Hey man, I'm Stuart Bennington. I'm originally from New York, but I recently moved to LA, to study here. I don't know man, I seen you around campus, and I have a really good feeling about you, and was wondering if you wanted to hang out today?"

Klaus feeing perplexed and puzzled, looked very strangely at Stuart. Klaus did not have any friends whilst he was at UCLA, and Stuart was just about the same. He had no idea of how to react or respond. So, he found it rather odd and peculiar that Stuart decided to come up and approach him. Let alone invite him to hang out, outside of school. Klaus prepares to walk towards the classroom door. While he's doing that, he responds to Stuart.

"Oh hey. My name is Klaus Kleinberg. I am from LA. My family is like a mix. I'm German, Lebanese, Jewish. Yeah, I'm actually busy, so unfortunately, I have to pass. But it was nice meeting you Stuart, and you take care man."

Stuart looks down at the ground, defeated. Feeling disappointed that Klaus did not accept his offer, he decides to give Klaus a second attempt. Hoping that probably this time, he will reconsider, and decide to give him another shot. With both men now in the hallway, Stuart decides to follow Klaus, and once again pushes his luck with him.

"I see. I understand that you're busy. But I'm busy too. Everyone is busy, we have tests and projects that are due. I'm sure we both are swamped with our other courses too. But let's take a break today, and just hang out. I know this arcade, that has a bar and..."

Klaus decides to put his hand on Stuart's shoulder, letting him know how he really feels, and decides to be extremely blunt and honest, with how his feelings currently are.

"Do you have a listening problem? I told you that I am busy today. I do not want to hang out. Now this is the last time, I'm gonna ask you to leave me alone. Take care, sir."

In this very moment, as Stuart is accepting defeat, and willing to let Klaus go, Klaus notices that Stuart has a sticker on one of his notebook binders. Klaus grabs Stuarts binder, and is shocked and amazed at what he sees. He then speaks to Stuart.

"Oh wow, you're a Grateful Dead fan. I never met another person in my life, who liked their music. Okay, you got lucky, only because you're a Deadhead, I'm gonna change my mind."

Stuart smiles back at Klaus, and can't believe he managed to luck out, at finding a common ground, between himself and Klaus. The both of them continue to walk down the hallway, into the outside courtyard of the campus. As the both of them continue out, Stuart replies back at Klaus, excited that they both share the same music taste.

"Oh yeah, I been a fan of theirs since I was young. I knew there was something about you, that we both shared. I'm glad I was lucky enough to find it, so about that arcade..."

Klaus stops and turns his direction towards Stuart. He then gives out a sharp reply.

"I never said that I wanted to hang out with you. I just said that I was gonna give you another chance, and what I meant by giving you another chance, is that I don't mind you walking with me. I never said anything about us going to arcades or bars or play dates. We're not friends. Just because we both like the Grateful Dead, doesn't mean we're best friends now. Come on."

Stuart smiles back at Klaus, and the both of the men continue walking around campus. Stuart doesn't completely believe Klaus is telling the truth, and his hiding his true intentions and feelings. Stuart then decides to bring up a strange coincidence to Klaus.

"Well, you know today is my Twenty First birthday today. I just wanted someone to hang out with today, that's all. Celebrating your birthday alone, is really depressing and sad. So, you're gonna reject a guy on his birthday? I see. Well, if that's how you feel, then I understand."

Klaus then begins to feel empathetic over Stuart, and has a complete change of heart. Klaus understands the tough spot that he is currently in. He cannot reject Stuart on his birthday, that would be very cruel and wrong. Klaus, although very timid and shy himself, understands that under normal and regular circumstances, he would not agree to spend time with Stuart, but only because it is his birthday, he is willing to make an exception.

"Damn, why do you have to do this to me. Okay, fine. We can hang out, but only because it's your birthday. Alright. Now where are we going, 'Chuck E. Cheese?' Ha Ha."

Stuart laughs hysterically back at Klaus, and after composing himself, he then responds back to Klaus, informing him of where he plans to go.

"Oh no, this is more mature, for grown people. It's this sports bar, with an arcade, and they have bowling, and they have really good beer and drinks. It's called 'Dave and Busters', and you're gonna like it. I been there before, and it's really fun."

Klaus is unsure, as to whether or not, he has attended this place before. He is sure that he probably has. Klaus seems optimistic and excited. Although his body language isn't saying that, and is showing a completely different feeling. Both of the men continue walking outside of campus, towards Stuart's car. They both get in, and during the car ride, Klaus can't believe how fast things are going. Up until a half an hour ago, he was an introvert, that wouldn't dare form any friendships, or relationships with anybody else on campus. Now he is deciding to celebrate a guy's birthday, he just met a short while ago. The location of the venue, is not far from campus, and both of the men arrive there, rather quickly. Feeling nervous and unsure of himself, Klaus reluctantly follows Stuart inside of "Dave and Busters". Stuart then speaks to Klaus.

"Are you hungry? I haven't had a thing to eat all day, and I figured that we could get something to eat first, then we can play the arcade games, and play some bowling rounds."

Klaus, still feeling confused and puzzled, realizes that he is quite hungry, and it wouldn't hurt for him to have a meal with Stuart. Klaus responds back to Stuart, letting him know, that he would like to eat, and both of the gentlemen, take a seat down at a table. As they are reading over the menu, which mostly consists of regular sports bar food, like Buffalo Wings, Burgers, Burger Sliders, Chicken Fingers,

Nachos, and other novelties, Klaus starts to make his mind up, as to what he wants to eat. Occasionally taking glances over at Stuart, and the both of them smiling, if they happen to make eye contact with each other. Stuart decides to order the Chicken Nachos, as Klaus decides to get an order of Buffalo Wings. The waitress comes over to take their order, and when she begins to walk away, Stuart and Klaus smile at each other, and Stuart starts to hold Klaus hand. As he is doing this, he silently responds back to Klaus, feeling happy that he accepted his offer.

"I'm very glad you decided to come here. I don't have any friends, and you're the first person at school, that agreed to hang out with me. I didn't lie, today is actually my Twenty First birthday, and I refused to spend yet another birthday alone. Thank you so much Klaus."

Klaus is truly feeling happy, that he managed to keep Stuart company on his birthday. Soon, both of their food arrives, and the men start to eat. When they are finished with their meal. Klaus decides to pay for the meal, as it's Stuart's birthday, and he wishes to treat him. Stuart thanks Klaus, and they then venture onto the video arcade, on the other side of the establishment. Klaus buys a card with credits on it, and himself and Stuart play the arcade games, by swiping the card on the machine. Both men arc having fun playing thc vidco gamcs, and Stuart is feeling like he is having one the best birthdays, that he has ever had. Soon after, Klaus and Stuart then play bowling, with Klaus offering to pay for the bowling rounds. Although Klaus is very skilled at bowling, and getting many strikes and spares, Stuart is not as skilled at bowling, and is getting many gutter balls. This is fine, as Stuart doesn't mind that Klaus is beating him at bowling. He's just happy that he has a new friend, and enjoying his birthday.

When the men are finished playing bowling, Klaus buys himself and Stuart a beer. Klaus hands Stuart a beer, while congratulating him at the same time.

"Happy Twenty First birthday man. This one is on me, and if you want another round, just ask. Just be happy I didn't ask them to send a dancing mouse, or a dancing dog, or cat, or a care bear or something, to sing 'Happy Birthday' to you. Ha Ha. Cheers man."

Stuart laughs back at Klaus, and both men drink their beers. This was the start of a very long friendship between the both of them. Stuart was eternally happy to spend his birthday with Klaus, and this was turning into a perfect, joyous day. Klaus orders Stuart a chocolate brownie, and he asks Klaus, if he doesn't mind sharing it with him, as the dessert portion was rather large. Klaus obliges, and they both eat the chocolate brownie together. They are both also watching a baseball game on the television. With it currently being the bottom of the ninth inning, The Dodgers versus, The Giants, with the Dodgers winning the game at the end. Being that it is getting quite late, both of the men decide to call it an evening. Stuart once again thanks Klaus for taking the time, to hang out with him. They both get back into Stuart's car, and he drops Klaus off at his apartment. As Klaus is getting out of the car, Stuart shouts back to him.

"Hey man, what are you doing tomorrow evening? Don't tell me you're busy with classes and homework. That's bullshit, you have to be free tomorrow. Let's go hiking. I won't take no for an answer. You told me you didn't have any afternoon courses tomorrow, so how's 3 p.m.?"

Klaus nervously scratches the back of his head, and is feeling uneasy again. He agreed to hang out with Stuart on his birthday, and didn't mind keeping in contact with Stuart, but wasn't altogether comfortable of Stuart suggesting that they hang out, the very next day again. Although, Klaus had a different feeling about Stuart, he agreed to go hiking with him.

"Yeah sure, I'll see you tomorrow at 3 buddy."

As Klaus is walking to his apartment, Stuart gets out of the car, and gives Klaus a big hug. Klaus nervously smiles back at Stuart, and tells him goodbye. Stuart then drives off down the road, and Klaus walks inside of his apartment. The very next day, Klaus attends his courses, earlier on in the day, knowing that come this afternoon, he promised Stuart, that he would go hiking with him. Klaus is now beginning to regret that choice, and wonders if that was the right decision to make. Klaus hasn't been hiking in years, and feels that Stuart is more physically figured to handle hiking. Klaus is a bigger man, and hiking isn't necessarily his forte. But he is willing to give it a try anyways, in order to make Stuart happy. 3 p.m. approaches, and Klaus has changed into appropriate attire for hiking. Stuart picks up him at 3 p.m. on the dot, and the both of them head off to the hiking trail. While they are driving there, Stuart speaks to Klaus.

"Yeah, hiking is one of my favorite hobbies. It's so relaxing, peaceful, you get to smell the fresh air and nature. Hiking around evening time is also great too. California is great for hiking and outdoorsy stuff. You feel the same, right Klaus?"

In actuality, Klaus did not feel the same. Hiking was something that before today, Klaus would have wanting nothing to do with, or take any part in. However, he didn't want Stuart to know this, so he responds back to Stuart, fibbing to him, about how he feels.

"Oh yeah, I go hiking all the time, it's fun. I enjoy it for the exact same reasons that you do. We're gonna have a great time. I am just glad to be here Stu."

Stuart is unaware that Klaus is lying, and Stuart feels happy and content. The men finally make it to the hiking trail, and Klaus starts to buckle under the pressure. Sweat is beating down his face, and he feels like fainting. This was probably a terrible mistake. Klaus isn't as active and fit as Stuart, and not even five minutes into the hiking outing, Klaus is already feeling like he wants to go home, and not continue. Despite that, Klaus decides to put on a façade, that everything is fine, as he doesn't want to upset Stuart, and worry him. The men continue into the hiking trail, and twenty minutes into the hike, Stuart is treading down the trail fast, with Klaus barely keeping up, and about to keel over. Klaus decides to take a rest at a bench on the trail, and struggles to catch his breath. He is completely winded. Stuart notices that Klaus is not behind him, and back traces himself down the trail, to notice Klaus, looking lethargic and tired. Stuart smiles at Klaus, and starts to pour water across his face. He then softly speaks to Klaus.

"You never been hiking before a day in your life, have you? Klaus you didn't have to lie, I could have taken you to a more beginner trail. Why didn't you bring any water either? Tell you what, we'll just do half the trail, and call it a day, because the other half of the trail is way too extreme and difficult for you, and Klaus, you need to also keep active more man."

Klaus smiles back at Stuart, but doesn't respond. He knows that Stuart was absolutely right. All throughout his life, Klaus struggled with his weight and body image, and was never into sports. Klaus did some weightlifting in High School, but he still wasn't the active and fit type. So, he didn't dare backtalk, or respond defiantly, or rudely back to Stuart, as he knew he was right. Klaus should never have lied to Stuart, that he wasn't skilled in hiking, so Klaus only had himself to blame. Klaus gets himself off the bench, and Stuart manages not to walk as fast, since Klaus isn't experienced in hiking, as he originally thought he was. The both of the men enjoy their hiking trip, despite the original hiccup, with Klaus not being ready or experienced for the trail. It was a good day, and it was yet another bonding experience, between them.

After the hiking trip, Klaus invites Stuart back to his apartment. They end up ordering pizza, and having beer. Also telling each other secrets, about their lives. Stuart explains to Klaus, his family moved from New York, and Klaus is explaining to Stuart, his upbringing, being born in Los Angeles. The both of them talk about their career aspirations. It was during this exact time, to where it was clear, that both Klaus and Stuart, wanted to become radio hosts. It was like a spiritual energy that came across the room, which sparked this interest with them. They both were studying Broadcast Journalism, and they both were interested in news and politics. It was strange and uncanny at first, but it was something that was purely meant to be. It was one of those strange occurrences and instances, to where it sounded very strange, but it still made sense, and it was something that was meant to be, and was supposed to happen. Klaus and Stuart, form a tighter bond, and from this day forward, they took a vow, that they would always be by each other's side, and look out for one another. They would be partners in life, with their main end goal, having their own radio show, and becoming world famous, from that.

Stuart was living on campus housing, and once Klaus and Stuart graduated through their programs, Klaus and Stuart decided to look for an apartment together. If they were going to be life career partners, they decided it made sense, to live together. Klaus and Stuart didn't have any romantic spark. They were not each other's type, and they both took dating and romantic relationships as something awkward, and as something they didn't talk about. Although they were both bisexual, they simply did not have any attachment like that. They were strictly, close friends, and also looked to each other as business partners. Klaus and Stuart, did manage to rent a two-bedroom apartment, and during the day, Klaus worked as a cable installer, and Stuart worked at a television advertising company. They were simply jobs the both of them took to pay the bills. As they were both taking post graduate classes for Broadcast Journalism. Although Klaus and Stuart did like their day jobs, they still had plans to start their own radio show. It was something that never left their minds, and it was something more than a pipe dream. It was something that they knew they had to accomplish soon, as they both were getting older, and if they wanted to break it into radio entertainment, they had to start young. They needed an immediate course of action, and a plan, as to how they were going to get their radio career started. This was something that they needed to concoct, and put together, very soon.

One evening, as Stuart was coming home, he looked extremely upset. Klaus could feel the anxiety off of Stuart, and by looking at his face, knew it was something bad. Klaus wondered what was wrong. Stuart informed Klaus of some devastating news.

"They let me go from the company today. They just have been laying people off, left and right, and I had a feeling I was going to be next. I just didn't know it was going to be this sudden. I don't know what I'm gonna do. I was promoted to coordinator, and assistant executive, and..."

Klaus who was sitting on the living room sofa, stood up. Klaus still had on his uniform from the cable company. Klaus flung off his nametag on his shirt, and silently spoke to Stuart.

"It's time. I don't want to work for that cable company anymore. They fired you for no reason, and I enjoy my job, but it's not what we're meant to do now. You know what time it is."

Stuart smiles back at Klaus, and knows exactly what he means. During this time, Klaus and Stuart began to devote their attention to their radio career. Klaus and Stuart would then create a demo reel, of Klaus reporting on issues surrounding the city of Los Angeles, with Stuart videotaping the segments, and vice versa, with Stuart acting as reporter, and Klaus filming all of the action. It was a joint effort, and Klaus and Stuart acted as joint co-hosts of the news program. Klaus and Stuart would upload their news segments to YouTube, although the views would not come in. Klaus and Stuart kept at this for a year and a half, with very minimal results. It wasn't until Klaus and Stuart, started reporting on more risqué issues, such as police standoffs, burning buildings, political unrests and rallies, and government conspiracy coverups, that views on their news segments, would pour in. Strictly living on their savings, being that they were both unemployed now, they were now getting donations and funds from social media, by uploading and broadcasting their content. Klaus and Stuart, with their aptly named, "S and K show", now amassed several thousand subscribers and followers. They assumed they were now ready, to make it big, or at least attempt to. After consulting several radio stations, getting doors slammed in their faces, being told no, laughed at, and that their dream of being radio personalities, are slim to none, Klaus and Stuart began to feel defeated. Klaus at his wits end, then decided to come up with a last-minute suggestion. One morning, while himself and Stuart were at IHOP eating breakfast, Klaus gave a proposition out to Stuart.

"Hey man, I know our YouTube channel is going big, and we tried to talk to the radio stations to give us a chance. They all said no right? Well, we're getting impatient, and we have to think of something else. Let them come to us man, we'll do our own podcast show. Yeah!"

Stuart takes a sip of his coffee, and nods his head in agreement with Klaus. That following night, Klaus and Stuart, with the few tools and equipment they had, set up their own news station, in their living room. With a greenscreen, lights, HD cameras, all on tap, and ready. They would start the first episode of their news show, right and direct from their own house. The show would start every Wednesday and Thursday, from 7pm to 10pm Pacific Standard Time. The best part, was that their viewers, fans, trolls, whatever; could call in, and speak their mind, whether they agree, or disagree as to what Klaus or Stuart said, or if they need life advice, or just wanted to call in, and act a fool, they didn't mind. As long as the viewers had a telephone number, they could call in. They also would have webchat and email available, for people that wanted to send in questions through that avenue as well. Klaus and Stuart already had their show planned out, and knew if they did this job well enough, the networks would consult them.

Klaus and Stuart, did their first show, without a hitch. It was a major success and hit, and they gained thousands of viewers and watchers. They also managed to rack up several new fans and followers. The following day, episode two, of their show commenced, and it was even better. It was an overnight success, and Klaus idea, turned out to be a very successful, and wise one. Only through the course of two episodes, have they managed to pull through, this unprecedented, success. The show did so well, that following Monday morning, several news outlets, wanted to get in touch with Klaus and Stuart. Networks such as People Magazine, US Weekly, TMZ, and MTV. That Monday, Klaus and Stuart were interviewed by several of these news networks, which as predicted, brought more exposure to their program. That next day, Good Morning America, and the Today's Show, also interviewed them Via Satellite, and remote, as well. By this point, Klaus and Stuart had really lucked out with their prestige. They continued on with their YouTube show for another month, when their dreams finally paid off.

One day, Klaus and Stuart received a call, that an "iHeartRadio" station, wants to give Klaus and Stuart, their own radio show. Upon hearing this news, Klaus and Stuart jumped all around their house, full of happiness and excitement. After signing the contract for the show, in the meantime, Klaus and Stuart, are still doing their YouTube show, but keeping the news that they were given a radio show deal secret, until everything was final, and so that they wouldn't be in breach of contract. Once the contract was approved, Klaus and Stuart, gave the news to their fans, letting them know they were now official radio hosts. Their show would come on "WBCT" Radio. A station that played 70s., 80s, 90s, and some early 2000s pop hits during the day. But during the early mornings, evenings, and nights, several different radio programs air. With Klaus and Stuart's show, "The DJ S. and K. show", airing Tuesday,

Wednesday, and Thursday, from 7 p.m. to 11 p.m. Their show was a huge success, and their fanbase, continued to grow and grow. Growing to the point of having celebrity guests, and Klaus and Stuart would even interview them. Life was starting to become great for the both of them, and they were each relishing into some sort of celebrity, through this journey of theirs. Although they sparked some controversies, here and there with their radio show, it was all water under the bridge mostly. Klaus and Stuart, made it known, their show isn't politically correct at all, and the viewers know exactly what they are tuning in for. If Klaus or Stuart, happened to say something that was disrespectful, their fanbase would understand, that they meant well, and it wasn't that big of a deal. The success of their show, powered on, and now for five years, the show has still been going on strong. Every week, from Tuesday, to Thursday, Klaus and Stuart meet up at the studio in Downtown Los Angeles, and entertain their listeners, and give a good show. Whether the show has a set topic for the night, or it's open discussion, and anything goes. Over the course of time, Klaus and Stuart now live in their separate apartments. They are still great friends, but Klaus has his own life, and Stuart has his, and they do hang outside of doing shows, but mostly, remarkably, they keep to themselves, when a show is not airing. However, they have never missed a show. Even if Klaus or Stuart isn't feeling well, they take some aspirin and Tylenol, and show up to the studio anyways, so their show is not disrupted. That was until, things fast forward back to the present, and, that was until tonight. Stuart for the first time ever, did not show up at the studio.

Klaus makes the difficult choice, to suspend the show, as he cannot do it without Stuart. For five years, he always had Stuart by his side, whenever they commenced their radio show. Now that Stuart is not here, it is going to be simply, too awkward and strange, for him to do the show on his own. Klaus starts to power off all the broadcasting equipment, and decides to play a loop of prerecorded pop songs, to take place through their delayed and cancelled radio show. As Klaus walks out of the studio door, he decides to step outside, to the upper deck patio of the studio. Klaus takes out his pack of cigarettes, and begins to light one. Klaus also takes out his phone, and begins to call Stuart, once more.

"Stu, it's me again. Yeah, I'm just wondering where you are man. Just let me know something. Call, text, do something. Don't leave me in the dark like this man. Alright. Peace."

Klaus finishes his cigarette, and still feeling apprehensive and worried, directs himself to the parking structure of the studio, and decides to drive out of the studio, heading home. Klaus, as well as Stuart, live in Redondo Beach, in the greater Los Angeles area. With both of their homes, being close, so they can keep in contact with each other, at all times. Redondo Beach is a beach town, located south of Downtown LA, the location of the radio station, where Klaus and Stuart do their show. Klaus told himself, that he would swing by Stuart's house, and see if his car was in the driveway. If his car was in the driveway, that would ease his mind. If his car wasn't in the driveway, he would probably feel more concerned and worried, and his mind wouldn't be at ease. Before heading home, Klaus decides to make a stop at Walgreens, to get himself some snacks, as he hasn't eaten all day. Klaus gets himself a Salisbury Steak TV Dinner, a Caesar Salad, and a pint of "Ben and Jerry's, Tonight's Show" Ice Cream. Klaus pays for his items, and heads directly heads to Stuart's townhouse, just to be sure. As Klaus drives by Stuart's residence, he notices that Stuart's car is not in the driveway. Feeling very anxious at this point, Klaus parks his car, and walks up to Stuart's door, and rings the doorbell. When after ringing the doorbell, and not having anyone come to the door, Klaus starts to sweat, and has a really uncomfortable feeling, in the pit of his stomach. He feels glued to Stuart's porch, and can't move for several seconds. He does manage to snap out of it, and return to his car. Klaus ultimately, has no idea where Stuart is, or what is happening, but all he can do is hope that everything is fine. Klaus then drives a short distance, around the block to his own townhouse. Klaus opens the door to his house. Proceeds to the kitchen to warm up his TV dinner in the microwave, put his ice cream in the freezer, and then makes his way to his living room, to watch television.

Klaus, still has not heard back from Stuart, and trying his best, not to worry about this anymore. If Stuart wishes to contact him, he will.

Klaus takes off his shoes and socks, and relaxes on his sofa, watching reruns of "The Walking Dead", one of Klaus, favorite programs. The microwave soon dings, letting Klaus know, that his TV dinner is ready. Klaus is ordinarily a moderately good cook, but for tonight, he was not feeling like cooking, and decided to get a frozen microwave TV Dinner. Just a simple Salisbury Steak dinner. Nothing too fancy. Klaus also got a side salad at the store as well, to go with the meal. Klaus heads back to his kitchen, and takes a Bud Light beer out of the refrigerator. Klaus then eats his dinner by himself, and watches his program. Klaus finishes his meal, and opens up the freezer, to take out the ice cream he bought. Klaus has a sweet tooth, and ice cream is one of his personal favorites. Especially, "Ben and Jerry's Tonight Show" flavored, which has chocolate chips, and cookie dough. Klaus sets his ice cream container on his coffee table, and opens up the drapes in his living room, which gives a view of the Pacific Ocean. Klaus then turns off the lights, and watches the 10 o'clock news, as he usually does, on days he doesn't have to do the radio show with Stuart. Klaus enjoys the news, so that way, he can be up to date on current events, when doing his show.

Klaus starts to eat this ice cream, feeling comfortable at the moment. Even though he hasn't heard from Stuart, he doesn't want that to worry or pester him. The news program continues to showcase, both uplifting, and more serious and devastating stories. To which Klaus is both interested in the good, and the bad news segments. Klaus eventually finishes the entire container of ice cream. He then lays down on the sofa, steadily watching the news. Klaus for some reason, starts to feel slightly drowsy, snoozing and dozing in and out during the news program. Klaus ends up taking a short nap during this. However, he manages to regain consciousness, when the female news anchor announces breaking news.

"We have breaking news, in the Downtown Los Angeles area. A man was robbed at gunpoint, earlier this evening. He was unfortunately killed during the ordeal. LAPD, and through the help of witnesses, later located the suspect, who resisted arrest, and was accosted by the police. We will give you more information about this story later, please stay tuned."

Klaus immediately sprung up from the sofa, and it was like powerful burst of energy, went through his entire body. Klaus, heartbeat was beating a million times a minute, and everything went completely blank for him. The only thing on Klaus mind, was he was just hoping that it wasn't Stuart. He felt the odds of that being that possible, weren't likely. But why was Klaus feeling this way then? He sadly knew, that yes, the possibly was low, the news story could have been talking about Stuart. Klaus immediately shuts the news program off, and walks off to his balcony, looking out towards the view of the beach and ocean. Klaus can hear the waves crash against the shore, in this very calm night in Redondo Beach. Klaus doesn't have the slightest idea of what to do, after hearing that news story. Feelings of guilt and shame run throughout his body, and it causes him to stand still and motionless. Klaus takes a final look at the ocean, and walks back into his house. Klaus takes out his phone, and once more, decides to give Stuart a call, and there is no answer. He sends a text message to Stuart as well. Klaus sets his phone down on the coffee table in the living room, and heads into his kitchen. He then starts to wash his dirty dishes, and tidies up the rest of his kitchen. Klaus has a modest design to his house. He has posters of rock bands like "Grateful Dead", "Kiss", "Rolling Stones", "ACDC", "Black Sabbath", "Def Leppard" and "Led Zeppelin", but also has some sports memorabilia, as Klaus likes Hockey and Baseball. Klaus also is a video game fanatic, so he has a lot of PlayStation, Nintendo, and Xbox games as well. Above all, Klaus is into media journalism, so he has his camera equipment, microphones, lights, tripods set up as well.

Klaus finishes the dishes, and heads back into the living room, and sits down on the couch. He picks up his phone, and notices that Stuart has not responded back to him. Klaus decides to turn to the television to ESPN, to look at a sports highlight show. Klaus relaxes himself on the couch, trying his best to clear his mind. Although the news story that he watched earlier, is still lingering in his thoughts. Fifteen minutes later, as Klaus is still watching his sports program, he receives a call on his phone. Feeling optimistic, that it's possibly Stuart. Klaus looks at his phone, and notices, the number says "Los Angeles Police Department." Klaus let's his phone ring without picking it up, for several seconds, feeling shocked and scared, but does ultimately decide to pick up the phone, and answer it. A male voice responds to Klaus.

"Yes hello. I'm speaking to Klaus Kleinberg, correct?"

Klaus responds to the man on the other end of the line.

"Yes, this is Klaus speaking. Is everything alright, did I do something wrong?"

The man responds directly back to Klaus.

"No sir, you didn't do anything wrong. My name is Detective John Ross. I'm with the LAPD. I just wanted to say, that sir, are you somewhere comfortable and safe right now?"

Klaus feeling very worried and tense, responds back to the detective.

"Yes sir, I'm at home, and I'm somewhere safe. What is going on? What happened?"

The detective then replies back to Klaus, very swiftly and directly.

"Well sir, unfortunately, I'm calling to inform you that your close friend, Stuart Pennington, he was killed in a robbery this evening. We managed to subdue the perpetrator, and he was taken down by officers. We are aware of your relationship with the victim. Sir, we..."

Klaus immediately screams and shouts back at the detective.

"What the hell? NO! FUCK! This can't be right! Stuart's dead! Oh no, I knew something was up, when I saw it on the news. Oh man, Stu. Why him? No."

The detective responds back to Klaus, attempting to mediate the situation.

"Sir, I understand how you feel. But I need you to calm down. We are gonna be in touch with you, as we do a thorough investigation. We are terribly sorry for your loss sir."

Klaus slams his phone down on the floor, and runs his hands through his face, feeling depressed and stunned. Klaus then can hear the audible sound of the detective on the other end, and picks up his phone, and responds back to the detective.

"Fuck your investigation, Stu is gone, and he's dead. I have no answers, I don't know what happened. He was my best friend. You have no idea. Oh man."

The detective then calmly speaks back to Klaus.

"Klaus, we understand that, we are going to keep in touch with you over this, and it's going to be okay. We are here for you, and again, we are sorry about your loss."

Klaus starts to slowly, but surely, understand the severity of the situation, and has some level of acceptance. He replies back to the detective calmly.

"Yes, I understand sir, thank you detective. Goodbye."

Klaus starts to play a Grateful Dead song on his phone, and sets his phone on the coffee table, and walks out to his balcony again. He takes out another cigarette, and watches the ocean. As the Grateful Dead song is playing in the background, Klaus begins to cry and sob heavily. He then silently lets out something under his breath.

"This was your song Stu, and I'm gonna miss you. I love you Stu."

CHAPTER 2:

MOVING ON

For the remainder of the evening, Klaus was unable to compose himself. Hearing the devastating news, about his best friend Stuart, caused his entire body to panic. Klaus entire professional life, centered around Stuart as well, as they were work partners. Klaus was unsure, as to how, or if, he was going to continue the show, without Stuart right there by his side. This was happening very sudden, and fast for Klaus, and he had no plans or ideas, as to what to do next. After speaking with the detective on the phone, all he wanted to do, was fade into the abyss. The reality was, that Stuart was no longer here, and Klaus had to accept this news. Klaus loves doing radio, but he feels that it doesn't seem right, if Stuart isn't at the station with him. He realizes that if he does choose to continue on working, it will be strange, with Stuart, no longer being present. Klaus has to get his priorities figured out, and understand what his next plan is going to be. He cannot just simply do nothing for the rest of his life. Stuart would have wanted Klaus to live happily, and not sulk over his death. Klaus is hurting, and he's grieving, but in the end, he has to realize, that he must move on, and for the sake of Stuart as well, carry on. Although this may take some time for Klaus to adjust, and get used to, it is ultimately something he must do, in order to advance further in his life, and so that he is living a proud and fulfilling life, to the best of his abilities. Dealing with sadness is not easy, and especially dealing with the loss of a close friend isn't easy either, but life must go on. Klaus must pick himself back up, and not stay stuck to his sorrows. He needs to rebuild himself, and keep going, as staying optimistic and positive about the future, is Klaus only option and hope.

Klaus found it very difficult to sleep that night. His mind was racing extremely fast, with a wave of thoughts. He was constantly having flashbacks, related to himself and Stuart. As much as Klaus wanted to fall asleep, he simply couldn't. The news that he was just told, was too much for his body to remain calm, and still. After struggling to fall asleep for hours, Klaus decided to get out of bed, and head over his computer. Klaus powers up his computer, and he starts a video editing program. In addition to video broadcasting, Klaus has another hobby. Video editing. Klaus always had dreams of being the next Steven Spielberg, or George Lucas, or Quentin Tarantino. So, he liked to think of himself as an ace, when it came to video editing and directing. Klaus liked to take his video camera out in the public, and film his own documentaries. With consent with the people, he filmed of course. He would later return home, and edit the footage that he shot. The editing part, Klaus liked the best, because he felt half of the production quality, lied in between the editing. Klaus has produced so many short documentary films, alongside with the help of Stuart, and it only further perpetuated, his love of media. Being in the city of Los Angeles, there are many opportunities and people, places, and things to film. A niche category that Klaus liked to film, was nature and outdoor settings. Forests, parks, beaches, deserts, mountains. Klaus liked to get it all on film, and he figured that having footage of God made things, was just simply fantastic and beautiful. It was a hobby Klaus enjoyed very greatly, and he knew that he had a future in the media broadcasting, and filmmaking business, because of his own craft and eye for detail. Klaus was very aware of all the techniques, and routines when it came to filming and editing, and it was at the point, to where he excelled at doing it. No matter what type of film it was, Klaus was able to create his vision out of it, and make a production, that he knew the audience would like. Above all, a production that he would like, and be satisfied with. A production that he would be proud to have his name next to.

What Klaus was intending to do now, was create a video, in remembrance of Stuart. Klaus felt that since he couldn't fall asleep, he might as well do something constructive, and also something that may simmer his mind down. This is something that he feels will help him get over the loss of Stuart easier, if he creates a movie, featuring moments of himself and Stuart, out doing their show, out having fun, and also pictures of them both. Klaus thought of it, as a nice farewell, to show that he will always have Stuart on his mind, but understanding fully, that he is gone, and no longer here. Klaus starts to put together more of the footage, sobbing while doing so. This activity is not only depressing for Klaus, but it's also at the same time, therapeutic, and causing him to feel better about the situation. Klaus is also adding some of Stuart's favorite songs, as background music in the film. Something such as that, to give the film more spice, and a better touch. Klaus is noticing as he's putting together this video, that he is losing track of time. This is not unusual or uncommon. When Klaus gets wrapped up in his computer editing, time seems to stand still. Minutes can turn into hours, which then turn into days, weeks, and months, of Klaus working on a particular project. So, Klaus has been working on this film, for quite some time now, and it is now creeping up on 5 a.m. Klaus is now starting to feel tired, and drowsy. Although he is only halfway done with creating the memorial film for Stuart, Klaus is now finding it hard to stay awake, and decides to save all that he has done so far, and walks himself back to bed. Making the film, made Klaus feel better about the recent events, and it allowed him to be able to go to sleep. He wasn't on high alert, or worried anymore. Klaus was able to drift off to sleep without any hassle, and was slowly and surely, beginning to accept everything, and Klaus was able to make it back down to reality, and tread on with whatever life has in store for him next. Klaus continued to doze off calmly, and softly.

Hours later, with it now being 1 p.m., Klaus frantically jumps out of bed, when he looks at his alarm clock in his bedroom. Even though Klaus and Stuart were contracted to do the show Tuesdays,

Wednesdays, and Thursdays; on Fridays, Klaus and Stuart usually go to the studio anyways, to do technical editing work. Klaus totally forgot about this, due to the wave of turmoil that just happened. Part of Klaus, wants to not report in for work, being that Stuart died the day before. The other half of Klaus, feels like showing up to work anyways. Although Klaus is primarily feeling that he shouldn't show up today. Already shocked and on edge, Klaus entire body trembles, upon looking at what the time is currently is. He is frantic that he overslept that long, and begins to freshen himself up for the day. After tidying himself up, Klaus directs himself to the living room coffee table, where his phone is situated. Klaus notices that he as an abundant number of missed calls, primarily from the radio station, and Klaus boss, Larry Weston. Mr. Weston, is a very strict boss, and he is the manager of the radio station, that Klaus and Stuart worked at. He is no nonsense, and if he tells you to do something, you had better do it. He doesn't give people second chances, and if you make a bad impression on him, and you end up on his bad side, he will not give you any chance to redeem yourself at all. Klaus, and Stuart as well, were very fearful of Mr. Weston. They knew that he was a man, that was not easy to talk to, and he had no intentions of being reasonable with you. Talking to him, was like pulling teeth, and Klaus and Stuart, tried their very best, not to get him riled up. As Klaus is scrolling through all of his missed calls, all of a sudden, he gets an incoming call, right at this moment, from Mr. Weston. Klaus was once again feeling stuck to the ground, and frozen in place.

Klaus was very adamant on answering the phone. He didn't know how Mr. Weston was feeling, or what he was going to say. Under normal circumstances, Mr. Weston should be aware that Stuart was killed yesterday, and maybe he will let Klaus off easy, despite the fact he is late for work. But Klaus knew the M.O. of Mr. Weston, and that's not how he operates. He is most definitely, going to be irate and angry at Klaus, and not reasonable at all. Nevertheless, Klaus knew that he had to answer the phone, because he will never know, unless he answers.

"Hello Mr. Weston. This is Klaus. How are you today Sir?"

Mr. Weston, quickly responds back to Klaus, in an unpredictable manner.

"Hey Klaus. I just wanted to say, I'm really sorry about the loss of Stuart. You don't have to show up to the studio today. I could never make you do that. You can take all the time you need, and we'll just air reruns of the show until you return. Don't take too long though. Ha Ha."

Klaus was very shocked, that for the first time ever, Mr. Weston talked to him, with an ounce of respect. He was totally expecting to be berated, and degraded, as he knew how Mr. Weston's entire personality was. It was actually the opposite, and Mr. Weston was very understanding of the situation that happened, and was willing to cut Klaus a break. Klaus can take an indefinite break from the studio, and the show, in order to grieve Stuart's death. Klaus was relieved and happy to receive this news, as he knows deep down, he is not completely ready to return to the show, just quite yet. If Klaus can have just a little bit more time to himself, and to reflect on everything that happened, it would do him justice. Klaus had no idea of how long his break was going to be, but it was going to be as long as he needed it to be, and he is not going to return back to the show, until his mind is fully clear, and he can carry on without Stuart, without any hassle or issues. Feeling very overjoyed that his boss was accepting of the much-needed break, Klaus little by little, was changing his entire mood. Things are going to be different indeed without Stuart, but Klaus has to be able to adjust to that, and understand that now. Radio and broadcasting are something Klaus truly wants to do, and he is very passionate about his calling, and what he feels, he was put on this earth to do.

Klaus responds back to Mr. Weston, in a calm tone.

"Oh yes sir, I will be back. I just need to take some time off, for myself, and after that, I'll be just fine. I am going to miss Stu very much, but it is what it is. Thank you so much sir."

Before the both of them disconnect the call, Mr. Weston responds quickly back to Klaus.

"Oh, and Klaus, if you need me, I'm here. I understand this is a difficult time for you, and I'm here if you need someone to talk to. If you need someone to go for a drink with, if you just want to stop by and just talk, I'm here, and I'm here for support."

Klaus is understanding Mr. Weston's sudden change of heart, and happy that his attitude has changed, to a more friendly and welcoming one. Klaus responds rapidly back to Mr. Weston.

"Yes sir, thank you for that. I need all the help that I can get. I'm struggling, but I'm going to make it. I just need to rectify some things, and I'll be alright. I'm just trying my best to carry on without Stu, but I'm sure he would have wanted me to be happy. Thank you, sir."

Klaus and Mr. Weston then end their phone conversation. Due to the fact Klaus no longer has to work, and has time to himself, he wonders, what will he do now. From his contract, Klaus will get paid leave time off, and that will make the fact he's not working easier. But Klaus also understands, that he will eventually have to get back to work someday soon. Radio is what he has to do, and what he is supposed to do. This break will only be temporary, and it's not going to be permanent. Klaus will get back to his calling, and his profession, but he needs more time to calm himself down. Not a whole lot of time, but just a little bit of time. Now that Klaus has good rapport with his boss Mr. Weston, he knows that on the business side of things, everything is peachy and golden. However, on the personal side of things, Klaus still has bouts, probably every fifteen minutes, of him missing Stuart, and wishing that he could talk to him again, or see him again. His best friend is still no longer here, and Klaus needs to realize that. Not only realize that, but accept, understand, and carry on with his personal life.

After speaking with Mr. Weston on the phone, Klaus continues to scroll through the other missed calls on his phone. He notices that Detective Ross has attempted to call Klaus, several times throughout the day. Klaus wonders if Detective Ross has something important to tell him, so he decides to get back into contact with him right away. Klaus immediately calls Detective Ross back, and he picks up the phone instantly.

"Detective Ross, LAPD, how may I help you please?"

Klaus for a few seconds, becomes anxious, and is unable to get words out. Police can make Klaus nervous, and he feels uneasy talking to them sometimes. Even though he just talked to Detective Ross the day before, and he still felt strange talking to the police. Klaus was still intrigued, as to what Detective Ross wanted, and why he called his phone.

"Ah yes, Detective. My name is Klaus Kleinberg. I spoke with you yesterday evening. I was Stuart Bennington's friend. He was involved with a robbery yesterday. You called me several times today, I overslept, and missed your calls."

The Detective quickly responds back to Klaus, is a calm, professional tone.

"Oh hey, Klaus. Yes. You know what, why don't you come down to the station, as there are a few things we wanted to talk to you about. We are the DTLA precinct, you know how to get here right? If not, we can send an escort out to get you..."

Klaus immediately responds back to the Detective.

"No sir, that's fine. I know exactly how to get there. I am on my way there right now. Thank you so much sir."

Klaus hangs up the phone, and starts to drive out to the police station. It is Friday afternoon, and it is very sunny California weather. It isn't too hot, and there are light clouds in the sky, with a slight breeze. This is a perfect day to go to the beach. However, Klaus cannot go to the beach, he must report to the police station, to see what Detective Ross wishes to tell him. More waves of thoughts rush through Klaus mind, as he is driving to the police station. He wonders what news the police want to tell him. He is sure that it has something to do with the investigation of Stuart's death, and situations surrounding that, but he doesn't know exactly what they wish to tell him. The suspense is really getting to Klaus, and he doesn't know if he will be able to handle the news. Even though the police station is only about a half hour drive from Klaus house, it feels like he has been driving for several hours. It is most likely due to the fact of him being anxious, and not being able to focus his mind right. Klaus does however, finally make it to the police station, and the tense feeling Klaus has, since he left his house, has not gone away. Klaus walks into the police station, and speaks with a female clerk.

"Hello, my name is Klaus Kleinberg, can I speak with Detective Ross please? He is expecting me, and it's really important that I talk to him."

The female clerk looks through her computer, and responds back to Klaus.

"Yes sir, if you can sit down over there, he will be right out. Thank you."

Klaus thanks the clerk, and he takes a seat in the lobby, waiting for Detective Ross to arrive. Five minutes, turn into ten minutes, turn into thirty minutes, which then turn into an hour. Klaus is feeling really puzzled at this point, and wondering what is keeping Detective Ross so long. Klaus is already impatient as is, and feels that he is unable to wait, for much longer. Klaus gets up from where he was seated, and speaks with the female clerk.

"Yes ma'am, I really need to speak with Detective Ross. You told me that he would be right out, and that was an hour ago. Am I going to be able to see him or not?"

The female clerk, then returns an attitude towards Klaus.

"Sir, this is a police station, and we are very busy, and you're not the only priority here. If you want to talk to Detective Ross, you have to wait. If not, you can come back later."

Klaus feeling angry and frustrated, shakes his head at the female clerk, and returns back to his seat. Finally, twenty minutes later, Detective Ross arrives in the lobby for Klaus.

"Oh hey, Klaus. I'm terribly sorry about the wait. Something came up last minute, and I had to deal with that. I appreciate you for staying and waiting. Follow me please."

Klaus shakes Detective Ross hand, and he follows him back, to a conference room at the station. On the way to the room, Klaus notices how dark the hallways in the police station are, and it gives off a very ominous vibe. Klaus sees many officers and detectives, walking through the hallways, in and out of rooms, and it seems like a scene off a television show, or movie. Klaus and Detective Ross finally make it to the conference room, and Detective Ross, shuts and locks the door behind them. Detective Ross has a notepad with him, and a separate folder. He sets everything down on the table, and starts to converse with Klaus.

"Alright, Klaus. We did our investigation. It seems it was unfortunately a random act of violence. Stuart was approached by a man, he was a transient, older Caucasian man. He noticed that Stuart was filming on a street corner, and robbed him of his equipment."

As Detective Ross is explaining the full details as to what happened with Stuart, Klaus then remembers, that sometimes before every show, Stuart liked to go out in the public, and do the same thing that Klaus enjoys doing, and that's filming different scenes in the Los Angeles area. Unfortunately, if you're in the wrong area, at the wrong time, you make yourself a target. Not only for people that do not wished to be filmed on camera, but also people that are thieves, and could steal your camera equipment. Klaus sometimes would worry when Stuart would go out and do this, and was concerned about his safety. But he never thought something like this would happen with Stuart, and that his safety, in regard to when Stuart would do his filming, was alright, and he had nothing at all to worry about.

Detective Ross continues on explaining the events.

"It seems from eyewitness statements, Stuart refused to give the man his equipment, and his wallet. There was some type of scuffle and fight. Stuart was able to overpower the man, but the suspect ended up taking out a handgun, and shooting Stuart in the chest. I'm really sorry."

Now that Klaus knows how exactly everything panned out, it seems in an opposite effect, Klaus who was on his way to acceptance and understanding, is now having a denial and anger stage. Klaus doesn't understand why Stuart didn't give the man his equipment, instead of fighting with him. That doesn't seem like the Stuart he knows. It seemed like an unwise choice, and Klaus feels, that if Stuart just handed the man his property, he would still be here. Klaus feel as though, the camera equipment can be bought again at a later date, however, your life cannot be replaced like that. Klaus is starting to be in disbelief as to how this panned out, and immediately stands up, and walks around the conference room. Klaus is sweating heavily, and his hands and fingers are shaking. He clamps his hands behind his head, looks up at the ceiling, shaking in head at the same time. Klaus then silently responds back to Detective Ross. Klaus is having difficulty thinking once again, and feels that Stuart, made a preventable mistake. Klaus knew that all Stuart had to do, was obey what the robber asked him.

"No way, Stuart would never do such a thing like that. How could he be so careless? I can't believe this. I mean, I knew Stu would do his filming before shows, but I always told him to be careful. I was robbed myself years ago. I just gave them my equipment. Can't believe this."

What Klaus said was correct. A few years ago, Klaus while doing his filming, and was approached by a man, who demanded Klaus hand over his wallet, phone, and his camera equipment. Klaus complied with what the robber wanted, as he felt it wasn't worth it, to fight with the robber. So being that Klaus was in this situation before, he doesn't understand why, Stuart didn't do the same thing. This was something Klaus would forever not know, as Stuart is deceased, and he isn't here to tell his side of the story, and explain why he did what he did. But the eyewitnesses wouldn't lie, and they insist, that Stuart was fighting the robber off. Klaus comes back to reality, and sits down on his seat. Detective Ross, tells Klaus more details of the crime. He shows a picture of the suspect, asking Klaus if he knows who the man is. Klaus has never met the man before. After signing a statement, and giving it to the detective, Klaus is told, that the case is officially closed, and that if he has any further questions, he can contact the police department. Klaus shakes Detective Ross hand once again, and leaves out of the police station. Being that it is only 4 p.m., Klaus decides to make an unpredictable stop at the radio station. Only because it is relatively close by the police station. Klaus decides to do something that nobody else is going to do, and that's pack up Stuart's things, that are located on his desk.

As Klaus is walking in the hallways of the radio station, he then notices, that Stuart never mentioned having any family. He didn't have a partner, didn't have any children. Stuart mentioned his father passed away young, of Lung Cancer, but he mentioned that his mother was still living. This reminded Klaus of his own situation. Both of Klaus parents, are now deceased and gone. Klaus father died of a heart attack when he was 18, and Klaus mother passed away soon after of Breast Cancer. Stuart was the only one there for Klaus, when he had to deal with the death of his parents. Klaus doesn't have any other extended family members. Only an Uncle, he hasn't spoken to in quite some time. So family is something delicate, and complicated for Klaus. But Klaus was more concerned over Stuart, and whether or not, he could get into contact with his family. He was hoping that by going through Stuart's belongings, he would be able to find this information. Although Klaus was also understanding of the possibility, of him not being able to accomplish this at all. His main goal, was to accomplish, clearing out Stuart's office.

Stuart kept his desk very cluttered and messy. He had an array of things all across his desk, from books, magazines, toys and souvenirs, and other knickknacks. In addition to photos of himself and Klaus. Stuart had his degrees from school hung up near his desk, at the studio as well. Stuart kept copies of the films he shot with his camera, on a shelf near his desk too. Klaus made several trips, putting Stuart's belongings in the back of his SUV. Klaus had one final trip to make, putting Stuart's things in his car, when he happened by chance, to come across Mr. Weston, who was walking through the hallways, sipping out of his coffee mug. Shocked to see Klaus at the studio, Mr. Weston responds to him.

"Klaus, what in the hell are you doing here? That was a short break. I didn't expect to see you here. Ha Ha. So, what's going on?"

Klaus who has a box of Stuart's belongings, that he is carrying, initially ignores Mr. Weston, and walks towards the elevator of the building. Klaus then responds back.

"Well Sir, I'm just gathering Stuart's things. I was his best friend, so I think it's only fair that I keep all of his things, and I keep them safe at my house. He is no longer going to be here right? So, I figured I go on ahead and do this, as I feel it's the right thing. You know?"

Mr. Weston nods his head, and responds back to Klaus.

"Alright, alright. I see. That makes perfect sense, and I understand. Oh, Klaus, I almost forgot. I spoke with Stuart's Stepmother. His mother unfortunately passed a couple years ago. I have a feeling he never told you that…"

Klaus sets the box of Stuart's belongings on the ground, touches the elevator button, and responds back to Mr. Weston, in a very confused manner.

"No, I thought his mother was still living. I also had no idea he had a stepmother."

Mr. Weston takes a sip of his coffee, and sharply responds back to Klaus.

"If you allow me to finish Klaus, I wasn't done. So, I was speaking with his Stepmother, and they already have a funeral planned out for him on Monday. I am not even going to ask, if you are going to attend. I already know what the answer is going to be, so yeah."

The elevator door opens, and Klaus picks up the box he was holding. Klaus wouldn't miss Stuart's funeral for the world, and he knew he had to attend. Klaus was satisfied, that Stuart did have extended family, and they were arranging a funeral for him, so his death would be honored officially. Klaus steps into the elevator, and responds back to Mr. Weston.

"Of course, I'll be there. I don't really like funerals, but Stuart was my best friend, and I have to show up for him. It's not going to be easy, but yes, I will be there."

Mr. Weston smiles at Klaus, and Klaus smiles back at him. They both say goodbye to each other, and Klaus returns to his car, with the last box of Stuart's belongings. Klaus reaches his residence, and starts to put Stuart's things, in the corner of his living room. Unsure as to what he is going to do with all of Stuart's stuff, for now, he is placing them in his living room. Immediately after that, Klaus proceeds to his kitchen, to open up his refrigerator. He pulls out a bottle of Bud Light, and sits down on his sofa. Klaus is already feeling nervous about Stuart's funeral. Funerals are not events Klaus enjoys, being that he has had to attend several in his life. Klaus wonders who's going to also be in attendance at the funeral, and if he is going to see Stuart's family, which of whom, he has never met. After he finishes his beer, Klaus heads to his bedroom closet, and pulls out a black suit, that he plans on wearing at the funeral. Klaus also is intending on giving a eulogy to Stuart. He wonders if he will improvise what he is going to say, or write everything down. Klaus gets a piece of notebook paper, and a pen, and begins to jot several things down on the paper, but he crumples up the paper, and throws it away. Klaus decides, that he isn't going to have a scripted and rehearsed eulogy. He will instead say what he has to say from his heart, and he will improvise his eulogy to Stuart. Klaus knew that for the rest of the weekend, his mind was going to be fully on the funeral, and also getting ready and prepared for that.

The funeral was going to be held Monday, at Noon. So, Klaus was slowly anticipating for the event to come. Klaus kept to himself the days leading up to the funeral. Not associating with anyone else, or doing anything else. He was going back and forth, from his usual calm mood, to his more tense, and depressive mood. Especially as the hours to the funeral were approaching closer, Klaus was feeling more anxious of attending. Before he knew it, Monday morning was here, and it was the day of the funeral. Klaus struggled to sleep the night before, and an array of thoughts were in his mind. Klaus started to get ready for the funeral, and began putting his suit on. Klaus didn't necessarily enjoy wearing suits, but he had to make sure he looked respectable and presentable, at Stuart's funeral. He was still optimistic at the people he was probably going meet there. Keep in mind, that Klaus is an introverted person, and during these types of events, he will most likely keep to himself, and not draw much attention to himself. Despite the fact, he will be giving a eulogy, in memoriam of Stuart. Klaus is all set for the funeral, and starts to drive himself there. The funeral is located near Klaus house. So, it is not a long drive at all for him to go through. The weather for today, is very cloudy and overcast. Which gives off a gloomy tone, to the overall atmosphere. Klaus has no issues at all, finding the funeral. It is located outside, with several chairs situated, in front of Stuart's body, which is in a closed casket. Klaus is shocked, when he notices, that there aren't that many people in attendance. The funeral was private, so fans of Stuart, and the show, were not able to attend. Including Klaus, there are seven people present. Klaus knew that Stuart had a haphazard relationship with his family, but had no idea, that the funeral would be this small. Klaus is both equally happy that the funeral is of a smaller capacity, so his social anxiety would be in order; but Klaus is also concerned, that Stuart didn't have that large of a family. Klaus takes a seat in the front row of the funeral. Meanwhile, Stuart's Stepmother Joan, introduces herself to Klaus. Klaus then meets Stuart's Aunts, Uncles, and Cousins, who make up, and consist of the other attendees at the event.

The funeral soon commences, and a pastor starts the proceedings. Klaus is very respectful during the service, and keeps his direction towards Stuart's coffin, located at the center of the funeral. Stuart's family members come up, one by one, and give their words. The pastor then afterwards asks, if there is anyone that wants to make any addition remarks. Klaus then stands up, and directs his way to the front of the funeral. He then starts his eulogy to Stuart.

"Hello. I'm sure some of you have no idea who I am. That's okay. I just wanted to introduce myself. I am Klaus Kleinberg. I was a very good friend to Stuart. I was his business partner. We had a radio show together. He was my best friend. I'm going to miss him."

Stuart's family members, are proud of the eulogy and message that Klaus is giving, and Klaus is doing an outstanding job, of remembering his friend. Even though Klaus is very tense, anxious, and depressed, he carries on with his eulogy, without any issues. Klaus begins to cry at one point in the eulogy. He is locked in his thoughts, and is speechless. At this point. Stuart's stepmother Joan, comes up to Klaus, to console and calm him down. A few minutes later, Klaus is able to carry on with his eulogy. Albeit, still feeling drawn out in his emotions, Klaus manages to power through his feelings, and give Stuart, the proper eulogy at his funeral.

"I'm going to miss Stuart very much. He was a great man, a wonderful person, a talented artist. The man was very kind to others. This is a devastating loss to us all. I love you very much Stuart, and I was so blessed to have you as a friend. I love you Stuart. Goodbye."

Klaus then takes his handkerchief out, and begins to wipe the tears from his face. Klaus steps away from the pulpit at the funeral, and proceeds back to his seat. The funeral lasted for about a half an hour more, with Klaus, and Stuart's family members, mourning his loss. The funeral was then over, and after saying goodbye to Stuart's family, Klaus directs himself straight to his car, and starts to drive home. During the trip home, Klaus is not able to control his emotions, and ends up pulling up to the hiking trail, that he and Stuart went to, when they first met. Still in his suit from the funeral, Klaus, although feeling tired and tuckered out, manages to walk the entire trail. Even though it was an overcast and cloudy day, it was still a beautiful sight, and trail to hike through. During his hike, he is using this as his last goodbye to Stuart. Klaus is feeling very lethargic, but manages to complete the entire hiking trail, knowing that he is making Stuart proud in spirit, and Klaus understands the emotional significance, of this activity. As Klaus makes it to the very end and of the trail, he stops and admires the view, whispering softly.

"Stu, this is for you man. I'm gonna miss you, and love you Stu."

Klaus begins to sob and cry once again, and takes his handkerchief out, to wipe his face. Klaus remains at the top of the trail for several more minutes, before finally walking off. Klaus arrives back at his car, and heads directly back to his house. Back at home, Klaus is once again, fearful of the unknown, and where he will go from here. He understands, that he cannot take his break from the show forever, but he still isn't ready to go back. This continued on for the rest of the week, and for the first time, the "DJ S. and K. show", did not air any live episodes, as Stuart is no longer here, and Klaus, was not mentally ready to return. Klaus remained in his house, and would only leave to go to the supermarket, and he would bring himself right back to his house directly afterwards. Klaus was unhappy, and starting to turn himself into a recluse. He was becoming a hermit, even though it has only been a week, since Stuart's death. It seemed like years to Klaus, and due to his mental strain and turmoil, he was losing all aspects of time.

Klaus has now taken his break for two weeks, and he feels now is the time for him to return, or attempt to. Klaus has had just about enough of being crawled up in his home, away from others. The show must go on, and he must continue the legacy, for himself and Stuart. It is Tuesday, and it's time for start the "DJ S. and K. show", except this time, "DJ S.", is no longer here. It is not going to be the same at all, with Stuart not being there, but Klaus has to carry on with the show. Being a radio host, is Klaus profession, and he can't let setbacks like this happen. Klaus felt his break was long enough, and it's time to simply move on. Klaus begins to get ready for his radio show. For the first time in two weeks, Klaus will be returning to the studio. For the first time ever though, without his partner. It will be a strange adjustment, and maybe an adjustment Klaus may never get used to. Although Klaus will try his best to manage the show without Stuart, it will of course, never be the same. Klaus while driving to the studio, has no idea how he will plan the show without Stuart. The whole point of the show, was that himself and Stuart would have back and forth banter with each other. Klaus feels like it's going to be difficult, managing the show without Stuart, as the both of them looked out for one another. It was a group effort with them. If Stuart was going off, and ranting too much, Klaus would step in, and tell Stuart to calm down. Likewise, and vice versa. If Klaus was going off topic and ranting, Stuart would step in, and remind Klaus to simmer himself down as well. So it was that common bond the both of them had, that will no longer be there. Klaus will be doing the show on his own, and it will be a solo effort. Something that Klaus feels, he is still not ready and prepared for.

However today, is just a trial run. Klaus will see if he is truly ready to do the show without Stuart. If he can make it through today, then Klaus will be able to handle all future shows, in honor of Stuart. The whole point of the show, was for Klaus and Stuart do to his together, but that simply cannot be the case anymore, so Klaus must think of another way and plan to get his ideas and plans across. Klaus has been brainstorming ideas, of how to do the show on his own, but he has yet to come up with a concise game plan. Klaus, while still driving to the studio, ponders whether he should hold auditions to replace Stuart possibly. However not even within ten seconds, Klaus shakes his head at that idea. There is no way that Stuart can be replaced. Even if he manages to find someone with the same rapport and vibe as Stuart, it is not going to be the same, at all. Klaus soon realized, that Stuart cannot be replaced, and that's going to be final. Even though Klaus pondered that this idea may make his job as host easier, by finding another co-host; Klaus is strict on the fact, he doesn't want a replacement for Stuart. Klaus approaches the parking lot of the radio station, and shuts his engine off. The show starts in less than an hour, and Klaus is shaking uncontrollably. He then whispers to himself.

"Stu, I can't do this. No. This was a mistake. I'm going back home."

Klaus then turns his engine back on, but thinks to himself for several seconds. He then understands, that Stuart would not have wanted him to act this way. Klaus then decides, that he's going to at least try, instead of quitting right here. Klaus pulls himself together, and shuts his engine off. He then gathers his things, and walks into the radio station, for the first time in two weeks, to do the very first live episode of "The DJ S. and K. show", without Stuart. Klaus walks to the station, with every step feeling like quicksand. Understanding how heavy and serious everything currently is. From this day forward, Klaus will be doing the show, without Stuart, and it's still not yet something clear and concise to Klaus. It still continues to be something that doesn't feel right, and Klaus feels incomplete. Klaus approaches the door of the studio, and places his hand on the doorknob. Klaus stands there motionless, and thoughtless. With a lot of hesitation, after a minute, Klaus does manage to open the doorknob. Upon seeing Stuart's empty chair, Klaus begins to cry, and feels depressed. Klaus takes a seat at his chair, staring deeply at Stuart's chair. Hoping that through some magic force or energy, Stuart will appear. The whole studio feels weird and strange without Stuart, and Klaus believes Stuart's presence, is still there. Klaus reluctantly begins to set everything up for the show, making sure all the audio issues are corrected, and doing all the pre-show prepping. Klaus is still feeling tense through all of this, and still not having a clue, as to how he's going to plan the show.

Klaus repeatedly feels nervous, over the fact the show will start in less than thirty minutes. Several of their viewers will be listening to the show, and for the first time, Stuart will not be a host of the show. Klaus has to find the correct way, on how to convey this, and get this across to the viewers. He is contemplating on whether or not, to go totally in depth on Stuart's death, or whether he should lightly discuss the matter, and carry on with the show as usual. This is something Klaus is still not sure, as to how he's going to deal with this, but he must figure out the method and fashion he wishes to take soon. As the show is going to start any minute now. With the show now going live in fifteen minutes, Klaus does final touches on getting the show ready. Taking out a notepad, and writing down ideas and topics for the show, and what he plans to discuss. Knowing that the audience are going to call in, and wondering what topic he should have for the night, for callers to discuss and talk about. With ten minutes to go, the pressure is now on, and Klaus is having second thoughts. Although, he feels it's much too late to back out now. He has made it this far, and he must continue on with the show. He can't quit now, as he already has gotten all the equipment ready for the show, and everything is set to go live. Although Klaus is unhappy, and reluctant. He has to go on with the show, and go through with it. He has to look deep into himself, and have strength to carry on. The show will start in five minutes, and Klaus is already fully aware of how awkward the show is going to be, starting the "The DJ S. and K. show", intro, with Stuart not being there. Klaus didn't have the time to edit the intro, so for now, it will stay. Klaus will have to come up with a professional way, to announce that Stuart is not here, and he will never be coming back. Stuart was killed, and Klaus started to realize how unfair everything was, and how things were starting not to make sense anymore.

Two minutes left until the show, and Klaus is still in disbelief and confusion. Every few seconds or so, Klaus goes from feeling confident, to feeling defeated and drowned. Klaus has no idea as to what he's doing, and he is scared that he is going to take it out on the show, and the callers. His performance is going to sink, and Klaus feels if he is going to put on a poor performance, he may as well cancel the show, and quit while he is ahead. In the end, Klaus at least wants to give it a try, and see what happens. If he quits offhand, then he will never know, and forever be doubtful. If he at least tries, and fails, and gives a bad performance, then at least he tried, and he understands, that he is not at all ready to proceed with the show. So, having that mindset, causes Klaus to move on with the show. The keyword, is moving on. Something Stuart wanted Klaus to do, move on. The show is starting in exactly a minute now, as Klaus watches the countdown timer, before things go live. Sweat pouring down his face, unable to move his hands, legs, or entire body. Klaus is overthrown with anxiety, and is feeling nervous. It is now crunch time, and as Klaus watches the timer for the show head to thirty seconds, it seems the entire world stops spinning. Klaus cannot believe he has made it this far, and he is proceeding on with the show, with Stuart not being present and there. All the memories are flashbacking, and fading by. Ten seconds remaining, Klaus feels like a statue, and he can't comprehend or understand anything that is currently happening. Time is still, and he is motionless. Five seconds remaining, feels more like five hours to Klaus. He is still completely zoned out. Klaus needs to clear his mind now, as the show is live, and the theme song, and intro plays. As Klaus hears Stuart's voice, in the intro, he uncontrollably starts and sob, and gets up from his seat. He cries in the corner of the studio for a few seconds, but snaps out of it, once he realizes that the show is live. Klaus wipes off his tears, and makes his way back to his seat. He then starts the show.

"Hello everyone out there. This is the 'DJ S. and K. show'. However, I have to take some time out, and acknowledge, that a key part of our show is no longer here."

Klaus buckles under the pressure, and pauses for a bit, but then composes himself.

"My fellow partner, Stuart, who you all know as 'DJ S.', is no longer with us. I am not going to go into incidentals. I'm sure you are all aware of the full details. I am going to miss him, and if you guys would respectfully allow me to have a moment of silence, I appreciate it."

Klaus shuts off his microphone, with the show still being live. He has a one-minute moment of silence to honor Stuart. The show would be in complete radio silence for a minute. At this time, Klaus continues to wipe sweat and tears from his face, calming himself down. Klaus is so far, doing a remarkable job of continuing the show, without the presence of Stuart. The silent memorial, gives the audience a chance to give honor to Stuart. During this time, Klaus, who still had no plan or outline for the idea of tonight's show, all of a sudden had a bright idea. Klaus decided to make this show, all about grieving. So, the show is still honoring Stuart, but it's also forming as a therapeutic tactic, that the audience and callers can participate in as well. Klaus was glad that he came up with this idea, and began writing down topics on his notepad, to discuss during the show. As the one-minute moment of silence was ending, Klaus turned his microphone back on, and started to announce the topic of the show to the audience.

"Alright, thank you everyone for that. I know you guys are all wishing the show well. I know you all have Stuart in your hearts. But the show must go on. Tonight, I decided in lieu of Stuart, we would have the topic be about grieving."

Klaus stops himself for about ten seconds, and the thought that he's actually doing the show by himself, reaps up again. This causes Klaus to feel scared and pressured, and become silent. Klaus felt that he was doing so well up until this point, but is now having second thoughts. Klaus then feels as though, there is no way he can continue on with the show, and he is fooling himself, if he believes that he can carry on, regardless. Klaus decides to give himself a five-minute break to think about it, and if after five minutes, if he doesn't feel comfortable, he's going to go home, and quit the show. Klaus abruptly speaks into the microphone, to the audience.

"But first, we are going to take a quick commercial break. We will be back shortly, everyone stay tuned. You are listening to the 'DJ S. and K. show.', Keep it locked."

Klaus immediately shuts off his microphone, and covers his hands with his face. He once again erupts in waves of tears and sadness. At this exact moment, Mr. Weston walks into the studio. He hands Klaus a bottle of water, and pats him on the back.

"If you're not ready man, you can go home. I don't think you're ready for this, and it's okay. You can take a longer break. I won't get mad at you. Health before wealth. Okay?"

Klaus nods his head at Mr. Weston, and takes several big swigs of water. Klaus doesn't respond to Mr. Weston, but instead keeps his hands covering his face, looking down, and having his usual defeatist attitude. As the commercials for the show are playing, Klaus still remains silent, with Mr. Weston watching him, with a very concerned look on his face. Klaus then reaches into a drawer of his desk, and takes out a bottle of Tylenol. He takes out two pills from the bottle and swallows them. With the show set to go back from commercial break in less than a minute, Klaus shakes his head, and finally responds to Mr. Weston.

"No, I'm not going home. I'm already here. I'm gonna give them a show of a lifetime, and I'm gonna give them the show that if Stuart were here, he would have wanted."

Mr. Weston nods his head, and pats Klaus on the back. He then walks out of the studio. At this exact moment, the show comes back from commercial break, and after taking the Tylenol, Klaus feels calmer and more collected to continue. Klaus turns his microphone on, clears his throat, and starts to speak to the listening audience.

"Okay, we are back, and as I said before, tonight's topic is grieving. I will ask if you guys could please refrain from directly speaking about Stuart. You guys are more than welcome to give condolences, but tonight's topic is about grieving in general, and not specific to Stuart."

Even though the topic of the show was grieving, Klaus did not want the focus to be totally on Stuart. He wanted this to be a group therapy activity. He was okay with callers indirectly talking about Stuart's loss, but the main objective, was to talk about the caller's experiences with grieving. Klaus felt this might make the situation altogether better. Klaus hoped that he made the topic of the show clear and concise enough, but was afraid that some callers would not fully respect the rules of tonight's show, and make it all about Stuart, when that wasn't necessarily the point, or the objective of the show. Klaus soon turns on the phone line, so listeners and callers can be connected to the show. Klaus was ready to take on the callers for tonight's topic. It was then, that Klaus started to gain his confidence back, and that he could actually truly do the show, on his own. Even though at times, Klaus would look at Stuart's chair, and be upset that he wasn't sitting to his right, Klaus understood that the show only features him now, and he has to be professional to the audience. Klaus continues normally with the show, with the phone lines currently being open. Klaus has a caller ready, and begins to push the button, to connect the first caller to the show, without Stuart there. Klaus, connects the caller, and brings them live onto the show.

"Hello caller, this is DJ K., you're live on the air. What's your opinion on the topic?"

Klaus then listens to what the caller has to say, noting that they are putting on a fake voice. This immediately upsets Klaus, as Klaus and Stuart are prone to getting prank and phony phone calls, but the fact the first caller of the show was a joke caller, didn't sit well with him.

"Ah yes, my name is Mike. My opinion on the topic, is I deal with grieving a lot. When Netflix takes a show off that I really liked, I get really fucking upset and mad. I can't…"

Klaus immediately disconnects the call. Nothing upsets Klaus more than a prank caller to the show, and also a prank caller, that isn't even creative or funny. Klaus mood took an extreme 360, and now his attitude goes back on quitting the show. Even though if Stuart were there, he would have boosted Klaus morale, and gave him support to carry on. The fact Klaus is on his own, dealing with that irritating prank caller, made him very upset and distraught. After disconnecting the caller, Klaus explains his feelings about him to the audience.

"Okay, if you guys are going to be assholes and jerks, don't even bother calling. This is your final warning. If we get another prank call, I'm ending the show, with the quickness. I don't have time for this shit, and you guys are grown ass adults doing this. Y'all need to stop."

To his recollection, this was the first ever time, that Klaus has actually raised his voice, and was stern and direct to the audience. Klaus was afraid that he would perform this way, when the show went live. Klaus didn't like having this tone, but he didn't appreciate, being pranked on his show either. Klaus notices that another caller is on the line, and reluctantly connects them live on the air. He also understands, that if this caller is a troublemaker, he is immediately ending the show.

Klaus then let's the caller know they are on the air, and starts to speak with them.

"Hello caller, you are live on the air. What is your opinion on tonight's grieving topic?"

Once again, a caller putting on an exaggerated voice, decides to prank the program.

"Yeah, my opinion is this show stinks and sucks. You need to bring Stu back, he was the funny one, not you. Oh wait, you can't bring him back. Ha Ha. Sucks to be you buddy. Hey..."

Klaus rapidly disconnects the caller, and slams the telephone switchboard down on the ground, which causes it to unplug. Klaus then snatches his headphones off, and throws them down on the ground as well. Klaus then puts the show on commercial break, and shuts his microphone off. Klaus gave an attempt to resurrect the show, with Stuart's absence. But it isn't working, and Klaus is truly done, and doesn't care anymore at this point. It's not worth continuing the show, and Klaus doesn't want anything to do with this, anymore. He is tired of it all, and is done, and has run out of options. Klaus continues his tantrum for several more seconds, feeling both angry and upset. Klaus starts to throw more equipment in the studio around, ripping up pieces of paper in the process. Klaus has truly lost control of his emotions. Upon hearing the ruckus and commotion, Mr. Weston walks into the room, and comforts Klaus. As Klaus and Mr. Weston are hugging, he softly whispers to Klaus.

"No, it's okay. I understand. You're not ready, you can go home Klaus. I won't be mad. Don't do this. Stuart wouldn't want you acting like this. It's okay. Go home Klaus."

Klaus and Mr. Weston continue to hug, for over a minute. Klaus then goes back to his seat, plugs the telephone switchboard back in, and puts his headphones back on. Klaus takes more giant swigs from his water bottle, and covers his face with his hands, shaking his head. Klaus then starts to laugh to himself, as a coping defense mechanism, to make himself feel better. Klaus then turns his direction towards Mr. Weston, and replies.

"I'll take one more caller. This will be my last ever caller. I swear, this will also be my last show. I'm not gonna let these prankers get to me. I'm not gonna go out like this. If I have to cuss every single one of them out, I will. I'm not gonna do Stuart's legacy like this. Hell no."

Mr. Weston nods his head in agreement, and walks out of the building. During this time, the commercials for the show end, and the show is back live. Klaus plus his microphone back on, and has no filter or control anymore. Klaus has lost his temper, and has had enough. He then starts to speak in the microphone, angrily to the audience.

"Okay, since you guys have jokes tonight, this is the last damn call I'm taking. So, whoever this is, you better be funny, because you're gonna be the main event, and final attraction. If you're not funny, well then, you'll still be the last call. Hello caller, you're live."

A man with a cool voice, then answers back to Klaus.

"Oh hey, yeah man. I want to apologize for all those other assholes pranking you man. I'm sorry about the loss of Stu. I'm a long-time listener of y'all, first time caller though."

Klaus for some reason, develops a safe feeling with this man, and allows him to continue talking. Klaus notices that the man has a "Happy Days", Arthur Fonzarelli voice, and seems drawn and interested to him for some reason. Klaus changes his mood, and responds to him.

"Alright. Yeah, they are just jerking. I'm hoping you're not one too. Thank you for being a long-time listener, and welcome to the show. Also, thanks for the warm wishes about Stu. If you don't mind me asking, may I have your name please?

The caller pauses for several seconds, and also laughs and chuckles to himself, which causes Klaus to feel puzzled. However, the caller does respond back to Klaus with his name.

"Oh um, well DJ K., you can call me The Bus Driver. Yeah, that's what they call me. They call me The Bus Driver. Well, I have other nicknames too, like Dax. But you can call me The Bus Driver, or Mr. Bus Driver. I don't care. Yeah, so that's my name"

Klaus immediately starts to laugh at this man, and for some unexplainable reason, feels entertained by him. Klaus has no idea why this particular caller interests him, but he wants to get to know him more, nevertheless. Klaus quickly responds back to the caller.

"Okay, that's nice. So, why in the hell, do they call you The Bus Driver? Enquiring minds want to know, and I feel that's a rather strange nickname, The Bus Driver. Tell me.

The caller hesitates again for several seconds, laughs to himself once more, and then responds back to Klaus, being honest, with the true intentions of his name.

"Well, because I'm a bus driver. I drive buses all across LA. I drive Metro LA buses, yeah. That's what I do, that's my job. I been listening to your guys show for years, and I listen to you guys every week during my shifts. It gets lonely and boring driving these buses at night."

Klaus feels really immersed with this caller, and is intrigued more and more. Klaus then decides to let the caller continue. Klaus responds back to the bus driver, asking him a question.

"So, I bet you have several stories to tell, being a night shift bus driver and all. Do tell."

The caller yet again laughs at Klaus, and responds.

"You have no idea, I don't mind sharing a few, right now in fact."

Mr. Weston, who is concurrently listening to show, is pleased. He knocks on the door of the studio, smiling, and giving Klaus a thumbs up. He waves his hand for Klaus, to speak with him. Klaus is feeling joyful that Mr. Weston is happy at the quick turn of events for the show, and Klaus also being happy, that he managed to get his mojo back, and get back on track. Klaus then responds back to the caller.

"Mr. Bus Driver, my boss is telling me to put the show on break, do you mind staying on the line for about five minutes. I want to hear those adventures and stories of yours. Please."

The caller yet again laughs and snickers to himself, but rapidly responds to Klaus.

"Yeah, I been listening to this show for years, and this is my first time on air, and getting lucky enough to make it through the lines. I can wait five minutes no problem. Ha Ha. I'm gonna tell you everything. I have stories that are so crazy, your head is gonna spin. I can wait. Ha Ha."

Klaus then happily responds back to the caller, and puts the show on commercial break.

"Alrighty then, we will be right back in about five minutes. We have The Bus Driver here, and he is gonna talk to us, about his adventures, being a nighttime bus driver. Stay tuned, stay put, don't go anywhere. You are listening to the "DJ K. Show". Keep it locked."

Klaus disconnects his microphone, and the commercials start to play. Klaus has fully moved on. He announced the show as the "DJ K. Show", understanding, that the ball is in his court now, and he can move on. Stuart absolutely, would have wanted Klaus to continue on like this, and put on an amazing show. Klaus finally accepts everything, and he is ready to rebuild his life, and turn a new leaf. Mr. Weston, who is still smiling outside the studio door, is continuing to knock for Klaus attention. Klaus responds back to him.

"Alright, alright. I'm coming. What is it?"

Klaus opens the door, and Mr. Weston gives Klaus a strong hug.

"I just wanted to say, I'm proud of you. Welcome back Klaus."

Klaus and Mr. Weston continue to hug, with Klaus having a wide smile on his face.

CHAPTER 3:

THE BUS DRIVER

After getting his motivation back, to resume the show, Klaus feels rejuvenated. He is back to his original self, and he is ready to bring things back to normal. Klaus would have never thought, that it would take this solitary caller, to change his mind. It was something about The Bus Driver, that made Klaus very attached to this man, and more intrigued and willing to hear his story, and where he came from. Klaus boss, Mr. Weston, is also pleased at Klaus attitude, and performance change. He was listening in on the program the entire time, and noticed how Klaus was not dealing with his emotions, in the correct way. However, Mr. Weston is pleased that Klaus managed to turn everything around, and things seem to be looking up.

Klaus is back to his old self, and he's ready to do what he loves doing best. Which is putting on a great radio show, and making sure the show is entertaining, and the audience is entertained. It took some time for Klaus to adapt himself back to who he was before, but he's back now. Nothing is going to stop Klaus, and whatever he wants to achieve and accomplish, he should be able to do it. He is feeling on top of the world, and he is feeling refreshed. Things are most definitely going to be different, but the show is still going to be great. Klaus is no longer feeling trapped like he was before, and is excited, as to what is in store for him next. The sky is the limit, to where he takes his radio show, and he is ready to take on this journey. Klaus, or "DJ K.", as he likes to call himself, is back in town, and he's ready to make up for the time he lost, when he was feeling down. His friend Stuart is gone, and nothing that Klaus, or anyone in the universe can do, can bring Stuart back. What Klaus can do, is carry on the show's legacy, so that Stuart would be proud. Klaus is on cloud nine, and knows that he will succeed.

Klaus continues to hug Mr. Weston, outside the studio. The show is still currently on commercial break, and Klaus is excited to hear the stories that, The Bus Driver caller, has to say. He knows that this caller is a special character, and will make tonight's show exciting. Mr. Weston and Klaus, direct themselves to the break room of the radio station. Mr. Weston pours Klaus a cup of coffee from the coffee machine, and speaks to him.

"See, I told you things were going to be okay. The show is back, and you're back. Here, it looks like you need this. You're gonna need your strength from this caller. I can sense it."

Klaus accepts up the cup of coffee Mr. Weston made for him, and takes several gulps of the coffee. Klaus is jittery and excited, and has a big grin on his face. Klaus takes more gulps of the coffee, and responds to Mr. Weston, in a jubilant way.

"Yeah, I was losing faith for a minute. I was just about to quit, and that caller came through, and changed my mind completely. I want to know everything about him. Yes!"

Mr. Weston pats Klaus on the back, and smiles back at him. Klaus then looks at his watch, and surprised at the time. He takes more sips of his coffee, and responds to Mr. Weston.

"Oh god. I have to get back, the show is gonna be live soon. Now if you excuse me, I have a show to do. Ha Ha."

Mr. Weston smiles at Klaus, and Klaus walks himself back into the studio. He puts his earphones on, turns his microphone on, and begins to start the show.

"Alright everyone, welcome back to 'The DJ K. Show', if you just tuned in, that's okay, you've made it right on time, we have a special caller on the line, called The Bus Driver. I'm just as excited, as you guys are excited. Let's hear his story. Bus Driver, are you there?"

Klaus awaits the caller on the line to respond. Klaus is concerned after the caller does not respond after several seconds. However, the caller does eventually speak.

"Hey, you bet I'm still here. I been a fan of you DJ K., for the longest, and I'm not gonna miss the opportunity to share my story with you. Hell yeah, I'm still on the line. Let's go."

Klaus is happy and elated, that the caller is still connected. Klaus starts to jot down notes on his notebook, of questions that he wishes to ask this man. Klaus seems to forget what he's going to say, if he doesn't write it down. The fact Klaus has an array of topics and questions he wishes to ask this man, makes him more determined to write what he wants to ask him down, so he is able to remember what to ask of the caller. Klaus skims through his notes, and decides what the first question he is going to ask to this caller, is going to be. Klaus clears his throat, takes yet another gulp of his coffee, and starts to ask The Bus Driver, a question.

"Alright sir, if you don't mind me asking, since this is my first-time meeting, well, not meeting you, but talking to you, where did you come from? What was your upbringing like?"

The caller hesitates for several moments. You can hear him audibly coughing, and grumbling to himself. The caller then makes an unrelated statement, before answering.

"Hey, I just wanted y'all to know, I'm actually calling from inside one of the buses. I'm on my last round, and last route before clocking out. When I get to the bus bay, I'll let y'all know. So, before I ask any questions, am I coming in clear?"

Klaus laughs and chuckles to himself for a bit. He is amazed at the caller's personality, and feels extremely safe with him. He knows that he isn't like any caller that has called into the show before. Klaus then reaffirms to the caller, that everyone can hear him fine.

"Yes sir, you're coming in very clear. Now, onto the question I asked please."

The caller yet again hesitates for a bit, but then starts to talk about himself, bluntly.

"Well. For starters, my name is Dan. That's my legal name. I'm not giving y'all my last name, Ha Ha. Well Daniel is my full name. But I just go by Dan. That's the name my parents gave me. I'm thirty-one years old. My Mom is from Mexico, my Dad is from The Netherlands."

Klaus takes a sip of his coffee, and cuts off the caller, quickly responding to him.

"Hey whoa, whoa. So, you're half Mexican, half Dutch? Wow. So, you're a multicultural butterfly like me then? Ha Ha. I'm sure if you're a fan Dan, hey that rhymes, Ha Ha, then you know that I'm Jewish, German, and Lebanese. So, we both come from mixed backgrounds. Ha."

Klaus seems even more connected to the caller now, after only simply learning about his heritage and culture. Likewise, with the caller, Klaus comes from several backgrounds as well. Klaus decides to the press the caller more, strictly on his background, and racial identity.

"So, Dan, or Bus Driver; I don't even know what to call you man. Ha Ha, but do you still keep in contact with your family? Being half Mexican and half Dutch? Let's hear it."

The caller Dan, let's out an audible sigh, but then responds to Klaus.

"Well actually no, I don't. Mom died of Skin Cancer, when I was 10. My dad, he was kinda an asshole, and I didn't talk to him. Well, he died when I was 16 in a car crash."

Klaus is silent for a short while, and feels devastated, upon hearing this news. Before Klaus is able to collect his thoughts and respond, the caller Dan, continues speaking.

"Yeah, that's why I called tonight. I miss my Mom a lot, so I can relate to loss."

Klaus continues to listen to the caller, and is attentive. Klaus has his hand over his mouth, in pure shock, as to how much connection and rapport there is, between himself and this caller. Klaus then responds back to Dan, giving a very heartfelt reply.

"I'm so sorry for your loss Bus Driver Dan. I'm sure your mother is very proud of you. As you know, I lost both of my parents young as well. So yeah, it's tough. Stay strong my brother. So, you don't talk to any of your other family I suppose?"

The caller Dan laughs at Klaus remark, and responds very quickly to him.

"No, I most certainly do not. I don't get along with them. They don't get along with me. I'm originally from Ohio, I moved here to LA, to get the hell away from them. I live alone."

Klaus is learning more and more about this man, as time goes on, and the more questions he asks of him. Klaus is understanding, that this Bus Driver character, is a very unique person. Klaus looks over his notes, and asks The Bus Driver, more personal questions.

"So, Dan, you don't have a Girlfriend or Wife, do you? Do you have any children at all?"

Dan responds to Klaus comment, in a swift and serious tone.

"I don't have a Girlfriend, no. I don't have a Wife either. I am single. I am actually Bisexual, but maybe that's another story for another time. Ha Ha. But I have no kids. Not really the fatherly type, so no. I ain't got no kids. Hey, are you gonna keep asking me stuff like this?"

Klaus then starts to feel nervous and anxious again. Despite the fact Dan, didn't mean any malice or ill intent, with what he said. He was simply being sarcastic. However, Klaus is unable to fully deduce this information, and mistakes the caller for being irritated or angry at him. Klaus then decides to remedy this situation, by quickly responding back.

"Oh no, I don't mean to be like that. I was just curious that's all. Please forgive me. If you want me to stop asking you questions, I will. I didn't mean to be in your business like that."

Directly after, Dan the caller, laughs at Klaus, and informs him that he's not bothered.

"Ha Ha. No, it's okay. DJ K., you know I'm one of your biggest fans. It's alright buddy. I got all night. I'm pulling up to the bus bay right now. Can I call y'all back, after I park the bus?"

Klaus is pleased that Dan is not upset at his questions, and wants to talk to his caller, for as long as possible. Klaus then replies back to Dan.

"Sure, take your time. I'll put you directly back on. In fact, we're actually going to take another break. When we come back, we're gonna hear more of the Bus Driver's stories. Yeah!"

Klaus then disconnects his microphone, takes his headphones off, and gets off his chair. He then dances around the studio, feeling ecstatic. Klaus knows that this is definitely the best show he has had in quite a long time. He has been talking to the Bus Driver caller for nearly twenty minutes, and already wants to know more about him. Klaus can't wait for the break to end, so he can get right back to his conversation with him. Klaus is also aware that Mr. Weston, more than likely is listening in on the program, and is pleased with the proceedings as well. As the commercials continue to play in the background, Klaus takes more gulps of his coffee. Knowing tonight, is the first show in a long time, to where he felt liberated and overjoyed. Eventually, the commercial break ends, and it's time for Klaus to continue the show. Klaus looks over his notes, and takes a gander at his questions, finding one he hasn't asked Dan, The Bus Driver yet. Klaus then puts his headphones on, and plugs his microphone on as well. The show then officially returns from break, and Klaus, asks Dan another question.

"Okay, we are back. We got The Bus Driver, or Bus Driver Dan. I am now about to grill him some more. Ha Ha. I'm gonna ask him another question. Why did you become a bus driver? Like, was that something when you were a little boy, you always wanted to be?"

The caller Dan laughs back at Klaus, and with no hesitation, answers the question.

"Well, when I was a little boy, I wanted to be an astronaut. But I think like every other little boy on the planet wanted to be an astronaut as well. Things didn't pan out like that. I hated school. Hung out with the wrong crowd. Dropped out of college. I just became a bus driver."

Klaus feels that what Dan said wasn't sufficient enough, and wants more information.

"So that's it? There's gotta be more to the story than that? Come on man. Be serious."

Dan the caller coughs and clears his throat. He then elaborates more on his story.

"Like I said earlier, I was living in Ohio. School wasn't my thing. So, I had to do something. I was a bus driver in Ohio. I later transferred here to Los Angeles, so I am now a Bus Driver for LA Metro buses, and I enjoy my job very much, and I love it. So, the rest is history."

Klaus feels more satisfied now, and understands the situation better. Klaus takes a sip of his coffee, looks at his note pad, and asks the bus driver, yet another question.

"So, be honest. What's the craziest thing you witnessed, as a bus driver? I mean, you drive buses at night, so you have to have real spicy stories. We want to know. Don't hold back."

Dan the caller, laughs heavily at Klaus, and pauses himself for a few seconds. He then quickly brings up something unrelated to the topic.

"Hey, I'm in the break room right now. I already parked my bus. Let me get in my car, because I don't want my coworkers to hear me. Y'all hold on for just a bit."

Klaus shakes his head in excitement. He cannot believe that this caller is a real person, and feels like this is yet another prank, but he knows that deep down, it's not. This is an actual genuine caller, and the experiences that he is talking about, are true. Klaus is putting on an amazing and entertaining show, and this is exactly why he got into radio, to entertain others. He knows that callers such as Dan, deserve the spotlight to share their stories. The whole point of Klaus program, was to bring opinions and voices together, in an entertaining way. While Dan is walking to his car, to have the remainder of the conversation in private, Klaus is unsure, as to how long this is going to take. But nevertheless, he speaks to the audience, reassuring them.

"Okay, so hold on everyone. We're gonna get Dan back in a minute. But man, is this guy entertaining or what? Just the stories he has, I'm just amazed at what this guy comes up with. I swear. So, if you guys could please wait for just a short while longer, I appreciate it. Thanks."

A short time later, and Klaus offering banter to the audience meanwhile, Dan, The Bus Driver, does manage to make it to his car, and is able to finally answer the question. Dan this time, is speaking in a more personal and quiet voice.

"Oh man. Well. I don't want to get too graphic. But I've had people do nasty and disgusting things in my bus. Drunk people, homeless people, drug addicted people. People throwing up, people overdosing on drugs on my bus, passengers having sex."

Klaus starts to laugh and giggle to himself, and writes several things down on his notebook. Klaus is treating this as a social experiment, learning more about this Bus Driver character, and the antics and situations he has to go through, and experience, on his daily life. Before Klaus has the chance to respond, the caller Dan, continues on explaining his story.

"So, there's that. I've had both women and men ask me out. I always say no. I'm not really the one to date passengers, and I don't know. I'm not the mushy, romance type. Let's see. Since we're on that topic. I have had stories of drivers dating passengers, dating other drivers..."

This time, Klaus manages to cut Dan The Bus Driver off, responding to him.

"Okay Dan, before I let you continue, I just want to let you know, not to mention any names, alright? That's a rule on this show. So, you can talk about this, but I don't want to get into trouble, so don't mention anyone by name please. Thank you. But keep going please. Ha Ha."

Dan laughs to himself, and ultimately carries on with his story, and his adventures.

"Yeah, I promise not to reveal anyone by name. I wouldn't do that. But yeah, just drama between us drivers, and the drivers dating passengers. I don't get it. It gets awkward. Some of the drivers then date, and sleep around with the coordinators and managers. What the hell? Ha Ha. But I try not to judge, that's them. I don't understand it, but there's a lot of monkey business."

Klaus steadily continues to jot down notes, as Dan continues to talk about his experiences. Klaus then looks at his separate sheet of paper, which has a list of questions, he wanted to ask Dan. He is noticing, that he is running out of questions, and is only down to two more questions left. Klaus asks one of the last questions he has on his list.

"So, uh, Dan. Do you have any friends? You have to have a bunch of friends, I mean, come on. A guy like you, so opinionated, whimsical, full of laughs. What about your friends?"

Dan the caller is silent for about five seconds, but then he reluctantly responds.

"I ain't got no friends. People find me weird sometimes. I mean, I think I'm a pretty good-looking guy, and people know I'm a handsome man. It's my personality, once they get to know me. They think I'm weird. I don't know. DJ K. you should relate, we're metalheads. Ha Ha."

Klaus smiles to himself, as he writes more notes down. It is true that Klaus is a metalhead, and enjoys metal music, and he, along with Stuart, have shared their musical taste on the show before. So, the caller Dan, used this opportunity, to relate himself more to Klaus, as they share the same liking of music. Klaus is also concerned that Dan doesn't have any friends, as he was expecting for him to give a completely different answer. He starts to ponder, about why Dan has trouble making friends, and forming connections with people. Klaus starts to feel that maybe it's something Dan can't control, or some type of quirk, or bad habit that he has. Klaus starts to figure out the best way to bring this up to Dan, and ask him why. Before Klaus can press him more about this, Dan unexpectantly, answers Klaus question for him, in a sense.

"I have a bad temper too. I didn't want y'all to know that. Ever since I was young, I was just a bad kid sometimes. Well, I wasn't a bad kid, just misunderstood. So, I lose my temper quite often, and I think that wrecks a lot of friendships. But I'm working on it. I go to therapy."

Now that Klaus has this information about Dan, things are making more sense. Klaus is soon understanding, that Dan has mood and anger issues, that causes rifts with his daily life. Klaus feels that this doesn't make Dan a bad person though, and he deserves to be treated like everyone else. Klaus continues to listen to Dan explain his woes, and struggles in his life.

"I mean, I don't hate people. I love kids. When I take morning bus shifts, I give the kids a ride to school, and the kids know I'm a nice bus driver. I feel I'm doing a great job, by getting people, where they need to go. But I don't know. I feel like I'm different from other people."

Klaus continues to be drawn by Dan's conversations, and learning about the problems that he faces. Klaus likes that Dan both has a funny side, but also a serious side. Klaus is also becoming unaware, that Dan has been on the show for a long period of time. He feels that possibly the other callers are angry and upset, that they aren't getting a chance to be on the show. But Klaus doesn't necessarily care, and feels like no other caller can match Dan, and can entertain the show as much as he is doing. Although Dan is hogging the show, he is making an entertaining show, that the listeners, and audience, are enjoying and loving. Klaus looks at his sheet of questions that he wishes to ask Dan, and notices, that he is down to his last question. This question, Klaus asks to every caller, before they are disconnected from the show. So, this question isn't exclusive to just Dan, but every caller gets asked this. Klaus and Stuart, would ask the caller, what are their three wishes, or what are three things that they want to change about the world. Klaus was very excited to hear what Dan had to say, and what his response was. Klaus prepares himself to ask Dan, his final question.

"So, Dan, as you know, you're a fan of the show, the last question we ask people, is what are their three wishes, or three things they want to change in the world. What are yours Dan?"

Dan stops for a bit, takes a deep breath, and then softly responds to Klaus question.

"Well, wish number one, is that I would like to find a group of friends. I don't always like feeling lonely, and I would like to make friends. Wish number two, I want a Mustang, Ha Ha. Wish number three, well, I wish for world peace, and peace on earth I guess."

Klaus is now feeling bittersweet, as he knows he has to disconnect the call with Dan, as primarily, this is the last question that they ask each caller, before the call ends. Klaus notices the switchboard is full of other callers, so he understands it's only fair for the other callers to call in, and talk about what is on their mind as well. But Klaus refuses to let Dan go, and wants to talk to him more. Dan simply isn't like other callers, and he has a certain edge to him, that no other caller in the show, had before. Klaus had an idea, that he knew was an amazing and spectacular one. He wanted Dan The Bus Driver, to be temporary co-host for the remainder of the show. Klaus knew he had to get permission of Mr. Weston first, but he was sure that he was going to say yes. This was a perfect plan, and Klaus would not only get to keep speaking with Dan, but in fairness, it allowed the other callers, trying to get through, to be on the air as well. Klaus then at this moment, decides to put the show on commercial break, while he hatches his plan.

"Okay, thank you so much Dan. I must say, you were an amazing caller. You gave us plenty of laughs, and I know the listeners enjoyed hearing from you. I hope you call the show again, and you take care man."

Dan then quickly responds back to Klaus, in a friendly tone.

"Anytime DJ K. Like I said, huge fan of yours, I feel this was a dream come true. I tried for months to get through the lines to call, and finally got lucky tonight. Peace man."

Dan is disconnected from Klaus, but Klaus realizes that he still has Dan's number, which was shown on the switchboard. As soon as the show goes to break, Klaus is going to contact Dan right back, and ask if he would like to be an acting co-host. He was sure that Dan's answer was going to be yes. Not only that, he knew the audience would appreciate this as well. Feeling happy with his plan set, Klaus then prepares to put the show on commercial break.

"Alright, time for another break. Here are some words from our sponsors, and people who paid the radio station to advertise their company, and we will be right back. Keep it locked."

Klaus takes off his headphones, and unplugs his microphone. He then starts to walk out of the studio, to Mr. Weston's office. Klaus then started to get second thoughts, that Mr. Weston, would not allow for Klaus plan to commence. But he was going to ask him anyways. The worst that could happen, is that Mr. Weston could say no, and it's no big deal. Klaus at least tried, and Klaus mindset, and agenda, is now about trying, and taking risks. Now that Stuart is not here anymore, Klaus is starting to become more of a risk tasker, and is being more optimistic with his thoughts. He is no longer keeping his ideas to himself, and wants others, to visualize his vision. Klaus is feeling equally glad, and nervous, while walking to Mr. Weston's office, to discuss what he wishes to do. Klaus opens up the door to Mr. Weston's office. Klaus takes a seat in front of Mr. Weston's desk, and starts to laugh to himself. This infectious laughter causes Mr. Weston to laugh as well, in addition to feeling confused. Klaus now believes how uncanny his idea is, and it's so strange, that he isn't even brave enough to explain it to Mr. Weston. It is only when Klaus realizes, that the show will return from break soon, that he doesn't have much time to tell him. Klaus is able to get himself together, and composes himself, and starts to explain his idea and plan to Mr. Weston.

"Sir, you know that Bus Driver caller, that I just spoke to?"

Mr. Weston nods his head. Klaus then excitedly, continues with what he has to say.

'Sir, let him be my co-host for the rest of the show. Come on. The viewers would love it. This guy is awesome, and I'll perform better too, because I'm used to a partner. Please?"

Mr. Weston then starts to laugh at Klaus, while shaking his head at the same time. Mr. Weston then gets up from his seat, and pats Klaus on the back. He then whispers to him.

"What the hell. Alright. Just this once though. If he pulls any funny business, it's going to be you, and not him. Well, what are you waiting for, the show is going to be live in a minute."

Klaus then springs up from his chair, and sprints out of the room. At the same time, while he's leaving the room, to go back to the studio, Klaus responds back to Mr. Weston.

"Oh, right. Thank you so much Sir. You won't regret this choice. I promise you."

Klaus races back to the studio, with only a few seconds to spare, before the commercial break ends. Klaus then has to quickly figure out a way, how to explain to the audience, that Dan will be a co-host, for tonight. Klaus doesn't know how he's going to do this, but he is sure, that he will think of something, and find the correct way to do it. Klaus puts his headphones on, turns his microphone on, and the show is now back live. Klaus speaks to the audience.

"Hey everyone, welcome back to the show. I have a special announcement to make. Dan The Bus Driver, will be co-host, for the rest of the show. Get this, he doesn't even know it yet. So, we're gonna call him now, and tell him the news. Everyone, wait a minute while I call him."

Klaus laughs to himself, and starts to look at the switchboard history, to find Dan's number. Klaus manages to locate it, and starts to immediately call Dan. Klaus manages to three way the conversation, live to the remote radio feed, so the viewers, in the same time as Dan, can hear the call. The phone rings several times, which causes Klaus to feel nervous. However, Dan eventually picks up the phone, and answers it.

"Hey. DJ K. is that you? What did I do? Did I win a prize or something? Did I get front row, and backstage tickets to the Radiohead concert? I want to know. Ha Ha."

Klaus snickers to himself at Dan's response, and directly responds back to him.

"No Dan, unfortunately, I got no Radiohead tickets. I wish man. But guess what. You did win something else though. You won the privilege of being my co-host for tonight's show. So, what do you say? I mean, if you don't want to, I understand..."

Dan immediately cuts Klaus off, and starts to scream and holler into the phone. Dan is very excited and happy, that Klaus offered to make him co-host. Dan continues to celebrate into the phone for several more seconds. He then calms himself down and responds to Klaus.

"Are you kidding me? I have to be dreaming. Fuck yeah, I'll be your co-host DJ K. Wow, this has gotta be a dream. I always wanted to be a radio host. So now what do I do? Ha Ha."

Klaus in the same instance, gets up from his seat, and dances around the studio. Even though he knew that Dan was going to agree to being co-host, the fact it was confirmed, made Klaus extremely happy. Although it was for tonight only, and just temporary, Klaus had another co-host. No, he wasn't Stuart, but he was Dan The Bus Driver, and Klaus, even though he has only known this man for an hour, it seemed much longer than that. Klaus then jots several more notes down on his notepad, and responds to Dan at the same time.

"Alright buddy. All you have to do, is just be my co-host. We're gonna take some calls, discuss some topics, and you're gonna be my sidekick. Just for tonight though, so don't get too crazy or carried away Dan. Hey, who knows, if you do well tonight, maybe you can come back."

Klaus then started to regret saying that. The plan was that Dan would be temporary co-host, only for tonight's show. However, Klaus slipped up and said that there is probably an opportunity for Dan to co-host again. Klaus didn't think anything of this slip up at the time, but he was worried, that he got carried away, and shouldn't have said that. He doesn't want to make Dan promises, that he doesn't intend on keeping. Nevertheless, Dan was the co-host for the show tonight. Immediately after that, Klaus started taking more calls from listeners, with Dan also chiming in, with his co-host duties. They both were hearing what the opinions of the callers were, offering them advice, and talking through whatever problems or issues they had. Dan was doing a great job as co-host, and himself and Klaus, although they have known each other, only earlier tonight, they were forming a strong connection with each other. Klaus couldn't believe how Dan was able to naturally behave as a co-host, and how well the show was doing, entertainment wise. The other callers had no issue at all, with Dan being co-host. Klaus feels as though, Dan essentially saved the show. Klaus was seconds away from quitting and going home. Dan was the last call he was going to accept, assuming he was a prank caller. It turns out, that he wasn't. The man was the saving grace to the program, and made everything better in the end.

Klaus next goal, was to get to know Dan, outside of the show. As Klaus continued to listen to Dan talk to the callers, writing down notes as well. Klaus had to get to know who Dan was, and form a friendship with him. It was a special feeling he had for him, and it was a feeling Klaus couldn't explain, or describe that well. The show was going to end in about fifteen minutes. Time was definitely zooming by, and the end time slot of the show was soon approaching. Klaus decided to take one final call, and then he was going to end the show. The final caller to the show, ended up being a prank caller. However, Klaus didn't mind, as the way Dan approached and dealt with the prank caller, was fantastic. Klaus wasn't worried at all, and while Dan was heckling the prank caller, Klaus was simply listening, laughing, and shaking his head. Happy that he didn't have to deal with the prank caller himself, and that his co-host Dan, was taking care of everything on his own. The prank caller soon decided to stop, and hung up. That was the final caller of the night, and it was now time for the show to end. Klaus still shocked at how the night went, and how everything was turned completely around. How the start of the show, Klaus almost permanently quit. To how things flipped, and Dan called in, and saved the day. With only a minute left of the show being live, Klaus then speaks to the audience.

"Okay, unfortunately, we are out of time. I want to thank all the callers. We had an amazing show. I know Stu would be so proud. I want to thank my co-host tonight. Mr. Bus Driver, Dan. Thank you so much for your help sir. We will be back tomorrow night, same channel, same time. We will see you then. Alright. Peace, and love everyone. Goodnight."

Klaus then takes off his headphones, disconnects his microphone, and turns the switchboard off. Klaus starts to congratulate himself. He looks up at the ceiling, smiling. He managed to do, what he thought was the impossible. Klaus carried on the show, in Stuart's legacy, and everything turned out great. Not even ten seconds into Klaus silent victory, Mr. Weston, rushes into the radio station. He opens his arms wide, signaling for Klaus to hug him. They both end up hugging, and Mr. Weston softly speaks to Klaus, kissing him on the forehead.

"I don't know how you did it, but you're a genius. You want to know the fun part, is that we are gonna do it all again tomorrow. Yeah baby. Go home, get some rest, see you tomorrow."

Mr. Weston continues to kiss Klaus on the head, also hugging him tightly. They both then say goodnight to each other, and Mr. Weston walks out of the studio. Klaus then noticed, that he wanted to talk to Dan, once more after the show. This time, Klaus calls Dan, from his personal phone. Klaus manages to get his number from the switchboard history. For some reason, Dan is not answering Klaus call. Probably from feeling tired, it didn't occur to Klaus to leave a voicemail or text Dan. Klaus simply decided that he would try to call Dan in the morning. In total disbelief of how the night went, Klaus starts to immediately gather his belongings, and prepares to go home. Upon reaching his residence, Klaus pulls a Bud Light beer out of the refrigerator, and relaxes on his sofa. Still feeling like this is all a dream. His career as a radio host is no longer doomed, and he's no longer scared or anxious, of what the next day brings. Klaus finishes his beer, and makes himself some soup.

After eating his soup, Klaus goes to bed. The very next morning, with it now being 9 a.m., Klaus once again tries to call Dan. It is important for Klaus to get into contact with him. Dan once again does not answer the phone, and Klaus for no apparent reason, decides once again, not to leave a text message or voicemail message. Klaus then starts to feel hungry, and wants to treat himself out to breakfast. He starts to prepare himself to leave home. Then, another strange idea sprouts in Klaus mind; he wonders if he can be able to contact Dan, to go out to breakfast, or possibly lunch with him. Klaus knew this was not going to be possible to accomplish, but Klaus decided to use his reporter skills, to make what seems like an impossible task, possible.

Klaus decided to then drive down to the Los Angeles Metro, Transportation Center. He was going to try to see, when Dan was scheduled to work, and surprise him. Klaus didn't see how this was a bad idea at all. Once at the transportation center, Klaus fibs, that he's a

Metro employee, so he's allowed into the employee area, to take a look at the schedule. Klaus notices there are three different Dan's, that are bus drivers on the schedule. One Dan, clocks in at 10 a.m., another Dan, clocks in for work at 11 a.m., and the third Dan, clocks in at Noon. Klaus decided he would wait and see which bus driver Dan, clocks in, and ask if he's the right Dan. Klaus can also tell by his voice. It's also possible, if Dan was a fan of his as he said, he would also recognize Klaus as well. Klaus knew this was sort of creepy, and possessive, but he didn't care. He was yet again, in his risk-taking mode, and was losing all of his inhibitions. Klaus had no idea how wrong, and incorrect this was, but he simply didn't care. 10 a.m. arrived, and the first bus driver named Dan, clocked in. It was an older bald Caucasian male, and Klaus figured he looked like an older version of himself. He asked the man if he was Dan from the DJ K. show. The man said no.

Klaus waited in the employee area for an hour. The second Dan, that clocked in at 11 a.m., was a handsome, short haired, muscled up, fit man. Klaus wasn't sure if this was the correct Dan, but felt it was possible he was. Klaus asked if he was Dan from the DJ K. show. The man said that he wasn't. Klaus then knew, that the third Dan, had to be the one. Klaus, yet again, waited another hour, and the third Dan clocked in at Noon. This Dan, was a tall, sort of haggard looking man, with short black hair. Klaus went up and spoke to him.

"Hey, are you Dan from last night? It's me DJ K. You have to be the right Dan. I been trying to call you, and you haven't been answering your phone. What's up co-host?"

This man was in fact the correct Dan, but he responded with a shocked reaction. Dan replied to Klaus, in a very hushed and silent, almost embarrassing tone.

"What the hell are you doing? You trying to get me fired? How did you get back here? Why are you here? Man, you're weird. Get the hell away from me, I'm gonna call security."

Klaus immediately felt strange that Dan reacted this way, and tried to calm him down.

"What about last night? I came to ask if you wanted to hang out, and I wanted to offer you a position to be my in-studio host. I thought you were a fan of mine? What happened?"

Dan then loses his temper, and begins to shout at him.

"Leave me the fuck alone! Man, I don't know you! You're getting on my nerves!"

Dan then picks Klaus up by his collar, and grabs him forward. At this same time, the supervisor of the transit agency, Mark Rosewood, notices Dan assaulting Klaus.

"Mendoza, that's it. I said if you had another outburst, I'm canning you. You can go home now, and don't bother coming back. Give me your badge please. You can go now."

Dan looks at Klaus, with a shocked and defeatist look on his face. Dan then snatches his badge from his chest, and throws it on the ground. He then responds to Mr. Rosewood.

"It's fine. I'll be okay. I'll find another better job. I was a good bus driver. If this is how you think of me, then I'll take my services elsewhere. I'm outta here. Goodbye."

Dan then walks out of the transit center. Klaus is feeling speechless, and motionless. He feels overthrown with guilt, that he just managed to get Dan fired from his job. Mr. Roscwood instructs everyone to get back to work, and to never mind what just happened. Klaus immediately runs after Dan, and calls out to him.

"Dan, wait! I'm sorry. Let me explain. I'm so sorry. Let me explain."

Klaus manages to catch up to Dan, and taps him on his back. Dan then punches Klaus on the side of his face. Dan then feels empathetic for what he just did, and is regretful.

"Oh man, shit. I didn't mean to punch you that hard. DJ K. are you alright?"

Klaus manages to compose himself. Although the punch from Dan hurt, Klaus is going to be fine. He laughs to himself, and quickly responds back to Dan.

"Yeah, but I'll feel better if you let me treat you to lunch. Do you forgive me?"

Klaus extends his hand out for Dan to shake. Dan with a smug look on his face, gives eye contact to Klaus, and shakes his hand as well. Dan then rapidly replies.

"Well, I'll forgive you by not only you treating me out to lunch, but you have to make me a permanent host now, because it's because of the shit you pulled, I got fired. It's only fair."

Klaus rubs the back of his head and smiles. He then responds back to Dan.

"Alright, I guess it's fair. I didn't mean to get you fired; I was just trying to surprise you. You can start tonight, I guess. You know we have a show tonight? So congrats, you're my new co-host Dan Mendoza. Now, where do you wanna go out to eat?"

Dan laughs, and agrees to join Klaus for lunch. Klaus and Dan, both decide to go to IHOP. It was a restaurant that Klaus would visit with Stuart, quite often. Once Klaus and Dan ordered their food, they begin to converse with each other. Dan then reveals devastating news.

"DJ K., well, I mean Klaus. Can I call you Klaus now? Ha Ha. Um, can I ask a big favor of you. Can you let me stay with you? I just got fired, and it's all your fault mind you, but I'm behind on my rent, and I was gonna move soon anyways. So, can I stay..."

Klaus immediately cuts Dan off. He responds to him, very angrily.

"Absolutely not. I don't even know you like that. The only person I ever lived with was Stuart, and that was different. Look, I'm sorry I got you fired, but my answer is no."

Dan angrily looks back at Klaus, and fires back at him.

"I can't believe you. I can't believe you at all. So much for being partners, and me being your co-host. I don't even know why I asked you, I don't want to be co-host no more."

Klaus then has a change of heart, and quickly reconsiders, and changes his mind.

"Okay, you can stay with me. But I have house rules, and you have to follow them, and if it doesn't work out, if I ask you to leave, you have to leave. I'm gonna regret this so much."

During this time, the waitress arrives at the table with their food. Dan takes bites of his pancakes, and very excitedly responds back to Klaus.

"This is gonna be fun. I'm roommates with DJ K. I can't believe this shit. Yes!"

Klaus looks down on the ground, covers his face with his hands, and shakes his head. He then starts to eat his meal. When both of the men are finished, Klaus spontaneously visits Dan's apartment, and helps him move his stuff out. Klaus felt this was all too sudden, and happening too fast. It was only yesterday that he met Dan, and they are now going to be living together. Klaus wasn't prepared for any of this. This was both exciting, and worrisome for him. Dan didn't have that much stuff, so the entire process went by quickly. When they both reach Klaus house, Dan is amazed at what he sees, and compliments Klaus residence.

"Wow man, you got a really nice place. So, you live in Redondo Beach? Very nice. Whoa, man you got a view from the beach with that balcony. I can imagine us having some cold ones, and looking at that view, just chilling. The both of us. Man this..."

Klaus immediately stops Dan, and replies back at him, abruptly.

"Yeah, that's not happening. I am allowing you to stay here, and that's it. This is not a party house. This is not a beach house. This is my home, and the rules are, if you dirty something up clean it. Don't touch any of my shit. Your room is the first door on the right."

Dan shakes his head, and laughs at Klaus. Dan then begins to carry his things to his bedroom. Dan then shouts back to Klaus, while he's in the room.

"Hey, there are no sheets on this bed man. Give a guy some bedsheets please. Ha Ha."

Klaus was able to hear Dan, and opens up a cabinet in the hallway. He then enters Dan's bedroom, and throws several sheets at him. Klaus then replies to him.

"Remember, we have a show at seven. So, we will be leaving for the studio later. Don't forget, you're still my co-host, and we have shows, Tuesday, Wednesday, and Thursday."

Dan starts to put the bedsheets on his mattress, and responds smugly to Klaus.

"I didn't forget nothin'. I know we have a show tonight DJ K. I mean, Klaus. I mean Boss. I mean, buddy. Ha Ha. Hey, thanks for helping me out man, I appreciate it."

Klaus, who had his head leaning against the door frame, shakes his head, and walks away. Klaus then walks into his bedroom, and pulls out of picture, of himself and Stuart, that was located on a shelf in his room. Klaus stares at the picture for several minutes, before he begins to cry. Klaus then puts the picture back on the shelf, softly speaking to himself.

"Stu, I know you're proud of me. I got this. I'm doing this for you Stu. I love you Stu."

Klaus then starts to get ready for tonight's show. He directs himself to the living room, and takes out his laptop computer, as well as a note pad. Klaus then starts to list down topics, and questions for the show. Dan, who is still wearing his Bus Driver uniform, walks into the living room, and is curious as to what Klaus is doing.

"Hey man, what you doing? What's all this shit? So, these are the topics that you're going to talk about tonight? So, you just write down notes for all the callers? That's interesting."

Dan picks up Klaus notepad, and Klaus quickly snatches it away from him.

"Hey, hey! What I tell you about touching shit that doesn't belong to you? This is mine; this is not yours. If you want to see it, just ask. Look man, I'm sorry. I'm not used to living with people, and just don't touch my stuff. Okay? Here, you can look at it if you want."

Dan takes the notebook, and raises his eyebrows, shaking his head, and laughing at Klaus in disbelief. Dan sits on the other side of the sofa, reading the notepad. Klaus continues to plan tonight's show on his laptop, while he gets a text message from Mr. Weston. It reads, that he is taking a vacation, and will not be in the studio for several weeks. This excites Klaus, as it saves him the anxiety, of asking Mr. Weston, if Dan can be an in-person co-host. Klaus believes that Mr. Weston would approve anyways, but there is a possibility, that he wouldn't be okay with it. That doesn't matter, as Klaus is off the hook, as Mr. Weston is on vacation anyways. Klaus then starts to be excited for the show, and how viewers will react, when he reveals that Dan is now a in person, co-host. It was only yesterday that he was a caller, and now he's an in-studio co-host. This was seeming like a dream to Klaus, but Klaus already positioned himself too far into this, so there was no going back now. The show was going to start soon, and Klaus would have a partner again. It wasn't Stuart, but it was Dan, or Bus Driver Dan, that Klaus had no idea who he was, until yesterday.

Klaus and Dan get ready for the show, as Dan changes into a more casual outfit. Klaus grabs his car keys, and Dan follows him out of the house. Klaus is trying to hold back his anxiety, and also hold back how crazy this all is. He is actually driving to the studio with Dan, as his partner, and as his co-host. Klaus while driving, couldn't stop thinking about how much of a bonanza this would be. How the ratings for his show would be. Nobody would believe that Dan, who was simply a caller yesterday, is now a co-host, inside the actual studio.

As Klaus is approaching the studio, Dan is amazed at what he is seeing.

"Ah, so this is where the radio station is. This is really top secret. I feel like James Bond, and I'm discovering, the top-secret lair. I'm so excited. We're gonna have a great show."

Klaus laughs and shakes his head. Klaus parks his car, and himself and Dan get out of the vehicle, heading to the radio station. With the show starting in an hour, Klaus tries his best, to give Dan a tour of the studio. Also being frank and direct with him as well.

"Yeah, so this is the studio. I doubt you know what any of these buttons do, so in other words, don't press anything. Keep your paws off all this. Don't touch shit. All you have to do, is talk into this microphone, and if you have any questions, just ask me. Sit back, relax. It's okay."

Dan nods his head, responding to Klaus. Dan continues to walk around the studio, gazing at everything. Dan then takes a seat at Stuart's former chair. For a moment, this causes Klaus to feel a certain way, but Klaus then understands, that Stuart wouldn't mind at all, if Dan sat there. It was only a chair. Klaus was soon over this, and it wasn't any issue anymore. Klaus then starts to prepare more for the show, with Dan asking several questions, about the studio. Klaus is quick to answer any concerns Dan has, to get him more adapted, and used to the studio. With less than thirty minutes to go until show time, Dan starts to feel nervous. Klaus tries his best to make him feel comfortable, and lets him know, that he is going to do fine. All he has to do, is act the same way he acted the night before, when he was a caller. Only this time, he is an in-studio co-host now. Klaus gave Dan a great confidence boost, and he was feeling much better, and ready for the show. Now with just fifteen minutes until the show is on the air, Klaus begins to take his notebook out, and starts to write more notes down. He then speaks to Dan.

"So, buddy. What should tonight's topic be? I was thinking, well since you're here, the topic should be about friendships, and meeting new people. What do you think about that?"

Dan nods his head, and shrugs his shoulders at Klaus. Dan then whispers back to him.

"Yeah, sure. That's fine with me. Whatever you want the topic to be, I'm fine with boss. I'm taking your lead. I'm learning from you. I mean, it's only my second day as host. Ha Ha."

Klaus shakes his head, and laughs at Dan. Klaus is in agreement, that the topic for tonight's show, will be able friendships, and making new connections. So, with the topic of the show already set, the men are ready to go. Five minutes are left until showtime, and Klaus is starting to get his usual, pre show jitters. Maybe it's the fact Dan is now here, that's causing these last-minute nerves for Klaus. Even though the show starts in less than five minutes, Klaus gets up from his seat, and starts to ask Dan a question.

"Hey man. Do you want a cup of coffee? Some snacks? Chips, pretzels, crackers?"

Dan who was looking down at the ground, directs his eye contact to Klaus, and responds.

"Oh well, yeah. I didn't know you guys had coffee and food. Yes, you can get me a cup of coffee, and some snacks. Thanks man. Good looking out."

Klaus nods his head, and quickly directs himself to the break room. He pours himself and Dan, both a cup of coffee, and also grabs a bag of pretzels. He hands Dan his cup of coffee. Dan thanks Klaus, and Klaus takes a sip of his coffee. Dan immediately then starts to gobble down some of the pretzels. There is only a minute left until the show starts, and after having his cup of coffee, Klaus isn't as tense as he was before. Klaus watches the countdown timer, until the show stars, and before he knows it, it is now time for the show.

"Hello everyone. Welcome to the DJ K. Show. I have a surprise for you all. Here, in studio, in person, we have, Bus Driver Dan, well, he's not a Bus Driver anymore, for undisclosed reasons, but that's okay. He's now my in-studio co-host, say hello to the viewers Dan."

Dan laughs to himself for a bit, and introduces himself to the listeners.

"Hey guys. Yup, it's true. You're not hearing things. I'm actually here, in the flesh. I'm DJ K.'s co-host, and I'm here, and we are ready to rock. We're gonna have some fun!"

Klaus smiles to himself, and then starts to speak to the audience.

"Alright, so tonight's show, because in a strange, cosmic turn of events, I have Dan here in studio, tonight's topic, is gonna be about friendships, and making new connections, and meeting new people. I feel this is an interesting topic. Phone lines are open. Let's go."

Dan then starts to speak to the audience, engaging in friendly banter, and quirky jokes. Klaus is amazed at how natural Dan's personality for radio is, and is not worried about him at all. Klaus continues to jot down notes on his notebook, as Dan is talking. Everything at this moment, seemed to be going great. For the first hour of the program, everything is going golden. There aren't any issues, and they are taking several callers, and the show is doing splendid. Klaus and Dan are making a perfect team, and they are putting on a spectacular show. It doesn't seem like there is anything out of place, or anything causing concern. That is, until halfway through the show, a suspicious character, accidentally walks into the studio. As Dan was interacting with a caller, a Caucasian man, who seems to be a janitor, walks into the studio. Klaus speaks out to him, slightly unaware for the moment, that his microphone is live, and the show is live.

"Sir, may I help you with something?"

With the show still being on the air, the man, seems confused and embarrassed. He is carrying a mop bucket. He looks down on the ground, and although the viewers could hear his voice, he very silently responds back to Klaus, as he is walking out of the room with his mop.

"Oh, I'm sorry. I don't know what's wrong with me today. I didn't get much sleep last night. I didn't mean to bother you guys. I'm just the janitor. Sorry about that folks. I'm gone."

Likewise, with the feeling he had with Dan, Klaus, also had some sort of strange attachment with this man as well, and wanted to get to know him more. Klaus gets up from his chair, and with the show still being live, he grabs the janitors mop bucket, shakes his hand also in the process, and responds to him.

"No, don't go. Stay. I knew there were janitors in this building. I have seen several, the many years I worked here, but I don't think I ever came across you. You seem interesting. Here, take a seat. This is my friend Dan. Who are you?"

The janitor shakes Dan's hand, and takes a seat, at a vacant chair next to Klaus, in the studio. The janitor then reluctantly responds to Klaus.

"Well, I'm the Janitor."

Klaus shakes and his head, and laughs. He then jokingly responds back to the janitor.

"I know that. I meant, your name. What's your name, Mr. Janitor?"

The Janitor scratches the back of his head, and responds softly.

"Oh, my name is Ernest. Ernest McDougall. Oops. Did I say my full name? Sorry. Ha Ha."

Klaus shakes his head, and writes more notes down. He then responds to the audience.

"We're gonna take a break folks. We'll be right back, to talk with Ernest the Janitor."

CHAPTER 4:

THE JANITOR

Klaus and Dan, continue to be in amazement, as this individual joins the studio. Klaus at this point, was willing to accept whatever is thrown at him. This man was just an ordinary janitor, but Klaus decided to do something unusual, and invite this man inside of the studio. The Janitor, is a very timid, and shy man. He mostly keeps to himself, and he doesn't bother others. He shows up to do his job, and he leaves. Klaus knew that there were janitors, and custodians that clean the buildings, but he has never in his life seen this man before. He has come across other janitors, but this janitor, seemed to be completely different, compared to the others. The Janitor was doing his daily rounds, when he accidentally opened the wrong door. He meant to go to the room that was adjacent, to the studio that Klaus and Dan are currently in. Little does The Janitor know, that his mistake, would end up being a beneficial one. The Janitor had no idea, that by entering this studio, his entire life was going to change, and new and exciting things were going to happen to him. So, who exactly is this janitor? What is his backstory? Where did he come from? What secrets is he hiding? Well, all of the above questions, Klaus wanted to know for sure. That is exactly why he invited him inside the studio, so he can find out. Klaus figures that this janitor, has a lot to say, and has experienced many things.

The Janitor takes a seat, right next to Klaus, still feeling nervous and out of place. The Janitor, is aware that the building he is in, is a radio station. So, he is not feeling uneasy, over that. However, he was not expecting Klaus to invite him inside the studio tonight. So, suffice to say, the janitor is not prepared, for what is about to happen. The Janitor, continues to gaze around the studio, as if it were a museum. He is in total confusion, as to what is exactly going on, but is willing to go along with everything, for the moment. After gazing around the room for nearly a minute, feeling speechless and lost, the janitor then gets out his seat.

"You know what, I better get back to work. I don't want to bother you two. It was a pleasure meeting you, but I really have to get back to work. Take care."

Klaus then grabs the janitor by his jacket, in which the timid janitor, immediately signals himself back to his seat. At this time, the janitor looks down on the ground, looking uncomfortable. Klaus then quickly ask a question to the janitor.

"Why do you want to leave? Do you know you're live, and thousands of people are listening to you right now on the radio? Why do you want to go back to cleaning? Stay here with us. We can make you a star. We can make you famous. So, why don't you stay then?"

The Janitor still seems very unsure of himself, and once again gazes around the room. This is totally out of his element. The Janitor actually suffers from Obsessive Compulsive Disorder, and he also has a severe case of social anxiety. Klaus and Dan are unaware of this, however. The Janitor doesn't feel happy here, but he is unable, at least at this time, to use his words to convey to Klaus and Dan, that he wishes to leave. The Janitor feels like he is being taken advantage of by the both of them, and he is being held hostage, against his will. The Janitor feels as though, he doesn't have a choice: and he must tag and play along, with whatever Klaus and Dan ask of him to do. The Janitor doesn't have any friends or family, and keeps completely to himself. He is a total recluse, and doesn't rely on anyone else for help. He has been a janitor for five years, however, he has only been a janitor at the radio station, for only a handful of months. Being a janitor, is the only thing he amounts to in his life. Especially, after he dropped out of University, for personal reasons. The Janitor's name is Ernest. He enjoys his job very much, and he feels he is making a difference with what he does. Making sure that buildings are clean, and he feels he has complete independence with his job. The Janitor has never listened to Klaus show ever. He is not one to partake in radio shows, or much entertainment. So he doesn't have a clue, as to how big of a name, Klaus actually is. All the Janitor wants to do, is leave out of the room, and return to work. But it doesn't seem like he is going to be given that opportunity, as Klaus and Dan, seem really attached to this man, and want to know everything, from A, to Z, about this janitor. The janitor then after a short while, speaks.

"So, what did you guys want to know about me? I'm simply a janitor. I'm thirty-one. I don't have anything interesting about me. I don't have any special talents. Can I go now please?"

Klaus as usual, begins to dart down notes in his notebook, and also gives Dan smirks, which Dan smirks at Klaus in return. They are both silently laughing at each other, and through body language, are letting each other know, how they truly feel about the janitor. The Janitor, although he struggles with social cues, and isn't the best at communicating with others, has an idea as to what's going on, and sharply speaks his mind on the current state of affairs.

"Hey, hey. You guys are making fun of me, aren't you? That's not nice. You both are a bunch of cowardly bullies, and I'm leaving for real this time. Good night gentlemen."

The Janitor once again grabs his mob bucket, and starts to direct himself out of the room. He has had enough of this foolishness, and doesn't wish to participate in this, a minute longer. At this point, Klaus knows that this is going to be ratings gold. People that are listening into the show, are loving this completely. He wonders if the viewers think that this is rehearsed and scripted, when in fact, it's not. This Janitor character, is an actual man, that works at the studio; and Klaus feels this is in a way, experimental art. Klaus can't afford to let this man leave, and he needs him in the studio, for as long as possible. This is now the second time the janitor has tried to leave out of the studio. Klaus has a lot of work to do, if he wishes to coax him to stay. As the janitor starts to open the doorknob to return to work, Klaus once again grabs the janitor by his collar, and while the show is still live and direct, Klaus softly speaks to the Janitor.

"No please, don't go. If you stay, you can be co-host. You'll be our guest of honor, and our special host. We're not making fun of you. We actually think you're kinda cool. Please stay."

The Janitor shakes his head, and looks down at the ground. Reluctantly deciding as to whether or not he wants to stay, or if he wants to return back to work. After about ten seconds of the Janitor deciding what he wishes to do, he ultimately decides to stay. He returns to his seat right next to Klaus, and is now obedient. Klaus feels that he yet again worked his magic, to get his way. His plan was to keep the janitor in the studio, for as long as he humanly can, in order for his show to get better ratings. It was almost as if Klaus didn't truly care about what the janitor felt, but more, he was concerned over his show. Klaus was showing more narcissistic traits like that. To where he is only caring about his own wellbeing, and his own agenda, instead of the feelings and thoughts of other people. As the three gentlemen sit in the studio, Dan continues his usual banter to the audience, although both he and Klaus sooner or later, wish to press the janitor. At this point, they are letting him calm down, and are moving onto other topics for the time being. Klaus and the Janitor, listen to Dan silently, as he is explaining current events, and news stories to the audience. Klaus is of course satisfied with this, and takes notes. The show is now turning into a free for all, and Klaus now not only has one partner, but two partners, to help him with the show. He has Dan, and he also has The Janitor. As Dan continues to talk to the audience for a couple more minutes, Klaus takes glances over at the Janitor. At this time, he seems to be calmer and more comfortable, than he was previously. This gives Klaus a confidence boost, as he doesn't want the Janitor, not to feel safe. He wants him to feel welcomed. As Dan finishes speaking to the audience, Klaus then tries again to interview the janitor.

"Okay everyone, so we have an in-studio guest. I swear to god you guys, I didn't make this up. He's not an actor. He's an actual, certified, janitor, that works in the studio. His name is Ernest, as you guys all know. Let's hear his story now. I'm sure you listeners want to know."

The Janitor remains silent, and Klaus and Dan, now start to get discouraged. The Janitor is not budging at all, and although his mood is calmer, he doesn't wish to participate, in what Klaus and Dan are doing. At this point, Klaus gets up from his seat, and walks to the break room, to get the Janitor a cup of coffee, in an attempt, that this will open him up. Klaus signals to Dan, to keep the show going while he is out. Dan then speaks to the janitor.

"So, Ernest. Don't be afraid man, this is a cool place. This is our radio show, and you're safe with us. We're not gonna hurt you. We just want you to have fun. Tell us everything."

Ernest the Janitor, nods his head, and looks down on the ground, still not wishing to fully express himself, quite yet. He feels comfortable with Dan, and thinks of him as a nice guy, but he is still trying to get himself used to the environment, and everything he is being presented with. At this moment, Klaus returns from the break room, and hands Ernest a cup of coffee. Ernest accepts the coffee, and starts to drink it. Ernest then finally speaks.

"Hcy, so is this some type of TV show or something? Is this candid camera? What's going on here? I think I get it now. It took me a while, but this is definitely Candid Camera, right? Ha Ha."

Klaus and Dan yet again, laugh at each other. They aren't laughing to make fun of Ernest, but they are laughing, at how entertaining Ernest is. Ernest finally is aware that they aren't making fun of him, and that they just think of him as quirky and strange. This time, he doesn't take offense to what they are doing. He has gotten used to the fact, it's a habit that Klaus and Dan exchange with each other, when they are pleased with something. Ernest understands, that they aren't directly making fun of him at all. Klaus then responds to the Janitor.

"No this isn't Candid Camera. Not quite. This is my radio show. You already know this building is a radio station, but yeah. This is my studio. This is my partner Dan. We talk about anything and everything. News, politics, entertainment, conspiracies, personal things. Yeah."

Ernest takes a sip of his coffee, and nods his head. He now totally gets the setup, as to what's going on. Once Ernest is able to deduce this, he then begins to laugh hysterically. This in turn, causes Klaus and Dan to laugh in unison with him. Ernest then speaks his mind.

"Ah, I get it. So, this is just talk radio? Ah. I'm so ignorant. So, this is some kinda pirate radio show or something? I got you now. So, you guys want me to be the Janitor character then?"

Klaus continues to jot down notes, and thinks of his show as a three-ring circus now. Things are just going to happen, the way they do. Klaus is willing to accept the unknown, and the strange, and as long as it's entertaining, he doesn't care what happens. As Klaus is continuing to write things down on his notebook, Dan decides to ask Ernest a question.

"So, Ernest, how did you become a janitor? What got you interested in doing janitor stuff? Was it something you woke up one day, and decided to do? I want to know. Tell me..."

Ernest takes a sip of his coffee, and shakes his head at Dan. He then responds.

"I don't know. I'm not good at anything else. I'm not good at anything really."

Dan seems confused and puzzled by what Ernest said, and asks him to elaborate more.

"Ah come on, you have to be good at something man. You have hobbies, right? You like movies, and music, and books, and sports, right? So, you became a janitor because, you aren't good at anything else? What kind of shit is that? I don't believe you. Tell the truth."

Ernest then starts to show an unhappy look on his face, and his entire body becomes tense. Sweating profusely, Ernest did not like the tone Dan gave to him. Ernest is becoming slightly agitated and angry over what Dan said. Ernest then takes Klaus water bottle, opens it, and splashes a great amount in Dan's face, getting him slightly wet. Ernest then starts to erupt with heavy laughter, with Klaus finding this hilarious as well. As Klaus is writing the proceedings of the show down in his notepad, Ernest then kiddingly responds back to Dan.

"Well, I'm good at that aren't I? No seriously. I'm not that book smart, I look kinda dorky, I mean, I have tv shows and movies I like. They are kinda old. I don't like anything new. I don't know. I'm weird, so I am a janitor. I clean buildings. Leave me the fuck alone. Ha Ha".

Ernest then starts to laugh to himself, as he takes another sip of his coffee. Klaus hands Dan some paper towels, so he can dry himself off, at the same time laughing at everything that is happening. Dan did not find this hilarious, and responds directly to Ernest.

"I'm gonna get you back for that. You like to throw water on people I see. Okay Mr. Janitor, I'm gonna get you back. I'm not gonna tell you when, but I am. You better watch out."

Klaus shakes his head, and chuckles to himself. Klaus is sure, that the janitor has many things to reveal and talk about. Klaus knows, that it's his job to get Ernest to speak about them, and tell everything about his life to the audience, so the show is entertaining and fun. Although the silliness and foolishness between them is nice, Klaus wants to quickly get down to business, and interview the janitor, more about his life. Klaus writes more notes down, and then he very quickly decides, to asks Ernest a question about his profession.

"What's the craziest thing you witnessed while being a janitor. You don't have to censor yourself, like our show is all about open talk, and being real. So, we want to hear the really juicy and weird stuff. Don't keep anything to yourself. We want to hear everything."

Ernest raises his eyebrows at Klaus, and begins to laugh. He takes yet another sip of his coffee. Ernest then takes his jacket off, and rolls down the top corner of his collar. In the process, he reveals a four-inch scar, that is horizontally across the right side of his chest. Ernest speaks.

"Well, for starters, this scar happened a couple years ago. I was a janitor at a bakery. I wasn't watching where I was going, and I was sweeping near this lift, that the bakers use to go up and down floors. I fell right through the shaft, about a good three stories. Yeah. But it's not so bad. I got this really cool, and sexy scar as a souvenir though. Ha Ha."

Klaus and Dan, yet again give eye contact to each other, and can't believe that all of this is real. But it is. After Ernest revealed his scar, Dan then asks Ernest a question.

"That is pretty gnarly, I must admit. So, you have that scar from when you fell? What about, like more disgusting stuff, we want to hear that. Like any body parts you find..."

Klaus then grabs Dan by the arm, and then speaks politely.

"I'm sorry, but Dan, that was really messed up. There is a way to ask a question like that, and doing it like that, was not it. You have to be professional and polite. He's not gonna..."

Ernest then quickly responds to Dan's question, never minding the fact, that Dan did not ask the question in the most respectful of ways.

"As a matter of fact, yes. This happened at the same bakery I fell at. This happened, well, actually like a couple weeks after I fell. I don't know if this bakery was haunted or what. But I was doing my rounds, and I just happened to find a toe. Yeah, someone's toe, on the ground."

Klaus and Dan snicker to themselves for a bit, which causes Ernest to respond.

"That wasn't supposed to be funny, so I don't know why you guys laughed. It was slightly irritating, because when something like that happens, I have to call the police, and biohazard has to come out, as I'm not necessarily trained to clean stuff like that."

Klaus is more and more intrigued about Ernest stories as a janitor, making sure he jots everything down for record, and is completely attentive to what Ernest is saying. Dan is even more intrigued, and feels more attached to Ernest. He then asks Ernest a question.

"So, who's toe was it? Did they ever find out where it came from? I mean, it's out of the ordinary, that a random toe will just appear on the ground, like that."

Ernest takes a big giant gulp of his coffee. He looks directly towards the ground. After several seconds of keeping himself silent, Ernest does eventually respond to Dan's question.

"Well, it belonged to one of the supervisors. He was injured the week before, and went to the hospital and they never did find the toe. I managed to find it, strangely enough. Unfortunately, it was too late to attach it back to his foot, but toe mystery solved. Ha Ha."

Klaus laughs at Ernest, and Dan is starting to feel confused. Ernest explained that the toe incident wasn't funny, but he just laughed at retelling the story. Dan doesn't feel this is fair at all, and decides to let Ernest know, exactly how he feels about this.

"Wait a minute, you told us that the toe thing wasn't funny, and scolded us for laughing, yet you just laughed right now. Don't be a hypocrite like that man. It's only fair. If you're gonna judge us for something, then you have to follow the same rules as well then. It's only fair."

Ernest then laughs at Dan, and has another sip of his coffee. Ernest then responds.

"Okay whatever. I told you guys it wasn't funny, and I laughed anyways. Lighten up. It's no big deal. I mean, he found it funny. Right big guy? Hey, what's your name again? I'm sorry."

Klaus writes more notes down on his notebook, and shakes his head. He then speaks.

"My name is Klaus. Or you can call me DJ K. Whatever you prefer. That gentleman over there, he can be a jerk sometimes, but he's cool, that's my co-host Dan."

Ernest nods his head, and continues to look around the studio more. Ernest then replies.

"Okay, I see. I won't forget this time. I'm terrible with names, so you have to forgive me. So, you're Klaus, and he's Dan? Yeah. It's etched into my memory now. So, you guys are the hosts of this wacky show I see. Wow, you guys are lucky. I have to clean, and you guys do this."

Klaus and Dan, yet again look at each other, silently laughing, which causes Ernest to laugh along with them. Klaus, likewise with Dan, was writing a list of questions that he wished to ask Ernest. He then comes across a question, he has yet to ask of him. Klaus speaks to Ernest.

"Ernest, you don't have any family, do you? No partner, no friends? You're just by yourself? I mean it seems like you are, but I wanted to ask and make sure. So, am I correct?"

For the first time, Ernest's mood completely changes to a more depressed and guilty mood. Ernest is silent for what seems like almost a minute, and Klaus and Dan are respectful enough, to let Ernest talk, whenever he is ready to do so. After some time, Ernest speaks.

"No, I don't have anyone. People don't like me. You guys already knew I don't have anyone. I never knew who my Dad was. My mom died when I was 10. She had cancer. I don't know where the rest of my family is. I doubt they care about me anyways."

Ernest then starts to sob, and tears are flowing down his face. Klaus hands Ernest some tissue to wipe his face, and pats him on the back. As Klaus is trying to console Ernest, Dan starts to feel empathetic to Ernest, and starts to cheer him up, by offering words of encouragement.

"It's okay man. We're losers as well. We don't have any support either. We'll be your friends. You can be our janitor friend. You're one of us now. Don't feel that way man."

Klaus continues to pat Ernest on the back, consoling him. Klaus speaks to Ernest.

"Ernest, whenever you want to come see us when we're doing a show, you're welcome to come in here man. I mean, I hope you don't get in trouble with your janitor job. But you know what I'm trying to say. You're welcome here anytime you want. So, cheer up buddy."

Ernest starts to smile, and changes his mood yet again. He then responds to Klaus.

"Hey, so that means I can be a host now? You guys said I'm welcome here whenever. So, I don't have to be a damn janitor anymore? I can be a famous radio host? Wow, thanks guys."

Klaus and Dan look at each other with shocked faces. Klaus did not mean at all, that Ernest could be a co-host. His intentions were to let Ernest know, that he's welcome here, whenever he wants a safe place to talk. Klaus did not mean at all, that Ernest can quit his job as janitor, and permanently be a host. That wasn't at all what the plan was, or what Klaus was trying to convey. Klaus feels he already has a partnership with Dan, and he doesn't wish to have another one. Dan also more or less, essentially, feels the same way. He doesn't necessarily want Ernest to be host either. Their agenda was never to make Ernest a host, but they wanted him to feel safe and secure. Klaus realizes that he cannot on air reject Ernest like that, with the viewers listening, letting him know that he cannot be a host. However, Klaus also probably feels, that maybe he should take another chance. Rather, he's been taking several chances as of late, so why not take another one. He already decided to make Dan a host, so why not make Ernest a host as well. Three hosts, are better than two, or so Klaus thought. In any case, it was time for yet another commercial break. Klaus knew that during the commercial break, he would make his mind up, as to what he really, truly wishes to do. Klaus speaks to the audience.

"Alright, so we have to take a quick break. Word from our sponsors, blah, blah, blah. You guys already know the drill. But we will be back soon. So please keep it locked."

Klaus takes off his headphones, and shuts off his, Dan's and Ernest's microphone. Klaus then covers his hands with his face, and leans back in his chair. He shakes his head and laughs. Klaus then jots more things down on his notebook, and says something to Dan.

"So, he wants to be co-host. What do you say? Shall we let him? I mean, he seems cool. How do you feel about it? I mean, I was against it originally, but now, I don't know."

Dan looks at Ernest, and shakes his head. He then focuses his attention on Klaus. Dan takes big gulps of his coffee, and while looking at Ernest, responds to Klaus.

"Damn, alright. What the hell, why not. He's one of us now. Damn. I was just getting used to it being us, now we have him. But he seems cool."

Ernest smiles at both Klaus and Dan. Ernest then gets up from his seat, and gives both Klaus and Dan giant hugs. Ernest returns to his seat, has another sip of his coffee, and responds.

"Oh man, thank you both so much. I no longer have to be a janitor. I no longer have to clean after people. This is the life. I'm gonna be a radio host. I'm so excited. Thank you."

Dan then scoffs to himself, and jokingly speaks back to Ernest.

"Alright, but now you have to pass the initiation to get accepted into the group. If you don't pass, then you can't join us. Those are the rules. So, are you prepared for that?"

Dan then starts to laugh heavily. Klaus smacks Dan across the side of his head, and gives him a disappointed look. Klaus then directs his attention to Ernest, speaking to him softly.

"He's joking, there is no initiation. We wouldn't do some shit like that. You're one of us now. You don't have to do any type of stunt, or anything. You just have to be an amazing host."

Ernest is happy that Dan was only kidding and joking. The show is set to return back from break in a minute, and Klaus puts his headphones back on. The show then returns, and once back from break, Klaus decides to give an announcement, to the listening audience.

"Okay everyone. I can't believe this. Things are happening very fast around here. Like a whirlwind. But I like to introduce you to our new co-host. Ernest the janitor, or rather, Ernest the former janitor, now co-host to the DJ K. show. Everyone be nice to him, he's new. Ha Ha."

Klaus pats Ernest on the back, and Klaus runs his fingers through Ernest hair. Ernest is glad that he is a host of the show, and for once in his life, feels included in something. Throughout his entire life, Ernest always felt excluded from everything. People never gave him a chance, and people only thought of him as a weird janitor. Well, that all changed today. Ernest has a new group of friends, and he is thankful, that he now has a group that appreciates him. After Klaus introduced Ernest as the new co-host to the show, Ernest speaks to the audience.

"Thank you. I am very blessed and thankful to be a host. I'll do a great job. Thanks."

Klaus and Dan laugh at Ernest, and officially consider him part of the team now. Ernest, in only this short time, managed to fit right into the show. The rest of the show continued, without any issues or problems. Ernest was answering callers fine. He was dealing with the usual ignorant prank calls, well. Klaus was accepting, of how everything was going. Earlier this week, Klaus was still grieving over the loss of his friend, and he didn't know if he was strong enough, to return to the show on his own. After on the brink of quitting for good, he managed to find Dan, which completely changed Klaus entire plans. Now that Klaus has yet another co-host with Ernest, it seems Klaus is out of excuses. Everything is coming into fruition for him, and Klaus can achieve anything that he wants, and can virtually do anything that he wants. He has a good team, with both Dan and Ernest, and there is no room to blame anything, or to turn to failure. Klaus has regained his energy, and can do his show, without any issues. There shouldn't be any complaints or worries. He needs to do his show, in memory of Stuart as well. Although the foundation of the show, was between himself and Stuart, Klaus respectfully has moved on with the show, and has a new direction for it. He has now met new people, and is finding new paths and horizons, with his work ethic. Klaus is confident, that whatever happens with the show at this point, will be beneficial and positive, and he also has a safe team working with him. Klaus isn't scared as to what tomorrow will bring, and it's all fine by him.

It is now time for the show to end again. The time slot is now over. For now, two shows in a row, a series of instant, and fast events have happened for Klaus. Yesterday, meeting Dan. Today, meeting Ernest. Klaus doesn't seem phased by anything anymore, and probably finds everything he's being encountered with, fun and exciting. Klaus then speaks to the audience.

"Oh damn, it can't be. Is it time for the show to end again? Unfortunately, yes. Don't worry. We will be back tomorrow. Same time, same channel. Take care. Peace everyone."

Klaus takes off his headphones, and shuts his microphone off. He also shuts the telephone switchboard off, officially closing the show. Klaus gives Dan a fist bump, and shakes Ernest hand. Klaus yet again completed a show, without any hassle. Klaus is finally getting used to how things are supposed to run on his show. Although the setup and format are different, and there are new faces and personalities along the way, that doesn't matter. It is still a show that Klaus is proud to have, and a show that Klaus is happy to have his name next to. A show that he knows is entertaining, and that people are enjoying and loving. Klaus starts to gather his things, and Dan does as well. During this time, Ernest speaks to the both of them.

"Okay guys. I'll see you tomorrow then. I gotta go, or they are gonna close…, I mean, I gotta put my supplies up, and I'll see you guys tomorrow. Okay. Nice meeting you guys. Bye."

Ernest then races out of the studio. This was very awkward and strange, the way Ernest was acting and behaving. Klaus and Dan look at each other, shocked. Klaus is aware that Ernest is hiding something. He doesn't know what it is exactly, but he knows it's something drastic, that Ernest doesn't want to reveal. Klaus is the kind of person, that feels it's his business to pry on others, and he can't let things go. Ordinarily, Klaus should mind his own business, and leave Ernest alone, but this time, he can't do that. Ernest is now a co-host, and he feels it's his job to find out what Ernest is lying about, and hiding. Klaus gathers all of his belongings, and looks at Dan for several seconds. Klaus then looks down on the ground, and softly speaks to Dan.

"He's lying about something. I don't know what, well, I have a slight idea as to what, but I'm not completely sure. But I do know that somethings up. Come on, follow me."

Dan quickly nods his head, and obeys Klaus. Klaus and Dan leave out of the studio. Klaus then patrols the building, on the hunt for Ernest. Klaus cannot find him anywhere. Klaus and Dan search floor, after floor, on the hunt for Ernest, coming up with nothing. Klaus is making it his mission to find where Ernest is, and he has a feeling, that he's still nearby. Klaus and Dan, then decide to leave out of the radio station. Klaus and Dan search outside of the building, outside the courtyard, and Klaus checks all the bus stops surrounding the station. There is no sign of Ernest. Klaus cannot believe that Ernest managed to disappear that fast, and as sudden as he did. Klaus then wondered, maybe he has to accept, that he is not going to locate Ernest, and he needs to let this go. Klaus wanted to try, just a little bit longer, to search and find where Ernest happened to go. Klaus and Dan search the opposite side of the area, and they notice a man, resembling Ernest, walking away from them. Klaus managed to luck out finding Ernest, and himself and Dan, race to catch up to him. It seems that Ernest is walking extremely fast, and Klaus and Dan, despite the fact they are running, are finding it difficult to keep up with him. Klaus felt pleased with himself, that he managed to locate Ernest, so he could talk to him. Although, the task of getting close to him, is not easy. Klaus and Dan are running even faster up to Ernest, and they are not going to give up. Dan manages to race ahead of Klaus, as Klaus starts to get fatigued from running. Dan is very close within Ernest, and finally managed to catch up to him. Upon reaching Ernest, Dan, heavily breathing and panting from running, grabs Ernest by his jacket, and speaks to him in a direct, friendly manner.

"Hey, easy, it's okay. Why you race away like that so fast? What's going on man?"

Ernest looks at Dan with an unhappy look, and remains silent. Ernest doesn't really have any intentions, on telling Dan anything. Ernest doesn't feel that it's any of Dan's business, and he feels that he doesn't deserve to explain anything to him either. Ernest feels scared, and uncomfortable, that Klaus and Dan were following him the entire time. By this time, Klaus has managed to catch up to Dan and Ernest, and slightly catching his breath, speaks to Ernest.

"Hey man, we were just concerned, because you zoomed off like that. Where are you going? We can give you a ride home. We're partners now. You don't do stuff like that. We were nice to you the entire night, then you just up and leave like that? Come on, that's not right man."

Ernest, who is still feeling unsure and uncomfortable, looks around the street. While he's looking out in the distance, Ernest reluctantly responds back to Klaus and Dan.

"Uh, that's okay you guys. I am going to catch the bus home. Thank you guys though."

Dan shakes his head, and laughs at Ernest. He is fully aware he is lying. Dan responds.

"No, you're not. The bus that runs in this zone is the 45 bus, and the last route for that bus, stopped running at 9 p.m. You would have to catch the Figueroa, 76 bus, but that's at least an hour walk from here. Stop lying. What's going on? You're hiding something from us man."

Ernest then begins to cry, and tosses his backpack on the sidewalk. He then starts to fall himself into Dan's chest, while still crying. Klaus is feeling concerned over this, and Dan is confused as to why Ernest is acting this way, but is consoling him. Ernest responds.

"I'm homeless. Alright? Okay? You guys happy now? I was trying to get to the shelter before they close in like 15 minutes. The janitor job at the station pays poorly. I had other janitor gigs with good pay. I could pay rent fine. Not anymore. Now leave me the fuck alone you guys."

Ernest then grabs his backpack off the ground, and continues to walk in the direction he was originally going. Dan then once again grabs Ernest by the collar, and speaks to him.

"Hey, it's okay. You can stay with us. Klaus has plenty of room, and I'm sure he wouldn't let a co-host of his, stay on the street. Hey, remember, we got to stick together now, as we're partners, and we have to look out for each other. We love you man. It's okay."

Dan then kisses Ernest on his forehead, and Dan and Ernest hug. Klaus at this point shakes his head and laughs to himself. Part of Klaus wants to speak up and say, that Ernest staying with him, is not feasible. He only met Ernest today, and this doesn't make any sense. But Klaus is having the silent approach. Klaus is in risk taking mode, and he's willing to let things happen, the way they happen. Dan, although he is speaking for Klaus, and it wasn't Dan's decision at all to make, as to whether Ernest can be allowed to say, Klaus knows he is right. If Ernest is going to be co-host, Klaus has to look out for him, and help him. Ernest lives on the street, and is homeless. Ernest's janitor job wasn't paying that well, and he was struggling to make ends meet, and it was tough for him. Klaus has to do the right thing, and look out for his new work partner. The three men then start to walk back to the studio, with Ernest, walking with Dan, with his head tucked under Dan's arm, and Klaus walking behind them, shaking his head, with his hands in his pockets. Klaus has had a long day yesterday, and he has had yet another long day today, and things are happening very rapidly, and strangely. The men, finally make it to the studio, and Ernest stops to tell Klaus and Dan something.

"I have to get my things from my work closet. I don't have a lot of stuff. It's okay."

Klaus and Dan understand, and allow Ernest to get all his belongings. Klaus and Dan, also help Ernest put his things into the back of Klaus SUV. Once they are done with that, Klaus, starts his car, with Dan sitting in the passenger seat, and Ernest sitting in the back seat. During the car ride, Ernest starts to cry, and Klaus can see through the rear-view mirror, that Ernest is unhappy. Klaus can sense, that things have been rough for Ernest, and he is possibly not used to this type of kindness. Not liking seeing Ernest in this condition, Klaus decides to do something, that will possibly cheer him up. Or at least Klaus was hoping it would. Once he reaches a stoplight, Klaus then decides to speak to both Dan and Ernest.

"Hey guys. I was just wondering. I'm sure you guys are hungry, as I'm hungry as well. Why don't we go to Denny's? I mean. That's if you guys want to."

As soon as Klaus mentioned this, Ernest attitude abruptly changed, from feeling upset and depressed, to feeling very pleased and happy. Ernest cheerfully responds to Klaus.

"Yeah, that sounds fun. I am kinda hungry after all. I don't know the last time I actually went to a restaurant. This is gonna be fun. Yeah, count me in."

Klaus looks over at Dan, and they both smile at each other. Klaus then heads directly to Denny's, so himself, Dan and Ernest can eat. The Denny's location that Klaus was going to visit, was the one that was closest to his house in the Redondo Beach area. That meant, the restaurant was still quite a drive, from where they were currently at in Downtown Los Angeles, where the radio station is located. During the car ride, Dan starts to play music through Bluetooth, on Klaus stereo. Dan is miming and dancing along the music that is playing. The music is a mix of Pearl Jam, Sublime, and Nirvana. All bands which Klaus likes as well. Due to the fact that Klaus and Dan had identical musical tastes, he didn't mind the type of music that Dan was playing.

Otherwise, he may have been slightly disturbed at the music. Being that it is late Wednesday night, after 11pm, there are not many cars on the road, so the trip to the restaurant, was going to be a quick one. If this were earlier in the day, traffic may have been more hectic, and heavy. However, during this time, traffic was lighter and calmer. During the car trip, Klaus and Dan exchange in small talk. They talk about television shows and movies that they have watched, and also other things related in the news, and other current events. Ernest remains silent in the back seat, not engaging in the conversation that Klaus and Ernest are having. As Klaus is getting closer to the restaurant, the hungrier, and ravenous that he becomes. Klaus enjoys food quite a bit, and has a big appetite. It was only earlier in the day, that himself and Dan had breakfast, so now once again, Klaus is hungry. Klaus will never pass up an opportunity to eat, and he is a guy that likes his food, and he enjoys eating.

Klaus finally manages to reach the Denny's restaurant, and he parks his SUV. Himself, Dan, and Ernest get out of the car, and direct themselves to the restaurant. Denny's, is a diner style restaurant, which usually serves American comfort food. Such as burgers, chicken fingers, steak, they also have a breakfast menu, which you can order any time of the day. The three men make their way inside of the restaurant, and a waitress, has them seated at a table in the back of the restaurant. The interior of the restaurant isn't anything special. Nothing too fancy, or anything that noteworthy to mention. The restaurant is simply average, and there are no extreme frills, or incidentals about it. The waitress has them situated at a booth table. Klaus and Dan end up sitting at the booth, next to each other, as Ernest sits alone on the other side of the booth. As the men are seated, the waitress hands them menus. As they are glancing at the menu, Ernest can't decide what he wants to eat. Ernest doesn't go to restaurants, and this is the first restaurant that he has been to, in quite a long time. Dan doesn't notice that Ernest seems out of his comfort zone at the restaurant, but Klaus quickly is able to deduce, that this is probably something new for Ernest. Klaus understands, that it's rare for someone to treat Ernest out for a meal, and that this is a blind, and new experience for him.

Klaus wanting to help, in an effort to show his kindness, softly speaks to Ernest.

"Hey man, you feeling alright? Do you want me to recommend something for you?"

Ernest looks up from his menu, and focuses his attention to Klaus. He smiles at him, and shakes his head. Ernest then directly goes back to leering over the menu. Klaus laughs to himself, and shakes his head, and looks over at his menu as well. It seems as though Dan has already decided what he wanted to eat, as he quickly set his menu off to the side, and starts to stare at the basketball game playing on the TV, near the bar. As he's watching the basketball game, Dan starts to shout out to the television screen, feeling very intrigued in the game.

"Yeah, let's go Lakers. Y'all got this. Celtics suck. Let's go Lakers yeah."

Klaus who is still reading his menu, shoves Dan on his side. Klaus knows that the game is not live, and is rather a reshowing of the game that was played live earlier. Klaus who figured that Dan knew this, was shocked at the way he was acting. Klaus then responds to Dan.

"Hey man, this game isn't live. They were playing when we were doing the show earlier tonight. The Lakers won. I checked the scores hours ago. Sorry to burst your bubble. Ha."

Dan shakes his head, and shoves Klaus back as well, and laughs. Ernest who was watching them both, finds this funny, and laughs at them. The waitress arrives back at the table during this time, and asks for their food order. Klaus decides to order a Steak and Mashed Potatoes, Dan orders a Bacon Cheeseburger and Fries, and Ernest decides to order the Country Fried Steak, and Mashed Potatoes. Soon, their food order arrives, and the gentlemen all eat. Klaus is happy to finally have food, and Dan and Ernest also seem happy. Klaus took a few moments, to enjoy the time he is spending with his new friends, that he met within the past couple of days. Yes, things were happening fast and sudden, but Klaus didn't care about that anymore. He had friends, and he had a group of people he could support and trust. Things were going great, and this is a new path for Klaus, and it's fine by him, and he doesn't feel worried. As the men finish up their food,

Klaus pays for the check, and leaves a tip for the waitress. They then head to Klaus car, and Klaus drives immediately home. As Klaus reaches his residence, he, along with Dan, start to get Ernest belongings, from the back of the car. It only takes a few minutes for them to get all of Ernest's things. Once all three men have accomplished that, Klaus heads to his kitchen, opens up his refrigerator, and pulls out three Bud Light beers. Ernest takes a seat on the sofa, in Klaus living room. Klaus hands Dan a beer, in which Dan quickly takes gulps of. Klaus then hands Ernest a beer, who reluctantly takes it. Klaus then opens up his beer, and takes swallows of it. Klaus then reaches in his pocket, and takes his pack of cigarettes out, signaling for Dan to join him on the balcony. The both of them head out to the balcony, shutting the door behind them.

Ernest glances at them from the living room, and takes sips of his beer. After a few minutes, Ernest is curious as to what they are talking about, and walks over to the balcony door knocking on it. Dan opens up the door, and Ernest joins the both of them, on the balcony. Once outside, Ernest then starts to speak to Klaus, softly.

"Hey Klaus. Hey man, can I bum a cigarette off you? I really appreciate it."

Klaus shakes his head, and reaches into his pocket, handing Ernest the pack. Ernest takes a cigarette from the carton, and gives the pack to Klaus. Klaus then hands Ernest a lighter, and Ernest lights up his cigarette. Klaus and Dan engage in trivial talk, with Ernest silently listening to them both, not contributing to the conversation. Ernest finishes his cigarette, and stays on the balcony silent for several more moments, listening to Klaus and Dan. Ernest then speaks.

"Hey Klaus. Another favor. Can I borrow a towel? I'm gonna take a shower."

Klaus shakes his head, and laughs. He then starts to walk out the balcony, directing for Ernest to follow him. As he is doing this, Klaus replies bluntly to Dan.

"I'll be right back man. I'm gonna help him out. I'll just be a minute man."

Klaus and Ernest then walk out of the balcony, and Klaus tells Ernest to wait in the living room. When Klaus returns, he hands Ernest a towel. Ernest then proceeds to the bathroom, to take a shower. While Ernest is showering, Klaus returns to the balcony. While Dan is looking out to the ocean, with his direction still facing forward, he softly speaks to Klaus.

"You know Ernest, he's a great guy. He's just a little weird that's all. Ha Ha."

Klaus takes a sip of his beer, and nods his head, silently laughing with him. During this time, Ernest has finished taking his shower. Ernest mistakenly heads into a what he believes is a guest bedroom, but is in actuality, Dan's room. There was actually a third vacant bedroom, Klaus was intending to tell Ernest about, but never got around to informing him about this. Feeling tired and lethargic, Ernest changes into his pajamas, and starts to fall asleep. Meanwhile, Klaus and Dan exit out of the balcony. Klaus heads directly to his bedroom, and prepares to take a shower. Dan walks to his bedroom, and is aghast, when he notices that Ernest is sleeping in his bed. Although shockingly, Dan lets Ernest rest. The bed is King sized, and it's large enough for two people. While Klaus is showering, in the bathroom located inside his room, Dan decides to shower in another bathroom. In total, Klaus residence contains three bedrooms, and a den/lounge, and there are also, three bathrooms in Klaus house. One is in the master bedroom, which is in Klaus room. The other two are located in the hallway of the house. Klaus finishes showering, and gets in his bed, and drifts off to sleep. Once Dan finishes showering, he walks back to his room, noticing that Ernest is not sleeping in the bed, as he was earlier. Ernest actually went to the kitchen, to get himself a glass of water. Dan is not aware of this, or cares, and drifts off to sleep. Once Ernest has gotten his glass of water, he directs himself back to the bedroom, noticing that Dan is sleeping in the bed. It dawns on Ernest, that this is actually Dan's bedroom, and he doesn't get back into the bed. He instead, decides to sleep on the sofa, in Klaus living room. Ernest dozes off to sleep, but wakes up, about an hour later. Ernest walks back to Dan's room, and lays down on the other side of the bed, covering himself up. Dan notices this, and kisses Ernest on his forehead, tucking him in. He then silently speaks to him.

"Good night man. Sleep tight. Sweet dreams."

The next morning, which is now Thursday morning, appears. It is a bright sunny day. Klaus is the first one to wake up. Klaus is walking to his kitchen, still wearing his sleeping outfit, a t shirt, and underpants. Klaus is about to prepare himself a cup of coffee. At the same time, he notices Ernest walking out of the bedroom. It then clicks to Klaus, he never told him, that he could sleep in the third bedroom, and that room is actually Dan's room. Klaus speaks to Ernest.

"Oh damn, I meant to tell you, the room on the other side of the hall is yours."

Ernest then laughs, and quickly responds to Klaus.

"Oh, that's okay. This room is just fine. I'm gonna sleep with Dan. He doesn't mind."

Klaus shakes his head, laughs to himself, and continues to walk to the kitchen. He then pours himself a cup of coffee, and offers Ernest a cup of coffee as well. Minutes after that, Dan, walks out of the bedroom, and Klaus and Dan, give each other a fist bump. Klaus then takes his mug of coffee, and sits in the living room, watching the morning news. Dan ends up fixing himself and Ernest, a bowl of cereal. With today being Thursday, that means tonight, is another show, and it's also the final show of the week. The show airs live Tuesday, Wednesday, and Thursday nights, at 7 p.m. So, the men still have quite a bit a time for the show. However, there was some technical issues in the studio, that Klaus noticed in last night's show, that he neglected to bring up. It is really important that Klaus fixes these issues, before they start to be an even bigger problem later on. Because of this, Klaus needs to leave for the studio, earlier than he usually does. He has also asked Dan and Ernest to accompany him at the studio, to which they agreed to do so. At 3 p.m., Klaus, Dan, and Ernest, leave out of Klaus house, heading straight to the radio station. Today is still a great sunny day, and it's typical, Los Angeles weather. Klaus arrives at the radio station, and he, along with the rest of the men, direct themselves to the studio. Mr. Weston of course is absent, as he is on vacation. Klaus instructs

Dan and Ernest, to remain in the studio room, as Klaus heads to the control room, to fix technical related issues. To pass up time, Ernest starts to read books, and Dan is watching videos on his phone.

Klaus is in the control room, and starts to mess with several wires, buttons, and terminals which are located in this room. Klaus noticed that in last night's broadcast, there were audio and lag issues, and he's hoping by modifying the settings in the control room, these issues will not occur for tonight's show. While Klaus is tampering in the control room, he realizes that he needs to go to the hardware store, to get more electrical wire. Klaus directs himself back up to the studio room, and informs Dan and Ernest, that he will be stepping out of the building.

"Guys, I have to go to Home Depot right quick and get something. I'll be back in a flash. Don't touch anything in this room. You guys get along, and just chill. I'll be back soon. Bye."

Dan and Ernest acknowledge that Klaus is leaving, and Klaus walks out of the studio. He walks down to the parking structure, and drives out of the station, heading to the hardware store. As Klaus is driving out of the station, he notices a short heighted African-American man, with a laptop, standing outside the front studio door. Klaus doesn't pay this man any mind, and continues to drive to the hardware store. Once Klaus is at the hardware store, he manages to find the item that he needs. He purchases it, and quickly drives himself right back to the radio station. Klaus is extremely shocked, once he sees that the gentleman he saw standing outside before, is now sitting on a bench, right outside the front door. Klaus immediate reaction, was that this man was a trespasser. Klaus was sure that he meant well, and didn't mean any harm. However, he was still a trespasser. Klaus wanted to give this man the benefit of the doubt, and that he was a tourist, that lost his way possibly. Instead of driving directly to the parking structure, Klaus instead drives up next to the man, pulling his car up to the sidewalk. The man notices Klaus pull over. Klaus then gets out of his car, and starts to speak to the man.

"Hello, can I help you Sir? Was there something you needed? Can I help you?"

The man then immediately sets his laptop on the bench, starts to smile, and covers his hands with his face. The man then starts to yelp and scream to himself. Klaus is confused, and puzzled, and finds this man strange. Seconds later, the man starts to hug Klaus tightly. Klaus is starting to feel uncomfortable in regards to this, and is motionless, and speechless. The man continues to hug Klaus, while screaming out to him.

"Oh my god! DJ K.! I'm your Number one fan! I've been listening to your show, since like, forever. I'm Jerome Montgomery. People also call me Einstein, because I really love knowledge and trivia. I told myself, today, was the day. I was gonna camp out to find you, and to get a glimpse of you. Don't ask how I found out the studio location. That's for me to know, and for you to find out. Ha Ha. May I have your autograph please, Sir?"

Klaus has a confused and puzzled look on his face. Klaus then scratches the back of his head, and starts to laugh out loud.

CHAPTER 5:

THE JOURNALIST

Klaus continues to feel shocked at this current time. He doesn't know who this man is, and why he decided to sneak up on him like that. This isn't the first time that Klaus has had fans, come up and confront him. However, this is the first time, to where a fan has approached him, in a manner such as this. A manner that made Klaus very uncomfortable. The fan decided to stalk the radio station that Klaus works at, until he saw him. Klaus thought of this as an extreme measure, that ordinary people don't generally do. It was something very unusual, and something that doesn't seem very trustworthy, from Klaus point of view. The fan, whose name is Jerome, was a short heighted African-American man. Although Jerome was 29 years old, he looked much younger than that. Almost as if he were High School aged. Klaus, although he was a very open-minded person, was shocked upon seeing Jerome. He didn't know what kind of person he was, and thought that his profile, and his stature, was one that you didn't see every day. Klaus is still trying to gather his thoughts, after coming across this man. How is he going to interact with him, in a professional and kind way? A big portion of Klaus, wants to just ignore this man. He is only a crazed fanatic, who had no business at all, standing in front of the studio, stalking him. Yet although, another part of Klaus, wants to be nice, and decide to be cordial and polite with the fan, regardless of everything considered. Klaus, and his self-proclaimed, number one fan, Jerome, continue to stand in front of each other for several seconds. Klaus decides to do what he thought was the correct choice at the time, and nods his head to Jerome, and decides to drive back in his car. Jerome immediately seemed shocked and disappointed, that Klaus didn't even acknowledge his presence at all. The only thing that he did, was nod his head. Jerome started to feel upset, that Klaus, a person that he idolized and looked up to, and was a fan of, was acting this way. Klaus quickly drives away, to the parking structure of the studio, on the other side of the building.

Jerome, still feeling upset and defeated, sits down on the bench, and begins to cry. He felt, all that effort, was for nothing. Klaus didn't even give him the time of day, and carried on. Jerome didn't want to accept this at all, and wanted another attempt to get Klaus attention. Jerome snaps out of his depression, and decides to follow Klaus, on the other side of the radio station building, where the parking structure is. Jerome's main plan, was to sneak into the parking structure, without Klaus being aware. He was going to have to be quick and swift, and stealth about this. If Jerome was not quick or fast enough, he wouldn't be able to achieve this sneaky stunt. Jerome races to the other side of the building, and with not even a nanosecond to spare, Jerome hides in front of the parking structure. Jerome waits until Klaus car has left the parking structure entrance, so he's not seen by him. Jerome also has to be careful he doesn't wait too long, before the structure gate closes. Using the advantage of his small stature, Jerome is able to crawl under the parking structure gate, until it closes. Jerome has successfully sneaked into the parking structure, and he did it, without being noticed or seen by Klaus. Jerome is starting to feel slightly excited and proud of himself, that he managed to do this. His next plan, was to somehow make it into the radio station; again, being stealth, and not being seen by Klaus, or anyone else that is in the building. Klaus has no idea at all, that Jerome managed to meander, and slither his way into the building. Klaus is also slightly regretting, that he should have maybe acted more civil to Jerome, and not did what he chose to do. However, Klaus feels he did what he thought, was the right thing, and he feels it's no use trying to feel guilty over it. Klaus figures that he is never going to see

Jerome again, so it's nothing for him to worry, or fret about. Klaus, now with the electrical wire that he bought from the hardware store, that he needed to fix the control room issue, proceeds to the control room, which is located on the first floor of the studio. Jerome, who is still in the underground parking structure, continues to sneak through the studio. With his main objective and mission, to find Klaus. Jerome locates the elevator, and chooses to stop at the first floor. Unaware that Klaus is also on this floor, but in the control room.

Now that Klaus is in the control room, he begins to tinker with the wires, trying to quickly assess, rectify, and fix the audio issue, before the show starts later tonight. Now that Klaus has bought the right part he needs, this is becoming an easier task for him, and he knows that he is going to be able to fix the issue, very shortly. Jerome continues to explore the radio station, looking for Klaus. Klaus studio, is actually located on the third floor. The radio station in total, has three floors. The third floor also contains the buildings break room as well. The first floor contains storage rooms, and also the control room, where Klaus currently is in. The second floor contains two radio stations, which consists of other radio shows, that the station airs throughout the week, and at different days. Klaus, Dan, Ernest, and now Jerome, are the only individuals in the studio at this time. As Mr. Weston, the studio manager, who is usually always present in the studio, is now on vacation. Also, Klaus program, is the only one that airs on Thursday evenings. So his studio, is the only one being occupied and used, during this time. Jerome continues to trespass, and roam through the first floor. Opening doors, that he shouldn't be opening, and noticing that all the rooms, are just storage rooms, containing equipment, and past tapes and archives of radio shows. Jerome is aware that the rooms he's exploring are storage rooms, as he is a big fan of Klaus program, and is also well versed on how radio stations work, from his own personal research.

Up on the third floor, Dan continues to look at videos, and watch sport highlights on his phone. Ernest is also continuing to read his book. On the first floor, Klaus is now just about finished fixing the audio issue, and starts to assemble, and screw everything back together.

Klaus is pleased that he was able to fix the issue he felt was wrong, and no longer has to worry about the show tonight, having audio issues or problems. Klaus then resets all the settings in the control room, double checks that all the ports, and connections, are where they need to be, and are accounted for. Klaus then grabs his tool box, and closes all the electrical port doors, and walks out of the control room, closing the door behind him. Klaus then starts to direct himself to the elevator, that is located on the other side of the first floor. As Klaus is walking to the elevator, he cannot believe what he sees at all. He notices that Jerome is walking through the studio. From Klaus perspective, Jerome is facing away from him. So Klaus knows that Jerome has no idea, that Klaus is right behind him. Klaus approaches Jerome sneakily, and then decides to pull on Jerome's ear, which startles and frightens Jerome, as he did not know Klaus was behind him. Klaus then ferociously grabs Jerome by his collar. Klaus then screams at him.

"What the hell are you doing in here? You're that kid I just saw earlier aren't you? Get out of here, this is private property, and you're lucky I'm not calling the police. Out!"

Jerome then begs out to Klaus, in a very soft and polite tone.

"DJ K., please? All I want is an autograph, and I'll go away. Please? I'm your number one fan. I've been listening to you for years, and it would mean the world to me. Please?"

Klaus looks down on the ground, and shakes his head. He then responds to Jerome.

"Okay, I'll give you your damn autograph. Then I want you out. Alright? Okay kid, what do you want me to sign? Hurry up, because I have a show I have to prepare for you know."

Jerome smiles back at Klaus, and then grabs a cover of "Wired" Magazine. A magazine about business technology, and information about computers, computer science, and the telecommunications world. The cover features a picture of both Klaus and Stuart. Upon seeing that magazine that Jerome pulls out, Klaus totally forgot that himself and Stuart were on the cover of that issue. This slightly shocks and amazes Klaus for a moment, and he smiles heavily. Jerome then also pulls out a marker pen. After this, he then shouts out to Klaus.

"This is the issue of Wired magazine you were on. I was at Target, and they had only one copy left on the rack, in the book and magazine section. I was a fan of you guys, and DJ S., god rest his soul. When I saw you guys were on this copy, I had to get it. Can you, will you, sign it?"

Klaus shakes his head, and grabs the magazine and pen from Jerome. Klaus with a wide grin on his face, then signs the cover of the magazine. Klaus then softly speaks to Jerome.

"Wow, you weren't lying. You really are my Number one fan. I don't even have this issue of Wired. I think this issue was kinda rare, and a special edition. Here you go kid. That's my John Hancock for you. Now as promised, you gotta leave, okay? Let me walk you out."

Klaus hands the magazine back to Jerome, and Jerome puts the magazine in his tote bag. Jerome and Klaus stare are each other for several seconds. Shortly after this, Jerome begins to dart and race down the hallways of the radio station, jokingly shouting back to Klaus.

"But you have to catch me first. Ha Ha. Come and get me. I dare you. Ha Ha."

Klaus then starts to become irate, and frustrated. He doesn't know why Jerome decided to do this, and he thinks this is petty, and immature. With an angry look on his face, Klaus starts to run after Jerome, although he unsuccessfully, is not able to find where he went. Jerome, who was hiding behind a corner in the building, notices that Klaus is facing away from him, and decides to make a run for the elevator. Jerome takes the elevator to the second floor, while Klaus continues so scope out the first floor, looking for Jerome. Klaus decides not to call the police, as he doesn't feel Jerome is a threat. Klaus believes that Jerome is just a High School kid, that's just a fan of the show. He has no idea, that Jerome is only a few years younger than him. Klaus is getting slightly agitated, that Jerome ran away, as he continues to look through rooms on the first floor, not locating him. Jerome, now on the second floor, explores the rooms, noticing that they are all empty radio stations. Jerome is respectful, and doesn't touch or mess with anything in the rooms. Once Jerome is done exploring the second floor, he then decides to go to the third top floor. As Jerome is heading up to the third floor, at this time, Klaus manages to make it to the second floor, looking for Jerome. He comes up unsuccessful, as he is too little too late. Jerome has already left this floor, and is now on the third floor. Klaus continues to be frustrated.

With Jerome now on the third floor, he walks through the building, exploring the rooms, like he did with the entire rest of the building. Jerome then comes across Klaus studio, and opens the door. Upon opening the door, Dan and Ernest look at Jerome, with confused and puzzled faces. Jerome at first, has no idea this is Klaus studio, and is motionless and shocked, and can't move. He is amazed at what he sees, and upon looking at Dan and Ernest, he finds their profiles interesting. After several seconds of awkward silence, Dan then shouts out to Jerome.

"Who the hell are you? What are you doing here? Can we help you kid? Are you lost?"

Immediately after this, Jerome puts his hands over his mouth, and starts to scream.

"Oh my god! Oh my god! I recognize that damn voice. You're the bus driver! Dan!"

Ernest then puts his book down, and starts to laugh, as Dan continues his puzzled look at Jerome. Dan then looks at Ernest, who is laughing at the situation. Dan responds to Jerome.

"Hey, how did you know who I was? Are you some kind of wizard, or something? Ernest, is this a friend of yours? Who is this kid, and how did he get in here? I'm scared now."

Jerome then starts to laugh, and takes a seat on Klaus chair. Jerome then puts his tote bag on the table, and then takes his laptop out. While he's doing this, he responds to Dan.

"First of all, I'm not a kid. I'm twenty-nine. I just have a growth disorder, that makes me look and sound like a kid, that's all. Number two, I'm DJ K.'s Number one fan. I've been listening to the show all week, and you're Dan, and you're Ernest. I can't believe this. Ha Ha."

Dan looks at Ernest, and shakes his head at him, while Ernest continues to laugh. Dan returns to looking at videos on his phone, and Ernest also resumes reading his book. Jerome can't believe that he managed to find Klaus studio. This feels like a dream come true to him, and he feels so lucky to be where he's at. Jerome is aware that he is trespassing, but he doesn't care. He feels it's totally worth it, to be disobeying, and doing what he's currently doing. Jerome then starts to type on his notebook. As he's doing that, he starts to speak to Dan and Ernest.

"Yes, this is perfect. I'm a freelance journalist, so this story is gonna be great. I can't wait to blog about this, and how I managed to get into DJ K.'s actual studio. This is exciting!"

Dan puts his phone down, and then starts to feel concerned. He asks Jerome a question.

"Hey, so does Klaus know you're here? You didn't sneak in here, did you? You did huh? Why you little. You little rascal. Get the hell out of here. Come on kid, it's time to go now."

Dan gets up from his seat, and Ernest tries to hold Dan back. Dan however manages to go over to where Jerome is seated, and grabs his shirt. Jerome then starts to beg at Dan.

"I told you, I'm not a kid. Here's my ID. See? I told you. I'm twenty-nine years old. Please let me stay. I'm DJ K.'s number one fan. Don't make me go. Let me stay. Please?"

Jerome hands Dan his identification card, and Jerome is telling the truth, that he's an adult. Dan shakes his head, and returns back to his seat. Dan then goes back to looking at his phone, and Ernest continues to read his book. Jerome then starts to laugh, and goes back to writing his blog diary, on his laptop. The three men in this room, stay silent to each other, and the atmosphere continues to be awkward and strange. However, five minutes later, Klaus, who this entire time was still on the lookout for Jerome, knows that the only room he hasn't checked yet, is his studio. Klaus opens the door to the radio studio, and low and behold, he manages to find Jerome sitting in his chair, in the studio with Dan and Ernest. Klaus is immediately angered by this, and before Jerome is able to react, or say anything, Klaus grabs him by his shirt.

"Didn't I tell you to leave? Damn it. Get out, before I call the police kid. I have had it with you. Now get out you little brat. I don't have time for this. It's time to go, get up."

Instantaneously, Dan manages to speak to Klaus, in an effort to defend Jerome.

"Hey man, he's not a kid. He's a grown man. He says he's a fan of yours. Come on, let him stay. He seems harmless enough. Hey, um, I never got your name, but show him your ID."

Jerome then in that exact moment, hands Klaus his identification card. While looking at it, Klaus shakes his head, and is in disbelief. He then laughs and while still looking at Jerome's identification card, silently speaks back to him, still slightly shocked.

"You're twenty-nine years old? Damn. I would have never guessed. You look like you're fourteen years old or something. That must really suck to look that young, but you're not. Hmm. Yeah, but you still gotta go though. You got your autograph, now you have to leave, okay?"

Dan once again, tried to beg and plead for Klaus, to let Jerome stay.

"Let him stay man, he's not hurting anybody. He's your fan. He's here to interview you, I think. You are here to interview him, right?"

Dan then winks at Jerome, and Jerome finally gets the hint, as to what Dan is trying to convey and get across. Jerome then starts to laugh, and swiftly responds.

"Oh, yeah. He's right. DJ K., like I said earlier, my name is Jerome Montgomery. I'm a freelance journalist, and I work for Buzzfeed, and I'm here to get an inclusive impromptu, candid, live and direct, remote interview. So, what do you say?"

Even though Jerome is a journalist, he does not actually work for Buzzfeed, and he didn't arrive to give Klaus an interview. He was simply a crazed fanatic, and wanted an autograph from Klaus. Klaus is also fully aware of this, and knows that Jerome is fibbing. Klaus unfortunately doesn't buy this charade that Dan and Jerome were trying to concoct. Klaus responds to Jerome.

"Yeah right. You're not here to interview me. You're just being silly now. You came here, because you wanted an autograph. You got one, and now it's time to go. I'm sorry for mistaking you for a kid, but you have to leave now. So, for the last time, it's time to go now."

Jerome then crosses him arms, and sits back in Klaus chair. Dan and Ernest immediately start to laugh, and find this amusing. Still seated, and having his arms crossed, Jerome responds.

"Well, DJ K. you have to carry me, and throw me out of here your damn self, as I'm not going anywhere. Dan and Ernest don't have any issue with me being here, do you guys?"

Dan and Ernest then agree with Jerome, and nod their heads in agreement, that they do not mind if Jerome wishes to stay in the studio. Klaus however, is still adamant on wanting Jerome to leave. Klaus with an angered look on his face, then loses his temper.

"Alright. That's it. I was being nice, but that's over with. Get out of my chair."

Klaus shockingly picks Jerome out of the chair, and carries him behind his back. Dan and Ernest watch in amusement, as Klaus, quite literally, carries Jerome away. During this time, Jerome equally finds this thrilling, yet exciting, and shouts out to Klaus.

"Hey, big guy, put me down. That's not fair. Put me down. Ha Ha."

Klaus then starts to carry Jerome out of the studio, and down the hallway. Klaus directs himself to the elevator, while still carrying Jerome. While standing outside, waiting for the elevator, Jerome then starts to shout back to Klaus.

"DJ K., I didn't know how strong you were. I mean, I know I'm a small guy, but damn. You smell nice too. I feel like I'm being carried by Hercules. Ha Ha."

Klaus doesn't know what came over him, but he immediately forms a change of heart, and begins to laugh hysterically at what Jerome just said. Klaus, unable to control his laughter, falls on the ground, which causes Jerome to fall on top of Klaus as well. The both of them stare at each other in this awkward formation, and they both soon laugh. Jerome then responds.

"DJ K., I didn't know you wanted to reenact a scene from Titanic too. Ha Ha."

Klaus and Jerome are still on the ground, with Jerome on top of Klaus. Klaus shakes his head, and laughs. The impact of the fall, caused

Klaus glasses to fall. Jerome notices this, and puts Klaus glasses back on his face. Jerome then whispers back to Klaus.

"DJ K., your glasses fell. Here, I would hate for them to break. There you are."

Klaus continues to shake and his head and laugh. This time, he responds to Jerome.

"Who are you? What are you? What do you want from me?"

Jerome laughs, and quickly responds back to Klaus.

"I told you who I was. My name is Jerome. I'm your number one fan. If by now you can't realize that, or see that, then I don't know what to tell you. People don't go around saying Number one fan for nothing right? This is like a dream. I never thought I'd meet you in my life."

Klaus, who is still pinned on the ground by Jerome on top of him, shakes his head. Klaus then sarcastically responds back to Jerome, in a direct, stern manner.

"Yeah, Number one fan or not. You have to leave though. Get your things. Time to go."

During this whole ordeal, Dan and Ernest watch from the other side of the hallway, shocked at what they are seeing, and motionless as well. Not able to react at all. Jerome, who is still on top of Klaus, continues to tease and laugh at Klaus.

"Well, I'm not leaving. You can't kick your Number one fan out like that. You just can't."

Klaus shakes his head, and laughs once again, while still giving Jerome eye contact. Still being pinned on the ground by him, Klaus decides to play along with Jerome.

"Tell you what. Since you're my number one fan, I'm gonna give you a quiz. If you pass the quiz, you can stay, if you fail, you have to leave, and I don't ever want to see you again."

Jerome then laughs at Klaus, and replies right back to him.

"Okay fine, I don't care. Try me. Quiz me. I'm not scared at all. I'm ready. Okay."

Klaus yet again shakes his head, and laughs at Jerome. He then replies back.

"Three years ago, Stuart and I did a remote broadcast in a location away from the studio. During this broadcast, we ended up meeting Arnold Schwarzenegger. Where were we at?"

Jerome immediately starts to laugh, and quickly replies back to Klaus.

"Really? That's easy. That was Las Vegas, you guys were doing a show at The Luxor. I remember that show like it was yesterday. DJ K., you gotta do better than that, come on."

Klaus shakes his head, and tries to think of a more difficult question. Klaus speaks.

"Alright. This one is tougher, so, you're not gonna get this. A show we did four years ago, Stuart and I revealed our favorite ice cream flavor, was what? "

Jerome then starts to tease Klaus for a bit, and responds back to Klaus question.

"Oh DJ K., that's a tough one. Not! Chocolate Chip Cookie Dough. Duh. I thought you said that this question was going to be hard. Think of a tougher one. Next. Ha Ha."

Klaus is now starting to feel strange and weirded out, that someone like Jerome, knows all about his history. Klaus would have never suspected that someone with the profile of Jerome, a short heighted, black, flamboyant man, that looks younger than he actually is, would know all the trivia related to his show. This was causing Klaus, to feel like he shouldn't judge others, as you never know what opinions people have, and what people know. Klaus then had one more question in mind. That only the biggest fans of his would know, or be able to answer. Klaus knew that if Jerome was able to correctly answer this question right, then he was indeed his Number one fan, and was worthy of that title. With Jerome still being pinned on top of Klaus, who is on the ground, Klaus then gives Jerome, one last question.

"Alright. This is for all the marbles. If you get this right, then I worship and salute you. You're not gonna get it though. If you get it wrong, you leave. If you get it right, well, you're not gonna get it right, so don't even worry about it. Here is your last question. Are you ready?"

Jerome again laughs at Klaus, and softly responds back to him.

"I'm ready. What's this all-important tough question, DJ K.? I'm ready to hear it."

Klaus laughs, and shakes his head once more. Klaus then whispers back to Jerome.

"On our very first ever show that Stuart and I did, we used to have a word of the day segment. We only said it once, and once only, during the show. We stopped doing it, because we found it cheesy, but what was our very first word of the day, that we did?"

Jerome then starts to have a concerned and worried look on his face. Klaus, then feels like he has finally stumped Jerome, and he finally found something that Jerome didn't know. Jerome continues to look puzzled and unsure. Klaus then teases Jerome.

"Ten seconds. Nine, eight, seven, six, give up? You don't know, do you? Ha Ha."

Jerome then has a grin on his face, and looks directly at Klaus. Jerome then laughs to himself, which causes Klaus to feel slightly worried. Jerome then responds to Klaus.

"Copacetic. Adjective. Definition; In order, cool, calm, okay, satisfied, satisfactory, alright, fine. DJ K. I'll use it in a sentence for you. 'The prime minister explained to reporters, that we don't need to go to war, everything is copacetic.'. Ha Ha. DJ K. I told you, I was your Number one fan, and you just have to accept that, and yeah. Ha Ha."

Klaus forms an angry look on his face, and silently whispers back to Jerome.

"Damn you. Good boy, what can I say? Okay, you can stay. What is happening? Ha Ha."

Jerome stands up, and starts to jump for joy. He can't believe that he managed to pass Klaus quiz. Jerome knows that he is for sure Klaus Number one fan. Klaus is still in disbelief, that Jerome answered all the questions correctly, and feels that he is worthy enough to stay, based on that. Klaus at this time, manages to get himself off the floor, and Dan and Ernest, who were watching the both of them the entire time, stare deeply at Klaus and Jerome. Klaus, who is feeling both equally amazed at Jerome, but angry at how strange recent events are happening, quickly loses his fuse at the moment, and shouts back at Dan and Ernest.

"The hell are you two looking at? Get back inside."

Dan and Ernest laugh at Klaus, and walk back into the studio. Klaus and Jerome stare at each other for several minutes, before Klaus extends his hand out, in the direction of the radio studio, for Jerome to proceed ahead of him. Jerome understands Klaus signal, and walks into the radio studio. Klaus remains standing in the hallway, still trying to gather his thoughts, and bring himself back to reality. This is now becoming the third day in a row, to where Klaus is experiencing a wave of new events, like a whirlwind. Things are happening very fast recently, and Klaus, is finding his own way to manage and deal with everything, that he is being presented with. Klaus understands that it's going to take some time to get used to Jerome, and he feels that he has a strange feeling about him, but also feels pleased, that Jerome knows so much history about the show. Klaus ultimately does eventually direct himself back in the studio. Klaus notices that Jerome is sitting in his chair. Even though it's just a chair, Klaus has always sat in that chair, for many years of doing the show. Klaus was feeling very defensive over the chair, and originally took offense of Jerome sitting on the chair. However, Klaus was willing to let Dan sit in Stuart's chair, so Klaus feels he shouldn't mind if Jerome wishes to sit in his chair. Klaus takes a vacant seat, next to Jerome's chair. Once seated, Klaus whispers to Jerome.

"Hey, Number one fan, that's actually my chair, and was my chair, since day one. But you earned it, it's your chair now. Congrats. Don't make me change my mind on this though."

Jerome who had no idea that he was sitting in Klaus chair, quickly retorts and responds.

"Oh no, DJ K., I couldn't take your chair. I didn't know. Here, I'll sit somewhere else."

Jerome stands up, and Klaus grabs Jerome by the wrist. Klaus stands up, and shoves Jerome back on the chair. Klaus then sits down, and with an angry and infuriating look on his face, gives eye contact back to Jerome, and softly responds back to him

"It's your chair. You're my Number one fan. It's yours. Sit down, and don't mention it again. It's your chair now. Sit down, and stop with all that. Before I change my mind. Sit."

Jerome nods his head silently, and opens up his laptop. Klaus shakes his head, and starts to write down notes on his notebook, like he customarily does. At this time, Jerome becomes more accustomed to Dan and Ernest, and they both engage in small talk. Klaus who is busy writing notes, eavesdrops on what Jerome is telling them. Even though Klaus is silent and not responding, he still feels fully engulfed in the conversation. Klaus then starts to feel sorry, and empathetic to Jerome, after Jerome explains his life situation to Dan and Ernest. Jerome was born with a growth disorder, that causes him not to age like other people, and he looks much younger than what his actual age is. When he was younger, he went through tests to reverse this, however, none were successful for him. Jerome's father abandoned him when he was very young, and his Mother who raised him by herself, died of Ovarian Cancer. Once Jerome's Mother died, he was in foster care, and lived-in group homes. He doesn't have any other family support, and once he turned eighteen, he went to University at USC, and graduated in Journalism. Jerome is also Autistic. Although Jerome has had several office, and clerk jobs, the occupation he has now, is being a freelance journalist. Jerome enjoys writing, and gathering information, and researching, very much, and it's his main hobby. Klaus also found out that Jerome is gay, and he doesn't have any friends, or a romantic partner at all. Once Jerome finishes explaining his past to Dan and Ernest, Klaus then feels an extreme wave of kindness towards Jerome, and responds to him.

"You know, we have a show starting soon, In a couple hours actually. I can't believe I'm saying this, but Jerome, Number one fan, would you like to be my fourth co-host?"

Dan and Ernest look at each other, with excited faces, and seem pleased at what Klaus just said. They already formed a great bond with Jerome, and they feel the same way as Klaus, and would love to have Jerome join their team. Jerome is speechless, with his hands covering his mouth, and doesn't know what to say. After about a minute of awkward silence, Jerome does finally respond back to Klaus.

"DJ K. I would, yes. Oh my god. I feel so lucky. I'm gonna pinch myself. This isn't real."

Jerome then gets up from his chair, and with Klaus still seated, he starts to tightly hug Klaus around his neck. Dan and Ernest start to laugh. Klaus then screeches back to Jerome.

"Alright, okay. You're officially a co-host now. Stop choking me. Jesus. God. Ha Ha."

Jerome quickly snaps out of it, and detaches himself from Klaus. Jerome then responds.

"Oh, I'm sorry DJ K. I just got a little carried away. God. Thank you so much. Really."

Jerome returns to his seat, and Jerome and Klaus stare at each other for a few seconds. They both exchange a smile towards each other. Jerome then continues to write his blog, on his laptop. Klaus looks at him with excitement, and curiosity. Klaus is aware that Jerome is writing a blog, and doing journalism work, but he still feels slightly intrigued. With Thursday night's show starting now in an hour, the radio station becomes shockingly quiet. Dan continues to look at videos on his phone, Ernest is reading his book, Jerome is doing work on his computer. Klaus is writing down his itinerary for tonight's broadcast, as well as making sure all the audio equipment is in working order; so when the show actually starts, they are all set to go. Klaus then gets up from his seat, and asks a question he usually does, before every show.

"Alright, we're gonna start soon. I'm gonna go and stop at the break room. As I'm gonna already be there, anybody want any refreshments? Coffee, water, chips, crackers?"

The rest of the men tell Klaus what they want from the break room, and Klaus quickly heads to the break room, grabs the refreshments and snacks, and walks back to the studio. He hands the men the snacks they asked for. During this time, the show will now start in thirty minutes. Klaus is getting the topic for tonight situated. Klaus decided that the topic is going to be about, not judging people, and that looks can be deceiving. This was triggered, due to the fact Klaus profiled Jerome incorrectly. Klaus assumed the polar opposite of what he thought Jerome was. After explaining the topic to Jerome, and asking if he's okay with it, Klaus made the topic of the show for tonight, official. Very quickly, Klaus informs Jerome, of how the radio controls work. Informing him that Dan and Ernest managed to get the hang of things easily, and he will as well. Klaus starts to write some final notes, in his notebook. Klaus continues to get everything in the studio set up, with it now only being fifteen minutes until the show starts. Klaus, and the rest of the guys, are feeling slightly tense and nervous. With Jerome especially, this being his first show. Jerome, like with Dan and Ernest, had no prior background in radio, so he feels this is quite strange, and not familiar to him. Ten minutes to go until the show starts, and the guys now have their undivided attention. Dan put his phone away, Ernest read through the ending of his book already, and stopped reading. Jerome also shut down his laptop. The only person that is still getting things prepared, is Klaus. He is doing last minute final touches, and audio checks, before the show starts. Five minutes left until the show, Klaus decides to get himself another cup of coffee, and asks the guys one last time, if there is anything from the break room they need. The rest of the men say no. Klaus quickly leaves out of the studio, to the break room. After getting himself another cup of coffee, Klaus swiftly returns back to the studio. Three minutes, turn into a minute, turn into seconds, of the show now officially starting. After the theme of the show plays, Klaus and the rest of the men, put their headphones on. Klaus then connects all of the guys microphones, and Klaus then speaks into his microphone, to the audience.

"Hello everyone. Welcome to the DJ K. show. This is Thursday night. Final show of the night. Yeah, I know, it's bittersweet. After tonight's show, you guys have to wait until Tuesday. But it's okay, because tonight we are in for an exciting show, and I have a new host today."

Klaus remains silent for a few seconds. He realized that every day this week, he announced a new guest host, with now Jerome being the third. Klaus laughs to himself over this trivial fact, and wonders if the listeners have picked up on this as well. Klaus is sure that they have.

Klaus then after coming to this realization, then quickly speaks back to the audience.

"I would like to introduce you guys to Jerome. He's like a walking computer. His nickname is Einstein, and I can see why. I met him today, and he's gonna be one of our new hosts, and I'm so happy. You guys are gonna enjoy him, like I do. Jerome, introduce yourself."

Directly following this, Jerome becomes nervous, as he was not ready for Klaus to put the spotlight on him like that. Jerome does realize that he is on live radio, and he knew exactly what he was signing up for, and getting himself into. Jerome then speaks to the audience.

"Hey radio world. As DJ K. said, I'm Jerome. I was born and raised in LA. I was a Journalism major at USC. Woot. Woot. I enjoy Sci-Fi stuff. I like Doctor Who. I like jazz music. I uh, I'm a huge fan of DJ K., you guys will soon understand later. Ha Ha, Nice to meet y'all."

After Jerome introduces himself to the audience, Klaus smiles at him in acceptance. Directly after this, Klaus then speaks to the audience, letting them know the topic of the show.

"Okay, so tonight's topic, is going to be about not being judgmental. The moral of, looks can be deceiving. You see, I met Jerome today, and I did something bad and incorrect. I judged him before getting to know him. I don't want you guys doing the same. So, let's explore this."

Klaus and Jerome again give each other eye contact, and smile at each other. The show then went on as regular, with both Klaus, Dan, Ernest, and Jerome, all equally contributing to the program. The men continued to take calls during the show, and were having regular discourse and dialogue, about the topic that was at hand. Time was zooming by rather quickly, and Jerome was naturally getting used to the show, and Klaus never once, felt uncomfortable with Jerome being there. Even though it was only the first day that they have met, and he also met Dan and Ernest recently as well, it was like Klaus had known his fellow co-hosts for years. They were getting along perfectly as a team, and this was how Klaus imagined, the show would be like indefinitely. Although Mr. Weston was not here, and was still on vacation, Klaus was sure that his boss would be proud of all that work that he is currently doing. Before Klaus even knew it, the time for the show to end, was already approaching. Klaus couldn't believe it at all. Klaus wishes he could let the show go on longer, but he cannot. Once the time slot of his show approaches, he has to by contract, end the show. He felt that it was only a few minutes ago, that he first started the show. Time seems to slip by faster, if you are having fun, and having a great time. Klaus, now understanding the show has to end, speaks to the audience.

"Oh gee, I can't believe the end of the show is here. No! Say it isn't so. Ha Ha. So, we all have to go. Thank you, all the callers, all the listeners. We love all of you. As you all know, we will not be back tomorrow night, we will be back Tuesday, 7 p.m. sharp. See you there. Peace."

Klaus then takes off his headphones, and unplugs his microphone. Klaus then shuts off the telephone switchboard. Klaus gives Dan a fist bump, and shakes Ernest hand. Klaus takes a look at Jerome, and simply nods his head to him. Jerome smiles back at Klaus in agreement. Klaus then stretches his arms out, and yawns. After doing this, Klaus gets up from his chair, and looks at his phone. Klaus then starts to speak to Dan, while scrolling to his phone.

"I'm starving, I have to get something to eat. Dan, you like 'In N Out Burger' right?"

Dan gets up from his seat, and quickly responds back to Klaus.

"I love 'In N Out Burger'. Yeah, that sounds good man. I'm hungry too."

Klaus continues to scroll on his phone. He then puts his phone in his pocket, and directs his attention to Jerome. He then softly speaks to him.

"Me and the guys are gonna go get some burgers. I don't know if you wanted to follow us. Do you have a car? If not, you can ride with us, and I can drop you off at home."

Jerome looks down on the ground, and whispers back to Klaus.

"I don't have a car no. I have my learners permit, but I'm scared to take the actual test. I went to this driving school, and they helped. But I'm looking for more people to teach me how to drive, so I'm not scared for the driving test, and I can pass. I took the bus here though."

Dan heard what Jerome said, and shakes his head. He then responds to Jerome.

"Oh damn. Yeah. That's too bad. You took the 45 bus, right? Yeah. Ha Ha. That bus stopped running. The nearest bus stop from here is the 76, and you have to transfer..."

Klaus immediately cuts dan off, and begins to shout back to him.

"Alright, enough of that man. Shit. I think he already knows he missed his bus. We're gonna give Jerome a ride home anyways, so it's okay. Alright, Jerome just follow us. Okay?"

Jerome nods his head in agreement with Klaus. Minutes later, Klaus manages to close up the studio, and shuts everything off, and disconnects all the equipment. All four of the men, then head down to the underground parking structure. During this time, as they are all walking, Dan then notices that he hasn't moved his car. He then speaks to Klaus.

"Hey man, tomorrow, can you drive me to my car? I know where I parked in. I just wanted to move my car to your driveway. That's alright with you right? Ha Ha."

Klaus doesn't say anything, but simply laughs and shakes his head. All the men are now in Klaus SUV, with Dan sitting in the passenger side, and Ernest and Jerome sitting in the second row. Klaus then immediately starts to drive to 'In N Out Burger'. Once Klaus reaches a stoplight, he then starts to ask Jerome a question.

"Hey man, where do you live? We're gonna stop and get the burgers, and you can just take your food home. I'm gonna give you my number, and we can talk later. Where do you live?"

Jerome hesitates for several seconds, but does eventually respond back to Klaus.

"DJ K. I mean, I can call you Klaus now, right? I live in North Hollywood."

Klaus then starts to become silent, as he knows that's in the other direction of where his house is at, in Redondo Beach. Klaus understands that he has to find a way to work around this. As Klaus is still gathering his thoughts, Jerome then responds right back to him.

"I live in a boarding house. It sucks. I hate it there. My housemates are awful. I have been trying to find another apartment in my budget. I wasn't having much luck, so yeah."

Klaus shakes his head, and while he is continuing to drive, replies back to Jerome.

"Don't worry about all that, it's okay. I'll get you home. I don't know how I'm gonna swing back, but I'll find a way, I guess. I'm gonna stop at the burger stand first, then drop Dan and Ernest off. They live with me, they are my roommates, and I'll take you home. Okay?"

Jerome nods his head, and seems to be in acceptance with this plan. It seems that Klaus has worked everything out, despite the fact Jerome lived in the opposite direction, then he was assuming. Eventually, Klaus makes it to the 'In N Out Burger' drive thru, and orders ten double-double burgers, and four orders of fries. After getting the food, Klaus drives a short distance to his residence. Klaus parks his SUV in the driveway of his townhouse, and he, along with the rest of the men, get out of the car. Being that this is the first time that Jerome is seeing Klaus residence, he is very happy at what he sees. He notices that Klaus has property, only located a couple blocks from the beach, in Redondo Beach. Klaus also has a nice modest townhouse. Jerome is pleased that Klaus has managed to be successful with his career, to own such a nice house. As the men get inside the actual residence, Dan and Ernest take a seat on the sofa, in Klaus living room. Jerome continues to be amazed, while inside Klaus residence. Klaus sets the burgers and fries on a counter in his kitchen. Klaus then opens up the refrigerator, and grabs two beers, and hands both to Dan, to which Dan hands Ernest the other one. Dan then turns the television on, in which the Jim Carrey movie, "The Cable Guy", is playing. Jerome continues to walk around the residence, looking at the band posters, and sports memorabilia, on Klaus wall. During this time, Klaus notices that Jerome is roaming about his house, and calls out to him.

"Okay Jerome, I'm gonna put your food in this bag, and I'm gonna take you home now. It's getting late, and it's a long drive to North Hollywood. Say goodbye to Dan and Ernest."

Jerome then takes a seat on the other end of Klaus sofa. He then crosses his arms, and starts to tease Klaus. With his arms still folded, Jerome sharply responds back to Klaus.

"What? I don't want to go home yet. I'll go home when I feel like it. It's not a school night. I don't have a curfew. I'm not a child. I'm a grown ass man."

Klaus is feeling shocked and appalled, that Jerome is once again presenting an attitude towards him. Klaus laughs and shakes his head. Immediately following this, Jerome gets up from the sofa, and walks into the kitchen. He opens up Klaus refrigerator, and pulls out of bottle of Bud Light. Jerome immediately twists open the cap, and takes several sips of it. Upon noticing this, Klaus successfully manages to snatch the bottle away from Jerome, snapping at him.

"Hey, no! If you want a beer, all you had to do was ask for one, and I would have given you one. That's not how we do things in this house. You may be an adult, but you're acting like a really immature, and defiant little boy. Now get your things, I'm taking you home."

At this time, Jerome notices that Dan and Ernest are walking out to the patio, to smoke a cigarette. Jerome then speaks back to Klaus, asking a request of him.

"Can I smoke a cigarette first, then you can take me home? Please?"

Klaus has an angered look on his face, but is willing to allow Jerome's request. Klaus nods his head, and Jerome directs himself to the balcony, with Dan and Ernest. The three of them all smoke a cigarette, with Klaus watching them all, from outside the balcony. Jerome continues to circulate with Dan and Ernest, as they are on the balcony smoking. Klaus is anticipating for them to finish, so he can drop Jerome off at home. Once Jerome finishes his cigarette, Klaus is waiting for him in the living room. Klaus then proceeds to get his car keys.

"Alright, you had your cigarette, now it's time to go. Jerome, if you're not doing anything tomorrow, we can hang out, and have fun. But you gotta go home now buddy, okay?"

Jerome nods his head, and starts to get his tote bag that was situated beside the sofa. Klaus then starts to walk to the front door with

Jerome. However, Jerome drops his bag next to the front door, and races back to the sofa, laughing in the process. This angers Klaus greatly, and he walks over to the sofa, and picks Jerome up with his arms. Jerome is laughing during this, but Klaus is not amused one bit. Klaus continues to carry Jerome behind his back, when Jerome decides to give a remark back to Klaus.

"Oh, my knight in shining armor is back again. Such a strong, virile man. Ha Ha."

This causes Klaus to laugh hysterically, and himself and Jerome, both fall on the floor. With Jerome once again pinned on top of Klaus, Klaus whispers softly to Jerome.

"You want to sleep over, don't you? You're acting like a big baby. Well big baby, I'm gonna feed you, and put you to sleep, and I want you to be quiet for the rest of the night."

Jerome laughs at Klaus, and plays along with him as well, and replies.

"Damn right. I'm a big baby, and I always get what I want. I'm your Number one fan, and if your Number one fan wants to stay, then I'm going to stay. You just have to deal with it. Ha Ha."

Klaus then gets up from the floor, and carries Jerome on his back yet again. Klaus then walks to his bedroom door, and throws Jerome down on his king size bed. Klaus then responds.

"You stay in here for the rest of the night, you're in time out. Wait, hold on."

Jerome takes his shoes off, and sets them on the side of Klaus bed, and seconds later, Klaus returns with the beer that Jerome opened earlier, and also a bag of burger and fries. Klaus sets the beer and food down the side table, and responds to Jerome.

"Now you be a good boy. Okay you big baby? I don't want to hear a word from you. You got your beer; you got your food. There is a TV here. Is there anything else you need?"

Jerome turns the television set on, and the television set is playing an episode of Crank Yankers. With his vision directed at the television set, Jerome whispers back to Klaus.

"Yeah, there is one more thing I would like. Can I have a kiss from Daddy?"

Klaus doesn't seem be feeling the same way immediately. Klaus, with an angered and disgusted face, growls back at Jerome.

"No, that's not what I meant. You also cannot. You've been bad, and bad boys don't get kisses. Only good boys get kisses. So no, you don't get a kiss. Now drink your beer, eat your food, and watch TV. I don't want to hear another word from you. Understood?"

Jerome then laughs, and nods his head. Klaus prepares to exit out of the bedroom, when he stops for a few seconds. He then makes his way back to Jerome on the bed. Klaus leans in closer to Jerome, and starts to laugh. Jerome starts to laugh as well. Klaus then whispers to Jerome.

"But you're being a good boy now. My Number one fan. So, Daddy will give you a kiss."

Klaus then leans into Jerome, and kisses him directly on the lips, for several seconds. Jerome then starts to laugh uncontrollably, which makes Klaus uncomfortable. Klaus then with an angered look on his face, shakes his head, and walks out of the bedroom, shutting the door behind him. Jerome, still laying on the bed, continues to look at Crank Yankers on TV, and takes a sip of his beer, and starts to his eat his food. Klaus directs his way to the kitchen, and opens himself a bottle of Bud Light. Before he leaves out of the kitchen, he takes out of handful of French fries from the 'In N Out' bag, and begins to eat them. Klaus then proceeds to the balcony outside, where Dan and Ernest are still talking. Klaus shuts the balcony door behind him. Dan then immediately hands Klaus a cigarette, and he lights it. Dan then speaks to Klaus.

"So, what about Jerome, you're not gonna take him home? What happened?"

Klaus takes a puff from his cigarette, and shakes his head. He then, while looking out towards the distance, looking at the view of the ocean, softly responds back to Dan.

"Uh no, he's gonna sleep over tonight. He asked me, and I said it's okay."

Dan takes a puff from his cigarette, and raises his eyebrows, nodding his head. Dan then looks out towards the same distance Klaus is, facing the beach, and responds.

"Okay, that's cool."

Dan then looks at Ernest, in which Ernest takes a puff from his cigarette, and rests his head on Dan's shoulder. Dan kisses Ernest on his forehead, and Dan and Ernest both laugh. Klaus who is still looking out towards the ocean on his balcony, takes another puff of his cigarette. Klaus shakes his head, and laughs to himself.

CHAPTER 6:

THE ARTIST

Klaus continues to remain outside on the balcony with the other men. As the three of them smoke their cigarettes, continuing to watch the night view of the beach in the distance, and in the horizon. Klaus tries to remain composed, as he tries to gather himself, in relation to all the recent events that he was recently faced with. This has been a very hectic week for Klaus, and things were going very fast at first, but Klaus has somehow managed to adjust himself through it all, and it is no longer an issue or problem for him. Thinking back how on Tuesday, Dan called into the show, and he came in contact with the first time. Also thinking that how on Wednesday, Ernest came into the studio, and both Klaus and Dan developed a friendship and relationship with him. Now Klaus is thinking of today, to where Jerome, his self-proclaimed, "Number one fan", stepped into his life. Klaus was even more shocked, when he found out that Jerome was actually right about being his number one fan after all. As Klaus continues to sit on the balcony, with his new friends, he takes this time to relax. Klaus is happy that they do not have return to the studio until Tuesday, but Klaus is going to visit the studio tomorrow, not to do a show, but to work on some technical issues. This is a wonderful night in the Los Angeles area. The sky gives off a nice light brown, mixed with a dark navy-blue color. The fact that Klaus lives relatively near the beach, the men are also able to smell the ocean from Klaus balcony. In addition to the therapeutic sights and smells of the sea, you can also hear the waves crash against the shore. So, it's very peaceful. Klaus, Dan, and Ernest continue to enjoy themselves on the balcony. They are having such a great time, at this location, that Klaus eventually decides to step into the kitchen, and grab the bag of food that they had ordered earlier, so they can enjoy it on the balcony. It seems that if they were to eat their meal out on the balcony, they would enjoy it much better.

The men eat their burgers and fries on the balcony, while Jerome continues to stay in Klaus bedroom, eating his food, and also still watching "Crank Yankers", on the big flat screen television in Klaus bedroom as well. It seems as though Klaus, Dan, and Ernest are losing complete track of time, and are having fun where they are. They don't want to leave this balcony, and wish that they could stay there indefinitely. They are having a calm time bonding with each other, and they are also losing track of time as well. It is now creeping up to 2 a.m., which is quite late. This shows, as Ernest starts to drift in and out of sleep, while Klaus and Dan are talking to each other. Klaus and Dan are not aware that Ernest has fallen asleep, as they are really engulfed in the conversation that they are having, which is a mix between discussion about entertainment, sports, and news and politics. Klaus feels very secure talking to Dan now, despite only meeting recently. Klaus sort of almost thinks of Dan, as a best friend at this point. So it's only natural that they are able to connect well by now. Klaus finally is able to tell how late it is getting, and understands that it is now time for the men to call it a night, and to head inside. Klaus also wants to check on Jerome as well, as he hasn't seen him in hours. Klaus and Dan hug each other, and Klaus walks out of the balcony. At this same time, Dan wakes Ernest up, and the both of them proceed to bed. Klaus directs himself to the kitchen, to throw the food bag, and beer bottles away. Klaus then walks himself straight to his bedroom.

Once Klaus is in his bedroom, he notices that the TV is now playing an episode of "Reno 911." Klaus also notices that Jerome is in the bed, deep asleep. Klaus smiles to himself, and decides to tuck Jerome in the bed, under the covers, also kissing him on the forehead.

Klaus then lowers the television volume down, basically putting the television on mute, as it is quite loud, and he doesn't wish to wake Jerome. Klaus then immediately after, then grabs the empty food containers that Jerome has eaten, and his empty bottle of beer, and throws them away in the kitchen. Klaus then starts to yawn, and feels extremely tired and fatigued. Klaus decides to fall asleep on his sofa. He takes his shoes and socks off, grabs a blanket from his hallway, takes his blanket back to the sofa, and drift to sleep. An hour later, Jerome gets out of Klaus bed, to grab himself a glass of water. Jerome gets his water, and while he's walking from the kitchen, back to the bedroom, he notices Klaus, is fast, and deep asleep on the sofa. However, Klaus was so exhausted, that he forgot to take his glasses off. Jerome is aware of this, and decides to take Klaus glasses off, and sets them on the coffee table. Jerome then kisses Klaus on the forehead, and also very silently, whispers out back to him.

"Good night, sleep well, DJ K."

Jerome then walks back into the bedroom, shutting the door behind him, and falls asleep minutes after this. Hours later, Klaus is awakened at the sofa, by the smell of someone cooking in the kitchen. Klaus checks his phone, and he notices that it is now 10 a.m. Klaus fully wakes himself up, and he notices that Dan is making waffles in the kitchen. This slightly angers Klaus, as the smell of the waffles, woke Klaus up. Ernest is also sitting by the kitchen counter as Dan is making the waffles, reading a book. Klaus shakes his head, and directly walks to his bedroom. Klaus sees that Jerome is still asleep, but doesn't decide to wake him, and allows him, continue sleeping. Klaus is now going to take a shower. He grabs the outfit he is going to wear for today, and a towel, and very quickly steps into the bathroom, to take a shower. During this time, Dan is continuing to make waffles, in addition to also making bacon, sausage, and eggs. Dan remarkably, is quite a good cook, and is not burning the food at all, and the food looks quite delicious. Klaus minutes later, finishes his shower, and walks back into the bedroom, with Jerome still being asleep. Klaus quickly gets his clothes and outfit on, and before leaving the bedroom, he walks over to where Jerome is on the bed, and wakes him up.

"Okay, time to get up. Dan is cooking something for breakfast, come on. Get up."

After waking Jerome up, Klaus then heads over to kitchen, and notices that Dan is just about almost finished cooking their breakfast. Dan, while cooking, then speaks to Klaus.

"Give me another five minutes, and everything will be ready. Ernest and I walked to the supermarket this morning, and we decided to make a surprise breakfast, why not? Ha Ha."

Klaus laughs and shakes his head, and walks back to the sofa in the living room. Following this, Jerome walks into the living room, and sits on the sofa, right next to Klaus. They both stare at each other for a few seconds, and smile at each other. Klaus then speaks to him.

"Did you have a good sleep? How are you feeling today?"

Klaus then turns the television on in the living room, which is showing the morning news. Jerome also directs his attention to the television as well, and replies back to Klaus.

"Oh yes, I did sleep well. Um, listen, Klaus. There is something I have to tell you."

Klaus then lowers the news program on the television, but still has his vision, pointed toward the television. Klaus laughs and shakes his head, and then replies back to Jerome.

"Now, whatever you're going to tell me, can it wait until after breakfast? Dan went through so much to make all that food, and you're not about to spoil my appetite, or the vibe or anything. So if it's something really devastating or bad, tell me after, okay?"

Jerome shakes his head, and gets up from the sofa, snapping back at Klaus.

"You know what, forget it. Wow. Never mind, just forget about it."

Jerome walks away from the living room, into the kitchen with Dan and Ernest. Klaus then once again, shakes his head, and laughs, and continues to watch television. Jerome remains in the kitchen, conversing with Dan and Ernest, and talking about mundane topics and issues. Very soon after during this, Dan is finished preparing breakfast.

All four of them sit in the kitchen, and enjoy their meal. While they are all eating, Klaus says something to all of them.

"Alright, once we get done with this, I'll drop Jerome off at home. After that I..."

Jerome takes a sip of orange juice, and eats his breakfast, quickly replying to Klaus.

"I'm not going back there, ever. I rather live on the street. I told you yesterday, it's a boarding house, and I share it with like twenty other people. The place is disgusting and dirty, the people that run it, are racist and homophobic. I tried to tell you this, but you wouldn't listen."

Dan and Ernest eat their breakfast, but decide to be nosy, and involve themselves in the sudden drama that has erupted at the table. Klaus then takes a sip of his coffee, and shakes his head, basically ignoring Jerome. Jerome then while looking down at his plate, responds to Klaus.

"I was hoping, you let me stay here. I'm not very big, and don't take up much space. Ha Ha. I mean, Dan and Ernest stay here, so why can't I? If you say no, I understand, but please?"

Klaus takes several bites of his breakfast, and has another sip of his coffee. Klaus then shakes his head, and laughs, like he customarily seems to do, and then whispers to Jerome.

"If you want to stay, you can stay. I guess. Fine. Whatever. I don't care anymore."

Jerome has a puzzled look on his face, and doesn't respond, or talk back to Klaus at all. Jerome just simply shakes his head, and returns to eating his breakfast. Dan and Ernest remain respectfully quiet, although they are amused by this whole exchange. For the next five minutes, it was complete silence around the table, as the men are totally concentrating on eating their breakfast. Klaus was wanting to bring several topics up, but decided for this moment, to bite his tongue, and wait until later to talk about them. Eventually, the men finish their breakfast, and Klaus does indeed say what he initially wanted to say, to all of the men.

"Alright, so I need to stop by the studio today, and do some technical stuff, so you all may as well come with me, and keep me company. I think first thing, I'll take Dan to pick his car up, then we'll go to the studio. After that, I'll let Jerome get his things, as he's moving in."

The rest of the men seem to be in agreement with this plan, and it sounds good to them. After breakfast, Jerome returns to the living room sofa, and does work on his computer. With Ernest sitting on the other side of the sofa, reading a book. Dan is in the kitchen, washing the dishes that he cooked. Klaus is also in the living room, sitting on his recliner, watching reruns of "Star Trek, The Next Generation." This seems like an ordinary slow day, but it isn't. The guys are all having quiet time at the moment, but they still have much to accomplish today. It seems right now; they have a little time to spare. This continues on for a couple hours, when 2 p.m. hits. The guys all immediately get ready to leave the house. Klaus, Dan, Ernest and Jerome, all head into Klaus car, and Klaus then drives to the Downtown Los Angeles area, where Dan's car is parked. Dan is able to locate his car, and is quite agitated, when he notices that he has a parking citation. Klaus decides that he is going to pay the citation for Dan, and tells him not to worry, or get upset about it. The men then proceed directly to the radio station, with Jerome riding in the passenger seat in Klaus car, and Ernest riding in the passenger seat, of Dan's car. On Fridays, Klaus usually does technical work around the studio, and it can be quite boring. He does this, so when it's time to do the show the following week, everything is in order, and there wouldn't be any issues or errors. The men gather inside the station, and head up to the third floor, where the studio of their show is. Klaus then tells all of the men, that he will be right back, as he is doing technical work. As Klaus is about to leave the studio, Jerome taps on the back of Klaus shirt, and speaks to him.

"Hey, you mind if I tag along? I have always been interested in the technical and electronic aspect of how radio stations worked, and I thought it be nice. If I can't it's okay, I..."

Klaus begins to laugh to himself, shaking his head. Not signaling that he means no, but he feels shocked at his current position right now, and doesn't know what to say. Klaus responds.

"Uh, I guess so. If you want to. It's very boring, but since you want to follow me so bad, let's go. I guess you might learn something too, I suppose. On your way out, you might as well, hand me that tool box while you're at it. Thanks, I appreciate it."

Jerome then grabs Klaus toolbox, which is situated on the other side of the studio. The both of them walk down to the ground floor, where the control room is, and Klaus begins to work. Jerome has his laptop with him, and is taking notes of everything Klaus is doing. As Klaus continues to work, he tries to educate Jerome, on exactly what he's doing right now.

"This studio uses fiber optics. It's kinda a new technology, that uses these very thin, almost string like connectors. I'm sure you're aware of that. In the good old days, they used coax cables, and A/V connectors, and shit like that. Not anymore. We upgraded to latest and greatest."

Jerome continues to type down notes on his laptop, and nods his head in agreement with Klaus. As Klaus continues to do more technical work, Jerome softly responds to him.

"I remember on the show, you talked about how you used to be a cable guy, and would install cable TV for people. That's kinda cool, and I can see it now. You're good with this stuff."

Klaus heard and understood what Jerome said, however, he doesn't respond, react, or emote, and continues to work. Klaus is very detailed at what he is doing, and he is very skilled as well. Jerome steadily writes notes down on his laptop computer, and watches carefully as to what Klaus is doing, being very interested in everything. Jerome is enjoying learning new things, such as electrical and technical related topics, in regards to how the radio station is run. Klaus then begins to wrap up working in the control room, and starts to assemble everything back together. As Klaus is completing his work, he takes a look over at Jerome, who's typing notes on his laptop. Jerome doesn't know, or realize Klaus is staring at him. Klaus simply laughs and shakes his head, as usual. Klaus has finished his work, and he and Jerome head up to the top floor, to let Dan and Ernest know they are finished. Even though Klaus is knowledgeable on his radio station technical work, it still took some time for him to accomplish his task. It is now 5 p.m., and that's rather late in the day. Klaus then decides to speak to all the men.

"Hey, you know what. Dan, you have your car now right? Here's the key to my place. I trust you won't burn my house down, or blow it up. Ha Ha. Why don't you and Ernest go back to my place. Y'all can just chill there until we get back. Jerome is gonna drive with me to get his stuff. I already know that Friday night traffic, to North Hollywood is gonna be bad, but yeah."

Dan is in agreement, and Klaus gives Dan a key. While Klaus is detaching the key from his keychain, he then speaks out to Dan, asking him to do something.

"Oh yeah, also go to the hardware store, and get a copy of that key. Make one for you, Ernest and Jerome. So that way we all can get in. We all live there now right? So yeah."

Dan once again is in agreement, and shakes his head. He takes the key, and Dan and Ernest, immediately head to the parking structure, and Dan drives himself and Ernest, to the hardware store, and then back to the house. Klaus and Jerome remain in the studio, wrapping things up. As Klaus and Jerome are closing up the studio, Jerome whispers out to Klaus.

"I wanted to say thank you for everything. DJ K. You're a very kind man, and I feel really lucky to have you as a friend, and thank you for giving me a chance."

Klaus heard what Jerome said, but does not react, or respond. Klaus, although he is not showing it, is very happy that Jerome appreciates everything that he is doing for him. Klaus and Jerome then exit out of the studio, and get inside of Klaus SUV. Klaus is dreading having to drive to North Hollywood, but he doesn't have a choice, as he wants to help out Jerome. During the long ride on the highway, Klaus and Jerome engage in small talk. Klaus speaks to Jerome.

"So, are the people there really that bad? Like, what do they do? Give me an example?"

Jerome, with his vision directly facing front towards the windshield, responds to Klaus.

"Oh, we could be here all day, but they are just evil people. They throw my property away. They say disrespectful comments to me. They lock me out quite a bit. Uh, what else, they don't clean the place up, and I try my best to tidy the house up, but why bother you know.

Klaus understands what Jerome means, but keeps his eyes towards the road, and doesn't have any type of reaction. Klaus then asks Jerome yet another question, that he is curious about.

"So you rather live with me, Dan and Ernest though. I mean, why? I mean, you don't find us weird or strange? Like, you're the complete opposite of us. I don't know. Whatever."

Jerome then turns his head towards Klaus, and smiles. Jerome then responds to Klaus.

"I don't know, I just feel, I don't know, safe. I guess safe is the right word. I've always been a fan of yours DJ K. I think, you guys are cool. You guys don't mind me right? Which it doesn't seem like you guys do, so yeah. I like all you guys, and I'm glad we're all friends."

Klaus then turns his head towards Jerome, and smiles. He then rubs his hand through Jerome's hair, and continues driving down the highway. Although it was a very long trip, Klaus does eventually make it to where Jerome lives. Klaus notices that North Hollywood is a very nice suburban area, but the property that Jerome was living in, was very decrepit. Klaus felt that they should be taking better care of the building, so it's not in the state, and condition, it's currently in. The outside lawn was in dire need of maintenance, several work needs to be done to the outside of the building as well. Klaus is now starting to see, that Jerome was not lying about his living situation. Klaus parks his car, and he alongside Jerome, go inside of the building. Klaus then realizes that Jerome was correct. The building is not very clean, and very dingy. He also notices the other housemates in the building look questionable and shady. Jerome opens the door to his bedroom, that has bunk beds, that he shares with three other guys. Jerome then starts to grab suitcases, and storage containers. While he's doing this, he speaks to Klaus.

"I try to keep all my stuff in order like this. I never know when I have to leave, or depart. I don't carry much stuff. This is pretty much everything. You can grab that, I'll grab this."

Klaus nods his head, and grabs what Jerome told him to pick up. In only one trip, Klaus and Jerome manage to get everything, and they put them in the back of Klaus SUV. Klaus then drives himself and Jerome, back south to Redondo Beach, where his house is. On the trip back, Jerome then decides to think of an idea, and explains it Klaus.

"Hey, you know Dan and Ernest made breakfast for us today. Why don't we surprise them ourselves, and gives them a pizza party? Why not? I mean, it's something nice right? I'm not that great of a cook. I know you can cook pretty well DJ K., but let's do it. Come on. Ha Ha."

Klaus laughs, and shakes his head, and agrees to the plan. Klaus and Jerome, then head to Pizza Hut, to pick up several pizzas, for all the guys to enjoy. Once they have got the pizzas, they both head back to house. Dan and Ernest are happy that they bought pizza. For the rest of the night, the guys eat their pizza, and socialize with one another. All of the guys are drinking beer that Klaus had in the refrigerator too. Klaus, Dan, Jerome, and Ernest, then play Mario Party, on Klaus Nintendo Switch video game system. They are having a great night together, and it seems, they are all happy. The men as usual, lose track of time, and it's getting quite late, with how much fun the guys were having. It is now 3 a.m. Dan and Ernest then head into the bedroom, to start getting ready for bed. Klaus and Jerome then help clean everything up. Once they are finished, Klaus decides to sit at the sofa in the living room, watching television. Jerome directs himself to Klaus bedroom, takes a shower, and then gets himself ready for bed. Jerome then falls fast asleep on Klaus bed. An hour later, Klaus drifts in and out of consciousness and sleep, and turns the television in the living room off. Klaus then takes a shower, changes into his sleep clothes, and falls asleep next to Jerome, in bed.

The next morning, being that it was a Saturday, was shockingly, very uneventful. Not much happened, and the guys, due to how much fun they had the night before, ended up oversleeping heavily. It was now Noon, and all of the guys were still in bed asleep. It wasn't until 1 p.m., in which Ernest was the first to wake. Ernest decides to walk into the kitchen, and prepare himself a cup of coffee. A half an hour later, Dan wakes up, and joins Ernest in the kitchen. Dan and Ernest simply engage in trivial banter, as Dan makes himself a bowl of cereal. A half an hour later, Jerome wakes up, but notices that Klaus is still deep asleep. Jerome kisses Klaus on his forehead, and gently gets out of bed, not to disturb Klaus. Jerome joins the other two men in the kitchen. Dan prepares Jerome a bowl of Honey Nut Cheerios cereal, to which Jerome thanks him for. Dan, Ernest, and Jerome, remain in the kitchen for several minutes, conversing with each other, and exchanging jokes. Not long after that, Klaus awakens, and walks himself to the kitchen. Dan notices Klaus, and starts to speak to him.

"Hey man, you want a bowl of cereal? Here sit, I'll pour you one."

Dan takes a bowl out of the cabinet, and Klaus grabs Dan's wrist, and puts the bowl back on the shelf. Dan gives Klaus a shocked look, and Ernest and Jerome are also shocked as well. Klaus then opens up a drawer in the kitchen, taking out some Tylenol. Klaus then opens the refrigerator to get a bottle of water. Klaus swallows a couple of the Tylenol pills. He then puts the Tylenol back in the drawer, and takes more sips of water. Klaus then responds to Dan.

"No, I don't want any fucking cereal. I'm not feeling well. Y'all need to keep it down, you guys are too damn loud. I'm not feeling well. I have a headache. You guys drive me crazy. Why do you guys have to be so loud like that? Ugh."

Klaus then takes more sips of his water, and with the water bottle in his hand, walks towards his room. Klaus then slams the door shut, once inside. Dan, Ernest and Jerome, all look at each other, and laugh. For the remainder of the day, all the men kept to themselves. Later on in the evening, Dan went to the supermarket, and bought ground beef, to make tacos. Klaus was still in his room, being secluded from the other guys. Once Dan finished making tacos, he knocks on Klaus door, to let him know that dinner is ready. Klaus doesn't respond, and continues to stay in his room. Dan, Ernest and Jerome eat the tacos that Dan has made. An hour and a half later, Klaus finally comes out of his room, feeling better. Klaus prepares a plate of the tacos Dan made, and quickly takes his plate back to this bedroom, and slams the door. The rest of the men, who are in the living room, who watched him do this, find this funny, and start laughing. Dan, Ernest, and Jerome, remain in the living room for the rest of the night, also playing video games, like they did the night before. When midnight approaches, Dan and Ernest go into the bedroom. Jerome remains in the living room by himself, watching "SpongeBob SquarePants." Jerome then notices that there are dirty dishes in the kitchen, so he decides to clean them himself. Once Jerome has finished with the dishes, he turns to watching cartoons in the living room. Jerome starts to get tired, and turns the television in the living room off, and walks himself to bed. Jerome notices that Klaus is deep asleep, and tries his best not to wake him up. Jerome then falls asleep. A couple hours later, with it being 3 a.m. now, Klaus awakens. Klaus doesn't disturb Jerome while he's sleeping, and Klaus walks outside to his balcony to smoke a cigarette. Klaus then has a drink of water, and returns to bed, with Jerome still fast asleep, not disturbing him. Klaus returns to falling asleep, seconds later.

The following day being Sunday, was just as slow. The men didn't do anything that amazing or spectacular. It was a slow rest day. The only difference is today, Klaus was feeling much better, and was interacting with the guys more. To make up for his foul mood from yesterday, Klaus decided to stop by the supermarket, to pick a few things up, and will cook a steak dinner for all the men. Klaus was an excellent cook, and the rest of the men, enjoyed his cooking very much. Klaus made a side of mashed potatoes from scratch, and also steamed vegetables, with Klaus own secret recipe for garlic bread. The men were very happy to have the meal Klaus prepared, and the morale of the group, was boosted back to normal. Ernest also decided to bake a cake for dessert. Klaus also managed to get some ice cream from the store, and the guys all had ice cream for dessert. Once the men were finished with dessert, Jerome cleaned up all the dishes, as none of the other guys were willing, or wanting to do so. Jerome didn't mind cleaning up the kitchen after dinner. Klaus and Dan, then were playing "Call of Duty", on Klaus Xbox in the living room. Ernest was also on the sofa, reading a book. Once Jerome was finished with the dishes, he joined the rest of the men in the living room, watching Klaus and Dan play the video game. The men all eventually got tired, and went to bed.

With the weekend now being over, and it now being Monday, the guys knew, that they have a show that will be going live, tomorrow night. Klaus wakes up at 11 a.m., and is the first person in the house, to do so. He makes himself a cup of coffee, and starts to work on his laptop, organizing for tomorrow night's show. Over the course of the next hour and a half, the rest of the guys wake up, and it's yet another slow day. For dinner, Dan ends up making a pasta like casserole, with the leftover ground beef, from the tacos he made the other day. The guys enjoy the meal, and thank Dan. Jerome starts to do the dishes, but Ernest offers to take the task away from him for today. Jerome refuses, and tells Ernest that it's okay, and he will do the dishes. Ernest decides to keep Jerome company anyways, and engages in small talk with him. Once the dishes are finished, Ernest and Jerome go on the balcony, to have a cigarette. Klaus and Dan are in the living room, and do what they normally do, and play video games, battling and competing with each other all night. Ernest and Jerome then join the rest of the guys in the living room. Eventually, it is time for the men to go back to bed, as they all become tired. All of the men say goodnight to each other. The men then, all go to sleep for the day.

It is now Tuesday, and today is the first day of the week, for the show to start. The show airs live every Tuesday, Wednesday, and Thursday night. Klaus wakes up, excited that they are having a show tonight, and can't wait to get to the studio. The rest of the men are excited as well, because they are happy to do the show, alongside with Klaus. Klaus ends up having a bowl of cereal, and Dan joins him in the kitchen soon after that. Klaus and Dan speak with each other, and are completely ready for the show that is going to happen later tonight. Ernest and Jerome soon wake up, and join them in the kitchen. The guys all eat their cereal together, and are ready to take on the day. Once breakfast is finished, the guys start getting dressed, and situated. Klaus has all his notes ready for tonight's show, which he decided the topic of the show for tonight, will be about giving people second chances, or forgiving people, that did something wrong. Klaus is sure that this topic is going to cause a lot of controversy to his show, and people will be very interested in it. The callers will storm in with their stories. Klaus always makes sure that he picks topics, that are going to be controversial, for this very reason. Klaus, doesn't want to have a boring show, and so in order to prevent that, he has to have engaging topics for the audience to enjoy. Klaus jots down several more notes down on his notepad, and is all set for the show tonight. Sooner and later, it is time for the men to head to the radio station, to start tonight's show. Klaus, Dan, Ernest, and Jerome, all get into Klaus SUV. He then drives them all down to the radio station, in Downtown Los Angeles. They all proceed like they normally do, to the top floor. Mr. Weston is still on vacation, and is not present at the studio. The show doesn't start for another two hours, but Klaus would rather arrive to the station earlier, rather than later.

Klaus then starts to power on all the equipment in the radio station, doing several sound checks, so there are no difficulties or issues, when the show starts. Klaus sees that everything is fine, and he has nothing to worry about. Now that he has gotten used to his new co-hosts, it seems there aren't any more pre show jitters that Klaus usually has. He is very comfortable with the guys he is working with, and he trusts them wholeheartedly. Dan is on his phone, watching videos. Ernest is reading a book. Jerome is on his laptop, writing his blog, and doing other computer work. As Klaus is also doing last minute preparations for the show, he looks at his co-hosts and smiles to himself. Klaus feels that he is lucky that he has this new found team. Klaus could have sworn that when Stuart died, that was going to be the end of everything. Klaus didn't feel that he had the strength to carry on with everything, and move on, after that. Klaus managed to somehow, someway do it. He was able to save his show, and he almost feels as if his show is even better than it was previously. It has definitely gone through a major development and adjustment, but Klaus knows that his show is entertaining. Klaus would never let the show go on live, if he wasn't happy with it, and if he wasn't satisfied with everything that was going on. With the show now coming on in an hour, Klaus doesn't have to do any more preparations. He is fine with the way everything is, and he knows that he's ready, and that his co-hosts are ready for what tonight's show will bring. Klaus is excited, and happy.

Before long, it is time for the show to start live. It is now 7 p.m., and it is time for Tuesday night's show to commence. Klaus, and the rest of the men put their headphones on, and Klaus also turns the microphones in the studio on. The theme song of the show begins to play. Directly following that, Klaus speaks into the microphone to the audience.

"Hello everyone. Welcome back to the show. I hope you all had an amazing weekend. It is Tuesday, so that means, well, it means the show is back on. Ha Ha. Tonight's topic is going to be about second chances, forgiving, forgetting. If you have any experiences, please call in."

Klaus then turns on the telephone switchboard, in which several callers are on hold to the line, and wish to call in. The rest of the men introduce themselves to the audience. Klaus continues to write down notes, and several questions. Klaus has that feeling again, that he felt the previous week. The same identical feeling. The feeling that tonight's show for some reason, is going to be different. Klaus has no idea what exactly about this show, was going to be different. He also had no idea whether this feeling was going to be bad or good. But Klaus knew that something was up. It was an energy that he felt. This was going to be an interesting show. At the start of every show, Dan usually starts off, by giving the audience random recent events and topics. As Dan is explaining the current events, and hot topics for this show, Klaus takes this time to think to himself, and to calm himself down, over what tonight's show will bring. That anxious feeling he has, is very powerful, and Klaus understands that it's a message trying to tell him something. It is a message letting him know, that something drastic is about to happen. Klaus is trying his best to ignore this, and part of Klaus wants to believe that this feeling is nothing, and that it is all in his mind. However, Klaus knows way better than that. He knows that this feeling is serious, and that this feeling can only mean one thing. It means that something is up, and something serious, is going to happen soon. This feeling wasn't wrong the other times he felt it all last week, so why would it be wrong now? Dan starts to wrap up talking about his current events. Immediately following that, Jerome now has a segment, to where he announces community events and groups. This was a segment that Klaus approved for the show. Klaus remains silent, as his co-hosts are speaking to the audience.

Once Jerome has finished explaining recent community events and activities. The next segment features Ernest, giving off his daily life hack. It's a segment in which Ernest gives the audience, tips on how to modify things in your life, so they serve another purpose. In this segment, Ernest is talking about how you can use a beer can, to make a scented candle. Once Ernest gets done with his segment, it is now time for the main show to commence. Klaus begins to compose himself in order to get ready for the show. Klaus clears his throat, takes a sip of his coffee, and starts to speak in the microphone, to the audience.

"Yes, so like I said. Tonight's show is about second chances. Forgiving, forgetting, moving on. Letting things slide. Not having bad blood anymore. Calling truce. So yeah."

Klaus then starts to jot more notes down on his notebook, and starts to write questions down in his notes as well. Dan, Ernest, and Jerome, then start to speak, and encouraging listeners to call into the show, if they have any experiences, or something they want to add. The switchboard is overflowing with callers that are on hold, and Klaus is just about ready to take his first caller. Klaus readies himself to accept the caller that is on hold, on the switchboard. Klaus then began to sweat, and doubts himself heavily. He was starting to feel as though, he shouldn't let this caller on. Even though it was only a few seconds, it felt as though it was longer before Klaus accepted the call. With his finger over the button, Klaus looks at Dan, who nods his head, gesturing for Klaus to accept the caller. Klaus then connects the caller to the station. Klaus clears his throat, and very reluctantly, responds to the caller who is now live.

"Hello caller, You're live on the DJ K. show. Tonight's topic is about second chances, forgiving, forgetting. Do you have any experiences, or any input to tonight's topic caller?"

The caller then begins to laugh and snicker to himself. Klaus is feeling irritated, but the rest of the men find this amusing. So therefore, Klaus does not disconnect the call. The caller continues to laugh for several more seconds, before Klaus through frustration, responds.

"Caller, I'm going to disconnect you, if you don't stop. Was there something that you wanted to add to the topic? If not, I'm going to go on ahead and end the call. Alright?"

The caller then decides to finally respond to Klaus.

"Hey, you remember last week? The caller that pranked you? Well, both those callers were me. I was using a fake voice. I was only joking, and just goofing with you."

Klaus then starts to understand why he had that feeling. Klaus cannot believe that he is talking to the jokester, that called during last week's show. Klaus is slightly angry at this caller, and has an angry look on his face. The rest of the men are silent, and can see that Klaus is not happy at this caller. Klaus then takes his headphones off, and covers his hands with his face. Seeing that he is distraught, Dan tries to mediate the situation, and speaks with the caller.

"Yeah, I remember you. You got on the line before me. So, both those callers were you. That was fucked up man, why you have to do that? You got my host upset right now, live on air. So, I want you to apologize to him right now, for that shit you pulled. Apologize to DJ K. now."

Klaus was then happy that Dan stood up for him, and defended him. Klaus smiles back at Dan, and decides to put his headphones back on, and quickly changes his entire mood. The caller who is still connected live to the show, starts to laugh, and responds.

"I'm not apologizing for shit. I've been a fan of the show for years. I'm sorry that DJ S. is gone, I kinda liked him better, but oh well. DJ K. is okay. You know what. I will apologize, my bad. I'm sorry for my behavior. My name is Paul. I'm sorry for pranking earlier."

Klaus then decides to give the caller Paul another chance, and lets him remain on the line. Even though Klaus is upset that this is the prank caller from the week before. He is forgiving him. Maybe it was coincidence that tonight's topic was about forgiving, and here Klaus is letting the man who acted a complete fool on his show the week before, a second chance, and forgiving him. Klaus smiles to himself, and shakes his head. Klaus takes a sip of his coffee, and during this time, Dan decides to speak to the caller Paul, asking him a question.

"Alright Paul. That was very kind what you just did. Although, how did you manage to call into the show, twice in a row? There have been listeners of this show for years, that have struggled to get to the station, and received busy signals and such. So, what's your secret?"

Klaus continues to take sips of his coffee, and smiles at Dan. Klaus is appreciative to how observant Dan is, and he knows that Dan is always asking and thinking of the same things, that Klaus usually, more often than not is as well. The caller is silent for a few seconds, and responds.

"Oh yeah. I'm not telling you guys that. It's just my own personal secret, so yeah. But anyways, yeah. The topic is about forgiveness, so do y'all forgive me? I'm truly sorry. Ha Ha."

Klaus takes yet another gulp of his coffee, and then responds back to the caller Paul.

"Yeah, we forgive you. So, Paul, tells us about yourself. Other than being an asshole, and a jerk, what else should the listeners know about you? Where are you from, what do you do?"

The caller Paul then starts to clear his throat, and quickly responds back to Klaus.

"Well, born and raised here in the LA area. San Pedro to be exact. I'm Jewish, but I don't tell anybody this, because that's nobody's business. So, we can relate right DJ K.? Ha!"

Klaus shakes his head and laughs to himself, as he continues to listen to the caller Paul. The caller is actually right, and that both Klaus, and himself are Jewish. Klaus wasn't going to let the fact that the caller was simply Jewish as well, excuse his actions. Klaus was glad that Paul was Jewish too, but altogether, that didn't mean much in the grand scheme of things. Klaus takes another sip of his coffee, and continues to speak with the caller Paul.

"Alright, so what do you for a living, other than call my show, and prank everyone?"

Klaus then begins to laugh, and the rest of the men in the studio, start to laugh as well. The caller then erupts in laughter too, along with the rest of the men. The caller Paul then quickly decides to respond, after slight hesitation, from all the laughing.

"Well, I'm an Artist. When I say Artist, I mean Contemporary Artist. Well, I'm actually a painter, a damn good one too. I do portraits, murals, street art, I've done some comics and cartoons as well. I'm talented. Just nobody knows who I am yet, but that's gonna change soon."

Klaus takes a sip of his coffee, but almost spits it out, once finding out that Paul is an artist. Klaus was shocked that someone such as Paul, would be the type of person to prank his show, and act that way. Klaus seems even more intrigued with the caller now. Before Klaus is able to ask a second question, Dan instead asks a question to the caller Paul.

"Wow man, that's pretty cool. Hey, do you have any social media or anything? A website where we can see your stuff? Because I want to check out your stuff. See if your being truthful. Because I don't know. How do we know, you're not lying or pranking us again?"

Klaus shakes his head and laughs at Dan. Dan returns a smile back at Klaus, and laughs. Ernest and Jerome continue to listen to the show, being very amused and entertained at everything. The caller Paul then immediately responds.

"Sure, I can give you guys my website, my social media, and all that jazz. No problem."

The caller Paul, then proceeds to give the guys at the station all his information online, to where the guys can check out his artwork. During this time, Klaus decides to call a commercial break, and during the break, the guys plan on seeing Paul's work. Klaus then speaks.

"Okay guys, this would be a perfect time for a break. We're gonna keep Paul on the line. We're gonna check out his stuff. See if he's the real deal or not. We'll be right back. Stay tuned."

As soon as the show goes on break, Dan then pulls up the social media information that Paul gave to them. It doesn't take long at all for Dan to find Paul's portfolio. Once locating this information, Dan is actually shocked to see how talented Paul is. Paul was indeed telling the truth, and that he does oil paintings, street art, murals, and also cartoon and computer animation, and Paul also knows how to draw comics as well. Klaus, Dan, Ernest, and Jerome, still can't believe that this man is actually Paul. Klaus more importantly isn't too convinced. But during the break, Klaus and the rest of the men, watch interviews that Dan has done for public television, and they then realize that the voice matches the same one, the caller has. This is the same man. Klaus then covers his face with his hands, and shakes his head. Still in total disbelief. The commercial break of the show, then ends at this time. Klaus then speaks to the audience.

"Alright, welcome back everyone. During the break, we saw Paul's artwork online. You guys, we can say with absolute 100 percent certainty, that Paul is telling the honest to god truth. This man is an Artist, and he's so damn talented. Shame he had a bad attitude, but yeah well. Ha Ha."

The caller Paul, who is still connected to the line, laughs at Klaus remark. The other guys laugh as well. Ernest and Jerome, still continue to silently listen to Paul speak to Klaus. The show is becoming very entertaining, dramatic, and exciting. The caller Paul, responds back to the guys in the studio.

"Yeah, the guy with the glasses, with the shaggy hair. That ugly man is me. Ha Ha."

Klaus looks at Dan, and they both shake their heads and laugh. Klaus then responds.

"How old are you Paul? If you don't mind me asking. I was just curious to your age."

The caller Paul is silent for a few seconds, and doesn't say anything. Klaus was then worried, that he might have offended the caller, and that he would hang up, and disconnect the call. That was Klaus worst feeling, that the caller would hang up. Klaus feels the show so far tonight, is very entertaining, and if Paul were to leave, that would ruin the mood. Klaus then began to regret asking Paul that information, and then decides to back track himself.

"Oh, never mind, I'm sorry. I had no idea how intrusive that question actually was. You're absolutely right, that is none of my business how old you are. I was just curious, that's all. You don't have to answer that, if you don't want to. I'm sorry."

Klaus then waits for the caller's response. Klaus, along with the rest of the men in the studio, wait for several seconds for the caller to speak again. They all remain in awkward silence. Eventually, the caller Paul after some time, finally decides to speak back to Klaus.

"Yeah uh, that is none of your business, and normally I don't tell people my age. But DJ K. I'll make an exception for you. I'm willing to move on. Like tonight's show is all about second chances and shit, right? So, I'll move on. Ha Ha. I'm actually, believe it or not, thirty-five years old. Oh no. I'm old. Ha Ha."

Klaus then begins to laugh hysterically, and takes a look at Dan, who is also laughing. Ernest and Jerome begin to laugh in addition as well. The infectious laughter continues for quite some time, and Klaus tries his best to pull himself together, and carry on. Klaus cannot stop laughing, and Dan decides to take this time to speak to Paul, while Klaus is calming down.

"Alright, so Paul. What else should we know about you? So, I don't mean to pry, but I noticed it said you're an art teacher at UCLA. So that's kinda cool. Is this true?"

The caller Paul coughs and clears his throat, and scoffs to himself. Paul then responds.

"I *was* an art teacher at UCLA. I was laid off last fall. Been unemployed since, basically being a literal starving artist. I eat sardines, ramen noodles, and peanut butter sandwiches. Hoping that one day, I'll make it big, and be the next Van Gogh, or Picasso."

Klaus then in a sudden mood change, starts to feel empathetic of Paul. Dan, and the rest of the men, change their tones to more serious ones as well, in regards to what Paul just said. As the men are still gathering their thoughts, Paul during this time, continues on explaining his life.

"My nickname is Picasso by the way. People would call me that all the time. So yeah. I do my art; I stay with a buddy of mine now. I'm trying to manage, and live day by day. So, I take my own frustrations out on others. I'm sorry for pranking you the other day DJ K. Sorry man."

Klaus then for the first time in the night, has fully let the past situation with Paul go. Despite the fact he pranked call his show last week. Klaus has fully forgiven him. Klaus takes a look at Dan, and they both smile at each other. Klaus then speaks back to Paul.

"I forgive you Paul. It's okay. You're really talented man. Damn. Remember that, okay?"

The caller Paul then laughs back into the phone, and responds back to Klaus.

"Aww, thank you DJ K. I know you mean that too. That means we're friends now right? Ha Ha."

Klaus then hysterically laughs, and shakes his head. Klaus then replies back to Paul.

"Yeah, we're friends. We're buddies now. So, Paul, you have a Girlfriend or Wife? Are you single? Do you have any children? Again, just my curiosity, I wanted to know all of this. You don't have to answer, but I figure since we are friends now, I can ask you this. Ha Ha."

Paul in return, laughs into the phone over what Klaus said, and quickly answers back.

"I'm single. I'm actually Bisexual, so yeah. I have no kids. How boring huh? Ha Ha."

Klaus snickers to himself for a bit, and responds to Paul rather quickly

"Hey, no. That's not boring. That's cool. You're a lovely man Paul. Ha Ha."

Paul laughs in return to Klaus, and responds back to him.

"You're too kind DJ K. I'm very flattered and honored. Thank you very much. Ha."

Immediately following this, Klaus, and the rest of the men, continued to talk to Paul. Minutes turned into hours, and time was quickly passing by, with Paul being the center of attention. It wasn't until the last hour of the show, that Klaus realized, that Paul was the first, and only caller of the night. Klaus was then starting to worry, that other callers would be mad, that they aren't having a chance to call in, and speak on the show. Klaus speaks to the audience.

"Hey, you know what. Paul, you're a really fun guy, but I think we're gonna let you go man. Thank you for showing us your art. We have to get to the other callers, the phone line is blowing up, and we have to take other calls. So, I'll chat you with later then, okay Paul?"

The caller Paul hesitates for a second, but then he quickly speaks back to Klaus.

"Aww, alright. I guess it's only fair. But wait, hey. DJ K., let me stay on the line, and I'll be a guest co-host. Please? I've been a fan of your show for years. You'd be foolish to say no. Please?"

Klaus then takes a look at Dan, Ernest and Jerome, who are all nodding their heads. Klaus still feels against this idea, and doesn't know if he should actually go through with it. Klaus feels that he has enough hosts, and adding Paul, doesn't seem like it would be a wise, or beneficial decision. Klaus then realized that Paul was on the show for several hours, so there is clearly some chemistry, between himself, and Paul, and the entire show itself. Klaus then leans back in his chair, looks up at the ceiling, with his hands behind his head. He is unsure as to what to do. Half of him is saying one thing, and the other half of him is saying another. Klaus knows that Paul is entertaining and engaging, but Klaus is still not sure. Klaus must make a decision now though, as they are live on the air. Whether the answer is yes or no, Klaus needs to give his answer, and Paul needs to know. Klaus then takes a look at the other guys, who are telling him to say yes. Klaus then decides to respond back to Paul, giving him his decision.

"Damn. Damn. Damn. What the hell. Everyone, our guest host for tonight, Paul!"

Paul then decides to shout back into the phone, very pleased and happy.

"Oh wow! Thank you, DJ K., I don't know what to say. Hey listeners, I'm gonna be guest host for tonight. I feel like a celebrity. Yes. Let's do this. This is so awesome. Great!"

Klaus laughs and shakes his head, and Dan at the same time, pats Klaus on the back. For the last hour of the show, Paul was a guest host in the program. The guys all answered more calls from the callers, and Paul was a natural, at being the guest host. The show then approached it's ending time slot. Klaus had to close off the show, and let the audience know.

"Damn it. We have to go; our timeslot is ending. Thank you, guest host Paul. We'll be back tomorrow though. Same time, same channel. Catch everyone later. You all take care, be nice to each other, and love one another. Peace and love. See you."

Klaus, and the rest of the men, take their headphones off. Klaus then disconnects all the microphones, and turns the telephone switchboard off. Not even a second later, Klaus starts to call Paul up on the phone. The phone rings several times, but Paul eventually answers.

"Hello, who is this?"

Klaus then immediately responds back to the Paul on the phone.

"Paul, I'm inviting you to the studio, to be a permanent host."

Paul then immediately screams into the phone, replying to Klaus

"What? Yes. Thank you DJ K. Oh man. Wow. Thank you, thank you, thank you."

Klaus shakes his head, and smiles. Klaus gives Dan a fist bump, and Ernest and Jerome seem to also be accepting of Klaus decision, to allow Paul to be a permanent host. Paul continues to remain on the line, and Klaus then swiftly responds back to Paul.

"You're free tomorrow, right? We can have lunch, and you can meet all the guys. It's gonna be fun. We can have our first in person meeting, and yeah.

Paul continues to stay on the phone and responds right back to Klaus.

"Tomorrow is fine. Lunch sounds great. Just tell me where to meet up, and I'll be there."

Klaus shakes his head, and laughs, and responds to Paul.

"Alright man, see you tomorrow. Congrats on being our next co-host. And uh, well, you have a good night, and you just keep on drawing, I guess. Ha Ha. See you tomorrow man."

Paul laughs at what Klaus said, and responds back on the phone to Klaus.

"Yes. You have a good night too DJ K. See you tomorrow. Goodbye."

Klaus then disconnects the call, and puts his phone down on the table. Klaus then covers his hands with his face, and laughs. Dan walks over to Klaus, and pats him on the back. Dan then softly whispers back to Klaus.

"You did the right thing. What you're feeling is normal. It's okay man. Ha Ha."

Klaus then stands up, takes a sip of his coffee, and grabs Dan, and shoves him under his arm. Klaus is giving Dan, a noogie on his head, with Dan laughing. Klaus then responds.

"I know I did the right thing. You don't have to tell me Dan. Ha Ha."

Dan laughs back at Klaus. Klaus and Dan then hug, and Dan kisses Klaus on the cheek. Klaus, and the rest of the men, then start to prepare, to close up the studio.

CHAPTER 7:

THE ARMY SERGEANT

Things are becoming more drastic for Klaus. There never seems to be a dull moment, and Klaus is always on high alert, when it comes to new events, and issues, related to his life. Klaus at first wasn't prepared to deal with any of this, but he now feels ready for everything. Things are rushing by rather fast and quickly, but Klaus just wants to be able to move on despite that. Klaus is now fully accepting everything, and in the past, Klaus would have thought of all of this as weird or strange. Now, Klaus seems to think of it as ordinary and common. Klaus doesn't feel pressured to face the unknown anymore. He has already faced the unknown quite a bit already, and he's ready to just deal with things, however they may come. Klaus figured his life before, was simple and ordinary. It was his dream to always make it big on radio. He wanted to fulfill that dream, without any problems. He had his business partner Stuart, and life was perfect.

However, Klaus felt he received the ultimate cruse or setback, when he heard the news that his best friend for life, and his radio partner Stuart, was killed. Klaus was adamant on closing himself off from the world indefinitely, and not caring about anything else in the world. Klaus wanted to crawl himself up into a ball, in a dark room, and never come out. He was in that much of a depression, and all Klaus wanted to do was sulk. He didn't care about anything else, not anymore.

Klaus wanted to vanish from reality. Never to be seen, or heard from again. But Klaus turned his agenda around, and he managed to find a new group of friends, and an even stranger network connection. Although he has only met these men for a short time, Klaus has an extreme trust and bond with them, and they have his back, and they will continue to look out for one another. Klaus is safe and understanding of that. Everything is okay for him.

The men all the leave the studio, after having yet another eventful show. The guys all planned and intended for this to be a regular show, but tonight's show, they managed to add yet another co-host to their team. Paul, the guy who pranked called Klaus on his first show, since taking a break. Klaus would have never thought he would come across this man again. What are the odds, he would encounter Paul again? Even though Klaus was agitated and angry, and wanted to disconnect Paul at first, Klaus decided to give Paul another chance. The theme of the show tonight was about second chances, and forgiving people for past mistakes. So that's exactly what Klaus did; he allowed Paul to remain on the show, and gave him the benefit of the doubt. It turns out, that was a wise choice, as Paul turned out to be a good guy. Not only was he a good guy, but Klaus enjoyed talking to him so much, that he decided to make him an in-studio co-host. To which the rest of the guys were very much in agreement, with this decision. As Klaus and the rest of the guys, continue to close up the studio, they all start to reflect on the events of tonight's show. Knowing that although the show had a lot of twists and turns, the show also turned out to be fun, and the guys also managed to meet a new friend through it all. Klaus, and the men, finally are done wrapping up and closing the studio, and they all walk out of the building. Klaus heads home, and once the guys are back at the house, Dan boils some hot dogs on the stove, and the guys all decide to have that as their supper, along with some potato chips. Dan finishes making the hot dogs, and the guys then eat. After the men ate their dinner, they immediately all go to bed. Klaus found it extremely difficult to rest tonight, as he knew he was going to be meeting up with Paul. Klaus was going to see Paul in person for the first time, and Klaus couldn't wait to meet him. He knew Paul was interesting on the phone, and knew it would be even more interesting to see him live, and in person. Klaus does eventually manage to drift off to sleep, but it was still difficult for him to do so. Klaus just simply couldn't stop thinking about Paul, and it was preventing him from concentrating on his sleep. Morning arrived, and it is now 9 a.m. Klaus gets out of bed, and notices Jerome is still asleep. Klaus smiles, and tries his best not to wake him up. Klaus walks to the kitchen, to where Dan and Ernest are already up, and conversing with each other. Klaus greets them, and then starts to pour himself a cup of coffee. After getting his coffee, Klaus then decides to walk over to the living room, and watch the morning news. Jerome awakens a half an hour later, and walks to the kitchen, and circulates with Dan and Ernest. Klaus then for a moment, forgot that they were meeting up with Paul today.

Klaus takes out his phone, and starts to text Paul, asking him if meeting up at 2 p.m. for lunch, is okay with him. Klaus waits for five minutes to Paul to respond to the text, and he doesn't. Klaus gets slightly agitated and worried, when Paul doesn't immediately reply back to the text. Klaus starts to shake with anxiety and concern. Klaus while still sitting on the sofa, crosses his arms, and looks out towards his balcony, shaking his head in frustration. Klaus can audibly hear Dan, Ernest, and Jerome, talking, exchanging jokes, and laughing in the kitchen. However, he is not fully listening or eavesdropping into their conversation. Klaus then returns his vision back to the television set in his living room, and watches the news. About ten minutes later, Klaus hears a notification sound on his phone, letting him know that he has a new text message alert. Klaus picks up his phone, and reads the text, and notices that it is from Paul. Paul replies back, apologizing for his late reply, and that he was busy. Paul also says that 2 o'clock is fine. Klaus while reading the text, has a wide grin on his face, and is very delighted. Klaus then replies back to Paul, texting him the restaurant that they are going to meet up at. Klaus decides that they all should meet up at Chili's. It's a restaurant specializing in American comfort food, and Tex-Mex food, and other specialties such as Burgers, Steak, Chicken Fingers, Fajitas, Quesadillas, Pasta, and Barbecue Ribs. This is one of Klaus favorite restaurants. He was sure that Paul was going to like it as well, and it was the perfect spot for them all to meet up for lunch at.

Klaus gets up from the sofa, and walks over to the kitchen, where the other men are. Klaus pours himself another cup of coffee. While he's doing that, he speaks to all the men.

"I just got off the phone with Paul. We're gonna meet him at Chili's at 2 p.m. We're gonna have lunch with him, and chat with him. Introduce ourselves to him. Y'all know the drill."

Klaus takes a sip of his coffee, and Dan, Ernest, and Jerome, nod their heads in agreement. Klaus then remains in the kitchen, and decides to chat with the other guys. They are all having friendly talk, and are simply bonding with one another. Klaus is anticipating for this afternoon, to where they will all go out to lunch, meeting up with Paul. The other men are also excited to meet Paul as well. Klaus finishes his coffee, and walks out of the kitchen. He then begins to get himself ready for the day, and picking out his outfit. The other guys follow suit, and also prepare themselves for the day. Klaus, and the other men also know, that tonight, is a show night. It's Wednesday, so they have to report to the studio. So the men all have a busy day ahead of them. They not only have to meet up with Paul, but they also have to report to the studio later tonight, as they have a live show as well. The men are totally prepared for all of this, and they don't seem scared, or phased by this at all. In fact, this is very much exciting for them all to deal with. Klaus, and the other men, are used to this by now, and don't seem to mind all the zany adventures that they have encountered, and came across, so far. Jerome has already gotten himself prepared, and sits on the edge of Klaus bed. Being slightly amused, as Klaus keeps changing his mind on what shirt to wear. Putting one shirt on, and taking it off for another one. Jerome tries to hold back his laughter, but is unable to. Klaus notices this, and speaks to him.

"I want to make a good impression for Paul, which one should I wear? I can't decide."

Jerome shakes his head and laughs. He then points to a blue plaid shirt.

"I think you would look cute in that one. Plaid really suits you. Go with that one."

Klaus looks at the shirt, and shakes his head. He then frowns at Jerome and responds.

"Really? I wear this one quite a bit, and I don't know. I wanted to try something different, but maybe, if it ain't broke, don't fix it, I guess. Are you sure I should wear this one?"

Jerome nods his head, and laughs. Klaus then shakes his head, and begins to put on the shirt, that Jerome recommended him to wear. Klaus then sprays come cologne fragrance on, and then jokingly sprays some on Jerome, who finds it funny. Meanwhile, Dan is helping Ernest shave in the bathroom. Although Ernest is scared that Dan might accidently nick him, Dan is doing a perfect job of shaving Ernest. Dan finishes shaving Ernest's face, and the men then continue to get ready. Eventually, all of them are now prepared and situated. They then begin to head out for the day. All four of them head into Klaus SUV, and Klaus drives directly to the Chili's restaurant, to meet up with Paul, like they earlier planned. The restaurant is not far from Klaus residence, so the men happen to make it there rather quickly and fast. Upon driving up to the restaurant, Klaus notices a lanky looking man, with shaggy hair, wearing glasses, wearing a green button-up shirt, and jeans and tennis shoes. Klaus knew that this man was Paul. Klaus biggest worry was that Paul would stand him up, but it turns out, Paul was a man of his word. Klaus and Paul did not make eye contact, so Klaus is not sure that Paul noticed them. However, Klaus did indeed locate and see Paul. Klaus was extremely happy and pleased, things were going smoothly, and correctly. Paul did indeed show up to the restaurant, and he was already there, before Klaus, and the rest of the men happened to arrive there. The other men in the car, realize that man is Paul as well, and are content that they happened to locate him. Klaus manages to find a parking spot, and parks his SUV. The men then all get out of the car, and start to walk to the restaurant, where Paul is standing in front of. A minute later, Paul notices the men walking up to the restaurant, and waves out to them. Klaus and Paul finally come in contact with each other. After a few seconds of silence, and both of them snapping out of the initial shock, Klaus speaks.

"Oh my god, it's really you huh? Wow, I can't believe you're real, and not some joke or prank. I'm DJ K., or Klaus, whatever you want to call me. This is my entourage. Ha Ha."

Klaus and Paul shake hands, and Paul begins to laugh. Paul then responds to Klaus.

"Well, I don't know. Maybe my name *isn't* Paul, maybe I'm not the guy you think I am. Maybe I'm some entity that doesn't exist, and this is all a figment of your imagination. Actually, no. I *am* the jerk that prank called you. Unfortunately, my name is actually Paul. Ha Ha."

Klaus shakes his head, and laughs, and can't believe how hilarious Paul is. The rest of the men, then introduce themselves to Paul, and shake his hand. Directly following that, the men all head inside the Chili's restaurant, so that they can have lunch. Once inside the restaurant, despite it being 2 in the afternoon on a Wednesday, the restaurant still has a handful of other patrons and customers. The waitress seats Klaus, and the rest of his party, at a table in the back of the restaurant. Klaus sits on the end chair, while Ernest and Jerome sit next to each other on the left side of the table, while Dan and Paul, sit on the right side of the table. The waitress hands all of the men menus, which the men all start to gaze at. Klaus then starts to speak with Paul.

"You can order whatever you want man. An artist has to eat right? Ha Ha. Whatever you want, it's on me. Whatever you're hungry for, you can get it."

While he is still reading the menu, Paul replies back to Klaus.

"I see. I think I have been here before years ago, with a friend of mine. So when you suggested Chili's, I figured I would easily make my mind up. But there are so many options, and I am kinda hungry, so it's more difficult to choose. Ha Ha. But I'll think of something I guess."

Klaus then shakes his head, as usual, and laughs at Paul. Klaus is also unsure of what to order himself. Klaus and the rest of the men, continue to look at the menu. Ernest looks up from his menu, and starts to stare deeply at Paul, and decides to reluctantly, ask him a question.

"Hey, uh, Paul? You wouldn't have happened to volunteer for Salvation Army before?"

Paul then raises his eyebrows, and he and Ernest then make eye contact. Paul then laughs.

"Hey, wait a minute. You're the guy that was serving punch at that event. No shit. Ha."

Ernest then smiles, and nods his head. Ernest resumes looking at his menu, and responds.

"Yup that was me. My memory is shoddy now, I'm getting older. But yeah. I was volunteering for that community outreach art event, in Downtown LA, near City Hall. You were one of the artists that were painting the skyscraper mural. I had nothing to do, so I volunteered with snacks and refreshments. I knew you looked familiar. Small world. Glad I met you again."

Ernest then looks up from his menu, and he and Paul exchange eye contact yet again, laughing at each other. Klaus who was listening to Ernest and Paul converse with each other, shakes his head, and laughs, and continues to read his menu. Dan also feels curious towards Paul, and decides to ask him a question as well.

"Yo, man? You wouldn't happen to do graffiti, would you? Just curious if you did."

Paul continues to read the menu, and then starts to silently laugh to himself. It seems as though Paul isn't going to answer the question, based on his slight hesitation. However, a few seconds later, Paul does indeed politely respond back to Dan's question.

"As a matter of fact, I do. I used to do graffiti more often when I was younger. Am I the best graffiti artist, no. Graffiti is tricky, because it's illegal, and it also has criminal ties to it. But graffiti is still art, and it's beautiful, and yes, I am quite skilled in it. Why?"

Dan then taps his fork on the table, creating a musical beat, and responds back to Paul.

"Oh, no reason. I was only curious. I figured the answer was yes, but wanted to be sure."

Paul then nods his head, while he's still reading the menu. Jerome then starts to stare at Paul, and likewise with the other men, wants to ask him a question too. Jerome speaks to Paul.

"I was just wondering. I'm not the best artist. I've always been fascinated with art, don't know much about it. I was wondering, if you could teach me, how to use an easel and stuff?"

Paul then laughs, and then starts to look at Jerome. Paul then softly responds to him.

"Sure champ. I can teach you art. Whenever you want, just call me, I'll teach you. Ha."

Paul and Jerome then smile at each other, and both Jerome and Paul, go back to reading the menu. The rest of the table is silent directly after this, as the men continue to look at the menu's, deciding what to eat. They all then decide what they are going to order. Klaus decides to order the Baby Back Ribs. Dan decides to order the Bacon Cheeseburger. Ernest decides to order the Chicken Sandwich. Jerome decides to order the Chicken Quesadilla, and Paul decides to order the same thing Klaus did, which was the Baby Back Ribs. After the men give the waitress their order, they resume having friendly talk with one another, with Paul especially immersing himself more with the group. Shockingly, Klaus is the least receptive person active in the conversation. He is simply nodding his head and smiling. Dan, Ernest, Jerome, and Paul, conversate heavily with one another, with Klaus listening. Actually, Klaus isn't even really listening or getting involved. He's too involved with his own thoughts, and simply notices them speaking as background noise. Klaus is daydreaming heavily, and also has his mind mainly on the show that is airing tonight. Paul is going to be a new host, and that's yet another person that's an addition to the show. Klaus isn't worried about this, but finds it interesting, that he has another host to add to his show, regardless. As Klaus continues to watch over the table, at his new group of friends, he decides to daydream some more. None of the other guys even notice that Klaus is being quiet, as they are too involved, with being friendly with one another. Klaus finds it amazing how all these men manage to get along, and connect with each other, without any issues. Klaus is taking advantage of the fact, the other guys are not noticing him zoning out, and daydreaming, and Klaus decides to continue doing it. Even though he and the rest of the men, are only doing something simple, as going out to lunch, Klaus doesn't see it that way. This is a time for him to reflect, and for him to see the bigger picture, with everything involved.

Klaus is interrupted by his daydreaming, when the waitress returns to the table, with all of the men's food orders. The guys then all start to eat. Klaus, who was extremely hungry, is happy, now that he has food, as usual. The rest of the men are enjoying their meal as well. As they are all eating, the men continue to talk with each other. As he is eating, Klaus is aware that the guys still have a bit of time, before the show starts later tonight. Klaus wonders if he and the guys are going to go straight back home, or if he is going right to the studio after they have lunch. Either way, he's happy with whatever happens. If the guys want to go back to the house, that's fine. If they want to go to the studio, even though it's still quite early, he's content with that as well. Klaus is willing to do, whatever the collective wishes to do as well. He is now a part of a group, and his opinion, isn't the only one that matters. He now needs to understand that the rest of the men, have a say in what the plan is as well. It's not that Klaus sees himself as the leader, but it was starting to seem that way. That simply isn't true. Klaus cannot simply think of himself as the leader, and himself only. Klaus has four other men that he has to consult first, and see how they feel about certain things prior. Klaus cannot be selfish, and he has to be aware, of the feelings and considerations, the other guys may have. Klaus continues to eat his lunch, remaining silent, as the other men, steadily talk with one another. Klaus doesn't feel left out, that he's being silent, and not contributing. He simply doesn't have anything to say right now. It's not that he's feeling uncomfortable, it's quite the opposite. Klaus is happy to be here. He's happy to meet Paul today, he's happy that he's with his new friends, having lunch. The fact of the matter is, Klaus doesn't wish to speak, or talk right now. His mind isn't set for that, and he rather stay silent and listen. Klaus eats his meal, and keeps his opinions and thoughts for himself.

The men all finish their plates, and they steadily talk with each other at the table. Minutes later, the waitress does arrive at the table with the check. As promised earlier, Klaus pays for the entire check, paying for not only his meal, but his friends' meals as well. Klaus also leaves a tip for the waitress. The men then all sit in silence, unsure as to what to do next. They all eventually then decide to get up from the table, and walk out of the restaurant. Once they are outside of the restaurant, the men continue to stand in silence. The five of them remain standing outside silent, not speaking. Klaus is finding this rather awkward, and feels as though, it is going to be up to him, to say or do something, to get out of this awkward scene. Klaus then decides to pull out his phone. While Klaus is doing that, he speaks to Paul.

"Hey, you know we have a show tonight? We start at 7 p.m. I'm gonna text you the studio address, and also the code for the parking garage. We can meet you there tonight. Okay?"

Paul who had his hands his pockets, notices that Klaus just sent him a text. Paul takes his phone out, and reads the text, which has the address to the studio on it. Paul nods his head, and puts his phone back into his pocket. Paul then whispers out to Klaus, directly after that.

"So, there is something I have to tell you. I hope you understand, and won't get mad."

Klaus starts to raise his eyebrows, and laughs. Klaus is already bracing himself, to hear something he is not going to like. Klaus knows that Paul is going to say something that is going to upset him, or change the mood. Klaus has gotten used to this feeling by now, but he rather not deal with it, or experience it. Klaus can also tell by Paul's face, that he's going to say something rather sensitive and delicate. It's going to be something Paul is probably embarrassed to admit and say. Klaus realizes that he could be incorrect, but he is sure, that what Paul is going to say or mention, is going to be something disruptive, or something possibly unfortunate. Klaus then decides to accept whatever Paul is going to say, and responds back to him.

"What do you have to tell me Paul? I won't get mad. Just tell me man. What's up?"

Even though Paul was directing his question to Klaus. Also, despite the fact Klaus and Paul were speaking each other very quietly and softly, Dan, Ernest, and Jerome, are also still present at the scene, and can hear everything clearly. They are also slightly intrigued and curious, as to what Paul wants to ask Klaus. Paul then looks down on the ground, with his hands in his pockets. Paul is silent for about a minute, before he finally responds back to Klaus.

"Can you let me sleep on your couch? My roommate and I, had a fight this morning, and I think it's best if I leave. I understand if you say no, but I have nowhere else to go. Please?"

Klaus then starts to laugh, and walks away from Paul. Klaus then shakes his head, and starts to walk back to his SUV. While he's doing that, Klaus whispers to himself, although Paul, and the rest of the guys, can hear what Klaus is saying audibly.

"Damn, I may as well just open a fucking hotel. I can't believe this shit. I knew he was going to say that too. I already predicted it. I cannot believe this at all."

Paul, looking defeated and depressed, puts his hands in his pockets, and looks down the ground. Paul was not expecting for Klaus to react that way, and was hoping that he would be more understanding, and that he would come across more friendly. Paul is disappointed, and upset, that Klaus behaved the way he did. While still looking down on the ground, Paul whispers out to Dan, Ernest, and Jerome, who are still standing at the scene.

"I take that as a no. It's okay. I didn't have my hopes up or down. It's okay. At least I tried and asked right? Ha Ha. I guess I'll see you guys at the studio tonight then."

Dan then walks over to Paul, and gives him a hug, and kisses him on the cheek. While he is still hugging Paul, Dan softly whispers to Paul.

"Actually, that was a yes. Klaus is just weird, and he acts like that sometimes. You can stay with us man. In fact, I'm gonna text you Klaus address, just go get your stuff right now."

Dan and Paul then smile at each other, and Dan gives Paul, Klaus address. Paul then once again hugs Dan, and he also gives Ernest and Jerome a hug. Paul then drives off, to start packing his things. Dan,

Ernest, and Jerome, then walk back to Klaus SUV. Klaus is sitting in the driver's seat, shaking his head, and trying to calm himself down. Once back in the car, Dan gets into the passenger seat, and Ernest and Jerome, sit in the back seat. As Klaus is turning on the ignition, Dan shakes his head at Klaus, and whispers to him.

"I told Paul he can get his stuff, and texted him your address. You didn't have to do that do him. You can be such an asshole and jerk sometimes man. Wow. Klaus. Jesus man."

Klaus doesn't look at Dan, and customarily shakes his head. Klaus then starts to drive away from the restaurant, and heads directly back to his house. Once back at Klaus residence, Klaus walks straight his to bedroom, and shuts the door. Dan, Ernest, and Jerome shake their heads at the way Klaus is behaving, and ignore him. A couple hours later, Paul, shockingly arrives back at the house, with all of his belongings, hauled into his Honda minivan. Even though Paul doesn't have that many things, he still has quite a bit of boxes and belongings. Dan, Ernest, and Jerome, all help Paul move his things into Klaus house. As Dan is helping move some of Paul's things out of the back of his car, Dan speaks to Paul.

"There is a vacant bedroom on the far side of the hall. You can take that one. Ernest and I share a room, and Jerome shares Klaus room. That's the way we been doing it. It's only fair we let you have your own room. So, you can take that one, since nobody else claimed it."

Paul, who was walking behind Dan, nods his head in agreement. Once inside of the house, Paul takes a couple minutes to look inside, and compliments how everything is. Paul continues to follow Dan. Once they are inside, Dan instructs Paul to follow him into the vacant room. Once they are inside of the room, Dan then speaks to Paul.

"Yeah, so this is gonna be your room. I'm sure all your stuff can fit in here. The bedrooms in this house are quite large, so I'm sure this is spacious enough for you."

Paul looks around the bedroom, and then while still walking around, speaks to Dan.

"Oh, this is perfect. Thank you guys so much. I'm gonna like it here. I think it's gonna be great, that since we are all working together on the show, we all live here. Thank you."

Dan smiles, and pats Paul on the back, he then walks out of the room. As Dan is walking out of the room, he responds back to Paul, in a friendly tone.

"If you need anything, just ask. We look out for one another here. All of us get along fine, and I'm sure you're gonna get used to how we run things here. Relax, kick back man. Ha."

Even though Dan has already left the vicinity, Paul looks at the direction Dan left, and smiles. Paul then starts to open the boxes that contain his belongings, and he begins to unpack. During this time, Klaus who was in his bedroom the entire time, has a feeling that Paul has arrived, and decides to leave to his room, to see if his suspicions, and assumptions are true. Klaus walks to the bedroom that was vacant, and isn't shocked to see Paul, unpacking his things. Once Paul realizes that Klaus is standing at the bedroom door, he is slightly shocked and scared, and stops what he's doing. Paul is motionless, and his body trembles in anxiety. Klaus and Paul stare at each other, with Klaus giving Paul an agitated look. Paul continues to stand in silence, and unsure of what to do, and scared to move or react. Klaus then whispers back to Paul.

"If you need any help, you can talk to the guys, and they will help you out. I have a spare 50 Inch TV in my garage. You can have it. It works fine. Kitchen, and living room, and balcony, is free for you to use. Dan usually cooks for us, but you can use the kitchen too. Okay?"

Klaus, with still an angered, and agitated look on his face, quickly walks away, not giving Paul a chance to respond, if that was even Klaus plan, to allow Paul to do so. Paul shakes his head, and resumes unpacking his things. Fifteen minutes later, Klaus does return with a large, flat screen HD television set. While Klaus is plugging up the set, he speaks to Paul.

"This TV works fine. See. It has streaming, movies, cable, Everything. I have a TV in my room, and Dan has a TV in his room, so

I thought it's only fair if you have one. We're gonna leave for the studio in about an hour. So if you don't finish packing, you can do it later."

Klaus, as he's finished successfully setting up the television, once again races out of the room, not allowing Paul to respond or speak back, if Klaus was even intending Paul to respond back. Paul yet again shakes his head, and returns to unpacking all of his things. Paul does manage to unpack all of his belongings, and put all of his art supplies in his bedroom, right on time. Klaus informs all of the men, that it is now time to report to the studio, as they need to do tonight's show. Dan, Ernest, Jerome, and Paul, all leave the house, and get into Klaus SUV. With Dan in the passenger seat, Ernest and Jerome in the second row, and Paul in the third row. Traffic was of course heavy and rough, on the way to the studio. Los Angeles traffic is like that usually. Being that it is rush hour, and primetime. It is the reason Klaus decides to leave from his house earlier, as he knows he will have to sit in traffic, and deal with all of that. Klaus has to adjust his commute time so he doesn't end up being late for his show. Despite the heavy traffic, Klaus manages to make it to the radio station, about an hour before the show starts. During this time, Dan, Ernest, and Jerome, direct themselves up to the top floor, while Klaus decides to give Paul, a tour of the entire studio, being that it's his first time here. Paul is amazed at how the studio is run, and is listening to everything Klaus is saying, so he is better situated, with how everything in the studio operates, and is run. After Klaus finishes giving Paul a tour, Paul then follows Klaus up to the top floor of the station, where the studio is.

Once inside of the studio, Paul is very intrigued at what he sees. Paul is excited that he's in an actual radio studio, and that he's a radio host now. Paul takes a seat on the far end of the table, sitting next to Ernest. Klaus continues to relay and instruct everything related in the studio, and Paul is listening closely. With it now being only thirty minutes until the show starts, Klaus then forgot that he has not set a topic for tonight's show. Klaus then takes his notebook out, and starts to brainstorm topic ideas, yet not many are clicking to him. Klaus then is able to quickly figure out a topic that he is comfortable with, and decides to make tonight's topic, about missed connections, friends, people, relationships, connections, that you would like to rekindle, or bring back. People whom you lost contact with, not necessarily over bad blood, or negative situations that happened. Mainly because the both of you were busy, or other trivial things came up. Klaus then smiles to himself, knowing that this is a great topic to bring up. Klaus continues to write down notes on his notebook, and how tonight's show is going to be run. Klaus then also understands, that all of the guys, each have a special segment they do for the show. Dan does his current events and hot topics, Jerome does his community event announcements, Ernest does his DIY life hacks. Klaus then informs Paul about this, to which Paul, decides, that his segment is going to be about "This Day In History." To where Paul will bring a fact about how today is coincidentally the same day of an important event that happened in yesteryear, or in the past. Klaus is in agreement with this, and allows for Paul to have this segment. Now that Klaus has this in order, he feels he is ready to proceed on with the show.

Things were going great, until Klaus yet again, gets that all familiar feeling, that he usually has. Klaus cannot believe that he is once again feeling this. The same feeling that he got when he got the unfortunate news about Stuart. The same feeling he experienced, when Dan first called into the show. The same feeling he was feeling when he first met Jerome, and the same feeling that he had yesterday, when he came across Paul. Klaus didn't want the other guys to know that he was experiencing this feeling. Not that they would understand, or relate to the feeling anyways. As this feeling is exclusive to Klaus. None of the other guys are feeling it, or understand the turmoil and anxiety he is feeling as well. The other guys will simply tell Klaus not to worry about it, or give him similar words of encouragement. They don't, and cannot, understand how severe this feeling is for Klaus, and how much stress it brings to him. The show will be starting soon, and Klaus needs to compose himself, or this will reflect on the show. Klaus cannot explain why he is feeling this way, and what's going to happen, as a result of this feeling. He knows that he is going to be presented with something strange, and something he's not expecting. Klaus however, has no idea when then is going to be presented, or how he's going to deal with it, once he is faced with this. Klaus looks around the studio. He notices that Dan is doing what he normally does; watching videos on his phone. Ernest also is customarily reading a book. Klaus notices that it's a Stephen King novel. Jerome is on his laptop, writing articles. Paul has a sketch pad out, and is doodling cartoons and drawings. Klaus shakes his head, and can't believe how calm the other guys in the studio are, compared to himself.

Klaus is starting to slightly become worried, and his fear of the unknown, is brewing more and more. With the show starting in only minutes, Klaus tries to calm himself down, by writing more notes, and plans of action, as to how the show is going to go. Also, looking at the other guys in the studio, and how collected they are, calms him down somewhat. But Klaus is still sure of himself, that something isn't quite right. Maybe this thing isn't necessarily bad, but it's still something that is plaguing and bothering Klaus greatly. Klaus does what he normally does, before every show, and is going to walk to the break room, to get himself snacks. He asks the guys if they need anything, and the guys exclaim out to Klaus, what that want from the break room. Klaus proceeds to the break room, still feeling nervous and anxious. Sweat beating down his face, feeling slightly disorientated while he's walking. Klaus ends up making himself a cup of coffee, which seems to calm him down a little. He then grabs the snacks the other guys asked for. Klaus then proceeds to walk back to the studio.

Once he is in the studio, Klaus still feels on edge. He opens a drawer under the table in the studio, and takes out a bottle of Tylenol. Klaus decides to take a couple of pill capsules from the bottle, and swallows the pills. He takes several gulps of water. Klaus leans back in his chair, and stares at the ceiling, with his hands covering his face. Dan, Ernest, Jerome, and Paul watch Klaus, feeling slightly concerned over the way he is acting. Dan then softly responds to Klaus.

"You feeling okay man? I'm just worried about you, that's all. You're fine right?"

Klaus takes several more gulps of water, and then whispers back to Dan.

"Yeah, I'm fine. I just have a headache that's all. I'll be okay. Don't worry, I'm fine."

Dan shakes his head, and returns to looking at videos on his phone, and doesn't bother Klaus. The rest of the guys, also don't press or pester Klaus more, and figure that he is telling the truth, when he says that he's fine. With the show coming on in ten minutes, Klaus realizes that he no longer has time to mope about. He has to change his mood to get situated on the show. The viewers are expecting an amazing program, and Klaus can't let his anxiety get to him. It is going to affect the show, and Klaus might experience a downfall, because of that. With five minutes left until the program starts, Klaus then double checks to make sure everything, technical wise is set. That all the microphones are calibrated correctly. That all the sound and audio issues are rectified. The last thing that Klaus wants, is an audio issue to happen during the show. Klaus feels comfortable, when he notices that everything is fine, and they are all set for the show to start. Klaus then starts to get the telephone switchboard ready, so that callers can be connected to the show. With three minutes to go until the show starts, the strange feeling that Klaus has, still persists, but Klaus is trying his best to ignore it, and not let it get to him that much. Klaus jots down final notes in his notebook, and prepares himself to go live.

Eventually, it is now time for the show to start. The theme song plays, and it's business as usual for Klaus. Klaus then speaks into the microphone to the audience.

"Hey everyone. Thank you all for tuning in for Wednesday's show. Here we go. I have some exciting news; seems like every day I'm adding a new host. Ha Ha. Well, here's another one. You remember Paul from yesterday right? Well, he's our new in studio co-host. Yes!"

Klaus then signals for Paul to speak into the microphone. Paul speaks to the audience.

"Oh, hey everyone. DJ K., is right. I'm Paul, you guys all remember me? I'm now a permanent host, and I love it. This is going to take some time to get used to, but I'm ready for it. I'm happy to be here, and we're gonna have so much fun. Thank you all."

Klaus then smiles, and the feeling he has is still lingering, but Klaus continues to ignore it. Klaus writes more notes down on his notebook. Klaus, then allows the other guys, to give their pre-show segments. Dan starts off the show, by doing his current events, and recent hot entertainment topics. Jerome follows him, by announcing community events, and other functions. Directing following this, Ernest then gives his DIY tip of the day, in which he tells the listeners, how they can make a coin purse, out of an egg shell. Once Ernest is done with his segment, Paul then explains his day in history segment. In which he explains that this week, Abraham Lincoln, was sworn in as the sixteenth president. Klaus finds this trivia fact interesting, and happy that Paul has this segment in the show. Once all the pre-show segments are done, Klaus readies himself to announce what the main topic of the show will be. Klaus starts to clear his throat, looks over his notes, and speaks in his microphone, to the audience.

"Okay everyone, tonight's topic will be about, missed connections. Is there a classmate or coworker that you miss? A friend, or partner, or lover that you miss? Lost family member? Any type of connection you regret that fizzled out, or you guys lost contact? Let us hear it."

Klaus then continues on his usual note taking, and ganders at the telephone switchboard, which has several callers on hold, wishing to call into the show. Klaus then starts to connect the first caller to the show, and the feeling he always seems to get, once again appears. Klaus starts to feel anxious, and can't move a bone in his body. Klaus begins to sweat, and feels pressured. Klaus is hesitating for a few seconds before taking the call, due to his overwhelming anxiety. However, Klaus is able to snap out of it, and allows the caller through. Klaus then speaks.

"Hello caller, welcome to the show. Tonight's topic is about missed connections and relationships. Do you have anything that you wish to add to the topic? What is your story?"

The caller then waits for a couple seconds, but then responds back to Klaus.

"Oh, hey. I'm just surprised I managed to get through. I've been trying to call this show for months, and I'm never able to get through. I'm shocked I'm actually live. Ha Ha."

Klaus shakes his head, and jots down more notes. He then responds to the caller.

"Well, believe it or not, you're live. Congrats on making it through the line. We have a lot of fans and listeners, so yeah, it's tough to get through the busy lines. So caller, as I said, the topic is missed connections, so we're all curious as to what your experience is. Tell us."

Klaus continues to jot down notes, as he waits for the caller to speak. Klaus has that strange feeling, seep up on him again, and Klaus still can't explain why he's feeling the way he is. During this time, the caller responds directly back to Klaus.

"Well, my experience is going to shock everyone. I wasn't expecting to get through the lines, and maybe it's coincidence tonight's show is about missed connections. Klaus, you don't recognize my voice do you? I thought you would have. Tell the audience who I am. Ha Ha."

Klaus takes a sip of his coffee, practically almost spitting it out. Klaus then tries to pick up his pen to write in his notebook, but he cannot. Klaus hands begin to freeze up, and his body begins to lock up as well. Klaus then takes a look at Dan, Ernest, Jerome, and Klaus, and they all look at him very puzzled and confused. Klaus then understands where that feeling was coming from, and the feeling then goes away. Klaus knows exactly who the caller is, and can't believe he's speaking to him on the phone. Klaus takes another sip of coffee, and shakes his head and laughs. Even though this whole ordeal is only ten seconds, it seems much longer, and in Klaus head, it was much longer. Klaus is then able to get himself together, and speaks to the caller.

"Uncle Bill, is that you? Oh my god. I haven't spoken to you in years. Man. It's so good to hear from you. I bet you're proud your nephew has his own radio show, aren't you? Ha Ha."

Klaus then starts to shake his head, and laugh. The rest of the guys in the studio also laugh, and are shocked that the caller is actually Klaus Uncle. The caller, who is Klaus Uncle Bill, is still connected to the show, and begins to laugh hysterically. Klaus is pleased, that he is having this sudden unexpected family reunion. After a few seconds, Bill then responds.

"You know it's me. I knew my Nephew would recognize me. You know I love you Klaus, and I haven't seen you in ages. God. I found out you're a radio star, and I been trying for months to get through, and I was unlucky. I have so much to tell you. God. Where do I begin?"

Klaus then starts to once again shake his head, and writes notes down on his notebook. The relationship Klaus has with his Uncle, is rather peculiar. Even though Klaus parents died when he was young, Klaus still had other family that was around. Including Klaus father's brother; his Uncle Bill. Bill is from Klaus paternal side of the family, and is of Lebanese descent. Bill is not Jewish, like Klaus maternal side is. When Klaus was younger, he would visit his Uncle Bill's house, and he would also go fishing, and do other outdoor activities with his Uncle as well. Unfortunately, Klaus lost contact with his Uncle when he went to college. Bill was also dealing with financial and personal issues, as he was in the military, and had a high rank of Sergeant as well. Bill was honorably discharged, after he injured his leg, when was doing a tour in Afghanistan. Due to his injury, Bill would never return to active military duty again. In addition to this, Bill experienced heavy PTSD, and other mental turmoil, as a result of his military days. Bill has been living on disability pay, and also working part time in a paint store, to make ends meet. Bill is still trying to deal with his PTSD, and former military days.

Klaus is aware of all of this, and understands how equally strange it is to have this reunion with Bill, but Klaus is also happy, to speak with his Uncle again. Klaus jots down more notes in his notebook, and shakes his head. Klaus then continues to speak with his Uncle.

"Where do you begin? Man, I don't know. How do you begin? Ha Ha. Uncle Bill. Man. Imagine had you not gone through the line tonight, you would have continued to try to contact me. I understand. It's tough, and it's confusing, I know. How else would you get me? Ha Ha."

Bill then quickly responds back to Klaus.

"Ha Ha. I know. I don't have your number, and this is the only information I have of you. I only found out about your show recently, and I'm like, that's my nephew. So I literally have been calling the show for months, trying to get through. Sorry about your friend Stuart."

Klaus shakes his head, and still continues to be stunned, at everything that is going on. The rest of the guys in the studio, are respectfully quiet, as Klaus is trying to rehash the relationship with his Uncle, that he hasn't spoken to, in a long time. Klaus has thousands of questions that he wishes to ask Bill. Klaus is treating this family reunion very delicately. Klaus also wants to meet Bill, and is so happy to speak with his Uncle again. As Klaus is gathering his thoughts, he then starts to ask Bill a question.

"So Uncle, how are you? How is life? How is your health? Is everything alright with you? Be honest with me. Don't go into full detail, but just summarize everything. How are you?"

Bill then quickly responds to Klaus, being directly honest with him.

"Well Nephew, not too good. My leg is still bothering me you know. Still on disability. I work part time. I don't have any friends, or anyone to talk to. I keep to myself, but I manage."

Klaus then nods his head, and writes more notes down on his notebook. As Klaus is about to ask Bill another question, Bill then carries on explaining his life, to his Nephew.

"The VA hospital doesn't do jack shit. They don't help me at all. My mood is all messed up, and I keep getting flashbacks and stuff. I'm 48 now, and I feel like I'm thirty years older, due to everything I've been through. It's tough. Again, I manage, and have my faith in God I guess."

Klaus again nods his head, and smiles. Klaus is extremely happy to be talking to his Uncle, and can't fully believe that it's actually him that he's speaking to. Bill has been on the line for over half an hour, and Klaus decides to put the show on a commercial break at this point. Klaus then speaks into his microphone, to the audience.

"Okay folks, we are gonna take a commercial break. The DJ K. show, becomes unpredictable, day by day it seems. My long-lost Uncle has called into the show everyone, and I'm just completely shocked. Uncle stay on the line, the listeners are loving this, Wow man."

The show then goes on commercial break, and Klaus then takes his glasses off, and sets them on the table. Klaus then runs his hands through his face, shaking his head. Dan walks over to Klaus, and starts to rub and pat him on the back, consoling him. Jerome then lays his head on Klaus shoulder, to comfort him as well. Ernest and Paul then walk over to Klaus, and huddle and comfort him as well. Klaus then starts to experience an unexpected emotional wave of feelings, and starts to erupt in tears. This in turn causes the other men to cry as well. Klaus did not ever believe, that he would be in contact with any of his other family members, ever again. Klaus was overjoyed, to finally speak to his Uncle again. Klaus calms down a minute later, and takes a sip of his coffee. The show is now returning from commercial break, and Klaus then starts to speak back to the audience, trying his best to hold back his emotions.

"Welcome back to the show everyone. I'm sorry, but during the break, me and the rest of the guys, got very emotional. I just can't believe this is happening. I would never in my life ever think I'd get back in contact with my Uncle. We have a lot to talk about. Uncle are you there?"

Klaus then waits for Bill, who is still connected on the line to respond. Bill then speaks.

"Of course, I'm here Nephew. I love you, and I'm sitting here crying. I know you're busy, but I just want to scc you soon. We can have a beer together, and hang out."

Klaus then starts to smile, and shakes his head. Still having so many thoughts in his head, Klaus continues to stay composed and calm. Klaus then decides to do something spontaneous, and something that he did, with the other men he recently came in contact with. Klaus then clears his throat, and starts to speak into the microphone, to the audience.

"Uncle, I want you to stay for the rest of the show, and be my co-host. You're my Uncle. I can't disconnect you from my show. I can't do that. Wow, I still can't believe it's really you."

Bill then immediately responds back to Klaus, in an excited tone.

"Nephew, I appreciate that. That's very kind of you. I'd be happy to stay on with you. I'm not gonna hang up, I'm here. I'm your Uncle, I won't let these callers bully you. Ha Ha."

Klaus shakes his head and laughs. He then replies back to his Uncle Bill.

"Ha Ha. That's the Uncle Bill I know. Always looking out for me, and protecting me. Alright Uncle, you're my co-host now, and just relax and enjoy the show. You're my family."

Bill then laughs back into the phone, in agreement with Klaus. For the rest of the show, Bill remained on the line, being another co-host to the program. Klaus knew that there wasn't a chance in the universe, that he wouldn't allow his Uncle, that he hasn't spoken to in years, not to remain on the show. Bill throughout the rest of the show, was very entertaining to the other callers, and had interesting stories, to his past military life. Even though Bill was in the military, and was a Drill Sergeant, he still was very friendly, neutral, and open minded to others. Bill was a great addition to the show, and Klaus knew his Uncle would help out with the show. Time was passing by very quickly, with the addition of Bill, and the show was very interesting and engaging. Klaus was having yet another fun filled show, and was glad. Klaus was slightly perturbed and upset, that the show was going to be ending soon. Klaus was having so much fun, that he once again, hated that the timeslot for the show was ending. Time continued to pass, with Klaus, and the rest of the guys, along with his Uncle Bill, having a fantastic time with the show. More and more minutes pass into the show. However, ending time has arrived. It was now unfortunately time for the show to end, and Klaus had to accept this. Klaus then speaks into the microphone, letting the audience know, the show is over.

"Okay everyone, that's it. This was yet another fun show. It seems every day, something new and exciting happens. Today definitely delivered. Uncle, thank you so much. Thanks to the rest of my co-hosts as well. Thank you callers. We will see you guys tomorrow. Peace and love."

Klaus then unplugs the switchboard, takes off his headphones, and unplugs his microphone. Klaus then immediately takes out his phone, and manages to locate Bill's number on the telephone switchboard. Klaus calls Bill's number, and the phone rings. Bill then answers the phone.

"Hello, this is Bill."

Klaus then begins to cry again, and the other guys in the studio start to cry as well. Klaus manages to composes himself, before responding back to Bill.

"Uncle, it's me Klaus. I, well I don't' know what to say, but I'm happy to have gotten into contact with you again. Thank you for helping out with tonight's show. If you don't mind, can I speak with you privately for a bit? Man, there is so much I have to tell you."

Bill then laughs, and softly speaks back to Klaus on the phone.

"Nephew, I love you, and I'm here. I'll talk to you all night if I have to. I haven't spoken to you in years, and we can take all the time that we need. I'm always here. I love you."

Klaus then begins to cry. Klaus then lets the rest of the men know, he is going to step out of the studio, and speak to his Uncle Bill in private. The other guys understand, and Klaus leaves the room, with Bill still on the line. Klaus then continues on his conversation with his Uncle, crying tears of joy, shaking his head, and laughing.

CHAPTER 8:

SHOW'S OVER

There are several unexplainable things that are happening recently. Klaus continues to battle and conform with all of the events that he sees. Klaus understands that he must be strong, and not let these things take control of his life anymore. It is obvious that by this point, Klaus has already automatically contorted his mind, in response to deal with anything strange, that he comes across. When Klaus decided to become a radio host, he already knew that his passion in life was going to be different. The opinions that he had, several people, were also going to be listening to them as well on the radio. What Klaus was not expecting, was for his own personal life to be intertwined in his radio career as well. Klaus was not prepared for that one bit, and at the beginning, it caused him a lot of stress, and turmoil to deal with. Klaus now feels suitable to take on whatever his mental capacity throws at him. Now that he has his team, he is ready to go on his with life regularly, and now minding if he is faced with yet another setback. Klaus feels like he can take on the challenge. Although he will feel uneasy about it at first, Klaus has the strength, and the will to succeed, and rise above any situation he has. Klaus is taking each day as its own. Also understanding that it sems that every single day, a new event happens in his life. Klaus doesn't have any time to rest or calm himself down, as he needs to always be on alert, all the time. Klaus has a stressful personality, and because of that, it can make dealing with his problems a challenge. Klaus will have to find a way to deal with both his career priorities, and also his personal agendas, and his personal feelings as well.

Tonight's show, of course, yet again was full of new adventures. The first caller to be connected to the show tonight, happened to be an estranged family member, that Klaus has not spoken to in a very long time. This family member, incidentally happened to be Klaus Paternal Uncle Bill. Klaus wouldn't ever believe that he would get into contact with his Uncle again. Tonight, it seems a miracle was watching over Klaus, and he was able to reunite with his Uncle. Klaus doesn't have much family support left. His parents passed away when he was young, and the rest of his family, he had a strayed relationship with. Realizing that his Uncle Bill is still around, gave Klaus the ultimate confidence boost, to feel happy and satisfied with his life. Klaus does have family support, and it's a great feeling, to know that you can count on your blood relative. Especially giving the fact, of everything that Klaus has had to deal with recently. Klaus is sure that his Uncle Bill will be a listening ear, and add to Klaus already growing recent support of friends. Klaus managed to have his Uncle Bill on the show, for the entire time slot. He has not interacted with his Uncle in a very long time so time was passing by rapidly. Klaus, very much still in shock to speak with his Uncle again, has so many questions that he wants to ask him. This is a very emotional moment, and the rest of the guys are aware of how Klaus is feeling too. They are giving him all the space that he needs to deal with all of this.

Despite being on the show, the entire time it was on air tonight, Klaus wanted to speak with him some more. Immediately after the show was over, Klaus dialed his Uncle Bill. Klaus was able to get Bill's number, through the switchboard history, in the studio. Klaus then excused himself from the studio, and started to have a very heartfelt, and emotional phone conversation with his Uncle. Klaus was trying to hold back his tears, and Klaus knew that his Uncle, was also trying to hold back his tears. Both of the men were emotional to finally come back into contact with each other. Emotions were running very high, and Klaus can't remember the last time, he felt this emotional. The rest of the guys remain in the studio, although some of them do peek out in the hallway at Klaus, who is roaming about the hallways of the studio, speaking to his Uncle on the phone. The guys are only curious, and do not intrude, or listen to the conversation. Klaus continues to speak with Bill, and minutes and minutes pass by. Klaus, becoming more aware that time is passing by, and after speaking with Bill for over a half an hour, decides to finally end the conversation with his Uncle, informing him that he can always speak to him.

"Uncle Bill, I have to go, and close up the studio. Oh god, I am still refusing to believe I managed to speak with you again. You have my number, I'm gonna text you my address. You can speak to me whenever you want Uncle Bill, we can do breakfast, whatever. I love you."

Klaus then gives Bill a text message, containing the address of his house. Bill receives the message back, and Bill then speaks back to Klaus.

"Aww, thank you so much Nephew. I'm gonna let you go then. I'll speak with you soon. You know that I love you Klaus. Alright, I'll see you. Bye Nephew."

Klaus then says goodbye back to his Uncle, and disconnects the call. Klaus then shakes his head and laughs, and scratches the back of his head. Klaus puts his phone back in his pocket, and directs himself back to the studio with the other men. Upon entering the studio, there is slight silence, with Klaus simply standing there, motionless and silent, for several seconds. Klaus then shakes his head, and puts his hands over his face, and yet again starts to cry. At this time, Dan, Ernest, Jerome, and Paul, stare at Klaus, and all of the men go up to hug and comfort him. Dan then softly speaks to Klaus.

"Your Uncle seems like a cool guy. I hope we can all meet him one day. I'm sure he has a ton of stories. I'm so happy you reunited with him man. Family is always important."

The rest of the guys, including Klaus, agree with what Dan said, and all of the men continue in their huddle of support for several minutes. The men then decide that is time for them to wrap up, and shut everything off, and close the studio off. It's time for them to leave, and all go home. Klaus and the rest of the men, then begin unplugging all the microphones, and Klaus begins shutting down all of the audio equipment. They are able to finish closing up quickly, and they all exit out of the studio, and proceed down to the parking structure. The men get into Klaus SUV, and originally head directly back home. However, Dan complained of being hungry, so Klaus stops at Taco Bell, nearby his home, and the men all order a bunch of tacos and burritos. Klaus then drives directly back to his house, and notices a strange vehicle in the driveway. The vehicle seems to be a shuttle like van. The vehicle, also seems to have its headlights on, and continues to idle in Klaus driveway. The other guys notice the strange car as well. They know it's not Dan's car, and it's not Paul's minivan, so who's vehicle could this exactly be? Klaus begins to sweat heavily, and his nerves strongly creep back up on him. Klaus grips, and squeezes the steering wheel tightly. Klaus hands, and his entire body is turning into stone. The further Klaus is approaching his driveway, the more anxiety he seems to feel. Dan, who is sitting in the passenger seat, is just as curious, and concerned as Klaus is, and whispers to him.

"Hey man, do you know who that is. Are you expecting company?"

Klaus keeps his vision forward, toward the windshield, and shakes his head at what Dan said. Klaus then steadily continues onto his driveway, still alerting himself, as to why this vehicle is in his driveway. Klaus full attention is directed at this vehicle, and he wants to resolve the mystery of this, as soon as possible. Klaus was not expecting anyone to visit, and the vehicle is not familiar to him either. This is all very strange and unusual for Klaus. Klaus at his vantage point, is able to see that two people are actually inside of the vehicle. Even though it is nighttime, and all Klaus can see is shadows, there seems to be a female in the driver seat, and there is a male in the passenger seat. It is still too dark for Klaus to see who is in the vehicle, and Klaus continues to feel concerned over this. Meanwhile through all of this, Klaus parks his SUV in the driveway, and is ready to find out, why this car is here. Klaus is probably hoping that this person is lost, and has the wrong address. That is the least that Klaus is hoping for. Klaus walks out of his SUV, and the rest of the guys follow out of the vehicle with him. Klaus starts to step over to the vehicle, with the ground feeling as though it's quicksand, due to how nervous and anxious Klaus is feeling. Klaus then approaches the car, and the female who was sitting in the driver seat, steps out of the vehicle. The woman is a young Asian-American woman, and she has hospital scrubs on. Klaus immediately starts to realize that this woman is a nurse. Before Klaus is able to fully get his feelings in order, the woman starts to speak with Klaus.

"Do you know this man? My name is Rose. I'm sorry, but he's been causing a disturbance at the facility, having loud phone calls, and laughing. He's being staying at the veteran's facility for several months, but he doesn't follow the rules. He gave me this address."

Klaus then looks around towards the ground, and is confused. He immediately at first doesn't know who this woman is talking about. It then dawns on Klaus, that the woman is probably referring to Bill. Once it clicks to Klaus, he starts to laugh and shake his head. Rose, the nurse, then continues on speaking with Klaus, about Bill.

"We've been trying to help him, get his treatment plan in order, but he's not cooperating, and tonight was the last straw. The residents are complaining that he's having very loud obscene phone calls, and I'm sorry, but he has to leave. He says you're his Nephew, is that correct?"

Klaus then laughs, and quickly responds back to Rose.

"If you're referring to Bill Kleinberg, yes. He is my Uncle. I'm sorry if he was disturbing others, but that doesn't sound like my Uncle Bill at all. He's a kind man. I was speaking with him on the phone earlier. So, I feel the loud phone calls, are me to blame, and partly my fault."

The nurse Rose, then shakes her head, and hands Klaus a large folder. Klaus then starts to skim through the folder. As he is doing this, Rose then responds back to Klaus.

"Well, that's his case history. As you can see, he has a history of incidents and events. Outbursts, episodes, arguments over politics with the other residents. I understand he's a veteran, and has PTSD, and our service has done a lot to help him and others, but I'm sorry."

Klaus then shakes his head, and gives the folder to Dan who accepts it. At this time, Bill steps out of the passenger side of the vehicle, and then screams out to Klaus.

"Hey! Nephew! Klaus. Come give your Uncle a hug. I'm so glad to see you."

Klaus then reluctantly walks over to Bill, and they both hug tightly. Klaus can see that Bill has on a baseball cap that says "ARMY" on it. A black t-shirt, green camouflage pants, and black tennis shoes. As Klaus and Bill are continuing to hug, Rose then opens up the back of the vehicle, and pulls out three large suitcases, which all contain Bill's belongings. Dan and Paul then start to grab the suitcases. At the same time, Rose the nurse, starts to speak with Dan.

"Okay, so you have his case information. This seems to be the right address. I have to get back to work now. If you guys have any questions, you can call us. Take care."

The rest of the men are silent, as Rose backs out of Klaus driveway, and drives away. Bill remains at Klaus residence, with all of his things. All six of the men, stand outside Klaus driveway in total awkward silence for nearly a minute. Finally, Bill manages to once again go up to Klaus and hug him, softly speaking to him.

"Man, Nephew, you have grown so much. You're taller than me. I remember when you were eight years old. I'm sorry for coming under short notice, they got mad when I was talking to you on the phone. I hate that fucking place. I figured you wouldn't mind if I crash here."

Bill then kisses Klaus on the cheek, and they once again hug very tightly. Klaus who has still not yet gathered his thoughts, starts to respond to Bill, but is unable to. Bill then responds.

"Thanks Nephew, I appreciate it. I knew you would help me out. So, why don't we all go inside, unless y'all want to stay out here in the cold all night. Come on, give me a tour. Ha Ha."

Klaus then shakes his head and laughs, and remains standing where is, still in complete total shock. Bill then walks with the rest of the guys, with Dan opening up Klaus front door. Dan, Ernest, Jerome, and Bill all walk into Klaus residence, with Klaus remaining outside his driveway, still shocked, and unable to move or react. With the rest of the men inside the house, Bill then starts to look around, giving his opinions on the layout of the residence.

"Oh man Nephew, you have a really nice pad. You have the place decked out nice."

During this time, Dan and Paul set Bill's suitcases in the living room. Jerome takes a seat on the living room sofa, and Bill sits down on Klaus recliner, relaxing himself. Bill and Jerome exchange eye contact, and Jerome smiles at him. Bill then speaks to Jerome.

"Oh, hey little man, you must be Jerome. Oh, I plum forgot. Forgive me, I'm sorry. You're the one my Nephew was talking about. You look 12, but are actually grown. I see."

Jerome doesn't verbally respond back to Bill, but simply reluctantly nods his head. Bill, feeling ashamed at his disrespectful comment towards Jerome, looks around the room for a few seconds. Bill then decides to make amends with Jerome, and calls him over. Jerome gets up from the sofa, and walks over to the recliner, where Bill is seated. Bill then responds to Jerome.

"Hey buddy, listen here for a second. I can be an asshole sometimes, and it's from my military days. I don't judge anybody, and any friend of my Nephew's is a friend of mine. So again, I'm sorry about all that. Please forgive me. I'm sorry."

Bill then kisses Jerome on the forehead, and rubs his hands through his hair. Jerome then laughs, and softly speaks back to Bill.

"It's cool. I know you didn't mean any harm. Would you like a beer?"

Bill then nods his head, and quickly responds back to Jerome.

Oh yes buddy, thank you. A beer sounds good right about now. Thank you very kindly."

Jerome then laughs, and walks over to the kitchen to get Bill a beer. At this time, Dan continues to look over Bill's documents from the veteran facility. Dan after reading through the papers, taps Paul on the shoulder. Dan then whispers out to him.

"According to this, he needs to have his back and leg medication. They reported that he hasn't taken it yet, and refused to when he was at the facility. Ugh."

Dan then shakes his head at Paul, and walks away. Paul remains still, unsure of what to do. Klaus now has walked back into the residence, and notices that Jerome is handing Bill a beer. Klaus then walks up near the both of them. Bill grabs the beer from Jerome, and thanks him.

"Ah, thank you Nephew. You don't mind if I call you Nephew. Well, all of you guys are my Nephews. I'm Uncle Bill to you all, and I love you all, and I'm here for all you guys."

Bill once again runs his hands through Jerome's hair, and smiles at him. Jerome laughs at Bill in return. Klaus then walks up from behind Jerome, and sets his hands on Jerome's shoulders. While he's doing this Klaus then whispers into Jerome's ear.

"Go into the bedroom, and stay in there. Go. Do as I say, and go. Now."

Jerome then becomes defiant, and with his vision still at Bill, responds.

"No, I don't want do. Leave me alone. I want to talk to your Uncle Bill."

Bill then becomes concerned, and notices that Klaus and Jerome are fighting. Bill then takes another sip of his beer, and then starts to speak to both of them.

"I know it's not any of my business, but if he wants to stay let him stay Nephew."

Bill then winks at Jerome, and Jerome winks back at him. Klaus then shakes his head and walks away from the both of them. Dan then grabs Klaus by the collar, letting him know that Bill needs to take his medication, and it's important that he does. After Dan informs him about this, Klaus while he's in the kitchen, grabs a beer out from the refrigerator. Klaus then takes several giant gulps of his beer, shaking his head, in the process. While he's still in the kitchen, drinking his beer, Klaus then shouts out to Bill, who is in the living room.

"Uncle, when I said you can call my anytime, I didn't mean you can stop by right now. You should have talked to me about this first. I'm gonna let you stay, because you're my uncle. Also, Uncle, you have you take your medication now, okay?"

Bill then takes another sip of his beer, and shakes his head. He then snaps   back   at   Klaus.

"No I don't Nephew. Those pills make me terribly sleepy, and I don't like them."

Jerome, who's sitting at the end of the sofa, near the recliner where Bill is, laughs at Bill's remark, and Bill smiles at Jerome, and pats him on the back. Paul continues to stand in the corner of the living room, with a puzzled look on his face, unsure of how to react. Dan and Ernest sit on the other side of the sofa. Bill then shakes his head, and speaks to Jerome.

"Hey sport, give Uncle his backpack over there next to the coffee table. Thanks."

Jerome nods his head, and walks over to get Bill's backpack. Jerome hands Bill the backpack, and Bill then takes out his medication. He swallows the pills, and takes large sips of his beer. Bill then sets the backpack down, on the side of the recliner. Dan then gets up from the sofa, and walks over to the kitchen. Dan grabs the bag of tacos and burritos, and sets them down in the coffee table in the living room. Dan then speaks to all of the men.

"Alright guys, we have some food here. If you guys are hungry, you can dig in."

Klaus, who's watching everything unfold from his kitchen, shakes his head, while he is looking down towards the ground. Klaus then grabs another beer from the refrigerator, and pulls out a pack of cigarettes, from his pocket. Klaus signals for Dan to join him out on the balcony. Klaus hands Dan the other beet, and they both walk outside to the balcony, and start to smoke their cigarettes, and are also conversing with each other. Bill, who is puzzled, starts to speak.

"What's up with them? What's that all about? Ha Ha."

Ernest takes a taco and begins to eat it. Ernest while he's eating, responds to Bill.

"Oh, they do that a lot. You'll get used to it. They have like their cigarette therapy group. They are gonna be out there for a while, so never mind them. Ha Ha. So, nice to meet you Bill."

Bill then nods his head, while looking across the room. Jerome then takes a taco, and starts to eat it. Ernest walks over to the refrigerator, and grabs three beers. He then hands a beer, each to

Jerome and Paul. Paul, who is still standing on the other side of the living room, feeling confused and puzzled, then starts to open his beer taking sips of it. Bill who notices how strange Paul is acting, starts to speak out to him.

"Hey, are you okay? Why are you standing over there, come here, join us."

Bill then starts to pat the empty recliner that's next to him, hinting for Paul to come join them. Paul takes more sips of his beer. Paul decides to stay exactly where he is, and doesn't move. Paul then silently responds back to Bill.

"Nah, that's okay. I'm fine here. You guys don't worry about me."

Bill then shakes his head and laughs, and shockingly, gets up from the recliner. Bill then grabs Paul by the arm, and places him on the adjacent recliner. Ernest and Jerome watch in amusement. Paul then remains seated on the recliner, and takes more sips of his beer. Bill then returns to his seat, stares at Paul, and laughs at him. Bill takes a sip of his beer, and speaks.

"I see you're a tough egg to crack. You're not like the other guys. It's okay. Ha Ha."

Bill continues to laugh, and grabs a taco, and eats it. Ernest and Jerome stare at each other and laugh. Ernest then turns the television on, and the men all watch "Ghostbusters 2". Ernest, Jerome, and Bill are all having fun watching the movie. Paul however, is silent, and is feeling very unhappy, and uncomfortable. Something is on his mind, that he is not relaying to the other guys. Klaus and Dan continue smoke their cigarettes, and talk out on the balcony. Throughout the movie, Bill is offering funny commentary, to which Ernest and Jerome are enjoying. However, the entire time, Paul is silent, and looks down towards the ground. Eventually the movie ends, and Klaus and Dan are still outside on the balcony. It is now 2 am, and quite late into the night. Ernest and Jerome decide to take themselves to bed, and say goodnight to everyone. Ernest walks into bed, and Jerome walks into bed as well. With the television now playing infomercials. There is awkward silence for quite a bit, with Bill and Paul, remaining in the living room. Bill nods his head, and looks around the room. Bill then gazes at Klaus and

Dan on the balcony, smiling at them. Then remarkably, Paul then shockingly starts to speak.

"Hey, my Dad was a veteran. He was in the Air Force. It really messed up his mind, and he was never the same. War and battle does strange stuff to people. My Dad passed away, but I miss him. You kinda remind me of him, and I'm sorry, I didn't want the other guys to know."

Bill then grabs Paul's hand, and squeezes it tightly. Bill and Paul then smile at each other. While still squeezing his hand, Bill whispers back to Paul.

"Ain't that the truth. I understand. I been through a lot myself, so it's   okay.

Bill then kisses Paul on the cheek, and Paul while looking down at the ground, smiles to himself. Paul then takes a taco, and starts to eat it. While he's eating, Paul then speaks.

"Uh, listen. Again, don't tell the other guys this. It's not that I have a uniform fetish or anything. Maybe I do. But you wouldn't happen to have your uniform, would you. Can I see it?"

Paul then stares at Bill, and Bill begins to laugh at Paul. Bill then responds back.

"Are you kidding? Of course, I have my uniform. Bring me the suitcase that's on the far end please. I believe it's in that one, if I'm not mistaken."

Paul quickly stands up, and garbs the suitcase that Bill asked him to bring. Bill thanks Paul, and starts to open the suitcase up. Bill then quickly pulls out two military uniforms. One is a more formal ceremonial suit, with awards and metals on the side, another is a camouflaged battle gear outfit. Bill lays bout of the suits on the sofa, which are wrapped. Paul responds.

"Wow, so much history. I'm not gonna ask you to open them. This is satisfying my crave enough. Ha Ha. I just love military uniforms. I never been in the armed forces myself, but yeah."

Bill laughs, and shakes his head. Bill then puts the uniforms back in his suitcase. At this point, Klaus and Dan exit out of the balcony. Klaus notices that Bill is putting his military uniforms away, and quickly snaps at Bill.

"Uncle, you're not boring with him military stuff, are you? Ha Ha."

Before Bill is able to respond, Paul, who is feeling slightly agitated and bothered, likewise how he was feeling earlier, replies back to Klaus, in a very angry tone.

"Actually no, he's not. I requested to see his uniforms. He was nice enough to take them out, to let me see them. I don't know why you assumed, that he was boring me. I notice you do that shit a lot Klaus, and wow. My God. How fucking dare you."

Paul then gets up from the sofa, and storms down the hallway, and into his bedroom, slamming the door shut. Klaus, Dan, and Bill remain shocked and silent. Klaus then takes a taco, and fist bumps Dan. Dan ends up taking a taco as well, and eats it. Dan then says goodnight to both Klaus and Bill, and walks into his bedroom. Klaus and Bill are now alone in the living room together. Klaus starts eating his taco, and walks towards his bedroom. Klaus then starts to speak.

"Well Uncle, good night. We'll talk more later, and I'll explain the house rules to you. You have now met the rest of the boys, and yeah. We all get along here. I don't know why Paul just did that, but whatever. I'm gonna go to bed now Uncle. Good night. Love you."

Klaus then walks over to Bill, and kisses him on the forehead. Bill then slaps Klaus on the behind, and Klaus laughs. Bill then softly responds back to Klaus.

"Alright. Good night, Nephew. You sleep well. Love you."

Klaus and Bill smile at each other, and Klaus walks into his bedroom. Bill then remains in the living by himself for about five minutes. Bill then hears audible crying, and is not sure where the sound is coming from. Bill turns off the television, originally thinking that it was coming from that source. However, when Bill notices that he still hears someone crying, he becomes more adamant to find out, where the crying is coming from. Bill then notices that the crying is coming directly from the bedroom that Paul is in. Bill quietly creeps up towards the door of Paul's bedroom, and without knocking, opens to door. Bill then sees that Paul is sitting on the edge of the bed, crying heavily. Paul notices that Bill has come into the room, and stares directly at Bill, and immediately snaps at him.

"Hey! Get out! What are you doing in here? Haven't you ever heard of knocking?"

Bill then starts to feel bad, and intrusive, and starts to close to door, and walk out of the room. As he's doing that, Bill whispers back to Paul.

"Oh, sorry sport. I didn't mean to do that. I went into the wrong room. It's my eyes, I didn't mean to disturb you. I'm sorry. Good night."

Paul then remarkably responds back to Bill, before he completely shuts the door.

"Hey, wait a minute. Come here. I need to talk to you about something."

Bill then walks back into the bedroom, and shuts the door behind him. Paul then slaps the bed, signaling for Bill to sit next to him. Bill obeys, and sits next to Paul on the bed. Paul then resumes crying, and keeps his head towards the ground. Bill then awkwardly looks around the bedroom, silently. Bill then decides to rub on Paul's back to comfort him. Bill then notices an easel that is located in the corner of the bedroom. Bill gets out of the bed, and starts to look at the painting, that is situated on the easel. Bill sees that it's a painting of The Queen Mary. An English ship, that is now permanently docked in Long Beach, California. Bill is fascinated by the painting, and understands that Paul is the one who painted. Bill then responds to Paul.

"This is pretty good. You're very talented. This is one of my favorite ships too."

Bill then starts to look at Paul's art supplies, and picks several paintbrushes, and canisters of oil paint up. Once Paul realizes that Bill is doing this, he gets out of bed, and grabs Bill's arm, putting the things Bill picked up, back where they were originally. Paul then responds.

No, don't touch any of that please. Don't touch my things. Thank you."

Paul then walks back to the edge of the bed, and has his head down on the ground, with his hands covering his face. Bill then laughs, and once again walks over to the bed, to sit next to Paul. Bill continues to look around the room, before getting off the bed, and speaking to Paul.

"Alright buddy. I'm getting tired, so I'm gonna go back to the sofa and sleep. Take care."

Paul with his head still facing the ground, grabs Bill's arm, and whispers to him.

"No, stay with me please. I'm not feeling well, and I need you stay."

Bill then shakes his head, and laughs. Bill then returns to the bed, and speaks to Paul.

"Ha Ha. I get it now. Alright. I'll stay as long as you want me to. I understand. Ha Ha."

Paul and Bill continue to sit next to each other in the bed for several minutes, until Paul does something very shocking. Paul then immediately positions his face towards Bill, and starts to passionately kiss him. Bill doesn't hold back, and the both of them fall on the bed. Paul and Bill stop kissing, and Bill starts to laugh at Paul. Paul then doesn't react at all, and sits back up on the edge of the bed, and remains silent, looking down on the ground. Bill whispers to Paul.

"Okay, that was interesting. I'll keep our little secret. I won't tell the other guys."

Paul then looks toward Bill, and smiles. Paul then looks back towards the ground, and laughs to himself. Paul then whispers back to Bill.

"Go get your things. I want you to sleep with me tonight. Make me feel Good. Ha Ha."

Before Bill is able to react, Paul once again, changes his direction, and spontaneously kisses Bill yet again. This time Bill is slightly agitated, and responds back to Paul.

"Alright, you made your point. I'll be right back; I'm getting my stuff. Just wait."

Paul shakes his head and laughs. Bill also laughs, and walks out of the room to get his suitcases that are located in the living room. Once all of Bill's things are in the bedroom, Paul then starts to change into his sleep clothes. Bill silently watches him, and Paul then crawls into bed. Bill then changes into his sleep clothes as well, and cuddles up next to Paul in bed. Both of the men soon fall asleep. The next morning, with it now being 9 am, Bill out of extinct, is the first to wake up. Bill notices that he is in bed with Paul. Bill kisses Paul on the head, and starts to prepare himself, to take a shower. Dan and Ernest wake up a few minutes later, and direct themselves to the kitchen. Dan then starts to prepare breakfast for the guys. Dan is preparing pancakes, bacon, eggs, and sausage. Bill walks out of the bedroom at this time, and Dan and Ernest notice that he walked out of Paul's bedroom, and the both of them stare at each other, and shake their heads, and start to laugh. Bill then walks into the shower. At this time, Jerome walks out of bed, trying his best not to disturb Klaus, who is still sleeping. Klaus joins Dan and Ernest in the kitchen. Jerome pours himself a glass of orange juice. While Jerome is taking sips of his orange juice, Dan, while he's preparing breakfast, starts to whisper to Jerome.

"Hey, Ssh. Paul and Bill are sleeping together. We just saw Bill leave his room."

Jerome almost spits his orange juice out, holding back his laughter, and responds.

"Ooh, you guys are lying. Well, I'm not saying anything. I think it's rather cute. Ha Ha."

Ernest then starts to laugh, and Dan laughs as well, and shakes his head. Several minutes later, Bill leaves out of the shower. Dan, Ernest, and Jerome watch him silently, as he walks back into Paul's room. Bill notices the men starting at him, and respectfully and politely speaks.

"Good morning gentleman, how are all you guys doing? Breakfast smells good."

Bill then walks into Paul's room, and shuts the door. Dan, Ernest, and Jerome, all erupt into loud laughter and heckling. Bill then puts his outfit for the day on, which is a blue polo shirt, and some black denim jeans. At this time Klaus has waken himself up, and walks out of the bedroom. Klaus joins the other men in the kitchen. Klaus gives Dan a fist bump, and pours himself a cup of coffee. At this same time, both Bill and Paul walk out of the bedroom. Bill is the only one who is fully dressed. The rest of the guys have their sleepwear on. Klaus is shocked to see both Bill and Paul leave out of the bedroom together. Bill directs himself straight to the recliner in the living room, and starts to read his newspaper. Paul then walks over to the kitchen, and without giving the rest of the guys any eye contact, pours himself a cup of coffee. The rest of the men remain silent, and Paul takes a sip of his coffee. Paul then snaps at all the men.

"What in the hell are you guys looking at?"

The men in the kitchen stay silent, and don't respond. Bill heard Paul shout at the other men, and puts his newspaper down, and calls out for Paul to join him in the living room.

"Hey buddy, leave them alone, come over here and sit with me. Leave them alone."

Paul listens to Bill, and Paul does indeed take his cup of coffee, and sits next to Bill on the sofa. Paul and Bill then begin to speak with each other. Klaus has a puzzled and confused look on his face. Dan then taps Klaus on the back, and whispers something to him. Klaus takes a sip of his coffee, almost spitting it out, and starts to laugh. Klaus then looks at Ernest and Jerome, who didn't hear what Dan whispered to Klaus, but have an idea of what he told him, and Ernest and Jerome both nod their heads. Klaus shakes his head, takes a sip of coffee, and speaks.

"Wow, I can't believe it. As long as they are happy, I'm okay with it. Ha Ha."

Klaus then is able to get the whole complete picture as to what's going on, and doesn't intrude or invade with Paul and Bill, and leaves them alone. Klaus continues to chat with Dan, as he continues to prepare breakfast. As Klaus is drinking his coffee, it is Thursday, meaning tonight is another show night. Klaus knows that eventually he will have to write down his plans for tonight's show. He still has quite a bit of time to do it, but he must do it soon. Klaus then looks around his house, and takes a look at his friends, and his Uncle. Knowing how he came into contact recently with all these men. It wasn't long ago, to where Klaus shared his home by himself. Now he is sharing it with five other people. Klaus is slowly, but surely, starting to become less of an introvert, and more of a social person. At this time, Dan has finished preparing breakfast. Dan yells across to the living room to Paul and Bill, that breakfast is ready. Paul and Bill grab their plates of food, but shockingly, go back to the living room. Klaus shakes his head, and laughs. Klaus, Dan, Ernest, and Jerome, remain in the kitchen, eating their breakfast. Dan once again cooked an amazing breakfast, and the men all enjoy it. As they are eating, Klaus starts to clear his mind, and using breakfast, as a method to once again bring himself back to reality. Klaus is comfortable that Bill managed to fit right in already, and Klaus of course doesn't mind that his Uncle, has decided to join them. Klaus is intending to bring Bill to the studio, as he's sure that Bill wouldn't mind being on the show with them. The men all finish their breakfast, and Klaus then starts to get himself ready for the day. Dan, Ernest, and Jerome, get ready for the day as well. Once Klaus is dressed for the day, he walks into the living room, and sits in the recliner, next to Bill. Klaus pulls out his laptop computer, and his notebook, and starts to write notes for tonight's show. Paul is also in the living room, drawing on his sketch pad. As Klaus continues to write down notes, Bill starts to curiously ask Klaus a question.

"Hey Nephew, what are you writing? Are you writing down your memoirs? Ha Ha."

Klaus while looking at his laptop and typing, laughs at Bill, and quickly responds.

"Ha Ha. No Uncle. I wish. I'm just taking notes for the show tonight. That's all."

Bill nods his head, and goes back to reading his newspaper. Klaus jots down more notes, and prepares more for the show later tonight. Klaus has still not yet come up with a topic for the show. Klaus then ponders as to whether or not he should do something that himself and Stuart have done in shows in the past, and that's deciding not to have a set topic for the show. To let the show be free for all, open discussion. In the end, Klaus does decide to do this, and the show will not have a designated topic. Callers can talk, and speak about, whatever they wish. Jerome is doing the dishes in the kitchen, with Ernest also at the kitchen counter, reading a book. Dan is out on the balcony smoking a cigarette, and listening to a podcast. Klaus then after taking his notes, decides to take a nap on the recliner. He leans his head back, and begins to rest. Klaus can audibly hear Paul and Bill having mundane conversation, but doesn't eavesdrop or listen at all to what they are saying. Klaus wakes up from him nap, sometime later. He feels rejuvenated after his nap, and feels better. Klaus looks at the time on his phone, and he notices that it's 4:50 PM. Klaus frantically then starts to get himself, and the other guys ready to leave. Klaus feels this is the perfect time to leave for the studio, so they are not stuck in traffic, and are late. Klaus then informs all the men, that it's time to leave for the show. Klaus gathers all his things, and he, and the other men, get into Klaus SUV. Dan sits in the passenger seat, Ernest and Jerome sit in the second row, with Paul and Bill, sitting in the third row. Klaus does manage to make it to the radio station in time, and the men still have a little over an hour before the show starts.

Klaus shows Bill around the studio, and Bill is glad, that he is able to see the radio station, that his Nephew works at. The rest of the guys, report directly up to the top floor, where the studio is. After giving Bill a tour of the radio station, Klaus directs Bill, up to the top floor with the rest of the guys. Bill then starts to see the inside of the radio station for the first time. Bill is amazed at what he sees, and proud of what Klaus is doing with his radio business. Bill then takes a seat, with the rest of the men, in the studio. With the show coming on very shortly, Klaus does his usual, final preparations for the show. Klaus takes out his notes, and looks them over accurately. Bill during this time, takes out his newspaper, and starts to read it. Ernest is doing what he customarily does before every show, and is reading a book. Jerome is writing his blog on his computer, and writing articles. Dan is watching auto mechanic videos on his phone. All of the men are keeping to themselves, and are being very civil. Time continues to pass, and the show will not start in thirty minutes. Klaus gets up, and asks the guys, if they want any snacks. The men tell Klaus what snacks they want, and Klaus reports to the break room. Klaus gets the snacks and refreshments, and also grabs himself a cup of coffee. Klaus returns to the studio, handing the men their snacks. Klaus takes more sips of coffee, and is not worried. The vibe of the studio continues to be calm. Klaus is very ready for the show, and the rest of the men are stable and comfortable too. With ten minutes to go, Klaus is doing final audio checks, as he normally does. Everything is fine, and there aren't any issues or problems related to that. The show will start in five minutes, and Klaus continues to be worry free. Unlike the past few shows, Klaus doesn't have any strange feelings at all. Klaus, along with his team are content with everything. With the show starting in a minute, the guys are all excited to begin. It is now show time. The theme song of the show begins to play. Klaus then puts his headphones on. The rest of the men put their headphones on as well. Klaus then speaks into the microphone to the audience.

"Hello everyone. This is the DJ K. Show. Another day, another guest we have in the studio. Ha. Ha. Today, we have my Uncle Bill. He's with us in the studio for moral support. Ha."

Klaus then signals for Bill to speak. Bill then starts to speak to the audience.

"Hey all you guys. You heard my Nephew, DJ K. He's right. I'm joining them in the studio tonight. I'm observing everything for now. We are all going to have fun though. Ha."

Klaus starts to laugh, and shakes his head at Bill. Then, the guys start to do their pre-show segments. Dan does his usual current events, and hot topics segment. Directly after that, Jerome does his community events and functions segment. After that, Ernest does his DIY and life hack segment, to where he talks about reusing paper milk cartons, as storage containers. Paul then does his day in history segment, to where he talks about how Georges Bizet's production of "Carmen", written by Prosper Merimee, Opera, premiered for the first time in Italy today in 1875. Klaus then allows Bill to give a segment if he wishes. Bill, not sure of what segment to add, then decides the only thing he can think of, which is to give the sports scores to the audience. The rest of the guys find this hilarious and laugh, and Bill laughs as well. Now that the pre-show segments are over, Klaus then is ready to begin the actual show. Klaus then clears his throat, and then starts to speak in the microphone to the audience.

"Okay, so let's get on with the show. Tonight, we have a big treat. There is no topic for tonight. You guys can call, and discuss whatever you want. It's open discussion. Let's go."

Klaus then turns on the telephone switchboard, which has several callers on the line, that are wishing to be connected to the show. Klaus, takes several callers, and himself, and the rest of the guys, have an entertaining show, speaking with the callers. Klaus Uncle Bill, like Klaus suspected, is handling the show well, and is being entertaining to the audience. Things seem to be going smoothy, and this was a great show for Klaus. The men made it through halfway into the time slot, with it now being 9 PM. The men are still carrying on with the show, and are having a blast, and a wonderful, and fantastic time. Things were going peachy and cool, until Klaus heard a knock at the studio door. Klaus, and the other men, directly look at the door, and notice that it's Mr. Weston, with an angry expression on his face. Klaus heart then immediately sank, and his whole body felt still. Klaus knew that Mr. Weston was unhappy, and that he was in trouble. The other men don't react at all. The show was still going live, as Mr. Weston knocks on the door, a second time, with his face even angrier. A caller was speaking to the men during this time, and Klaus signals for Dan and the others to keep going. Klaus gets up from his seat, and walks out of the studio, to go and speak with Mr. Weston. Klaus walks out of the studio, and shuts the door, with Mr. Weston crossing his arms, angry, while Klaus is doing this. Mr. Weston, and Klaus then give each other eye contact. Mr. Weston angrily responds back to Klaus.

"I want you in my office, right now."

Klaus entire body continues to sink, and feel heavy. With Klaus heart beating fast, sweat pouring down his face, and every step Klaus taking feeling like his feet are stuck in cement. Klaus feels very anxious and nervous currently. He doesn't know why Mr. Weston is angry, or what he wants. Mr. Weston continues to walk behind Klaus, staring at him menacingly. Even though Mr. Weston's office is only a short walk, it seems much longer, due to the anxiety Klaus is going through. Klaus arrives at Mr. Weston's office, and takes a seat in front of his desk. Mr. Weston keeps his eyes locked on Klaus, giving him an angry look, as he's taking a seat at this desk. Mr. Weston then pulls out a large envelope full of documents. He then spreads the documents al across his desk, and continues to leer at Klaus. Mr. Weston then responds.

"You see this? These are all FCC complaints. I go to a business convention for two weeks, and you fuck my entire studio up. Who the fuck are those men in the studio with you? They have no broadcasting credentials, and I want them all out now."

Klaus gathers his thoughts for a while, and then softly speaks back to Mr. Weston.

"Sir, those are my co-hosts. They are great guys, you just gotta get to know them. I know I should have told you, but you were away, and figured you be fine with it. I don't know what those complaints are, but I promise you sir, that we didn't do anything too bizarre. I'm sorry."

Mr. Weston shakes his head, and continues to angrily stare at Klaus. Mr. Weston speaks.

"I don't give a damn about all that. I want them gone. You know what, I don't like your smug tone, and smart-ass attitude, and backtalk. Yeah. Don't act like I don't see through this. Since you like them so much, you can go with them. DJ K. The show is cancelled. You're fired."

Klaus then smiles and shakes his head. Klaus then laughs, and stands up. He then stares Mr. Weston directly in the face, and silently speaks back to him.

Okay. Well fuck you sir, and have a great day. Me and my boys will go elsewhere. Bye."

Mr. Weston shakes his head at Klaus, and doesn't respond. Klaus then walks out of Mr. Weston's room, shutting the door behind him. While walking back to the studio, Klaus shakes his head and laughs.

CHAPTER 9:

THE TEACHER'S STRIKE

Klaus continues to stand outside of Mr. Weston's office. Part of Klaus, doesn't yet fully comprehend what was told to him. Klaus wants to falsely believe that possibly Mr. Weston was joking, or being silly or funny with him. Mr. Weston just informed Klaus, that he is fired from the studio, and that he and the rest of the men, must leave out of the studio, right now. Making the show also essentially over, finished, and cancelled. As much as Klaus tries his best to make it seem that Mr. Weston was pulling his leg, and being funny, that's simply incorrect. Mr. Weston was indeed very serious, when he wanted Klaus to leave. When Mr. Weston was on vacation, he had no idea that Klaus was going to completely change the show. Mr. Weston was also not intending for Klaus to add five additional men, that do not have any radio experience on, as hosts of the show. Mr. West had returned from his vacation today, and was not expecting to return to this news. Maybe Mr. Weston has behaved and acted too quickly, but that didn't matter. His decision was final, in that Klaus, and all of the other guys, simply had to leave. Mr. Weston was not going to change his mind on this, and the decision was locked. Mr. Weston had received far too many complaints, about how the show is being run. This greatly concerned Mr. Weston. Once finding out that Klaus has added Dan, Ernest, Jerome, Paul, and his Uncle Bill to the studio, Mr. Weston then started to put the puzzle pieces together, and it made perfect sense, as tow why the show received the complains and backlash it did. This is complex and torn, as Mr. Weston is right. The show did receive some complaints from the FCC and other media board organizations. However, the complaints were about level pegged as they were, when Klaus and Stuart were doing the show. So, it's not like the show received more complains now. It's essentially about the same as it was originally, before Klaus changed the setup of the show.

Also, yes there were some negative complaints and reception. However, there were also many positive reviews of the show, and many listeners were tuning into the show as well. So, if Mr. Weston is making it seem that Klaus was putting on a show that wasn't entertaining, that is simply not the truth. Klaus was doing an amazing job at the show. Radio was his calling, and Klaus, despite the fact he came across his new group of friends, who actually brought Klaus up from the dumps and ground, Klaus still had the same magic and talent, for radio. Klaus continues to stand outside of Mr. Weston's door, starting at the carpet. Klaus becomes slightly disorientated, and is scared, and anxious, as to how he is going to tell the news to the other guys. How disappointed, and upset they are going to be, once they realize that they all have been fired from the station, and the show is over, and they all need to leave. Klaus was dreading walking back to the studio, and explaining this. He could imagine how upset they would be. Klaus was willing to stall how long he relayed this information to them, by walking slowly back to the studio. Klaus figured the slower he walked, the slower he would have to talk to the other guys about the show being cancelled. Klaus takes his glasses off, and cleans them with his shirt, and shakes his head. Halfway through walking back to the studio, and from Mr. Weston's office, Klaus stops in his direction, and is completely still. Klaus then begins to cry heavily, and still can't believe what is currently happening. Klaus was fired from what he loved doing best, and his calling. And not only that, his friends are also being dismissed from the show as well. So, all of this was extremely though to deal with. Klaus still believes this was unfair of Mr. Weston to do, and should have given Klaus a chance; letting him continue on with the show. Klaus refuses to believe that Mr.

Weston is going to let the over five years of Klaus doing the show, go down the drain, and not mean anything anymore. This was turning into a nightmare for Klaus.

Klaus starts to wipe the tears of his face, and manages to be strong enough, to carry on back to the studio, to inform the men, that the show is cancelled, and that they have all been fired. Klaus reaches the door of the studio, and stands outside the door for nearly a minute. Klaus is still anxious to turn the doorknob and enter. Klaus then realizes that he was to tell the guys this information, and he can't keep stalling. Klaus then shakes his head, and open the door. Once Klaus is inside the studio, he notices that the show is still going on live, with Dan speaking with a caller. Klaus had a sudden angered impulse, and lost his anger. Klaus immediately snatches the microphone away from Dan, and then starts to angrily shout into the microphone, live on air.

"I'm sorry everyone, but my boss just informed me, that I'm fucking fired, and so are the rest of the guys. He also told me the show is now cancelled. So, if you guys want to write or send any complaints, you can send them to Larry Weston, as he's the guy who fired us. So yeah."

The rest of the guys in the studio, stare at Klaus in shock, and unable to speak. At this time as well, Mr. Weston races down the hallway, straight to the studio. Mr. Weston walks into the room, right as Klaus is about to make another statement on air. Mr. Weston then snatches the microphone away from Klaus, and Mr. Weston speaks to the audience on air.

"Yes, I'm Larry Weston, you guys can send your complaints. It doesn't matter. DJ K. has broken all the stations rules, and he must be dismissed for that. The show is cancelled. We will also not be airing reruns of the show, DJ K. will have nothing to do with this station anymore."

Mr. Weston then immediately starts to unplug the switchboard, and turns off all the equipment that is located in the studio. As Mr. Weston is doing all of this, he speaks.

"All of you must immediately leave the premises now. You are not permitted to be here, as you are fired. DJ K. you're fired, so you must leave. The rest of you guys, you guys don't have any credentials or any certifications to be in this studio, so you guys have to leave too."

Mr. Weston then decides, that instead of asking Klaus for the keys to the station back, Mr. Weston reaches where Klaus is sitting on the table and grabs the keys. Upon noticing this, Klaus attempts to grab the keys back, shouting at Mr. Weston in the process.

"Hey, wait. I have to get all my things in storage. If you want me to leave, that's okay, but I can't leave without getting all of my stuff first. That is simply not fair, and you know it."

Klaus and Mr. Weston stare deeply at each other for several seconds. Mr. Weston who has the keys to the station in his hand, then silently responds back to Klaus.

"What makes you think I care? I don't. You have to leave, and whatever property you have in this building, it belongs to me now. It's written in the contract somewhere. I don't have time to tell you the exact line and section, but believe me, it's there damn it. Now leave."

Klaus then shakes his head, and starts to gather his belongings. Klaus then responds.

"You know, you're really fucked up. You know that? What a fucked up man. I swear."

As Klaus is still gathering his things, Dan then starts to speak to Mr. Weston.

"So, all of those years, Klaus worked for you, not mean anything now, what an evil man you are. Whoever takes our place is gonna be boring, you know what right? Shit."

The guys all remain in the studio, with Mr. Weston watching over all of them. Klaus continues to gather his things, while the rest of the men sit, in shock that the show is over, and that they are all being asked to leave the studio. Bill then starts to lose his temper, and is upset at the way Mr. Weston, is treating his Nephew. Bill is usually an even minded guy, but certain situations trigger to him. Bill then gets up, and grabs Mr. Weston by the shirt. As Bill is still grabbing and holding onto Mr. Weston. Klaus quickly notices this, and he, along with Dan and Paul, try to restrain Bill from hurting Mr. Weston. Bill then shouts to Mr. Weston.

"You motherfucker. My Nephew has a great show, and you're gonna can him. You're probably just jealous, that's probably what it is. You give my Nephew his job back you loser."

Klaus, Dan, and Paul, successfully manage to detach Bill from Mr. Weston. Directly after this, Mr. Weston starts to shake his head, and laughs. Mr. Weston then responds to the men.

"Yeah, I am definitely making the right decision. By the way you all are acting, this is proof that you guys shouldn't be here. You guys are not fit to work in radio. For the last and final time, you all need to leave the studio. I will call the police if you guys do not leave."

Klaus has finished gathering all of his things at this point, and turns his direction towards Mr. Weston. Klaus stares at him silently for a short while, and then responds back to him.

"We're gonna leave, and we're gonna prove you wrong. You made a very unwise decision. You are gonna reap what you sow, and you are a terrible fucked up man. Goodbye."

Klaus then picks up his things in his arms, and speaks, while staring at Mr. Weston.

"Guys come on, let's get the fuck out of here. We don't need this. We shouldn't be somewhere where we don't belong, and somewhere that we aren't appreciated. Let's go."

Without much hesitation or struggle, the rest of the guys immediately obey and follow Klaus orders, and walk with him outside of the studio room. Mr. Weston simply shakes his head, as all six of the guys leave. The men then all head directly down to the parking structure, and get into Klaus SUV. Once they are all inside of the vehicle, the men remain silent. Klaus then decides to drive back home. Klaus decides to immediately drive home, still shocked that his dreams seemed to be crushed. This is a terrible thing that just happened. The show that Klaus feels that he was worked so hard to get, and the show that he knew his friends were also happy to be a part of, was gone. It was never coming back. Klaus was also additionally fired from the studio. Being fired was something that Klaus was not happy or comfortable with. Klaus figured that he had an amazing relationship and bond with Mr. Weston. That all completely changed, and Klaus has no idea why Mr. Weston was not in agreement with the new changes of the show. Klaus continues to shake his head, as he is driving, and starts to wonder, that maybe if he is cursed. First, the death of his parents. Then, the death of Stuart. Now, Klaus has to deal with the fact, he is now fired, and the show is over. The main thing Klaus enjoyed doing, he won't be able to do anymore. Klaus couldn't stop thinking that he was being punished, or cursed. Klaus was also feeling for the other guys as well. Knowing that they were disappointed and upset to. They all were having such amazing fun doing the show, and things have now come to a halt. The show is cancelled and has come to an end. There is nothing the guys can do to change this.

Klaus manages to make it back to his residence, and himself, and the rest of the men, immediately get out of the car, and walk inside. Once inside of the house, Klaus walks himself to the kitchen, and garbs a beer of the refrigerator, Klaus then walks outside to the balcony. Ernest, Jerome, and Paul, take a seat on the sofa. Bill takes a seat at the recliner. Dan walks over to the balcony where Klaus is in, but doesn't open the balcony door. Dan stares at Klaus in concern. All of the men are silent, and looking down towards the ground. Dan then decides to open up the balcony door, and walks out to join Klaus, on the balcony. Dan shuts the door, and sits down on the chair on the balcony next to Klaus. Dan begins to speak to Klaus.

"Hey man. You don't mind if I keep you company, do you? Everything is gonna be fine."

Klaus, with his vision still looking out towards the balcony, responds back to Dan.

"I do mind. Leave me the fuck alone. Go back inside. I don't want to talk to you man. It's nothing personal, I want to be left alone. We'll talk later Dan, just go away. Don't bother me."

Dan then shakes his head, and gets up from sitting at the balcony with Klaus. Dan then walks back into the living room, and speaks with the rest of the guys.

"Well, I tried. Let's just give him space you guys. It might take a few days, it might take a week god forbid, but give him his space. I'm gonna cook some Spaghetti, okay?"

Dan then walks to the kitchen, and starts to prepare dinner for the guys. As Dan is in the kitchen, Ernest, while looking down at the floor, starts to nod his head, and speaks.

"You know, even though our show is cancelled, I am still thankful that Klaus gave us the opportunity. All good things must come to an end. I'm still happy to have met all of you. Ha."

Jerome then agrees with Ernest, and also begins to speak to all of the guys.

"Ernest is right you guys. I know. DJ K.'s, Klaus show, got me through a lot of tough times. The fact I got to finally meet him, and he's now my close friend. I'm just happy for that."

Paul then takes out his sketch pad, and starts to draw animations and cartoons, like he normally does. As Paul is continuing to draw on his sketch pad, he responds.

"I had a feeling this was gonna happen. I don't know why, but I was scared that the show as gonna end soon. What we were doing was kinda revolutionary and weird. So, I kinda get it."

Bill then pulls out his newspaper, and starts to skim through all of the articles. With his vision directly focused on the newspaper, Bill then speaks to all of the men.

"My Nephew had an amazing show, and that stupid boss of his, doesn't know what he's talking about. Klaus is gonna bounce back. I know he is; he always does. It's not over."

Dan continues to prepare dinner in the kitchen, although he is hearing everything that the rest of the guys are talking about, loud and clear. Dan then says something to the guys.

"I'm just happy that Klaus gave each of us a chance. You guys know, that before we all came along, he didn't have anybody. No friends, nobody. He was recluse. The show is over, and nobody knows where we are gonna go from here, but that's okay. Look at the whole picture."

The rest of the guys, nod their heads at what Dan said. The men are all currently in this rut to where they don't know where to go next. The show was just unexpectantly cancelled by Mr. Weston, and they are unsure of what they should actually do next. The guys are starting to accept that they aren't going to be returning to the show, but it's still very though for them to get used to the fact, there is no more show. What are they doing to do at this point? The biggest fear that Klaus is feeling, is that it's going to ruin his creative energy. Doing the show, was Klaus main ambition and passion. Especially after the death of Stuart, the show had an even bigger impact. Klaus decided to carry on with this show, knowing that is what Stuart would have wanted. The fact Mr. Weston decided to cancel the show, without putting Stuart in mind, Klaus was really upset and angered over. Klaus knew that there wasn't anything for him to do. That's the part that really tore him up. If there was something that Klaus could do, to return the show, he would do it. However, the only thing Klaus can do, is accept the fact, that he, and the rest of the guys, will never go back to the studio, and the show has ended. Klaus remains outside in the balcony, trying to gather his thoughts, and his plan as to what he is going to do next. For the first time, since being dismissed from the studio, Klaus hatches a brand new idea. Although he is still feeling quite upset from being let go from the station, Klaus starts to slowly cheer himself up.

Klaus has the idea, that he should start his own independent show, with the rest of the guys. Likewise, the same type of content he did with Stuart. It wouldn't be a radio studio show, however, Klaus would have live broadcasts, out in the public, and out in street. Klaus figured that this would be perfect, and with the help of the other guys, this idea would be great. They could broadcast their show on YouTube, and online, and gain so many viewers. They could cover things, ideas, places, that other people are afraid to. Push the limits, when it comes to getting content across. Klaus continues to sit outside the balcony, and takes more sips of his beer. Happy that he was able to come up with this idea. Klaus starts to smile to himself, and realizes, that he doesn't need the radio station. Mr. Weston probably did Klaus a favor, and yes Mr. Weston took Klaus position at the station away, and cancelled the show. However, Mr. Weston did not take Klaus talent away, and he did not take Klaus prestige, and his name away. Klaus is still DJ K. and he still has several fans, that are willing to listen to him, and follow him, no matter what avenue he may choose. So, although Klaus is no longer at the radio station, that doesn't mean that Klaus can't find other methods to get his show across. Upon realizing this, Klaus entire mood changes, and he no longer feels upset as he was. The only thing was explaining this to the other guys, and if they were going to be on board, and agree to go along with the plan as well. Klaus is very sure that they will. Klaus was glad that he was bouncing back, so quickly. It seemed for a moment that everything was all lost and gone.

Klaus then decides to walk out of the balcony, to let the other guys know of his plan. Once Klaus is in the living room, the men all stare at him, curious as to what he's going to do or say. Klaus then begins to smile, and starts to speak with the rest of the guys.

"Hey, I have an idea. I got fired from the station. Alright. We lost our show. Okay. But guess what? We're still here, and we can still do a show. We don't need that damn radio station. We can make our own show. Tape it, and stream it ourselves. This is only the beginning."

The guys all look at each other, and confused at Klaus at first. However, after several seconds, it seems the guys have managed to get what Klaus is talking about. Paul then speaks.

"So, you want to have our own independent show? Alright. I understand now."

Klaus then nods his head towards Paul, and quickly responds back to him.

"Exactly, and not only that, we are going to have it live and direct. We will go out in the street, to whatever events are happening, and record and capture it live. We can be our own news station, and news network. Fuck doing radio and podcasts, let's get out where the action is."

Jerome, who is excited about this plan, responds back to Klaus with concerns.

"This sounds like fun; however, it might be dangerous. I don't know Klaus. I mean I'm on board, but I just want to explain the dangers in something like this. I'm only concerned."

Ernest then pats Jerome on the back, and starts to speak with all of the guys.

"Klaus wouldn't do that to us. He would make sure that we are all safe, and nobody gets hurt. I'm on board with this too. This is great, and would be even better than our radio show."

Bill who is reading his newspaper, then responds to the idea that Klaus just brought out.

"Nephew, whatever you want to do, you can count me in. I said I would support you, and be there for you whenever you need me to be. I mean it. I support this idea, and it sounds great."

Dan, who is still preparing dinner for the guys, is still very engaged in the conversation, and has also heard the idea, that Klaus has brought out. Dan then speaks to all the guys.

"Klaus, I don't know how you come up with these heinous ideas. That is absolutely fantastic, and only a genius would think of something like that. You know I'm on board. Yes."

Klaus then looks down on the ground, and smiles to himself. So, it seems to be settled. All of the guys are in agreement with the new idea and plan Klaus has. So the worry that the men would not agree to the idea, is gone. Klaus knew they would all agree, but the fact it's official, and they are all happy with it, Klaus is okay with. So now that the whole group has agreed to the idea, Klaus has to now figure out how he is going to put it in all in formation. Although Klaus is still unsure as to how he is going to get everything set up. Klaus feels that he has plenty of time to sort that out, and get his ideas all down. For now, Klaus was happy that the idea and thought was agreed on, and approved by the whole group. Klaus still doesn't wish to think of himself as the leader, and doesn't wish to be selfish like that. Any idea that he has, he still wants to run it through the rest of the guys first, and see what their opinion of the matter is, before he proceeds. Klaus feel the worst thing that he could do, is cause any rift or friction within the group. Yeah, there are times to where the guys will have petty arguments or gripes, but usually, the entire group gets along well with each other, and are able to relate well with one another.

At this time, dan has finished preparing the spaghetti dinner. One by one, the men all grab a plate of food. Klaus, and Bill, brings their plates back to the living room, and Klaus sits in the recliner, with Bill sitting in another recliner, next to Klaus. Jerome, and Paul grab a plate of food, and they both sit on the sofa in the living room. Dan and Ernest, both eat at the kitchen counter. With all the men eating their food, Klaus soon starts to forget, that Mr. Weston fired him today, and ended the show. Klaus was going to move onto his other ideas, and not let that bring him, or the rest of his team down. As Klaus is eating the spaghetti, he is amazed at how good of a cook Dan is. The pasta tastes amazing, and the rest of the guys, are pleased, and enjoy the meal as well. The television in the living room, is playing the movie "Commando", an Arnold Schwarzenegger action movie. Even though Dan and Ernest are in the kitchen, they can still see and hear the movie that is playing in the living room, from where they are. All six of them are watching television, and they soon start to forget everything that happened earlier tonight. With the show coming to an end. Klaus wanted to forget all of that, and move on, and be happy. He had other fish to fry, and other things on his list that he wanted to get to. He didn't care that Mr. Weston dismissed them. Klaus was simply trying to get all of that. It didn't bother him anymore, and it wasn't that big of a deal to him. Klaus continues to eat his dinner, and is calm and collected with everything. The mean all finish their dinner. For dessert, Ernest happened to bake a cake, and the cake is finished at this time. The guys all eat the cake, and they all thank Dan and Ernest for dinner and dessert. One the men are finished with dessert, Jerome without hesitation, or being asked, decides to clean up all of the dishes, like he normally does. As Jerome is washing the dishes, Paul and Bill say goodnight, and they both walk into the bedroom. Ernest, shortly after, says goodnight as well, and walks into the bedroom. At this time, Klaus and Dan decide to have a cigarette on the balcony, and walk out there together. Jerome finishes all of the dishes, and walks into the bedroom. Klaus and Dan remain on the balcony speaking to each other. Klaus takes a puff of his cigarette, and speaks to Dan.

"Hey man, I'm sorry about earlier. I get like that sometimes, and I apologize. I just can't believe that asshole fired me, and after everything I did for that man. I can't believe this."

Dan takes a puff of his cigarette, and pats Klaus on the back. Dan then speaks to Klaus.

"It's okay. I know you were upset, and I know who you act now man. I have gotten used to it. Ha Ha. Everything is gonna be okay. We got this. You're not a quitter. You got this."

Dan pats Klaus on the back again, and Klaus looks down on the ground, and smiles. Both of the men remain outside the balcony for several more minutes. Eventually, Klaus and Dan walk out of the balcony, and go back into the house. Dan walks into his bedroom, and Klaus walks into his bedroom. When Klaus walks into his room, he notices that Jerome is fast asleep. Klaus covers Jerome up, and tucks him in, and kisses him on the forehead. Klaus then starts to change into his sleepwear, and gets into bed, and drifts off to sleep. Klaus didn't have any issue falling asleep. He was extremely tired, and experienced so much recently, with the drama surrounding Mr. Weston, and being dismissed from the show. With Klaus now having a "Plan B", and a backup plan, he feels more secure with his agenda, and his next plan of attack. When morning arrives, Dan, Ernest, and Bill, are already awake. Bill is in the living room, reading his newspaper. Dan and Ernest are in the kitchen, both eating a bowl of cereal, and talking with each other. It is a Friday, and the weather is perfect for Los Angeles. The sun is shining brightly, and there are very few clous in the sky. Dan and Ernest notice how nice the weather is, as they look out the windows from the kitchen, staring outside. At this time, Paul wakes up, and joins Bill in the living room. Not long after this, Jerome wakes up, and walks over to the kitchen, to speak with Dan and Ernest. A half an hour later, Klaus, who is usually the last to wake up, joins the rest of the men, inside of the living room. Klaus immediately begins to pour his custom cup of coffee, and starts to take sips of it. Klaus then takes his cup of coffee, and joins Bill and Paul in the living room. Klaus takes another sip of his coffee, and notices that the television is showing the morning news. Klaus continues to look at the news broadcast intrigued.

The news is having a live breaking news segment, on a LAUSD, which is the Los Angeles Unified School District, having a teachers strike. This interest Klaus greatly, and he is totally and completely drawn to the news story. The strike is over the fact that teachers are not getting equal pay, or great benefits. Teachers are also having to deal with unruly students, students with special circumstances, gifted students, that aren't given the proper education, and classes and programs. As a result of the strike, several schools are closed, and teachers are out of work. Students are also missing class, and being bussed into schools that are farther away. Klaus then starts to take his notebook out, and jots down notes of what he sees during the news program. Klaus then has yet another bright idea. Klaus is confident, that this would be the perfect time to act out on his plan. Klaus is noticing how there aren't that many news stations present at this strike, and because there are so few people reporting on this story, this would be perfect for Klaus, and his men, to report on it. The strike is also not located far from Klaus residence. Klaus didn't see any reason to pass this up. Klaus takes another sip of his coffee, and grins to himself. Klaus cannot believe how easy it is, for him to come up with these schemes and ideas. The news program then shifts away from the teachers strike, and moves onto another segment. Klaus continues to smile to himself, and shakes his head. Klaus then shuts the television off, and stands up. The other men all look at Klaus, giving him their undivided attention. Klaus then speaks.

"You guys just heard that teachers strike thing, right? Let's go right now, and cover it. This will be like out test pilot. Ha Ha. Hey, you guys did say you were on board with this. We'll capture everything, interview all of the teachers, get the information on everything. Let's do it!"

Dan raises his eyebrows at Klaus, and then swiftly replies back to him.

"You mean right now? Like, you want us to up and leave, and get down there now?"

Klaus then shakes his head and laughs at Dan. Klaus takes another sip of his coffee, and while he's drinking his coffee, speaks to Dan.

"No, I mean next year. Shit, of course right now. Let's go. We're wasting time. Time is money, and the longer we mope around here, the less time we have to cover the story. Come on."

Dan shakes his head, and the rest of the guys are puzzled for a few seconds. They soon understand that Klaus is not joking or fooling around, and wants the guys to report to the location of the teacher's strike, immediately. All of the men start to get prepared and dressed, and it doesn't take them long to get ready. Klaus manages to get all his equipment, his microphones, his camcorders, his tripods, his camera lights, and also his wireless hotspot router, as the guys are going to be doing a live remote broadcast. As Klaus is sorting all of his equipment, he thinks to himself a bit, about how he's back in action. He is not going to let what happened to him yesterday, mean anything. He didn't care at all of Mr. Weston's opinion. Klaus wishes to prove him completely wrong, and Klaus is going to continue on like normal. Klaus knew this was his passion, and nothing at all was going to stop him. When one door closes, another one opens. This is another opportunity for Klaus to spring into action, and to entertain others. Although this was simply a test, and a spur of the moment thing, it was of course good enough for Klaus. Eventually, Klaus has everything he needs, before all the men set out. Although they are all still skeptical as to what's going on, and what they are trying to accomplish, the men are still happy and excited. The men all get into Klaus SUV, as he begins to drive to the location of the teachers strike. Klaus has partly no idea as to what he's doing, with the other part of him, confident that he will have a clear setup and plan, to all of this. It is not long before Klaus manages to reach the teachers strike location, Klaus parks his car a few blocks away from the action.

After he is parked, Klaus immediately gets out of the car, and starts to grab his equipment. As he's grabbing his equipment, Klaus then starts to speak.

"Dan, I'm gonna hand you this microphone. Ernest you take this camera, and film everything Dan is doing. You guys are gonna cover the west side of the strike. Uncle Bill, you're gonna take this camera, and Paul, here's a microphone. Uncle film everything he picks up."

As Klaus is handing all the equipment to the guys, Dan is puzzled, and speaks to Klaus.

"Hey wait a minute, hold on buddy. What do you want us to do? So, I'm gonna report, and you want Ernest to record what I report? You also want to have Bill record, what Paul is reporting as well. I understand. This is all so sudden, but fun. Okay. I got it now. Ha Ha."

Klaus and Dan then fist bump, and then Klaus hands dan another piece of equipment.

"Oh, I almost forgot. Here's a network hotspot. This allows you to connect to our viewers live on YouTube. I already calibrated the cameras so they go live to our network. If you have any questions, you guys all have my number, and text me. We will meet up at the end of the event."

Dan and Ernest then immediately walk away, with Ernest acting as cameraman, and Dan acting as reporter. Klaus then quickly let's Bill know how to work the camera; which Bill remarkably is able to figure out rather quickly. Klaus then gives Paul the wireless hotspot, and both Paul and Bill walk away. Klaus and Jerome then remain at Klaus SUV together. Jerome slightly puzzled, then starts to speak in a jokingly tone, to Klaus.

"IIey, what about me? Ha Ha. What do you want mc to do?"

Klaus then grabs another microphone, and hands it to Jerome. Klaus then speaks.

"You're gonna be my reporter. You're my number one fan right. We'll number one fan, use that lovely personality of yours, and be my reporter. Don't worry, you'll do great. Ha Ha."

Jerome then laughs, while looking at the microphone. Klaus then takes a camcorder, and wraps it around his neck, and starts to test it. Klaus also puts another wireless hotspot in his pocket. He, along with the rest of the guys, are now connected live. Klaus has a separate device connected to his camcorder, that gives him a view of both Ernest, and Bill's camera feed, both video and audio. Klaus can also have a look at the live chatroom on YouTube, their show is being broadcasted on. With everything now set, Klaus starts to speak with Jerome.

"So, be honest. How do I look? Do I look professional now? Do we look legit? Ha."

Jerome once again laughs, and nods his head towards Klaus. It is now show time. Things are happening rapidly, and the guys are having to adjust and get through this quickly. Dan and Ernest direct themselves to the west side of the event, covering that area. Paul and Bill, direct themselves to the North side of the event. Klaus and Jerome, direct themselves to the south side of the event. Once all the guys are that the teachers strike, the entire event is very loud and chaotic. There is a lot of unrest, and unhappy people, and there is much commotion. There are several teachers holding up signs, yelling and shouting, and the teachers feel that the way the school district is handling this, is incorrect. There is a lot of commotion, and outrage, and Klaus knew that this would be a perfect event to capture. Klaus takes a quick gander at the camera feeds from the other guys. He notices that Dan and Ernest feed seems fine, and they are already getting great footage. Klaus glances at Paul and Bill's camera feed, and everything looks good, coming from them. Klaus takes a look at the video stream, and notices that they already have two hundred people watching live. It may not seem much, but Klaus is very happy with that. Klaus and Jerome continue to walk through the event. Klaus is also surprised, that there aren't many other reporters, or news networks, covering what is going on at all. However, not even ten minutes into Klaus and Jerome being there, they are approached by a police officer. The police officer is an older Caucasian man, with a thick mustache, and wearing sunglasses. Jerome immediately feels anxious, and unsure as to what to do. Klaus also feels scared, and all of his thoughts become jumbled. Klaus didn't explain to the men, what their game plan was, if they were to be approached by the police. Klaus is well aware that he, and the rest of the guys, do not have any press passes, or any media credentials, to be covering the event.

Klaus also feels, that they shouldn't need any of that. As long as Klaus, and his team, are covering things in public property, which the outside of a school district building is, then Klaus has every right to do a news story. Klaus immediately responds to the police officer.

"Oh, hello officer. We are with Fox 11 News Los Angeles. This is my on the field reporter, and I'm his cameraman. We are just doing a news story officer. Thank you."

The police officer then directs him attention to Jerome, and Jerome speaks to the officer.

"Yes, hello officer. He's right officer. This is my cameraman, and I'm a reporter. We work for Fox 11 Los Angeles News. We are simply doing a news story."

The officer doesn't respond, but smiles, and walks away from them. Klaus and Jerome give a sigh of relief, that they managed to get pass the police. During this time, Klaus starts to worry that Dan, Ernest, Paul, and Bill, will come across the same issue. Klaus then sends a mass text message to them all, letting them know, to just tell the police, that they are with the news. The other guys managed to get the text message, and are aware of the memo. Klaus was happy that he managed to slither himself out of that situation. Klaus couldn't believe that he already had to go through that, not even a few minutes into them arriving at the location. Klaus tries his best to ignore that, and he didn't feel good lying to the police, but Klaus felt he had every right, for himself, and the rest of his team, to do a news story. Klaus and Jerome continue to walk through the event, and Jerome stops Klaus, and asks if he can interview one of the teachers. The teacher that Jerome decides to interview, is an elderly woman, holding up a sign, in the strike. Jerome then starts to introduce himself to her, and begins to interview her.

"Hello ma'am. My name is Jerome. We're a news station, doing a story on today's event. If you don't mind me asking, you can explain why you here at this event please?"

The elderly woman continues to hold up her sign, and responds directly to Jerome.

"I have been a teacher for over fifty years, and I'm sick and tired of the bullshit, that the school district decides to pull. We are sick of it, and aren't going to take it anymore."

As Jerome is interviewing the teacher, Klaus cannot believe he is actually going through whit his plan. He's making his own news program, and it's going exactly the way he envisioned, and the way he exactly planned. Klaus understands that this is perfect, and Klaus is loving this very much. Klaus continues to capture the event, smiling to himself. The whole universe stops, as Klaus is putting all his feelings in order. Time usually seems to stop, as Klaus is gathering his thoughts. This feels like a dream, and Klaus is doing all that he can, to tell himself that this is real, and this is happening live. Klaus steadily continues to broadcast the vent live, and is also takes note at the viewers, which has raised from two hundred people, to now six hundred people are currently watching. Jerome continues to interview the woman.

"I see. I can imagine how stressful this is for you. I always felt teachers were one of the most underpaid professions, and the most undervalued people. Thank you for sharing ma'am."

Jerome ends up shaking the woman's hand, and both Klaus and Jerome continue to walk about the event, getting the complete coverage of what they are picking up live. Meanwhile, Dan and Ernest are managing to get fantastic coverage. Dan ends up talking to a tall middle-aged man, that has short hair, and a goatee. Dan walks up to the man, and interviews him.

"Hello sir. My name is Dan, I'm with Fox News LA. I wanted to ask you a few questions please. May I ask why you are here with the event. What are you demanding to change?"

The man, who is holding up a picket sign, responds swiftly pack to Dan.

"I work with special needs students, and I feel the district has done nothing to help these students, and I feel that's unacceptable. These kids depend on us, and the district has failed."

Ernest manages to do a perfect job of capturing Dan, and getting the event out live. Dan then continues to speak with the man he's interviewing.

"Oh yes sir. I really appreciate you sharing that with us. It seems you truly care about your job as a teacher, and the difference that you make with you students. Thank you, sir."

Dan continues to interview the teacher, and once Dan finishes interviewing him, he shakes his hand. Klaus, who was intermittently watching Dan and Ernest's feed, smiles to himself, and pleased that

Dan and Ernest are doing an amazing job. Klaus still tries to bring himself to reality, that they are actually doing this. Things are going smoothly and fine. Klaus shuts off Dan and Ernest's camera feed, and then is curious as to what Paul and Bill are doing. Paul meanders through the event, with Bill doing an excellent, and satisfactory job, capturing the proceedings live. Likewise, with the other men, Paul is going to interview the teachers that are on strike at the event. Even though there is a lot of noise, and commotion at the event, the men are finding it second nature, to deal with it all. Paul walks up to a younger blond woman, who is holding up a sign. Paul then decides to interview her.

"Hello ma'am. My name is Paul, I'm with Fox 11 news LA. We are out here, trying to get information on this event and strike. Can you tell me why you are here please?"

The teacher, likewise with the other teachers, is holding up a sign and protesting as well. She then quickly responds to Paul interviewing her, and answering his question.

"Yes. I run an afterschool program. I teach the kids music therapy. We do homework help, arts and crafts, sports, and other activities. The district cut this program. That's not right."

Paul carries on interviewing the woman, and understanding her struggle, and can see why this woman is here, protesting with the other teachers at this event. Paul then responds.

"Oh yes, that is very terrible that the district is doing that, and I understand completely why are you fighting for that. Ma'am thank you so much for sharing that with us."

Paul ends up shaking the woman's hand, and Paul and Bill carry on through at the event. Klaus continues to have a wide grin on his face, and feels more pleased, once noticing that Paul and Bill are doing great, and getting excellent live coverage as well. As minutes carry on, and the men remain at this event, the viewers of Klaus broadcast, increase, and increase. With the viewers now at a thousand people, Klaus shakes in head in disbelief. Jerome, Dan, and Paul, interview several more teachers, and figure out their purpose at the event, and what they are exactly fighting for, and wishing and wanting the school district to change. These teachers are clearly angry, and they want others to know how upset they are. As Klaus is continuing to capture everything at the event, with Jerome with his reporter, he continues to look at how chaotic this event is. How angry these teachers are, and how they have had enough. To the point to where they are having this protest, demanding for things to change. The men have all been at this event, for a few hours now, capturing a lot of footage for their news program. At this point, several of teachers have left, and the event is slowly dying down. The strike is not over, and the teachers will be back, to carry on the protest. They will keep going until the district listens to them and responds to their complaints and their issues. Even though several of the protestors have left the event, Klaus, and the rest of the men, stay at the event. Klaus feels there is still quite a bit left to over, and they don't have to leave quite yet. With it now being late into the evening, Klaus remains at the event, and views of the show slightly go down, as the men aren't capturing anything else that is noteworthy or exciting. Klaus decides that if this continues for another hour, which Klaus is thinking to himself that it probably will, he will call it day.

Klaus assumptions were correct, and the event never picked up steam, the way it was, when the men first arrived at the scene. Most of the teachers have gone home, and put their protesting on hold for today. Although this strike is far from over. Klaus and Jerome walk across the event, and due to the fact, the crowd has dissipated, and most of the action has subsided, they come across by chance, Paul and Bill. Upon noticing each other, they laugh for a bit. Klaus and Paul then speak to each other, and talk about all everything that they managed to capture today, and how wonderful the show is. Klaus takes a look at the broadcast, and the viewers are now at a hundred people. This figures, as what they guys are currently recording live, isn't that eventful, but Klaus is happy that the majority of the show was exciting, and that his plan of his worked out in splendid way, like he knew that it would. The event has slowed down, and there are not many people present anymore. Ten minutes later, with Klaus, Jerome, Paul, and Bill roaming about the event, they manage to come across Dan and Ernest. All six of the men have reunited with each other, and are pleased with what they were able to come up with. This was their first ever live remote show, and the guys felt confident, to do these a thousand more times. Klaus, and the rest of the men walk around the event, and although there are still a few teachers protesting, the event is virtually over, and most of the action and drama is done. Klaus then decides to end the live broadcast, and Klaus, Ernest, and Bill, all shut their cameras off. The men are all walking back to Klaus SUV. On the way there, Dan then starts to speak to Klaus.

"I don't know how you come up with these ideas man. You're the only person that would have thought about this. Not only was the idea crazy, but it worked. How do you do it? Ha Ha."

Klaus starts to look at the settings on his camcorder. While he is doing that, Klaus decides to softly speak back to Dan

"I don't' know. I guess I'm magic. Ha Ha. If I can dream it, I can do it, I guess. Ha Ha."

Dan laughs, and shakes his head towards Klaus. The guys all continue to walk toward Klaus SUV. Once they reach the vehicle, Klaus grabs all of the equipment, and sets them in the back of the vehicle. The men then all get into the vehicle and Klaus drives off. While Klaus is driving off, he is still overjoyed in his emotions, and grinning heavily. At this time, when Klaus reaches a stoplight, he decides to speak to the entire group.

"I'm so proud of boys. I really am. I mean, I knew you guys could do it, but the fact we actually did it. Yes. We are back in action, and we got this. Why don't we celebrate. Let's all go to Red Lobster. I'm hungry, and haven't had anything to eat. My treat you guys."

The rest of the guys are all in agreement, with Klaus plan, to go to Red Lobster. Klaus then drives directly to the Red Lobster restaurant, and all of the guys get out of the vehicle. Because it's Friday night, the restaurant is quite crowded with customers, and Klaus and the other men, must wait a while, before they are able to secure table. The guys manage to wait outside of the restaurant, talking and conversing with each other, and exchanging jokes, to pass the time. Eventually, a table does open up for them. The waitress then seats all of them at a table, at the back of the restaurant, in which gives the guys a view of the beach, which the restaurant is located in walking distance, in front of. Klaus, and Bill both take the end seats, with Jerome and Ernest sitting on the left side of the table, and Dan and Paul, sitting on the right side of the table. The guys then all read their menu's, deciding on what to order. The men are able to give the waitress their bar drinks, while the guys are still deciding what meal they want. As the guys continue to stare at the menu's, Dan then decides to speak with Klaus.

"Hey man, thanks for treating us out. I know you get tired of us thanking you, and being all like this, but I think I speak for all the guys when I say this. Thank you Klaus. I mean it."

Dan and Klaus fist bump each other, and Klaus returns to looking at his menu. Klaus was tired of the guys constantly taking him, and giving him gratitude, but he was also happy that the guys were pleased with what he is doing. Klaus is enjoying that he has friends, and a support system. This was something that he didn't have previously, so Klaus is also thankful in that regard. The men soon decide what they want to eat. Klaus, Dan, Paul, and Bill, all decide to get the surf and turf, lobster and steak meal. Ernest and Jerome, order something similar, but get the steak and shrimp surf and turf. The waitress soon arrives, with the guys food order, and the men then all start eating. Along with the meal, the guys are also given Cheddar Biscuits, which are a personal favorite with Klaus. The men are all enjoying their food, and also talking with one another as they are eating. Once the men have finished eating, the waitress arrives back at the table, with the check. Klaus pays for the meal, as he promised, and leaves a tip for the waitress. Shortly after, the men all get up from the table, and leave out of the restaurant. Before going back to the car, Ernest asks if they can all get ice cream, at Baskin Robbins, which was located nearby the restaurant. Klaus agrees, and the men all go into the ice cream shop. Ice cream is one of Klaus favorite foods, so he wasn't going to pass that up. Klaus decides to order his chocolate chip cookie dough ice cream. Dan orders Rocky Road ice cream. Ernest has rum raisin ice cream. Jerome decides to get butter pecan ice cream. Paul gets strawberry ice cream. Bill decides to order, Mint Chocolate Chip ice cream. After getting their ice cream, Klaus, then decides to surprise the guys, by driving to the beach, which was also close by. Upon reaching the beach, Klaus, and the rest of the men, then get out of the car. All six of them sit outside, facing the beach, eating their ice cream. They are all happy together at this moment. Klaus watches the ocean, and hears the waves crash. He can smell the sea as well. The sun is also setting during this time, which makes this an even more beautiful scene.

The men remain at the beach, for quite some time, enjoying their ice cream, and looking at the ocean. As the sun starts to set, and it's getting more closer to dusk, and nighttime, and it now creeping up after 7pm, Klaus decides that they all should return home. Klaus and the rest of the men, throw away their ice cream containers in the trash, and they all get back into Klaus SUV. Klaus then immediately drives back to the house. Once they have arrived back home, Klaus gathers all the camera equipment, and stores them in the den of his house. Dan sits at one of the recliners in the living room, and Bill sits in the other recliner in the living room. Ernest and Jerome remain seated at the sofa in the living room. Paul walks into his bedroom for a minute, then walks back out to the living room, with a grin on his face. Klaus at this time, managed to make his way back into the living room, and notices that Paul is standing in the living room, with a wide smile. Klaus who is curious, starts to speak to him.

"Hey, what are you smiling at. What's so funny. What happened? Ha Ha."

Paul then sticks his hands in his pockets, and looks down on the ground, smiling and laughing to himself. Paul then takes something out of his left pocket. Klaus watches as Paul does this and notices that Paul takes out a bag of marijuana. Klaus starts to take off his glasses, and begins to clean them with his shirt, as if his eyes are deceiving him. The rest of the guys, also look at Paul in amusement, not expecting for him to do that. Klaus puts his glasses back on, and continues to look completely stunned, at the bag of marijuana that Paul is currently holding. Klaus walks over to Paul, and quickly snatches the bag out of his hand.

"Hey, you dirty bird. You been smoking this shit in my house, weren't you?"

Paul then changes his expression to a more serious tone, and shakes his head. Klaus raises his eyebrows at Klaus, and looks at him with disbelief and doubt. Paul then responds.

"No. I swear I haven't. I wouldn't do something like that without your permission. I don't know if the rest of you guys are 420 friendly. I was saving it for the perfect time for us all."

Klaus then starts to laugh, and hands the bag back to Paul. Klaus then responds.

"Ha Ha. Okay. So, you guys wanna get high then? Paul has some pot, so yeah. Ha Ha."

The rest of the men are in agreement, and Paul starts to laugh and smile. Paul then sits down on the sofa, and rolls two marijuana joints, rather quickly. Paul then keeps a joint for himself, and hands Klaus the other one. Paul lights the joint he has, taking several puffs, and passes the joint to Bill, who takes puffs of the marijuana joint. Bill then passes the joint, to Ernest, who takes puffs of it. Klaus then lights to joint he has, taking several puffs, and passing it to Dan. Dan takes several puffs of marijuana, and hands the joint to Jerome. Jerome takes puffs of the marijuana joint, and hands it back to Klaus. At this time, Dan starts to cough from smoking the marijuana. Dan then turns the television set in the living room on. The television is playing the Adam Sandler movie, "Happy Gilmore." Dan starts to laugh, and speaks to Paul.

"Man, this is some good strong shit. You were hiding this the whole time. Man. Ha Ha."

Paul takes more puffs of the marijuana joint, and laughs at Dan's comment. The six of them continue to smoke for several more minutes. Klaus, and the rest of the men, start to get slightly buzzed from the marijuana, and are feeling comfortable. Klaus hands the joint of marijuana that he and the rest of the guys were smoking, back to Paul, as there is not much left to smoke of it left. Paul puts the end of the joint back into the bag of marijuana. Ernest, hands back Paul the other joint end, and Paul also puts it away. Klaus walks over to his kitchen, and gets two bottles of beer. Klaus, along with Dan, then do what they normally do, and walk out on the balcony, and chat with each other.

Ernest, Jerome, Paul, and Bill, remain in the living room, watching the movie. Klaus and Dan start to drink their beers on the balcony, and Dan begins to light himself a cigarette. While Dan is looking and facing forward, he speaks to Klaus.

"Oh man, that was some strong shit. I swear Paul, that guy is unpredictable I swear. I haven't been this high a long time. I don't know what he had, but that shit was good. Jesus. Ha."

Klaus then lights himself as cigarette as well, and starts to smoke it. Looking and facing forward out of the balcony as well, Klaus then responds back to Dan.

"Oh, I knew he smoked weed. I can tell. I just didn't know he had any. That pot was good. Sharing is caring, so it is nice that he had enough for the whole class, so yeah. Ha Ha."

Dan shakes his head and laughs at Klaus. The both of them continue to hang outside the balcony for several more minutes. At this time, both Ernest and Jerome, are feeling slightly faded, yet they are still alert. They manage to rest on the sofa, silently. Paul and Bill watch the movie on the television, acting extremely hyper, and being loud. Once the movie has finished, Klaus and Dan, are still outside on the balcony, conversating with one another. The rest of the men, remain all together in the living room. Ernest then decides to take himself to bed, and says goodnight to all of the men. Ernest then walks into the bedroom. A few minutes later, Jerome does the same, and walks himself into the bedroom. Paul and Bill, as well as Klaus and Dan are still active, and aren't as lethargic, as Ernest and Jerome were, and they remain where they are. Bill calls Paul over to give him a back message, and Paul obliges. As Paul is giving Bill a massage, he teases him, by kissing his neck, and caressing him, which Bill doesn't mind. Klaus and Dan continue to remain on the balcony, exchanging jokes with one another and circulating.

Eventually, the rest of the guys start to become tired as well. Paul and Bill, then direct themselves to the bedroom. Shortly after that, Klaus and Dan leave the balcony, and are slightly shocked, when the notice that the other guys have went to bed. Klaus and Dan are unaware, of how they lost complete track of time. Klaus and Dan fist bump each other, and they both say goodnight. Once Dan is in the bedroom, his kisses Ernest who is sleeping on the head, and Dan changes into his sleepwear, and gets into bed. Klaus walks into his bedroom, and notices Jerome, deep asleep. Klaus kisses Jerome on the head, and changes into his sleepwear. Klaus then gets into bed, and immediately and quickly, drifts off to sleep.

CHAPTER 10:

THE WINGMAN

After having an amazing night of fun, the guys are now faced with the morning after. Yesterday was a very eventful day, much to Klaus chagrin. Klaus was informed by Mr. Weston, that he was not just fired from the radio program, but that his show as going to be cancelled as well. This rightfully angered Klaus, and made him seep into a dark depression. The main thing that Klaus loved more than anything else in the world, was doing radio. So the fact it was slipped away from him, in a quick instant like that, made Klaus extremely upset. Klaus felt betrayed very much by Mr. Weston, and couldn't believe that their prior relationship, didn't mean anything, or come into the equation. Klaus spent great time on that show, so the fact the show is gone, and cancelled, is very severe and difficult for Klaus to manage. Klaus also was concerned about how his friends, and the rest of the guys were going to feel about the news as well. Klaus didn't want to only think of himself, and he was trying not to be selfish. He had five other men, his new group of friends rather, that were working for him. They would have to leave as well. Klaus was surprised to find out, that the guys actually took the news well, and were accepting. So Klaus realized that if the other guys were taking the news well, then he could deal with the situation as well. Klaus didn't want to make a big fuss or fight, and even though Klaus has a strong dislike for Mr. Weston at this point, he decided that he, and his friends, should leave out of the studio quickly. That's exactly what Klaus did, and he wanted to move on. Mr. Weston had already made his mind up, so Klaus didn't really feel that it was worth it to argue or fight with him. Klaus, and the rest of his crew, simply left the studio.

Following that, Klaus was upset for a sting, and he went back to closing himself to the world, likewise how he used to do, before he met the rest of the guys. However, Klaus knew that being upset and feeling down about yourself, accomplishes nothing. Klaus had to snap himself out of this depression he was in, and think of another plan, quickly. Klaus was indeed able to do is, and he came up with the idea, for the guys, to start their own show. Klaus was going to produce his own independent news show. He didn't need Mr. Weston's help, and he also didn't need a radio station. All that he needed was his solid and core group of friends to help him run the show. Once the idea was sparked into Klaus mind, nothing was going to stop him, and he was determined to go along with his idea. Although the idea did sound sort of strange, and unusual, Klaus didn't care. He wanted to fulfill his new idea, at all costs, and by any means necessary. Klaus started to understand, that this is the internet and technology age, and his idea of going independent, was a very wise and beneficial one. Klaus figured that the true fans of his radio show, would also tune into his new independent show. Once Klaus figured this tactic out, his mood completely changed, and he was happy and pleased with himself again. He couldn't wait to tell his plan to the other guys. Once Klaus explained his idea, of course, his group was accepting, and were willing to do Klaus plan as well. Once Klaus found out that his friends were on board with the idea as well, Klaus wanted to start his show, as soon as possible. Klaus was very excited, and in tuned with this idea. He didn't want to waste any needed time, and wanted to get straight to producing it, and putting everything together. Klaus had all the right equipment, and he had his crew, so there weren't any excuses, as to why he couldn't do the show, the way he wanted to do it. Klaus would soon get his wish, with wanting to start the show soon, and he wouldn't have to wait that long.

The next day, Klaus was watching the morning news, and he noticed a Teacher's Strike, that was happening, at the Los Angeles School District Building. The light bulb stroke into Klaus head yet again, and another idea sparked. He immediately asked the guys, to follow him down to the strike, so they can do a test episode of their show. Klaus figured that there was no time like the present, and this was the ample opportunity they needed, to showcase their show. Klaus noticed the array of angry teacher's that were there, and the unrest that they were all feeling. Most importantly, Klaus noticed that there were not that many news avenues that were covering the event. So especially over that fact, Klaus and his men, had to get themselves down there, to cover the event, immediately. Klaus didn't waste any time doing this, and he took all his equipment, and started to do his own independent amateur show. Even though things were hectic at first, and Klaus was Jerome were stopped by the police, asking why they were filming the event, they were easily able to weasel themselves out of the situation, and everything was fine, in the end. Klaus, and the rest of his group, managed to put out an amazing show, and even though it was only intended to be a test episode, the guys were confident, and secure of themselves, that they could most definitely do this again, and continue this new format of their show. Afterwards, the men decided to celebrate, and it was rightfully deserved. They yet again bounced back, and managed to get themselves out of the corner, that they painted themselves in. Klaus has his mojo and attitude back, and he's extremely happy, and Klaus feels, that the only way is up for him. Going forward, and advancing forward, is the only option and choice. Klaus is going to definitely continue on with this show, with his guys. If not if, it's as matter of when, they will do their second episode. Klaus continues to feel excited over this, after they successful completed their first independent show, and nothing is going to stop him, or any of the other guys either. Klaus went to bed that night, the happiest that he's ever been. Without any worries, or concerns, and now very optimistic to what the next day brings, and what's next for him.

The morning continues on, with today being Saturday morning. The day is perfect, and clear. Light clouds in the sky, blue clouds, sunny comfortable weather. Very wonderful Los Angeles weather, for today. Bill is the first to wake up today, and he gets himself out of bed, and directs himself to the kitchen, to pour himself a cup of coffee. After Bill gets his coffee, he then walks to the living room, and sits down the recliner, like he usually always does, and starts to read his newspaper. Bill remains in the living room for a half an hour, before Dan, and Ernest, wake up as well. Dan walks over to Bill, and they both fist bump each other. Dan then walks into the kitchen, and starts to prepare breakfast for the guys; something that Dan does quite often. Dan continues to prepare breakfast, speaking with Ernest in the process. At this time, like clockwork almost, Paul wakes himself up, and directs himself to the living room, to sit on the sofa, and starts to speak with Bill. Paul turns the television set on, and he starts to watch documentary about wild Apes and Monkeys. About ten minutes later, Jerome awakens, and he joins Dan and Ernest in the kitchen as well. It seems as usual, that Klaus is customarily the last person to wake up. Several minutes later, Klaus wakes himself up, and walks to the kitchen, with the rest of the men. Klaus gives Dan a fist pump, pours his usual cup of coffee, taking several large gulps and sips of it. While Klaus is drinking his coffee, Dan speaks to him.

"Hey, so what's your schedule for today, what do you plan to do. Nothing? Ha Ha."

Klaus laughs, and shakes his head at Dan. Klaus takes another sip of coffee and speaks.

"Well, I guess so. Today was gonna be a rest day. I don't really have anything planned."

Klaus takes another sip of his coffee, and Jerome, starts to stare at Klaus. Jerome then while looking at the ground, starts to silently speak to Klaus.

"DJ K., I mean Klaus, do you want to go hiking today. We can all go, it would be fin. This is the perfect day to do it. I love hiking, don't you. I know this amazing trail nearby too."

Dan while cooking the breakfast, then starts to quickly respond back to Jerome.

"Aww Damn. You know I would buddy, but I promised Ernest me and him would go to this function together. It's just gonna be us. We can do a rain check though, we can go hiking some other time, okay. Why don't you ask Paul and Bill? They might want to go with you guys."

Jerome nods his head, and gives a slight disappointed smile to Dan, and looks down on the floor. Jerome then walks over to the living room, and speaks to Paul and Bill.

"Hey guys. Um, I wanted to know if you wanted to go hiking today. I asked Dan and Ernest, they are busy. I asked Klaus, he didn't respond. What about you guys. What do you say?"

Paul with his vision still directed at the documentary, responds to Jerome.

"Oh, um. Hiking is not really my thing, I'm not a hiking type of guy. I would hate to be a poor sport. Tell you what, I can do an art project with you later to make up it for it, okay?"

Paul then starts to rub Jerome's hair, and smiles and laughs at him. Jerome then laughs and smiles at Paul in return, and Jerome immediately walks over to speak with Bill. Before Jerome can even answer, Bill knows exactly what question he is going to ask, and responds.

"I'm sorry buddy, in my glory days, and younger years, I would have absolutely said yes. But my leg is bothering me quite a bit today, I'm really sorry."

Bill then grabs Jerome and kisses him on the forehead, and pats him on the back. Jerome laughs and smiles at Bill, but disapprovingly walks back to the kitchen area, with Klaus, Dan, and Ernest. Jerome is feeling really upset, that all of the guys had rejected his offer to go hiking with him. Dan, while still preparing breakfast, notices how upset Jerome is, and walks over to comfort and console him. This makes Jerome feel slightly better at the situation, and he manages to cheer himself up. Dan then returns to preparing breakfast, and speaks to Klaus.

"Hey man, go hiking with him. It's not like you're doing anything, or have anything else to do. Also, you could really use the exercise. Go hiking with him. Ha Ha."

Jerome then then gives a convincing desperate and upset look towards Klaus, which Klaus doesn't originally fall for or accept, but does eventually give into it.

"Damn it, okay. Only because the other guys refused and didn't want to. Also, Jerome you can never say I never done anything nice for you after this. Damn. Ha Ha."

Klaus returns to sipping his coffee, and Jerome unexpectantly, runs up to hug Klaus, very tightly. Klaus feeling surprised and shocked at this, doesn't respond. Jerome speaks to Klaus.

"Oh, thank you so much Klaus. We're going to have so much fun. I can't wait."

Klaus then laughs and shakes his head, and sips more of his coffee. Jerome then returns to his seat, and is quiet and obedient. Dan eventually finishes breakfast, and the guys all start to eat. Once breakfast is over, Jerome starts to immediately do the dishes, like always. While he is doing the dishes, Jerome is excited, that he is going hiking with Klaus. Klaus however, is not quite feeling the same way about the event, and slightly scared and nervous. Hiking isn't really Klaus forte, and he remembers when he went hiking with Stuart, the first time they met. It was slightly a disaster, and Klaus was not ready or prepared, for what he had to deal with. Klaus sits on his recliner in the living room, wondering if he made a terrible mistake. At this point, Klaus no longer feels interested in the hiking outing, and doesn't want to go anymore. Klaus is starting to regret agreeing to go hiking with Jerome, and is slightly thinking about telling him, that he changed his mind, and he no longer wishes to go. Klaus then understood, that this would be devastating, heartbreaking, and upsetting for Jerome, so Klaus decides not to do it, and he is sticking with the promise that he made Jerome, and is going to go hiking with him. Klaus knows that he's not probably going to fully enjoy it, but he wants to make this day, special for Jerome, so Klaus is going to play along regardless, and go on hiking.

Jerome finishes the dishes, and both himself and Klaus, then start to get themselves ready for the hiking trip. Klaus decides to pick out a green plaid shirt, and some black cargo pants, with sneakers. Jerome decides to wear a polo shirt, with cargo shorts, and also wearing sneakers as well. Now that both of the men, have their outfits together. Jerome then starts to pull out a backpack. Jerome then starts putting water, crackers, and a first aid kit in the backpack. As he's doing that, Jerome then softly speaks to Klaus.

"This is kinda my safety pack. When I go hiking, which I do quite often, I take a pack with him like this. I try to keep it light, and not too heavy, just essential stuff. You know?"

Klaus, who's sitting on the edge of his bed, watching Jerome pack everything, silently nods his head. Even though Klaus didn't care for hiking that much, Jerome enjoyed hiking very much, and Jerome has been hiking several times. Jerome was slightly unhappy that the other guys couldn't go hiking with him, as he wanted this to be a group activity, but he is happy that Klaus managed to agree to go hiking with him regardless. Jerome then starts to put the safety pack, backpack, around his back. Klaus and Jerome then awkwardly stare at each other for several seconds, before Jerome starts to whisper out to him.

"So, are you ready? I'm ready when you are. Come on let's go, we're wasting time."

Jerome then laughs, and attempts to grab Klaus arm, to pull him off the bed. Jerome is far too weak to lift Klaus up, and is unsuccessful. Klaus simply silently gives Jerome a cold stare. Jerome the notices that Klaus is joking or fooling around, and then whispers back to him.

"Oh no. Don't tell me you don't want to anymore. I knew it. Never mind. Forget it."

Klaus did indeed, seem to instantly change his mind on wanting to go out hiking. It was something that Klaus wanted to give a try at first, but later realized, that it's best for him if he didn't. Klaus realized that Jerome would be upset, but if Klaus didn't wish to go hiking, that was going to be his choice. Klaus didn't know the exact way to explain this to Jerome, so he decided to remain silent, and was hoping that Jerome would get the hint. Klaus watches as Jerome takes his backpack off, and tosses it on the bed; with Jerome having a disappointed look on his face. Klaus then once again shifts his mood, when he notices how disappointed Jerome looks, and starts to feel guilty and empathetic. Klaus starts to get a soft spot for Jerome. At this time, Jerome starts to walk out of Klaus bedroom, but Klaus instantly without Jerome being aware, puts Jerome's backpack on his back, and Klaus picks Jerome up, also carrying him on his back. Jerome not expecting this, starts to laugh, and Klaus softly speaks back to him.

"You wanna go hiking, we're gonna go hiking damn it."

Klaus then continues to carry Jerome throughout the house, on his way to the driveway. The other guys notice this, and start to laugh. Once Klaus and Jerome are outside in the driveway, Klaus sets Jerome down. After doing that, Klaus throws the car keys to Jerome, in which Jerome has a puzzled and confused look on his face. Klaus and Jerome then stare at each other for several seconds. With Jerome still being confused, Klaus starts to speak to him.

"Remember you told me you didn't have your license yet? You only had your learner's permit? Well since you want to go hiking so bad, drive us to the hiking trail. I know you can drive, you just need more experience, and right now is perfect. Believe in yourself. Ha Ha."

Jerome then starts to feel anxious, and doesn't feel like Klaus plan or idea is wise. Jerome doesn't feel as though he's ready to drive. While holding Klaus car keys, Jerome responds.

"Actually, I'm not that great of a driver. I actually failed the test two times already, and I don't think driving is for me. You better drive, I don't think this is a good idea."

Jerome then starts to walk towards Klaus, and Jerome extends his arm out, to hand Klaus the keys back. Klaus does not reach for them back, and instead, responds back to Jerome.

"Well if you don't drive, I'm not going hiking. So make your choice. Either you start driving, or I'm going back in the house, and we're not going anywhere. The choice is yours. Ha."

Jerome then starts to frantically look around, anxious and unsure of himself. After a few seconds, Jerome does decide to drive the car. Jerome opens the driver's side door, and Klaus sits in the passenger seat. Jerome once inside the vehicle, stares at Klaus, and Klaus smiles to him. Jerome smiles back to Klaus, and feels more confident with himself. Jerome puts his seat belt on, checks his mirrors, and turns the ignition on. Klaus is steadily watching Jerome like a hawk during this entire process, making sure that he's doing everything correctly. Jerome then puts the car into reverse, and starts to back out into the driveway. Jerome then immediately, puts the car into drive, and directs himself down the road. At this time, Klaus decides to turn the stereo on the car on, in which Klaus is playing a Radiohead song, from his phone. Jerome shockingly, is doing is an amazing job, as Jerome continues to drive toward the hiking trail. As Jerome continues to drive, Klaus wishes to test Jerome's ability to parallel park. Klaus then speaks to Jerome.

"Hey, you see those two cars? Pull up in between those cars, and park. You can do it."

Jerome then covers his mouth with his hand, and starts to feel worried. Parallel parking is something Jerome wasn't able to succeed accurately at yet, when it came to driving. Jerome is not sure he is going to be able to accomplish and complete this task. Jerome then puts the car into reverse, and as he's backing the car up, Jerome responds to Klaus.

"You want me to parallel park now? Okay. I'm not good at this. I'm gonna try."

Klaus laughs and shakes his head. During this time, Jerome starts to parallel park Klaus SUV, and is doing it fantastically. Jerome successfully parallel parks the car, and shuts the engine off. Jerome starts to celebrate to himself, by screaming and hollering to himself.

"Oh my god! Yes! I have never been able to parallel park before. Yes! I did it!"

Klaus then shakes his head and laughs, and pats Jerome on the back. Klaus then speaks.

"You did do it buddy. So, I guess now this means, you're gonna let me take you to the DMV on Monday, and you're gonna do the driving test, and get your license right? Ha Ha."

In this instance, Jerome's mood instantly changed from being jubilant and celebratory, to a more serious and anxious tone, after hearing what Klaus just said. Jerome then starts to feel nervous, and realizes that Klaus is being serious. Jerome doesn't immediately respond to Klaus. Jerome then shuts the engine back on, and proceeds to back the car out from the parking spot, and onto the road. As Jerome is doing this, he then softly speaks back to Klaus.

"Oh, so that's what this was about? You want me to get my license. Okay, I'll go to the DMV with you on Monday, but I'm not sure. You'll let me take the test in your car right?"

Klaus, with his vision directed forward at the windshield, laughs, and responds to Jerome.

"Of course I will. You'll pass the test with flying colors. You'll do fine. It's okay."

Jerome as he's continuing to drive to the hiking location, smiles over what Klaus said. Jerome does feel more confident to pass the test, and get his license. Klaus was the confidence boost that Jerome needed, in other to become prouder of himself, in relations to his driving. For the remainder of the crap trip, Klaus and Jerome are silent, and do not speak. The only noise is coming from the car stereo, playing music. Jerome has caught the bus, and has caught an Uber to the hiking trail many times, so he knows exactly where it is, and will find the hiking location, without any issues. It doesn't take long at all for Jerome to arrive, at the hiking location. As both of the men reach the hiking spot, they both get out of the car. Klaus carries the backpack Jerome packed around this back. Jerome then starts to walk ahead of Klaus, and speaks to him.

"This trail can get rough, but you should be okay. Just follow me. If you need me to stop, or if you want to take a break, Klaus, let me know. It's okay. Don't be modest about it. Okay."

Klaus simply nods his head at what Jerome said, and the both of them carry on through the trail. The weather for today is extremely sunny, and the climate is perfect. This is a splendid day to go hiking, and Jerome was happy that he managed to pick a such a great day to do it. Jerome is having a great time hiking, and he as hiked through this trail several times, and is used to the terrain and the experience. Klaus however, is not skilled at hiking in the first place, and also is not used to this trail. Klaus as he suspected, is finding it hard to go through with the trail, and is becoming winded, and exhausted very quickly. Klaus notices that Jerome is trekking ahead of him, and doesn't want to become a burden or issue with Jerome, so he doesn't call out for him to slow down, so Klaus can be able to keep up. Klaus is getting slightly disorientated, and he takes his glasses off, to clean them with his shirt. Klaus carries on with the hike, in an attempt to catch up with Jerome soon. Even though both of the men have only been on the hike for about ten minutes, it seems like ten hours for Klaus. This hike is turning out exactly the way Klaus knew it would, with him being tuckered, and tired out. Jerome who has proceeded several feet away from Klaus on the trail, looks behind him, and notices Klaus, but sees he's quite a distance away from him. Jerome shakes his head, and laughs, and waits for Klaus to catch up to him. Klaus, eventually does manage to walk his way up to the hike with Jerome, but Jerome can see that he is very, clearly exhausted, and tired. Klaus manages to catch his breath, and stands next to Jerome for nearly a minute. During this time, Jerome shakes his head, and reaches into the backpack that Klaus is carrying, and takes out a bottle of water. Jerome then speaks to Klaus.

"Here, have some water. You look like you need it. You doing okay so far. This is only the beginning of the trail, so we still have a long way to go. We can take a break now though."

Klaus accepts the bottle of water, and begins to heavily drink it. As he is drinking the water, Klaus nods his head yes, to what Jerome said, approving to go on ahead with the hike. Once Klaus is finished drinking the water, Jerome has a drink of water as well. Directly after that, the men then continue on ahead with their hike. Even though Klaus told Jerome that he was fine to continue on with the hike, the actual fact was, Klaus was not feeling okay. Klaus was very tired, and exhausted. However, Klaus didn't want to disappoint Jerome. Klaus was starting to remember, how he and Stuart went hiking, and Klaus pretended to enjoy the event, in order to please Stuart. Klaus is now realizing, that he is rehashing all of that now, with Jerome. Klaus is not entire happy hiking, and is only doing this to please Jerome. It shows how much Klaus has improved his own personality, by putting others, before himself. Klaus, even though he's not liking the actual hike, does appreciate that today is a wonderful day, and that the sun is shining nicely, and the plants and the nature all around the hike is lovely. Klaus can feel the fresh air from the trees on his skin, and it's very lovely and pleasant. Klaus can also hear the birds chirping as well. So yes, Klaus is very tired from the hike, but he still is glad to be outside, and he is happy that he is experiencing nature. As Klaus is going through the hike, for the second time, he notices that he is trailing far behind Jerome. Klaus is becoming more disorientated and tired, as more minutes pass, with him walking down the hike. Jerome, who is a considerable distance ahead of Klaus, notices that Klaus is not in his vision anymore. Jerome becomes worried, and starts to back track down the trail, in order to find Klaus. Jerome walks back down the trail, and is shocked when he notices that Klaus is walking rather slowly up the trail. Jerome quickly runs back down the trail, to check on Klaus, and speaks to him.

"Hey, are you sure you're okay. Take it easy alright. I'll stay close to you from now on."

Klaus nod his head, in agreement with Jerome, letting him know that he's fine. Jerome is not all together sure that Klaus is being truthful with his actual feelings. Klaus is indeed hiding the fact, that he's feeling extremely exhausted from the hike, as he doesn't want to upset Jerome. Klaus is trying his best to deal with the rigors of hiking, which is not an activity that Klaus gets along with that well. Jerome has decided to hike alongside Klaus from this point forward, pacing himself slower, as Klaus is not as experienced in hiking, as Jerome is. As time passes on, with the men now being on the hike for over an hour, and reaching the halfway point of the hike, Klaus is feeling slightly better, and he feels his body has gotten used to the conditions. Although Klaus is still feeling tired and sluggish, it seems he might be developing a tolerance for hiking. Due to the fact Klaus seems to be doing much better with the hike, Jerome decides to pick his pace up, and proceeds farther above from Klaus. Immediately after Klaus notices that Jerome is no longer in his vision, Klaus once again starts to lose himself, and becomes disorientated. This time, was not like the other times though. It seems Klaus has over worked himself, and pushed himself far above his own limit. All of a sudden, Klaus, as he was walking down a sloped part of the trail, loses his balance, and faints. During this, Klaus glasses fall off his head, and Klaus slightly rolls down further in the trail, with a tree breaking his fall. Klaus, although he took a terrible fall, will be fine, and once Klaus realizes that he's not in extreme danger or hurt, tries to get himself up, but is too weak to do so. Klaus doesn't scream out for Jerome to help him. When Jerome looks back, and notices that Klaus isn't behind him anymore, Jerome suddenly has a strange feeling that he should go back and check on Klaus. Jerome walks back on the trail, and is mortified, when he sees Klaus fainted and slouched on the ground. Jerome screams out to Klaus.

"Oh my god! Klaus hold on. I'll be right there. I'm gonna help you right now."

Klaus can hear Jerome clearly, but is too weak to respond back. Jerome approaches Klaus, and then tries his best, to sit Klaus up from the ground. Once Jerome manages to sit Klaus up, Jerome opens up the backpack, and takes out a bottle of water. Klaus then starts to drink. As Klaus is drinking the water, Jerome starts to search the area around Klaus. Jerome then speaks.

"Your glasses fell, I'm gonna try to find them right now. Oh, found them. Here they are."

Jerome manages to find Klaus glasses, and hands them back to him. Klaus then puts his glasses back on. Jerome then smiles at Klaus. During this time, Jerome notices that Klaus has a large tear on his shirt, coming from his left arm. Jerome starts to feel worried over this, and lifts Klaus arm up, revealing a slight bloody scar. Klaus notices and is aware of Jerome doing this, but doesn't say anything or react. Jerome starts to panic, and screams out to Klaus.

"Oh no, Klaus. What happened? What did you do? Are you alright? Are you okay?"

Klaus, who is starting to get himself back together, responds back to Jerome.

"I'm fine, it's just a scratch. I'll be fine. Don't worry about me. I'll be just fine."

Jerome gives Klaus a concerned look, and shakes his head. Jerome then reaches into the backpack, and pulls out a first aid kid. Jerome then pours rubbing alcohol on Klaus injury, and also tries to clean the wound. Once Jerome is done tending to Klaus, he then speaks to him.

"Do you want to go home now? I really wanted us to do the whole trail, but you got hurt, so maybe we should go now. I'm sorry, I should have known hiking wasn't your thing."

Klaus then takes more sips of water, and signals for Jerome to sit next to him. Jerome does obey Klaus, and joins him, sitting with him on the trail. Klaus then speaks.

"No, we're gonna finish the trail, and then we're gonna go home. I can't keep quitting and giving up. I fucking hate hiking, but I'm not gonna quit. Come on let's get going."

Klaus then kisses Jerome on the forehead, and hugs him. Jerome laughs, and both Klaus and Jerome begin to hug. Shortly after that, both of the men carry on with the hike. Klaus for the rest of the hike, didn't have any further issues, and was being strong, and powering through everything. Jerome noticed that Klaus was doing much better, and was keeping up with him. Both of the men carry on with the hike, and after two hours, they managed to each the end of the hike. Klaus couldn't believe it. He actually managed to walk through the entire course of the hike. Although he did have a slight hiccup and slightly hurt himself, Klaus was still proud that be managed to complete the hike. Jerome was also proud of Klaus as well, that he managed to get everything done. As Klaus and Jerome are walking to Klaus SUV located in the parking lot of the hiking trail, Klaus then jokingly responds to Jerome.

"Hey, don't you ever, ever, in your life ask me to do this again. Okay? Ha Ha."

Klaus then reaches up from behind Jerome, and hugs him. Jerome then laughs. Klaus gets into the passenger seat of the vehicle, and Jerome gets in the driver seat, and starts to drive away from the hiking trail. While Jerome is driving, Klaus then starts to speak with him.

"Hey, why you don't stop and get us something to eat? I am in the mood for some Fried Chicken. I don't know why. Ha Ha. Let's get some KFC for the guys. They would like that."

Jerome shakes his head, and starts to laugh. Jerome then immediately drives to KFC, and orders chicken for them to enjoy. After getting the chicken, Jerome drives directly to Klaus house, and parks the car in the driveway. Klaus and Jerome get out of the car, and walk into the house. Upon arriving inside, Klaus notices that Paul and Bill are playing chess in the living room, with The Beatles music playing through a music app on the television. Jerome sets the chicken down in the kitchen table, and starts to grab plates from the cabinet. Klaus walks over to the living room, and Klaus and Paul make eye contact. Paul simply awkwardly nods his head at Klaus, and Klaus nods his head in return to Paul. Klaus then walks over behind Bill, and starts to hug him. Bill then starts to laugh, and pats Klaus on the back. Bill then speaks to Klaus.

"Hey Nephew, did you guys have a nice hike? Hey, what happened to your arm?"

Bill notices the tear on Klaus shirt, in which Bill lifts up Klaus shirt, revealing a slight scar that is on Klaus left arm. Bill then looks concerned. Klaus then quickly responds to Bill.

"Oh Uncle, I just tripped that's all. Luckily Jerome was there to help me. I'm okay."

Bill and Klaus smile at each other, and Bill shakes his head, and laughs to himself. Bill then returns to the chess game he is playing with Paul. Klaus then looks around for a bit, and notices that he doesn't see Dan and Ernest. Klaus takes out his pack of cigarettes, and with the intentions of chatting with Dan for a bit, starts to walk to Dan's bedroom door. Paul is able to hint at what Klaus is doing, and with his vision directed at the chess board, Paul responds.

"If you want to hang out with Dan, you're gonna have to wait until later. He and Ernest left, to go to some party, or function, or something. They didn't say when they will be back."

Klaus then looks down towards the ground, slightly disappointed that Dan is not home, but accepts this news. Klaus nods his head, and starts to quickly walk out to the balcony. Klaus then starts to smoke his cigarette, whilst, he is out on the balcony. At this time, Jerome has gotten all the plates and silverware out, and walks to the living room to speak with Bill and Paul.

"Gentlemen, I have some chicken in the kitchen for you guys. Come and grab a plate of food, I know you guys are hungry. Dan and Ernest can eat when they get back, I guess. Ha Ha."

Paul and Bill temporarily suspend their chess game, and proceed to get them a plate of food. Jerome, Paul, and Bill, all take their plates back to the living room, and Paul and Bill resume their chess game. Jerome turns on the television, in which the movie Space Jam, with Michael Jordan is playing. Klaus continues to remain outside in the balcony, calming himself down and smoking a cigarette. Klaus then wishes that he could hang out with Dan, but understands that if Dan wants to hang out with Ernest that's fine. Klaus is respectful about that, and doesn't mind. Klaus, Jerome, Paul, and Bill, remain comfortable at the house.

Meanwhile, Dan and Ernest, did decide to hang out together. They left when Klaus and Jerome were out on their hike. Dan did mention earlier to Jerome, that he was planning on hanging out with Ernest, which Jerome was aware of, but Klaus forgot about, and as he was on the balcony smoking his cigarette, it later dawned on him, that Dan did mention this earlier. Dan, using his own car, drove with Ernest, about a half an hour before Klaus and Jerome arrived back. Dan decided that he was going to take Ernest to this mixer, so Ernest can improve his social anxiety. Dan noticed that Ernest has an issue talking with other people, and meeting others. Dan is hoping that his event will boost Ernest confidence and that he will possibly make new friends at this event. The mixer is located in Santa Monica, which is located adjacent to Redondo Beach, where Klaus residence is. As Dan is driving on the highway to the event with Ernest, Dan can see that Ernest is rather tense and nervous. Dan then tries to make Ernest feel more comfortable.

"Relax, alright? Just stick with me, and I'll be your Wingman, okay? You need to get out more, and talk with people. Circulate. Stop being a wallflower man. We're gonna have fun!"

Ernest smiles at what Dan said, but is still unsure of himself, and feeling anxious. Ernest keeps his vision directed down on the ground, and doesn't initially respond to Dan. As Dan continues to drive to the event, Ernest starts to look out the window, slowly feeling more comfortable, and collected traveling with Dan. Ernest remains silent, and keeps to himself for a bit. Eventually, after being calm enough to talk, Ernest then decides to ask Dan a question.

"Okay, but if I don't feel comfortable, I have the right to leave. Is that understood?"

Dan with his vision still directed forward and driving, laughs, and responds to Ernest.

"Hmm, Okay. If you're not feeling the people here, then I'll respect that. But you're gonna have fun though. You have nothing to worry about. Just stick with me, you'll do great."

Dan then turns to look at Ernest, and smiles at him. Ernest looks at Dan as well, and also gives him a smile. Dan carries on his way to the event, which is being held at a bar and lounge type club, in Santa Monica. As Dan gets off the highway, and onto the surface streets, he is noticing that being that it's the weekend and Saturday, traffic is quite hectic. Dan forgot about how rough traffic is, and realized that he and Ernest should have let the house sooner, to avoid all the traffic. Dan is becoming slightly agitated trying to drive through traffic, with his main goal being to reach the event and venue. Ernest is noticing how tense Dan is while driving through traffic, but decides not to speak with him. Being that this is Santa Monica, there are a lot of ritzy shops and venues that are located here. There are also many tourists that have come to visit, and to be at the beach. There are several upscale shops, and it's a very upper-class atmosphere. Ernest continues to look at window, noticing how preppy the pedestrians look, and is starting to second guess, as to whether or not, he should attend this event with Dan. Ernest doesn't feel like he can compete with these people, and they seem to be in an altogether different league. Dan continues to drive through the streets on his way to the venue. As Dan is continuing to drive through Santa Monica on this lovely evening, Ernest starts to feel nervous, about the impression he is going to have, with the others that will be present there. Dan has been to many mixers and social events, and he also doesn't care what people think of him. Ernest doesn't feel the same, and still continues to feel like he doesn't belong, and that this isn't meant for him. Ernest is more concerned about what people think of him, and he doesn't like to be in environments, to where he feels that he is not in the same league as other people. Ernest feels as though, he cannot compete. Ernest doesn't feel that it's worth it, to put himself in that situation, and to humiliate and embarrass himself like that. However, Ernest doesn't want to let Dan down, and he is going to let Dan be his Wingman, and help him through the event, and be his plus one, and someone he can turn to for help. So only because Dan is there with him, Ernest is going to try to have fun at this event, although, he doesn't want to be there at all.

Before long, Dan manages to find the venue. Dan notices that there are several people standing outside the door, and this sight starts to worry Ernest. Dan then speaks to him.

"Oh, don't worry. We're gonna get in. We're on the list, I called earlier. It's okay."

Ernest, who was feeling anxious at the huge queue and line of people outside the venue, felt better, once Dan let him know, that they don't have to worry about not getting in. Even though Dan was able to find the venue rather easily, the more difficult part, was finding a place to park. Dan was trying to find a parking spot, that was located near the venue, but was having much difficulty finding one. It was the weekend, and Santa Monica had a lot of visitors this evening, so it was making parking more difficult. Being fed up, that he wasn't able to find any parking spots, in the adjacent and surrounding curbs of the venue, Dan had no choice, but to pay for parking, and park his car in a private lot. This was something that Dan was trying to avoid, but at this point, he doesn't have much of a choice. Dan manages to find a private parking lot, situated reasonably close by the venue, and pays the ten dollar parking fee to park his car. Dan is still angered that he had to pay for parking, but tries his best to get over it. Dan is easily able to find a parking spot, as there are plenty of spots available in the private lot. Dan then parks his car. After parking his car, Dan immediately opens up his glove compartment, and takes out a jar of cologne fragrance. Dan sprays himself with it, and also sprays Ernest with it. Ernest seems reluctant of this, and Dan starts to laugh. Dan then speaks to Ernest.

"This stuff is like magic. You spray this on, and people come crawling to you. Ha Ha."

Dan puts the jar of cologne back into the glove compartment and shuts it. Dan and Ernest then immediately get out of the car, and direct themselves a few blocks to the venue. The parking structure wasn't that far from where the venue was located, but it was still quite a distance, being that it was eight blocks. As Dan and Ernest are walking through the streets, Dan is feeling cool, calm, and collected, while Ernest is looking completely out of his element. Dan notices how tense and nervous Ernest looks, and decides to adjust his collar, as they are both walking down the sidewalk. This causes Ernest to chuckle to himself for a bit, and Dan also smiles. Both of the men continue to walk down to the venue, basically window shopping in the meantime, and looking at all the store fronts. There is the scent of many restaurants, and also the scene of the ocean as well, in this area. There are many people that are dressed to the nines, and have their best outfits on. Ernest still believes that he shouldn't be here, and that he doesn't belong, and has no business being in this area. Dan is fitting in slightly better though. The gentlemen continue to walk towards the venue, with it now only being a few blocks away. They are so close, that they can now see the queue of people lining up. So, they know that's the location of the venue.

Eventually, Dan and Ernest make it to the venue, and they join the back on the queue and line. While they are waiting, Ernest starts to frantically look around, very anxious. Dan pats Ernest on the back of the neck, and starts to massage his back. Dan then whispers to Ernest.

"Hey, what I tell you. Don't worry. I'm your Wingman. Everything is going to be just fine. Just stick with me, and everything will be okay. Stop worrying man. Ha Ha."

Ernest then gives a confident smile, and laughs at Dan. For the first time tonight, Ernest is starting to let himself loose, and put all his faith and trust in Dan. Ernest is realizing that Dan is right, and there isn't anything to worry about. As both the men continue to stand in the queue, they are getting closer to where the bouncer is located, and the entrance of the club. Ernest, feeling more collected isn't worrying anymore, and Dan is also standing directly next to Ernest in line, keeping him company, and making him comfortable. The men reach closer, and closer to the end of the line. As both Dan and Ernest get closer to the door of the club, the more excited and happier they feel. They are both anticipating getting inside, and can't wait for the wonderful time they are going to have. Ernest especially, now being slightly more optimistic than he was previously, trying to expand his social network, and improve his social anxiety. The men eventually teach where the bouncer is situated, and the bouncer, who is a very overweight, tall, bald, Caucasian man, with a beard. has a large clipboard in his hand. The bouncer then gives both Dan and Ernest, a stern and strict look, and then begins to speak with them.

"Alright, if your name is on the list, you can go in, if not, y'all have to leave. Got it?"

Dan then nods his head, and smiles at the bouncer. Dan gives his name to the bouncer.

"Okay, yeah my name is Dan Mendoza. I should be on the list. I called earlier. Yeah."

The bouncer raises his eyebrows, and skims through several pages of this list. Ernest at this time, starts to have a bad feeling in his body, and is worrying again. Dan is confident and sure that he is on the list, so he doesn't have any reason to worry or be afraid. The bouncer however skims through all of the pages on his clipboard, and quickly responds back to Dan.

"You said Mendoza right. Yeah, there ain't nobody on this list with that name sir."

Dan then looks around, with a shocked and confused look on his face. Dan then reluctantly starts to speak with the bouncer again, this time in a softer manner and tone.

"Can you check once more please sir? My name is Dan Mendoza. I know I'm on there."

The bouncer gives Dan a very angry and agitated look. He then skims through all of the names on the clipboard once again, and after he reaches the final page, he then responds to Dan.

"Yeah, that name is not on this list at all sir. You're not on my list."

Dan laughs and shakes his head. Dan then at his wits end, takes his wallet, and flashes a hundred-dollar bill in front of the bouncer. Dan then starts to joke with the bouncer.

"Okay, I see. Alright. So, will this make my name appear on this list or not? Ha Ha."

The bouncer is not amused, and gives Dan a cold strict stare. The bouncer then responds.

"No, but it will make my fist go across your scrawny face. You're trying to get me fucking fired? Now you guys really have to leave. You're not getting in my club. Fuck off."

The bouncer then immediately grabs Dan and Ernest by the collar, and pushes them out of line. Dan simply shakes his head at the bouncer, and Ernest holds Dan back. Dan and Ernest walk away from the line, and they both feel defeated for a moment. Dan then silently speaks.

"I don't know what happened, maybe the club is at max capacity, and they removed my name from the list. It's okay, we're gonna get into this fucking club. Follow me, and be quiet."

Ernest nods his head, and directly follows Dan. Dan starts to walk on the other side of the venue, noticing that one of the back loading doors, that the bartenders used to carry liquor, wine and draft beer through is open. Dan puts his finger to his mouth, signaling for Ernest to remain quiet, and he does. The both of them silently, and inconspicuously, try to sneak into the club. Unluckily during this time, the bouncer that they just encountered, is taking a cigarette break, in the same area. The bouncer smokes his cigarette, and in the right moment and instance, notices Dan and Ernest sneak in. The bouncer drops his cigarette, and starts to chase the both of them.

"Hey! You little shits! Come here! I'm gonna beat the fuck out of both of you. Hey! You get your asses back over here! Don't go through that door! Get over here! Come here!"

Dan and Ernest quickly notice the bouncer, and race through the door. Trying their best for him not to thwart them. Once inside, Dan and Ernest shut the door behind them, fully closing the door, and locking it. Dan and Ernest hi five each other, and happy they managed to sneak in. Seconds later, the bouncer manages to reach the door, but notices that it's locked. The bouncer bangs on the door, but due to how loud the venue is, his knocks are not heard. The bouncer punches the door frustration, and starts to walk back to the other side of the club. Once inside of the club, Dan and Ernest realize how crowded and packed it is. There is loud electronic music playing, which makes it hard to talk, and for someone to hear you. Dan immediately began to feel as, he felt the venue was more low key and intimate and personal. It's not, and it's a rather loud function and venue, with loud music and lots of noise. Dan and Ernest still remain close to each other, as Dan directs himself to the bar. Dan orders himself a Jack and Coke, while Ernest decides to order himself a Gin and Tonic. Dan and Ernest sit at the bar, looking at everyone around. Dan then starts to understand how Ernest was feeling earlier, and Dan also feels out of place. The Bartender then finishes making their drinks. Dan takes a sip of his drink and talks.

"Man, you were right. This place is full of fucking yuppies. I thought this place was cooler, like Jazz club kinda deal you know. Nope. All these people are conformed and ritzy."

Ernest takes a sip of his drink, and nods his head at Dan. As Dan and Ernest remain at the bar, enjoying their cocktails, they now realize that coming to this place was not a good idea. Both Dan and Ernest feel like they don't belong here, and it's way too much of a commercial, and hip place for them. After they both finish their drinks, Dan and Ernest get up from the bar. They continue to walk around the club, with the loud electronic music booming. Dan then speaks.

"We're just gonna have fun at this point. We're not gonna meet anybody here man. But let's just chill, and have fun. I'll still be your Wingman if you want me to though."

Even though the loud music in the club was playing, Ernest could hear Dan fine. Ernest smiles right back at Dan, and the both of them continue walking through the club. During this time, Dan walks up to an old classmate of his, that happened to coincidentally be at the venue. Dan shouts to the man, and the man waves to Dan. Dan walks up and speaks to him, and they hug, and both begin to talk. Ernest watches as Dan converses with this man, and because Ernest doesn't know him, and due to how antisocial Ernest is, he doesn't intrude at all on Dan's conversation, and continues to walk through the venue. Ernest notices how people in the club, are giving him strange and weird looks, and this in turn causes Ernest to feel uncomfortable, and Ernest starts to feel anxious again. Dan who has been talking to his old classmates for several minutes, then realizes that Ernest is not by his side anymore. Dan says goodbye to his old schoolmate, and starts to look for Ernest in the crowded club. Dan finally locates Ernest, and sneaks up from behind him, and grabs him by the collar. Dan then speaks with him.

"Hey man, what I tell you, stick with me. I'm your Wingman. You don't know anybody here, and if you stick with me, you'll stick out less. Alright. Don't worry. I got your back. Ha."

Dan then lightly slaps Ernest on the cheek, and smiles at him. Ernest, who can still hear Dan speaking despite the loud music in the venue, gives off a reluctantly smile in return, and walks off with him. Dan and Ernest remain in the club for a half an hour more. During this time, Dan walks up to a group of guys, that he feels comfortable talk to. Dan introduces himself to these men, however, although the group is content with Dan, they start making fun of Ernest. The group isn't making it a secret how much they find Ernest weird, and are insulting him, right in front of his face. Dan then decides to walk away from the group, once they started to insult and disrespect Ernest. Dan didn't appreciate the group doing that, and quickly grabs Ernest, and walks away from them. Ernest starts to feel slightly upset, but Dan then takes Ernest off to a side area of the club, and starts to rub and pat him on the pack. Dan then responds to Ernest.

"Don't pay them any mind. They are just a bunch of drunk idiots. They didn't mean that. You're still having fun right. Remember, I'm your Wingman okay. Just stick with me."

Ernest, although finding it hard to hear Dan with the loud music, understands him completely. Ernest yet again changes his mood to a calmer one, and gives Dan a smile. Dan and Ernest continue to walk through the club, although their night is going the way they hoped at all. Dan's main objective and goal, was to get Ernest more socialized, and to meet people more, and to make connections. The venue not only ended up being that Dan wasn't expecting, but Dan was fearful, that Ernest was not enjoying himself at all. Dan notices that the people who are in attendance at this venue, are very closed minded, and not very welcoming to new people. Dan was happy that he was able to see his old schoolfriend, but other than that, the night hasn't gone that great, for either of them. As Dan and Ernest continue to walk through the crowd, Dan notices that there isn't anybody else in the crowd, that he feels comfortable walking up to, and speaking with. Everyone seems to be with their own cliques and groups, and Dan doesn't wish to disturb them. As Dan and Ernest walk through more of the crowd, all of a sudden, Dan notices the bouncer they dealt with earlier, running straight in the direction, himself and Ernest are standing at. Dan also notices that there is now a second bouncer of identical stature. With the second bouncer being a bearded African-American man. Upon noticing both bouncers running to them, Dan quickly grabs Ernest by the collar, and Dan starts to run away from them. As Dan and Ernest are running, the bouncer they interacted with earlier, starts to yell.

"Hey you! Get the fuck over here! I've been looking for you! Get over here now!"

The rest of the patrons at the venue, watch in amusement as Dan and Ernest, are trying to run away, and escape from the bouncers. Dan then tries to think ahead, and realizes that if they try to leave out of the front, there would be more bouncers and security there. So Dan knew the only way to leave, was through that door. Dan then grabs Ernest, and they both make a run for the back door, they came in from. Dan and Ernest are lucky enough to make it to the door they sneaked out of, and quickly open it, and run outside. Dan and Ernest continue to sprint outside the back alley of the club. At this same time, both bouncers open the door, and chase down the alley, towards Dan and Ernest. The African-American bouncer however stops the Caucasian bouncer that Dan and Ernest dealt with earlier, and starts to speak with him.

"It's not worth it man. We know their faces; they aren't ever allowed back here."

The Caucasian bouncer then tries to catch his break, and screams to Dan Ernest.

"Damn it! You fucking punks! Ugh! Don't ever bring your asses back here again!

Dan and Ernest continue to sprint down the alley, away from the club. Both of the bouncers shake their heads the African-American bouncer, pats the Caucasian bouncer on the back. They both then walk back inside. Dan and Ernest continue to run, until they finally reach a park, that's located near the club. They both then catch their breaths, and Dan speaks to Ernest.

"I think we lost them. I don't see them anymore. Ha Ha. Hey man. I'm so sorry."

Ernest then looks around, and when he notices the bouncers stopped following them, he starts to feel happier and calmer. Ernest then softly speaks back to Dan.

"Sorry about what? Man, this is the most amazing and fun night I ever had. I had so much fun. Thank you Wingman, for being there for me. You definitely made the night better. Ha Ha."

Dan still trying to catch his breath, gives Ernest a puzzled look, and laughs at him. Dan was not expecting for Ernest to react that way, and thought that Ernest wasn't having the best night. Upon realizing that Ernest was having fun, Dan no longer felt concerned over this. Dan wanted Ernest to be happy, and if Ernest is happy, Dan is satisfied. Dan then wraps his arm around Ernest's neck, and begins to silently speak to him.

"Well, I'm glad I was able to help. I'll be your Wingman anytime you need me to be. Yeah tonight didn't go exactly as planned, but that's okay. We still had a grand fun time, didn't we?"

Ernest looks down at the ground, and silently nods his head towards Dan. Dan and Ernest continue to walk through the park, noticing how beautiful the scenery is. The park is located right in front of Santa Monica beach, and you can see a direct view of the ocean, through the park. Ernest decides to take a seat at a bench, and starts to look out towards the distance. Dan is confused at first, but decides to sit next to Ernest on the bench. Ernest continues to look out towards the ocean, and starts to shake his head. Ernest then whispers out to Dan.

"This is an amazing night, and nobody has ever done this to me before. You've always been a great friend Dan, and thank you for giving me a chance, and treating me."

Dan shakes his head and laughs, and looks down on the ground. Dan responds to Ernest.

"Oh, it's no problem. Anytime you want to hang out. I'm here. Whatever you want to do, wherever you want to go, I'm here. I'll always be your Wingman. Ha Ha."

Ernest then turns his direction towards Dan, and whispers back to him.

"Well, I hope you don't mind if I do this then. Wingman."

Ernest then reaches up to Dan's face, and kisses him directly on the lips. Dan accepts Ernest kiss, and they embrace for several seconds.

Ernest then rests his head on Dan's shoulder. Dan simply shakes his head and laughs, and runs his hands through Ernest hair. Both of the men sit for several minutes at the park. Ernest then speaks back to Dan.

"Okay, I had my fun. I want to go home now Wingman."

Dan once again shakes his head and laughs, and rubs Ernest on his back. Dan and Ernest then start to walk themselves out of the park, and back to the house.

CHAPTER 11:

KEEPING IT ALL TOGETHER

After having a great night together, Dan and Ernest start to go back to the house. The night did not go at all, the way Dan hoped, and planned that it would. However, both of the men still had a great time together, and it was a great experience all around. Dan's main objective and plan, was for Ernest to become more socialized with others, and to get out of his comfort zone, and not to be such a wallflower like he usually is. Dan wanted to take Ernest to the club, so he can be more open and extroverted with himself. It turns out that despite Dan already making a reservation to enter the club prior, for some reason, his name was not on the list. This originally flustered Dan, and he didn't understand why this was the case. With his mission towards Ernest, still on his mind, he decided that they both would sneak into the club. After successfully doing that, they found out the club wasn't as fun as they were hoping. The people that were inside, were mostly stuck up, and not as welcoming to others. Even though Dan did manage to find a former classmate of his, most of the people at this venue, were not friendly at all. Dan even noticed that some of the people were making fun of Ernest, and that upset him very much. So Dan decided not to speak with those people, who were disrespecting Ernest. At that point, Dan and Ernest were simply at the club, to enjoy themselves, and they didn't care that they weren't socializing or circulating with other people, as they weren't connecting or meshing well with them anyways. Things were going great, until the bartender spotted them, as the two guys that sneaked into the club. At that point, Dan and Ernest knew that it was time to go. They were finally caught for sneaking in, and the party was over, and the fun was over. Dan and Ernest managed to successfully run away and escape. They then managed to arrive at a park. Whilst they were at the park, Dan and Ernest have some alone time, and kiss.

It was then that Dan knew that Ernest was fine, and Dan also knew, that Ernest didn't need to conform himself to people, and change the person that he is. Dan realized that he was the person that Ernest felt most comfortable with, and the person that Ernest looked up to, as his closet friend, and Dan was now a companion, boyfriend, and partner to Ernest. Dan was willing to accept this, and as long as Ernest was happy and satisfied, Dan was happy. It was essentially the same view point, from Ernest. Ernest didn't want to try to fake himself with other people, and Dan is the person that he feels happy and safe with. When Ernest kissed Dan at the park, he felt extremely safe and confident with him, and Ernest was happy having Dan as a boyfriend, and a close friend, and he knew that Dan was trustworthy for him. Dan and Ernest enjoyed the time that they spent together, and are going home happy. The night was unpredictable and crazy, but both of the men still had a wonderful time. As Dan and Ernest arrive back at the house, they both notice that Jerome, Paul, and Bill, are all in the living room. Jerome is watching the Rick Moranis movie, "Little Shop of Horrors.", to which Jerome is singing along to the musical numbers. Paul and Bill continue to play chess in the living room too, with both of them being level pegged, and even, as far as skill. Paul wins one match, and Bill wins the next one they play, and vice versa, and so on, and so forth. Klaus is on the balcony, watching ESPN on his phone. Dan and Ernest also notice, that there is a bucket of KFC chicken, that is located in the kitchen. Dan and Ernest grab some chicken, and Ernest takes a seat on the living room sofa, next to Jerome. Dan decides to walk out on the balcony, and join Klaus. Once Dan is on the balcony, Klaus and

Dan fist bump, and Dan then takes a seat on the balcony, eating his chicken. Klaus laughs at him, and with Klaus vision directed at this phone, he speaks to Dan.

"So, did you guys have a great time. You guys were gone for quite a bit. You have fun?"

Dan continues to eat his food, and laughs silently towards Klaus. Dan then responds.

"Yeah, we had fun. We went to this club; my name wasn't on the list. Me and Ernest, sneaked in anyways. The people in there were assholes and jerks. The bouncer later figured out we sneaked in, and he kicked us out. Ernest and I then chilled at the park by the beach."

Klaus nods his head, while still looking at a sports highlight show on his phone. Klaus then decides to ask Dan another question, that he is curious about.

"Why did you take Ernest to a club though? That doesn't seem to be his style at all."

Dan still eating his food, doesn't initially respond back to Klaus, but after some hesitation and silence, Dan does decide to reluctantly speak to Klaus, while still chewing his food.

"Well, I was trying to get him to be less timid and shy. You know how Ernest is. That was what I was trying to do. But the club was awful. People sucked there, so it didn't work out."

Klaus then nods his head, and this time Klaus looks up from his phone, and has his vision towards the ocean, that is facing his balcony. Dan then continues to speak with Klaus.

"But that's okay, as I want Ernest to be himself. We went to this park after, and we kissed for a bit, and I don't know. I guess maybe Ernest is fine the way he is, and that's okay."

Klaus then starts to laugh, and shake his head. Klaus then starts to take his pack of cigarettes from his pocket. Klaus then lights one, and begins to smoke. Klaus then speaks to Dan.

"Aww, how sweet. That was really cute to hear. But you already knew Ernest liked you."

Klaus then takes puffs of his cigarette, and starts to laugh. Dan then finishes the last bits of food he has left on his plate, and while still chewing his food, responds to Klaus.

"Yeah, but not like that. We were just friends, and now I think I was blind and ignorant before, and I didn't see the signs or hints, that Ernest really likes me. I'm cool with it though."

Klaus shakes his head and laughs, and takes more puffs of his cigarette. Klaus, with his vision steadily facing the ocean, then starts to softly respond back to Dan.

"Alright, well, you take care of him though. You make sure, that you look out for him."

Klaus again laughs to himself, and Dan laughs as well. By now, Dan has finished all the food on this plate. At this exact time, Klaus yet again reaches into his pocket, and takes out his pack of cigarettes. This time, handing one of them to Dan. Dan accepts the cigarette, and begins to smoke it. While taking puffs of the cigarette, Dan then silently speaks back to Klaus.

"You know I will, I will always have Ernest back. I mean, all six of us are a team now, and we are going to look out for each other always, but I will definitely be Ernest's Wingman."

Klaus then takes another puff from his cigarette, and starts to laugh at Dan.

"His Wingman? Ha Ha. Okay. I thought a Wingman, was the guy who is running everything, and can make everyone in the club, speak to you. You're not a good Wingman. Ha."

Klaus then starts to laugh to himself, however Dan, does not find this funny. Dan playfully socks Klaus in the arm, and Dan shakes his head, and takes more puff of his cigarettes. Dan knew that Klaus was being silly, but he still didn't find what he said funny at all. Both of the men continue to smoke their cigarettes, out on the balcony. Shortly after this, Paul and Bill start to get tired, and finally abort their chess playing. Both Paul and Bill, won an equal amount of chess matches, so it wasn't like one person was more skilled. It was nice for both Paul and Bill, that they both didn't feel intimidated with each other, by playing chess. Both men, were equally matched at chess. They were playing for fun anyways, so that didn't really matter. Paul and Bill then say goodnight to Ernest and Jerome, and they then direct themselves into the bedroom. Shortly after this, Ernest decides to prepare himself for bed, and hugs Jerome, and says goodnight to him. Ernest then walks inside of the bedroom. At this time, Jerome, who was watching episodes of cartoons on the television, notices that Klaus and Dan, are still out on the balcony. Ordinarily, Jerome would ignore the both of them, and think nothing of this. Jerome is well aware that Klaus and Dan both have a strong friendship, and they usually hang out on the balcony, socializing with each other. However this time, Jerome was far too curious, and wanted to know what they were both talking about. Jerome turns the television off, and walks out onto the balcony, to join Klaus and Dan. Upon realizing that Jerome has joined them, Klaus responds.

"Hey, get back inside the house. Dan and I are having a private conversation. Go!"

Jerome then shakes his head, and grabs Klaus pack of cigarettes that were positioned on a table, in the balcony. Klaus doesn't react and is silent, and Dan has his view out, towards the ocean. Jerome then takes a cigarette out of the carton, and begins to smoke it. Jerome then takes a seat on the balcony, sitting in the middle, between Klaus and Dan. Jerome then speaks.

"No, I want to hang out here with you guys. It's not fair how I can never hang out here."

Klaus then takes a puff of his cigarette, and softly responds to Jerome.

"It's not that you can't hang out here. Dan and I are talking. That's all. Behave yourself."

Dan with his vision still directed forward, finds the quarrel that Klaus and Jerome having hilarious, and starts to laugh to himself. Dan takes another puff from his cigarette, and remains quiet. Jerome then lays his head down on Klaus shoulder. Klaus then starts to speak to Jerome.

"You know we are still going to the DMV Monday morning, so you can take your driving test, right? Don't forget. We're gonna do some more practicing tomorrow, so yeah."

Jerome then starts to form an agitated face, and Jerome takes a puff from his cigarette. Jerome then starts to speak in a bothered tone towards Klaus.

"Ugh, not that again. Yeah I know I did well driving today, but watch when I take the test, I'm gonna fail. I already failed it twice before, so what makes you think I'll pass this time?"

Klaus with his vision directed forward, shakes his head, and laughs to himself. Klaus then takes another puff of his cigarette, and starts to whisper back to Jerome.

"You're going to pass this time, because, well, you're my number one fan. That's why."

Klaus then runs his hand through Jerome's hair, and then kisses him on the forehead. Klaus then starts to laugh, which causes Jerome to laugh as well. Dan finding Klaus and Jerome's interactions amusing, begins to laugh with Klaus and Jerome as well. At this time, Dan then gets up from the balcony, and says goodnight to the other men. Dan then walks into his bedroom, and starts to go to bed. Klaus and Jerome remain out on the balcony for several more minutes, but they both eventually walk out, and direct themselves to bed. The following day, with it now being Sunday, most of the men are already up for the day. Dan is in the kitchen, and he is doing what he seems to do often, and it's make breakfast for all the guys. Ernest is also in the kitchen keeping him company, and reading a book. Bill is also in the living room, reading his newspaper, but a golf match is also playing in the background, which Bill is also listening to, while reading his paper at the same time. As Dan continues to get breakfast prepared, Paul joins the other men, and takes a seat in the living room, joining Bill. This seems to be a common and typical morning routine, with all of the men, yet it seems the men might not even notice this. Not long following this, Jerome joins Dan and Ernest in the kitchen. Jerome then has a conversation with both Dan and Ernest. Klaus, of course, is the final man to join everyone, and he immediately directs himself to the kitchen, pouring himself his usual cup of coffee. Klaus and Dan fist bump, and start to speak to each other. Sunday is usually a slow and quiet day for all the men. Nothing eventful, or that noteworthy usually happens. However, today, Klaus does intend to take Jerome out for last minute driving practice. Klaus is still adamant on Jerome getting his driver's license, and passing the driving test. After seeing Jerome drive himself in action, he believes that he is ready to take on the test, and that Jerome shouldn't have anything to worry about at all. Now that Klaus has his agenda set for today, he feels calmer. Dan then finishes preparing breakfast, and the men all then begin to eat. Dan has cooked his usual breakfast, of pancakes, sausage, eggs, and bacon. All of the guys enjoy Dan's cooking, and enjoy the breakfast that Dan has prepared. After the men finish eating, Dan and Ernest walk into the living room, to watch episodes of "Star Trek, The Next Generation.", while Paul and Bill are in the living room as well, doing what they did the day prior, and playing their chess game. Jerome is also doing what he commonly does, and starts to wash the dishes. As Jerome is washing the dishes, Klaus who is still at the kitchen area, is watching sports highlights on his phone. Klaus, with his vision still directed at his phone, starts to softly speak to Jerome.

"So, are you ready to do more driving practice today, so you can do the test tomorrow?"

Jerome continues to wash the dishes, and although he doesn't verbally respond back to Klaus, Jerome reluctantly nods his head. Klaus then at this time, looks up from his phone, and watches Jerome do the dishes. Klaus simply shakes his head, and returns to watching the sports highlights. Jerome eventually finishes washing the dishes, and Jerome then takes a seat at the kitchen counter, with Klaus. Jerome stares at Klaus for several seconds, before speaking to him.

"I know yesterday it seemed I was good at driving, and usually I am. However, I know I'm gonna flunk the driving test, because I always choke, and make a careless mistake. Ugh."

Klaus then takes a sip of his coffee, and pats Jerome on the back. Klaus then speaks.

"That's because you didn't believe in yourself, and you were probably too nervous. Most likely from lack of practice and experience. I know you can do it. Believe in yourself, that's all."

Jerome looks down on the ground, and nod his head, and smiles. Jerome knew that Klaus was right, and that if Jerome applied himself, and was calmer and more collected when taking the driving test, there would be no reason that he wouldn't be able to pass. Although Jerome at times, wasn't that confident in his driving abilities, Klaus knew that Jerome was ready, and that he has all the potential, to pass the driving test, and get his license. Soon after this, Klaus and Jerome then leave out of the house, to continue on Jerome's driving practice. Jerome gets into the driver's seat of Klaus SUV, and Klaus sits in the passenger seat of the car. Klaus then continues to allow Jerome to practice driving, as they take strolls down different streets and blocks. Klaus once again tests Jerome's ability to parallel park, and he is able to do it, without any hassles or issues. Jerome is doing a marvelous, and splendid job driving. Jerome also seems more comfortable and happier with himself, and isn't tense or scared to drive. Klaus is taking note of this, and realizing this. Klaus doesn't see any reason at all, why Jerome would fail, as he is sure that Jerome's driving abilities are very satisfactory. Jerome continues to drive, and decides to make an unexpected stop at a cemetery. Klaus who is slightly confused and puzzled, doesn't say anything, but realizes that Jerome has stopped here, for a good reason. Jerome continues to drive through the cemetery, and pulls the car over, at a specific section. Jerome then stops, and parks the car, and turns his direction towards Klaus, and speaks.

"I hope you don't mind if I stopped here. I wanted to show you something. Follow me."

Klaus nods his head, and Klaus and Jerome get out of the car. Klaus follows Jerome, as he walks through the cemetery. A couple minutes later, Jerome then stops walking, at a particular area in the cemetery. Jerome then sits down on the grass, in front of a gravestone. Klaus then catches up with Jerome, and sits down with him at the gravestone as well. Jerome then starts to sweep grass, weeds, and leaves off the gravestone with his hand. Klaus who hasn't read the name on the gravestone yet, starts to clean his glasses with his shirt, and puts his glasses back on. Klaus is then able to read the name on the gravestone. At this same time, Jerome, who is still sweeping off the gravestone, starts to softly speak.

"This is my Mom's grave. This is where she was buried. She passed away when I was young, and I wish I got to interact with her more. I loved her, and miss her very much."

Klaus then starts to feel sad for Jerome, and starts to rub Jerome's back, to comfort and console him. Jerome then starts to cry, as he's staring at the gravestone. Jerome the responds.

"But I know she's proud of me. She's happy for me. I know that she's watching over me. She is proud of everything that I have accomplished and done. Rest in peace, Mom. I love you."

Klaus then gives Jerome time to reflect, and is fully aware of the situation. Klaus then wipes Jerome's tears with his shirt, and wraps his arm around Jerome, continuing to comfort him. Klaus and Jerome remain at the cemetery for quite some time. Klaus is allowing Jerome to take all the time he needs, as this is a very delicate and sensitive event and situation. Jerome remains in front of his mother's grave for several more minutes. Eventually, Jerome and Klaus start to leave out of the cemetery. Jerome is happy that he was able to see his mother's grave, and he is also happy that Klaus was understanding as well, and was there to comfort him. As Klaus and Jerome are walking back to the car, Jerome still feels slightly upset, and starts to remember the times that he had with his mother, and wishes that she was still around. Jerome also understands that his mother would be very proud of him, and happy for him. This gives Jerome the strength to carry on. Klaus and Jerome make it back to the vehicle, and they both get inside. Jerome then starts the engine, and proceeds to drive away from the cemetery. Now that Jerome is back on the road, the remainder of the car ride is rather silent. Klaus is being respectful, and not bothering Jerome, after stopping at the cemetery. However, minutes later, Klaus does decide to break his silence, and speak to Jerome.

"Hey, I'm really sorry. I know what it's like, and I can relate. Both my Mom and Dad are gone. They are buried in Thousand Oaks though. I have to take you to their grave one day."

Jerome nods his head in response to Klaus, and continues to drive. At this time, Klaus feel that Jerome has practiced enough of his driving, and informs Jerome, that he can go back to the house. Jerome does head back to the house, and feels confident in his driving, and he feels ready to take the test tomorrow. Klaus and Jerome arrive back at the house, and Jerome directs himself to the living room sofa. Ernest is also on the sofa reading a book. Paul and Bill steadily continue on with their chess game. Klaus then notices that Dan is out on the balcony, and ordinarily joins himself on the balcony with dan. Klaus and Dan fist bump each other, and start to talk and converse with each other. The rest of the day, being that it was Sunday, was an easy and slow day. The guys all kept to themselves doing their own thing, and remained in the house. When dinner time arrived, Dan and Klaus walk out of the balcony, and Dan heads over to the kitchen. Dan then starts to prepare dinner, which is Baked Ziti pasta, with cheese. As Dan is making dinner, Klaus and Dan continue to speak to each other, talking about sports and politics. The other men remain in the living room. Once Dan is finished with dinner, all of the men start to grab their plates. Paul and Bill take their plates back to the living room, and continue their chess game, as they are eating. Ernest and Jerome grab a plate, and report back to the living room as well. Klaus and Dan however, decide to eat at the kitchen counter, carrying on with their trivial discussion and conversation. For dessert, Ernest decides to bake another cake, and the guys all enjoy the cake that Ernest has baked. Once dessert is finished, Jerome directs himself to the kitchen to wash dishes. Likewise, with earlier in the morning for breakfast, Klaus remains at the kitchen counter, gazing at Jerome, as he is doing the dishes. Klaus is unsure, whether or not to speak to Jerome, or remain silent. Klaus then decides to speak to Jerome.

"So, are you ready for your driving test tomorrow? Don't be nervous. You'll do fine."

Jerome continues to do the dishes, and starts to smile to himself. Jerome then responds.

"I'm ready yes. I practiced enough. I really do hope that I pass this time.

Jerome remains doing the dishes, as Klaus continues to stare at him. Klaus shakes his head, and starts to laugh. Once Jerome has finished doing the dishes, he joins the rest of the men in the living room. Klaus then joins Dan, who is out on the balcony, and Klaus and Dan, then both start to smoke their cigarettes out on the balcony. As the night goes on, the men in the living room, start to excuse themselves. Ernest says goodnight, and walks into the bedroom. Jerome, feeling tired, then says goodnight, and walks into the bedroom. Paul and Bill lose track of time, and didn't notice how late it was, due to how embraced they were in their chess game. Paul and Bill then direct themselves to bed. Eventually, both Klaus and Dan fist bump each other, and say goodnight, and direct themselves to bed as well. The following morning, being now Monday morning, arrives. Klaus wakes up, and notices the time on his phone states that it is 9:20 a.m. Frantically, Klaus springs out of bed, and starts to jolt and shake Jerome who's in bed.

"Hey get up! We're late! Your appointment is at 10 remember. Hey! Get up!"

Jerome then quickly wakes himself up, and jumps out of bed. Jerome then speaks.

"Oh god, how did I oversleep. See I told you I have bad luck on my driving test day."

Jerome starts to gather his outfit for the day, while Klaus shakes his head. Eventually, Klaus and Jerome manage to get ready, and start to leave out of the house, towards the DMV office. Klaus notices that remarkably, none of the other guys have woken up yet. Klaus then gets into the driver's seat, deciding to drive; allowing Jerome to calm himself down before his test. On their way to the DMV, Jerome starts to experience bouts of nervousness. Jerome is second guessing himself, and doubting himself, and the confidence he had earlier, is gone. Jerome was sure that on the day of his test, he was going to do fine, and all of his nervousness, and jitters would go away. However, Jerome is starting to lose his confidence, and is scared that he is once again going to fail the test. Not only letting himself down, but letting Klaus down as well. As Klaus continues to drive to the DMV, he notices that Jerome is feeling more tense and scared. When Klaus reaches a stoplight, he then rubs his hands over Jerome's back, and responds.

"Hey, buddy. You're going to do well. Don't worry. You're gonna pass this test."

Jerome, while looking down towards the ground, starts to smile to himself. Jerome remains nervous about taking the test, but the reassurance and positive energy from Klaus, makes him feel slightly better, about the situation. Klaus shortly after his, arrives at the DMV office. Klaus is slightly concerned when he notices, that despite it being 9:50 a.m., there is still a long line of people at this DMV office, and the line stretches out of the building, and wraps around, the adjacent sidewalk of the DMV office. Klaus was assuming that this was the non-appointment line. Klaus and Jerome then step out of Klaus SUV. They both start to proceed to a DMV attendant, who is a young Caucasian woman with blonde hair, who standing in front of the building. Klaus also assumes this is the right person to speak to, and this is the check in clerk. Klaus then pulls out Jerome's paperwork, and speaks.

"Yes, hello ma'am. My friend is here to take his driving test. He's gonna be taking the test in my car. Here is his learning permit, and all his information. He has an appointment."

The DMV clerk looks directly at Klaus, and quickly responds back to him.

"Okay sir, even with an appointment, you need to stand in that line over there. The DMV office opens at 10 a.m. we will check everyone. Those with appointments will be serviced first."

Klaus then starts to form an angered look on his face, and responds to the clerk.

"Yes ma'am, but as I said, I had an appointment, and I don't see why I have to..."

The clerk then cuts Klaus off, and starts to swiftly respond back to him.

"I understand that sir, but you should have left earlier. Those are rules. I don't make them. Now sir, go stand in that line, and you will be serviced as soon as possible. Thank you."

Klaus then shakes his head, and Jerome who was listening to the clerk, also understands the procedure, and follows Klaus to the back of the line. Once they are in line, Klaus and Jerome talk to each other, and are patiently waiting in the line. Now that Klaus and Jerome have been waiting in line for an hour, they both start to become bothered. Although the line is moving, Klaus and Jerome, are still quite a way from the end of the line. They both continue to patiently wait, and another hour passes, and it now being noon, Klaus and Jerome, finally reach the front of the line. This time, it is a different clerk they are approached with. It is a middle aged, African-American female. Klaus starts to gather Jerome's paperwork, and speaks with her.

"Yes, hello ma'am. My friend is taking his driver's test. He's taking it in my car. Here is my information, and here is his learner's permit, and all his documents. I have an appointment."

The clerk then enters all the information into her computer. She then quickly responds.

"Yes sir, I managed to bring you up. Here is your number, they will call you shortly."

The clerk also hands Klaus additional information, along with his number. The clerk then directs her vision to Jerome, and smiles at him. Jerome smiles back at her. The clerk then speaks.

"Also, good luck on your driver's test. You both can wait over there. Thank you."

Both Klaus and Jerome thank the clerk, and sit at the area, she instructed them to. Now that Klaus and Jerome are both seated, they remain quiet. Klaus assumed that they were going to be called quickly, however, it was another hour wait at this point. Eventually, it was Klaus and Jerome's turn to proceed forward. They reach other clerk, a middle aged, Hispanic woman, in which she hands Jerome a paper, and instructs him to drive to the driver's test area at the back of the DMV building. At this point, Klaus hands Jerome his car keys, and he gives Jerome and hug. They both tightly hug for several seconds, and Klaus kisses Jerome on the forehead, and speaks.

"Hey, don't be nervous. This is it. Just relax, and don't worry. Stay calm. You can do it."

Jerome then silently nods his head, and Klaus and Jerome walk out of the DMV office. Klaus takes a seat on a bench, on a designated area outside the DMV office, along with other people, waiting for the person who is taking the test in their car, to complete their test. Jerome looks back at Klaus, and Klaus gives Jerome a thumbs up. Jerome reluctantly smiles back at him, and walks towards Klaus car. Jerome reaches the car, and quickly turns the ignition on. Jerome them drives to the driving test area, and waits, along with the other test takers. Jerome, continues to wait for several minutes, trying to calm himself down, and not being nervous. Jerome then notices that several different examiners, all of different profiles and appearances, are being assigned to the test takers. Jerome's examiner then arrives on the scene. Jerome notices that he is an older elderly Caucasian man with glasses, looking very similar to Bernie Sanders. Jerome starts to wonder whether the examiner would be nice and friendly to him. The driving examiner then takes a look at his clipboard, and starts to introduce himself.

"Hello, my name is Otis. I'll be your driving examiner for this afternoon. I won't tell you to do anything illegal or unsafe. We're gonna start, with common knowledge of the vehicle."

Jerome nods his head, and the driving examiner asks Jerome to point to several different buttons in the car Including asking him where the hazard lights, where to turn on the head lights, and high beams, asking him to press on the break, and also to turn on the turning signals. After successfully doing that, the driving examiner writes in his clipboard, he then tells Jerome, what the hand signals are. Jerome correctly is able to show them to the examiner. At this point, the examiner gets into the passenger seat, and Jerome continues on with his driving test. Jerome takes several deep breaths, as he drives out of the DMV office, and proceeds down the road. Jerome is noticing that the examiner is writing down several things in his clipboard, which cause him to feel nervous. Jerome is scared that he is doing something wrong, as why else would the examiner be writing things off on his clipboard. As the test carries on, the examiner asks Jerome to drive in a residential area. Once in this area, the examiner then speaks to Jerome.

"Okay, I would like for you to parallel park in that space right there please."

Jerome takes another deep breath, and notices that this part in particular, was one in prior test attempts, to where he failed, and was not able to succeed. However, Jerome is confident that he has practiced enough, and that he will be able to parallel park this time. Jerome, knowing that he can't let himself down, and he can't let Klaus down, begins to parallel park. With it now becoming second nature and common for Jerome, he very quickly maneuvers the car into a parallel park position. Upon completing this, Jerome starts to smile and silently celebrate to himself. The examiner then continues to write things on his clipboard down, and Jerome drives out of the parking spot. The examiner gives more instructions to Jerome, and the rest of the test seemed easy, and simple for him. Before Jerome even knew it, the test was over, and the instructor directed Jerome back to the DMV. The test lasted for about over 20 minutes, like the same length, as Jerome's previous driving tests. Once Jerome parks the car in the holding area at the end of the test, Jerome starts to feel more nervous. This is the part he dreads, to where he is told that he has failed. Even though Jerome knew he did a great job, and there wasn't any chance that he failed, Jerome was still worried, that it could be a possibility that he did not pass. Jerome and the examiner remain in the car, as the examiner looks over his clipboard, making more checks and notes. The examiner then sets his clipboard down, and speaks to Jerome.

"Alright, okay, so I did notice several errors. I'm gonna chalk it down to you being nervous, and I understand. You drive pretty well. With that being said, congratulations, you scored enough to pass. Take this paper inside, and hand it to the clerks. Take care."

Jerome, who was trying his best to contain his emotions, couldn't help himself, and starts to dance and scream, feeling very delighted and overjoyed. The driving examiner starts to laugh, and hands Jerome a piece of paper. Jerome shakes the driving examiners hand, and the driving examiner gets out of the vehicle. Jerome stays inside the car, still in disbelief, and shock. Jerome cannot believe that he finally did something, which he felt he could never accomplish. Jerome managed to get his driver's license. Jerome stays in the car for another minute, but then composes himself to walk towards Klaus, to tell him the news. Jerome decided that he was going to play a trick on Klaus, and make it assumed he failed yet again, when in actuality, he passed. Jerome starts to walk to the area where Klaus is, forming a depressed and sad face. Klaus, who was reading articles on his phone, looks up, and notices Jerome, with an upset face, walking towards him. Klaus then starts to feel concerned, and speechless and motionless. Assuming that Jerome has failed his test. Jerome walks close to Klaus, still looking defeated and upset. Seconds later, Jerome still with an upset look on his face, starts to softly speak to Klaus.

"Damn, ugh. I cannot believe this. I passed!"

Klaus then starts to form an agitated face, and pulls Jerome's ear. Jerome then starts to laugh, and Klaus starts to change his mood as well, understanding that Jerome was being silly and funny, with this fake out prank and trick. Jerome then pulls out the paper the examiner gave him, which states that he passed his test. Klaus then hugs Jerome, and kisses him on the forehead. Klaus is extremely proud of Jerome, and glad he finally managed to pass his driving test. Jerome is of course happy as well. Happy he managed to finally achieve this, and also, he didn't let Klaus down, after all the help he has given him. Klaus and Jerome walk back into the DMV office yet again, and this time, they didn't have to wait at all. There was a special area of the DMV the driving test applicants report to after passing, and there is no wait at this section at all. Jerome hands the paper, incidentally to the same African-American female clerk they saw earlier. The clerk then starts to type on her computer, and responds to Jerome.

"I knew you would pass. I had faith in you. Here is your temporary driver's license. You will get your physical license by mail, in two weeks. If not, come back to us. Congratulations."

Jerome grabs a document, containing his temporary driver's license from the clerk. The clerk thanks Jerome, and Klaus and Jerome thank her back. The both of them then leave out of the DMV. Klaus decides not to let Jerome drive, as he is too excited from passing, and wants him to calm down. Klaus is extremely proud of Jerome, and wants to treat him, for passing his driving test. As Klaus gets into the driver's seat, and Jerome gets into the passenger seat, both men start to drive down the road. When Klaus reaches a stoplight, he starts to speak to Jerome.

"I am so proud of you. You're a driver now. You never thought you be one, would you? Ha Ha. Let me give you a treat, since you were such a good boy. Where do you want to eat?"

Jerome then starts to laugh to himself, and shakes his head. Jerome while looking straight forward towards the windshield, responds back to the question Klaus asked.

"Well, I want to go to The Olive Garden. I like their food. Yeah. That's what I want."

Klaus turns his head towards Jerome, and starts to laugh. Klaus was going to allow Jerome, to eat anywhere that he wanted, as a treat for passing his driver's test. Jerome wishes to go to Olive Garden, and Klaus has no issue or problem with that at all. Both of the men continue to the Olive Garden restaurant, which was a short distance from the DMV office. When they arrive at the restaurant, they get out of the vehicle, and start to walk inside. The waitress seats Klaus and Jerome at a booth in the far side of the restaurant. Klaus and Jerome sit on opposite sides of the booth, staring at each other. It is lunch time, and there are several customers inside of the restaurant, but the restaurant isn't that crowded. Klaus and Jerome start to stare at the menu, and the waitress arrives, to take their bar drink orders. Jerome orders a strawberry margarita, and Klaus orders a Budweiser beer. After ordering their drinks, both the men continue to read over the menu. At this time, Klaus starts to speak to Jerome.

"I can't remember the last time I been to The Olive Garden. It's been a while; I know that's for sure. I don't know what I want to order. You can get whatever you want Jerome."

Jerome continues to look at the menu, and as he's doing that, Jerome responds to Klaus.

"I can't either. That's why I wanted to come here. Ha Ha. I already know what I want."

Klaus stares at Jerome, and shakes his head, and laughs. At this time, the waitress returns to the table, with their bar drinks. Klaus and Jerome have also decided what they wanted to eat. Klaus decides to order the Stuffed Ravioli. Jerome decided to order the Fettuccine Chicken Alfredo. The waitress then leaves the table, and Klaus and Jerome continue to speak, and reflect with one another. Jerome is happy that Klaus treated him out to lunch. Klaus is as well pleased to have lunch with Jerome. Before long, the waitress walks back to the table, but not giving the men their main course. Instead, she hands them breadsticks, and salad. Klaus and Jerome then eat their appetizers, and continue to converse with each other. Not much long after this their main food arrives at the table, and they begin eating. The men are enjoying their food, and this occasion and outing, is nice, for both Klaus and Jerome. Klaus asks Jerome if he wants anything for dessert, and he says that he does. Klaus and Jerome then decide to order some strawberry cheesecake for dessert, and they are enjoying that as well. Once the men are finished with dessert, the waitress comes back to the table with the check. Klaus pays for the meal, and leaves a tip for the waitress. Klaus and Jerome then get up from the table, and walk out of the restaurant. Klaus again feels that Jerome is too excited to drive, so Klaus drives the both of them back to the house. Once back at the residence, Jerome is excited to tell the guys that he got his driver's license. Dan and Ernest are sitting in the living room; with Ernest reading a book, and Dan watching The People's Court, on the television. Even though Dan and Ernest heard Klaus and Jerome enter, they do not initially respond, or acknowledge them. Jerome then walks over the living room, and in a very excited tone, tells the news to the men.

"Hey guys, I finally did it! I passed the driving test, and I have my license."

Jerome then hands the paper, containing his temporary license to Ernest. Ernest starts to read and look over the paper, and smiles to himself. Ernest then responds to Jerome.

"Wow man, congratulations. You have your license like the rest of us. Ha Ha. Congrats."

Ernest then hands Jerome back his temporary license. Jerome then gives the paper to Dan, and Dan starts to take a look at it as well. Dan while reading the paper, then speaks.

"This is really cool. I'm proud of you. Congrats buddy, I knew you could do it. Ha Ha."

Dan then hands the paper back to Jerome, and Jerome continues to read the paper, although feeling shocked, he is very pleased and happy. Klaus then notices that he doesn't see Paul and Bill, and walks over to the living room area, and speaks to Dan.

"Hey, do you know where Uncle, and Paul went? Strange they aren't here."

Dan with his direction still watching the television, quickly responds back to Klaus.

"Oh shit, that's right. Bill had a doctor's appointment, and Paul took him there. Don't know when they left, they were already gone when Ernest and I woke. So yeah."

Klaus looks down on the ground, and shakes his head and laughs. Klaus then playfully smacks dan on the back, and takes a seat on the recliner in the living room. Klaus is not sure why his Uncle Bill, and Paul, didn't tell him, that Bill had a doctor's appointment today. Klaus figured that they felt he didn't need to know this information, or that it wasn't relevant. Klaus thought that all the guys would be in open communication with each other, and would let the whole group know, what their agenda and schedule was for the day. Klaus feels that he should have been aware of Bill's doctor's appointment, but for whatever reason, he was not informed over this. Klaus is also concerned that Paul and Bill are still gone, and haven't come back home yet. Giving the fact Klaus and Jerome were at the DMV for most of the day. Klaus decides to let this go, and figures that Bill would be alright with Paul. Klaus, and the rest of the guys, remain in the living room. Meanwhile, congruently during this time, Paul and Bill, are indeed out of the house together. Bill did in fact have a doctor's appointment today, but the appointment wasn't until 1 p.m. Paul decided to drive Bill to his appointment in his minivan. The distance to the veteran's hospital, where Bill's appointment was, happened to be quite a distance from Klaus residence. So therefore, Paul had to leave earlier, and also deal with Los Angeles traffic. Paul manages to arrive at the hospital for Bill's appointment, just in time. Hospitals make Bill extremely nervous, and he doesn't like to go to them. Bill doesn't like to deal with doctors, and talk to them about his health. Bill can be stubborn in this regard sometimes. Paul understood this, and managed to go with Bill, to make him feel better. Paul and Bill walk through the very large veterans' hospital, that has many departments and buildings. Paul has never been inside of this hospital before, but bill has several times, and instructs Paul as to where to go, which Paul accepts. Paul and Bill direct themselves to the information kiosk. Paul then approaches the information kiosk, and notices a middle-aged Brunette Caucasian nurse, working there. The woman is typing on her computer, and doesn't notice them. Paul then speaks.

"Yes, hello ma'am. I have an appoint for Bill Kleinberg at 1 p.m."

The nurse returns to typing on her computer, and then responds back to Paul.

"Oh yes. Please report to building D, and go to floor two. Just wait in the lobby, there won't be any receptionists present. Doctor Simpson will then see him soon. Thank you."

Paul thanks the nurse, and Paul and Bill then direct themselves to building D, with Bill guiding Paul as to where to go to reach there. Paul and Bill manage to arrive at building D, and take the elevator up to the second floor. They both then decide to wait in the lobby. While they are both seated, Paul then grabs a magazine, that is located on a side table, and starts to read it. Bill then frantically looks around the lobby, and there are a few other patients in this room, waiting. Paul continues to skim through the magazine, but takes a look at Bill, and notices how nervous he seems. Paul then sets the magazine down, and proceeds to speak with Bill.

"What wrong? Are you okay? Do you want me to get you some water or something?"

Bill then angrily continues to look around the lobby, feeling uncomfortable. Bill simply shakes his head towards Paul, and carries on glances around the room. Bill then responds to Paul.

"No, I'm not okay. I don't like hospitals. They put me on edge, and the doctors, every single damn time tell me some bad news, so I already know they are gonna say something bad."

Paul then starts to rub and massage Bill's back. Paul softly responds to Bill.

"Well, the doctors are only concerned about your health, that's all. It's okay."

Paul continues to rub Bill's back, and is trying to comfort him. Paul and Bill wait for several more minutes in the lobby, and Paul returns to reading his magazine. The longer that the both of them wait in the lobby, the more nervous Bill becomes. After a half an hour of them both waiting in the lobby, a young Hispanic nurse, calls Bill's name. Bill and Paul both start to follow the nurse, to the exam room. While in the exam room, the nurse begins to speak to Bill.

"Alright sir, I'm just going to get your height, weight, and blood pressure.

Bill, still feeling very upset that at his doctor's appointment, allow the nurse to take his height and weight, and check his blood pressure as well. The nurse then speaks to Bill.

"Okay sir, Dr. Simpson will be right with you in a few minutes. Thank you very much."

The nurse then walks out of the exam room. Bill and Paul remain in the exam room, quiet, and not speaking to each other. Bill remains seated on the exam table, while Paul is sitting on a chair in the corner of the room, reading a magazine. A few minutes later, Dr. Robert Simpson, who is a short, slightly chubby man, with balding blonde hair, walks into the room. Dr. Simpson then sets his clipboard on the counter, and starts to wash his hands in a sink, located in a corner of the exam room. While Dr. Simpson is doing this, he starts to speak to Bill.

"Hey Bill. How are you. It's been a while. I see you have a friend with you."

Bill then looks down on the ground, and shakes his head. Bill responds to Dr. Simpson.

"Yes, this is my very good companion Paul. He's here for moral support, and yeah."

Dr. Simpson then finishes washing his hands, and walks over to Bill. Dr. Simpson then uses his stethoscope, and puts it on Bill's chest. Dr. Simpson then asks Bill to open his mouth, and Bill obeys. Dr. Simpson then gives bill more commands, and orders, to which Bill also follows. Once Dr. Simpson is finished with all this, he then walks to the other side of the exam room, and starts to write on his clipboard. Paul respectfully stays silent in the corner, watching everything. As Dr. Simpson continues to write in his clipboard, he softly speaks to Bill.

"Bill, you have been taking all of your medications right? Be honest with me now."

Bill, while still looking down the ground, and feeling unhappy, responds to the doctor.

"Yes, I'm taking all of my meds doctor, like you ordered and asked me to."

Dr. Simpson finishes writing down his notes, and pulls out a document, that was located inside Bill's medical record folder. Dr. Simpson glances at the paper, and then speaks to Bill.

"Alright Bill. The blood test you took a couple weeks ago, we got your results. Your cholesterol is very high, and we're concerned with. Your blood pressure, it could be better. EKG results aren't that good, and we're concerned with that. Bill, this is not looking good."

Bill shakes his head, and looks down at the ground. Bill then starts to feel grumpy and bothered, and was expecting this news from the doctor. Bill then swiftly speaks to the doctor.

"So Doc, what are you trying to tell me. Get to the point, what's wrong with me?"

Dr. Simpson writes in his clipboard for a bit, and once he's finished writing, he stares directly at Bill for a few seconds, and softly responds to him.

"Bill, the point is. You could have a stroke, or heart attack very soon."

Paul who was listening to the doctor, starts to run his hands over his face. Paul is feeling very concerned over Bill's health. Paul then decides to ask the doctor a question.

"So, Dr. Simpson. I'm actually close friends with Bill's Nephew. Had I known it was this serious, I would have invited him here. I thought this was a routine visit. I had no idea."

Paul then stands up, and walks over to Bill, rubbing his back, and comforting him. Bill continues to have this vision down towards the ground, being silent, and feeling upset. Dr. Simpson then returns to writing more notes, and responds to Paul.

"Well, this was intended to be a routine visit, but I have to be honest with you. Bill is at very high risk for a stroke, and a heart attack. I'm gonna change his medication, and were gonna do different treatment plans. Maybe arrange an exercise program for him. That's the plan."

Paul nods his head at what Dr. Simpson said, and Dr. Simpson hands Paul a piece of paper. Paul takes a look at the paper, and notices that it's a prescription. Dr. Simpson speaks.

"Okay, for now, make you get this prescription filled. Continue his usual meds, but I'm gonna add these medications for him. This will help him greatly. We want him to be healthy."

Dr. Simpson then pats Paul on the back, and also pats Bill on the back. Paul thanks Dr. Simpson, and Dr. Simpson thanks Paul as well. Bill does not respond or speak to Dr. Simpson at all. Once Dr. Simpson has left the room, Bill quickly speaks to Paul.

"See, what I tell you. They always have something horrible to say. Take me home, now!"

Paul nods his head, and Paul and Bill then walk out of the exam room, and proceed to go the pharmacy at the hospital, to get Bill's medication prescription. Paul and Bill wait for a half an hour at the pharmacy lobby, not speaking with each other. When Bill's medication is ready, Paul picks it up. Paul and Bill then directly drive back home. Throughout the entire car trip home, Bill is silent, and doesn't speak to Paul. However, when Paul manages to reach the driveway of the house, Bill does decide to finally speak. Bill starts to squeeze Paul's arm, and Bill and Paul look directly at each other. Bill begins to silently speak to him.

"Don't tell any of the guys what the doctor said. Please. Promise me you won't?"

Paul simply nods his head towards Bill. Paul and Bill then get out of Paul's minivan, and walk inside of the house. Once inside of the house, Jerome notices them, and walks up to them. Jerome then pulls out his temporary driver's license, and shows it to bill. Jerome then speaks.

"Uncle Bill, look, I passed my driver's test today. Klaus helped me. I can't believe it."

Bill reads the paper Jerome handed to him, and starts to smile. Bill then speaks.

"Oh wow Nephew, you sure did. I'm really proud of you. Great job."

Bill then rubs his hand through Jerome's hair, and kisses him on the forehead. Paul remains silent, and remembers the promise he made to Bill in the car, not to talk about the news, the doctor shared with them. Jerome then walks back over to the living room area, and Paul and Bill, also walk to the living room area as well. Bill takes a seat on the recliner next to Klaus, and Paul sits down on the sofa. Klaus stares at Bill for several seconds, and then speaks to him.

"Hey Uncle, what did the doctor say? Why didn't you tell me you had an appointment?"

Bill then sits back in the recliner, and shakes his head. Bill then speaks to Jerome.

"Hey Nephew, can you go get Uncle a beer from the refrigerator please?"

Jerome quickly gets up, and walks to the kitchen, to grab Bill a beer. Jerome returns to the living room, and hands Bill the beer. Bill opens the beer, and starts taking several sips. Klaus has an irritated and frustrated expression at Bill. Bill then speaks.

"Thank you Nephew. Oh god. The doctors didn't say anything. Just the usual stuff. They don't know anything. They put me on this new medication, but that was it. They said nothing."

Klaus looks down on the ground, and shakes his head. Dan and Ernest are silently listening to this entire exchange. At this point, Paul starts to feel guilty, and can no longer keep this information concealed. Paul knows that he promised Bill that he wouldn't speak of this, but Paul cannot bring himself to keep this information hidden from Klaus, and the rest of the guys any longer. Paul then stands up from the sofa, and starts to speak to the guys.

"I'm sorry Bill. I know you told me not to tell. I just can't keep this a secret. Klaus, the doctor gave us really bad news. His blood pressure is high, and his cholesterol is high. His EKG results were not good. Doctor said he's at very high risk for a stroke, or a heart attack."

Klaus then immediately gets up from his seat, and is extremely angry. Bill then looks at Paul with a disappointed look in his face. Bill takes a sip of his beer, and speaks to Paul.

"Hey scout, you promised you wouldn't tell. I trusted you. Damn. Why did you do that?"

Paul then covers his hands with his face, and sits down on the sofa, and starts to cry. Ernest then walks over to Paul, and comforts him. Jerome at this time, starts to feel guilty, that Klaus was at his driving test, instead of being at the hospital. Jerome then speaks.

"Oh no, I feel so bad. Had I known Bill had a doctor's appointment, I would have told Klaus to postpone my driving test today. Klaus should have been with his Uncle today. Oh God."

Bill then rubs his hands through Jerome's hair, and softly responds back to him.

"Aww, that's okay Nephew. Don't feel bad. It's my fault, I didn't tell you boys, other than scout, that I had a doctor's appointment, so y'all didn't worry I'm proud of you Nephew."

Jerome then starts to smile at Bill. At this time, Klaus starts to feel worried over Bill's health. Even though Bill is not upset that Klaus chose to spend the day with Jerome, Klaus still wishes that he went to the hospital, instead of Paul. During this time, Bill takes more sips of his beer, as Paul continues to have his head down, crying on the sofa. Bill then speaks to Paul.

"I thought I could trust you scout. I ain't mad at you, but why did you do that? Man."

Klaus then looks around the room, with an angered look on his face. Klaus walks over to Bill, and starts to rub him on his back. Klaus then silently speaks to Bill.

"Uncle, anything related to your health, we all have to know. I care about you, and we're gonna get you healthy, okay? All of us, alright? Uncle, don't keep secrets like this from us."

Bill nods his head, and then slaps Klaus on the behind. Klaus shakes his head, and walks away from Bill. Bill laughs and responds back to Klaus.

"You're right. I'm so sorry Nephew. I won't keep secrets like this from you guys again."

Bill then gets up from the recliner, and starts to walk behind the sofa towards Paul. Paul still has his hands covering his face and crying, being comforted by Ernest. Bill then reaches from behind Paul, and Bill begins to massage Paul's neck. Bill then whispers to Paul.

"I'm sorry scout. I didn't mean to get mad at you. I wish you didn't tell the boys that, but I guess I'm glad you did. Please forgive me. I love you scout. I lost my temper, and that was wrong of me to blame you It's my fault. It's not your fault. Cheer up, I love you scout."

Bill then kisses Paul on the cheek, but Paul continues to keep his head down on the ground, crying. Bill then shakes his head, and returns to the recliner. Jerome sits and watches everything respectfully, staying quiet. Ernest continues to comfort Paul. Klaus then starts to feel anxious, and pulls out his pack of cigarettes. Klaus then walks up to Dan, who was silently watching everything. Klaus taps Dan on the shoulder, signaling for him to join him on the balcony. Dan agrees, and Klaus and Dan walk out on the balcony. Klaus pulls out a cigarette, and hands Dan a cigarette as well. Dan lights his cigarette, and has his vision head. Klaus starts to light his cigarette, but instead starts to cry. Dan notices Klaus is upset, and starts to hug him from behind. While Dan is comforting Klaus, he softly speaks to him.

"It's gonna be okay man. Just calm down. Everything is gonna be fine. It's okay."

Klaus then fist bumps Dan, and Dan returns to his seat. Klaus then whispers to Dan.

"Yeah, I know it will. But Damn. You're right man. Everything is gonna be okay."

Dan and Klaus then stare at each other, and smile. Klaus then lights his cigarette and takes a puff from it, with his vision facing forward. Klaus shakes his head, and laughs.

CHAPTER 12:

THE AMUSEMENT PARK

Klaus continues to remain on the balcony with Dan, in an attempt to calm himself down. Klaus is still slightly agitated, that Bill kept the information related to his health, a secret from the other men. Especially giving how severe the information the doctor explained to him. Bill, due to how weak his blood pressure, and his heart is, has a very high risk of having a stroke, or a heart attack. Klaus had no idea that his Uncle was in this bad of health. Klaus doesn't also understand why Bill didn't ask him to visit the hospital with him. He instead asked Paul to go. Klaus is slightly feeling less worried, after Bill seemed to have his reasons for not asking Klaus to come to the hospital with him. It was mainly because Bill didn't wasn't Klaus to feel upset or worried, as Bill was well aware, that the news the doctors were going to was going to be bad, and it was going to be devastating news. So Bill knew that Paul was comfortable enough, not to share the news with the other guys, so the whole group, and collective, weren't worried. Klaus instead spend the time, helping Jerome get his license, which Klaus was proud of. The other guys, including Bill, were very proud that Jerome managed to pass his driving test, which in the past, he has failed at succeeding from passing. So Klaus was happy this event happened, and he was able to help Jerome. Upon returning home from the hospital, Bill told Paul, not to tell the guys, what happened at the hospital, and what the doctor said. Paul originally agreed on this plan, however at the last minute felt that Klaus deserved to be told this information, and that I was too serious to keep to himself. Once Paul revealed Bill's secret, relating to his health, Bill was angry at Paul. Klaus was angry as well. This in turn caused Paul to get guilty for bringing it up, and Paul became upset. However, both Klaus and Bill seemed to forgive Paul, although Paul, still seems to be feeling guilty about it.

Klaus continues to stay at the balcony, smoking his cigarette, and chatting with Dan. Unsure of what he is going to next. Klaus then speaks softly to Dan.

"I don't know what I'm gonna do about Uncle. I'm just worried about him that's all. I wish I knew more about his health history, and I want him to be healthier, that's all."

Dan then takes another puff of his cigarette, and nods his head. Dan then speaks.

"You have to get him more active, and make sure he's taking his meds. All of us are going to help him, he's going to be fine. Don't worry about anything. It's gonna be okay."

Klaus while looking down towards the ground, nods his head in response to Dan. Klaus and Dan are silent for several minutes, and Klaus starts to think to himself. Klaus understands that he needs to get his Uncle started on an exercise, and fitness program. Bill hasn't been the most advantageous and interested in this before, but Klaus is going to have to try to make Bill become more active, so that his health is better. Bill will have a stroke or heart attack, if he does not improve his health. Klaus starts to brainstorm ideas, on how to get his Uncle to become more fit. Klaus then thinks the best way to get his Uncle to be more active, is to just start slow, and to take him out on a walk, first thing tomorrow morning. The walk won't be that grueling, just a very simple walk through the park. Klaus knows that this idea is grand, and it's a great way to get his Uncle to be more fit. Klaus isn't even going to let Bill now prior, that he is going to take him out on this outing. This will be spur of the moment, and very unpredictable. Bill is probably not going to like the unplanned morning walk, but Klaus doesn't care, and he knows that his Uncle's health is more important. Klaus has already made his mind up, and he is going out on this walk with Bill, whether Bill likes it, or not. Klaus explains his idea to Dan, to seems to be on board, and in agreement. Klaus and Dan stay out on the balcony, for a couple more hours, while the rest of the men, are in the living room together. Dan eventually leaves the balcony, and starts to prepare dinner for all of the men. Dan, feeling concerned after hearing about Bill's health, decides for tonight, to make a healthier meal. Dan is deciding to cook a grilled chicken salad with mushrooms, and also a tomato bisque on the side. Dan gets started immediately on dinner, and Klaus remains outside on the balcony, thinking to himself.

Dan manages to finish dinner, and the guys are all excited to taste it. Dan decides to make Bill a plate first, and Dan walks over to the living room, and hands it to Bill, speaking to him.

"Okay Uncle, I made this dinner special for tonight. It's something healthier. Let me know if you like it. Although it's healthy, it should still taste great. Enjoy Uncle."

Bill accepts the plate of food from Dan, and then replies to him.

"Oh, thank you Nephew. This does look very delicious. I appreciate it. Thanks."

Bill then starts to eat the food on his plate, and seems very pleased with it. Dan is happy that Bill likes the meal, and Dan walks back into the kitchen. The other men then start to take a plate, and are all enjoying dinner that Dan has prepared and made. While the guys are eating dinner, they are watching Family Guy on the television in the living room. This seems to be, yet again a nice bonding time for all the guys to enjoy, and they are all comfortable with each other, having dinner. Even though Dan made a health alternative to the dinner, the men don't seem to notice, or care. They simply enjoy the food. Once all the men are finished with dinner, Ernest decides to do something that he often does, and that's bake a cake for dessert. Ernest decides to bake a butter chocolate cake with frosting, which the guys also enjoy greatly. After having dessert, Klaus and Dan report back out to the balcony, and mingle with each other. The other guys stay in the living room, watching television. As always, as the night continues on, the guys start to excuse themselves off to bed. Starting with Ernest, followed by Bill, followed by Paul, and then lastly, followed by Jerome. Once Klaus and Dan notice that all of the men have drifted off to bed, Klaus and Dan fist bump each other, and say goodnight. Dan walks into the bedroom, and Klaus walks into the bedroom as well. All the of the guy then go to sleep.

The next morning, Klaus was determined to do what he planned, and that's take Bill out on a walk. Klaus, although usually he is the last guy to wake up, this morning, he made sure that he was the first, by setting his alarm clock at an earlier time. Klaus is wide awake at 8 a.m., and gets out of bed, not disturbing Jerome, who is still sound and fast asleep. Klaus then starts to get dressed, and prepare himself for the day. After he is doing that, Klaus walks into the kitchen, and has is usual cup of coffee. Klaus knew that Bill was going to be the first one to wake up, and that was when he and Bill were going to go out for their walk. This was not up for discussion, and even if Bill didn't want to do it, Klaus was going to make Bill go on the walk anyways. Fifteen minutes later, Klaus prediction was right, and Bill wakes up, and walks out of the bedroom. Bill then starts to walk to the kitchen with Klaus, and once Bill notices Klaus, he speaks to him.

"Hey Nephew. This is the earliest I have seen you up. What's going on here? Ha Ha."

Klaus takes a sip of his coffee, and shakes his head and laughs. Klaus has his vision pointed at the floor, and is reluctant to speak to Bill. Klaus then responds to Bill.

"Well Uncle, I am concerned about your health, so, how about you and me go for a walk in the park this morning. You have to get more active. I'm gonna talk to Paul, and the guys too."

Bill pours himself a cup of coffee, and then has an angered look on his face. Bill takes a sip of the coffee, still with an angry expression, and then responds to Klaus.

"Oh no Nephew, that's alright. I'll be okay. Those doctors don't know anything. You don't have to do that. I appreciate it but I'll be alright. Don't worry about me Nephew."

Klaus takes another sip of his coffee, and shakes his head. Klaus then starts to grab Bill.

"No Uncle, we're going right now. Come on. I knew you were going to be difficult, but it's okay. I was already prepared. Come on Uncle. We're wasting time. Let's Go."

Bill takes another sip of his coffee, while Klaus is grabbing him. Bill quickly sets the coffee cup down on the counter, and laughs. Bill then responds back to Klaus.

"Alright Nephew, I guess I can't say no now. Let's go out on this walk. Ha Ha."

Klaus starts to laugh and shake his head, and Klaus and Bill walk out of the house, and into Klaus SUV. Klaus then decides to drive a few miles down to a park, with a nice walking path, close to the beach. Klaus arrives at the park, and himself and Bill, get out of the car. It is an extremely sunny and clear day. Hardly any clouds in the sky. The temperature is amazing, and it is neither too cold or too hot, despite it being early in the morning. Bill, who was very reluctant, and not willing to go on the walk at first, now seems to be more agreeable, and happy. As Klaus and Bill start their walk, they start to have cordial conversation with each other. They are both talking about family events, that the other guys would not be aware of. Klaus and Bill while continuing to stroll and walk through the park, are talking about family events they had. Even though Klaus maternal family was Jewish, and German. Klaus paternal family, which includes Bill, was Lebanese, and so it was a nice cultured mix, for Klaus to experience. Klaus was experiencing, a nice wave of nostalgia, by talking to his Uncle, about their family history. Bill was well aware of both sides of Klaus family, and was involved in both cultures, even though Bill is not Jewish, like Klaus maternal family is, he still kept a close bond, and relationship with both sides of Klaus family. Even though Klaus and Bill were mainly talking about happy and pleasant times, the conversation did swift. Eventually, Klaus and Bill happened to talk about more depressing and upsetting times, and family situations and events, that weren't so pleasant. Klaus and Bill then discussed and talked about, deceased family members that are no longer living, and the memories that they had with them. This causes the both of them to feel somewhat upset, although strangely happy at the same time as well, by thinking of the happy times, to cover over the fact, these family members have died, and passed away. Through it all, Klaus and Bill are having a fantastic time together, and they continue to both talk about the bad, and good memories and experiences that they both have, and speaking about their true intentions to each other. Klaus and Bill are having such a great time speaking with each other, that Klaus has forgotten, how long they have been on the walk. For nearly two hours, Klaus and Bill continue to walk through the park, losing complete track of time, due to how strong their bond is.

Klaus does eventually decide that Bill has had enough exercise for the day. As Klaus and Bill are walking back to Klaus SUV, Klaus then pats Bill on the back, and smiles at him. With Klaus and Bill continuing to walk back to the vehicle, Klaus softly speaks to Bill.

"Hey Uncle, how about we try do to his more often. Not every morning, but we can try to do it, maybe a few times a week. If you aren't feeling up to it, I understand. But yeah."

Bill, with his vision down towards the ground, shakes his head, and laughs. Both of the men are silent for a few minutes, as they continue to walk back to the car. However eventually, Bill then pats Klaus on the back as well, and speaks to him.

"Alright Nephew, I don't mind making these walks a regular thing. I'm okay with that."

Klaus and Bill then smile at each other, and they hug tightly. Klaus and Bill continue to hug for nearly a minute, with Bill patting Klaus on the back, during the hug. Klaus feels very happy to have the support of his Uncle, realizing that it's all the family Klaus has left. So that is why Klaus is more concerned about Bill's health. Bill is also happy with this Nephew Klaus, and everything that he has managed to do. Not only helping him, but helping the rest of the guys as well. Klaus is becoming less selfish of himself, and putting others before him, and that's a great quality to have. Klaus and Bill then get into the vehicle, and Klaus starts to make his way back to the house. Once they arrive,

Klaus notices that Dan is preparing breakfast in the kitchen, and is speaking to Ernest, who is at the same time reading book, at the kitchen counter. Jerome is in the living room, and playing a video game on Klaus Xbox. Paul is also in the living room, drawing comics down on his sketch pad. Bill then walks over to the living room, and creeps up from behind Paul, who is still drawing on his sketch pad. Bill wraps him arms around Paul, and Paul doesn't react or respond. Bill then runs his hands through Paul's hair, and speaks to him.

"Hey scout. Good morning. I'm still sorry about yesterday okay. Don't be sad."

Bill then kisses Paul on the cheek, and smiles, and walks into the kitchen with Klaus, Dan, and Ernest. Even though Bill couldn't see his expression, Paul does give a light smirk to Bill. Klaus continues to remain in the kitchen, and is speaking to Dan, as Dan continues to prepare breakfast, which is waffles, eggs, and sausage. This seems to be a very typical morning. Even though Klaus and Bill went out for a walk this morning for Bill's exercise, it seemed at first, that this was going to be a typical morning. Maybe it was because of the downtime, but it was during this time, that Klaus started to wonder, when the guys were going to do their next live show. Klaus is very excited, to continue on with the next edition of their show. Klaus was understanding that the fans of the show, were probably wanting more, and are expecting the guys to put out another show. Klaus then starts to think back, about how the teacher's strike was an amazing Broadcast, and Klaus couldn't believe how he managed to do it. It turned out to be more successful than he imagined. The fact the other guys were on board with the program as well, and it went without a hitch, made Klaus more eager to try it again. Klaus was waiting for the perfect opportunity, and story to break, to make this possible. Right now, he was fine with taking a break. The guys were all happy. Dan is happy, Ernest is happy, Jerome is happy, Paul is happy, his Uncle Bill is happy, and Klaus was happy. So even though Klaus and the guys were of course going to get back to their live show, Klaus was okay for taking a break right now. Klaus hasn't forgotten about the show, he just simply wants to take a break.

As the men continue to stay in the kitchen, the radio station app, that Dan was playing, which consisted of mostly pop songs from the 80s, 90s, and early 2000s, took an advertising break. Dan usually liked to put the radio on when he was cooking. Usually when radio advertisements, on the radio app come up, Dan ignores them, and doesn't pay them any mind. Dan sometimes also turns into another station, so that he can listen to more music. However, Dan was far too occupied with cooking breakfast, and did not turn the radio station app station, during the advertising break. Dan continued on with cooking breakfast, and speaking with Klaus, and Ernest. The radio station app continued to play more advertisements, when one particular advertisement came on, which intrigued Jerome, who was playing a racing video game, on Klaus Xbox. The advertisement featured a woman with a high-pitched voice.

"Hello Spotify listeners, it's time for our daily morning trivia. Be our first caller, to answer three trivia questions, based only a category we give, you will win our prize for day. Our prize for today is, a six pack of tickets to Disneyland resort!"

Upon hearing this announcement, Jerome shuts the video game off, and runs into the kitchen. Dan and Klaus watch him do this, and laugh at him. Jerome then stands by Dan's phone playing the announcement, and starts to smile to himself. The advertisement voice continues.

"So the category for today is, since the prize is Disneyland tickets, the category is Disney history. So I hope you guys know about Disney. If you do, you win those tickets. Be the first caller to call this number, and if you give me the correct answers you win. Good luck everyone."

The announcer then informs the listeners, as to what number to call. The advertisement then ends, and Jerome then starts to pick up Klaus phone, to dial the number. As Jerome is dialing the number, Klaus and Dan look at him, very puzzled. Jerome then speaks to them.

"I listen to this trivia show every morning when Dan plays it. I always get the answers right, and always kick myself for not calling in. Not today. I'm a trivia master. I got this. Ha Ha."

What Jerome said, was true. Multiple times, this trivia segment has come on up the radio station app that Dan listens to, and the other guys don't pay it any mind. However, Jerome always listens to it, and is able to get all the correct answers. Jerome always feels guilty for never calling into the show, and he no longer wishes to do that. Jerome is confident that he is going to win the trivia, and also win the tickets. Jerome is very knowledgeable on Disney history, so Jerome is sure that he is going to get the questions right. Jerome is disappointed, when the first attempt at him calling, results in a busy signal. Jerome then once again dials the number on Klaus phone, with Klaus shaking his head, and Dan also laughing as well. On the second attempt at calling, the phone rings, and it seems as though Jerome has been connected. This is further confirmed, when the trivia segment feed is also playing live on the radio app. Jerome starts to feel very excited, and then speaks to all the guys.

"Oh my god you guys, it's ringing. I think I got through this time. Yes!"

The phone continues to ring for several more seconds, until the female announcer that was on the radio advertisement picks up the phone, and starts to speak.

"This is Spotify trivia. Congratulations, you're the first caller to play. Who's this?"

Jerome then hears the voice on the other side of the phone, and very quickly speaks.

"Yes, my name is Jerome, and I'm from Redondo Beach. Am I live, oh my god!"

Upon hearing Jerome's voice on the radio, all of the guys are shocked, and are speechless, as to what's currently going on. Dan turns the radio down, knowing that there is a feedback delay, and starts to shake his head. Klaus as well starts to shake his head, and can't believe this is actuality happening. Ernest, Paul, and Bill, are stunned as well, and are amazed at Jerome. Not even a second later, the announcer then starts speaking to Jerome.

'Well Jerome, congrats. All you have to do is answer three trivia questions related to Disney, and you win those tickets. If at any time you give me a wrong answer, or fail to answer in three seconds. you don't win anything I'm afraid. We're gonna take the next caller. Okay?"

Jerome was already well aware of the rules, as he has listened to this segment several times, so nothing that the announcer was saying, was foreign or strange to him. Jerome didn't feel that he had to worry, as he knew he was going to get all the answers correct. Jerome speaks.

"Yes, I understand all the rules. I listen all the time. I'm ready."

The announcer then starts to quickly ask Jerome question number one.

"Alright, here is your first question. Can you tell me what Mickey's original name was?"

Jerome has to answer all the questions within three seconds. This is to prevent people from cheating, and looking up the answers online. Jerome knew that people did this anyways, but Jerome was assuming that people were answering legitimately and didn't have to cheat. So Jerome was not going to ask the guys to look the answers up online. Jerome felt that would be cheating, and he wanted to win the trivia, fair and square. So not only does Jerome have to know the right answer, there is a time limit, and he must come up with the correct response, in a very quick and swift amount of time. Jerome knew exactly what the answer was to this question, and in a quick fashion, gave his response to the announcer.

"Mickey Mouse original name was Mortimer Mouse!"

The announcer then quickly responds back to Jerome.

"That is correct. You only need to answer two more, and you win those tickets. We are going to go immediately to question number two. Tell me the name of three Disney dogs."

Jerome was slightly stumped, as he knew the answer to two, but was not able right away to come up with a third dog. Jerome understanding that he only had three seconds, had to quickly come up with the complete correct response, Jerome then luckily managed to think of three.

"Goofy, Pluto, and Slinky Dog from Toy Story!"

The announcer then quickly speaks back to Jerome.

"Yes, that's correct. You only need to give me one more correct response, if you get it wrong, then you don't win anything. If you get it right, then you win the tickets. Are you ready?"

Jerome then takes a deep breath, and looks at all the guys, who all are happy for him, and want him to win. Jerome would feel devastated if he did not win, after giving two correct responses, and he was that close from wining the tickets. Jerome wouldn't be able to deal with himself, and he would feel like he failed. Jerome wanted to win this trivia, and he was not going to take losing. Jerome has listened to this program several times, and knows that he can win, and that he can accomplish this. Jerome then quickly speaks right back to the announcer.

"Yes. I am ready for the final question."

The announcer then directly after this, gives Jerome his final question."

"Okay, here is your final question. Remember, if you get this right, the tickets are yours, fi you get it wrong, you win nothing sadly. Your final question is, what Disney moving, taking place in Los Angeles, deals with Judge, wanting to eliminate all toons."

Jerome again took a second to think about the answer. Also minding, that he had a thirty second time limit to answer, so he needed to come up with a response fast. Jerome was starting to worry after a second passed, and he still hasn't been able to think of the correct answer yet. However, after two second have passed, the answer clicked to Jerome, and Jerome knew he only had a second to give his answer, before he reached his time limit, and the announcer counted that as an incorrect response. Jerome then quickly shouts his answer in the phone.

"Who Framed Roger Rabbit!"

Jerome is confident that he has the right answer. The rest of the guys remain silent, waiting for the announcer to confirm whether Jerome is correct. The announcer then responds.

"That is correct! You are a Disney trivia legend! You have won the six pack of tickets to Disneyland. You earned them; you definitely know your Disney history! Congratulations!"

Jerome then dances around the kitchen, and upon hearing the news, Klaus picks Jerome up, and carries him around his back. The other guys start to laugh, and are happy for Jerome. Jerome has done it. Jerome managed to get all the trivia answers right, and he won the tickets to Disneyland. Jerome also managed to do it without cheating, or using Google to look up the answers, which Jerome is mainly proud of himself for. Jerome then starts to calm himself down, and speaks back to the announcer on the phone.

"Oh my god! Thank you so much! Thank you, Spotify Trivia! I listen every morning, and I always kick myself for never calling, as I get all the answers right. Thank you."

The announcer then continues to play celebratory sound effects, and speaks to Jerome.

"Okay, stay on the line, I'm gonna get your information, and get those passes to you. Congrats, and I hope you and your friends have fun at Disneyland. This has been Spotify Trivia."

The trivia segment on the radio then ends, and Jerome continues to shake his head, and celebrate. Jerome knew that he was going to win the trivia, but when he actually won it, he still couldn't believe, that he actually managed to make it happen. Jerome continues to stay on the line, as promised by the announcer. Seconds later, the announcer starts to speak to Jerome, and she informs him, that he has two options, with claiming his prize. The tickets can either be mailed to him, or he can go to the corporate office, which is a moderate drive from Klaus residence, and pick up the tickets in person. Jerome decided to opt to pick the tickets up in person. Jerome gives the announcer his information, and the announcer tells Jerome the address, as to where he can pick his winnings, and prize up. Jerome then hangs Klaus phone, up, and then returns to dancing around the kitchen. Celebrating to himself. Dan then speaks to Jerome.

"I don't know what in the hell just happened, but wow. Great job buddy. Ha Ha."

Dan then rubs his hand through Jerome's hair, and smiles at him. Klaus then shakes his head, and looks down on the ground and laughs. Klaus then softly responds to Dan.

"This little guy is some type of machine or computer. He can't be real. Ha Ha."

Jerome then takes a sip of his orange juice, and laughs, and responds to the men.

"For your information, I am real. I'm breathing. I'm human. I'm just weird. I like to shock people about what I know. I do a lot of research, and I want to know everything. Trivia is something that I'm really serious about. I don't know everything, but I know some stuff. Ha Ha."

Klaus shakes his head, and laughs at what Jerome said, and Dan does the same as well. Even though the men were glad that Jerome won the trivia contest, they caried on with the rest of their day s normal, and went back to what they were doing before. Dan finishes making breakfast, and the men all then start to eat. Jerome continues to feel excited at winning the Disneyland tickets. Jerome asks Klaus, if they can go to pick up the tickets at the office later. Klaus agrees to this, and this in turn, makes Jerome happy. Jerome felt as if, the sooner that they can get the tickets, the better. Jerome, didn't mention this, nor were the other guys assuming this, but Jerome was planning on using those tickets, to take all the guys out to Disneyland. Jerome felt that it would be an amazing trip, for them all to experience, and go to. While the men are all still eating their breakfast, Jerome takes this time, to explain to the men, his intentions.

"You know you guys, I thought with the Disneyland tickets I just won, why don't we all go to Disneyland, All of six of guys. I mean, did win six tickets, so why not? It will be fun."

The guys all look around, not feeling sure of how to respond or react. Not assuming that Jerome was going to offer or suggest that plan, of them going to Disneyland together. They were happy that Jerome managed to win the tickets, but were not assuming for Jerome to suggest that they all go there together. The men all continue to stare and look at each for several minutes. Jerome notices how silent the other men are, and starts to feel disappointed. Klaus notices is, and gets up, and walks over to comfort Jerome. Klaus then walks up behind Jerome, and hugs him, and kisses him on the cheek. Klaus then softly speaks to Jerome.

"That's a great idea. We all would be happy to go. Right guys?"

The rest of the guys look at each other, slightly puzzled. But they all respond in agreement with Klaus. This made Jerome feel happy, that the other guys were willing to go along with the Disneyland trip, that Jerome suggested. Even though the guys were reluctant to go to Disneyland with Jerome, they did feel that they should be proud of Jerome, and agree with his plan. Paul and Bill, weren't the biggest fans of amusement parks, but were willing to go anyways. Dan and Ernest were caught by surprise by Jerome mentioning, that he wanted to go to Disneyland, and found it random, but then realized it's only fair that they go, to congratulate Jerome for winning the contes. Klaus felt as though he was the voice of reason, and not that he was the leader, but Klaus felt that he needed to be the person to mediate, and facilitate the situation. Once the guys realized that Klaus was on board, they were sure to agree with it. Now that it was settled, the guys were going to visit Disneyland on Saturday. Later that day, Klaus and Jerome, drove down to the radio office, and managed to get the Disneyland ticket passes. For the remainder of the week, Jerome was extremely excited about the Disneyland trip, and it was all that he could think about. Jerome's mind couldn't think about anything else, but that. Jerome started to think about how much fun he was going to have, riding all the rides. Meeting all of the costumed Disney characters. Seeing the Disney parade, and all the other Disney attractions. Jerome was giving into his Peter Pan syndrome, and wanted to be silly and have fun. Above all, Jerome was happy that all six of them were going to be doing this together.

Klaus was slightly optimistic about the trip. Even though Klaus had a higher tolerance for amusement parks, he did find the thought of the idea, initially strange. Klaus felt that it was sort of unusual, for all of them to go to Disneyland, but Klaus wanted to make the event fun. At least he was going to be spending time with his friends, and they were going to be doing something, that people don't really do that often, and that's visit an amusement park. The days leading up to the Disneyland trip carried on, and all of the guys couldn't wait for it to come. It was an otherwise ordinary and typical week up until then, with the guys anticipating the Disneyland outing. The night before the trip, Jerome was excited, more than he ever was. Jerome even took the extra distance, to go online, and come up with a plan, based on the map of the park. Jerome, and the other guys have been to Disneyland before, but it was been a while. The Disneyland amusement park has also changed greatly, since they last all attended. Jerome did more studying on Disneyland, and figured out what rides and attractions that he wanted to see first, and did more research online, as to what attractions have a longer wait time than others. Jerome felt that if the guys wanted to split up, they could. However, Jerome also suggested that after every three hours, the guys would all meet up in a predesignated area, just as a safety precaution. The guys were in agreement with the plan Jerome had. Klaus was impressed that Jerome managed to plan everything accordingly. Klaus knew that Jerome was treating this event very seriously, and he wanted Jerome to have a great time. Klaus then had yet another one of his usual, bright ideas. Klaus figured this would be nice, if he could take his cameras, and they could do a prerecorded broadcast, of their time at the amusement park. Klaus knew that this would be excellent content, and it would also be nice, to have a record of the trip they all took together.

The night before the Disneyland trip, all of the guys remain in the living room, content with each other. Jerome is on the sofa, on his laptop, continuing figuring out his plan for the Disneyland trip. Paul and Bill, are playing chess. Dan and Ernest, are watching The Simpsons on the television. Klaus is reading articles on his phone. Klaus then starts to stare at all of the men, and figures that now is the right time, for him to announce his idea. Klaus then speaks.

"Hey you guys, I was wondering, why don't we make our trip into a show. I think it would be a great idea, and it would show our sillier side to or audience. Don't you agree?"

The guys all look at each other for several seconds, and they all nod their heads. They agree with Klaus, that the idea is wonderful. Dan then decides to respond to Klaus.

"Yeah man, that sounds great. We'll capture everything and turn it into a fun show."

Dan then gets up from the sofa, and walks over to the recliner where Klaus is sitting. Klaus and Dan then fist bump each other. Jerome also is happy with Klaus idea, and speaks.

"Yeah, I like that idea. I feel it will make this trip even better. Yes."

Klaus then smiles at Jerome, and Klaus runs his hand, through Jerome's hair. Paul and Bill accept this idea as well. The men are all now comfortable, and the men are understood, as to what their plan at Disneyland will be. They will not only have fun at Disneyland, but the men will also take this opportunity to capture all the proceedings, turning this into a show as well. So they are accomplishing two tasks at once. The men will be having a great outing together, and they will also be making this event, part of their show as well. The men carried on as usual for the rest of the night, knowing that they will all get up early tomorrow, so they can go to Disneyland. The guys were having difficulty falling asleep, feeling excited, that they are all going to Disneyland. However, the men do manage to get some sleep. The following Friday morning, at 8 a.m., the guys all wake up and start to get ready. Once all the men are dressed, they all get into Klaus SUV. Instead of having breakfast at the house, Klaus decides to stop at McDonalds, and the guys all get breakfast from there, and eat it in the car. Once the men are finished with their breakfast, Klaus throws all their trash away in the trash can, and gets back into his car, and proceeds to drive to Disneyland. Even though the Amusement Park doesn't open until 10 a.m., Klaus, and the rest of the group wanted to get there early anyways, so they can take advantage of the amusement park hours. As Disneyland closes at 10 p.m.

Klaus manages to reach Disneyland, and is already shocked at how many people are there, being that it's only a little bit after 9 a.m. Klaus is slightly more frustrated, when he is not able to find a parking spot for several minutes. Dan tries to calm Klaus down, which helps Klaus compose himself, and he doesn't feel as frustrated as he was. Klaus does eventually find a parking space, which pleases Klaus. Klaus, along with the rest of the guys, then get out of the car, and Klaus then walks to the back of his car, opening the back trunk. At this time, Klaus starts to grab his camera equipment. Klaus hands Ernest a camera, and he also hands Bill a camera. The men then, all start to walk to the entrance of Disneyland. Klaus is noticing that today is a perfect day. Very normal California weather. The sun is shining bright, and there are slight clouds in the sky. Perfect temperature, and a great day to visit an Amusement Park. Klaus, and the rest of the guys, continue to walk towards the Disneyland entrance, with Klaus being slightly agitated, that there is a line of people standing outside. Crowds can frustrate Klaus at times, but he is learning how to tolerate himself better to crowds. The men reach the front entrance of Disneyland, and continue to wait outside the front entrance, for the amusement park to open. With it now being 9:30 a.m., the guys don't have that much long to wait, however, they cannot enter the park, until 10 a.m., as that's when guests are allowed to go inside. During this time, the men continue to talk and converse with one another. Eventually, 10 a.m. opening time arrives, and the gates to Disneyland open. The men all hand the Disneyland employees their entrance pass, and the guys are all now officially inside.

According to Jerome's plan that he already mapped out, once the men were inside, all six of them would split up into groups. Jerome would be alongside Klaus. Dan, would be alongside Ernest. Paul, would be alongside Bill. The men all agreed to this plan, and the six of them, did indeed split up. During this time, Klaus starts to power on his camera, and starts to film everything. Klaus and Jerome start to walk around the park, and Jerome following his itinerary, decides to choose the first attraction that he and Klaus will get on. Which is the Pirates, of the Caribbean Ride. Klaus and Jerome then directly make themselves to that attraction. There isn't a long line at all for the ride, and Klaus and Jerome, start to walk through the empty queue. Klaus has his camera out, and is filming the artistic elements of the queue.

Klaus understands that he cannot film once he's on the ride, per Disneyland rules. Klaus shuts his camera off, once he and Jerome reach the loading dock of the ride. Klaus and Jerome instantly, get on the ride. They are having fun, and they also get lightly soaked, being that it's a dark water ride. Once the ride is over, Jerome continues to follow his game plan, and decides that he wants to ride, The Haunted Mansion attraction next. Klaus obliges and agrees, and they then walk over to that ride. Klaus once again, starts to film the decorations of the queue. This time, the line is slightly longer, as more people are waiting for attractions in the park. After some time, Klaus and Jerome, manage to make it to the inside of the ride, and Klaus yet again, turns his camera off. Klaus and Jerome get on the ride, and have fun at this attraction. Once the ride is over, Jerome then follows his agenda yet again, and the next ride he wishes to get on, is the Indiana Jones ride. Klaus takes out his camera again, capturing everything, as he and Jerome walk to the attraction. Klaus is noticing that the lines for the rides, are getting longer, and longer, as the day carries on. Klaus and Jerome then reach the loading dock of this ride, and Klaus shuts his camera off again, Klaus and Jerome also have a great time on this ride, and are enjoying themselves.

Once Klaus and Jerome leave this ride, then then decide to look at other attractions, and see many costumed Disney characters, walking around the park. Jerome then stops at a cotton candy cart, and Klaus buys Jerome a bag of cotton candy. Klaus decides to get a bag of popcorn. Klaus and Jerome sit down on a bench, enjoying their snacks. At this time, being that it's now 1 p.m., according to the rules they already planned out, after every three hours, the guys would meet at a predetermined place, to check in with each other. Klaus and Jerome then make their way to this location. Meanwhile. Dan and Ernest have just gotten off the Matterhorn ride, and have also ridden other attractions as well. They are having a blast together, and are having much fun. Dan and Ernest then realize it's time to meet up at the spot, and they make their way there. Paul and Bill, decided to ride the Railroad attraction, and are also having fun together. Paul and Bill visit other attractions, and they too notice it's time to meet up at the designated spot. The men then all meet up at the spot, and they are all glad that everyone is accounted for. The men talk about what attractions and rides they visited, and they all exchange banter with each other. After noticing that all the guys are accounted for, the men then go back to their separate groups. Jerome at this time, wants to visit Mickey's Toontown, and he, along with Klaus, start to walk their way there. Once in Toontown, Klaus and Jerome look at several attractions, and ride the Roger Rabbit Car Toon Spin Ride. Klaus continues to gather footage, and film everything. Directly after this, Klaus and Jerome make their way to Splash Mountain. This is another water ride, and Klaus and Jerome get wet, as a result of riding it. Directly after that, Klaus and Jerome get on, It's A Small World ride. Klaus and Jerome continue to have fun, but notice that it's now 4 p.m., and time again for another check in. Klaus and Jerome then start to walk to the check in area. Paul and Bill decide to check out more attractions, and are also happy. Paul and Bill ride the Tom Sayer Sailboat ride, and also check out more attractions. When they both realize it's 4 p.m., they then start to walk in the check in area, with the other guys.

Dan and Ernest were having fun, until they decided to ride the Teacups attraction. After riding, Ernest started to feel slightly ill. Even though Ernest was going to be fine, he experienced a bit of motion sickness afterwards. Dan and Ernest sit down on a bench, with Dan comforting Ernest. They knew had to meet up with the other guys at the spot, but Dan wanted to let Ernest rest, as he was not feeling well. At the check in spot, Klaus, Jerome, Paul, and Bill, all meet up, but Dan and Ernest are not present. Feeling slightly worried, Klaus then speaks.

"You guys seen Dan and Ernest. They were supposed to meet us here."

Paul and Bill shake their heads. Klaus then starts to call Dan, but Dan doesn't recognize his phone is ringing, and doesn't pick it up. At this time, the guys reluctantly decide to split up against each other again, hoping that Dan and Ernest are okay. Klaus is slightly perturbed that the guys didn't follow the plan, of meeting up after every three hours, but moves on. At this time, Jerome wants to visit Tomorrowland.

Klaus and Jerome ride Space Mountain. The line for this attraction was rather long, and it was the longest ride they had to wait for. After this, Jerome and Klaus rid ethe Star Tours attraction. Klaus continues to film the decorations of the ride, feeling that he has great footage of everything. Klaus and Jerome then ride the attraction. Klaus and Jerome then experience more attractions, and Klaus buys some souvenirs, and also buys Jerome some souvenir toys as well. Time continues to pass, with it now being 7 p.m. Klaus and Jerome make their way back to the meetup point again. Paul and Bill start to ride more attractions, and check out the Country Bear attraction. Paul and Bill then realize it's time for the guys to meet up again, and start to walk and make their way to the meetup point.

Dan is still trying to comfort Ernest, who is not feeling well. Even though Dan and Ernest are taking things slower than the other guys, Ernest is still having a great time. Dan and Ernest understand that the guys are worried, but Dan doesn't want Ernest to feel uncomfortable, so they once again decide not to meet up at the spot. Klaus, Jerome, Paul, and Bill, once again, are present at the meet up location, but Dan and Ernest are not there. Klaus again starts to feel worried, and flustered. Klaus then starts to speak to the guys.

"I don't know where the hell they are at. They can't follow a simple instruction. I thought it was crystal clear, that we all were going to meet up here, and catch up with each other. Wow."

Jerome, Paul, and Bill all nod their heads at Klaus. Feeling extremely concerned, Klaus yet again takes out his phone, and tries to call Dan. The phone continues to ring, and Dan does not answer the phone. Klaus leave a voicemail, and also a text to Dan. Klaus doesn't know why Dan is not responding, and he doesn't know that the issue is either. The men wait at the area for fifteen minutes, and when Dan doesn't respond, the guys decide to stay together for the rest of the trip. Klaus, Jerome, Paul, and Bill, all proceed to the Disneyland adjacent park, which was next in Jerome's agenda anyways. The adjacent park is, Disney's California Adventure. The park features more rides and attractions, and is an expansion to the park. If you have a Disneyland ticket, you are allowed to visit this park as well. The four men then start to get on more attractions, and continue to have fun. They visit Cars land, and they also ride The Incredibles roller coaster. The lines at California Adventure, weren't as long as in Disneyland, so the guys were able to spend more time, riding more attractions. As it was now creeping up past 9 p.m., in the back of Klaus mind, he was still worried, that he hasn't heard from Dan and Ernest. The other men were just as equally as concerned. At this time, Paul decides to take a stop at the Ghirardelli Bakery, and decides to buy dessert sweets for all of the guys. The four men continue to walk around the park, very happy at the day they had. Even though they had lost Dan and Ernest, the men were still happy that they managed to see so much at the park.

Shortly after this, a voice comes on the speaker, letting the guests now, that the park is now closed, and all guests have to leave. Klaus, and the rest of the guys, then walk out of California Adventure, and wait at the entrance of Disneyland. Klaus then pulls out his phone, and yet again calls Dan. Dan does not pick up the phone, and he does not respond to any texts either. Paul then rubs Klaus on the back to comfort him. All four men, take a seat on a bench outside the entrance of Disneyland. Jerome rests his head on Klaus shoulder, with Klaus having his hands covering his face, feeling anxious. Paul is rubbing and massaging Bill's back. Luckily, twenty minutes later, Klaus notices Dan and Ernest walking outside the entrance, Klaus out of impulse, then gets up, and starts to scream at Dan.

"Hey man, you know we were trying to get in touch with you all day. Where were you?"

Dan is shocked at the way Klaus is acting, but manages to respond.

"Ernest got sick, and I was taking things slow with him. Man. Chill. What's wrong with you. Klaus that temper of yours, I swear. You have to fix that."

Klaus then throws his hands up in the air, and shakes his head towards Dan. Klaus then returns to sitting down on the bench, and Ernest then starts to speak to all the guys.

"Yeah, I wasn't feeling well earlier. Still kinda don't. But I'm okay you guys. I'm sorry for not meeting up with you guys, but I was feeling sick, and I didn't want you guys to worry."

Jerome then notices how tense this current situation is, and decides to speak to the guys.

"Okay, okay, gentleman. Everyone is here. Everyone had a great time right? Let's not start all that, we are all friends and cool with each other. I still had fun today."

Jerome then walks up to Ernest, and starts to hug him, and Ernest hugs Jerome back tightly. The six of them remain in this area for a few more minutes, with Klaus remaining silent. Eventually, the men all decide to all get up, and leave the amusement park. Even with the slight issue of Dan and Ernest, Klaus was willing to accept, that he had a great time. Klaus knew that Dan was also right, and that Klaus needed to manage his temper better. Klaus still felt that Dan should have at least called, or sent a text message to him, explaining what happened. However, Klaus started to feel guilty and regret coming across the way he did to Dan. Klaus didn't want to wreck the friendship and bond that they had formed. The men all continue to walk back to Klaus SUV, with the rest of the guys speaking with each other. However, Klaus, is deciding to remain silent at the moment. When the guys reach the vehicle, Ernest, Jerome, Paul, and Bill all get inside. Klaus and Dan remain outside of the vehicle. Klaus then pulls Dan aside and speaks.

"Look, I'm sorry about that man. You're right. I get hotheaded sometimes. That's an issue I need to work o nyes. However, you should have called me though. It's okay."

Dan then starts to feel bad and guilty, and quickly responds to Klaus.

"Oh, well you see, my phone died. Forgot to charge it. Ernest left his phone at the house. That's why you were calling me, and couldn't get back. Oh, no wonder. I'm sorry man."

Klaus then starts to rub the back of his head, and starts to laugh. Dan then starts to laugh alongside Klaus. The both of them fist bump each other, and Klaus and Dan get inside of the vehicle. Once inside, Klaus seems more content and happier, that the reason Dan ignored the calls, was justified. It was a simple misunderstanding, that Klaus wasn't aware of. Klaus soon let this whole situation go, and forgives Dan. Klaus then decides to treat the guys all out to something to eat, before they head back to the house. Klaus makes a stop at Denny's, that is located near the amusement park. The rest of the guys were not expecting Klaus to do this, and are happy that he is treating them out to eat. Once they have arrived at the restaurant, the men all get out of the vehicle. They then walk inside, and a waitress, places them at a table. Klaus sits on one end of the table, where Dan sits on the other end. Jerome and Ernest sit next to each other on one side of the table, and Paul and Bill sit together on the other side of the table. The men then look at their menu's deciding what they want to eat. During this time, Klaus and Dan stare at each other, and smile. Dan then decides to say something to Klaus.

"Klaus, you're a great man. You can be rough at time, but I know you're still a gentle and caring man at the end of the day. I speak for all the guys, when I say, thanks man. Ha Ha."

Klaus simply smiles back at Dan, and doesn't respond. Klaus shakes his head and laughs, and agrees exactly with what Dan said. Klaus then returns to looking at the menu. Eventually, the men have all decided what they want to eat. Klaus decides to get the Steak Dinner. Dan decides to order the Country Fried Steak. Ernest decides to get a Club Sandwich. Jerome orders the Chicken Finger Meal. Paul decides to order the Bacon Cheeseburger, and Bill decides to order the Salmon Dinner. After the men place their orders with the waitress, they then all converse with one another. Their food soon arrives to the table, and all the men start to eat, enjoying their meal. Once all the men have finished eating, the waitress returns to the table with the check, and Klaus pays for the meal, and leaves the waitress a tip. Klaus and the rest of the guys, then get up from the table, and leave out of the restaurant. Klaus then drives directly back to the house. When Klaus and the men arrive back home, the men all get out of the vehicle. Klaus walks to the back trunk area of his car, also gathers all his camera equipment from the back of his car. Once inside, Klaus sets all the camera equipment up in his den.

Klaus then leaves the den, and immediately walks to his refrigerator, and pulls two beers out, setting both beers down on the kitchen counter. Klaus then starts to yawn, and stretches himself. Dan walks over to Klaus, and talks with him in the kitchen. Ernest who is feeling tired, says goodnight to the guys, and walks into the bedroom. Paul and Bill are feeling tired and fatigued as well, and also say goodnight, and walk into the bedroom. Jerome walks over to the living room, and opens up his souvenir bag, looking at all the toys and gifts he got at Disneyland, including a Buzz Lightyear doll, that Klaus bought for him. Klaus who is watching Jerome do this, starts to shake his head and laughs. Klaus then walks over to Jerome, and starts putting the souvenirs and toys, back into the bag. Klaus speaks to Jerome while doing this.

"Hey, why do you be a good boy, and take your toys in the bedroom. Okay?"

Klaus then hands Jerome the souvenir bag. Jerome then gets the hint that Klaus wants to talk to Dan in private, and agrees to leave the room, without any fussing or argument. Jerome understands that Klaus and Dan have a close friendship, and are going to allow the both of them to talk. Jerome grabs his souvenir bag, and while he's walking away to the bedroom, he speaks to the men.

"Alright, I get it. I'll leave you guys alone. I'm going, I'm going. Ha Ha."

Dan walks over to Jerome, kisses him on the forehead, gives him a hug, and rubs his hair. Klaus as well walks over to Jerome, does the same thing Dan did. Klaus rubs Jerome's hair, and gives him a kiss on the forehead. Jerome says goodnight to both men, and walks in the bedroom. Klaus and Dan then grab their beers, and start to walk outside to the balcony. While on the balcony, Klaus takes out his pack of cigarettes, and puts one in his mouth. Klaus hands Dan the carton as well, and Dan also takes a cigarette. Klaus lights hits cigarette, and Dan lights his cigarette too. Klaus then starts to look out to the ocean view from his balcony, taking puffs form his cigarette and shaking his head. Dan is looking out to the same view, and also takes a puff of his cigarette. Klaus takes several sips of his beer, while looking forward, which in turn, Dan starts taking sips of his beer as well. Dan then starts to laugh to himself, and speaks.

"Ha Ha. Yet another crazy day huh? Man, this is the life. I swear. Such a nice night. I'm chilling with my best friend. I had an amazing day today. I can't complain right?"

Dan takes another sip of his beer, while looking forward. Klaus takes a sip of his beer as well, with his vision facing forward. Klaus then softly responds to Dan.

"No man, you can't. I'm the one that does all the complaining it seems. Ha Ha."

Dan then playfully pushes Klaus, and laughs. Both Klaus and Dan fist bump each other. Dan continues to laugh. Klaus shakes his head, and feels Dan's laugh is infectious, and also laughs with him.

CHAPTER 13:

IN ACTION

The following Saturday morning, Klaus resumed his routine once again, to walk with his Uncle Bill through the park, in an effort to better his health. Even though the men are still slightly wired out, from the amazing day that they had before, Klaus doesn't want to waste any time, and plans to take Bill on a walk anyways. As soon as Klaus wakes up, he walks himself directly to the kitchen. This morning, Klaus is the first of the men to wake up. Klaus then makes himself a cup of coffee. This isn't anything out of the ordinary at all. Klaus takes several gulps of his coffee, feeling rejuvenated, and ready to take on the day. Klaus waits for Bill to wake, so Klaus can take him on another surprise health walk. Klaus doesn't have to wait long, only about ten minutes, for Bill to finally wake up. Bill acknowledges Klaus, and also walks to the kitchen, to get hem a cup of coffee. Klaus and Bill are silent for nearly a minute, before Klaus then second guesses himself about asking Bill for a walk and decides, that maybe Bill can have a break this morning. Klaus goes back and forth as to whether he is going to give Bill a break or not, staying silent until he makes up his mind. Klaus then ultimately decides, that he is not going to bother Bill today, and he won't pester him to go out for a walk. Klaus doesn't say anything to Bill. Klaus shakes his head, and takes more sips of his coffee. Klaus then walks into to the living room, and sits down on the recliner, and stretches his body back.

Bill watches Klaus closely, and also takes sips of his coffee. Bill is aware that Klaus was probably intending to ask if he wanted to go on a walk this morning. Maybe it's family member intuition, but Bill knew that Klaus meant to invite him on a walk, but for some reason, declined to do so this morning. Bill then takes his cup of coffee to the living room with Klaus, and starts to speak with him.

"Nephew, I know you wanted to take me out for a walk. You don't have to feel scared to talk to me about that. I want to improve my health. So, what are we waiting for? Let's go. Ha."

Klaus then stares at Bill, and shakes his head and laughs. Klaus takes more gulps of his coffee, and continues to sit on the recliner, relaxing himself. Klaus then softly speaks to Bill.

"Uncle, if you don't want to go on the walk, you don't have to. I mean it."

Bill then starts to walk behind Klaus, who is sitting on the recliner, and begins to squeeze and massage his back. While Bill is doing this, he whispers out to Klaus.

"Nephew, please. I want to start making healthier choices. Last time we went on the walk, we had fun right? Today is a nice day. Nice and early. So let's go on the walk, alright?"

Klaus then nods his head, as Bill continues to message his back. At this point, Klaus will obey his Uncle's orders, and go on the walk with him, like he originally planned to do. Not even a minute later, Klaus and Bill exit out of the house, and get inside Klaus SUV. Klaus then starts to drive directly to the park that himself and Bill went to previously. One Klaus arrives at the park. He and his Uncle, then start their walk. Likewise with the previous time, Klaus and Bill are also having conversations about their family life, and Klaus and Bill are also having trivial mundane conversations. Bill also stops to talk to Klaus, if he notices Squirrels and Rabbits that walk across the path. The park, which is located by the beach, not only has the scent of fresh air, and nature, grass, and tress; there is also the scent of the ocean and sea nearby. The sound of the waves crashing against the shore, can also remarkably, be heard from the park. As the both continue on with their walk, on this very clear and sunny day, Klaus has a very positive feeling, walking with his Uncle, in order for his health to get better. It seems that during this walk, time is flying rather fast, and Klaus and Bill have been on their walk, for over and hour. However, it seems that Bill could go on this walk with Klaus all day, and he isn't showing any signs of feeling tired, lethargic, or fatigued. So due to this, Klaus decides to continue on the path with Bill. Klaus and Bill continue on with their walk, until they reach an area that is located on a hill, on top of the path at the park. From this vantage point, you can see the entire ocean. Klaus and Bill stop to notice this area for a few minutes. After this, Klaus and Bill decide to go home.

Once arriving back at the house, after having another amazing walk through the park together, Klaus and Bill walk directly to the living room, and Klaus sits down on one recliner, with Bill sitting down on the other recliner. During this time, Dan is making breakfast for all the men, and talking with Ernest, who is reading a book, in the kitchen. Paul is sitting on the sofa, drawing sketches of skyscrapers and buildings on his sketch pad. Jerome is in the living room as well, and is on his laptop. Even though he didn't inform Klaus that he was going to do this prior, Jerome is starting to edit all of the footage from their Disneyland trip, in a video editor. Klaus notices this, and walks over to Jerome, rubs his hand through Jerome's hair, and pats him on the back. Jerome notices this and smiles at Klaus, and Klaus smiles back. Klaus then walks into the kitchen, with Dan and Ernest, and Klaus watches Dan cook breakfast for a few seconds. Hearing the bacon sizzle in the pan, and also smelling the biscuits Dan is baking in the oven. Klaus can't wait for breakfast to be done, so he can eat. During this same Dan starts to speak to Klaus.

"Hey, Good Morning buddy. I hope you are hungry, because I'm making an epic breakfast, as usual. Did you and your Uncle have a good walk?"

Klaus starts to pour himself another cup of coffee, and then replies to Dan.

"Of course we did, I always have a great time with my Uncle. This walk was longer than the one with took before but we still had fun, and it's great spending time with Uncle."

Dan continues to cook breakfast, but takes quick glance up at Klaus, and smiles as him. Klaus takes more sips of his coffee looking down on the ground, and thinking to himself. Klaus remains silent for a couple minutes, with his vision directed down towards the ground. Dan is nearly finished preparing breakfast, when he glances over at Klaus. Dan is curious about Klaus, and while Dan is continuing to cook and prepare breakfast, whispers out to Klaus.

"Hey man, what are you thinking about? Ha Ha. You're thinking about somethin' what?"

Klaus continues to look down on the floor, and takes another sip of his coffee. Klaus then laughs to himself, and shakes his head. After taking another gulp of coffee. Klaus responds.

"I don't know. I'm thinking about today, Thinking about tomorrow. Thinking about next week. Thinking about next month. Thinking about five years from now. Shit. I don't know. Ha Ha"

Dan yet again laughs, and shakes his head at Klaus, and Dan makes his final touches, in preparation for breakfast. In actuality, Klaus was thinking about quite a bit. Klaus was wanting for the guys to go back to their show soon. Klaus doesn't want to wait that much longer. Klaus is happy that the guys all had fun yesterday at the amusement park. But Klaus wants to get back to business, and get back to doing the show, as quickly as possible. Klaus was overflowed with excitement, and wanted all the guys to do another live remote show. It was all Klaus could think about at this moment, and he was totally invested, and interested towards that. Even though Klaus simply told Dan he was thinking about the future, Klaus indeed was thinking about that; However, Klaus was thinking of much more, and he had an array of ideas and feelings in his mind. Klaus feels that time is way too precious to waste, and that he wants to use all moments of the day, to his advantage. Although Klaus is unsure of the future, he is willing to accept the unknown, and the ambiguity, of what event he will be faced with next. Klaus is far too secure with his team, and only wants to move, and proceed forward. Klaus takes more sips of his coffee, and continues to think to himself, gathering all of his thoughts, and feelings. Dan then finishes making breakfast, and the men all grab a plate, like they usually do. Ernest, Jerome, Paul, and Bill, take their plates back to the living room. Bill is watching a golf match on the television, like he usually does on Saturday's. Klaus and Dan however, remain in the kitchen. Klaus then starts to eat his breakfast. Klaus was hungry, so he was happy and pleased to have food. As Klaus and Dan are eating, Klaus, through spur of the moment, reveals something on his mind to Dan.

"Hey, I was thinking that we should do the show again soon. It has been a while, and I feel now is the right time. There were several stories I read about on the news. I even been checking my police scanner app, and there were stories we could have covered. So yeah."

Dan takes several bits of his food, and nods his head at Klaus. Dan then speaks.

"You're right man, we have to do another news show. I feel you. We had our break, but it's time to get back to business. Whenever you're ready for a story, we're here for you man."

Klaus and Dan do their custom fist bump, and return to eating. It was official for Klaus now. The next story that he comes across, Klaus isn't going to waste any time. He, along with the rest of the guys, are going to immediately go cover it live, and do a remote news show. Klaus now had to be patient, and wait for the perfect time to strike. Klaus can't force news and events to happen, he has to be presented with them. Klaus starts to be nosier on news events. Klaus pays close attention to the news, and media, and his police scanner app, that lets him know if a major event is happening in the community. These events don't have a set schedule. It's up to fate, to if, and when they happen. That's the only downside, negative to everything. Klaus however, is willing to be patient just a little bit longer, so he can be presented with the right scoop, and the right story to cover and broadcast. Klaus continues to eat his breakfast, happy that he yet again managed to get everything in his mind sorted out. Klaus has his game plan already set-in order, and now, Klaus must wait to but his plans into action. The men all finish their breakfast, and the rest of the day continued to be typical. The guys remained in the house, doing what they seem to normally do. Paul and Bill are playing chess in the living room. Jerome is playing a video game on Klaus Xbox, also in the living room, Ernest is reading a book in the living room, and Klaus and Dan are out on the balcony, chatting with each other. The day seemed to pass by rather quickly. Dan cooked dinner for the men, which was Meatloaf and mashed potatoes, and the guys enjoyed the meal. After dinner, the men reported to bed.

The following day, being Sunday, which is usually always a slow, rest day for the guys, didn't have anything eventful happen at all. Today, Klaus and Bill did not go on their walk. Klaus overslept, and Bill chose not to wake Klaus up. Instead, Bill, still wanting to get his exercise, jogged around the block by himself, and didn't want to wake up the other guys, who were still sleeping. Once Bill was finished with his jog, he directed himself back into the house, and took a seat down in the living room. Bill then began to read his paper. After an hour, Dan and Ernest wake up, and Dan walks over to the kitchen, and starts to make himself a bowl of cereal. Dan isn't going to cook breakfast today, and is going to allow the men to make whatever they want. Dan, does however, make a Bill a bowl of oatmeal, with blueberries in it as well. After making the oatmeal, Dan hands Bill the bowl, and Bill thanks him. Dan, then walks back into the kitchen, and eats his cereal with Ernest, chatting with him about mundane topics. A half an hour later, Paul then wakes up, and stats to make himself a bowl of cereal. Paul takes his cereal back to the sofa, and sits and chats with Bill. The morning routine remains the same, as Jerome is the next to wake up. Jerome then makes himself a bowl of cereal. Jerome is chatting with Dan and Ernest at the kitchen. Fifteen minutes later, Klaus, like usually always wakes up last, and joins the rest of the men, in the kitchen. Klaus and Dan fist bump each other, and Klaus has his, almost mandatory and vital, cup of coffee. Klaus then starts to make himself a bowl of cereal. The men then eat their breakfast, with this day of course, being rather slow. Klaus again, doesn't have anything on his agenda for today. It is after all Sunday, and the men typically always use this as a slow day, and as relax day. As assumed, nothing that noteworthy happened today either, and the men did the same thing they did, the day before. The men all remained inside of the house, doing what they normally customarily do, and keeping to themselves. For dinner, Dan decided to make a special beef chili, with leftover ground beef, from the meatloaf, that he made the night before. The men always enjoy Dan's cooking, but it was this meal in particular, that the men seemed to really love and enjoy. The men all eat their dinner, and once they finish eating, they all remain in the living room. Eventually the men all drift to sleep.

The next day, which is Monday morning arrives. The day started off like it was ordinary. It was a nice sunny day, and there was perfect California weather. The most unusual thing about today, was that Klaus was the first one to wake up. This is not usually the case. Klaus, more often than not, is the last person to wake, between the entire collective of the men. However, in any case, Klaus was the first one to get up. Klaus walks out of bed, not disturbing Jerome, who is still asleep. Klaus then does something very ordinary, and walks to the kitchen, and gets his cup of coffee. Klaus starts to take sips of his coffee, while staring out of the kitchen window, admiring, how nice of a day it is today. Klaus, in the back of his mind, was secretly hoping that okay would be a day, that the guys could go out and do a show. It is all dependent on whether or not, a noteworthy event happens in the community. If it doesn't, then Klaus and the guys will not go out and do their show. If it does, then they will do another live remote broadcast show. At this time however, Klaus is enjoying the morning, and waking himself up. Klaus then takes his coffee mug, and starts to relax on his recliner in the living room. Klaus then turns the television on, and proceeds to watch the morning news. A half an hour later, Bill then walks out of the bedroom, and into the living room. At this time, Klaus started to take a nap on his recliner, and is not conscious. Bill notices this, and slaps Klaus on the face with his newspaper. As a result of Bill doing this, Klaus awakens, and starts to stretch himself. Bill then laughs, and speaks to Klaus.

"Good morning Nephew. Nice to see you up at this time. Did you sleep well?"

Klaus continues to stretch himself, and Bill then sits on the recliner next to Klaus. Bill then starts to unfold his newspaper, and begins to read it. Klaus then responds to Bill.

"Oh yes. Good Morning Uncle. I did have a good sleep. Thank you."

Bill then laughs and shakes his head, and continues to read his newspaper. Klaus continues to watch several of the morning news segments, while Bill is reading his newspaper. The rest of the morning, seemed to go like it customarily does. Dan and Ernest are the next to wake, and Dan decides to make breakfast for all the guys. Soon after that, Paul wakes up, and joins the rest of the guys. Not long after that, Jerome, in addition, joins the men. Now that all of the men are woken up, it seems the day has officially started. Klaus, after noticing that nothing on the news is important, or worthy of his attention, gets up, and walks out of the living room, towards the kitchen. Klaus and Dan give their usual fist bump, and start to talk with one another. Again, seems to be a very typical day between the whole group. Klaus and Dan continue on with their chatter and mingling, with Dan preparing breakfast, and Ernest reading a book at the kitchen counter. Klaus continues to listen to Dan ramble and talk, but Klaus is not really responding back to Dan. Reason being, is that starts to have ideas in his head. Klaus has a feeling, that today is going to be the day, that the men return to doing their show. Klaus doesn't know exactly how the events will pan out, but he is sure that the guys will be doing another show today, and that this day won't exactly be as typical and ordinary, as it's seeming so far to be. Dan soon finishes cooking breakfast, and the guys then eat. During breakfast, Klaus continues to have a feeling, that something eventful will happen today. Maybe the feeling is incorrect, and perhaps Klaus is probably overreacting, or rather, overthinking. However, the feeling seems too real and genuine to ignore, and the feeling, is the same feeling Klaus felt when every other recent event happened. So therefore, Klaus is taking this feeling rather seriously, and knows that it's real.

When the men are all finished with breakfast, the day goes on back to being ordinary. The men all return to doing their usual custom routines. This was when Klaus started to second guess himself, and that maybe his feelings and emotions are wrong. Maybe today isn't going to be different at all, and the feeling was lying to him. Klaus refuses to accept this, and he is very sure, that the feeling was correct, and the feeling didn't lie to Klaus before, so why would it now? As the day continues on, with it now being 4 p.m., Klaus, who has spent most of the day watching television, and reading articles on his phone, becomes more worried, when nothing meaningful happens during the day, and time passes on. Klaus steadily reads the news headlines, and also listens to his police scanner app, waiting for an opportunity to strike. However, nothing seems to be happening that he feels are worth the guy's time. Klaus is starting to feel very discouraged and angry, and it seems that the feeling was incorrect, and that nothing worthwhile is going to occur today, no matter how much Klaus wishes that it would. Klaus not knowing what else to do, thinks about taking a nap. Feeling drawn out from reading several news articles and headlines on his phone, sets his phone down on the coffee table, and starts to sit back on his recliner, and relaxes. Klaus rests his eyes, and continues to lean back on the recliner. Paul and Bill are playing their usual chess match. Jerome is on his computer, doing work on his blog, and doing research on the internet. Dan, and Ernest are in the kitchen, talking with one another. This is a very peaceful, and quiet time, and nothing is out of place, or unusual. Things seem to be extremely normal, and satisfactory.

Suddenly, while Klaus is continuing to rest his eyes on his recliner, and relaxing, the 5 p.m. evening news comes on. For some strange reason, Klaus felt intrigued to watch the news program, although initially, Klaus is still feeling drawn out, from paying attention to all the news headlines, in an effort to find a story that the guys can cover. Klaus full undivided attention, is at the news program. However, Klaus starts to again feel discouraged, when none of the stories being covered, are sparking his internet. Klaus still holds onto hope, that his feeling he had, since the day started, will come true. Klaus is sure that there is a story out there, that will break today, and it will be something exciting and entertaining enough, for the guys to do their show over. About halfway into the news broadcast, a female anchor then makes an announcement.

"We have breaking news to report. There is a man that has stolen a gasoline truck, and police are currently in pursuit of the suspect, travelling Northbound, on the 5 freeway. This is a slow speed chase, and the man seems to not be following the officer's orders."

Klaus then jumps out of his recliner, and starts to stand in front of the television. Klaus has a wide smile over his face. This was the feeling that Klaus felt the entire day. This was the event that he, and the rest of the men were waiting for. Klaus continues to grin heavily, and watches the breaking news story, of the man, with the stolen gasoline truck, as if it were an action movie. However, it is not an action movie. It's an actual real life crime news story happening. The breaking news segment continues to air, with police still congruently on pursuit with the suspect. Although to Klaus, this wasn't just a news story. This was something much more. For Klaus, this was entertaining and fun, and something that he wanted to cover immediately. Klaus stands motionless, and frozen in place. Klaus gathers his thoughts, and his plan, as to how he wishes to approach this story. Klaus then speaks to men.

"You guys, we have to get down there. This is what we've been waiting for. This story is perfect, and can you imagine all the views were are gonna get. We have to get down there guys."

Although Klaus is very jubilant and excited about the news story, the other guys do not feel the same way. They simply stare at Klaus, feeling puzzled and confused. Klaus starts to feel slightly agitated, that the other guys are not as happy as he is, and with an angered look on his face. Klaus walks out of the living room, and into his den, to grab his camera equipment. Klaus then sets all of the camera equipment down in the living room, and speaks to the men.

"Come on you guys, I thought you all wanted to continue the show? This is our moment; this is our time to shine. Nobody else is going to be covering this but us. Come on guys."

The rest of the guys continue to stare and look at each other in silence, not sure of what to do. Eventually, the guys then all reluctantly decide to follow along with Klaus, and agree with his plan. Within minutes, with the news broadcast of the police pursuit still being shown live, Klaus gets all of his camera equipment ready, and hands Ernest a camera, and hands Bill a camera. Klaus then takes a camera for himself. This is the same identical fashion and method, the guys used to produce their show last time. With Klaus, Ernest, and Bill, acting as cameraman, and Dan, Jerome, and Paul, acting as reporters. Klaus continues to feel excited and happy, although the other men are not feeling the same way, and are hesitant. The other guys now seem to look up to Klaus as a leader, and are following his command and orders. Even though the other guys feel slightly hesitant, and were not prepared for Klaus to start the show, right now at this instant, the rest of the guys, do feel slight excitement. Due to the fact they had an amazing experience with their last news broadcast show, the guys are ready, and willing, to do it again. They also know that Klaus is right, and that they need to produce another show, and this event seems like it will bring exposure and attention to their show. With not much time to spare, the guys then in an impromptu manner, start to leave out of the house, and proceed to the location of the pursuit. All six of the men get into Klaus SUV, and very swiftly, Klaus starts to drive to the location. With the help of Dan, who is sitting in the passenger seat, Klaus is able to keep up with the police helicopters, and where the pursuit is happening live. Klaus plan, and the main reason why Klaus decided to go on ahead with covering the story, is to use the fact, the suspect is driving slow against the police, and having a slow police pursuit, to their favor.

Klaus will pick an area he already preplanned, to cover all of the action. The fact the suspect is going slow, the men will be able to capture more dramatic events. After Klaus explains the plan to the guys, they are very accepting and understanding of it. The second worry that Klaus was beginning to have, was how far the police pursuit was. It was quite a drive, and that is not to mention, the evening rush hour Los Angeles traffic that is also going on. However, Klaus is adamant that he will make it to the police pursuit location, despite the traffic, and also despite the distance to get to the action will be. Through determination and will power, Klaus does manage to finally make it to the scene. In the entire car ride, the guys were silent. Possibly due to the fact they were equally as anxious and excited. When Klaus reaches the location of the police pursuit, Klaus then starts to find the spot, he and the other guys will capture their action at. Klaus drives a couple more minutes, in an area off to the side of the highway, with mountains in the background. The police pursuit with the suspect is happening on the 5 Freeway. The suspect continues to flee away from the police, driving the stolen gasoline truck, extremely slow. There are several mountains and valleys, on the side of the highway, which is where Klaus and the men, will situated themselves at. Being that it is not 6 p.m., it's evening time, however the sun is still shining, so the guys are lucky enough, to have some sunlight currently. However, if the police pursuit still continues to go on, darkness will soon seep, and it will become dark, making the entire process of doing their show, much more difficult. Klaus parks his SUV, in a separate secluded area of the highway, and Klaus shuts off the engine. Klaus then starts to speak.

"Alright guys. Just follow me, and do as I say, and we won't have any problems. This is going to be so exciting and entertaining. Do what you all did last time. Don't worry. Let's go."

Almost through instinct, the guys immediately agree with Klaus, and they all right away, get into action, and start their show, without really much of any interaction between them. Klaus, and the rest of the men, then start to walk away from the SUV, and walk about a quarter of a mile, to the vantage point, which is further west, that Klaus and Jerome are going to be shooting their footage from. Dan and Ernest will report from an adjacent area, further south, and Paul and Bill, will report from the vantage point that is further north. Now that all of the men are directing themselves, to the positions that they should be at, Klaus is very secure, that their show is going to be flawless, and there shouldn't be any issues. Klaus and Jerome walk to their section, and once there, Klaus starts to position his camera, and records the action. Jerome alongside, is also reporting the proceedings, and all the information as well. During this time, Klaus pulls up his separate camera feed, which lets him view what the other guys are recoding. Klaus then starts to look at Dan and Ernest's feed, and Klaus starts to call Dan's number on the phone. When Klaus and Dan are connected, they then speak to each other.

"Hey man, just checking in on you guys. You guys are doing great. The guy should be pulling up in about five minutes or so. You guys stick tight for a minute. We're just in time."

Dan has his full attention to Klaus on the phone, with Ernest still recording all of the events. Dan and Ernest continue to walk through their vantage point, and Dan responds.

"Alright man, sounds good. We're doing okay. If we run into any problems, we will let you know man, but we shouldn't. Everything is going perfect so far. Catch you later man."

Klaus then thanks Dan, and hangs the phone up. Klaus then checks on Paul and Bill's camera feed, and Klaus notices that they seem to be getting great footage as well. Klaus then starts to call Paul on the phone, to simply check in on him. The phone rings, and Klaus speaks.

"Hey, I was calling to let you know, that you and Uncle are doing a great job. Keep it up. You guys are getting amazing footage. The truck should be coming in five minutes. Okay?"

As Paul and Bill continue on recording their footage and content, Paul replies to Klaus.

"Okay, that's great to hear. We're trying to give you a good show. If we need anything, we will give you a call. We're doing okay for now though, and we got everything covered."

Klaus thanks Paul, and disconnects the call. At this time, all the men can do is wait, until the suspect in the gasoline truck, reaches the vantage point that all the men are at. Klaus estimates that this could take five minutes, but it could be sooner if the suspect drives faster, or slower, or rather never, if the suspect drives slower, or is accosted by police before then, and doesn't reach the vantage point. Klaus remains sure, that in due time, and very soon, the suspect will arrive where they are at, and Klaus will be able to cover the entire news story. During this time, Klaus then starts to check the internet stream on YouTube, and on other sites their story is currently being shown live. The viewers are pouring in, with already 500 people being interested. This is what Klaus envisioned, and what he wanted. An audience, and not only an audience, but an audience that was willing to watch his content, and what he was putting out. This makes Klaus happy, knowing that he is entertaining others, by simply doing what he does best, and what he loves doing, and that's entertaining others, by broadcasting, and by showcasing media to others. Klaus, and the other men, continue to wait on the side of the highway, steadily capturing the news footage. Waiting at any second for the suspect being chased to arrive at the scene. At this time, Jerome then starts to notice white headlights appearing down the highway.

"Oh god. I think that's them. It has to be. It's the gasoline truck, going very slow."

Klaus then immediately listens to Jerome, and turns his camera direction, showing headlights in the distance on the highway. While Klaus is recording, he then starts to speak.

"Oh shit. Yes, that is them. We finally made contact. Yes! Slow speed pursuit it is. Yes!"

Klaus continues to capture all the footage, taking note of the extremely slow speed, the suspect is driving on, and the wave of police cars, slightly behind the suspect. Klaus then starts to call Paul back on the phone, informing him that the suspect has arrived at their vantage point.

"Hey man, the Truck is now here. Get your cameras ready, because it's show time."

Paul and Bill then quickly run in the direction of the truck, and Paul responds back.

"Alright, you don't have to tell me twice brother. We're on it right now."

Klaus then hangs up the phone, and starts to call Dan, informing him of the truck. The phone rings for a few seconds, but Dan does eventually answer. Klaus then speaks to him.

"Yes, the truck is right here man. Hurry, they are the closest to you and Ernest. Go!"

Dan then starts to run, with Ernest steadily keeping up with him, recording. While Dan and Ernest are running, trying to keep his breath, Dan responds to Klaus.

"Oh Damn, okay. I see the headlights now. They are very close. We're going there now."

Dan then hangs up the phone, and Klaus continues to form a wide grin and smile on his face. The action is now starting, and the men are direct in the center of it. Klaus was waiting for an event like this to happen, to where the guys are live and direct with the action. The ball is in their court, and they are recording and capturing all the news footage. Even though the news helicopters are now starting to circle in the area, Klaus and his men, are the only people that are at the center of it all, and are level with the truck in pursuit. Although, Klaus is heavily excited, he is slightly nervous as well, as the guys do not have any business being where they are. They are taking a huge risk, mainly with their safety, from doing the show at this location, at the side of the highway, recording from the mountains and valleys. It was due to all of the excitement, and being in the moment, that the guys didn't take the time to realize this. Klaus wasn't concerned or worried about this at all. His main concern, was to get an entertaining show that was action packed. Dan and Ernest continue to head in the direction of the gasoline truck. Klaus, Jerome, Paul, and Bill, who are at their vantage points, also shift their direction to get a better view. Minutes go on, and the suspect steadily continues to drive the gasoline truck, slow through the highway. Things seem to be going smoothly, until Dan and Ernest's video feed starts to lag.

This upsets Klaus very much, as he knows this will affect how the show is being broadcast. The viewers do not want to see a laggy feed. This is evident, as Klaus notices that the viewers of the show are decreasing, and Klaus knows it's because of the bad quality of the live broadcast. Klaus isn't sure why the feed is laggy, but Klaus thinks that maybe Ernest has to refresh his FPS on his camera. Klaus then starts contact Dan, to tell Ernest to fresh the camera setting. Klaus dials Dan's number, but Dan doesn't respond. Klaus then starts to feel very frustrated and angry, that Dan is not responding to him. Directly after that Klaus, while still walking with Jerome, towards the other side of the highway, where the truck is heading, starts to call Paul on the phone. Unlike Dan, Paul, who is walking with Bill through the valleys, and mountains on the side of the highway, moving away from their vantage point, and heading where the truck is, answers the phone rather quickly.

"Yeah man, what's going on. Everything alright. Are we doing a great job?"

Klaus doesn't immediately respond back to Paul. Klaus continues to run and walk alongside Jerome, to the vantage point where Dan and Ernest are. Klaus then speaks to Paul.

"You guys are doing fantastic. However, I'm worried about Dan and Ernest. Their feed is laggy, and it's not only bad for the show, but it's also bad, because I can't monitor them. We're all gonna stick together from now on. Meet us at the point where Dan and Ernest are, okay?"

Paul and Bill continue to run through the side of the highway. Paul responds to Klaus.

" I see. Alright, understood then. We're going now. We will meet you guys over there."

Klaus then hangs up the phone, and continues to walk to the south vantage point where Dan and Ernest are. Klaus tries once again to call Dan on the phone, but he is not answering. Klaus continues to feel terribly worried for the both of them. Things make a turn for the worst, when Dan and Ernest camera feed disconnects and turns offline completely. This doesn't sound good at all, and Klaus doesn't know what is happening, in regards to Dan and Ernest. Klaus then tries to get to the vantage point Dan and Ernest are in, even faster. Right now, Klaus focus isn't even on the police pursuit anymore really. His main priority, is trying to get back into contact will Dan and Ernest, and hoping that they are safe and alright. During this time, the sun is setting, and it's slightly dark in the area. This makes running through the valleys and mountains on the side of the highway, much harder for the men. Klaus continues to look around the dusk sky, and the empty highway next to them, which is closed off the police, for the pursuit. Klaus, and Jerome make it to the vantage point that Dan and Ernest were assigned, however Klaus does not see neither Dan, nor Ernest. Klaus starts to shake his head, and runs his hands through his face. Jerome also feels worried and concerned, by not seeing Dan and Ernest as well. Klaus continues to look carefully for Dan and Ernest in this area, but they are simply not here. Klaus continues to look around, trying to find them, but is unsuccessful. A few minutes later, Paul and Bill arrive at the vantage point as well. At this time, Klaus makes the difficult decision to end the show, as he doesn't feel comfortable or safe to continue, with Dan and Ernest missing. Klaus then starts to speak to the audience viewing the show.

"I'm sorry guys, but we have an unprecedented emergency. Dan and Ernest are not here. We don't know where they went. I know you guys saw their feed go down. We hope they are alright. We're sorry this wasn't the fun show we hoped, but we'll catch you guys later. Bye."

Klaus then shuts off the video feed online, and also cuts off his cameras. The other guys agree with Klaus decision to end the show, as finding Dan and Ernest, is a bigger, and more important priority for right now. After shutting all the cameras off, Klaus then shakes his head, and looks down on the ground. Klaus then starts to speak to the guys.

"Okay, were gonna walk back to the car, put all the equipment up. Then we are gonna try to find Dan and Ernest. They have to be here somewhere. Man, I don't know what happened."

Jerome, Paul and Bill obey Klaus, and walk back to Klaus SUV, and the men put all of their equipment back in the car. The show is not going well now, and it wasn't a success as their previous show at the Teacher's Strike. This show is now turning into a crisis situation, now that Dan and Ernest cannot be located, and they are on the valleys and the mountains on the secluded highway. It is also getting darker, and deep into the night. Klaus, and the other guys, then proceed to walk down the other direction of the highway, looking for Dan and Ernest. Klaus starts to feel frustrated and angry, and starts to grumble to himself.

"It's always something with them. Everyone else can stick together fine. It's always them. Ugh. I was hoping this wouldn't happen, but it did. They had one job, which was to stay in that location, and they couldn't even follow that. Wait until I get my hands on Dan. Ugh."

The other men notice how angry and upset Klaus is, and Bill walks over to Klaus, and starts to rub and massage his back. Bill then softly speaks to Klaus.

"Nephew, calm down. All of us are worried about them, but calm down Nephew."

Klaus simmers down, after Bill comforts and consoles him. The men continue to walk down the highway, bear in mind, the police pursuit is still going on. This shows, as Klaus and the men, notice the suspect driving extremely slow with the gasoline truck. Klaus then starts to have hope, that maybe Dan and Ernest are hiding, and are still in the vicinity. Klaus and the men start to run faster in the direction of the gasoline truck, both looking at the pursuit, being amazed by it, and also on the lookout for Dan and Ernest. As the men continue to walk through the highway, something unusual happens. The suspect all of a sudden, stops the gasoline truck. Klaus, and the men, watch this happen live, and are stunned. Although they are supposed to be looking for Dan and Ernest, Klaus can't help but watch how the police pursuit took this dramatic turn. Klaus and the men then decide to watch the pursuit, and look for Dan and Ernest later. Klaus continues to watch as the suspect remains in the gasoline truck, with the officers having their guns drawn towards the suspect in the truck. Klaus and the men are at a point to where they are hidden from the police, and aren't seen, but can still hear the orders the police are giving the suspect.

"This is LAPD! Get out of the truck, and put your hands behind your head, now!"

Klaus and the rest of men, continue to be stopped in their tracks, as they are having a front row seat, to all of the action with this police pursuit. Klaus slightly regrets putting all his camera equipment up, as he knows that this would be amazing footage to capture. Several more minutes pass, and the suspect is not complying with police, and is remaining in the gasoline truck. The standoff between the suspect and the stolen gasoline truck, and the police, remains. Klaus and the men are close enough to where they can see the windshield of the truck, but Klaus cannot get a visual image of the driver, as it's nighttime and dark, and the headlights of the truck, are glaring, making it impossible to see who the driver is. Klaus biggest concern is that the driver is going to do something unpredictable or dangerous. However, Klaus feels that himself, and the rest of the guys aren't in any danger, and they have nothing to worry about. As Klaus continues to stare at the police pursuit, Klaus then hears a voice calling his name.

"Klaus! Hey Klaus! Hey man! Klaus!"

Klaus then focuses his vision, towards the direction he heard the voice. The other men heard the voice as well, and start to look in that direction. Right after this, Klaus notices Dan running up to the other men, continuing to shout Klaus name. Klaus and the other guys then run towards Dan. Once Klaus gets into contact with Dan, Klaus then throws Dan on the ground. Dan and Klaus then begin to wrestle and tussle. Klaus then starts to yell at Dan.

"Where the hell have you been? All of us are worried sick. Where is Ernest? You know how long that we've been looking for you? God, I've really had with it you this time Dan."

Dan and Klaus continue to wrestle, with Paul and Bill trying to break them up. Jerome who was watching everything, starts to cry, and is feeling upset and concerned. Paul and Bill break them up. Bill is holding Klaus back, and Paul is holding Dan back. Dan then speaks.

"You know what man, fuck this. I quit. I'm done. You and your temper aren't worth it. I don't know where Ernest went man. He said he wanted to get a better camera view, and that's the last time I saw him. I tried to stop him, but he wasn't listening to me."

Dan then shakes his head, and puts his hands behind his head. Dan then starts to pace himself away from the group. Klaus has an angry look on his face, crosses his arms, and shakes he head. Klaus then paces himself away from the group as well, in a opposite direction of Dan.

Klaus and Dan are extremely angry and upset at each other, and can't even look at each other either. At this moment, all of the men remain speechless and motionless, and trying to reflect on what just happened. Dan continues to pace himself away from the group, with his hands behind his head. Klaus essentially does the same, and paces himself away from the other men, with his hands in his pocket. A minute later, this setting is interrupted, when Paul starts to yell.

"Oh God! Oh shit! Oh my lord! Guys. Ernest!"

Paul then starts to point out to adjacent side of the highway, where Ernest is standing, recording the police standoff, with his camera. Klaus and Dan, immediately snap out of their angered mood, once they notice this. All of the men then start to walk down the side of the highway they are on, calling out Ernest name. Ernest however is not responding to them. It is possible that Ernest doesn't even hear them. The guys continue to yell and scream out for Ernest, although he continues to not respond. Klaus then starts to shake his head, and speaks.

"What the fuck is he doing over there? How the hell he even get over there?"

Dan then decides to walk down the hill, closer to the highway divider. Upon noticing Dan doing this, Klaus then treads himself down the hill as well, and manages to catch up to Dan. Klaus then starts to grab Dan's shirt collar, and screams out to him.

"Are you fucking nuts? You're gonna hurt yourself. I know Ernest is out there, but don't do that. It's not like were friends anymore, but I still care about you. Don't walk out there."

Dan then realizes that Klaus is right, and does not decide to walk past the divider, between the mountains and valleys, the guys are on, and onto the actual highway. At this point, both Klaus and Dan continue to scream out to Ernest, but they again are unsuccessful. Klaus then shakes his head, and looks down on the ground. Klaus while looking at the police standoff, which is still going on, starts to speak silently to Dan.

"I'm gonna call 911, and tell them Ernest is over there. I don't know any other option."

Dan nods his head, and understands that Klaus idea is the most sensible one to go with. Klaus then starts to pull out his phone, but at the same time, something unthinkable happens. As Klaus is getting his phone from his pocket, Ernest starts to walk out onto the highway, with his camera. Klaus and Dan notice this, and start to scream Ernest name, to get his attention. Klaus and Dan have no idea, why Ernest decided to do this, as it's very unsafe. Concurrently, Klaus and Dan are also shocked and mortified, when the driver of the gasoline truck, decides to all of a sudden, start moving forward. Ernest managed to hear Klaus and Dan shout out to him, and Ernest turns his direction to them. Klaus and Dan scream at Ernest to get out of the highway, and also motion for him to do this. But Ernest is not able to hear clearly what Klaus and Dan are saying, and he's not able to understand their body language, and motions either. Ernest remains standing in the area he's in, until the driver of the gasoline truck, notices Ernest, and has his intentions on running him over. The suspect driving the truck proceeds forward, and Klaus and Dan, along with the other guys, can do nothing but watch in fear, shock, and horror. The police notice Ernest is on the road, and assume he's an innocent bystander or hostage.

The police are careful by not shooting the gasoline truck, to avoid an explosion. They instead try to shoot the tires of the truck, so the tires would flatten, causing the driver not to proceed that much farther. The driver still manages to go forward, with Ernest still stuck in his position, unable to react fast enough. When Ernest does happen to realize the situation he's in, he tries to sprint out of the way of the truck. The unfortunate happens, and the gasoline truck fatally strikes Ernest, and runs him over. Dan immediately starts to scream and yell, and cannot control his emotions. Dan tries to walk across the highway divider, with Klaus holding Dan back. The other guys were watching the entire thing happen, up above on the hill. Jerome starts to cry, and puts his head into Paul's chest, while Paul is crying as well, and comforting Jerome. Bill in turn, pats Paul on the back, and then walks away with his hands covering his face. The men all continue to take in the devastating, and horrible events that just happened. As Ernest deceased body remains on the highway, Klaus continues to hold Dan back from walking out there, and is comforting, and consoling Dan. While the men are still taking in what just happened, the suspect of the gasoline truck, which happens to be a middle-aged Caucasian man, walks out of the truck, and starts to run down the highway. A few seconds later, the police fatally shoot the suspect, and he falls down on the ground. The men all watch this happen as well, and continue to feel shocked. Dan is still trying to escape from Klaus, and Dan yells and screams at Klaus.

"Man, get the fuck off me! I have to go down there. Man let go of me!"

Klaus then continues to successfully hold Dan back, and Klaus speaks back to Dan.

"I know you don't like me right now, and I don't like you either, so it's even. But I'm not letting you go, it's not safe. Calm the fuck down. Okay? We all feel the same man. Calm down."

Dan continues to fight against Klaus restraint, and cries. Klaus, while continuing to restrain and hold Dan back, starts to see all the police sirens, Ernest's, and the suspect's deceased bodies on the street, and several police officers walk out onto the highway. Klaus also notices the Police helicopter up in the air as well. Klaus steadily holds onto Dan, who's fighting against him to walk on the highway. Klaus still continues to successfully restrain, detain, and hold back Dan. Klaus then starts to laugh to himself in disbelief, and shakes his head.

CHAPTER 14:

NOW WHAT

The men all continue to remain at this devastating scene. Part of them are still trying to fully understand the magnitude, as to what exactly happened. One of the most horrific things that could happen, did actually happen. One of the members in their group, just died. None of the guys would ever think that such an event as this would happen, but it did. The guys did not agree to go on this adventure, with the chance that one of them could actually die as a result. They were all very adamant that nobody would get hurt during this, and they would all be safe. This is not the case, as someone in the group, is now gone. The guys are all in shock most likely, but they will eventually come to realization, to everything considered. The guys were only trying to have fun, with their show, but unfortunately, something drastic occurred. This event is making all of the men think, and think deeply. Perhaps this idea wasn't so wise, and they are not learning the hard way, that trying to get too involved, in matters that don't pertain to them, might not be the best idea. The guys were trying to give an entertaining show to the audience. None of the men really cared about how extreme their actions were. Their only concern was to make their show fun and engaging. Because of this, the men we're all in, over their heads. The men were not able to think this whole ordeal through and plan everything accordingly. In turn, they paid a cost for this mistake, and now they must live with it, and also accept the result. Guilt, regret, sorrow, are all of what the men are currently feeling. What shall they do from this point? What is the next plan for them? How are they going to move forward from this? None of the men have any idea, and that is the concerning part through all of this.

The fact of the matter, Ernest is now dead. There is nothing that any of the men can do about this. Ernest is now gone, and no longer here, and that's one thing that is for certain and true. However, what the men choose to do next, and where they go from here, would be up to them. Whichever methods they choose to accept or grieve this news, is up to however each man wishes to cope with it. This is all very unfortunate, and upsetting. Ernest was a person that all of the men got along with greatly, and they enjoyed the friendship that they had with him. The men can't fully comprehend how one of the guys in their group is not here anymore, and the guys truly don't feel that they will able to recover, or bounce back from this. The guys in addition feel guilty, that they started to become very carless. They feel as a result of their carelessness, Ernest was the unfortunate scapegoat with that. The person that is feeling the most guilt, would have to be Klaus. Klaus feels that if he never met Ernest in the first place, Ernest would never have this happen to them. So although each of the men are dealing with guilt in their own way, Klaus is definitely feeling it the most, and is starting to regret everything, starting from the beginning. Klaus is starting to realize, that perhaps this was indeed a terrible mistake. Klaus did not intend for any of the guys in his group to get hurt, and he was sure that they would be safe. Klaus did not manage to keep that promise or guarantee, as Ernest is dead. Klaus continues to gather his thoughts at this current situation, and is still unsure as to what his next plans are going to be. Klaus simply can't get his thoughts in order right now, and his mind is racing too fast. Klaus can't even think straight at this time, and continues to feel guilty. It then dawns on Klaus, that this is yet another person that he has formed a close bond with, that is no longer here. Klaus starts to think back to how he lost his business partner Stuart. Klaus is starting to feel as though he is cursed, whenever he tries to make social connections. The people that he seems to latch onto, and form personal bonds with, eventually end up slipping away from him.

Dan is not able to control himself right now either. Dan formed a special relationship with Ernest, so he is not taking this event well at all. Dan doesn't think that he is going to be able to control and compose himself, and deal with the news of Ernest's death. They were very close friends, and Dan feels that it's unfair that Ernest is dead. Dan also feels anger and hostility towards Klaus, as he feels that this whole entire thing, is Klaus fault. Dan trusted Klaus, and it turns out that Klaus wasn't dependable, and that one of the guys in their group, died during the live show they were doing. Dan is sure that he will not trust Klaus ever again, and the friendship he has with Klaus, is no longer. Dan completely flips his entire relationship with Klaus, and wants nothing to do with him. Dan can't even look Klaus in the eyes; that's how upset and angry he is at him. Dan feels that Klaus betrayed him greatly, and he can't understand it, and will not forgive Klaus for any of this. Dan starts to feel extremely depressed, while he continues to have thoughts of Ernest run through his mind. Dan understands that he will never see Ernest again, and all the past memories that the both of them have experienced, start to rush through his mind. As Dan continues to think about all of the fun times that he and Ernest went through, this makes him even more upset, and unable to control himself. Dan refuses to believe that Ernest has died, and wishes that this wasn't the case, however it is. Dan has to accept this news, and it is okay and alright for him to feel sad, but Ernest isn't coming back. While Dan is thinking about Ernest, he is also having much hatred for Klaus, and will continue to feel that this is all of Klaus fault. Dan went from a very close friendship with Klaus, to what now seems, arch enemy, and hatred. Klaus continues to hold back Dan, who wishes to go out onto the road to get closer to Ernest. Klaus is not allowing for Dan to do so, and successfully manages to restrain him from proceeding any further. Actually, all of the men are still continuing to stand in the area of the mountain, still trying to adapt their minds, as to what actually happened. It was during this time, that Dan is not able to control his emotions anymore, and even though Klaus is restraining him very tightly, Dan tries to think of a way to get Klaus away from him. Dan then takes his elbow, and strikes Klaus in the abdomen, with much force. Klaus then is stunned by the blow, and starts to put his hands over his stomach, due to the pain. Dan then starts to shout at Klaus.

"You motherfucker! This is all your fault! Ernest is gone because of you! I hate you!"

Klaus continues to feel pain, from Dan hitting him in the stomach. The rest of the guys saw all of this happen, and then walk down the hill, to join Klaus and Dan. As the men are starting to walk down to Klaus and Dan, Dan continues to shout at Klaus.

"Ernest trusted you, and you said none of us would get hurt! You fucking liar!"

Klaus continues to recover himself from Dan hitting him, and remains silent. Due to the noise that Dan was making, whilst he was shouting at Klaus, this attracted the attention of the police officers, who are down below on the highway. One of the police officers that notices the men, starts to shine his flashlight at them. The guys then all direct their attention to the police officer, standing on the highway. The officer then starts to shout at all of them.

"Gentlemen! Hey! What are you guys doing up there? Stay right there!"

At this time, the guys decide that they could either remain where they are, or they could decide to run away from the police. Dan was not trying to attract the attention of the police, but he unfortunately, by shouting at Klaus, managed to do so. Even though none of the guys are talking to each other, they all glance and look at each other, and through body language, it seems that the guys are all going to remain at the scene, and not run away. The guys then start to panic, that they might be in trouble. They all know that they have no business being in this area. The men are most definitely trespassing, and they could get into much trouble for this. A few officers then start to walk up toward the mountain the guys are all standing on. During this time, Klaus, who still feels pain from Dan punching him, then speaks to all of the guys.

"Hey, just tell them that we work for the media. Ernest is a friend of ours, and we all decided to split up, and he got lost. If we all have different stories, they will get suspicious."

Dan then looks at Klaus, and begins to shake his head. Dan then starts to rush towards Klaus, and while he is doing that, Dan starts to loudly shout at him.

"Fuck you! Ernest is gone, and it's all your fault, fucker! Shut the hell up!"

The rest of the men manage to hold Dan back from Klaus, Dan continues to give Klaus cold and angry stares. A few moments later, several police officers start to arrive at the area the rest of the men are at. The police officers shine their flashlights in the guy's faces. The light of the flashlight the officer is shining on them, is rather bright, and the guys seem blinded, and they are also disorientated as well. Police officer then starts to talk to all of them.

"Gentlemen, I would like to see some identification please. What are you guys doing out here? You know you guys can't be here right? So what's going on here?"

The men then start to hand the officers their identification. Several officers then start to look at their identification. As the officers are doing this, Paul then starts to speak.

"Officer, we are a news media program. We cover news events. We heard about the police chase, as he wanted to cover it. The civilian that was just hit, he was our close friend. So we are kinda shaken up about it. Officer it's the truth. We're not bad guys at all."

The officer then starts to give Paul a puzzled look, and the officer continues to look at the guys identification. The guys decide not to speak, and through the tone of their body language, seem to agree with the story that Paul gave the officers. After several more moments of silence, the officer is then handed the other guys identification, that the other officers obtained. The officer then puts all of their identification in his pocket, and then starts to speak to them.

"Gentlemen, I'm going to have to ask you to come with us. We just have to interview you all separately, and understand what's going on. You're not arrested, but you are detained. We are just gonna take you down to the station, and ask you a few questions. It's alright."

The guys then all start to feel scared, and anxious, after the officer says this. The men then start to believe that they will get into much trouble. Even though Klaus originally explained that they should all each have the same story, and have the same explanation as to why they are there, the fear that the police will try to catch the guys in a lie, and trip them up, is possible. Paul was the only person, that managed to go along with Klaus warning, and told the police a summary as to what happened. Even though Paul was not that far from the truth, the authorities are still hesitant, and unsure, as to whether the guys are actually telling the truth. The police wishes to take all of the guys to the police station, and interview them, and investigate this situation more. The guys are not arrested, but instead, they are all asked to go inside a police van, that is located a short walking distance, from where they all were. The men all get inside of the van, with Klaus and Dan sitting next to each other in the first row of the van, and Jerome, Paul, and Bill, sitting together in the back row. The driver of the van, then directly proceeds to the police station. As the men are riding in the van, they all continue to feel on edge, and slightly scared. The men remain silent, and are facing forward, motionless. This whole entire night is becoming very hectic. Just slightly earlier, they had to deal with the death of Ernest, and now the men are being detained by the police. This was not at all how they hoped the night would go, and the guys are now starting to see the consequences, and repercussions, to all of the behaviors, and actions they were exhibiting. What originally started as a faun experiment, doing the show, now turned into catastrophe, and disaster. As more minute's pass with the men riding in the van, Klaus, then starts to look over towards Dan, who has his head facing towards the ground. Klaus then decides to tap Dan on the shoulder, to get his attention. Dan doesn't respond, or emote back, to Klaus. Klaus then starts to look down on the ground, and shakes his head. The van continues on the road for several more minutes, with the men all remaining quiet. Klaus then once again, decides to get Dan's attention, by tapping him once more. Dan then shoves Klaus on the shoulder, and Dan stares at Klaus, giving him eye contact. Dan shakes his head, and speaks.

"Man, what? I don't even want to ever see you again in my life. What is it? Damn?"

Klaus then starts to laugh, and looks down on the ground, shaking his head. Klaus is silent for several seconds, but he does eventually, silently, respond back to Dan.

"I wanted to say sorry. I miss Ernest too. Dan, I know you're mad at me, and that's fine. I accept that. But I am sorry, and I miss Ernest as well. We all miss him. I'm sorry Dan."

Klaus then starts to rub Dan's shoulder. Dan continues to have his vision down towards the ground, and starts to shake his head. Dan, for the first time since Ernest dying, starts to slowly, but surely forgive Klaus. Dan realizes that his anger was slightly on impulse, and Dan understands, that Klaus didn't mean for what happened, to have happened. Dan, while he is still looking down towards the ground, silently responds back to Klaus.

"You're right man. I'm still trying to adjust, you know. I loved Ernest, and well, I don't know. Just don't talk to me now. We'll talk later man. Alright?"

Klaus who was looking at Dan this entire time, then softly speaks back to him.

"Okay, I guess we'll talk later then. Dan, again, I'm really sorry man. For everything. I feel maybe this was a bad idea, and I'm sorry for Ernest, and I do miss him too. I'm sorry."

Dan does not respond to Klaus, and continues his vision down towards the ground, being silent. Klaus as well remains silent too, keeping his vision down on the ground as well. The rest of the guys also are silent, and are not speaking. During this time, the men continue to think about what they are going to tell the police. The men are all understood, that they will follow Klaus orders, and all give the same details and story, as to why they are all at the highway. They were doing their news show, about the police pursuit, and Ernest split up from the rest of the guys, in an effort to get a better view of the scene. During this, Ernest was unfortunately ran over by the suspect. The men all saw what happened, so there was no reason for them to slip up on their story, or on their explanation as to what happened. The men minutes later, do eventually arrive at the police station. Once the van is parked, the officers all escort the men, into different directions. With Klaus going one way, Dan going into another, Jerome going into another separate direction, Paul being asked to walk in a different direction, and Bill going into another direction as well. As the men are now being split into different directions of the police station, it is clear that the police are wishing to interview them all individually.

Klaus continues to follow the officer in the direction he was asked. Klaus then arrives at an interrogation room, and the officer then shuts the door behind him, as he walks out. Klaus looks around the room, and notices that there is a camera located in the corner of the room, situated on the ceiling. There is also a two-sided mirror window, located on the other side of the wall, in the room. Klaus feels slightly nervous inside this interrogation room, and he has no idea what the police are going to tell him. Klaus waits for several more minutes, until someone walks into the room. Klaus is slightly shocked, upon seeing who the person who walked in was. It was Detective Ross, who Klaus dealt with, previously, during Stuart's death. Upon realizing this, Klaus shakes his head, and starts to laugh to himself. Detective Ross is drinking a cup of coffee, and sets up coffee down. Detective Ross, also understands that he has met Klaus before, and as Detective Ross is setting his notebook on the table, he starts to jokingly speak to Klaus.

"Hey, I know you. You look familiar. Wait a minute, you're the radio DJ right?"

Klaus while looking down on the ground, starts to laugh, and shakes his head. After a few moments of silence, Klaus then starts to respond to Detective Ross.

"Yes, I spoke with you before. I was a radio DJ. Not anymore. I actually got fired. I actually don't know what the hell I am anymore, or what I'm even doing with my life."

Detective Ross then starts to read several documents, and takes a sip of his coffee. Detective Ross, while still reading the documents, speaks back at Klaus.

"I'm sorry, that's unfortunate. Hey, could I get you anything. Coffee, Orange Juice, soft drink? Are you hungry? Did you want me to get you something to eat?"

Klaus, with his vision still down towards the ground, responds directly to the detective.

"Oh, no thank you sir. Thank you for offering, but I'm fine thank you. Sir, if you don't mind me asking, how long is this gonna take? Because my car is back at the scene, and if this is going to be a while, that's fine, I just wanted you to know about my car."

Detective Ross takes another sip of his coffee, and responds back to Klaus.

"Oh, this won't be that long. We just want to ask you a few questions as to what happened, and I'll let the other detectives know, that your car is back at the highway, and they will give you guys a ride back, unless something comes up, but I don't think that it will."

Klaus then looks up from the ground, and starts to give the detective a strange look.

"Something comes up? What do you mean by that?"

Detective Ross takes another sip of his coffee, while he is staring at all of the documents, as he is staring at the documents, Detective Ross then responds directly back to Klaus.

"Well, from what we gathered, this was just an unfortunate freak accident that happened. We are aware that the victim was a friend of yours. We pretty much already have the details, but we want to make sure we have all the stories and events correct, so that nobody is lying."

Detective Ross then sets his cup of coffee down on the table. At this exact moment, Klaus then starts to look at the camera that is located at the corner of the ceiling. Klaus then takes another look at the two-way mirror on the other side of the room, and he continues to feel nervous and anxious. Concurrently the rest of the guys, are also being interviewed, and interrogated by other detectives. The police simply want to make sure, each man has the same story, and that there are no discrepancies, or any contradictions, as to what happened. Detective Ross, starts to ask Klaus several questions, about how the entire night went. Detective Ross asks how Klaus met Ernest, and the purpose for all of the men being there. Klaus is bluntly honest with the detective, as to how everything panned out the way it did. Klaus gives the detective web links, of the show that himself, and the rest of the guys produce. Klaus, does not tell any fibs to the detective, and gives him an honest relay, and description, as to everything that happened. Klaus was very confident, that the other guys were giving the police the same story. Klaus wasn't worried at all that their stories would be flipped or mixed, which in turn, would get himself, and the rest of the guys, probably into trouble. As Klaus continues to answer the questions that Detective Ross gives, Klaus still tries to get his mind used to the fact, that Ernest isn't here. It's still sudden, and Klaus has to simply understand and accept this. After speaking with Detective Ross, for over an hour, the detective explains to Klaus, that he will be right back, and leaves the room. Detective Ross returns to the room several minutes later, and speaks.

"Okay, so the suspect doesn't seem to have any next of kin, or any family. So, if you know of any relatives of his that we are unaware of, let us know."

Klaus then starts to look down at the ground again, silent. Klaus then starts to remember, that Ernest mentioned to him, that he did not have any family. Klaus then feels very upset, and he realizes that virtually, himself, and the rest of the guys, acted as Ernest family. So the fact that they were the only support system that Ernest had, it made feel Klaus even more guilty and depressed, that Ernest passed away, through indirect actions, from the other guys. Klaus then starts to gather his thoughts for a bit, and he eventually responds back to Detective Ross.

"No, he didn't have any family. We were kinda like his family, and he didn't have anybody else. He was a janitor, that kept a solitary life. He was a very kind and nice man."

Detective Ross takes a sip of his coffee, and then starts to speak back to Klaus.

"I see. Well in that case, as he had no other family, we will hand the death rights over to you, as after talking to your friends, it seems the situation all matches. I'm really sorry."

Detective Ross, then once again excuses himself out of the room, and is gone for several minutes. Klaus still tries to calm himself down during this time, and continues to feel very uncomfortable, inside the interrogation room. Klaus feels much pressure, and this entire situation at the police station, is giving Klaus much anxiety and turmoil. Klaus continues to patiently wait for Detective Ross to come back, wondering what he is going to ask him, when he returns. Detective Ross then arrives back into the room, and hands Klaus several documents. As Klaus is reading the documents the detective handed to him, Detective Ross then starts to speak.

"Here is a copy of the investigation report. Your friend is being examined by the coroner, and we will give you a full report of that later. Again, I'm really sorry for your loss, sir."

Klaus then nods his head, and shakes Detective Ross hand. Detective Ross then speaks.

"Alright that's about it. We talked to your friends, and it doesn't seem like you guys are hiding anything, or we're up to no good. This just seems like an unfortunate situation. Again, I'm sorry for your loss. You have my number, if you have any additional information. Thank you."

Klaus once again nods his head, and Detective Ross, walks out of the room. Klaus then starts to look down on the ground, and shakes his head. Klaus remains in silence for several minutes, still not having much idea, as to what is currently going on. Klaus wishes that he could turn back time, before any of these events started. Klaus wishes that Ernest never walked in front of the truck. Altogether, Klaus wishes that he never even agreed to cover the police chase anyways. Klaus will always feel a type of guilt over this. It was because Klaus wanted a story that was entertaining to the viewers to cover. It was because Klaus was simply thinking about the attention and coverage, and reception, and prestige, that he didn't stop to think, about the safety of the other guys, would also be a concern. Klaus remains looking down on the ground for several more minutes, until a police officer walks into the room, and informs Klaus, that he is free to go. The police officer hands Klaus his identification back. As Klaus is walking out of the room, he sees, Dan, Jerome, Paul, and Bill, standing in the lobby of the police station. The men, are not speaking to each other, and all decide to remain silent at this time. Directly after this, the men all get back into a police van, and drive back to the location, where Klaus vehicle is. Once the men arrive back at the location, still remaining silent, they all get into Klaus SUV. Dan sits in the passenger seat. Klaus starts the engine, and heads directly back to the house. This was a very awkward, and silent car ride, with the men still under much pressure and stress. The ride back to the house was rather quick, as it is now late, and traffic is light. Once Klaus reaches his residence, the men all get out of the car, and walk into the house. Klaus immediately directs himself to the kitchen, and grabs a beer out of the refrigerator.

Jerome, Paul, and Bill, all take a seat in the living room, extremely silent. Klaus, who is still in the kitchen, takes several gulps of his beer, and starts to shake his head. Dan, who is in the kitchen as well, stares deeply at Klaus, and shakes his head. Klaus doesn't acknowledge Dan, and simply walks into the living room, with the rest of the men. Klaus takes a seat on his recliner, and Klaus starts to sit back, calming himself down. At this time, Dan who is in the kitchen, starts to open up the kitchen cabinets, Dan then starts to act erratically, and starts to throw several dishes on the kitchen floor, shouting during the process.

"Fuck! Ernest! I love you Ernest! Ernest! It's not fair. Fuck! I love you Ernest!"

Upon realizing this, Paul and Klaus get up, and leave the living room. Jerome and Bill watch Dan, feeling disappointed. Paul and Klaus then start to console Dan. Dan and Paul then hug tightly, while Klaus grabs a broom, and starts to clean up the large mess Dan has made, by smashing the dishes on the ground. Klaus while sweeping up the mess, notices Dan has cut his hand, as a result of throwing the dishes. Klaus then gives Dan a warm towel, and hands it to Dan. Klaus then shakes his head, and returns to sweeping. Klaus then, speaks to Dan.

"Dan, I understand you're upset man. Go in the living room with Paul, okay?"

Even though Dan does not respond, he does obey Klaus orders, and walks out of the kitchen with Paul, into the living room. Paul continues to comfort Dan. Klaus, as he is sweeping the cups, bowls, and plates, Dan smashed on the floor, starts to shake his head and laughs. Klaus it not angry at Dan, despite the fact he smashed several dishes on the ground. Klaus realizes that Dan is upset over Ernest's death, and is allowing him to grieve and accept this. So Klaus is not angry or mad at Dan for the scene that he caused, with throwing the dishes. Klaus manages to finish sweeping up the mess Dan made, and throws all the broken pieces of dishes, away in the trash. Klaus then immediately returns back to the living room, with the rest of the men. Klaus then takes a seat back on his recliner, and leans back on the recliner, relaxing himself. The men remain quiet for several minutes, until Dan decides to speak to all the men.

"So, we're gonna have a funeral for Ernest right? It's like you guys don't even care that he's gone. Like when we left the house, Ernest was still alive. He's not now. Y'all don't care."

Klaus who is sitting in his recliner, looks up, and shakes his head. Paul continues to comfort Dan at this time, and Paul starts to rub Dan's back. Paul then softly speaks to Dan.

"It's okay, we all are missing Ernest Dan. We do care, it's just, we are in shock, like you're in shock. Take all the time you need Dan. We're here for you and everything is fine."

Dan then shoves Paul off of him, and then starts to loudly shout to all of the men.

"What the hell? Everything is fine? Ernest is dead damn it. He's not coming back. His stuff is all in that bedroom, and I have to look it at. He's fucking dead. Ernest! No! Why?"

Dan then starts to get up from the sofa, and walks into his bedroom. Dan slams the door shut behind him. The rest of the men, remain silent at this. The men remain silent for nearly an hour. They are allowing Dan to grieve, and are going to give him space. As time continues on, Bill eventually excuses himself off to bed. Paul then soon directs himself to bed as well. Not long after that, Jerome directs himself to bed too. Klaus is the only person left in the living room, and continues to sit on his recliner. Klaus, unlike the other men, does not head off to bed. Klaus instead, takes out his pack of cigarettes, and walks out onto the balcony. Klaus, while out on the balcony, lights one of his cigarettes, and stares out of the distance, looking at the night sky. Noticing how the sky gives off a light brown color. Klaus uses this time to reflect, and recap, how everything happened tonight. Klaus remains looking at the calm night sky, and looking at the ocean view as well. This was truly an unfortunate night, and it is yet another event Klaus has been faced with, that he must deal with, and overcome. Klaus remains on the balcony smoking his cigarette, also feeling concerned about Dan. The death of Ernest, is causing much strain towards Dan, and Dan is accepting this, and grieving. Klaus eventually leaves from the balcony, and walks into his bedroom. Klaus then changes into his sleep clothes, and drifts off to sleep.

The next morning, Klaus awakens rather earlier than he usually does. It is 9 a.m., and Klaus gets up out of bed, trying not to wake Jerome. Klaus then starts to walk towards the kitchen, to get himself a cup of coffee. Remarkably, Klaus notices that Dan is in the kitchen as well. Dan is in his sleep clothes, sitting at the kitchen counter, silently looking down. Klaus does not speak to Dan at all. Klaus starts to prepare his coffee, continuing to ignore Dan. At this time, Dan, while still looking down at the ground, softly speaks to Klaus.

"Hey man. Tell the guys I'm sorry about last night. I just really miss Ernest. I don't know how I'm gonna accept this, or deal with this, but I have to. I'm sorry for how I acted. I'm sorry."

Dan then immediately gets up, and starts to hug Klaus from behind. Klaus turns around, and returns the hug as well back to Dan. Klaus and Dan continue to hug tightly, for several more moments. Dan then starts to walk away from the kitchen, and speaks to Klaus.

"I'm gonna go back to bed. I didn't get any sleep last night. Catch you later."

Klaus takes a sip of his coffee, and nods his head. Dan then walks into his bedroom, and shuts the door. Klaus then takes his cup of coffee, and walks into the living room. Klaus takes a seat on his recliner, and starts to relax himself. This is now the morning after the events which happened last night. Tensions are still currently high, and the guys are still trying to adjust and wrap their minds around as to what happened. Klaus then starts to remember that Dan wanted to give Ernest a funeral, and Klaus agrees, that would be a great send off for Ernest, to have an event to remember Ernest's life. At this time, Klaus starts to brainstorm ideas, as to how the funeral is going to be planned. Klaus ultimately feels, that the final decisions should be up to Dan, but nevertheless, Klaus continues to brainstorm, more funeral arrangements. Klaus is willing to pay for Ernest's funeral, as Klaus also understands, that Ernest did not have life insurance, or any funeral coverage. Klaus continues to get his thoughts in proper order, and waits to talk about the funeral further later, with Dan. The rest of the guys soon wake, and being that this is the first morning at the house, without Ernest, things are very awkward and silent. The guys feel as though something is missing with Ernest not being there. Dan continues in his room, resting, while the other guys are going on about the day, rather silently. It was also now, that Klaus realized, that he would also have to tell their viewers, that Dan is gone. In the show that the guys did the night before, the live feed was cut off, before what happened. Klaus is unsure as to whether or not Ernest death, was covered in the news. Klaus then decides to make an announcement regardless, on social media, informing their audience that Ernest is no longer here. Klaus is amazed at the support of the viewers, offering their condolences. After making the announcement in regards to Ernest's death, Klaus carries on with the day, silent likewise, with the rest of the men. Later that evening, Dan awakens from resting, and joins the men in the living room. Dan takes a seat on the sofa, and steadily stares down at the ground, still feeling upset. Klaus notices how dejected Dan is, but decides to softly speak to him.

"Hey, so, we're gonna have a funeral for Ernest. The guys and I, are gonna let you plan how it goes. I'm gonna pay for it, so don't worry. You just tell me what you want to do. Okay?"

Dan, while his vision is still looking down, nods his head in agreement to Klaus. Klaus then stares at Dan, and smiles to himself, and Klaus returns to relaxing in his recliner. Time continues to pass on through the evening. Being that the men are hungry, Klaus decides to have pizza delivered for dinner, in an effort to cheer Dan up. Klaus is fully aware, that Dan is the person that usually does the cooking for the house, but Klaus is wanting to give Dan a break this time. The pizza arrives, and the men, including Dan, all start to eat. It seems that maybe for the first time, the men have recovered, and although they are still grieving over Ernest, his death seems to be understood at this point. Dan is still feeling upset and silent, although, he is calmer and content, that he was previously. The men finish their pizza, and they all remain in the living room, for the rest of the night, still in silence towards each other. The men then all eventually direct themselves to bed. The following morning, Klaus and Dan are in the living room, writing down the itinerary and plans for Ernest's funeral. Dan has decided, that he wishes to have Ernest's funeral private. The only people in attendance, would be the rest of the guys. Dan is allowing fans to send in sympathy and memorial message, but Dan doesn't want any fans, or audience members of their show to attend the funeral. Dan also wants Ernest to be buried. Although this is going to take a lot of planning, to pick out a coffin, and grave for Ernest, Klaus is willing to accept Dan's orders, and take care of everything.

Klaus then arranges a date for Ernest's funeral, which would take place the following Friday. In the meantime, Klaus and Dan, then make several errands, trying to get everything planned in order, for Ernest's funeral. Dan manages to pick out a coffin for Ernest, and Dan also picks out a grave marker for Ernest. Klaus and Dan, then make a stop at the flower shop, to pick out flower arrangements for the funeral. Now that most of the major plans of the funeral are out of the way, the men simply have to wait until the day of the funeral to arrive. Several days later, it is now the date of Ernest's funeral. The guys all wake up early, and have on suits. Although this is a private funeral, and they would be the only ones in attendance, Dan, and the rest of the guys, still wanted to dress formal, and appropriate. The men all get into Klaus SUV, and Klaus starts to drive to the cemetery, where the funeral will be held. The cemetery is located a moderate distance from the house. The climate for today is rather peculiar. The sky is overcast and gloomy, and it is not the typical California weather. Klaus approaches the cemetery, and parks his car. The men proceed to get out of the vehicle, to the funeral location. There are several flower pieces around Ernest's coffin, which is closed. Although the guys did manage to see Ernest's body at the mortuary earlier, in which the embalmers dressed him, for the actual funeral, Dan requested that Ernest have a closed casket. Even though Klaus and the men are the only visitors at the funeral, Klaus did hire a rabbi, to officiate the funeral. Although Ernest was not Jewish, Klaus is sure that Ernest would not mind, the rabbi being there. Not long after the men approaching the location, the guys all take a seat, sitting in front of Ernest's coffin, with the rabbi being situated at the pulpit, located in the center. Soon directly after, the funeral officially starts. The rabbi then makes a silent prayer in front of Ernest's coffin, and then speaks to the men.

"Hello Gentlemen. Although I do not know the deceased personally, I am terribly sorry for your loss. I know he was an amazing and fantastic man, that will be missed. I'm sorry."

The rest of the guys listen to the rabbi, as he continues on officiating the funeral. The funeral seems to be rather solemn for the rest of the guys. Dan is trying his best to keep himself together, although it's only natural for him to feel upset. Dan starts to cry heavily, as the rabbi continues speaking. Klaus notices that Dan feels terribly upset, and Klaus starts to rub Dan's back. Jerome, Paul, and Bill, silent listen to the rabbi officiate the funeral. Several more minutes pass of the rabbi giving his respects to Ernest. Eventually the rabbi then speaks to the men.

"Okay, if there is anyone that would like to say any final words at this time. Please do."

Klaus then immediately gets up, and walks to the pulpit. Klaus is silent for a few seconds. Klaus takes off his glasses, and Klaus starts to rub his eyes. Klaus then starts to erupt in tears, and is unable to speak. The guys watch Klaus, feeling upset as well. Klaus continues to gather his emotions for several more seconds. Klaus puts his glasses back on, and then speaks.

"Ernest was a lovely man. Although the circumstances as to how I met him, were strange. He was a janitor at my radio station, and went into my studio my accident. The rest is history, and he was an amazing, kind, wonderful, and lovely man. I am going to terribly miss him."

Klaus then takes of his glasses once more, and once again, starts to cry. Klaus remains at the pulpit for nearly a minute. Klaus then returns to his seat, and continues to sob. Directly following that, Jerome decides to walk up to the pulpit, and starts to speak.

"Ernest was the nicest guy I ever met. He was very funny, and his energy and spirit, were lovely. This guy didn't have a mean bone in his body. He was just that kind. I had a great friendship with Ernest, and we are all going to miss him deeply."

Jerome then returns back to his seat, crying heavily. Paul is the next to get up and speak. Paul walks up to the pulpit, and takes his glasses off. Tears are running down Paul's face, and he struggles to get his words out. Paul puts his glasses back on, and speaks.

"Ernest, man. I admit that Ernest and I, didn't know each other long, and I'm now wishing and regretting I spend more time with him. But the memories I have with him, he's just an all-around delight. He was a lovely man. We miss him. We all love him. Goodbye Ernest."

Paul then starts to wipe more tears from his face, as he continues to cry. Paul then returns back to his seat, and Bill is the next to get up, and say his peace, towards Ernest.

"Ernest. Like with Paul, I didn't get to interact with him, as much as I wanted to. But he was very kind, and nice. He was very polite and kind, and he was a joy to be around. We are going to miss him, and we love him. Rest in peace, Nephew. We love you."

Bill then walks over to Ernest coffin, and starts to rub the top of it. Bill then returns back to his seat. Once Bill is seated, the guys all remain silent. At this time, Dan is the only one left, not to say his final words to Ernest. However, a minute passes, and Dan remains at his seat. The guys continue to remain silent, and assume Dan will walk up to the pulpit, when he is ready, and when he is comfortable. Dan then eventually does get up from his seat, and walks over to the pulpit, to say his final words to Ernest. Dan then approaches the pulpit and speaks.

"I never would though I would be doing this. Losing Ernest, I am still shocked, beyond belief, and I refuse to accept any of this. But, I know Ernest would have wanted me to be strong. I love you Ernest. I will remember you always. I'm your wingman, remember Ernest? Ha Ha. I love you Ernest. You rest and sleep well. I love you Ernest. Goodbye friend. Goodbye buddy."

Dan then walks over to Ernest's coffin, and starts to lay his head on top of it, rubbing it as well. The rest of the guys don't disrupt Dan, and give him his time, to be with Ernest. Dan continues to lay his head on Ernest coffin, for several minutes. Dan then starts to cry heavily, and has a wave of sadness, run through his entire body. Dan then calms himself down, and starts to pat the top of Ernest's coffin, nodding his head. Dan then kisses the top of Ernest's coffin and continues to rub the top of the coffin. Dan then silently speaks to himself.

"I love you Ernest! Goodbye. I love you Ernest!"

Dan then while looking down, and continuing to cry, returns back to his seat. Klaus then starts to rub the back of Dan's back, to comfort him. The men have all said their final words to Ernest, and have properly given him, the final send off. The men, Dan especially, continue to feel sad, and full of emotions. The rabbi at this time, starts to say his final words, giving Ernest a more official send off. The rabbi then concludes the funeral. Klaus, and the rest of the men, shake the rabbi's hand, and the rabbi leaves the funeral. Klaus, Dan, Jerome, Paul, and Bill, all remain at the funeral, still in their emotions, and feeling deep sadness. The men continue to sit at the funeral for quite some time, still silent. Eventually, after all the silence, Dan eventually gets up from his seat, and starts to speaks to all the men.

"So, I don't know about you guys, but I'm starving, and I'm really hungry. So why don't we all get something to eat? Klaus, it's on you, and you're paying though right? Ha Ha."

Klaus looks down at the ground, and laughs, while shaking his head. Soon after, the rest of the men all get up, and start to walk out of the funeral. The men all get into Klaus SUV, and Klaus immediately drives to TGI Friday's. A restaurant that specializes in American comfort food, and also barbecue food. The restaurant is not that far from the funeral, and Klaus soon approaches the restaurant. The men all walk inside, and a waitress situates all of them, at a table, located in the back of the restaurant. As the men are seated, they start to all silently read their menu's. Klaus would take glances at Dan, taking note of how Dan seems to be calmer, and collected, than he was previously. Klaus had no issue at all, treating Dan, and the rest of the men to a meal. Klaus was happy he was able to give Dan a funeral as well, and Dan was allowed to properly grieve over Ernest. As Klaus continues to read the menu, Klaus, although he is happy that he, and the rest of the men are together at the restaurant for the moment, and for now, Klaus has no idea, as to what the men are going to do now. Is the show going to go on? What are the men now going to do without Ernest? Klaus doesn't have the answers to these questions at the moment, but for right now, he just wants to enjoy his meal with the rest of the guys. The waitress arrives back at the table, and the men all give the waitress their orders. Klaus orders a Steak Dinner, with Mashed Potatoes. Jerome orders the Buffalo Wings. Paul orders a Bacon Cheeseburger with French Fries. Bill orders the Grilled Chicken Dinner with Rice. Dan orders Barbecue Ribs, and Mashed Potatoes. The men start to have small talk with each other, directly after this. The waitress then returns back to the table, with the food the men ordered. The guys then all start to eat their food, and they are enjoying their meals. The men are happy and pleased, and they continue to eat their food, and are happy bonding with each other.

The men then soon finish eating, and the waitress returns to the table, with the check. Klaus pays for the check, and leaves a tip for the waitress. The men then directly get up from the table and leave out of the restaurant. Once the men are all back into the car, Klaus starts the engine, and proceeds down the road. While driving, Dan then turns to Klaus, and speaks.

"Hey man, how about we get some dessert? How about some Ice Cream? That's what Ernest would have wanted right? This is also on you too right? Ha Ha."

Klaus then looks over at Dan, and smiles at him. Klaus then directs his vision back towards the road, and shakes his head, and laughs. Klaus then responds back to Dan.

"Okay, you want Ice Cream Dan? I'll get you Ice Cream. You feel better now? Ha Ha."

Klaus and Dan then share eye contact with each other, and they both laugh. Klaus then drives to the same Ice Cream shop that the men all went to previously. The men order their Ice Cream, and Klaus then drives to a park, located near the beach. The day is still overcast and gloomy, but it is still makes a very picturesque and lovely scene. The men enjoy their Ice Cream at the park, and are having trivial talk with one another. The men finish their Ice Cream, but they remain at the park for several more minutes. This park gives a nice view of the ocean, and the guys continue to be amazed at the view. Eventually the men do get up, and leave out of the park. Klaus pats Dan on the back, and the men all walk back towards Klaus SUV. Klaus then starts to head directly back to the house. Once Klaus has arrived back at the house, Klaus starts to stretch himself. Klaus then immediately walks to the kitchen, and starts to take a beer out of the refrigerator. Klaus sets the beer down on the counter, and starts to loosen his neck tie. Klaus then opens up the beer, and takes several sips of it. Klaus then starts to watch what the other men are doing. Jerome, Dan, and Paul, walk themselves to the living room. Jerome starts to play a video game, on Klaus Xbox console. Paul and Bill, then start to have their custom chess game. Bill takes a seat on the recliner, with Paul sitting on the end of the sofa, adjacent to Bill. Paul starts to situate all the pieces on the board. Klaus then looks directly in front of him, and notices that Dan is sitting at the kitchen counter, with his vision pointing down. Klaus is slightly concerned over Dan. Klaus takes a sip of his beer, and then speaks to Dan.

"Hey man, are you alright? Just checking up on you, that's all. Ha Ha."

Dan then looks up, and gives Klaus a smile. Dan then walks over to the refrigerator, and pulls out a beer. Dan starts to take several gulps of the beer, and responds to Klaus.

"Oh, yeah. I'm alright. Hey. Let's go out on the balcony. I have to tell you something."

Klaus then nods his head, and takes another sip of his beer. Klaus and Dan then immediately seem to do what they do normally, and they both direct themselves towards the balcony. Once on the balcony, Klaus shuts the door behind them. Klaus then takes out his carton of cigarettes, and takes a cigarette out. Klaus then hands the carton to Dan. Dan takes a cigarette out of the carton as well. Klaus starts to light the cigarette, and Klaus then hands Dan the lighter. Klaus and Dan, both start to smoke their cigarettes, being silent to each other. At this time, Klaus pulls out his phone, and starts to look at sports scores. While having his vision directed to scrolling on his phone, Klaus then starts to speak to Dan.

"So, what did you want to tell me? What was so important, that you had to bring me all the way out here, to tell me? Ha Ha?"

Dan takes another puff of his cigarette, and has his vision facing forward. Dan then gets up, and starts to fix Klaus shirt collar. Klaus, still has his vision still directed at his phone, and laughs. Dan finishes fixing Klaus collar, and returns to his seat. Dan then speaks.

"I wanted to tell you, that your shirt collar was crooked. Don't worry. It's okay man. I fixed it for you. You're looking really dapper in that suit Klaus. Ha Ha."

Klaus shakes his head, and laughs. Dan laughs as well. Klaus takes another puff of his cigarette, and while still looking at his phone, Klaus speaks to Dan.

"Ha Ha. Okay. But that wasn't it. No, seriously. What did you really want to tell me?"

Dan takes another puff of his cigarette, and starts to look out towards the distance. Dan then looks down on the ground, and runs his hands through his hair. Dan then speaks to Klaus.

"I wanted to say, that you're my best friend in the world. Thank you DJ K. Really."

Klaus then finishes looking at his phone, and put his phone in his pocket. Klaus then gives Dan eye contact, and they smile at each other. Klaus and Dan then fist bump each other. Dan takes a sip of his beer, and laughs to himself. Klaus as well takes a sip of his beer, laughing as well. Klaus then has his vision facing forward, and silently responds to Dan.

"I appreciate that. Thanks man. I'm really sorry about Ernest. If I could turn back time, I would, but I'm sorry man. Forgive me. Dan, you're my best friend man, and I love you. We all have to stick together now, being that Ernest is gone. We got this though. Right buddy?"

Dan then turns his vision towards Klaus, and nods his head, and laughs. Dan then starts to cry, which when Klaus notices Dan crying, he cries as well. The both of them are crying tears of joy however. Klaus and Dan have officially reconciled their friendship. Klaus then responds.

"That's right buddy. Oh, by the way. Just so you know. The Dodgers beat the Red Sox. It was a close game throughout, and it ended up being Extra Innings. Ha Ha"

Dan then starts to laugh, and Klaus laughs as well. Klaus and Dan then first bump once again. Klaus and Dan then turn their direction towards the ocean. Klaus then shakes his head, and laughs.

CHAPTER 15:

ELECTION NIGHT

The following morning, Dan is the first of the men to wake up. For the first time since Ernest's death, Dan decides to make breakfast for the guys. It seems that Dan is now the honorary chef, and cook for the household. Although the guys sort of already inadvertently made this the case. The other guys do cook from time to time, but Dan is the one that does most of the cooking for the guys. The men always enjoy Dan's cooking anyways, so it's a win/win situation. Dan has planned, and sorted out a very large breakfast for the men. Dan has decided to cook the guys pancakes, with eggs, bacon, sausage, and biscuits. Dan has also gone to the supermarket and bought some fresh pineapple for the guys to enjoy as well. While Dan is cooking the breakfast, he starts to look at the "Good Mythical Morning" podcast, with Rhett and Link. Dan enjoys the podcast very much. Both he, and Ernest, would listen to it quite often. As Dan continues to cook, Klaus eventually awakens. Klaus notices that Jerome is asleep, and he gently gets out of bed, trying not to disturb Jerome. Klaus ends up tucking Jerome, who is still sleeping in the bed, with the covers. Klaus then smiles to himself, and walks out of the bedroom. Klaus directs himself to the kitchen, where he notices Dan cooking. Dan then speaks to him.

"Good morning man. How are you feeling? Got your coffee already made right here."

Klaus then approaches Dan, and gives him a fist bump. Klaus then starts to pour himself a cup of coffee. Klaus takes sips of his coffee, and looks outside the window of the kitchen. It is a nice sunny day. The climate is neither too hot, or too cold, and there are light clouds in the sky. It is a wonderful day, and typical California weather. As Dan continues to cook, he decides to tell Klaus some news he recently found out about. As Dan is preparing breakfast, he speaks to Klaus.

"Oh yeah, um. I was going through my phone, just reading random stories today. You're not gonna believe this. But, your boss, well, your old boss, Larry Weston, he died. It said it was in a car wreck on the highway last night, and it was pretty bad. Just thought you show know."

Klaus then takes another sip of his coffee, and looks down on the ground. His initial reaction is one of silence, and Klaus doesn't know what to think. Although Klaus did have a good mutual professional relationship with Mr. Weston at first, the fact the fired him from the studio, made Klaus not appreciate him anymore, and more hatred over him, began to form. Klaus feels torn, as he knows he did not leave on the best of terms with Mr. Weston. Klaus was never able to recover from that, and now that Mr. Weston is dead, there is nothing Klaus can do, except deal with it, and live with it. On the other hand, Klaus feels deep sorrow, and sadness, for Mr. Weston's death, and despite how they left on a sour note, Klaus also has to put into consideration the positive and happy experiences, that he had with Mr. Weston. Klaus doesn't even know that much about Mr. Weston's family, or whether or not there are funeral plans arranged. Klaus continues to sip his coffee, and while Klaus is staring at the ground, he speaks to Dan.

"I see. That's unfortunate, and I know his wife and kids are upset. I think he has a son that's thirteen, so wow. Aww man. Thank you for telling me this."

Dan continues to prepare breakfast, and nods his head. Klaus has decided to read, and check in about Mr. Weston's death at a later time, although he is still taken back by hearing this. Klaus takes his cup of coffee, and walks into the living room, and takes a seat on the recliner. Klaus then starts to sit back, and relax in the recliner, resting his eyes. About twenty minutes later, Bill awakens, and joins the rest of the men. Bill takes a seat on the other recliner in the living room, next to Klaus. Once Bill has taken a seat, he opens up his newspaper and starts to read it. As Bill is skimming through the newspaper articles, he starts to speak to Klaus.

"Good morning Nephew. So, are we going to do one of our walks today? It's a great day, it seems perfect. After breakfast, let's take a walk. Does that sound good to you Nephew?"

Klaus, who is still relaxing in his recliner with his eyes closed, nods his head. Klaus is silent for several seconds, but he does respond softly back to Bill.

"Of course Uncle. If you want to take a walk, that's okay. Sounds like fun."

In actuality, Klaus wasn't in the mood to take a walk with Bill. Klaus does understand that Bill enjoys the walks to he takes with him, so for the sake of making his Uncle happy, Klaus decides to go along with the walks, and outings with this Uncle, regardless. Klaus also comes to realization, that the weather for today is fantastic, so Klaus is running out of excuses, to get out of going on the walk with his Uncle Bill. During this time, Klaus informs Bill, that his boss Mr. Weston has passed away. Bill respectfully responds to the news, offering sympathy and prayers, to Mr. Weston's family. Klaus continues to relax on the recliner, as Bill, steadily reads his newspaper. Dan is still preparing breakfast. This is seeming, that today is going to be an ordinary, and typical day. Despite the fact of Klaus becoming aware of Mr. Weston's death, it seems that news didn't affect, or disrupt the overall energy of the day. About fifteen minutes later, Jerome awakens, and joins the rest of the men. Jerome walks into the kitchen, and pours himself a glass of orange juice. Jerome then directs himself to the living room, with Klaus and Bill. Once he is in the living room, Klaus informs Jerome of Mr. Weston's passing. Jerome is sorry to hear the news, and gives well wishes to Mr. Weston's family. A few minutes later, Dan has now finished preparing breakfast, and Klaus, Jerome, and Bill, all walk into the kitchen to grab a plate of food. Congruently at this time, Paul also wakes up, and instinctively, he walks into the kitchen, and grabs a plate of food. The guys all start to eat breakfast at the kitchen counter. While they are eating, Klaus then informs Paul of Mr. Weston death. Paul respectfully understands this news, and gives proper respect to Mr. Weston's family. The men all eat their breakfast in silence, and they are all calm, and content with each other.

After the men have finished eating, Bill gets up, and puts his plate in the sink. Following that, Bill then starts to stretch himself, and speaks to Klaus.

"That was a good breakfast. Thanks Dan. So Nephew, are you ready for our walk? I'm gonna go take my medication, and then I'll be all set to go. Okay?"

Klaus, who staring out the window, takes sips of his coffee, and silently responds to Bill.

"Alright. Okay Uncle. Just let me know when you're ready, and we can go."

Bill nods his head, and walks away from the kitchen. Directly following this, Jerome starts to gather all of the guys plates, and does the dishes, like he customarily does. Dan and Paul walk into the living room, and Paul takes out his sketch pad, and starts to draw. Dan starts to relax on the sofa, and watches the television, which features a car customization reality show, in which mechanics modify cars. Klaus remains in the kitchen, and watches Jerome do the dishes. Klaus smiles to himself, and then directs his vision out the window. Minutes later, Klaus and Bill, leave out of the house, and go the park for their walk. Klaus arrives at the park, which is not that far from the house, and Klaus and Bill, get out of the vehicle. Once again, the both of them walk through the trail, at the park. Klaus and Bill converse with one another, and are having a nice time. Klaus was happy that he and Bill decided to go for a walk this morning, and it was simply, too lovely of a day, not to do it. Time is passing by rather quickly, with Klaus and Bill bonding during another one of their walks. As they are both approaching the top vantage point of the trail, Bill starts to take a look at the view, in which you can see the ocean. Klaus who is standing right next to Bill, also is amazed at the view. The both of the men continue to rest at this point, and look around, being amazed at the environment. As this is happening, Bill starts to each into his pocket, and pulls a metal out. While staring at the metal, Bill speaks to Klaus.

"Nephew, I don't know if you remember, but I was injured pretty badly during the war. I got shot in my shoulder, and I guess I'm lucky to be here. Figured the war, is what would take me out. Actually, it's my cardiovascular system that might. Ha Ha."

Klaus who is looking out towards the distance nods his head, and responds to Bill.

"I remember you telling me that Uncle. You're a military man, so I know you have a lot of stories to tell, and you experienced so many adventures. You're still here though Uncle."

Bill stares deeply at the metal he's holding, and grabs it tightly. Bill then grabs Klaus hands, and gives the metal he was holding, to Klaus. Klaus who is puzzled, looks down at the metal. Bill then directs his vision back towards the distance, and he softly speaks to Klaus.

"Nephew, I want you to have this. This is my purple heart. They give this to all the soldiers who get injured during battle. It's not that I don't trust Paul, I do. I trust you a little more than him, and I know you'll manage to keep it safe. I appreciate it Nephew."

Klaus then stares at the metal Bill handed to him, and quickly responds back.

"Tell you what Uncle. I'll put this in the living room shelf, and that way you know it's gonna be safe, and all the guys can look at it. Is that alright with you Uncle?"

Bill, who is still looking away out towards the distance, responds to Klaus.

"Alright Nephew, I'm fine with that. You know, I might not be here for much longer. Paul and I went to the doctor, and they told me bad news. My heart is bad. So, I'm gonna try to stick around for as long as I can, but I love you Nephew, and I love all you boys. So yeah."

Klaus then puts Bill's purple heart metal into his pocket. Klaus walks up to Bill, and starts to massage Bill on the back. Klaus then wraps his arm behind Bill, and softly speaks.

"Uncle, you're not going anywhere. You're going to be fine. Don't say things like that. Me, and the rest of the guys are gonna take care of you, and you're going to be okay."

Bill silently nods his head in agreement with Klaus. Both of the men remain at the top of the trail for several more minutes, looking at the beautiful view. Eventually, they both continue back down, to the end of the trail. Once they are finished with their walk, Klaus and Bill, get back into the vehicle, and direct themselves back to the house. Once they are back into the house, Klaus, as promised, puts Bill's purple heart award, on the living room shelf. Congruently, Bill takes a seat on the recliner in the living room, and starts to read his newspaper. Once Klaus is finished putting the metal on the living room shelf, Klaus speaks to Dan, Jerome, and Paul, who were staring at Klaus the entire time, he was doing this.

"Don't move this. This is Uncle's purple heart award. It's a big deal and special. Okay?"

The rest of the guys nod their heads in response to Klaus. After putting Bill's metal on the shelf, Klaus takes a seat on his recliner, and relaxes. The men seem to be doing their own thing, and not many eventful, or noteworthy things are happening. Until ten minutes later, Dan, who is continuing to watch his vehicle customization and modification show on the television, goes to commercial break. During the commercial, the guys notice the announcer speaking.

"Attention everyone. For today only, the U.S.S. Iowa, is having friends and family day. Any active duty, or military veteran, can bring guests, for a complimentary tour of the U.S.S. Iowa, Battleship. There will be a banquet dinner, and an open bar. Today only. Be there!"

The commercial then ends, and Jerome gets up from the sofa, and walks over to Klaus who is sitting on his recliner. Klaus, who wasn't paying much mind to the commercial, didn't seem that intrigued or interested. Jerome then starts to excitedly speak to Klaus.

"Hey, you saw that commercial right. Uncle is a veteran, so we can go to the event right? We aren't even doing anything anyways. Let's get out the house, and go. Please?"

Bill, as he is reading his newspaper, then starts to respond to Klaus, defending Jerome.

"Nephew, he's got a point. I'll go, if you boys want to go. Say yes Nephew. Ha Ha."

Klaus then starts to look down on the ground, and shakes his head. Klaus then laughs to himself, and he runs his hands through Jerome's hair. Klaus then speaks to all of the men.

"Ah, alright. Why not? What the hell. Event doesn't start until 4 p.m. so we still have some time though. But around 4, we'll start to head out, and we can go to the event."

Jerome then immediately starts to jump up and down, and hugs Klaus. Jerome is very pleased and happy, that Klaus has agreed, for all the men, to attend the event. While Jerome continues to hug Klaus tightly, Klaus laughs in response to this. Jerome remains hugging Klaus, at the same time, happily responding to him.

"Oh, thank you Klaus so much. You're such a nice guy. Very reasonable, very kind, and understanding. Very forthright. Very gentle. Thank you, Thank you. Thank you. Ha Ha."

Jerome then walks over to where Bill is seated, and starts to hug him tightly as well. Bill then runs his hands through Jerome's hair, and smiles at him. Dan and Paul watch all of this, and smile. For the rest of the day, the guys anticipate going to the military museum. Eventually it is time for all of the men to leave out of the house. The men get into Klaus SUV, and they go to the U.S.S. Iowa Battleship, which isn't located that far from where the house is. Upon arriving there Klaus wasn't expecting the large amount of people to be present at the event. Klaus noticed, that there were hundreds of people there, and Klaus started to slightly second guess attending. Klaus normally doesn't like giant crowds, and it gives him much social anxiety. However, Klaus is willing to overcome this, and be a good sport, for the sake of the other guys. Bill seems to be happy to attend this event, and it gives him a chance to reflect on his military culture. Due to the fact Bill is as veteran, he, along with the other guys, are allowed admittance into the event. The event will feature a tour of the U.S.S. Iowa Battleship, which is followed by a banquet dinner, and also an open bar. The tour, which would be tour hours, would not start until 5 p.m. Until then, there is a promotional exhibition held, in which several companies and organizations have booths. These booths are asking people to sign petitions, or they are wishing for people to sign up, or register on their company or business. Klaus, and the rest of the guys walk through the exhibition booths, mainly to kill time before the tour starts.

5 p.m. approaches, and it is now time for the battleship tour. There are several different tour guides, and the tours are split up into several groups, with each group being properly spaced away from each other. This is so the tour doesn't become too crowded, and each group has an equal amount of time, to experience all aspects of the ship. Klaus, and the rest of the guys, are a part of the same tour group. During the tour, the men all are educated on military history and Bill feels nostalgic during the tour, and is the most proud and happy to be there, out of all the men. The battleship is quite hold, and has a lot of history. The men continue on with the tour, with the tour guide pointing out specific locations and areas. During the tour, guests are allowed to see the ships engine room, the cafeteria of the ship, the upper deck of the ship, the Captains Quarter's area, the brig of the ship, the area where the soldiers slept, and they were also allowed to see the crew room of the ship. The guests were given a full thorough tour of the battleship. The tour, which lasted for several hours, allowed the guests of the tour, to be embraced, in a full experience of military culture. Once the tour was finished, the guys all left out, feeling glad, that they were educated, and immersed in the experience. Bill especially was pleased, and he was informing the guys about facts during the tour as well. The event was followed by a banquet dinner, which was free of charge, for all the quests. The banquet was held outside, and it was a nice venue, in which guests got a nice view of Wilmington, and the Los Angeles Harbor. The dinner included appetizers, main courses of chicken and side dishes, and there was also dessert. In addition to the meal, there was an open bar, in

which a bartender could prepare you a mixed drink, or bottled beer, free of charge.

Klaus manages to get himself a plate of food, and also gets himself a Vodka Cranberry cocktail. The other guys grab a plate of food as well, and also get themselves something to drink. Klaus takes a seat at the table, along with his other friends, and starts to eat. During their meal, the men continue to talk and speak with each other, and they continue to bond. Bill gives Paul a kiss on his cheek, and runs his hands through Paul's hair. Klaus starts to speak with Dan and Jerome, having trivial discussion. The men steadily eat their food. The day at the battleship, turned out to be a nice outing. The banquet meal that all the men got to experience afterwards, was a nice additional touch. The men soon start to eat their dessert, which consisted of your choice of either chocolate cake, or apple pie, topped with ice cream. As the men are all eating dessert, Klaus takes several glances over at Bill, and they smile at each other. Bill then gets out his seat, and walks over to the open bar, and gets himself another bottle of beer. Once Bill reaches the table with the rest of the guys, he wraps his arms around behind Klaus, and hugs him tightly. As Bill is hugging Klaus, he starts to whisper to him.

"Thank you Nephew. This evening was really fun, and I had a great time. Thank you."

Bill continues to hug Klaus, and Klaus takes a sip of his drink. Klaus then responds.

"Uncle, you know I'd do anything for you. I'm glad you're happy. You're welcome"

Bill then pats Klaus on the back, and returns to his seat. Klaus continues to enjoy the night, he is having with the rest of the guys. This was a moment they all needed. This was proof, that the group was somewhat getting back to normal, and that they were still strong together. The bond was still there, and the friendship they all have, still remains. Klaus continues to chat and mingle, with the other guys, as they eat their dinner, outside the dock of the battleship. As the men are finished with their dessert, they remain at the event for a little while longer, and they all continue converse with one another. Eventually, the men do decide to go home, when they notice that most of the other guests at the event, have left. Klaus, and the rest of the guys, get back into Klaus SUV, and Klaus directs himself straight home. Once they are back at the house, Paul walks into the living room, and grabs the chess set, located under the television. As he's setting the chess board up, Paul, while putting the pieces on the board, starts to talk.

"Bill, you owe me a match remember. Get over here, so I can beat you again. Ha Ha."

Bill then laughs to himself, and walks over where Paul is situated, and speaks to him.

"Are you kidding me? You mean so I can beat you. It's on. I'm ready. Let's go. Ha Ha."

Paul and Bill then start their chess match. Jerome walks into the living room as well, and starts to play on Klaus Xbox console. Klaus is in the kitchen, watching the rest of the guys, go on about their business. Dan who is in the kitchen as well, shakes his head, and is looking down at the ground. Dan then lethargically speaks to Klaus, as he continues to look down on the ground.

"I'm gonna go to bed man. I just feel really tired for some reason. Catch you later, okay?"

Klaus and Dan then fist bump, and Dan, who is clearly exhausted and tired, starts to walk to his bedroom. Klaus then pulls out his carton of cigarettes, and walks out to his balcony. While out on the balcony, Klaus starts to watch sports highlights on his phone, like he usually does. The rest of the night, aside from Dan going to bed early, seems typical. As hours go on, Paul and Bill then dismiss themselves off to bed. Jerome does the same, and goes to bed as well. Klaus remains on the balcony for quite some time, but he eventually follows suit with the other men, and goes to bed as well. For the following two weeks, things were very typical and normal. Klaus and Bill would continue to do their walks, every morning, well, almost every morning. Dan would continue to cook meals for the guys. Paul would continue doing his artwork, also playing chess matches with Bill in the meantime. Jerome would do his blogging, or he would play video games. Klaus typically kept to himself, and didn't bother the rest of the guys, and was the quietest, and reserved. However, one thing that remained on Klaus mind, was whether or not, the guys were going to return to their show. It was something that each guy was thinking about, but for no apparent reason, none of the men, brought it up publicly. Klaus started to become aware, that they have not done a show since Ernest passed away, and he feels that now is the correct and right time. They have taken a long enough break, and the time is now for them to return to their show. Klaus feels the only thing that's stalling and keeping them, is an event that Klaus feels is exciting enough for them to cover. Klaus would soon get his wish, as there was a very prolific event that was going to be in the news headlines soon. It was the election for Mayor of Redondo Beach. It wasn't a major election, like for President of the United States, or for Governor of California, or even for Mayor of Los Angeles. It was strictly an election held for the region, and area that Klaus and his group reside in, which is Redondo Beach.

Although, this event originally was intended not to be that notorious, it seems it has sparked controversy, as both candidates running for Redondo Beach Mayor, each have a level pegged support group, directed at them both. Both candidates identify as Democratic, but both have a very different political stances, and again, have different groups of supporters. Both candidates are currently council members of the city of Redondo Beach. The first candidate is Blake Nordstrom. Council member Nordstrom, is a middle aged, half Caucasian, half Mexican man, with salt and pepper hair. He is a handsome man with both a geeky, yet professional charm about him. His stances are more liberal leaning, and slightly open minded. He believes more on helping those in need, with community programs, offering free healthcare to citizens, and also his main stance, is making public transportation, and parking on city streets, more convenient. Council member Nordstrom, lives with his wife and young children. The other candidate, is William Greenwich. Council member Greenwich, is an older, gray haired man in his 60s, who wears glasses, and he's been in politics for a long time. His views are slightly more conservative, and old fashioned. His stances are more business related, and infrastructure related. His political stances, are to make city resources better, direct more business and companies to Redondo Beach, and better institutionalize, the overall business and conglomerate aspect of the city. Council member Greenwich lives with his wife, and has several adult children. Both candidates have done an equal amount of campaigning, and have done several events to sway voters. As a result, they both managed to gather an equal number of supporters for their campaign.

What's interesting, is that both candidates, seem to be favored by different guys in the group. Council member Nordstrom, is favored by Klaus and Dan. Council member Greenwich, is favored by Paul and Bill. Jerome doesn't favor any candidate, and is neutral, and doesn't plan to vote for either one, as he has not made his mind up yet. So with the Mayor election happening soon, this event is on everyone's mind. Including Klaus, and the rest of the men. Tuesday morning, the morning of the Mayor election arrived, and Klaus awakens early. Klaus walks into the kitchen, being the first of the guys to wake up today. Klaus has his usual cup of coffee, and takes several sips of it. As Klaus is sipping his coffee, he gets yet another bright idea. Klaus knows that the time to return to their show is now. Today, being that it's the day of the Mayor election, is the absolute perfect time, and it's going to be a major event in the city. Klaus knows that both sides are equally matched, and either candidate could win. Furthermore, bringing additional drama, and exposure, and controversy to the entire topic and event. As Klaus smiles to himself, knowing how wonderful this idea is, Dan awakens, and joins Klaus in the kitchen. Klaus and Dan fist bump, and Dan starts to pour himself a bowl of cereal. As Dan is making his cereal, Klaus continues to smile to himself, and starts to laugh. Dan gives a puzzled look to Klaus. Klaus steadily looks down towards the ground, and laughs to himself. Dan then speaks to him.

"Hey man what's so funny. What do you know, that I don't? Come on, tell me."

Klaus takes another sip of his coffee, and while looking down at the ground, speaks.

"Today is the mayor election, and I was thinking, that this would be a perfect time, to start our show again. We can report on the entire coverage down at City Hall. Both candidates are going to be there, on both sections of the City Hall building, so we can report on both sides."

Dan starts to eat his cereal, and continues to give Klaus a puzzled look. Dan then speaks.

"Yeah, no. I don't think so. Now is not a good time man, being election night. Yeah."

Klaus and Dan then give each other eye contact, and Klaus has an angry, disappointed look on his face. Although Dan is in agreement, that they should carry on with the show at some point eventually, Dan doesn't feel the election night, is the proper event to do so. Dan continues to eat his cereal, and he then asks Klaus a question, he is curious about.

"So, who are you voting for anyways. You're voting for Nordstrom, right? He's the only one out of the two, that I agree with. Nothing against the other guy, but I can't support him."

Klaus takes another sip of his coffee, and as he is walking to the living room, he speaks.

"Of course. I don't know who the rest of the guys are voting for, but I think they are gonna vote for Nordstrom as well. He is more up our alley, and yeah. It's a close race though."

Klaus takes a seat on his recliner, and starts to scroll through his phone. Klaus is not happy that Dan did not agree to cover the political event today, in an attempt to revive their news program. While Klaus is brainstorming some more, Jerome wakes up and joins the rest of the guys. Jerome directs himself to the kitchen and prepares himself a bowl of cereal. As he is doing that, he takes a seat at the counter, next to Dan. Jerome starts to speak to all of the men.

"Good morning boys. So, what's on the schedule for today? I can tell that you guys have something planned. I can feel your energy and aura, that you guys are hiding something. What?"

Klaus shakes his head, and remains quiet, as he is looking through his phone. Dan eats more of his cereal, and runs his hands through Jerome's hair. Dan then responds to Jerome.

"Oh nothing. Klaus just thought of a really stupid, and dumb idea. That we should do our show again tonight, and cover the Mayor election happening tonight. Yeah, I don't think so."

Jerome then stares at Klaus, who is still scrolling through his phone. Jerome simply silently nods his head in response to Dan, and returns to eating his cereal. Klaus, who heard both Dan and Jerome in the kitchen, shakes his head, and laughs. For several more minutes, the guys remain in silence, not speaking with each other. Klaus by the way, still is not willing to accept Dan's rejection, or refusal of doing the show. Klaus feels that he's going to act out his idea and plan, one way or the other. Not long after this, both Paul and Bill awaken, and join the other guys. Bill takes a seat on the recliner next to Klaus, and reads his newspaper. Paul walks into the kitchen, and makes himself a bowl of cereal. Dan fixes Bill a bowl of oatmeal, with strawberries in it. Dan hands the bowl of oatmeal to Bill. Bill then speaks to Dan.

"Oh, thank you Nephew. That was kind of you. I appreciate that."

Dan then pats Bill on the back, and returns to the kitchen. Before Bill starts to eat his oatmeal, Bill reaches into his pocket, and takes out two pill bottles. One bottle has one capsule left in it, whilst, the other bottle is empty. Bill seems alarmed, and concerned, at the empty pill bottle, but simply shrugs his shoulders. Bill puts the empty bottle into his pocket, and swallows the last pill from the other bottle. Klaus, out of curiosity, was starting at Bill open up the pill bottles. Klaus then returns to scrolling on his phone, and speaks to Bill.

"Everything alright Uncle? Is something wrong? You need me to get you something?"

Bill puts the other pill bottle into his pocket, and starts to eat his oatmeal. Bill continues eat his oatmeal, initially ignoring Klaus. Bill while still eating, swiftly responds back to Klaus.

"Oh yes. I'm fine Nephew. Thanks for asking. If I do need something, I'll let you know."

Klaus continues to look through his phone, and shakes his head and laughs. During this time, Paul gets up from the sofa, and puts his empty cereal bowl in the sink. Paul then remarkably has the thought of the election on his mind, and he speaks to all of the men.

"So, you guys are aware that it's election night tonight right? I know it's impolite to ask who you are going to vote for, but Bill and I are voting for Greenwich. He's more qualified."

Dan immediately turns his direction towards Paul, and starts to shout at him.

"What the hell? Greenwich is a bigot, and he's a jerk. What are you talking about? Nordstrom better win, and he's going to win. He's the better guy, and he needs to be Mayor."

Paul then takes his glasses off, and sets them on the kitchen counter, and crosses his arms. Dan and Paul menacingly stare at each other for several seconds. Paul then responds.

"You heard what the fuck I said. Greenwich is more qualified. Nordstrom doesn't know dick about politics. He's the people's puppet. His opinions don't matter, and he's gonna lose."

Dan then shakes his head at Paul, and Dan puts his bowl into the sink. Dan then speaks.

"I can't believe you man. Why the hell would you vote for that horrible man. Wow."

Jerome who is sitting at the kitchen counter, decides to speak to both Dan and Paul.

"Hey, hey. Gentleman. Alright. This is exactly why I hate politics. I'm not voting at all."

Paul puts his glasses back on, and massages Jerome on the back. Paul then walks back over to the living room, and sits on the sofa. During this time, Dan looks down on the ground, and shakes his head. Dan then smiles to himself, and starts to shout out to Klaus.

"Hey man. You want to do the show tonight at the election? Let's do it. Only so I can see the look on Paul's face, when Greenwich loses. This is perfect. Ha Ha. We're doing the show."

Klaus gets up from the recliner, and walks over to the kitchen where Dan is. Klaus and Dan stare at each other for several seconds. Klaus then hugs Dan tightly, and then gives him a fist bump. Klaus then returns back to the recliner in the living room, and both Dan and Klaus are smiling. Klaus then explains the plan he had, ever since he woke up today. The plan of him wanting to resume the news show that they all had, and covering election night, at city hall. It didn't take much convincing or coaxing at all, for Jerome, Paul, and Bill to also agree on the plan. Now that all the men are in agreement to resume the show, Klaus is happy his plan came into fruition. Another one of Klaus ideas managed to spring through. Although Dan was hesitant about the idea at first, it was his quarrel with Paul, that made him quickly change his mind. Dan understands how divided this event is, and how much controversy, and reception, this would give to their show. The guys kept their mind focused, to election night. The rest of the morning remained quiet, with Dan and Paul, refusing to speak to each other, after their argument over the political candidates. The election results were going to be read at 7 p.m., but the guys wanted to get down to city hall, slightly before that. The hours leading up for the guys to leave, Klaus started to get his equipment all situated. Klaus also went online, and made an announcement to their views and fans, that the wait is finally over. They are going to be doing another show, after long last. Although, Klaus on purpose, did not mention, that they were going to be at City Hall, as he wanted to keep the location of their broadcast, under suspense, and a secret for now.

The rest of the day, seemed to carry on rather fast. It was most likely due to the fact, the guys were all excited, to finally go back to doing their show. It was something they never thought they would be able to do again, but the time is now. The last show they covered, Ernest unfortunately passed away. Klaus feels he needs to keep the show going, out of legacy of Ernest. With it now being 4 p.m., the guys are now leaving the house, to start their show. It is now time for the action to begin, and the guys are ready, and prepared. The men all get inside of Klaus SUV, as Klaus drives to City Hall. Upon arriving at City Hall, the men all decide to cast their votes first, with the only exception being

Jerome, who is not voting. Klaus and Dan, vote for Nordstrom. Paul and Bill, vote for Greenwich. After the men have finished voting, they all return back to Klaus vehicle. Klaus then starts to get all of his equipment, likewise as he did with their previous shows. Although events are happening rather sudden, the guys are already fully aware of how the setup works. Klaus hands Bill a Camera, and hands Paul the microphone equipment. Paul and Bill will cover the West side of City Hall, in which Greenwich supporters are situated. Klaus hands Dan the microphone equipment. Klaus, as well as Dan will be situated on the East side of City Hall, where Nordstrom supporters will be. Jerome is not voting for either candidate, and is neutral. However, Jerome decided to initially go with Klaus and Dan, although again, he is neutral, and not in support of either side. As all of the men split up into different sections of City Hall, the event has remarkably garnered quite the crowd. There are several people at this event. Both candidates do indeed have an equal number of supporters, with both sides showing dedication and support to the candidate they prefer. People have picket signs, and other banners up, in support of the candidate they like, and also with insulting, and degrading signs, banners, and posts, for the candidate they do not like. Klaus immediately starts the live feed, and gets his feed, and Bill's camera feed calibrated correctly.

Klaus checks in on the live feed room, noticing that already two hundred people have tuned in, and they haven't even been live for a few minutes. Klaus starts to smile to himself, feeling delighted, at how much attention the show is getting already. Klaus, Dan, and Jerome, continue to walk through the eastern side of City Hall, with Klaus and Dan, feeling happy to be on the side of the Nordstrom supporters. Jerome however, doesn't feel any type of way about it. Jerome simply takes notes on the ordeal, being neutral. Klaus continues to capture everything at the event, and signals to Dan, that they should interview some of the other participants at the election night rally. The men happen to stumble upon a bald man wearing glasses, wearing a T-Shirt, with council member Nordstrom's name on it. Dan then decides to interview him.

"Hello sir. We are news program, covering election night. If you don't mind me asking, why have you decided to support Nordstrom, and why are you voting for him over Greenwich?"

The man then puts up a satirical cartoon sign of Council Member Greenwich and speaks.

"Because Nordstrom is the guy we need. He understands people. Greenwich is a clown."

Dan interviews the man, and asks him more questions, and Klaus continues to capture everything. Dan finishes interviewing this man, and thanks him. Several more supporters hold up banners and signs. The men then continue on through the City Hall, and Dan interviews more Nordstrom supporters. Klaus looks at the live feed room, and notices the viewers are now at one thousand people. Klaus continues to feel jubilant over his decision to cover the election night event. Out of curiosity, Klaus then starts to look over Paul and Bill's camera feed. Over at the western side, where the Greenwich supporters are, Paul and Bill, continue to go through the crowd. Paul, likewise with the guys on the other side, decides to interview, one of the participants at the political event, who is older man, that is wearing a Greenwich T-Shirt.

"Hello, how are you sir. We are doing a news story for election night. I wanted to ask you please, why are you voting for Greenwich, and why should he win over Nordstrom?"

The man then grabs a satirical cartoon sign, and waves it in the air. The man speaks.

"Greenwich cares about the people in the community. Nordstrom is a fake phony."

Paul steadily asks the man more questions, and continues to interview him. Bill remains capturing everything. Paul thanks the man for the interview, and Paul interviews more of the Greenwich supporters. Klaus continues to look over that the other guys feed, and once he notices that Paul and Bill seem to be doing fine, he closes their live feed. Klaus then focuses on his own direction of the event, and he alongside Dan and Jerome, continue to get more coverage for their show. As the event lingers on, it is getting closer to count all the votes, and reveal the winner. This is going to be the most pivotal, and intense part of the event. The side of the winner is going to be happy, and they are going to celebrate and riot, for their candidate winning. The side of the loser, is going to be unhappy, and they are going to riot and complain. So it's going to be a reaction, either way. Klaus was happy to get coverage, regardless of the outcome. Although he would like for Nordstrom to win, and Klaus is confident that Nordstrom is going to win, he would be satisfied, and would deal with the result, if Greenwich were to win. Klaus, Dan, and Jerome continue to remain on the eastern side of City Hall, and Paul and Bill stay on the western side. With the polls being closed, and the votes being counted, in only five minutes, everyone on either side, is very alerted. Before long, it is now 7 p.m., and the polls have officially closed. The officials inside the city hall building start to count every vote. Police start to swarm the event, for precaution, as they know the announcement of the winner of Mayor, would spark a reaction, either way. Klaus continues to capture everything on the Nordstrom side, and Bill as well captures everything on the Greenwich side. Both sides anticipate who the winner will be.

After half an hour passes, the votes are still being counted, and the vibe outside of City Hall, shockingly remains quiet, as they wait for the new Mayor to be announced. At this time, over at the Greenwich side, Bill who was capturing everything with the camera, starts to set his camera down on the ground, and starts to hold his chest. Paul notices this, and speaks to Bill.

"Hey, are you okay? Bill? Do you want me to get you some water? I'll get some water."

Bill doesn't respond to Paul, and Paul walks away to get Bill some water. Bill takes a seat on a bench, and shuts his camera off. During this time, Klaus being too involved on the other side of City Hall, doesn't check to see that Bill's camera feed was inadvertently cut off, when Bill set his camera down. On the Greenwich side, Paul manages to get Bill some water, and Bill starts to drink it. Paul is not aware that Bill's camera feed is off, however that isn't his main concern. Paul decides to comfort Bill during this time. Paul takes a seat next to Bill, and starts to rub his back. Bill continues to drink more water. Bill, feeling very weak, then speaks.

"Thank you. I'm not okay no. But I don't want to let you guys down. They are about to reveal the winner, so maybe I'm just nervous or anxious. I guess I'll be fine though. I'm okay."

Bill kisses Paul on the cheek, and runs his hands through Paul's hair. Paul reluctantly smiles back at Bill, and the both of them silently sit together, awaiting the results. About ten minutes after this, the votes have all been officially counted and verified. Several city officials, then start to walk on a podium, situated on the center of City Hall, in between both sides. A female, who is one of the city officials, stands at the podium, preparing to speak. Supporters on either side of City Hall, start to hush and quiet themselves, and police are also on standby, as they are prepared for any outbursts, that shall happen as a result of the announcement. Once the crowd is silent, the female city official at the podium, then starts to speak.

"Good evening everyone. I want to thank all the Redondo Beach citizens who have voted. Although, I am here to announce that although the vote was close, after verifying the votes, Nordstrom received 48% of the vote. Greenwich received 52% of the vote."

Immediately after the city official woman said this, the crowd had an equal amount of cheers coming from the Greenwich side, and several boos and moans, coming from the Nordstrom side. As police start to survey the crowd, the city official woman continues to speak.

"William Greenwich, is our new Mayor of Redondo Beach. Thank you and good night."

The city officials quickly leave the stage, as several of the crowd members begin to throw objects at the stage, and chaos immediately erupts. The Greenwich supporters are glad that their candidate won the election. The Nordstrom supporters, are not making it a secret, at how much they do not agree with this outcome. Klaus and Dan are extremely upset at this, and they, along with Jerome, start to walk out of the Nordstrom side of City Hall, to avoid the chaos and rampage. At this time, Klaus turns on the live feed, and notices that Paul and Bill's feed has gone off. This alarms Klaus, and Klaus starts to call Paul on the phone, in which Paul does not answer, as he cannot hear his phone ring, due to all the commotion at the election results. At the Greenwich side, in which the supporters are happy. Paul is pleased at the result. Bill is happy as well, although he is feeling extremely weak. Bill then speaks to Paul.

"Greenwich won. Yes. Although Nordstrom had a good campaign too. Yes. Greenwich won. I'm so happy. I, uh, I, ah, ugh. Paul, please, call Klaus right now. Ah, ugh."

Bill then starts to lean on his side, clenching his chest. Paul then shouts at Bill.

"Oh my god! Bill! Bill! Oh no! Somebody help me please! I need some help. Please!"

Immediately after saying this, several men walk up to Paul, and start to assist Bill. One of the men that walk up, who is an older Caucasian man with a mustache and flap top buzzed hair, start to take Bill's shirt off, and lays his upper body flat. The man speaks.

"My name is Isaac. He's having a heart attack. I used to be an EMT. I'm gonna try to keep him stable and calm, but he's gotta get to a hospital right now."

Isaac continues to aid Bill, and Paul stands by, watching in horror, with Paul having his hands over his face. Isaac then calls 911 on his phone, and speaks to the operator.

"Yes. I'm at City Hall. I have a gentleman that's having cardiac arrest. Please hurry." At this time, Paul takes out his phone, and starts to call Klaus. However, likewise when Klaus tried to call Paul, Klaus cannot hear his phone ring, because of all the outrage and noise. Paul then tells Isaac that he will be right back. Paul then races to the other side of City Hall, to find Klaus. Paul manages to locate Klaus, and starts to shout back to him.

"Bill is having a heart attack! Oh my god! We have to get him to the hospital quick!"

Paul then starts to cry heavily, which in turn causes Klaus to immediately feel sunken in his feelings. Klaus, Dan, and Jerome, immediately start to run and follow Paul. Upon reaching the area Bill was at, at this time, paramedics have arrived at the scene, and have put Bill on a stretcher. Klaus notices this, and immediately starts to cry, and starts to scream and shout.

"Uncle Bill! No! That's my Uncle! Uncle Bill!"

Dan and Jerome start to cry as well, and the men all try to race to area, where the paramedics are carrying Bill away. Klaus and the men get closer, but Klaus is detained by a police officer. Klaus then starts to speak with the officer, who is not letting him through.

"Officer, that's my Uncle on that stretcher. You have to let me pass. Please!"

The officer continues to detain Klaus, not allowing him to get closer. The officer speaks.

"Wait here, and I'll go speak with the paramedics. I cannot let you pass sir. I'm sorry."

Klaus shakes his head, and another officer goes to speak with the paramedics. The officer that went to speak with the paramedics, returns and speaks to the officer that is detaining Klaus, and the rest of the guys. During this time, Klaus notices that the paramedics continue to carry Bill in the stretcher further away, and are heading towards an ambulance. Before Klaus can get the rest of his feelings and thoughts in order, the officer detaining him, then speaks.

"Alright, they are taking him to Seaside Memorial. They believe he's having a heart attack, and they are gonna take him to the hospital, as a precaution to see if he's okay."

Klaus then immediately runs in the opposite direction of the officer, and Dan, Jerome, and Paul, who picked up Bill's camera, follows him. They then within a minute, get into Klaus SUV, and immediately head to Seaside Memorial Hospital. During the entire trip to the hospital, although it was only a few blocks away, it felt like it a was a few hundred blocks away. Klaus has tears running down his face. Dan, Jerome, and Paul, also are crying heavily. Klaus reaches the hospital's emergency room, and all of the men, race out of the vehicle. Klaus then speaks with the receptionist, who is a young brunette nurse.

"Yes. My name is Klaus Kleinberg. I believe my Uncle, Bill Kleinberg, was admitted here. They said that he was having a heart attack, and I just want to know if he's okay."

The receptionist looks on her computer, and then responds.

"Sir, he's in room E3. They just brought him in, he was having a heart attack. Reports are saying he was having cardiac arrest. I see that he's in critical condition. I..."

Klaus immediately runs past the receptionist, and the rest of the men follow him. The receptionists gets up from her desk, and starts to shout out to Klaus.

"Sir, you can't go in there right now. Sir."

Within seconds, Klaus reaches the room Bill is in. Klaus is mortified, when he sees several doctors trying to revive Bill, who is flatlining. Klaus starts to cry and sob more, as he is standing in the doorway of the room Bill is in. Within several more seconds, after several attempts of trying to revive Bill, he doesn't manage to recover. Bill is now declared dead. Several doctors huddle around Bill and start to close the curtain in the room. Klaus immediately throws his glasses down on the ground, in which the impact causes Klaus glasses, to break very badly, damaging the frames and the lenses. Klaus then starts to scream out loud.

"Fuck! No! Uncle Bill! No! Damn it! Uncle Bill!"

Klaus then starts to lean against the wall and cries heavily. At this time, Dr. Simpson, who was Bill's doctor, notices Klaus crying in the hallway and comforts him. Dan and Jerome who were on the other side of the hallway, cry deeply. Paul who was standing right next to them, falls down on the ground, unable to control himself. Dan and Jerome comfort him. Dr. Simpson continues to comfort Klaus, who is still crying strongly. Dr. Simpson speaks to Klaus.

"I'm sorry. I'm sorry about your Uncle. I'm sorry."

Dr. Simpson steadily comforts Klaus. Klaus then continues to cry.

CHAPTER 16:

HIGH TENSIONS

It appears, that there has been yet another devastating, and tragic event take place. It seems the men have just dealt with a similar experience, and now they have been encountered with yet another death. Another death of someone that was in their group. Another death of a friend, another death of a member of their brotherhood. It seems that these unfortunate, heartbreaking, and depressing events, seem to happen like clockwork. The main objective, and intention for the guys all being there, was to cover the proceedings. The guys had no intentions of getting involved with any of the side drama, or any of the other issues or situations that were present there. The guys wanted to revive their show, and they managed to do that. But unfortunately, yet again, their show ended on a terrible note. It was almost as if history was repeating itself. Not to beat around the bush, but the guys recently had to deal with losing Ernest at the police chase they covered. The guys all thought, that could have been the end of it there. It seemed as though things were done. Klaus and Dan, had strong conflict with one another, and it was very awkward for the men to continue, after witnessing what happened with Ernest. However, the guys managed to pull through, and carry on. Usually for the sake that they would carry on to honor Ernest's legacy. The guys soon bounced back, and calmed themselves down over the Ernest situation. Although plans to revive the show weren't for certain or guaranteed, it was something on the guy's mind. As to whether or not, the show would go on, and they were going to continue. After heavy reflection, between them all, the guys did manage to come to an agreement to continue on the show. It was a spur of the moment thing. Klaus took advantage of it being election night, and figured it was the ample opportunity, for them to resume their news program, as the event would be very notorious and prolific. This was also further fueled by the fact, that the guys themselves were at disagreement towards the event as well. This was a trivial coincidental detail, that played a pivotal role, in the situation.

The fact was, Dan was not originally in the mood, or interested in going to the event. Perhaps it was a feeling that he had, that was informing him, that this was a terrible idea. Dan had no problems with the guys carrying on with their show, but Dan didn't believe that the political event was safe for them to attend. Again, it was a feeling that Dan was harboring, that was probably telling him, that they shouldn't proceed. Dan and Klaus, were in favor of Council Member Nordstrom, to win the election, to be Mayor. They agreed with his stances, and views more. However, a strange paradox happened. Paul and Bill, were in favor of the opposing candidate, which was Council Member Greenwich, as they agreed with his stances, and his views as well. So the guys were torn, and divided, between the two candidates. Jerome was the only person who didn't want to get involved with the politics of the situation, and was neutral. Jerome was not in support of either candidate, and was not voting. Due to this, Dan, and Paul, began to get into a heavy argument, and conflict, being that they supported different candidates. It was because of this fight, that Dan quickly changed his mind, and decided that they guys should in fact, continue on with their show, and cover election night.

Things, as the guys suspected and originally hoped, went smooth at first. The guys were all together doing their news broadcast show, and they were all excited to be at the event. Because the guys were split between the candidates, Klaus and Dan, went in one separate direction, and Paul and Bill, went into the other direction. Jerome, even though he was neutral, decided to go with Klaus and Dan. The guys were covering all aspects of the event, and the viewers that were online, tuning into the show, was reflective of that. The broadcast, and show, was very entertaining, and the guys, of course, were putting on a fantastic show. The guys weren't having any issues or problems with the show. Everything was perfect, and the reception from the show, was excellent. Even though the guys also were aware, that once the winner of the election was announced, there would be outrage. It was suspected that the vote would be close, and both candidates have an equal number of supporters. Klaus, and the rest of the men, were looking forward to this though, and they figured, this would be the exciting part. Having to cover the divided reactions. From the supporters from the candidate who won, feeling happy, to the supporters of the candidate who lost, feeling upset and dejected. In the end, the vote was indeed close, and the winner of the election, becoming Mayor, was Greenwich. Klaus and Dan, were upset at the news, but quickly accepted it, and realized that the best candidate was the one who received the most votes. Paul and Bill, were happy that their candidate won.

However, things took an extreme turn for the worst, when Bill started not to feel well. Bill began to clench his chest, and complain of pain. Upon seeing this, Paul stepped into action, to get Bill help. Paul quickly alerted Klaus, and the rest of the guys. Things were happening very quick and everything was turning out to be, very traumatic, and stressful, for all the guys. Bill, was then transported to a nearby hospital, in critical condition. This was all happening in minutes, although it seemed like it was happening in hours. Klaus, and the rest of the men quickly directed themselves to the hospital, to check on Bill. Not long after arriving at the hospital, the men discovered that Bill had passed away, as a result of his heart attack. Through all of this, Klaus was so upset, that he threw his glasses down on the ground. Klaus glasses ended up being severely damaged, with both the frames, and lenses being damaged. By coincidence, Dr. Simpson, who was Bill's, primary care physician, was also present doing rounds at the hospital. Even though Klaus and Dr. Simpson have never met before, Dr.

Simpson quickly deduced, that Klaus was Bill's Nephew, from the way he was acting, and behaving. Dr. Simpson tries to comfort Klaus, during this delicate and traumatic ordeal, understanding that Klaus is hurting, over the death of his Uncle Bill. Klaus continues to feel upset, and depressed.

At this current time, Dr. Simpson continues to console, and comfort Klaus. By chance, Dr. Simpson happens to look down towards the ground, and notices Klaus broken glasses. Dr. Simpson picks them up, and hands them to Klaus. Dr. Simpson then speaks.

"Here, you broke your glasses. Why don't you follow me, to a more private room? Let's get out of this hallway. I understand you're hurting. Let's go to a more comfortable area. Okay?"

Klaus doesn't react, emote, speak, or respond. But Dr. Simpson starts to frown, and pats Klaus on the back. Even though Klaus did not respond to Dr. Simpson, as Dr. Simpson starts to walk down the hallway, Klaus obediently follows him. The rest of the guys, manage to follow Klaus as well. Dr. Simpson directs all of the guys into an empty waiting room. Klaus, Dan, Jerome, and Paul, all walk into the waiting room, and they each take a seat. Once all of the men are seated, Dr. Simpson tells the guys that he will be back shortly, and then walks out of the waiting room, shutting the door behind him. Following this, the men remain the waiting room silent, and not speaking to one another. Klaus continues to feel upset, and clenches his broken glasses in his fist. Dan and Jerome, both are quietly crying as well. Paul is very upset, and along with Klaus, is heavily crying. The men continue to feel upset, being silent in the waiting room. A few minutes later, Klaus then finally decides to speak.

"I cannot believe this. Uncle was doing so well with his health. I was going on walks with him, he was doing so well. I mean I know the doctors warned him, but. Oh god."

Klaus continues to look down on the ground, shaking his head, and crying. Klaus decides to put his broken glasses into his pocket. Because Klaus has broken his glasses, his eyesight is poor, and in addition to him crying, it's making Klaus vision very shady. At this time,

Paul strangely gets up from his seat, and starts to pace around the room, with his hands in his pocket. Paul continues to cry, and pace around the room, with his vision directed down. Paul speaks.

" I never forget that day I took him to the doctors, and how uncomfortable he was. I was sure that Bill would recover, and his heart condition wouldn't be a concern. Ugh. Why?"

Paul continues to pace around the room, feeling very upset. The guys have now been in this waiting room, for a half an hour, and Dr. Simpson has not yet returned. With Paul still pacing around the room, Dan at this point, gets up from his seat. Dan then speaks to the men.

"Hey, I'm gonna go to the cafeteria to get us all some coffee. I'll be right back, okay?"

None of the guys respond to Dan, to which Dan is slightly shocked that none of the guys said anything. Dan doesn't make a big deal about this, and understands that the guys are still most likely probably in shock, and dealing with the news. Dan nods his head, and walks out of the waiting room, and he proceeds to the hospital cafeteria. As Paul is pacing around the waiting room, out of anger and depression Paul then starts to kick a vacant chair in the room, and kicking the chair against the wall. Klaus and Jerome watch him do this, and Jerome starts to shake his head, he continues to cry. Klaus immediately gets up from his seat, and starts to comfort Paul. As Klaus is doing this, Paul is trying to push Klaus off him, but Klaus continues to console him. Klaus and Paul then start to hug, with Paul reluctantly trying to free himself from Klaus. As the both of them are hugging and consoling each other, Klaus then softly speaks to Paul.

"Hey man. You gotta calm down okay? Uncle was the only family I had. Like I'm not exaggerating that. Like he was all that I had left. So I understand you're mad Paul. But that shit is not helping, and you gotta calm down. Everyone's upset. Go take a seat, alright man?"

Paul then shakes his head, and starts to walk back to the seat. When Paul is seated, he looks down towards the ground still feeling very upset. Paul then responds to Klaus.

"I don't care. Fuck calm. I loved Bill very much, and, ugh. Why is everything bad happening to us. Like we are cursed it seems. First Ernest, now Bill. Fuck this shit."

Paul then unexpectantly gets up from his seat, and starts to walk to the door of the waiting room. Klaus then immediately gets up, and tries to stop Paul by grabbing him, but he is slightly too late, and Paul walks out of the room. Klaus walks right behind Paul out of the room as well. Jerome instinctively follows Klaus out of the room too. As Paul continues to walk down the hallway, Paul suddenly stops, and leans his head against the walls of the hallway, and cries. Klaus and Jerome eventually catch up to Paul, and Klaus starts to hug Paul. Klaus speaks.

"Hey, let's go outside and have a smoke alright? Let's just get some fresh air, alright?"

Paul takes his glasses off, and starts to wipe the tears off his face. Directly following this, Klaus, Jerome, and Paul, start to walk out to the courtyard of the hospital, so that they can all have a cigarette break, and calm down. In between all of this, while the men are directing themselves outside, Klaus remembers that Dan went to the cafeteria, to get the men all some coffee. Before Klaus can figure out what to do, as to whether or not he should go to the cafeteria, to tell Dan that they are going outside for a smoke, or text him to let him know where they are going; Dan suddenly walks down the hallway, in the opposite direction of the guys, carrying a cup holder, that has four cups of coffee. Upon seeing Dan, Klaus signals him over, and Klaus informs Dan, that they are all going to go outside, to smoke a cigarette. Dan understands this, and joins the guys, and walks with them as well. All four of the men, then proceed to the outside courtyard of the hospital. One they are all there, they all start to smoke their cigarettes. The men also start to take sips of their coffee, that Dan managed to get for all of them. Dan takes several puffs of his cigarette, and starts to look down on the ground. Dan then speaks.

"Damn, I told you man that we shouldn't go. It was just a feeling I had, and I should have just listened, to that feeling, and Damn. I just knew going to that event was a bad idea."

Paul then takes a puff of his cigarette, and then responds to Dan.

"That wouldn't have made any difference. His heart was just in really bad condition, so even if we didn't go to that event, I think he would have eventually had an attack anyways."

Dan doesn't respond to Paul at all, and Dan takes another puff of his cigarette. Klaus doesn't respond either, although he feels what Paul said was possibly right. The event virtually, might not have had anything to do with Bill's heart attack. Although, what was for certain, was that the event made Bill's heart attack, more of a stressful ordeal. The guys were simply intending on doing their show, without any problems or concerns. Unfortunately, Bill did have a heart attack, and passed away because of his heart problems, and the heart attack. This in turn, shifted what was supposed to be a happy and exciting event, into something that was very upsetting, and unfortunate, and devastating. Bill is now gone, and he is dead. The rest of the guys will have to accept this, and as there is nothing else that they can do. The men continue to smoke their cigarettes in the courtyard, and are calming themselves down. As the men remain outside in the courtyard, Jerome takes a puff of his cigarette, and starts to speak.

"I'm sorry for the loss of your Uncle Klaus. We all loved Bill. I am sorry Paul, as I know you and Bill were very close. This is really sad, and I'm gonna miss Bill greatly."

Klaus then smiles to himself, and runs his hands through Jerome's hair. Paul remarkably does the same, and smiles at Jerome, and runs his hands through Jerome's hair as well. For a few minutes, the guys remain quiet in the courtyard, smoking their cigarettes. The men still strongly feel upset over the death of Bill, but are trying to use coping and defense mechanisms, to calm themselves over the event. The guys still continue to be quiet for now, still being peaceful, and being calm with all of their thoughts and emotions. This goes on for a several more minutes. Dan then takes a sip of his coffee, and starts to scratch the back of his head. Dan then decides to break the silence that all the guys had, and he speaks to Paul.

"Hey man. I'm sorry about the fight we had earlier. I don't know what I was thinking. I feel it was very petty and childish, and I feel guilty. I'm sorry Paul for arguing with you."

Paul takes a puff of his cigarette, and nods his head. Paul then responds back to Dan.

"I forgive you, and I'm sorry too. I was also being a jerk, and we started the whole division thing, and I feel really bad about it too. Just forget about it man. We're cool now."

Dan and Paul then fist bump each other, and they have both made amends with their friendship. Klaus who was watching, and listening, Dan and Paul apologize to each other, smiles to himself, and shakes his head and laughs. Not long after this, the men decide to leave the courtyard, and report themselves back to the waiting room. Once all the men are back in the waiting room, they notice that Dr. Simpson is sitting down with a folder in his hands. The guys all take a seat in the waiting room, and Dr. Simpson quickly speaks to them.

"Oh, there you guys are. I assumed you guys stepped out for a minute, that's fine. Listen, Klaus. I'm terribly sorry for the loss of your Uncle. Here are all of his medical documents. Your Uncle was a veteran, so here's veteran resources, they will arrange a funeral for him. I'm sorry."

Klaus accepts the documents that Dr. Simpson hands to him, and he quickly scans them over. At this point, Dr. Simpson tells Klaus, that he and the rest of the guys can go home. Klaus, and the other men, shake Dr. Simpsons hand, and the men all leave out of the waiting room. The men then start to walk to Klaus SUV. Despite the fact that Klaus was quickly dealing with the death of his Uncle, it seemed that Klaus mood quickly shifted, when he started to come back to realization, that Bill is gone, and he has passed away. As the men are standing outside Klaus vehicle, Klaus starts to feel upset again, and starts to cry. Klaus thoughts have been reset, and he is back to feeling sorrow over Bill's death. Klaus continues to cry, and he is not able to move. The other guys sense this and start to cry as well. After a minute, the men are able to compose themselves, and they get inside of the vehicle. Klaus prepares to start the engine, but remembers he has broken his glasses, which he needs in order to see to drive. Klaus then takes the car key out of the ignition, and hands the key to Dan. Klaus then speaks.

"Dan can you drive? I broke my glasses, and I can't drive without my glasses."

Dan immediately understands, and agrees. Klaus gets out of the vehicle, and so does Dan. Klaus directs himself to the passenger side, and take a seat. Dan then gets into the driver's seat, and starts the engine. Dan then drives the rest of the guys, straight to the house. Although the house is located a short distance away from the hospital, the ride felt as though it was much longer, due to all of the turmoil the guys are experiencing. Dan does eventually make it back to the house, and it's a very upsetting time for all of the men. As they get out of the vehicle, the men all start to walk inside of the house. Once they are all inside, Paul immediately directs himself to his bedroom. Jerome takes a seat on the sofa, and looks down towards the ground. Dan who is in the kitchen, opens up the door to the refrigerator, and has an unhappy look on his face. Dan then closes the refrigerator, without taking anything out. Klaus, who is in the kitchen as well, directs himself to the other side of the kitchen, and Klaus opens up top cabinet in the kitchen. Klaus then takes a large bottle of Smirnoff Vodka from the cabinet, and sets it on the counter. Klaus takes a shot glass from the counter, and starts to take a shot of Vodka. Not even a second later, Klaus takes another Vodka shot. At this time, Paul returns from his bedroom, and walks into the living room, with a shoebox. Klaus stares at Paul, as Paul begins to open the shoebox. Inside the shoebox is marijuana, and rolling papers. Paul starts to make a marijuana joint, and upon realizing this, Klaus walks into the living room, and quickly grabs the paraphernalia away from Paul, who is stunned and doesn't initially react to Klaus doing this. Dan and Jerome watch everything silently. Klaus then walks back into the kitchen and sets the shoebox on the counter. Paul who was sitting on the sofa, shakes his head, and walks to the kitchen to grab the shoebox. Klaus picks up the shoebox before

Paul is able to get it. Klaus then makes himself a third Vodka shot and drinks it. While he's holding the shoebox, Klaus speaks.

"You're not gonna smoke that shit right now. You're gonna be acting loopy and stoned. Go back in the living room, and sit down. You're not getting this box back."

Paul then has an angry look on his face, and tries to wrestle the box away from Klaus. Dan notices this, and walks over to break them up. Jerome remains on the living room sofa, crying. Through the scuffle, Paul manages to grab the shoebox, and returns to the living room. Klaus tries to follow after Paul, but Dan manages to restrain him. Paul then sits down on the sofa, and resumes making his marijuana joint. Paul then starts to speak.

"Klaus, you're not my fucking Dad. You're such an asshole sometimes, I can't believe it. You got some nerve saying I can't smoke weed, and you had like several vodka shots already. Yeah I'm not stupid. Fuck you, and don't say shit to me for the rest of the night. Got it?"

Paul finishes making his marijuana joint and takes a puff of it. Paul then hands the marijuana joint to Jerome, and Jerome takes a puff of it. Klaus stares deeply at Paul, and shakes and his head and laughs. Klaus then takes a fourth Vodka shot, and Klaus puts the Vodka bottle, back on the top shelf. Paul continues to smoke his marijuana joint in the living room, and Klaus continues to stare at him. Klaus then once again, shakes his head and laughs. Klaus then speaks.

"You know what. This is ridiculous. Fuck this. I can't even. This is bullshit. I swear."

Klaus then immediately walks out to the balcony, and slams the balcony door shut behind him. Dan who was in the kitchen, shakes his head, and shockingly, does not follow Klaus on the balcony, and leaves him be. Dan instead, joins Jerome and Paul, in the living room. Dan takes a seat on the sofa, and Paul hands Dan, the marijuana joint. Jerome is already feeling buzzed from the marijuana, and he is sitting quietly on the sofa. Dan takes a puff of the marijuana joint, and gives a thumbs up to Paul, and hands the marijuana joint back to him. Dan then turns on the television, and starts to watch, the Eddie Murphy movie "Norbit". Paul takes another puff of the marijuana joint and is watching the movie on the television. Paul then laughs, and speaks.

"I swear, if he gets into my face one more time like that, I'm beating the fuck out of him. That's not the first time he came incorrect at me either. I swear to god he's gonna learn today."

Unluckily, at this same congruent time, Klaus opens up the balcony door, to go to the kitchen to get himself a beer from the refrigerator. Klaus heard everything Dan said, and speaks.

"You're gonna do what? I like to fucking see you try. I would mop the floor with you. Smoke your pot and leave me the fuck alone. Don't fuck with me, you will regret it Paul."

Probably because they are buzzed from the marijuana, Dan and Jerome simply laugh at this exchange. However, within a split second, Paul gets up from the sofa, and starts to tussle with Klaus. In turn, Klaus starts to tussle and wrestle with Paul. Both of the men are taking jabs at each other, and they both end up tussling on the ground. At this point, Dan and Jerome realize that Klaus and Paul are being serious, and get up from the sofa, and start to break them up. Klaus and Paul stop fighting, and Klaus shake his head and laughs, and Paul as well shakes his head. Klaus then immediately starts to walk to the kitchen, and gets a beer from the refrigerator. Paul returns to the sofa, and takes another puff from his marijuana joint. Klaus then proceeds to walk back out to the balcony, and as he is opening the door, Klaus speaks.

"Let me try some of that. That pot clearly has you twisted and fucked up. Ha Ha."

Klaus then walks up to Paul and snatches the marijuana joint from him. Paul does not budge, and allows Klaus to take it. Klaus takes a puff of the joint, and hands it back to Paul. Klaus then starts to cough heavily, and Klaus directs himself to the balcony door, and speaks.

"Oh damn, that's some good shit Paul. I guess you are a great guy. Thanks man. Ha Ha."

Paul then turns his head towards Klaus, and flips him off. Klaus in turn flips Paul off as well, and walks out onto the balcony, shutting the door behind him. Dan and Jerome laugh as a result of this. Paul shakes his head, and resumes watching the "Norbit" movie, with Dan and Jerome. Several more minutes pass, and the guys continue to watch the movie, and Klaus remains by himself, out in the balcony. Dan then decides to speak to Jerome and Paul.

"Hey, that pot is gonna give us the munchies. I'm gonna go in the kitchen, and there isn't much in the fridge. I have to go shopping tomorrow, but there is some leftover Chicken Breast, so I guess I can make some Chicken Nachos. I'm gonna go get that situated right now in fact."

Jerome and Paul continue to watch the movie on the television, as Dan walks into the kitchen, to prepare the Chicken Nachos. As Dan is in the kitchen cooking, Jerome and Paul continue to laugh at the movie that they are watching. Dan soon finishes the meal, and let's Jerome and Paul know the food is ready. Jerome and Paul both grab a plate of food, and return to the sofa in the living room. Dan walks over to the balcony door, knocks on it, and alerts Klaus that he has made some Chicken Nachos. Klaus steps out from the balcony, and grabs a plate, and takes his plate of food, and quickly directs himself back to the balcony. Dan watches Klaus scurry back out to the balcony, and Dan shakes his head and laughs. Dan then walks into the living room, and joins Jerome and Paul, and they both continue to watch the movie on the television. Once the movie is over, Dan explains that there is some cookie dough in the refrigerator, if the guys want any cookies. Paul decides to obey Dan's suggestion, and immediately starts to bake some cookies, using the cookie dough. Once the cookies are finished, Paul, Dan and Jerome all eat the cookies that Paul has made. The guys continue to watch television; they are now watching episodes of Family Guy. Klaus walks into the kitchen to get himself a glass of water, and eats one of the cookies Paul baked. Klaus gets his water, and returns back out to the balcony. It now seems hard to believe, that it wasn't that long ago, in which the guys had to deal with Bill's death. The men are taking this time to grieve in their own way, and are trying to go through, and deal with all the trials and tribulations that they are faced with. The men are upset over Bill's death, but right now are using a unique coping strategy.

An hour later, Jerome starts to drift in and out of sleep. Paul then without saying anything, gets up from the sofa, walks into his bedroom, and directs himself to bed. Dan, likewise, doesn't say anything, turns the television off, and walks into his bedroom, and directs himself to bed as well. Fifteen minutes later, Klaus who is feeling tired himself, walks out of the balcony, and shuts the balcony door. Klaus notices Jerome half asleep on the sofa, and Klaus smiles to himself. Klaus then picks up Jerome, and carries him behind his back. Klaus walks into his bedroom, and sets Jerome down on the bed. Klaus then reaches into his pocket, and sets his broken glasses down on his dresser. Klaus then gets onto the other side of the bed, and closes his eyes, and starts to rest. The following morning, Klaus is awoken by someone calling him on his phone. The time is currently 7 a.m. Klaus is startled by his phone ringing, and the sound also wakes up Jerome. Klaus feeling sluggish, and tired, grumpily, sits up in bed, and starts to speak.

"Really? Now who the fuck could that be calling me at this hour. Ugh."

Klaus looks at his phone, and notices the number is from a local area code. Because of this, Klaus answers and accepts the call. He wouldn't have otherwise. Klaus then speaks.

"Hello, this is Klaus. What can I help you with?"

The person on the other end of the line, waits a few seconds to respond, but speaks.

"Oh, Good Morning. Sorry for calling you so early. I realized after I made the call, that this seems like an ungodly hour to call. I'm just an early person. Ha Ha."

Klaus, still feeling half awake, shakes his head, and angrily responds to the caller.

"That's for damn sure. Okay, what the hell did you want? What is this?"

The caller once again hesitates for a few seconds, and then responds.

"Oh I'm sorry. Where are my manners? My name is Emilio Martinez. I was a close friend of your Uncle. I work for the Los Angeles Veteran's Association. I'm terribly sorry about your loss. I just called to ask, if we could meet up today please? It's very important I speak with you."

Klaus starts to rub his eyes, and wakes himself up. Klaus then responds to Emilio.

"Oh, thank you. I can meet up today. That's fine. What time did you want to meet up?"

Klaus then starts to grab a notepad and pen situated on his dresser. Emilio then speaks.

"Well, as soon as possible really. If you can meet up now please, that would be great."

Klaus agrees to this plan, and Emilio then gives Klaus the address to the Veteran's Association office. Klaus thanks Emilio, and hangs up the phone. Klaus then immediately starts to gather things and wakes Jerome up by shaking him. Jerome awakens and Klaus speaks to him.

"Hey, I haven't gotten my glasses fixed yet. I can't drive without my glasses, I can't see. I'm not waking Dan or Paul up. So can you please drive me. I appreciate it."

Jerome continues to wake himself up, and nods his head. Minutes later, Klaus and Jerome leave out of the house, and Jerome gets into the driver's seat, and Klaus sits in the passenger seat. Jerome then starts to drive to the Veteran's Association office, so that Klaus can speak with Emilio. The day is overcast and gloomy, and there is also slight morning fog. Jerome arrives at the office, and Klaus and Jerome get out of the car, and walk inside. While inside, Klaus informs the person at the front desk, that he is here to speak with Emilio. The front desk clerk tells Klaus to wait in the lobby. Klaus and Jerome then take a seat, and wait in the lobby. Minutes later, Emilio does arrive, and Klaus and Jerome shake his hand. Emilio is a half Irish, half Mexican man, that formed a friendship with Bill. Emilio is an Army veteran and he works as the Veteran's Association, as president of Veteran's family affairs. Emilio is an average heighted man he wears glasses, and he has grey thinning hair. Klaus and Jerome follow Emilio to his office. Once they are inside of the office, Emilio then starts to speak.

"Good morning gentleman. Thank you for meeting up with me. Again, Klaus, I'm really sorry for the loss of your Uncle. I knew Bill personally, and he was quite the character, but he was the nicest guy I have ever met. Okay, there was a few things I wanted to discuss."

Emilio then reaches into his desk, and starts to pull out several papers. As Emilio is setting the papers down on his desk, he pulls out a pen, hands it to Klaus, and Emilio speaks.

"Alright. So because your Uncle was a veteran. We are going to provide a military style funeral. Your Uncle will have the gun salute, flag folding. Do you have any of his uniforms?"

Klaus starts to skim through all the papers. While he's doing that, Klaus speaks.

"I do. My Uncle had a companion. He's a friend of mine as well. He has his uniforms."

Emilio starts to grab more papers from his desk, and sets them down. Emilio then speaks.

"Great. So that way he can be buried in his service uniform. That's quite common. So these are just legal papers, most of it is jargon. I just need you to sign these documents please."

Klaus nods his head, and immediately starts to sign all the papers. As Klaus is signing all of the documents, Jerome starts to gaze around the room, and looks at Emilio's awards and metals, that are adorned and hung up on the wall. Klaus finishes all the documents, and hands them to Emilio. Emilio then checks all the documents, and puts them in a file cabinet. Emilio leaves the room, saying he'll be right back, and arrives back a couple minutes later. Emilio then gives Klaus photocopies of the documents he signed. Emilio then pulls out another document.

"Alright, if it's fine by you, we will have Bill's funeral set for Friday. Is that okay?"

The document Emilio handed Klaus, was a conformation document, which if Klaus signed, will make Bill's funeral officially take place the following Friday. Klaus silently nods his head in response to

Emilio, and starts to sign the document. Klaus hands the document to Emilio, and Emilio gives Klaus a copy of this document, to keep for himself. Klaus and Jerome then say goodbye to Emilio, and walk out of his office. Now that Bill's funeral is set for Friday, Klaus feels comfortable and satisfied with that. Bill will be having a traditional military style funeral. As Klaus and Jerome get back into the vehicle, Klaus informs Jerome, to stop at the eyeglass shop. Klaus wants to get his glasses fixed, immediately. Klaus and Jerome arrive at the eyeglass shop, and Klaus tells the employees there, he wants his glasses repaired. The optometrist, who is a young Asian woman, takes Klaus glasses, and tells him to wait. Klaus and Jerome wait, and the optometrists is finished repairing Klaus glasses. Klaus tries the glasses on, and they are good as new, and fully repaired. Klaus pays the optometrists for fixing his glasses, and Klaus and Jerome leave out of the optometrist's office. Due to the fact that Klaus has his glasses fixed, he can drive again, and Klaus gets into the driver's side, and Jerome gets into the passenger side of the car.

Being that Bill's funeral is in two days, Klaus, and the rest of the guys, have to quickly get themselves ready for that. Klaus directs himself straight home. Once Klaus and Jerome make it back to the house, Dan and Paul are sitting in the living room, watching the morning news. Klaus informs the both of them, that Bill's funeral is on Friday. Klaus also informs Paul, if he could get Bill's military uniform, as that's the outfit he is going to be buried in. Paul agrees to get Bill's uniform, and Paul also offers to drop it off at the Veteran's Association office himself, which Paul does end up doing shortly after Klaus and Jerome arrive back at the house. Paul gives Emilio Bill's military uniform, and Emilio thanks Paul. Even though Bill is having a military style funeral, Klaus is not allowing any of the audience members, or viewers of their show, to attend. Klaus is only allowing some of Bill's military associates, to be there. Likewise with Ernest, the viewers of their show, give condolences to Bill. Friday, which is the day of Bill's funeral, arrives, and the guys are all prepared and ready. Klaus, is yet again having to attend another funeral. This time, the funeral is that of his Uncle. The only family that Klaus still was in contact with. Klaus must give an official goodbye and farewell to Bill. Klaus, and the rest of the guys wake up, and start to get dressed. Klaus puts on a suit, and Dan, Jerome, and Paul, all wear suits as well. Once all of the men are dressed, they all meet up in the living room. Eventually, the men then all leave the house, and start to drive to the Veteran's Cemetery, in Rancho Palos Verdes. It is located a slight moderate distance from where the house is.

Like with the day before, the weather for today, is overcast, and gloomy. This isn't the best weather, and Klaus feels it's almost reflective of the situation. Klaus does not enjoy funerals, and this is yet another one, he has to experience. The guys are emotional, and full of sadness. Funerals can bring out strong emotions, and the guys definitely are going through all of that. Klaus continues to drive to the cemetery, and Klaus starts to wonder how many people would be there. This is a private service, but Klaus is allowing some of Bill's military friends to be at the service as well. So Klaus is not sure as to how many people would be in attendance. Before long, Klaus manages to arrive at the funeral service. Once Klaus sees that there aren't that many people there, he starts to feel more comfortable. Klaus notices that Emilio, and a handful of other gentlemen, who Klaus believes are friends of Bill, are seated at the funeral. Klaus parks his car, and he, Dan, Jerome, and Paul, all get out of the vehicle. The men all sit in the front row. Once they are seated, Klaus starts to look around, and notices the flower arrangements on top of Bill's coffin, which is closed, with an American flag draped over it. Several minutes later, the actual funeral service commences. Emilio then gets up to the pulpit, and begins to speak.

"Hello everyone. It's unfortunate that we all have to gather here. We are here today to honor the life, of a wonderful man. A loving Uncle. A close friend of mine, and to others, Bill Kleinberg. Bill was a great man, and he had a kind spirit. We will miss him very much."

Emilio continues to speak, as Klaus starts to feel extremely emotional, as like he usually does during funerals. Klaus has his vision directed down towards the ground, and starts to cry. As the funeral service carries on, Emilio then asks if anyone wants to say any final words. Several of Bill's military friends walk up to the pulpit, and give their Eulogy to Bill. Once all of Bill's military friends have finished doing that, the guys then understand, that it's time for them to say their piece, and to give their final goodbye to Bill. Jerome is the first to speak. Jerome gets up from his seat, and walks to the pulpit. Jerome starts to cry, and he says his final words to Bill.

"I wanted to say, that Bill was a sweet man. I think about all the fun times we had together. Bill was very nice, and he was very open minded, and respected everyone. I am going to miss Bill, and I will remember him always. Goodbye Uncle Bill."

Jerome continues to cry, and he returns to his seat. Dan is the next to say his words to Bill. Dan gets up from his seat, and walks to the pulpit. Dan while crying, says his words to Bill.

"Oh man. Uncle Bill. I tell you, this guy was really something. He always made us laugh. If there was something on our minds, we could talk to him about it. Bill didn't judge anyone, and he was a great, nice man. Uncle Bill, we are all gonna miss you. Goodbye."

Dan wipes the tears from his face, as he continues to cry. Dan then returns back to his seat. It is now time for Paul to say his words to Bill. Paul starts to cry heavily, as he walks up to the pulpit. Paul pauses for a few seconds, as he continues to cry. Paul struggles to speak, and continues to stand in silence at the pulpit crying. Paul takes his glasses off, and wipes more tears from his face. Paul then composes himself, and he gives his words to Bill.

"I loved Bill very much. He reminded me so much of my father. Bill was the nicest man I met in my life, and I can't believe this. Bill and I had many deep conversations. I loved playing chess with him. I bonded a lot with Bill. I love you Bill. Sleep well. Goodbye."

Paul continues to cry deeply, and starts to walk back to his seat. Once Paul is seated, it is now Klaus, to say his final words to his Uncle. Klaus remains seated for several seconds, trying to get his thoughts and emotions clear. Klaus then gets up from his seat, and starts to walk to the pulpit. Like with Paul, Klaus is feeling terribly emotional over Bill's death, and he is frozen upon reaching the pulpit. Still overthrown with sadness, Klaus is not able to get his thoughts and words out. Klaus remains at the pulpit for a minute, in total silence. Klaus steadily cries, and wipes the tears from his face. Klaus manages to calm down, and gives his final words to Bill.

"Okay. Uncle Bill. I remember, wow, I can go back when I was nine years old. This man. I remember Uncle Bill at family functions. He was always a delight. I think I get most of my wit from him. I know I do. Ha Ha. Uncle Bill, you know I'll always have you in mind. You taught me so much. Uncle, I want you to sleep well okay. I miss you. I love you. Goodbye Uncle."

Klaus then cannot control his emotions, and starts to once again cry deeply. Klaus walks away from the pulpit, and returns to his seat, still not able to stop crying. Once Klaus has finished giving his Eulogy to his Uncle, the rest of the service continues. Bill is then given the gun salute, which is done by other military veterans. Directly following that, the flag folding is done, again, by other veterans. Emilio then hands Klaus, Bill's flag. After this the service is now officially over. Bill was given a proper, and formal military send off. Bill is then put to rest, and Bill's military friends, start to walk up to Bill's coffin, leaving flowers. Klaus, and the rest of the men stay seated, as they watch Bill's military friends, give their final respects to him. Klaus, and the other men, respectfully sit, and stay silent during all of this. Bill's military friends then walk up to Klaus and the rest of the guys, offering their sympathy and condolences. Emilio then walks up to Klaus, and the guys, and offers his sympathy, and condolences. Emilio then hugs all of the guys. Emilio hugs Klaus last, and as Emilio is hugging Klaus tightly, he whispers to Klaus.

"If there is anything that you need, anything at all, please call me. Even if you need someone to talk to, when you're feeling down. If you want to go for coffee or a drink. I'm here."

Klaus and Emilio continue to hug, and Emilio then kisses Klaus on the cheek. Emilio then leaves and drives away from the service. Klaus, and the other guys, remain at the cemetery, still full of emotions. Klaus turns his vision to Bill's coffin, which has several flowers on top of it. Klaus takes his glasses off, and again starts to cry. This causes the other men to feel upset as well. Klaus and Paul then walk up to Bill's coffin, and start to rearrange the flowers. Paul then kisses Bill's coffin, and Klaus kisses Bill's coffin as well. The men all remain at the cemetery for several more minutes, being silent around Bill's coffin. Dan then starts to speak.

"Okay, I think it's time we go now. We are getting too emotional, and yeah."

The other guys agree, and Klaus, and the men, all leave away from Bill's coffin. Klaus, and the rest of the guys get into Klaus SUV, and Klaus drives away from the cemetery. Klaus continues to drive. When he approaches a stoplight, Dan then starts to speak to Klaus.

"Hey, why don't we all stop and get something to eat. We can all reflect, calm down, wind down, eat some nice food. Talk. What do you say man, does that sound good to you?"

While still at the stoplight, Klaus starts to laugh and shake his head, and responds to Dan.

"You can have whatever you want Dan. I'll take you out to eat man. It's okay. Ha Ha."

Dan then shakes his head, and laughs at Klaus. Klaus as well shakes his head at Dan and laughs. Jerome and Paul, who were silently sitting in the back seat, heard Dan's suggestion, and are in agreement with it as well. Klaus then directly starts to drive to Sizzler, which was one of Bill's favorite restaurants. Sizzler is a restaurant, that specializes in steak, seafood, and other comfort dishes. Klaus approaches the restaurant, and the men all get out of Klaus SUV. Once the men are inside of the restaurant, the waitress seats all of them at a booth. Klaus and Jerome sit on one side of the booth, and Dan and Paul sit on the other side of the booth. The men start to read their menus, and start to figure out what they are going to order. While they are reading their menu's, Paul looks up at Klaus who's reading his menu. Paul then starts to speak to Klaus.

"Hey man. I wanted to apologize for the other night. I know you and I don't always get along, but I feel that wasn't cool of me to do that. I'm sorry Klaus, and please forgive me."

Klaus, with his vision directed down at his menu, responds silently back to Paul.

"Oh that. Yeah. It's cool. I'm sorry too. I was being a jerk as well. Forget about it man."

Klaus then looks up from his menu, and stares at Paul. Klaus and Paul give each other eye contact, and smile at each other. Shortly after this, the men have all decided what they want to order. Jerome decides to order the Steak and Shrimp, Surf and Turf, meal. Paul decides to order, the Bacon Cheeseburger and Fries. Klaus and Dan order the same thing, which is the Prime Rib Dinner. The food the men have ordered arrives, and they all begin eating. As they are eating their meal, the men customarily converse with one another, but having mostly lighthearted conversation. They are also talking about fun and happy times they had with Bill, and flashback to all of the positive and happy memories of him. Once all the men have finished eating, Klaus pays the check, and leaves a tip for the waitress. The men then get up from the table, and leave out of the restaurant. Klaus, and the rest of the men, then get into Klaus SUV, and Klaus heads directly back to the house. As Klaus arrives back home, the men quickly get situated while inside. Paul, and Jerome walk into the living room, and are seated down at the sofa. Klaus and Dan remain in the kitchen. Klaus is holding the flag from the funeral in his hand. Klaus walks into the living room, and puts the flag on the shelf in the living room. Klaus then speaks.

"I have to get this framed later. It would look really nice. I'll put it here for now."

While Klaus is in this area, he picks up Bill's Purple Heart medal, and starts to stare at it. Klaus smiles to himself for a bit and puts the metal back on the shelf. Klaus then starts to loosen his necktie, and he walks himself back to the kitchen. Klaus then opens up a top cabinet in the kitchen, and pulls out a bottle of Smirnoff Vodka. Klaus then takes two shot glasses out of the cabinet, and sets them down on the kitchen counter Klaus then pours Vodka into both of the shot glasses. Klaus signals for Dan to come over to where he is, and Dan obeys. Klaus hands Dan the other shot glass. Klaus raises his shot glass, and Dan instinctively raises his. Klaus then speaks.

"My buddy. My best friend. I can always count on you. This is for Uncle. Cheers Man."

Klaus and Dan then bring their shot glasses together, and do a cheers. Klaus and Dan then drink their Vodka shots. Klaus then starts to stare at Jerome and Paul in the living room. Jerome turns the television on, and starts to play a video game, on Klaus Xbox console. While the video game is starting up, Jerome notices that Paul is drawing in his sketchpad. Paul sets his sketchpad down momentarily, and Paul stretches himself on the sofa. Jerome then starts to gaze at the sketchpad, and out of curiosity, picks the sketchpad up, leering at it. Jerome then speaks.

"Hey, what are you drawing. I forget how talented of an artist you are. I really enjoy your artwork Paul. You don't mind if I take a look do you? Wow, these monsters look cool."

Paul then immediately snatches the sketchpad away from Jerome. Paul shouts at him.

"Hey, what are you doing? Did I give you permission to touch that? I didn't. You don't touch other people's property. You should know better than that. What's wrong with you?"

Jerome then looks down on the ground feeling guilty. Jerome then softly responds.

"I'm sorry. I just wanted to see what you were drawing. I won't touch your stuff."

Paul shakes his head, stretches his neck, and loosens his tie. Paul then reaches over to Jerome, and hands his sketchpad out for him to see. Paul then responds to Jerome.

"Here, just ask next time man okay? Yeah, this is an original series I'm doing. It's about these monster creatures that start business. They are smarter than the humans and stuff. Ha Ha."

Jerome smiles, and starts to look through Paul's sketches. Once Jerome is finished looking through the sketchpad, he thanks Paul for letting him look at his sketches, and hands it back to him. Paul then continues to draw on his sketchpad. Jerome starts to play video games on the Xbox Console. Klaus and Dan were watching this entire event happen, and they both smile at each other. At this time, something unusual, and unordinary happens. As Klaus and Dan are still in the kitchen, the doorbell starts to ring. Klaus immediately is puzzled, and starts to shout.

"Now who in the hell could that be?"

Dan starts to laugh, and Klaus laughs in return as well. Klaus then immediately proceeds to his front door, to see who is ringing the doorbell. Klaus opens the door, and is surprised to see Emilio, holding a large white box. Before Klaus is able to respond, Emilio speaks.

"Oh, hey again Klaus. Again, sorry about your Uncle. Uh, me and Bill's friends decided to give you a token of appreciation. Well, sort of. Ha Ha. It's triple chocolate cake, with chocolate, white chocolate, and fudge chocolate. From the best bakery in LA. Enjoy!"

Klaus shakes his head, and starts to laugh. Klaus accepts the cake that Emilio bought, and Klaus and Emilio hug again. Emilio kisses Klaus on the cheek, and says goodbye. Klaus shuts the front door, and walks back into the house. Klaus then directs himself to the kitchen, and sets the cake box on the kitchen counter. Dan looks at the box with a puzzled look, and speaks.

"Who was at the door. What's in the box?"

Klaus doesn't immediately respond to Dan, and Klaus starts to smile and laugh. Klaus opens up the refrigerator, and pulls out two beers. Klaus sets the beers on the kitchen counter, next to the cake box. Klaus then looks down on the ground, and shakes his head. Klaus speaks.

"Oh, well that was Emilio. He decided to give us a gift. He said it's a triple chocolate cake, from the best bakery in LA. This cake looks huge. Let's open it up, and see what we got."

Dan then shakes his head and laughs. Klaus opens up the cake box, and as promised, it's a triple chocolate cake, that looks extremely delicious. Dan then yells to Jerome and Paul.

"Hey guys, there is some cake in here, if y'all want some. Come and get it. Ha Ha."

Jerome pauses the video game, and Paul sets his sketchbook down. Both of them walk into the kitchen, and Dan cuts them up, each a piece of cake. Jerome and Paul take their cake back to the living room, and they start to eat it. Klaus and Dan who were staring at both Jerome and Paul, start to laugh. Dan then starts to cut another piece for Klaus, but Klaus stops him.

"Oh no, thanks man, but I'll get a piece a little bit later. That cake isn't going anywhere, look at it, it's like the size of a truck. That cake does look good though, I must admit. Ha Ha."

Dan then shakes his head, and laughs, and starts to close the cake box. As Dan is putting the cake into the refrigerator, Dan grabs his beer that was on the counter, and then speaks.

"Yeah, I'll get a piece later too. That cake is definitely gonna last us a while. Ha Ha."

Dan then starts to open his beer, and takes several sips of it. Klaus does the same, and opens his beer, and starts to drink it as well. Klaus then takes his cigarette carton out of his pocket, and signals for Dan to follow him out onto the balcony. Jerome continues to play on the Xbox video game, and Paul steadily draws on his sketchpad. Dan obeys, and follows Klaus on the balcony as well. Dan shuts the balcony door shut, once both he and Klaus are out on the balcony. Once both the men are out on the balcony, they both look at the evening overcast sky. This is rather peculiar weather for California, but it is still a nice beautiful sight. Klaus starts to light his cigarette, and takes a puff from it. Klaus hands Dan the lighter, and Dan lights his cigarette as well, and takes puffs from it. Klaus then looks down at the ground, and shakes his head. Dan, who is staring at Klaus, starts to laugh. Dan then takes a puff of his cigarette, and turns his vision facing forward, looking at the overcast sky, and the view of the ocean. Klaus and Dan can hear the seagulls, that are situated at the ocean, and they can hear the waves as well. Dan takes another puff of his cigarette, and with his vision facing forward, he speaks.

"Man, how many times were gonna do this? This never gets old does it? This is the life, I swear man. Ha Ha. Damn. Uncle. We keep your spirit alive, and we know you would have wanted us to be happy, and to do what we are doing now. We miss you very much Uncle."

Klaus looks ahead out to the distance as well, and shakes his head. Klaus speaks.

"No Dan, it never gets old. This is heaven. This is magical. So peaceful. I'm here, as always with my best friend in the world. I'll miss him, yeah. You're right Dan, Uncle would have wanted us to stay strong, and do exactly what we're doing now. Ha Ha. Miss you Uncle."

Klaus and Dan stare at each other, and erupt in laughter. Klaus and Dan then fist bump each other, and they return to looking at the distance. Dan takes another puff of his cigarette. As Dan is looking out forward towards the distance, Dan speaks.

"So Klaus. DJ K. What are we gonna do next? Now what do we do? Ha Ha."

Klaus takes a puff of his cigarette, and responds to Dan.

"I have no idea. I have no fucking clue. Ha Ha."

Dan starts to laugh hysterically, which Dan's laughter becomes infectious, causing Klaus to laugh as well. Klaus shakes his head, and continues to look forward, laughing.

CHAPTER 17:

THE SECRET SOCIETY

The morning after Bill's funeral, Klaus is the first of the men to awaken. What's strange, is that previously, Klaus was normally the last of the guys to wake up. Not there is a reverse effect; Klaus is typically the first of the men to wake up each morning now. Klaus gets out of bed, and Jerome remains deep asleep. Klaus directs himself to the kitchen, and has his, what is likely almost his required, and mandatory, cup of coffee. Klaus takes sips of the coffee, and despite it being 9 a.m., the weather is extremely hot. Possibly in the late 80s, as far as temperature. This weather is more usual to California, compared to the very gloomy, and overcast climate, that happened the day before. Klaus notices how warm the day is, and turns the air conditioning in his house on. Klaus takes more sips of his coffee, and stares out of the window. Following this Klaus walks over to the living room, and has a seat on his recliner. Klaus then starts to feel slightly upset, when he notices Bill's newspaper, that is situated under the coffee table in the living room. This was something that hasn't dawned on Klaus yet, and he begins to feel very emotional, and strange, knowing that Bill is no longer here. Klaus takes the newspaper, and sets it on the living room shelf, next to other books and magazines. Klaus then returns back to his recliner, and starts to lay back and relax. Klaus tilts his head back, and closes his eyes. Klaus isn't necessarily napping or sleeping, but he is resting his eyes, and relaxing. A half an hour later, Dan awakens, and notices Klaus relaxing on the recliner, and does not bother him. Dan smiles and laughs to himself, he walks straight to the kitchen, and starts to make himself a bowl of cereal. Once Dan has finished making his cereal, he walks into the living room, and sits on the sofa. Dan then immediately starts to eat his cereal, staring at Klaus, during this same time. Dan then turns his directions away from Klaus, and continues to eat his cereal. Dan again laughs to himself. Klaus, with his head back, and eyes closed, starts to speak.

"What's so God damn funny? Is there a spider, or an octopus on my head? What happened?"

Dan doesn't immediately respond, and he continues to eat his cereal. Dan quickly finishes eating his cereal, and gets up from the sofa. As Dan is walking to the kitchen, he speaks.

"We are all out of cereal, and the other guys are gonna hate me, for eating the last of it. I don't care/ I bought this box. If they want more, they can take their asses to the store. Ha Ha."

Klaus, still relaxing back in his recliner, shakes his head, and starts to laugh. Dan then put his bowl into the sink, and Dan walks back to the living room, taking a seat on the sofa. Dan then turns the television on, watching the morning news. While watching television, Dan speaks.

"So, what do you have planned for today? Nothing right? Ha Ha. You're always up to nothing, right man? Oh damn. Paul left his box of weed supplies here. He must have forgot it."

Klaus then sits himself up on the recliner, and starts to watch the news on the television. While Klaus has his vision directed at watching the news, he responds to Dan.

"Well, I guess we will see. I don't have anything officially planned. I guess today is going to be a rest day, and an off day. But you never know with me. Ha Ha. Just wait I guess."

Dan, who is still watching the news, laughs, and shakes his head. Klaus and Dan remain in the living room for several more minutes. An hour later, Jerome wakes up. Jerome doesn't acknowledge or speak to Klaus and Dan. Instead, he walks straight to the kitchen.

Jerome opens up the pantry, and is disappointed and unhappy. Jerome with an angry look, then starts to shout.

"Hey, what the hell? There is no cereal, and there isn't any milk either. You guys ate all the breakfast cereal, ugh. There is like no food in this damn house, I swear to god. Ugh."

Klaus and Dan start to laugh, which Jerome doesn't find amusing, and has an angered look on his face, while he's watching Klaus and Dan laugh. Dan then starts to speak.

"There's some oatmeal in there, eat that. Or you can go to the store. The choice is yours."

Jerome stares deeply at Dan, still with an angry look on his face. Jerome grumbles under his breath, and starts to slam the pantry doors shut. Jerome then takes out a container of oats, and proceeds to make himself a bowl of oatmeal. Once Jerome finishes making his oatmeal, he walks into the living room, joining Klaus and Dan. Jerome sits on the sofa, and begins eating. There is silence for several minutes during this time. Dan steadily watches the news on the television, Jerome is eating his breakfast, and Klaus, went back to relaxing on his recliner. While Jerome is eating his oatmeal, Klaus, who is still relaxing, with his eyes closed, speaks.

"Oh, by the way, young man. I want those fucking dishes cleaned, okay? Don't act like you didn't see those dishes in the sink, stacked like Mount Everest. You understand me?"

Jerome continues to eat his oatmeal, and starts to laugh. Jerome then silently responds.

"Yes Daddy, I'll clean the dishes up, don't you worry. I'll be a good boy. Don't worry."

Dan, who has his vision directed at the television, starts to laugh, and shake his head. Klaus, who is still relaxing back in his recliner, with his eyes closed, sternly responds to Jerome.

"You know what, don't have to be here, you know. You can live out on the street, or go with live with Peter Pan in Neverland. Everyone does their part around here, including you. Don't get fucking smart with me, as you can leave. I want those dishes done now Damn it!"

Dan again laughs at what Klaus said, and Jerome laughs as well. Jerome finishes his bowl of oatmeal, and gets up from the sofa. Jerome then walks up behind Klaus, and starts to hug him. Klaus doesn't seem very receptive, or comfortable, but doesn't emote or react. Jerome speaks.

"Okay, okay. Damn. I'm on it. Jesus Christ. I just woke up, and it's early. Alright?"

Klaus doesn't say anything, and Jerome kisses Klaus on the forehead. Dan yet again laughs and shakes his head, and Jerome walks over to the kitchen sink, and proceeds to do the dishes. While Jerome is doing the dishes, at this time, Paul manages to wake up. Paul, immediately walks over to the kitchen, not acknowledging Klaus or Dan. Once Paul is in the kitchen, he is very angry, when he notices that there isn't anything to eat. Paul speaks.

"Yeah, there isn't any food in here. Like, at all. Is this a prank or something?"

Jerome, as he is doing the dishes, and has his attention focused on that, speaks to Paul.

"Hey, don't look at me. I was upset, and puzzled just like you. There is oatmeal still left in there, I had that. There are some blueberries in the fridge as well."

Paul, starts to look through the refrigerator, very angry and upset, and takes a container of blueberries out of the refrigerator. Paul then opens up the pantry, and grabs the container of oats, and begins to make himself a bowl of oatmeal. Once Paul finishes making his oatmeal, he joins Klaus and Dan, in the living room. While Paul is eating his oatmeal, he speaks to the men.

"We really need to go to the supermarket. Like we don't have any food. That's not okay."

Klaus and Dan simply laugh at Paul, and do not respond to him. Once Paul realizes that Klaus and Dan, don't appear to be in agreement with him, he doesn't engage, or speak with them any further, and continues to eat his oatmeal. When Paul finishes his oatmeal, he returns to the kitchen sink, and hands Jerome his empty bowl. Jerome smiles at Paul, and Paul smiles back at Jerome, and Paul runs his hands, through Jerome's hair. Paul then immediately returns back to the sofa, with the rest of the guys. Jerome continues to tidy up all of the dishes in the sink. The guys all stay in a very awkward silence, for several minutes. Dan stays watching the news on the television, and Klaus remains relaxed in his recliner. Paul starts to take glances at both of them, and smiles to himself, and nods his head. Paul then looks down on the ground, remaining silent. Paul continues to stare deeply at both Klaus, and Dan, not saying anything. Paul is probably waiting for the both of them to say something, but it doesn't feel as though that is going to happen. The men continue to be silent, during this time. Paul continues to stare at the both of them, at the same time, gazing across the room. Paul then decides to speak.

"Good morning. You guys aren't hiding, or keeping something from me, are you?"

Dan, with his vision facing towards the television, watching the news, responds to Paul.

"Yes, we are hiding something. We are hiding that you need to shut the hell up. Ha Ha."

Dan starts to laugh hysterically, which due to the way Dan is laughing, makes Klaus laugh hysterically as well. Paul does not find this amusing, and shakes his head. Paul then gets up, and walks over to the shelf in the living room. Paul grabs his sketchpad, and starts to draw in it. As Paul is drawing animated characters in his sketchpad, he starts to hum Beatles songs to himself. Dan, who is trying to watch the news on the television, finds Paul humming annoying, and is agitated by it. Paul carries on with his humming, slightly being aware that Dan doesn't care for it. Paul has now been humming for five minutes, and Dan has just about had enough.

"Hey yo man, cut that out. You're gonna have to go in the other room or something if you're gonna do all of that. Klaus and I are trying to watch the news, and you're just being a jerk right now."

Paul does not respond at all to dan. Actually, he hums even louder, and Paul starts to laugh and chuckle to himself, teasing and annoying Dan further, as he continues his humming to the Beatles songs. Paul carries on humming for a few more minutes, and Paul speaks to Dan.

"Fuck you. I don't care what you think. What makes you think I care? I don't, at all."

Klaus, who remains laying back in his recliner, relaxing, shakes his head, and speaks.

"Okay, okay. Paul, stop humming, alright? It's annoying. Dan, you fucking quit it too."

Paul shakes his head and laughs, and obeys Klaus, and refrains from humming. Dan shakes his head, and laughs as well. Both Dan and Paul, stop quarrelling and squabbling, and carry on back to what they were doing. Dan resumes watching television, and Paul goes back to drawing in his sketchpad. Shortly after this Jerome finishes washing all the dishes, and returns to the living room, with the rest of the guys. Once he is in the living room, Jerome walks up from being Klaus, and starts to massage the back of his neck. Klaus tries to shove Jerome off him, but Jerome continues to play and tease with Klaus, by massaging his back. Jerome then speaks.

"Okay, I did all the dishes. You happy now? Do I get a gold star on the board? Ha Ha."

Klaus continues to shove and push Jerome off of him. As he's doing that, Klaus responds.

"No, you don't get a gold star. You get the satisfaction of doing what I asked you to do."

Jerome starts to laugh, and walks away from Klaus, and sits down on the sofa. Now, all of the guys are in the living room, quiet with one another. Dan and Jerome, watch the news on the television, Paul carries on drawing in his sketchpad, and Klaus, relaxes back on his recliner. This scene remains the same for several minutes, and an hour passes, and the guys still remain in this current state. So this very well might be a typical, slow day. The guys, aside from their usual mockery and antics, seem to be getting along fine and great with one another. The men are all content, and comfortable, with what they are currently doing. The weather outside, also is very warm. There doesn't seem to be any cause of concern, and things are going smooth. Well, at least they were. At was during this exact time, Klaus started to get that familiar feeling. The feeling that something is about to happen, and that something is going to alter the way things currently are, greatly. Klaus started to feel anxious, and he opens his eyes, and gets up in his recliner, becoming more alert. Something was definitely, and absolutely, going to happen soon. As much as Klaus didn't want to believe this feeling was accurate, it had to be. It was never wrong before. Klaus then focuses his vision directly down to the ground, feeling extreme anxiety all across his body. Klaus takes off his glasses, and starts to clean them with his shirt, and he remains nervous. Klaus looks around the room, and notices how calm, Dan, Jerome, and Paul are. Due to the fact the other men seem calm and happy, Klaus does not tell them, that he has something on his mind, and that he's concerned about something. Klaus doesn't want them to feel scared or unhappy. Klaus simply nods his head, and smiles to himself.

The awful thing was, this feeling was not Klaus doubting himself, or overreacting. So the option of Klaus simply ignoring this feeling, wasn't available. Klaus knew that something was going down very soon, and there was nothing he could do about it. This feeling was correct every single time before, so it's not incorrect all of a sudden now. Klaus simply has to wait, brace himself, and prepare for whatever happens, as a result of this energy he feels. Klaus decides to go back to relaxing, and although he's not ignoring the feeling, and he ready, and is alerted at any moment's notice, he wants to calm himself down for now, so when the feeling does come, he's able to comprehend and accept it, without any issues. Several hours actually pass, and all four the men, remain in the living room. Paul continues going about his sketches, Dan and Jerome flip through several channels, and converse with one another, making fun, and adding their own commentary to the programs that they are watching. Klaus steadily remains in his recliner chair, relaxing himself. Knowing the feeing he has still emanates around his body. As Dan and Jerome continue to flip through channels on the television, Dan works his way back to the local channels, and the news is covering a breaking story. For no apparent reason initially,

Klaus gets up from the recliner, and immediately directs, and focuses his attention on the television. Perhaps it was by coincidence or chance, but as soon as Klaus directed his attention to the television, the breaking news story went live, and a female news anchor, starts to speak.

"We have breaking news. It seems there is police stake out. Police believe they have located a residence, which is this mansion you see here, located in the Hollywood Hills, belonging to an organized crime group. Suspects inside, are not complying with police."

Klaus then forms a wide grin on his face, and Klaus immediately gets his notepad situated on the coffee table, and starts to jot down notes. Dan, Jerome, and Paul, out of instinct, stare at Klaus, as he is doing this. This was the feeling that Klaus felt. This was the opportunity that Klaus was waiting for. This was it, and this was the answer, for the question he was seeking. Klaus wanted to get down at the scene, and cover this event. Likewise with the teachers strike, likewise with the police pursuit, likewise with the election night, Klaus wanted to be there. While the breaking news story, is still being shown on the television, Klaus starts to go to his den, and grabs all of his camera equipment. Dan, who has an idea of what Klaus is doing, follows Klaus into the den. Klaus continues to grab all his cameras and microphones. Dan then speaks.

"What in the hell do you think you're doing? You're not thinking about going down there are you? Don't even think about it. No way. Stop. Klaus, don't do anything stupid. Come on."

Klaus remains having a wide grin on his face, and continues to gather all the equipment. While Klaus is doing that, still with a grin on his face, Klaus starts to softly respond to Dan.

"Oh, you bet your boots we're going down there. What are you, chicken? Ha Ha. We can't pass this one up. I been having this feeling all day, and I was waiting for this. Yes."

Dan shakes his head, and walks out of the den. Dan returns to the living room, and sits down on the sofa, and stares down at the ground, with his arms covering his face. Jerome and Paul, stare at him concerned, but do not say anything. At this time, Klaus returns back to the living room, and he has all of his equipment with him. Dan continues to feel hesitant and unsure, while Jerome and Paul remain alerted. Klaus then starts to speak to the men.

"Alright you guys, we have to hustle. We gotta get down there now. I know exactly where that house is. I researched about that mansion before. This is a really big crime group."

Dan gets up from the sofa, and gives a disappointed stare towards Klaus. Dan speaks.

"We're not going down there. You never learn do you. Now is not the time man. Don't."

Klaus shakes his head, and has a wide grin on his face, as he stares at Dan. Klaus speaks.

"You know what. Let's a take a vote. You're cool with that right? Okay. Who wants to go, and who wants to stay? The most votes win. I say we go, what do you guys think?"

Dan shakes his head, and takes a seat on the sofa. Dan then looks down, and speaks.

"You already know what I think. My answer is no. I don't think it's a good idea. No."

Jerome then starts to look around the room, and then speaks to the other men.

"Well, my vote is gonna be split. I'm a neutral vote, both yes, and no. I'm not sure."

Paul looks around the room as well, and after thinking to himself for a bit, Paul speaks.

"Hmm. I say we go for it. What the hell, why not. So I agree with Klaus. My vote is yes."

Klaus and Paul then fist bump, and Klaus then starts to reach into his pocket. Klaus pulls out a nickel coin and holds in it in his hand. Klaus then turns his direction at Dan, and speaks.

"Alright. You say no. Jerome is a split vote. Paul says yes. To make it more official and final, we're gonna have a coin toss. Whatever is lands on, is what we'll do. You call it Dan."

Dan laughs and shakes his head. Klaus grins back at him, and flips the coin. Dan speaks.

"Tails."

Klaus catches the coin, and turns his hand over to reveal what side it landed on.

"Damn, too bad, it's heads. So I guess we're going. Come on let's go. Don't waste time."

Dan starts to shake his head out of frustration, but is willing to accept the outcome of what happened. Within the next few minutes, the guys all then prepare to leave the house, to go to the mansion house, featured on the breaking news story, that is the focus of a stake out by the police. The residents of the house, are actually a prolific crime group. Klaus is well aware of the origins of the house, and has done extensive research on this mansion in the past. Even though the news did not relay, or talk about this information, Klaus is well aware, that the mansion belongs to the Diamond Mafia crime group. They are called that, because despite the fact, they do all types of crime, from robbery, to drug trade, even to ritual killings and murder, the group normally gets by doing overnight jewelry store heists, stealing over millions, in expensive jewelry, gold and diamonds. So because Klaus knew the entire history, and all of the incidentals of this group, he definitely was going to go down to the scene, and capture the event.

The men get all of their camera equipment, and leave out of the house. Klaus cannot stop smiling and grinning, and he feels very excited. Jerome and Paul, are fine with going to the scene. Dan however, is very hesitant, and feels it's no use trying to reason or argue with Klaus, to convince him not to be nosy, and cover the event, Dan remains quiet. Dan remains his stance, and conviction, that this is not the right time for them to resume their show, and Dan doesn't feel this is a safe story to cover. However Dan, because he knows there is just simply no reasoning with Klaus, doesn't say anything, and keeps his thoughts to himself. Klaus steadily drives down the highway, taking the drive to the Hollywood Hills, which is moderately spaced out, where his house is located at, in Redondo Beach. Dan remains quiet in the passenger seat, looking down, still feeling anxious and unsure, as

Jerome and Paul, who are sitting the back row, seem to be attentive to the situation. Minutes pass by, and Klaus has the breaking news report playing on his phone. The house is still on stake out by the police, so Klaus is certain that they will make it in time to the scene. Keeping in mind, that Klaus has been driving, on his way to the location, for quite some time by this point. Eventually, Klaus does arrive in the vicinity of the event. Klaus parks his SUV a few blocks away from the house, so they do not draw any suspicion from others. Once Klaus parks and turns the engine of his vehicle off, he immediately gets out of the car. Klaus then starts to gather all of his production equipment. Klaus grabs his camera, and grabs another camera, handing it to Paul. Paul accepts the camera Klaus hands him. Klaus then gives Jerome a microphone, to which Jerome accepts the microphone. Klaus then starts to hand Dan a microphone, but Dan does not accept it. Dan shakes his head, and speaks to Klaus.

"You guys go on. I'm just gonna wait here it's okay. Y'all go on ahead. I'll be fine."

Klaus shakes his head, and forces the microphone into Dan's hand. Klaus then speaks.

"Oh no you don't. Don't give me that shit. Be a man, and stop feeling scared. Stop it."

Dan shakes his head, and accepts the microphone that Klaus hands him. The four men then all start to walk away from the car, directing themselves to the mansion that the police are still staking out the suspects for. The men continue to follow Klaus lead, as Klaus, who remarkably seems to be very familiar with this area, starts to walk through a park. Klaus informs the men that the park is a shortcut, to another hillside area, where the guys will get a good vantage point of the house being on stake out. Klaus studied heavily this area before, and has the upper hand, and advantage during this situation. At this time, while the men are going through the park, Klaus starts up the live feed, in which the audience who follow or subscribe are automatically notified, that they guys are doing a live news show. As Klaus suspected, there are already two hundred people, tuned in live to the show, and he has only been live for exactly a minute. Klaus calibrates Paul's camera as well, and both camera feeds are connected. The men continue to walk through the park, heading to the shortcut, that Klaus suggested. The guys then reach the shortcut, which leads the guys to a bluff mountain area, very close to the mansion. Unluckily, Klaus doesn't remember a fence being installed where the shortcut entrance was. Although fortunately, the fence is broken at the bottom. Klaus, and the rest of the guys, crawl under the fence opening, to the other side. Once the guys are on the other side of the fence, with Klaus leading the way, the men all then walk across the side bluff, and mountains, in the Hollywood Hills. The men getting closer, and closer to the mansion. A few minutes pass, and the men have an extremely good vantage point of the mansion. At this time, Klaus instructs for Dan and Paul to go on the northern side of the mansion, while himself and Jerome, would be on the south side of the mansion. Dan and Paul agree, and they direct themselves, over to that area. Klaus and Jerome, then start to walk over to the southern side of the mansion, with Klaus capturing everything on his camera, and Jerome speaking to the viewers, using the microphone.

Klaus and Jerome reach the spot they are going to report at, and start their coverage of the event. Klaus can hear the police shouting demands at the suspects, who are hiding inside of the house, and are refusing to come out. With it now being 5 p.m., in the evening, Klaus wonders how long this stake out will last, and if the suspects will ever comply with the police. It doesn't matter in Klaus vision, as he knows the longer the stake out is, the more entertaining his show will be. More viewers tune into the show, with now a thousand people watching the coverage of the stake out, that Klaus, and the guys are broadcasting live. For about an hour, things are very uneventful, and it was then that Klaus had a slight feeling of regret, and maybe he shouldn't have decided to cover the stake out. Klaus assumed that things would be more exciting and engaging. This is deciding to show, as some of the viewers are not starting to sign off of the live broadcast, and the audience which was at a thousand people, is now down to five hundred people who are tuned in. Klaus starts to check into Dan and Paul's feed, and things are virtually the same. The feed and coverage that Dan and Paul are showing isn't eventful either. Klaus is very disappointed that things are turning out to be, terribly boring. Klaus then decides to call Dan, and tells him, that if nothing exciting happens, within the next half an hour, they are going to call it a day, and go home. Dan is in agreement with this plan, and hangs the phone up. Klaus continues to stay with Jerome, sticking with his promise, that if things don't turn around, they are going to leave.

Surprisingly, things do happen to become more eventful. Not even a minute after hanging up the phone, after speaking with Dan, one of the suspects, is seen trying to sneak out of an upstairs window, located on the northern side, where Dan and Paul are covering. Klaus instantly has a wide smile on his face, and feels glad. The viewers of the live feed, go up, as the guys continue to capture the suspect who is trying to escape from the second story window. The suspect continues to slither out of the window, and climbs out the side of the house. However, it is not long, before the swat team spots him, and when the suspect continues to resist and escape and run, he is shot and killed by the police. Dan and Paul managed to get all the coverage live. The swat team instantly start to climb up to the second story of the mansion, where the suspect sneaked out of. Now that the police know the area the suspects are trying to run out from, that gives them probable cause to get into action, and force themselves in. As the swat team enter the house, Klaus is pleased, when on the southern side, where himself and Jerome are, police start to climb up, and swarm throughout the house. Klaus can see shadows of the swat team, as they are inside. Klaus continues to cover everything, and things are becoming more intense. However, Klaus is then approached with a very familiar issue. Klaus looks at Dan and Paul's feed, and notices that is it offline, and not live. Klaus becomes slightly worried, but at this time, react. Klaus instead continues to stay with Jerome on the southern side, capturing everything. Not even a few seconds after this, in a very flash instant, Klaus feels what appears to be a burlap sack, cover his face. The burlap sack smothers him greatly. In addition to that, Klaus can also feel himself being struck with a needle, in the back of his left shoulder. Instantly, Klaus loses consciousness, and everything turns dark. The darkness remains for a minute, then five minutes, then what seems like twenty minutes, to eventually, in Klaus mind, what could realistically be an hour, of total darkness, and unconsciousness. Although, the darkness Klaus was experiencing, then turns into faded light, with a slight buzzing and ringing sound, in his ear.

The faded light, and buzzing and ringing, lasts for what seems ten minutes, and now Klaus can hear perfectly clear, but his vision is slightly blurry. Klaus notices that someone put his glasses inside his shirt pocket. Klaus has a feeling, although his vision is poor and bad, that his hands are tied. Klaus managed to move his hands through his shirt pocket, and Klaus, finds a way to successfully his glasses on. Once Klaus has his glasses on, and his vision has fully returned, instantly sees that someone has taken his shoes and socks off, and he is barefoot. Klaus also notices that his hands are definitely tied in front of him, with rope. As Klaus starts to come to, and become more aware the situation, Klaus can also tell, that he is in, some type of warehouse, or factory. The entire setting is slightly dark, with a couple of lamps on the ceiling. The building is extremely cold, and there is an ambient echo sound, throughout the entire building. Klaus, even though his hands are tied behind his back, manages to stand up, and walks around the building. Not even thirty seconds of walking around, Klaus notices Paul, who also had his shoes and socks confiscated, and his hands are also bound and tied together, is looking disorientated, and sprawling on the ground. Klaus, not trying to draw attention to himself, starts to silently creep and walk up to him. Klaus then whispers to Paul.

"Paul. Paul. Wake up man. It's me Klaus. Paul. Wake Up."

Paul simply remains disorientated on the ground, and Klaus approaches him. Klaus shoves Paul, using his shoulders, to get his attention, and wake up him. After a minute, Paul does manage to come to his senses, and starts to speak, although sounding weak.

"What. Klaus, is that you? Where the hell are we? What happened. I remember like someone putting a bag on my head, and they injected me with something. What's going on?"

Klaus then tries to untie Paul's hands. As he's doing that, Klaus silently responds back.

"Same thing happened to me. I think Dan and Jerome are also here too. If we help each other we can get these ropes off, and get the fuck out of here. Stay quiet though."

Paul nods his head, and Paul manages to get his glasses out of his shirt pocket, the same method and way, that Klaus managed to do it, and now that Paul has his full vision and eyesight, he starts to help untie Klaus ropes. Klaus does the same and tries to untie Paul, but is having difficulty. Although it took a while, Paul seems to be really advanced in knots, and is more skilled at untangling knots better than Klaus, and remarkably, is able to free Klaus.

"Whoa man, how did you do that? I'm free. Ha Ha. If only I can untie you. I'll try."

Paul silently laughs at Klaus, and shakes his head. Paul then whispers back to Klaus.

"I don't know. I was in boy scouts when I was younger, so I know some stuff. Ha Ha."

Klaus silently laughs back at Paul. Luckily, Klaus, through his slight knowledge of knots, not as good as Paul, but through his prior experiences with knots, is able to free Paul as well. Now that both Klaus and Paul are free from their hands being tied, they continue to walk around the building. A couple minutes later, they come across Jerome, who like with the other guys, had his shoes confiscated, and his hands are also tied. Klaus silently walks up Jerome, waking him.

"Jerome, hey. Wake up. It's gonna be okay. I'm here. Wake up buddy. It's okay."

Jerome manages to wake himself up, and immediately starts to cry and feel scared. Klaus starts to hug Jerome tightly, and kisses him on the forehead. Paul then starts to untie Jerome. Klaus continues to hug Jerome tightly, and Jerome then silently speaks.

"What the hell? What is this, where are we? Where's Dan? What's going on?"

Klaus continues to hold and hug Jerome, and Klaus silently whispers back to him.

"We don't know, but it's alright now. We're gonna find Dan, and get out of here."

Jerome silently nods his head, and at this same time, Paul manages to free Jerome. Paul notices that all of the ropes the guys are tied with, are done with separate knots, all with extreme difficulty. So in order for the guys to have been able to free themselves, they would have had to be experts at knots, in which by luck of god, Klaus and Paul both were. Once Jerome is free, the men continue to walk around the building, looking for Dan. After a couple of minutes, of walking through the dark factory, the guys unsuccessful in finding Dan, and start to feel worried. However, the guys do manage to spot Dan, after careful searching. Likewise with the other guys, Dan is barefoot, sprawling on the ground, with his hands tied. Klaus silently wakes Dan up.

"Hey man. Wake up. Stay quiet. We're gonna get out here, just stay calm okay?"

Unlike with the other guys, Dan doesn't take the situation lightly or calmly, Dan starts to yell and scream, however Klaus manages to cover Dan's mouth within a millisecond.

"You have to stay quiet, keep your voice down. Just stay calm. It's gonna be okay."

Dan obeys Klaus, and doesn't speak. During this same time, Paul starts to untie Dan. Like Paul started to already suspect, realize, and notice, Dan's knots seem to be the hardest and most difficult out of all the guys. This shows, as Paul spends about half an hour, trying to untie Dan, but not being able to fully untie him. The rest of the guys start to feel anxious and nervous, that Paul isn't going to be able to free him. Luckily, after about forty-five minutes of Paul messing with the knots, he's able to find what knot was used, and strategically and successfully untangles the knots, Dan was tied with. Dan, is now free. Once Dan is untied, all four of them, then continue to walk about the factory, trying to find a way out. The men feel as though they are trapped, and getting out seems hopeless. Although, things quickly turn around. Five minutes later, Klaus notices an open window, as the guys walk around a corner in the factory. Klaus, and the rest of the guys, also notice a stack of pallets, located slightly nearby. The guys then start to drag the pallets against the wall, forming a platform, turning it into a makeshift ladder, flight of steps, and staircase, so they all can reach the window, and crawl out of it. The guys, simply using teamwork, and working together, manage to position the pallets accordingly, and very quickly start to climb on top of the pallets, to escape. The men, one by one start to crawl out of the window. Klaus is the first, followed by Paul, followed by Jerome, followed by Dan, who is the last to crawl out of the window. Now that the men have reached outside, they now continue on with their escape. The men walk along the outside of the factory, although with it now being nighttime, and dark, it's quite difficult for the men to see where they are going.

Klaus, and the rest of the men, then come across what looks like an unguarded gate. Without wasting anytime at all, the men all start to dart at the gate, until they hear shouting.

"Hey! Hey! You guys! Stop right there, or we will fucking kill you!"

The men then all immediately stop, and remain motionless. The guys then notice, that there are three heavy set guards, two Caucasian, and one African-American, pointing large semi-automatic rifles, with flashlights, and scopes on them. Not even a few seconds after this, a slender Caucasian man, with short styled black hair, wearing a three-piece suit, walks from behind the three heavy set men. The man has his hands in his pocket, and starts to walk closer to the guys. As the suited man walks to the guys, one of the Caucasian heavy-set guards speaks.

"Hey Boss. Blow their fucking brains out like promised right? You got it."

Then, this same guard, starts to step closer to the guys, with his gun aimed at then. The suited man, then reaches into his suit jacket pocket, and takes out a pistol. He then speaks.

"No, change of plan. How about I blow your brains out, for letting them escape idiot."

Within an instant, the suited man shoots the guard in the head, killing him. The other guards stand motionless, as the suited man then starts to shout and speak to the guards.

"You guys are gonna be fucking next. How the fuck did you guys let them escape like that. You idiots. Put those guns down, and do as I fucking tell you, or your ass is grass. Got it?"

The guards immediately nod their heads, and put their rifles down, and obey the suited man. The suited man, then puts his pistol back in his suit jacket pocket, and starts to walk up to the guys. The suited man then starts to walk up to the guys, and starts to speak to them.

"Now, I'm gonna ask you all ne question, and one question only. I don't repeat myself, and I don't like to be ignored. Now, who is the leader, and how did you escape? ANSWER!"

Not even a nanosecond after this, Klaus immediately starts to speak to the suited man.

"Sir, I'm the leader. My name is Klaus. These are my friends. We're video bloggers. We know how to untie knots, and there was an open window. We put some pallets against the wall to escape. Please have mercy on us. We don't mean any harm."

The suited man then starts to laugh to himself, and with his hands in his pockets, starts to approach Klaus. Klaus stands in fear, not showing any reactions, and trying to stay calm. The suited man gets to a very close distance within Klaus, and stares at him. The suited man speaks.

"Okay. You have to be the luckiest man in the world. We were like five minutes away from going down there, to kill all of you. We just had other fish to fry. So we let you guys suffer down there until then. Don't know how you got through those knots. Ha Ha."

Klaus, and the rest of the guys remain silent, and motionless. The suited man then pulls out a walkie talkie from his jacket pocket, and then starts to speak in code.

"Papa, Foxtrot, Whiskey. Papa, Foxtrot, Whiskey. Echo, Delta, Hotel. Echo, Delta, Hotel. I like to put crackers in my Tomato Soup. I like to put crackers into my Tomato Soup."

Klaus and the other guys continue to stay silent, and motionless. The person on the other end of the walkie then responds with various other code words. The suited man speaks to Klaus.

"My name is King Shark. You can call me King Shark, King, Shark, or Boss. Don't call me anything else, or you're gonna get whacked in a heartbeat. Again, you guys are the luckiest sons of bitches ever. I like you guys; you guys are smart. So, I want you to work for me."

Klaus and the rest of the men, stay silent. Continuing listening to King Shark speak.

"You guys are now members of Diamond Mafia. Whether you like it or not. Not up for discussion. You guys reveal you're in the group. Whacked. You guys cut up. Whacked. You guys don't come correct. Whacked. You don't obey my orders. Whacked. Alright Gentlemen?"

King Shark then pulls out his walkie talkie and says more code words to person on the other end. King Shark then turns his vision towards Klaus, smirking at him. King Shark speaks.

"This is why it doesn't pay to be nosy. Curiosity killed the cat, remember? You're social media guys. Cops scoping out one of my houses. Y'all wanna play Columbo I see. Ha Ha. I'm gonna give you guys a second chance, as I like you. If you fuck it up, you already know."

King Shark again pulls out his walkie talkie, and says more code words to the other person. King Shark then takes out his phone, and texts someone. King Shark speaks to Klaus.

"I want you guys to do something for me. Since you guys managed to break out easily like that, you guys should have no problem at all, sneaking into an aerospace center, and stealing a hard drive. That hard drive contains classified information, and I need it right now."

Two additional armed guards arrive, and King Shark signals for the armed guards, to grab the rest, escorting them away from the location. Klaus and the men, being forced by gunpoint, remain following King Shark, as he pulls out his walkie talkie again, saying code words, and other code phrases. Klaus and the rest of the guys have no choice, but to remain silent. Klaus, and the men remain scared, silent, and obedient, as they are taken into a room, which looks like a tattoo shop. Once all the guys are in the room, one of the guards shuts the door and locks it. King Shark walks on the other side of the room, and pulls out four manilla folders. As he's doing that, King Shark speaks again to Klaus, and the guys.

"We can't just exchange information through the post office or UPS. No, that's really stupid, and also, we may as well write on the envelope 'We're a crime group, and this is illegal contraband'. Ha Ha. As what's the difference? So we have to use fronts and be slick about it."

King Shark continues to write on several documents, sticking them into the manila folders. As King Shark does that, he pulls out another packet of documents. King Shark speaks.

"So, this is like an initiation almost. How you guys manage to get the hard drive, is up to you. But I have the information here, the key codes for the lock doors are here. There is a map. So yeah. Get the hard drive, get it back here before sunrise, and I don't kill you. Got it?"

Klaus, and the rest of the guys, stay totally quiet, listening to King Shark. King Shark then sets the four manilla folders he took, out and takes out a marker pen. King Shark speaks.

"Two things left, and I'll set you guys out, so you can go and do your mission and task. Number one, you guys have to be given a nickname. All guys in Diamond Mafia have one. You guys have five seconds to think of one. If not, I'll kill you, and nickname you myself. Ha Ha."

King Shark then asks the guys to provide him a nickname. Klaus goes first, and says "DJ K.", Dan goes next, and says, "Dax", Jerome goes next, and says "Einstein", Paul is last to give King Shark his nickname, and he says, "Picasso". King Shark writes all their nicknames, on the top of every manilla folder. King Shark then puts several documents inside the manilla folder, and puts the folders, on the side of the table. King Shark then looks at the men and speaks.

"Alright. Last thing. Now this is really important. Yeah. Listen here, listen good boys."

King Shark takes off his suit jacket, and rolls up his shirt, revealing a three-inch tattoo, of the face of a tiger growling, with a large blue diamond behind the tiger. King Shark then speaks.

"Every Diamond Mafia guy has to get tatted. You guys don't have to get the tattoo no, but I'm gonna fucking kill you if you don't. So the choice is your boys. The longer you take to make your mind up on the tattoo, the less time you have for the task. Remember you only have until sunrise. That's it. Good luck on your journey. You guys will need it. Ha Ha. Bye boys."

King Shark instantly walks out of the room, followed by several guards. Klaus, and the rest of the guys, remain in the tattoo room, motionless. Seconds later, two bald Caucasian man, with several tattoos over their body, walk into the room. They each stand beside two barber's chairs. Klaus and the rest of the men, stay speechless, thoughtless, and motionless. At this time, the African American guard, that the guys saw earlier, then starts to speak.

"I don't know what you boys are waiting for. Just go and get it over with."

Strangely, not even a second later. Klaus and Paul, instantaneously, go sit at the two barber's chairs. Dan and Jerome simply watch, as their turn is going to be next. The tattoo artists, then immediately start inking Klaus and Paul. The tattoo is three inches, and must be on the guy's upper left arm. Klaus, although he is quiet, feels the pain of the tattoo needle, and also starts to wish everything that has happened within the past several hours, was a dream. It was now that Klaus realized that he should have listened to Dan. After about an hour, the tattoo artists finish both Klaus and Paul's tattoos. Paul looks down at his tattoo, and starts to cry. Paul shakes his head, and takes a seat where Dan and Jerome are sitting. Paul keeps his head down, shaking his head, crying. Klaus looks at his tattoo, and is emotionless, and is still in disbelief. The pain of the tattoo needle, although it's very much temporary, remains in Klaus mind. Even though Klaus is looking at Paul, he can tell he is unhappy, and is crying. It is now Dan and Jerome's turn, to get their tattoos. They both sit in the barber's chairs, and the tattoo artist, gives Dan and Jerome, the same tattoo, that was given to Klaus and Paul. Jerome, although he is clearly upset, and crying, and is uncomfortable, remains silent while getting his tattoo. Klaus starts to cry himself, as he is watching Jerome. Klaus then turns his vision to Dan, who is also congruently getting his tattoo done. Dan simply has a look of anger, and an almost, 'I told you so', expression on his face. Dan and Klaus give each other eye contact, and stare at each other, and Dan simply shakes his head. As a result of this, Klaus bows his head down, continues to cry, and shakes his head.

Another hour passes, and Dan and Jerome, have also completed getting their tattoos done. At this time, Dan and Jerome return seated, alongside Klaus and Paul. At this time, one of the tattoo artists, reaches on the desk, and pulls out the document packet, related to the hard drive, King Shark, ask the guys to steal. The tattoo artist hands Klaus the packet and speaks.

"Good luck you guys. The guards are gonna drop you guys off, a mile away from the location and you guys are gonna have to find a way to get there, and reach the building from that point. It will be too suspicious, if we drop you guys right in front. Be safe guys. Go tigers."

Go tigers, was a saying, meaning good luck, and well wishes to all the members. Klaus holds the packet in his hands, as the guards escort all the guys out of the tattoo shop, and into a van. While in the van, Klaus and Dan are seated in one row, while Jerome and Paul, are seated in the row behind them. The van then proceeds to the aerospace building. Klaus turns to look at Dan, who has both an angered and upset expression. Dan gives eye contact to Klaus and speaks.

"I fucking told you so man. Wow. I fucking told you so."

Dan then returns to looking down on the ground, shaking his head. Klaus then shakes his head, looks down on the ground, and laughs.

CHAPTER 18:

THE TASK

Something unpredictable, and frightening has just happened to all of the guys. Taking time to reflect everything that has happened. During some time, as the guys were covering event, there was someone, and that someone was part of the Diamond Mafia, that was watching the guys cover the story. Klaus, and the rest of the men were drawing a lot of suspicion to themselves, and the Diamond Mafia, who was spying on all the men, figured that they were up to no good, and were possibly a rival gang. The Diamond Mafia members, managed to sneak up to Klaus and the guys, and covered the faces with burlap sacks, and injected them, with some type of medicine, that managed to instantly make the men fatigued. Hours later, the men all start to wake up, and come to their senses. They notice that they are in some type of factory, and their hands are tied, and someone has taken their shoes. The men start to figure out a method, as to how they are going to escape, and get out of this. Klaus managed to locate Paul, with Klaus knowledge of knots, he was able to untie him. Through Paul's even more intensive knowledge of knots, and untangling difficult knots, Paul managed to untie Klaus, in which the knots that Klaus was tied with, was more complicated and difficult. The guys then located Jerome and Dan, and untied them as well. Now that the men were all untied, they quickly tried to find a way to get out of the building. The men came across an open window, and decided to use pallets, that were located nearby, to use a platform, so they can escape. The men successful do this, and it seems they were home free, and have escaped. Unfortunately, the men are stopped by several guards, and a frozen in fear. Klaus and the men, have no choice but to obey and comply. Shortly after that, the Diamond Mafia boss, King Shark, approaches the scene. King Shark kills one of the guards, out of anger, for allowing Klaus, and the guys to escape. King Shark, after finding out who Klaus and the guys are, manages to develop a slight ounce of sympathy, and allows the men to have a second chance.

King Shark will not kill the guys but the catch is, the guys must become members of Diamond Mafia. They must get tattooed, like the other members have, and they also must past an initiation task. If they are able to pass the task, King Shark will allow the guys to live. The men continue to feel fearful of this situation, and are hoping it's all a dream. Unfortunately, it isn't. It seems Klaus curiosity, and his knack for wanting to be nosy and involve himself in affairs that doesn't pertain to him, finally caught up to him. Klaus has stepped into something extremely bad, and the guys are in much trouble, and things are looking terribly dim for them all. The guys have no choice but to agree with King Shark, and stick with the program. The guys are all quickly given a nickname, as they are now members of the Diamond Mafia. Klaus is called "DJ K.", Dan is called "Dax", Jerome is called "Einstein", and Paul is called, "Picasso". Now that all of the guys have gotten nicknames, it is now time for them to get tattooed. This is not up for discussion, and all members up the group, must get a tattoo. The guys, again, not having any choice to refuse or decline, all get their tattoos, further completing the process, to become members of the secret society. After the guys are all tattooed, the guys now must go on, and complete their initiation task. Which failure to do so, will result in King Shark, killing them.

The task that King Shark wants the guys to do, is to steal a hard drive, which contains passwords, cryptocurrency accounts, and other classified information on it. The hard drive is located inside an Aerospace Technology business. Diamond Mafia, cannot ship, mail, or transport things, like ordinary civilians do. They must come up with another routine, as this would bring much suspicion to their group. Instead, Diamond Mafia, decides to exchange information with one another, by using planted, and fronted locations, so there is less suspicion. There is a Diamond Mafia employee, who works at the Aerospace building, and has already pre planted the hard drive earlier. Although initially, the employee was going to leave the hard drive there, and after the information was transferred to the hard drive through the internet, the employee was going to pick it up later, and return it to headquarters; King Shark decided to use this opportunity, to test the guys, and allow them to pick the hard drive up themselves. Not only that, they must do it after hours, and avoid being caught, and drawing suspicion. If that isn't difficult enough, the men must accomplish this task, and bring the hard drive back before sunrise. If the men are able to do this successfully, they will gain the full respect of Diamond Mafia, and King Shark, is going to spare their lives. The men are handed a packet, which contains all the information that they need, in order to complete the task. Klaus, and the rest of the men, are then thrown inside of a van, driven by a Diamond Mafia member to the location of the Aerospace building. During the van ride, Dan gives a very disappointed look towards Klaus, and as the men continue on to the Aerospace building, Dan eventually speaks to Klaus.

"I told you so man. I tried to tell you, but you wouldn't listen. I told you so."

Dan shakes his head, and looks down at the ground. Klaus then knew that Dan was right, and he should have just listened to him from the beginning. The men have really destroyed any chance of getting out of this situation, and there is nothing they can do. Klaus starts to deeply regret, not agreeing with Dan's original decision and choice, of them not leaving the house, and going to the location. The van continues to drive to the building, and Klaus cannot get his thoughts situated, and he has no idea how the men are going to accomplish this task. Klaus heart continues to beat and race very fast, and his nerves are of course causing him stress. Before long, as if it were within seconds, the van approaches a dark side street, that is situated a mile away from the Aerospace Building. The van driver shuts of the engine, and speaks to the guys.

"Alright guys. This is where I have to drop you guys off. I wish you guys luck, as you guys are going to need it. Ha Ha. Oh, here are all of your shoes back. King Shark didn't want you using your shoes to attack us, so he confiscated them. Alright guys. Go Tigers!"

The van driver then hands Klaus a black hefty trash bag which contains all of the guys shoes. Klaus goes through the bag, and takes out his shoes, and also gives the guys, their shoes as well. The guys then start to put their shoes on, and proceed to get out of the van. Once the men are all out of the van, the van driver starts the engine, and then speaks to the guys.

"Okay, once you guys have the hard drive, push this device, and I'll swing around back and pick you guys up. Again, good luck guys. Go Tigers!"

The van driver hands Klaus a GPS device, and the driver quickly speeds off down the road. Klaus looks down at the GPS device, and holds it tightly in his hands. Klaus then puts the device into his pocket, and shakes his head. Directly following that, Dan, Jerome, and Paul, start to feel very puzzled and confused, and look around the area, unsure as to what they shall do next. Klaus then starts to skim through the packet, and although he has not an idea in the world, as to how the guys are going to complete this task, he starts to attempt to brainstorm. Klaus, using his logic, and strategic skills, realizes that the best plan for all the guys to use, is to create as many diversions and distractions, as possible. There are four of them, so they can absolutely manage to do this. As Klaus continues to read through the packet, which contains a map, and a location of the hard drive, and other code keys, and locks, and elevators and staircase, he then starts to puts the puzzle together, as to how they are going to manage this task, and heist. Klaus first step of the plan, is to have Dan, act as an intoxicated drunk belligerent man. This would alreadly put the security guards on alert, over the way Dan is acting outside. Klaus has to understand, that security would most definitely call the police, so the men must act fast, before police arrive.

While Dan is causing a scene outside the front entrance, Jerome, would then walk into the building, and explain to the security at front, that he doesn't have a ride home, and he left his phone at home, and if he can use the phone. This would add yet another distraction.

Now that Dan, and Jerome, are acting out on their diversions, this would then allow, for Klaus, and Paul, to sneak into the building. Klaus notices that there are two separate staircases, located at the front entrance of the building, that the guys can go through. However, Klaus then has an idea hatch into his mind. Although this wasn't mentioned in the packet, or by King Shark either, Klaus starts to believe, that the building has surveillance cameras. Klaus then understands, that he must find a way to disable these cameras somehow, so the guys are undetected by them. This causes Klaus to feel more cognizant of the situation, and that he now needs to find a plan or method, to disable the cameras. Klaus, with his prior knowledge of hacking surveillance security cameras, feels like he will be able to accomplish this. Klaus just has to hope, that the building uses an obsolete system for their security cameras, as if they don't, Klaus will not be able to hack, or disable them, as he cannot hack the newer, and updated security systems. After Klaus manages to disable, and also reset the security cameras, so the camera doesn't pick up Dan, or Jerome in the building as well. Klaus and Paul, will then start to head to the second floor, to get the hard drive. Once the men have the hard drive, Klaus and Paul will walk to the front of the building, and give a signal to Dan and Jerome, letting them know, they have gotten the hard drive. With the plan now all set, although he is still feeling very unsure and doubtful, Klaus is satisfied with this plan, and he feels that as long as the guys act swiftly, there is no reason, as to why they can't accomplish it. Klaus prepares to explain the plan to the guys. Klaus then starts to fold the packet up, and after folding it, he places it in his pocket. Klaus then takes his glasses off, and cleans them with his shirt. After doing that, Klaus starts to speak to the guys.

"Okay, now listen to me. This is either going to go smooth like butter, or this is going to be rough like nails. If you guys follow my plan, we should be able to do this, without any issues, and do what we have to do, and get out of there. But you guys need to listen to me, alright?"

The men all remain silent, towards Klaus. Klaus then speaks to the men about the plan.

"Dan, what I need for you to do, is act like a drunk. I don't mean any drunk, you need to be really convincing, and act like as shitface drunk man. Use your imagination, and don't hold back. The more wild you are, the better we are going to pull this off. Okay?"

Dan nods his head, and Klaus then turns his vision towards Jerome. Klaus speaks to him.

"Okay, now you. Here's what I need you to do young man. Go into the building, and tell the security guard, that you are lost, and you missed the bus, and need to call your Dad to come pick you up. Tell the guard that you don't have your phone. Use your imagination. Okay?"

Jerome then nods his head, and understands the plan. Klaus then turns to look at Paul.

"Alright, now, what I need you to do, is kinda be my backup. It's gonna be me and you, that are gonna go and fish this hard drive. So you're just gonna be my backup eyes. You're gonna follow my lead, and I'm gonna disable the cameras. We will then go to the second floor."

Paul nods his head, to Klaus plan as well. Klaus then starts to look down on the ground, and starts to shake his head. Klaus then starts to cry, which causes the other men to cry as well. While the men are continuing to feel sad and depressed, Dan then starts to speak to Klaus.

"We don't have a chance in hell at pulling this off. This is all your fucking fault Klaus. All you had to do was listen to me, and we wouldn't be here. We can't do this. No way. Ugh."

The men continue to feel upset, and at this time, and take in what Dan just said. Dan was correct, and that the men should have never left the house, as they wouldn't be in this hopeless situation. The men are still feeling emotional, and Jerome starts to speak to the men.

"We have to at least try. If this is it, and this is how we all go out, and if King Shark ills us, at least we tried. So I'm willing to at least try you guys."

Paul then starts to look down on the ground, and speaks to all the men.

"Yeah, let's give it a try, and we'll see what happens. I think we have a chance of doing this, and I think if we just follow Klaus plan, everything is going to go fine. So yeah."

Understanding that the men do not have much time to complete this task, they must get going now. They also know, that they cannot call or inform the police, as the device Klaus was handed to by the driver, contains a live GPS tracker, so King Shark would know, if the guys are walking to a police station, or end up going somewhere other than the location of the building. With Dan still being reluctant, the guys without much discussion or hesitation, start to walk to the Aerospace building. During their walk, Klaus continues to recap his plan in his mind, and how everything is going to be mapped and plotted out. Klaus gave each of them a separate role in doing this task, and along with the diversions and also all of the distractions, Klaus is very confident, that the men are going to be able to succeed, at getting the hard drive, and leaving out of the building with it, in a swift fashion. Also considering, that Klaus is going to disable the security cameras, so it would be just as if, the guys were never there, and there would be no evidence of them being in the building at all. The guys are feeling slightly nervous, and anxious, but that's normal and typical. It would be strange, and impossible, for them not to feel that way. Although, if they are not able to control their nerves and anxiety, they are not going to be able to finish this task, and accomplish it successfully. The men are now half a mile away from the building, and they carry on with their walk, still having their plan figured out. The street the guys are walking on to the building is dark, and also quiet. Klaus at this time, now starts to second guess himself deeply, and he wonders if Dan is possibly right, and they are not going to finish this task, and that the results for all of them are going to very grim. Even though Klaus was sure that he had all the details of the task figured out, there is still the chance of mistakes or error happening, which could be a very devastating for the guys. Klaus just has to hope, that nothing goes wrong, and things go identical to his plans, and happen the way he imagined and hopes. Klaus knows that it's going to be up to destiny, fate, and chance, as to whether or not the guys manage to do this, or they come up short, and are unsuccessful. Time will always tell, and they are going to have to wait and find out, what the results of everything will be. Before long, the guys are in direct vision and view of the building. The Aerospace building, is a two floor, commercial building, which although the building isn't that large, it's not a small building either.

The building, in which a Diamond Mafia employee works there, has never been used as a front, to exchange information and items, between other members. This is the first time it's being done, as a Diamond Mafia member, is an employee here, so it works out. The police wouldn't have any suspicion, of the hard drive, the men are attempting to steal and obtain, has vital information. The goal for the guys, is to get the hard drive, and hand the hard drive back to King Shark, without being caught in the process. The men walk closer to the building, and Klaus is fully aware, that he needs to get his plan in order, right now. While the men are relatively close to the entrance of the building, Klaus stops all the men, and doesn't allow them to keep walking. Klaus then starts to look around, and begins to brainstorm ideas. Klaus doesn't want all of them to stick out, and cause more attention to themselves. At this point, Klaus is going to let Dan walk ahead of them, and start to do his part of the diversion and distraction. Klaus wants to give the impression, that Dan is not with their group, and that he's a random drunk man. Klaus is pleased, and satisfied, once he is able to think of this. Klaus then starts to tap Dan on the shoulder, and begins to explain to him the plan.

"Alright man, I'm gonna need you to go on ahead of us, and start to do, what you need to do. Dan, I really need you to act as drunk as you can. Please. Like be creative. Please."

Dan then nods his head, and looks down on the ground, and shakes his head. As Dan starts to walk, and tread away from the other men, he silently responds back to Klaus.

"You know, this is still all your fault. Remember that. This is all your fucking fault."

Klaus then shakes his head, and starts to laugh, as he watches Dan walk away. At this time, Klaus tells the other men, to stay where they are, and allow for Dan to walk ahead of them. The guys must wait for the right time, to continue on with the diversion. The other guys understand Klaus plan, and obeys him, and remains away from the entrance. Dan continues to walk closer to the entrance of the building, while he starts to get his theatrics, and plan in order. Dan has to play off a very convincing drunk man, so the security guard is distracted, and has his full attention to him. Dan tries to think of how he is going to pull this off, understanding that he doesn't have much time to accomplish this. Now that Dan has approached the entrance of the building, the security guard notices Dan, and they both make eye contact with each other. Dan quickly looks away from the guard, and tries not to draw further attention. The security guard, is an older, middle aged, Caucasian man, with short buzzed hair, and a beard. Dan then puts his hands in his pockets, and starts to doubt, if he can even do this. Dan starts to feel hatred towards Klaus, and Dan wonders, if he should blow the cover, and tell the security guard, to call the police. Dan then realizes, that he, and the rest of the guys, would all be killed, if he does that. Dan has no choice, but to follow the plan that Klaus set out. Dan then starts to begin his intoxicated act. At this time, Dan starts to yell and scream at the top of his lungs, and starts to jump up and down, repeatedly. Dan continues to make a scene, and spectacle of himself, which in turn, catches the attention, of the security guard, that is in direct view of Dan. The security guard initially doesn't respond or react. Dan notices this, and starts to become slightly agitated, and this act, at this point in time, doesn't seem to be working, and the guard is not buying it. Klaus, and the other guys, who are back at a vantage point that the guard can't see, also notice that the guard has not yet come out of the building, and respond to Dan's charade.

Dan ups the ante, and starts to act more belligerent. Dan walks up to the glass door of the entrance, and starts to give the guard rude gestures, and is also saying disrespectful comments. In addition to the fact, that Dan continues on with this antics and behavior. This finally makes the guard react to the way Dan is acting, and the guard gets up from his post. Dan then starts to walk away from the entrance, and back to his original location. Dan was thinking ahead, and is aware, that he wants to make sure the guard is far away from the entrance as possible. The guard then steps out of the out the building, and starts to approach Dan. The guard then speaks.

"Sir, you have to leave, and get out of here. This is private property. Leave now sir."

Dan continues to act drunk and belligerent. With slurred speech, he responds.

"Yeah, I'm just waiting for my roommate to pick me up, can I just wait here. He's gonna be here any minute, yeah. I'm not causing any trouble. I'm not hurting anybody. Come on man."

The guard continues to tell Dan to leave, and Dan carries on with his drunk act. Klaus, and the rest of the men, continue to watch, Dan's diversion. Klaus has a wide grin on his face, and he feels, that this plan might actually work. Now, Klaus instructs Jerome to walk directly to the building. Klaus and Paul, stay behind, and remain backed away. As Jerome is walking towards the building, Dan carries on acting wild, and distracting the guard. Dan continues his yelling, shouting, cursing, and drunk speech. Jerome tries his best not to stare at Dan, or the guard, and give any suspicion to himself. Jerome continues to walk closer to the entrance, and then walks inside. As Jerome waits inside of the building, from the way the guard was positioned, trying to deal with Dan, he didn't even notice Jerome walked in. Klaus is very pleased when he notices this as well. At this time, without any time to waste, Klaus instructs Paul, to follow him, to the building. Dan and the guard continue to deal with one another, and Dan, who is aware that Jerome already walked in the building, steps further away from the entrance, knowing that the guard is fully distracted. Dan can also tell that Klaus and Paul, are not creeping up towards the building as well. Dan then takes his act to a deeper level, screaming and shouting even louder, and acting even more drunk. The guard becomes more distracted.

At this time, Klaus and Paul have walked inside of the building. Carrying on with the plan, Jerome does not stare at them at all, and pretends not to know who they are, and acknowledges them. Klaus and Paul waste no time, walking to the back of the first floor, where the security control panel room is. Klaus and Paul make sure they are very stealth, and aren't drawing any unneeded attention to themselves. Klaus is very sure that the guard, was the only other person in the building, so they have no worries of being caught, as long as the guard doesn't come back into the building, and reports to the control panel room. Meanwhile, Dan continues to act irate to the guard, and Dan, who knows that the other guys are already inside of the building, drops down to the floor, and starts to roll his body down on the ground. The guard then starts to finally have enough, and proceeds to walk back inside the building, to call for backup. While the guard is walking to the entrance door, he notices Jerome standing inside. This causes the guard to become slightly puzzled, and disorientated. The guard then opens the entrance door, and Jerome doesn't stare at him, so the guard doesn't feel more suspicious at him. The guard then starts to approach Jerome, thinking he is much younger, and speaks to him.

"Hey kid. What are you doing here? Can I help you with something? Are you lost?"

Jerome then starts to look around the entrance of the building, and softly speaks.

"Yes sir. Um, listen. May I use the telephone please? I was hanging with some friends at the mall, and I missed my bus. Can I call my Dad to come pick me up please?"

Dan, who is aware that Jerome is inside, doing his part of the distraction, continues on with his drunk charade, being more obnoxious. The guard, who can hear Dan shouting and screaming, from inside of the building, starts to stare at him. While the guard is looking out the entrance door, watching how erratic Dan is acting, the guard speaks softly back to Jerome.

"Okay kid, you can call your Dad. But be quick, okay? I have to call the cops on that drunk idiot that's outside. Pick up the phone, and press pound, then dial nine, and the number."

Jerome nods his head, and starts to walk to the guard's desk, to dial the phone. Jerome picks up the phone, and starts to dial random numbers, to stall time. The security guard, noticing Dan, who is acting stranger, excuses himself from Jerome, and walks out of the building. Jerome continues to dial random numbers, doing his part of the distraction. At this concurrent time, Klaus and Paul managed to reach the security camera control room. Klaus immediately sits down, and starts to hack into the security feed. Klaus hopes and prays, that the system is an older model, and that he is able to get into the system, and not only disable the cameras, but erase any archive footage, of the men entering the building. That way, there isn't any incriminating evidence, of the guys ever being inside of the building. As Klaus is powering up the security camera feeds, he is delighted, when he notices that the building is using an older system. Paul who silently watches, as Klaus messes with the camera feed, is amazed at Klaus skill of this. Within a minute, Klaus has successfully disabled, all of the security cameras in the building. The next plan, is for Klaus to now erase the footage of he, and the rest of the guys entering the building. Klaus understands, that this is going to be a more difficult feat, as rewinding the camera footage, requires a more complicated setup. But Klaus manages to do it anyway. Klaus soon within thirty seconds, is able to erase any camera footage of the guys, and continues to leave the camera feed shut off. Klaus then turns to Paul, and they both fist bump each other and laugh. Klaus has successfully managed this part of the plan, and he, and Paul, quickly walk out of the control panel room, and start to walk up to the second floor of the building. With Klaus and Paul, each taking a separate staircase, to not draw more attention.

Meanwhile, Dan is still acting wild with the security guard, and being obnoxious with him. Jerome continues to dial random numbers on the phone. The security guard, notices that Jerome is still on the phone, and walks away from Dan, and proceeds to direct himself inside, to speak with Jerome. Jerome continues to dial random numbers, and the guard responds to him.

"Hey, have you called your Dad yet? I need to use that phone kid. That drunk guy outside, he is getting out of hand, and I need to call backup, okay?

Jerome starts to feel anxious, and tries his best to stall the guard. Jerome then speaks.

"My Dad isn't answering the phone, he has like two different numbers. Just give me a couple more minutes, please Sir. I'm sure that I'll reach him in a minute. Please."

The guard shakes his head, and doesn't respond verbally to Jerome. The guard instead, walks out of the building and returns outside, to where Dan is. Dan continues to put on his drunk act, and distract the guard. Jerome steadily goes back to dialing random numbers on the telephone. At this time, Klaus and Paul are now walking on the second floor of the building, trying to find the office, that contains the hard drive. The map of the building that Klaus was provided, seems to help greatly, and Klaus is able to figure out what room is the correct one, for him to proceed to. Paul catches up to Klaus on the second floor, and they both continue to silently meander through the building. Following the map, Klaus is able to locate the room, that the hard drive is situated in. The room requires a code key to enter, which the packet provided the correct code. The door opens, and Klaus and Paul, enter the room. The packet mentioned that the hard drive, would be located inside of a drawer, in a computer desk. Klaus at first thought this wouldn't be difficult, and that they simply would need to open a drawer to get the hard drive. However, what the packet failed to mention, was it didn't say, there were actually, ten different computer desks in the room. Upon realizing this, when Klaus and Paul go inside the room, Klaus starts to feel slightly frustrated, and worried. Although, trying not to waste any time, Klaus and Paul, immediately start to go through every drawer, searching intensively, looking for the hard drive. As Klaus and Paul are now in the hard drive room, Dan continues to act wild, and Jerome steadily remains at the front security desk, dialing random numbers on the phone.

The guard at this time, seems to have had enough of Dan, and walks back inside, in an effort to use the phone, to call for backup, over the situation. The guard realizes that Jerome is still on the phone, and the guard becomes agitated. The guard then speaks to Jerome.

"Hey kid, you have to get off that phone. You haven't called your Dad yet? I'm sorry, but I gave you plenty of time to call him, so kid, you I need to use that phone right now."

Jerome then realizes, upon looking down at the security desk, that the cameras are disabled. Jerome is aware that Klaus has already turned them off. Knowing this fact, Jerome then decides to allow the guard to use the phone. Jerome hangs the phone up, and speaks to the guard.

"Well, I left my Dad a voicemail, but I was trying to call his other phone. I can't reach him. Sir, can I stay in here, because I'm scared of that drunk man outside. Please?"

The guard then looks over at Dan, who remarkably, is keeping up his drunk act. The guard nods his head, in response to Jerome, allowing him to stay inside the building, and Jerome walks away from the telephone. Jerome then stands in front of the security desk, and the security guard walks over to the phone. However, the guard is shocked, when he notices the cameras have been disabled. At first, the guard doesn't pay this much mind or attention, and decides to walk to the control room later. The guard then starts to call for backup, in regards to Dan.

"Yes, I'm down at Platinum Aerospace. I'm the only guard on duty tonight. I have a really drunk and belligerent man outside. Can you guys please send police assistance? Thanks."

The guard then hangs up the phone, and then is curious about the fact the cameras in the control room have been disabled. The guard, without speaking to Jerome, starts to walk away from the security desk, to the control room. Jerome, who is concerned and scared, after the guard starts to walk away, thinks fast, and tries to convince the guard, not to leave the area.

"Sir, I saw the drunk man reach into his pocket, and he's acting really weird. I think he has a gun or knife or weapon or something. I'm scared. Guard, can you watch him please?"

The guard then turns in the opposite direction, and shakes his head. The guard then walks out of the entrance, and approaches Dan. The guard tries to frisk Dan, to see if he has any weapons. When the guard notices that Dan is unarmed, he starts to walk back into the building. At this same time, Klaus and Paul, continue to search through all of the desks in the room. Finally, Klaus manages to open the drawer in one of the desks, and finds the hard drive. Klaus heart continues to beat fast, and he can't believe that he managed to locate the item, that they were looking for. Klaus then puts the hard drive, into his pocket, and signals to Dan, that he has found it. Klaus and Dan then fist bump each other, and they start to sneakily exit out of the room. As Klaus and Paul are stealthy trying to escape out of the building, it was at this time, that Klaus has an idea, that they should turn the cameras back on, so they wouldn't draw suspicion. Klaus tells Paul, that they are going to report back down to the security control room, to disable the cameras. Klaus has to be very swift and quick about this, of course. However, shockingly, and remarkably, Paul offers to disable the cameras himself, saying that the knows how to do it, and understands what buttons to push. Klaus then realizes that turning back on the cameras isn't difficult, in fact, it's much easier than hacking them off. Turning the camera back on, requires only one button to be pushed. Klaus continues to insist to Paul, that he doesn't have to do that, but Paul isn't allowing Klaus to say no. Klaus then informs to Paul, that when he turns the cameras back on, to put the delay timer on for five minutes. That way the guys would have already left the building, when the camera reset. Paul understands clearly. Klaus is sure that Paul can do it, although Klaus is reluctant. Knowing that they don't have much time to waste, Paul starts to walk to the control room, and tells Klaus to proceed on ahead. After slight hesitation, Klaus does allow Paul to split up from him. Paul then carries on to the control room, and Klaus then starts to walk to a back emergency exit door.

Klaus immediately starts to race to this door, and successfully manages to open the door, and leaves out of the building. Once he is out of the building, Klaus starts to walk back over, to the entrance of the building. At this time, Klaus also pushes the button of the GPS tracker, letting the driver of the van know, the he has successfully obtained the hard drive. At this exact time, Dan is continuing to act out in the front of the building. Noting, that the guard has already called for backup, which should be on their way to the location. The guard, who is now back inside of the building, starts to walk back to his desk, double checking, and reaffirming to himself, that the security cameras, are off. The guard notices the cameras are off, and starts to walk to the camera control room, where Paul currently is. Jerome again, tries to think of a way to stall, at this time, Jerome notices Klaus, walking outside the entrance. Jerome then screams out to the guard.

"Oh, guard. That's my Dad right there. Oh thank god. Thank you so much sir."

The guard has a puzzled look on his face, and believes Jerome is fibbing. Jerome then walks out of the building, and runs up to hug Klaus. The guard still puzzled, starts to speak.

"Excuse me Sir, is this your son? Are you his Dad? I just want to make sure. That's all This man right here is acting erratic and drunk, and I was worried. This is your son right?"

Jerome continues to hug Klaus, and Dan, who has finally stopped his act, looks at Klaus, Jerome, and the guard. Klaus, who is slightly confused, then starts to speak to the guard.

"Oh yeah. I'm his Dad. Okay son, sorry that I'm late. Let's get out of here. Because you were such a good boy, we're gonna go to McDonalds okay. Alright, let's go buddy. Okay?"

Klaus and Jerome then start to walk away from the location, but Dan remains where he is, to avoid suspicion to himself, and the other guys. As Klaus and Jerome continue to walk further away from the building, the security guard laughs, and shakes his head. At this time, the security guard tells Dan to wait where he is, and the guard walks back into the building. Following this, at this time, the guard walks back to his desk, and sees that shockingly, the cameras have been reset back on, the same instance, in which the guard looks at the security screens. This causes great cause of concern for the guard, and he proceeds to walk to the control room, where Paul still is located. At this exact time,

Dan is certain, that Klaus already found the hard drive, and starts to walk away from the location. Dan then starts to catch and meet up, with Klaus and Jerome. Inside the building, the guard walks closer and closer to the control room. Paul then quickly finishes backtracking, and rewinding the cameras, and uses the camera delay as well, so it doesn't capture the guys, as they are leaving out of the building. Paul opens the door of the control room, and in the same exact instance, the guard is standing on the other side of the door. Paul starts to feel extremely nervous, and the guard as well, is shocked to see him as well. Both of the men, stand staring at each other, being very quiet, and there is awkward silence. The guard then starts to reach for his gun, and Paul starts to sweat heavily. The guard keeps his hand over his gun, as he stares deeply back at Paul. Both of the men, remain silent, and aren't speaking to each other. This continues for a minute, as Paul stands frozen in fear, not knowing how to react, or what he shall do next. Paul then looks down on the ground, and quickly starts to run past the guard. The guard however is able to tackle Paul down on the ground, and speaks to him.

"Hey, hey. Who the fuck are you? What are you doing in there? Answer me right now."

Paul doesn't respond and the guard continues to tackle Paul. At this time, Klaus and Jerome start to walk towards the van, but Klaus starts to feel concerned over Paul. Klaus then starts to look back, and tells Jerome to follow him back closer to the entrance. As Klaus reaches a vantage point between the front entrance of the building, and a secluded area where himself and Jerome can't be seen, Klaus starts to gaze around the area, looking for Paul. Klaus still cannot find where Paul is. Klaus at this same time, also notices, that Dan isn't at this area either. Klaus gets slightly worried, and the fact he already pushed the button to alert the van driver, he knows that he must locate the other guys fast. Dan, who walked ahead, notices he doesn't see the other guys either, and decides to instinctively walk back to the area, yet keeping a safe distance. A minute later, Dan does manage to locate Klaus and Jerome, and silently speaks to him.

"Hey man, did you get it? Ha Ha. Where is Paul? We need to get out of here now man."

Klaus and Dan then fist bump, and Klaus reaches in his pocket, and takes out the hard drive, for Dan to see. Klaus and Dan fist bump again, and they both laugh at each other. Klaus puts the hard drive back into his pocket. After doing that, Klaus then silently speaks to Dan.

"Yeah I got it. I knew we could it do it. I don't know where Paul is, but he should be stepping out, any second now. Once we see Paul, we can head back out."

Dan nods his head, and the men all stay in this secluded area, keeping their vision towards the entrance of the building, waiting for Paul to come out or appear. However, Paul does not. The guys continue to wait for Paul for a few minutes, and they now start to feel concerned. Klaus now starts to regret, allowing Paul to walk inside the control room, to turn the cameras back on. Klaus is very sure, this is what is keeping Paul. Inside the building, the guard is still tackling with Paul, with Paul trying his best to fight the guard off him, so he can run, and escape out of the building. However, the guard is not allowing Paul to get away. At this time, Paul, and the guard, managed to tussle their way out of the camera control room, and they are both starting to direct themselves to front entrance. The guard and Paul continue to wrestle, and fight with one another, as they are now in front entrance. Klaus, and the other men, notice this, and Klaus starts to immediately feel shocked. Klaus starts to walk towards the building, but Dan grabs him.

"Hey. Hey. No, man, no. Just wait. Chill. Wait for a minute. Alright. Stay here for now."

Klaus then looks down on the ground, and shakes his head. For another minute, the guys all watch, as Paul continues to wrestle with the guard. The men then start to feeling upset, that there isn't anything that they can do for now. The men simply watch, as they hope Paul can escape from the guard. Klaus simply cannot watch Paul being accosted by the guard and speaks.

"Come on, we have to help Paul. He's really in trouble guys. Come on, let's go."

Klaus, and the rest of the guys, start to walk towards the entrance, but are instantly stopped, when they hear loud police sirens in the distance. Within seconds, the sirens seep closer, and the police, instantly arrive at the scene. This causes Klaus, and the other guys to go back to the point they were originally at, out of fear. Without hesitation, Klaus, Dan, and Jerome, watch, as the police start to run out of their cars, and notice the guard and Paul, tussling. The police mistake Paul, for Dan, and think he is the drunk man, the guard was referring to. The police then know they have to act fact, in order to diffuse the situation. The police then make Paul their prime suspect, in regards to this situation. The police then all run into the entrance of the building, and have their guns drawn at Paul. Klaus and the rest of the men, continue to watch from a distance, seeing how things have took a drastic turn. Knowing that there isn't anything they can do right now. The guys still remain in fear, and in shock. With the police still inside of the building, they aim their guns right at Paul, and start to shout at him.

"This is LAPD. Sir, please lay down on the ground, and put your hands up now."

Paul then tries to comply with the police, but the guard steadily pins, and tackles Paul to the ground. The police mistake this as Paul resisting arrest, and become more agitated him. Within the next few seconds, more unfortunate events happen. At this time, the guard, who is still tackling Paul on the ground, not allowing him to get away, starts to put his gun back into the holster, but unfortunately, at this exact time, a police officer, again, thinking Paul is resisting, crawls down on the ground, to detain Paul. With a police officer down on the ground, directly following this, the guard, who was simply trying to put his gun away, accidentally fires a shot, at the police officer, that's down on the ground with them. The shot ends up striking the officer in neck, in which the officer out of instinct, assuming that Paul shot him, aims his gun at Paul. However, the officer, due to the fact Paul and the guard are still tussling on the ground, ends up shooting both Paul, and the guard in the head, instantly killing them both. The officer then starts to lose consciousness, after being shot in the neck, by the guard. The rest of the officers then start to rush over to the scene, noticing that Paul, and the guard are dead. Officers then try to do CPR, on the officer that was shot, although the officer is losing a lot of blood. Unfortunately, the officer quickly loses consciousness from his bullet wound, and is presumed dead instantly as well. Klaus, and the rest of the guys, watch, as these drastic events happen. Klaus, Dan, and Jerome, all being to cry, understanding that Paul is now dead. In this same time, the van driver immediately pulls up to the secluded location that the guys are at. Although the men notice the driver has pulled up, they continue to look at the entrance of the building. The driver speaks.

"Hey, you guys got the hard drive right? Wait, why is there a bunch of cops here. I thought there were four of you too. Where is your other friend? King Shark is not going to like this one bit. You guys are in a lot of trouble. Damn. Get in this van right now. Fuck."

Klaus and the guys, continue to cry, and erupt in tears, but they understand their only option is to get into the van. Klaus, Dan, and Jerome, get inside of the van, and the van driver immediately starts to drive away from the scene. As all of the men are inside of the van, on their way to report back to King Shark, Klaus then starts to feel very depressed and upset. Klaus, and the men, now have lost Paul. Klaus doesn't necessarily feel that the mission was accomplished, as not only were the police notified, but Paul was killed during this task. The van steadily starts to drive further away from the scene. Klaus turns to look over at Dan, who has a disappointed look on his face. Klaus and Dan give eye contact to each other, and Dan silently speaks to Klaus.

"Didn't I tell you so? I told you so right? You sick sadistic bastard. Don't you ever say another fucking single word to me ever in your life. I fucking hate you with a passion, you asshole. You're lucky I'm not gonna knock the daylights out of you now. Fuck you Klaus."

Dan then returns to looking down on the ground, and shakes his head. Klaus then looks down on the ground, shakes his head, and laughs.

CHAPTER 19:

DEEP, DEEP TROUBLE

Things continue to spiral out of control. The guys remain their streak, of turmoil happening to them. Now realizing, that the men have reached a very pivotal point; a point to where it sees, there is no going back, to fix, rectify or remedy this. The guys are all heading back to the Diamond Mafia headquarters. The men don't have any time to react to Paul's death, and this seems very unfair and cruel to them all. The task, wasn't completed in the way they hoped. Not only were the police alerted, which the guys feared, King Shark, would not appreciate this at all, but Paul is now deceased. Things did not go the way they hoped, and it was awful. While the guys are all in the van, reporting back to the Diamond Mafia group, Dan is extremely irate and angry, and doesn't keep it a secret, that he does not like Klaus. Dan angrily speaks.

"Don't ever talk to me again man. You're a sick sadistic bastard. I wish I never met you. I don't ever want to see your face in my life again. This is all your fault. I told you so."

Klaus understands the hurt Dan is going through, and understands that although he has gotten into several arguments and conflicts with Dan before, it seems as though this time is different. Dan truly wants nothing to do with Klaus anymore, and this seemed to have been the final straw. Having Paul killed at the end of their task, solidified that fact. At this time, all Klaus can do, is do his usual habit, whenever he feels nervous, or unsure of himself. Klaus looks down at the ground, shakes his head, and laughs. Jerome, who is sitting in the row behind Klaus and Dan, remains silent, and is crying heavily. Jerome is not able to control his emotions, and doesn't speak. Klaus, continues to feel scared, as to what King Shark is going to say. Klaus knows that they will eventually reach headquarters, and the men, will have to face King Shark's wrath then. Klaus feels that this is it, and he is most likely going to kill all of them, for not following the proper orders of the task. Because the police were alerted, Klaus is sure, that King Shark will get mad over this, and the guys will all get into trouble, as a result. The van dries closer and closer to headquarters. Eventually, the van does arrive at the Diamond Mafia factory. The van driver turns off the engine, and several guards start to stand outside the van. Klaus, Dan, and Jerome, are then escorted out of the van by the guards, and they are directed to King Shark's office inside. Minutes later, once all the men are seated inside the office, one of the guards walks out of the room, and locks the door. The guard remains outside the door, gun in hand, should any of the guys run out and escape. The men remain in the room silent. Dan, while looking down, speaks.

"When I see you in Hell Klaus, don't speak to me. You give me so much turmoil and stress here on Earth, I can't stand to look at your fucking face in the afterlife. Fuck you man."

Klaus who is also looking down on the ground, doesn't respond to Dan. Klaus simply shakes his head, and laughs. Jerome remains sobbing heavily, and is silent. It is so quiet, that you could hear a feather drop on the ground. Klaus can hear the wall clock in King Shark's office ticking loudly. Several minutes pass, and the men all stay in King Shark's office, awaiting him. Eventually King Shark does walk into the room. A guard follows him, but King Shark stops him.

"No, it's okay. If I need you guys, I'll let you know. I'll handle these Bozos. It's okay."

The guard then obeys King Shark, and remains outside of the room. King Shark locks his office store, and stares at all the guys, whilst he's doing that. The men do not look at King Shark, or give him any eye contact. King Shark then takes a cigar from his jacket pocket, and starts to light it. After lighting the cigar, King Shark takes a seat at his desk, and opens a drawer in his desk. King Shark takes out a container of hair gel, and starts to primp himself. The guys remain with their vision down, not looking at King Shark. Following this King Shark, takes puffs of his cigar, and stares at Klaus deeply. King Shark takes another puff of his cigar, and speaks.

"Hey, Doughboy? Did you get the hard drive? If you didn't, you already know. Whack. Ha Ha. Enough bullshit. The driver didn't tell me if you guys got it or not. Let me see it please."

Klaus then looks up, and gives King Shark eye contact. Klaus then reaches into his pocket, grabs the hard drive, and hands it to King Shark. Following this King Shark, has a wide grin on his face, and starts to plug the hard drive, into his computer on his desk. King Shark examines the hard drive through his computer, making sure the guys snagged the correct one. Once King Shark realizes the guys managed to get the correct hard drive, he speaks.

"What? How the fuck did you guys do this. Damn it. I was hoping this was a decoy or dud or something. This is what I was looking for yes. Okay look. I know the fuzz was at the scene. I'm willing to forgive that, as I know one of your buddies got shot."

King Shark takes another puff of his cigar, and unplugs the hard drive from his computer, and puts it inside the drawer of his desk. King Shark then looks at Klaus, and continues to speak.

"I'm really sorry you guys. So because I'm in a mushy mood, you guys are so fucking lucky, I'm gonna give you another break. Alright, so you guys are official Diamond Mafia members now. Ha Ha. So, as a reward, this one is on me boys. Drink up, put hair on your chest."

King Shark then opens up another drawer on his desk, and takes a large bottle of Jack Daniels whiskey out. King Shark then sets four shot glasses down on his desk. King Shark pours the whiskey into the shot glasses. Klaus, and the rest of the men, then grab the shot glasses. Once King Shark swallows his shot, Klaus, Dan, and Jerome, drink their whiskey shots as well. The room is in total silence for quite some time. The men oblige along with the toast that King Shark decided to give them. They continue to remain completely silent. Directly after this, King Shark gets up from his desk, and starts to speak to the guys.

"You guys can go home now. But I know where you live, so no funny business. Okay?"

King Shark holds up Klaus, Dan, and Jerome's identification, and starts to laugh. King Shark then hands their identification back to them. King Shark also hands them their phones, and keys as well. King Shark then takes another puff of his cigar, and speaks to the guys.

"Alright, now with your friend, he doesn't exist anymore, and never existed, okay. We burned his identification and phone. Nothing that happened tonight, ever happened. Okay? You guys run and tell the police anything, anything at all. Whacked. Don't tell the police shit. Okay?"

Klaus and the rest of the men remain silent, as King Shark takes more puffs of his cigar, and walks around his office. King Shark, then starts to fix Klaus shirt collar, and speaks to him.

"You, Doughboy. I'm gonna need your help soon okay? There is a rival group, starting shit, and since you were so good with this task, I ranked you and your buddies up to 2nd level Tigers. That never happens, and that's like a rank below me. Don't make me regret that. You guys have our protection as fellow Diamond Mafia. Tigers look out for each other."

King Shark continues to take puffs of his cigar, and starts to walk to the office door. King Shark puts his hand over the doorknob, and stops to look at Klaus. King Shark then speaks.

"But you guys fuck up, and don't do as I say, I will ice, and cap each and every one of you. That's not gonna happen though, at least I hope not. You boys seem obedient. Remember, you're 2nd level Tigers, so I'm gonna take things easier on you guys. Good night gentlemen."

King Shark then opens the door, and walks out of the office. Klaus, and the rest of the men stay silent in the room, not knowing what to do next. Not even a few seconds after King Shark steps out of the room, one of the guards opens up the door to the office. The guard that opens up the door, is the African-American guard, that the guys met earlier.

"Okay guys. Boss said you guys are free to go. We're gonna take you back to your car, and y'all are free to go now. Boss is giving you guys a break, he will contact you soon though."

Klaus, Dan, and Jerome, then quickly walk out of King Shark's office. They follow the guard back to a van, and they get inside. Once inside of the van, they are then driven to the location of Klaus SUV. The men get out of the van, and the driver of the van, quickly storms off. Seconds later, Klaus gets into his vehicle, and Dan sits in the passenger seat with Jerome sitting in the back seat. Klaus then starts the engine of his SUV, and starts to drive, heading home. Remarkably, despite everything that has happened recently, it is only 11pm. Although what the guys went through, was only a handful of hours, it seemed that everything took place, over the course of several days. During the car trip, Klaus would take glances over at Dan, who has his vision down towards the ground. Klaus gets on the highway, heading straight back to the house. As Klaus is driving on the highway, Dan, starts to look out of the windshield. Dan puts his hand over his mouth, and starts to shake his head. While looking out of the windshield, Dan speaks.

"Paul dying is your fault. You know that right? You're gonna have to live with that shit."

Klaus continues to drive, as he shakes his head. Klaus then immediately responds to Dan.

"I don't want to talk about it. I thought you hated me, remember? Since you hate me so much, you can get all your shit, and leave. Jerome, that goes for you too. Y'all can go talk to King Shark or whatever. Maybe you guys can stay with him. I'm not running Motel 6 anymore."

At this time, Dan turns his direction back to Klaus, and silently responds back to him.

"You're such an asshole, I swear. Not only that, you're a psychopath, you're a sadistic bastard, you're narcissistic, you're selfish. You're two faced. You treat me, and Jerome badly. It's your fault Ernest is gone. It's your fault Bill is gone. It's your fault Paul is gone."

Klaus shakes his head and laughs, and continues driving down the highway. Jerome continues to feel upset in the back seat, crying, and remaining silent. Dan doesn't speak to Klaus for the remainder of the trip. This was a very awkward car ride. Due to the fact it's later into the night, the trip back to Klaus house, isn't long. The men arrive back at the house, and Klaus, and the rest of the men, then walk inside. Once they are inside of the house, Klaus walks into the kitchen, and pulls out a bottle of Smirnoff Vodka. Klaus doesn't get himself a shot glass, and instead, drinks directly from the bottle. At this time, Klaus watches Jerome sit down on the sofa. Jerome points his head down towards the ground, and continues to cry. Dan remains in the kitchen, standing next to Klaus. Klaus takes a swig of the vodka, bottle, turns to Dan and speaks.

"Get the fuck out of my eyesight. You have some nerve. Why aren't you packing up?"

Dan then shakes his head at Klaus, and slaps Klaus glasses off his face. Klaus then reaches up to Dan, and balls up his fist. Jerome watches them both. Klaus then speaks.

"If you had any sense, you be a man, and just leave me alone. Fuck off Dan. Wow."

Dan shakes his head, and walks to his bedroom, and slams the door shut behind him. Jerome continues to cry on the sofa. Klaus then picks up his glasses, that Dan smacked off his face, and puts them on. Klaus takes another sip of the vodka bottle, and walks over to Jerome on the sofa. Klaus then smacks Jerome roughly across the face. Klaus silently speaks to Jerome.

"Young man, you need to go and get your stuff out my room, and pack. You and Dan are evicted. I wasn't joking you guys can go stay with King Shark. Go ask him for a place to stay, as y'all can't stay here anymore. Nope. I said go and pack your things right now. I'm not playing."

Klaus then sets the vodka bottle down on the coffee table, and picks Jerome up. Klaus then escorts Jerome into his bedroom, and throws him down on the bed. Jerome then speaks.

"Okay, you don't have to be a jerk about it. Fuck. I'm packing my things now. Jesus."

Jerome then starts to gather all of his things. Klaus shakes his head, and walks out of the bedroom, shutting the door behind him. Klaus then directs himself back to the living room, and grabs the vodka bottle that was on the coffee table, in the living room. Klaus takes another swig of the vodka bottle, shakes his head, and sets it down. Klaus then takes a seat down on his recliner. Klaus leans back in the recliner, and closes his eyes. A few minutes later, Dan walks out of the room, and starts to walk to Klaus bedroom door. Klaus, still relaxing, and having his eyes clothes, doesn't see anything, but can hear everything. Dan knocks on the door, and speaks.

"Jerome, get out. Stop packing. We're gonna have a household meeting. Come here."

Klaus then immediately springs up from the recliner, and gives an agitated look at Dan. During this same time, Dan gives Klaus a disgusted look at well, and shakes his head. Jerome soon joins the rest of the guys in the living room. Jerome, still sobbing heavily, takes a seat on the sofa. Klaus then shakes his head, and returns to sitting on the recliner. Dan then speaks.

"Hey man. Look. At least let us stay tonight. Jerome and I, will pack our things, and leave first thing tomorrow. We had a really rough night, like, it's almost midnight. This is like nightmare, night from Hell, but just give us tonight. Please Klaus. I never ask for you anything."

Klaus then starts to look at Jerome, who has a sad look on his face. Klaus looks down on the ground and starts to shake his head. Klaus gets up from the recliner, and reaches for the vodka bottle. Dan then grabs Klaus arm, and sets the bottle back down. Dan then speaks.

"Oh no Zangief, you already had enough of that. So, Jerome and I are gonna stay for tonight, and first thing tomorrow, we'll leave. You don't want us here, that's fine. Jerome and I understand, and it's your house, you're rules. But at least gives us tonight man. Alright?"

Klaus then stares at Dan, and starts to smile at him. Klaus then starts to laugh to himself, and walks away. Klaus then proceeds to the kitchen area, and pulls a cup out of the counter. Klaus then takes out a large bottle of water from the refrigerator, and pours it into the cup.

Klaus then starts to drink his water. Klaus then grabs his keys, and starts to walk to the front door. Dan and Jerome stare at Klaus deeply, not sure as to what exactly he's doing. Klaus then speaks.

"I'm gonna go to the park. I just need some fresh air. I can't even think right now. You guys are getting on my fucking nerves, and I am trying to control my temper. Don't follow me."

Klaus then immediately steps out of the front door, and walks away from the house. At this time, Dan looks down and shakes his head. Dan then notices that Paul's shoebox of marijuana paraphernalia, is located under the coffee table. Dan then opens the show box, and takes out some marijuana, and joint papers. Jerome watches as Dan does this, but does not respond or react. At this time, Dan then taps Jerome on the shoulder, and softly speaks to him.

"Hey, I know Klaus said not to follow him, but I have an idea. Follow me. Don't worry."

Dan then smiles at Jerome, and Jerome then smiles right back at Dan. Dan and Jerome then walk out of the house, and Dan locks the front door behind them. Upon leaving the house, Dan and Jerome then spot Klaus, walking rather slowly, ahead of them. Dan and Jerome finally catch themselves up to Klaus, and Klaus turns his vision back to them. As the three of them continue to walk alongside the sidewalk, they remain silent. Klaus while walking, speaks.

"I thought I told you guys not to follow me. You guys are so fucking hardheaded I swear. You guys are obsessed with me or something. Go back to the house and leave me alone. Damn."

Klaus then continues to walk faster, ahead of Dan and Jerome. They however don't listen to Klaus, and remain following behind him. Klaus once again looks back and notices that Dan and Jerome, remain walking behind him. Klaus then looks down, and shakes his head. Dan then catches himself up to Klaus, and starts to wrap his arm behind him, hugging him. Dan then grabs Jerome, and wraps Jerome's arms around Klaus, with Jerome hugging him as well. The men then form a tight strong, group hug. Klaus however is slightly reluctant. Dan then softly speaks.

"Look, I'm sorry. I'm sorry for everything. We have to stick together man. Me, this young, intelligent man right here. This is all we have man. Klaus. This is all we got now."

At this moment, Klaus then starts to cry, and proceeds to take his glasses off. The three of them, remain in this group hug for several minutes. Klaus knew that Dan was correct, and that they have to stick together. Dan, and Jerome start to cry as well, and the three of them continue to hold, and hug each other tightly. Eventually, Klaus starts to speak to the men.

"You're right guys. Tonight has been really heavy and intense. I'm sorry Dan. I'm sorry Jerome. I'm a jerk, and I don't know what I was thinking. It's all this King Shark bullshit, and we're like criminals now, and I don't know. I love you guys, and I'm so sorry."

Klaus then kisses both Dan and Jerome on the forehead. Klaus then puts his glasses back on. As the three of them continue to hug, then then starts to softly speak.

"It's not too bad. Think about it. At least we got free tattoos out of it right? Ha Ha."

This causes both Klaus and Jerome to laugh, and Dan steadily laughs with them. All three of the men, engage in infectious laughter, and continue to comfort each other. The men then all stop hugging, and they remain standing in the sidewalk, looking down at the ground towards each other. Klaus then puts his hands his pockets, and begins to walk in a circle. Dan, who is staring deeply at Klaus, then starts to ask Klaus a question.

"So, where were you heading to anyways? I have an idea, but I'm curious. Tell me now."

Klaus continues to look down to the ground and starts to laugh to himself. Klaus then looks up, and stares down the distance of the sidewalk, facing the beach. Klaus then speaks.

"I was gonna go to Seaside Park I guess. I was gonna go there to calm myself down. It's a nice park, you guys been there before right? I was gonna look at the ocean and think I guess."

Dan then starts to reach into his pocket, and pulls out the marijuana, and joint papers. Upon seeing this, Klaus starts to shake his head, and starts to laugh. Klaus is fully aware that the marijuana materials Dan is holding, belong to Paul. Dan then softly speaks.

"Damn, I knew you were going to Seaside Park. Something told me you were. I know you Klaus. Well, in Paul's honor and memory, how about we smoke of this chronic shit at the park. We can chill, relax. Think about this King Shark crap. Come on, I know you want to."

Klaus then smiles to himself, and stares at Jerome. Jerome smiles and nods his head. Klaus then once again looks out towards the distance, and laughs again. Klaus then speaks.

"Oh, what the hell. I guess it's the last I can do to make up for me being a jerk a while ago. Come on though, because it's getting late, and I'm kinda tired. Let's go to the park I guess."

Klaus shakes his head, and laughs. Dan and Jerome walk right behind Klaus, as they direct themselves to Seaside Park. Despite it being fifteen minutes until midnight, the night still feels strangely early. It is a nice night, with the night sky emanating a dark blue, and light orange color. The moon is rather full, and the climate is neither too cold, or too hot and humid. The men continue heading to Seaside Park, which is only located a few blocks away from Klaus residence. Before long the men arrive at the park, and they all take a seat on the bench. Jerome takes a seat on the bench first, Klaus sits next to him in the middle, and Dan sits next to Klaus. Once the men are all seated, they all stare out towards the ocean, where the waves are crashing against the shore. As the men stare at the Pacific Ocean, noticing the sounds of the waves, the smell of the sea, and the humidity of the beach, wafting to the park, they becoming calm with one another. During this, Dan reaches in his pocket, and starts to make a marijuana joint.

"This is for you Paul. We're gonna miss you man. Rest easy my good friend. Goodbye."

Jerome continues to watch the ocean, while Klaus stares at Dan make the marijuana joint. A couple minutes later, Dan has finished getting the marijuana joint situated. Dan takes a lighter out of his pocket, and starts to light it. However, Klaus quickly snatches the joint away from him. Dan then shakes his head, and starts to laugh. Klaus laughs, as well, and lights the joint.

"Excuse me, I'm the leader, I get to take the first puff. You can go next sir. Ha Ha."

Dan shakes his head again at Klaus, and laughs. Klaus then takes several puffs of the marijuana joint. Klaus then hands the joint to Dan. During this time, Klaus takes out his phone, and starts to play an internet radio station. The station plays 90s pop hits. The song that is currently playing, is The Sign by "Ace of Base". Klaus sets his phone down on the bench, as the music continues to play. Dan takes several puffs of the marijuana joint, and then hands to it Jerome. Dan then looks out towards the ocean, and starts to speak to Klaus.

"On a scale of one to ten, how much trouble are we in? Like be honest man. Like, we're in this secret illuminati crime group right? The tattoos are proof. Like, we're screwed right."

Jerome takes puffs of the marijuana joint, and hands it back to Klaus. Klaus takes several puffs of the marijuana joint, and starts to shake his head. Klaus looks at the ocean, and speaks.

"Man, damn. Like it's past ten. Like it's at one hundred. We are totally screwed, but it's okay. It's our bed, we made it, and we have to lie in it now. But we are gonna stick together from here on. I don't know what's gonna happen to us form this point, but we're staying together."

Dan nods his head, and Klaus passes the marijuana joint back to Dan. The three of them continue to remain at the park, calming down, and bonding with one another. Jerome speaks.

"So that means Dan and I can stay right? Thank you Klaus, for being understanding."

Klaus then looks at Jerome, and smiles at him. Klaus then starts to run his hands through Jerome's hair. Jerome then laughs back at Klaus. Klaus looks towards the ocean, and speaks.

"Yeah you guys can stay I guess. I don't mind having you guys around. Ha Ha."

Klaus then again, kisses both Dan and Jerome on the forehead. Dan and Jerome laugh in return to Klaus. All of the men, continue to remain at the park, taking in everything this sentimental moment, is bringing to them. The night is beautiful, the park is peaceful, the ocean in front of them is very calm. It was then, that Klaus was thankful, that despite all the issues the guys were faced with, even from the very beginning, Klaus was happy to have both the friendships and relationships, that he has with both Dan and Jerome. Klaus realizes that the rash decision he made earlier, to kick Dan and Jerome out, was incorrect. This is not the time for them to fight, or cause rifts between one another. They are going to have to keep their bond strong. Considering the fact, they are in essence, marked men at this point. The men are indefinitely indebted to King Shark, and the Diamond Mafia group. The men are criminals, and every move they make is now tied to the Diamond Mafia group. The future is not clear with the guys now, and anything is possible, and anything could happen. They already had to shockingly deal with Paul being killed, and it was something the guys had no control over. The guys cannot report to the police, or talk to the police about anything. In fear that King Shark would punish the guys for that, by killing them. The guys also do not know, what is going to happen with Paul's body. Whether the police are going to investigate, and figure out what happened to Paul, and tie this back to the Diamond Mafia group, or not. The guys couldn't do anything about this now, and they would simply have to wait, to see what happens, in regards to this news.

The guys continue to remain at the park, winding down, everything that happened. The music continues to play through Klaus phone, and the guys also continue smoking the marijuana joint. At this time, the guys are slightly buzzed from the marijuana, and are feeling better about themselves. Klaus and Dan then start to engage in trivial small talk, and exchange jokes with each other. While the internet radio is playing music on Klaus phone, Jerome is miming all the lyrics to the songs. Jerome gets up from the bench, and starts to dance to the music that's playing. Klaus and Dan notice him, and laugh, but they carry on, with their conversation and banter, with Jerome continuing to dance in the background. With the guys now being at the park for an hour, time is passing by, rather quickly. The men simply are too comfortable to leave, and despite all the hectic activity that happened, they for a moment, forget any of that happened. They are in their own world, and fantasy right now. They are trying to visualize, and imagine themselves, at a different setting. It has seemed to work, as the guys feel calmer than they were previously. The guys realize, that their lives are at jeopardy. They are members of the Diamond Mafia group now, and there is nothing that they can do to get out of it, or remove themselves from the secret gang and group. Klaus, Dan, and Jerome, have to obey everything the group asks them to do, or they will be killed. The guys come to accept this, and it's rather bittersweet. The guys know the amount of trouble they are in. It's not that they don't care, as they actually don't care, but they are learning to accept everything considered.

They are still feeling upset that Paul is gone, but the guys can't react to that. The fact this was a direct consequence of them joining the group, and the fact of the matter is, that any one of them could be next. If they don't follow the orders of the gang, and the group, they will be next. King Shark decided to cut the guys several breaks, so they shouldn't be thankful for that. Although, it's still upsetting, the guys are still tied to the group. The men cannot go to the police either, so they are in a very complicated spot and situation. Klaus, Dan, and Jerome, all lead a law abiding live, up until this point. Well not anymore, they are criminals. Earlier tonight, they already managed to go ahead with the task of stealing the hard drive, making their place in the Diamond Mafia group official. They have to accept the fact, they are members of the crime group, and if the group wishes for them to do something, they have no choice but to do it. Klaus is now starting to understand and reflect, that his old life, is possibly over. This is the price that he is paying, for letting his curiosity, get to the better of him. Klaus then starts to laugh at himself, and realize, that this, inadvertently, was what he wanted. Klaus wanted to be nosy, and learn about everything he could. Well, he got his wish. He's now a member of the Diamond Mafia, and so are Dan and Jerome. Klaus starts to wonder, if it was all worth it, to get involved in details, and situations, that didn't pertain to him.

Klaus, and the other guys, stay at the park, for a few minutes more, and they continue to look at the night sky, and also look at the ocean, in front of them as well. The men have no idea how much longer they are going to remain in this area. If they could stay here, until the end of time, they would. Being at this park, allows the men to feel free, and liberated. It takes their minds off the Diamond Mafia drama, and situation. It allows the guys to calm down, if only for a moment. The men all know that life as they knew it before, from this point on, doesn't exist anymore. The guys must come to understand this, which it seems they already have. Klaus, Dan, and Jerome, continue to stay at the park, relaxing themselves. By this point, the marijuana joint, that all the men were smoking, has gotten too short, for them to continue using it. Dan puts the end of the marijuana joint, into the bag of joint papers. Dan puts the bag into his pocket. The guys have finished smoking, yet they remain at the park. This scene is far too peaceful for them to leave, and they are steadily, going to stay at the park, for as long as they need to. Klaus starts to stare deep out into the ocean, as he, along with Dan, notice several boats and ships in the water. Dan turns his head towards Klaus, who is still looking at the sailboats, and yachts in the sea. Dan then starts to look out towards the ocean as well. Jerome, is still continuing to mime, and dance to the music that Klaus is playing on his phone. The radio station then comes across a song that Jerome doesn't like. Jerome picks up Klaus phone, and it skips to another track. This song, Jerome does enjoy, and he returns to miming, and dancing along to it. Klaus and Dan simply laugh at Jerome, as he's doing this. Klaus and Dan also continue to look out to the beach, noticing the array of boats. Klaus starts to shake his head, and then silently speaks to Dan.

"You think maybe if I ask King Shark for a yacht, He'd buy me one? Ha Ha. I always wanted to own a yacht or sailboat. You, me, Jerome, we all go out, have a guy's trip. Yeah. Ha."

Dan, who is also looking out towards the yachts and sailboats in the ocean, speaks.

"Yeah, I don't think so. King Shark is not going to buy a yacht. You can forget about that man. Ha Ha. But yeah. That would be the life. I can picture that now. Us out at sea. Yeah man."

Klaus shakes his head, and continues to look out towards the ocean. Klaus and Dan continue to look at the boats in the water for several more minutes. Klaus then starts to pick up his phone, and notices that it is now after Midnight. Klaus then starts to yawn, and he starts to stretch. Both Dan and Jerome, ignore Klaus, and Jerome continues to dance along to the music that is playing on Klaus phone, and Dan remains looking out towards the ocean. Klaus, then realizes that Dan and Jerome want to stay at the park longer, so Klaus doesn't say anything, and asks if they want to go home, and leave. This carries on for another ten minutes, with the men remaining at the park, calm and quiet with one another. Klaus yet again checks his phone, noticing how late it is. This time, Klaus wishes to leave, and go home at this point. He feels that Dan and Jerome have had enough fun, and that's it's time for them to go. As much as Klaus would like for them to stay at the park forever, that simply isn't possible. Klaus turns to look at Jerome, still dancing the music. Klaus then directs his vision at Dan, who continues to watch the boats in the ocean. Klaus then looks down on the ground, and shakes his head. Immediately following that, Klaus stands up from the bench, and starts to stretch himself, and yawns. Klaus turns off the internet radio station, and Jerome gets the hint that it's time to leave, based on Klaus doing that. Jerome then gest up from the bench. Dan however, remains seated, as he remains watching the boats, out on the ocean. Klaus feels slightly bad, for having to disturb Dan, but it's time for all the men to leave. Klaus taps Dan on the shoulder, to get his attention, that it's time to leave, but Dan ignores Klaus. Klaus laughs, and then pats Dan on the back. Dan smiles, as he continues to look out towards the ocean. Klaus pulls out his phone again, checking the time. While Klaus is staring at his phone screen, he silently speaks to Dan.

"Okay man, it's time for us to go. We had fun, but we gotta go home now. Alright?"

Dan, while looking at the boats in the ocean, one final time, nods his head. Dan then gets up from the bench. Klaus, Dan, and Jerome, all leave from the park, and start to walk back to the house. As the men are walking, Dan, while looking down at the sidewalk, speaks to Klaus.

"Hey, you know I'm like really starving. Maybe it was because of that weed, but I don't know. So, why don't we all go to Taco Bell. Sounds like a nice cure of the munchies. Ha Ha."

Klaus, who is also looking down at the sidewalk, nods his head, and laughs at Dan. The men all continue to walk down the sidewalk, feeling very happy, and comfortable with each other. Eventually, the men all reach Klaus SUV, and Klaus gets into the driver side. Dan gets in the passenger side, and Jerome sits in the back seat. Klaus then drives a short distance, to the Taco Bell drive thru. Taco Bell stays open late, despite it being past Midnight. Upon arriving at the Taco Bell, Klaus orders several Tacos, and Burritos, for the guys. Klaus then gives the cashier his credit card, and pays for the meal. Klaus grabs the food, and hands the bag of Tacos, and Burritos to Dan. Klaus then heads directly back home. Once back at the house, Klaus parks his car, and he, Dan, and Jerome, get out of the vehicle. As the men are inside, Klaus puts the Taco Bell food, on the kitchen counter. Dan then puts the marijuana supplies, into Paul's shoebox. Dan stares at the box for several seconds, taking deep breaths, and shakes his head. Dan then takes the shoebox, and puts it in Paul's bedroom. Jerome walks to the living room, and takes a seat, down on the sofa. Klaus who is in the kitchen, reaches into the refrigerator, and grabs three beers. Dan at this time, walks over to the kitchen, where Klaus is, and grabs the bag of Taco Bell. Dan takes the bag, and sets it on the coffee table in the living room. Dan then takes a Burrito out of the bag, and sits down on the sofa next to Jerome, and starts to eat it. Jerome then takes a Taco out of the bag, and begins eating. Klaus, who is staring at both Dan and Jerome, smiles to himself. Klaus then walks into the living room and hands a beer to Dan and Jerome.

Klaus then takes a seat on his recliner, and closes his eyes, and relaxes. Dan turns his direction over to Klaus, and while taking a bite of his Burrito, starts to speak to Klaus.

"Hey man, you're not hungry? You're not gonna eat? Come and get some food man."

Klaus, with his eyes still closed, relaxing on the recliner, then laughs, and starts to shake his head. Klaus then gets up from the recliner, and walks over to the coffee table, where the bag of Taco Bell is. Klaus then reaches into the bag, and takes out a Burrito. Klaus returns to his recliner, and starts to munch on the Burrito. Dan then turns the television set on, which coincidentally, is tuned into the news. The men all watch, as a female news anchor speaks.

"We have a developing story tonight. There was an officer involved shooting. Reports are saying, that an intoxicated man, was at the Platinum Aerospace building, causing a disturbance. Officers fatally shot the man, as he was resisting arrest. An officer and guard died as well."

At this second, Klaus gets up from the recliner, grabs the remote from Dan's hand, and immediately cuts the television off. Klaus then tosses the remote back at Dan. Klaus returns to his recliner, and continues to eat his Burrito. Klaus then lifts up the left side of his shirt, staring at the Diamond Mafia tattoo, on his upper arm. Klaus simply shakes his head, and continues to eat his Burrito. Dan and Jerome, do not respond to Klaus. Klaus then eats his Burrito and speaks.

"Jerome, be a good boy, and eat your food in the bedroom. I need to have a chat with Dan, and it's kinda private. Go in the bedroom and watch SpongeBob or something. Okay?"

Jerome leaves the sofa, and grabs two Tacos, and a Burrito from the bag. Jerome speaks.

"Sure. That's okay. I'll leave you guys alone, and let you both chat. Good night boys."

Dan then kisses Jerome on the cheek, and Klaus kisses Jerome on the cheek as well. Jerome then walks into the bedroom, and shuts the door behind him. Klaus finishes eating his Burrito. Klaus then reaches into his pocket, and takes out his carton of cigarettes. Klaus then grabs his bottle of beer, and gets up from his recliner. Out of habit, Dan immediately gets up off the sofa, and Dan grabs his beer as well. Klaus and Dan give eye contact to each other for several seconds, and they both then start to laugh. Klaus and Dan then fist bump each other, and hug. As they are hugging, Klaus starts to whisper into Dan's ear, softly.

"Things are gonna be different for us now. You understand, Jerome understands, I understand. We work for King Shark now, and that's the way it is. But it's gonna be okay man."

Klaus while still hugging Dan, kisses him on his cheek. Dan smiles, and responds.

"It's okay man. Whatever happens from now, we'll manage. I know we will. We have each other, and that's the important part. So, you ready to step out to the patio now man? Ha Ha."

Klaus continues to hug Dan tightly, and starts to laugh. Klaus nods his head, in agreement with Dan. Klaus and Dan stop hugging, and they both start to walk outside to the balcony. Klaus takes a seat on the balcony, and Dan follows Klaus out to the balcony as well, shutting the door behind him. Dan takes a seat on the balcony next to Klaus. With it now being 1 a.m. it is very late into the night. Klaus starts to light his cigarette, and he hands Dan the lighter. Dan then lights his cigarette as well. Klaus and Dan, rightfully go back to their familiar, and comfortable custom, with the both of them having their balcony cigarette session. Klaus and Dan smoke their cigarettes, as they stare at the late-night sky. Klaus takes his glasses off, and starts to clean them with his shirt. Klaus at this time, again, pulls up his left shirt sleeve, and looks at the Diamond Mafia tattoo. Dan, takes a puff of his cigarette, and notices that Klaus is analyzing his tattoo. Dan then starts to shake his head and laughs. Dan pulls up his left shirt sleeve, and starts to speak.

"Hey Klaus look. I got the same tattoo. Hey, I talked to Jerome, and guess what, he's got that same tattoo as well. What? No! Really? Ha Ha. Face it man, you better own that tattoo now. You don't have a choice. King Shark owns us now, and that's just the way it is man. Ha Ha."

Dan puts down his sleeve, and takes a puff of his cigarette. Dan then starts to look forward, looking at the ocean. Klaus shakes his head, and rolls his sleeve down. Klaus then takes a puff of his cigarette, and stares out forward, looking at the ocean as well. Klaus takes a swallow of his beer, and starts to look down towards the ground. Klaus then silently speaks.

"Yeah, I guess you're right man. I still wish all of this is a dream, but it's not right? Paul is actually dead, and we're in this damn group now right? Fuck. We are so stupid. Ha Ha."

Dan then takes a puff of his cigarette and starts to pinch Klaus on the arm. Dan then starts to laugh, and Dan's laughter, makes Klaus laugh as well. Dan then looks forward, and speaks.

"No, it's not a dream. This is unfortunately the way it is man. It's okay. Yeah. Ha Ha."

Klaus then pinches Dan on the arm as well, and the both of them laugh yet again. Klaus takes a sip of his beer, and looks forward toward the ocean. Klaus then silently speaks.

"Yeah man. That's true. That's just the way it is. That's just the way it is. Ha Ha."

Klaus and Dan then fist bump each other. Klaus takes another swallow of his beer, and has his vision facing forward. Klaus then shakes his head, and laughs.

CHAPTER 20:

THREATENED

By now, the men are fully aware of the situation, that they each are in. They managed to make it this far, taking note of the many mistakes, and issues that they dealt with, along the way. At first, the mistakes, and hardships the men were going through, could be measured up, to the fact they were inexperienced, and didn't know any better. It could also come down to the fact, that they were experimenting with themselves, and learning more about themselves. So, it made sense at that particular time, for them to make the mistakes that they did. However, the men cannot use that excuse anymore, and they need to realize that their mistakes at this stage, are due to their own poor planning, and from not fully thinking their decisions fully. The men carry on about their journey, and adventure, still not sure what things will hold for them, or what they will be introduced next. The guys have already accepted the dire position they are in, and by joining the crime group, they already managed to accept the fact, that they are going to adapt themselves to being criminals, and doing ill gotten things, in order to please the Diamond Mafia group, and also to please King Shark. There isn't any way for the men to get out of doing this, so there is no use in complaining or feeling upset. This was the price the guys had to pay, for being nosy, while doing their news story, on the Diamond Mafia Group. King Shark will kill them, if they don't follow his orders, and if they don't do exactly as they say. So now that it's set-in stone, that they men will not live life, the way they were doing it before, the men simply conform themselves to this. It is too late for them to go back and fix this, so they must overcome this anyways.

The men are now starting to regret their choices, but it's far too late. Not only is it far too late, but it's impossible at this point, for the men to redeem themselves, after the poor choices that they made. Their curiosity was the main priority for the men, and they must deal with it. They must come to grips, that this is how things are going to be now. Things such as this, were causing great conflict, and difficulties within the group as well. Starting with the fact, Klaus lost his temper, and wanted to kick Dan, and Jerome out of his house. He didn't want to associate with them any longer, and Klaus felt as though, he had enough. Klaus was acting very rash, because of the death of Paul, and his emotions were not under control, and stable. Klaus and Dan, managed to have conflict, and it caused their friendship to break, yet again. Although luckily, it seemed that Klaus and Dan were able to make amends with their friendship after all, and things were forgiven.

Dan, shifts his perspective, on the fact that he felt that most of this, is Klaus fault. Dan feels Klaus in a way, ruined his life. Dan had a great life as a bus driver, and he enjoyed his job, and he liked helping others. Listening to Klaus radio show, was just a hobby of his at the time, and Dan didn't want to take it that serious. Little did Dan know, that he would become more involved into Klaus life, that he ever envisioned, and imagined. One thing led to another, and Dan and Klaus, formed a tight friendship. Now being the best of friends. So Dan was willing to forego the fact, that Klaus shifted his life greatly, and managed to turn everything around for him. But Dan has lost his patience, and emotions with Klaus several times. Dan feels that Klaus can be self-centered, arrogant, manipulative, and his personality can shift, turning him into a very mean, and uncaring person. Although, Dan also feels that Klaus has a kind side, and he is willing to primarily focus on that aspect of Klaus. That is the only reason why Dan has given Klaus the number of chances he has, and continues to hold onto his friendship with Klaus, despite all the previous issues, that the has had with him. Klaus and Dan, manage to forgive each other, and through the hardships, and situations that they both had to experience. Now that the men are members of the Diamond Mafia group, Klaus and Dan both understand, this is not the time for them to have conflict, and arguments with each other. Their friendship must remain strong.

Jerome on the other hand is acting more as a neutral spirit. Jerome tries his best, not to get involved with the conflict the other men in the group have. Jerome was strictly someone who was soft spoken, and non-judgmental. Jerome keeps his opinions to himself, and his opinions usually were kind hearted, and from good faith, and good value. Jerome had a complicated upbringing, and he was abandoned by his family as well. Jerome had to live life, knowing that he looks younger than his actual age, which he managed to quickly manage the difficulties of this. Also managing the fact, that he was black and gay. Having all of that on his plate, caused great emotional pain for Jerome. The one thing that brought peace, clarity, and serenity to Jerome's life, was listening to Klaus radio show. Although Jerome knew that he was far from the primary demographic of Klaus show, that didn't matter. Jerome always enjoyed researching about topics, even about topics that others would never assume he would be knowledgeable about. Jerome simply wanted to get Klaus autograph, being that he was his self-proclaimed, number one fan. The rest ended up being history, and Jerome formed a strong bond with Klaus. Jerome, is willing to accept the consequences of his actions, that he, and the other guys have performed. Jerome is fully aware that he is now in the Diamond Mafia group with the other guys, and they are now stuck with the group and gang, and nothing is going to change that. Jerome knew what he was getting himself into and although Jerome feels emotional, he has learned to accept this.

As usual, the men do not know, what is going to happen to them next. They must stay on high alert, as they know that King Shark, would contact them at any moment's notice. If that should happen, the men do not have a choice, but to report strictly back to him, immediately. King Shark has promoted the guys to a higher rank of the group, due to how well they managed to do the previous task. Even though the police were called, King Shark managed to forgive the men for that. King Shark was also probably feeling sympathetic, after finding out that Paul died during the task, and wanted to be considerate, giving that fact. So at this point, all the men can do is wait. King Shark, knows exactly where Klaus lives, and if Klaus, or any of the other guys, report to the police, King Shark will absolutely get angry with them, and dangerous things are for sure going to happen, in response to that. Klaus, and the other guys, try to find a way to distract them, from these new realizations, from joining the group. For example, the guys all went to the park, located in front of the beach. The men had a relaxing time together, and it was a beautiful event for them all. The guys know that their lives are more at risk, working for a criminal group and gang, so they want to take advantage of the nice, and calm times that they have left together. All in all, the guys still must remain ready at any time, for things to quickly shift,

Klaus wakes up, following what could possibly be, the worst day of Klaus life. Everything started, with Klaus looking at the news story, and feeling nosy, wanting to cover the event. Klaus in hindsight, and in retrospect, knows that he should have never agreed to visit the location, of the house, belonging to the Diamond Mafia group, in the first place. Klaus knew, that he should have just initially listened to Dan, who was telling Klaus, not to go there. Klaus didn't listen, and the men all paid dearly, for this terrible mistake. A mistake, that Klaus wishes that he can go back, and fix, rectify, and remedy, but he simply can't. The guys were kidnapped, about to be killed, but were saved, when they became members of Diamond Mafia. They were given an impossible task, which the accomplished, but they also had to deal with the death of Paul. Klaus continues to reflect that hectic day. Klaus then tarts to wake himself, and notices that Jerome is laying down on his chest. Klaus smiles to himself, and looks out his bedroom window, nothing that it is a bright sunny day today. The weather, and temperature is also nice. It is now 9 a.m., and it is still relatively early in the morning. At least Klaus considers it early. As Klaus continues to wake himself up, he is startled, when he notices that his phone is ringing. The sound of Klaus ringtone, wakes Jerome up as well. Klaus then starts to complain.

"Who the hell is it now? Nobody calls me at this hour. Who is calling my phone now?"

Klaus reaches over to his side dresser on his bed, and puts his glasses on. Klaus then starts to look at the number on his phone screen, and his phone says that it is from an unknown caller. Ordinarily, Klaus wouldn't answer the phone, but reality quickly dawned on Klaus. He knew that it could possibly be King Shark, or someone else from the Diamond Mafia group, who is trying to get into contact with the men. Once Klaus deduces this, he answers the phone.

"Good morning, this is Klaus. Is there something I can help you with?"

The person on the other end of the phone, doesn't immediately answer. Klaus can hear audible noise in the background. He is sure that it's a restaurant. The person on the phone speaks.

"Yes. This is King Shark. Good Morning. Look, I know I said I was going to give you guys a break. I am. Which is why I'm treating you guys out to brunch. One of my guards is going to pick you boys up. I just need a favor from you guys. So meet me for brunch okay?"

Before Klaus is able to respond, King Shark quickly hangs up the phone. Klaus then starts to rub his eyes, and shakes his head. Klaus gets out of bed, and speaks to Jerome.

"King Shark, want us to meet him for brunch right now. We don't have a choice, so wake up. They are going to pick us up any minute. I'm going to go tell Dan now. I can't believe this."

Jerome nods his head, and continues to wake himself up. Klaus walks out of the bedroom, and walks over to Dan's bedroom door. Klaus then knocks on the door, and shouts.

"Hey man, time to get up. King Shark wants us to meet him, it's very important. Get up."

Dan shouts back out to Klaus through the door, affirming he understood him, and Klaus then walks back into his bedroom, to get himself ready. All of the men then start to prepare themselves, to have brunch with King Shark. As Klaus is getting ready, he starts to feel nervous, as to what King Shark wants to tell them. Klaus isn't sure, if this is some type of trick. King Shark might have told them, that he wishes to treat them out to brunch, but this could also be some type of set up or trap. Klaus nevertheless, doesn't have a choice. If he decides not to go, because he thinks King Shark is lying and he's actually going to kill them all, he, and the rest of the guys are going to be killed by King Shark anyways. If Klaus and the men decide to go, and it's a trap, well then it doesn't matter, as the other scenario, would be bad for them too. So logistically, it seems that Klaus doesn't have a choice, and his best course of action would be for him, Dan, and Jerome, to meet up with King Shark for brunch. Even if it is a trick, and there is on brunch, and it's actually something else, that King Shark has planned for the men. Eventually, all of the men finish getting ready, and they all wait in the living room, waiting for the driver to pick them up, to take them to see King Shark. Klaus remains sitting in his recliner, looking down on the ground shaking his head. Dan and Jerome sit on the sofa, likewise doing the same. At this time, while still looking down on the ground, Dan shakes his head, and starts to speak to Klaus.

"I don't think he's taking us to any fucking brunch man. King Shark isn't that nice of a guy. I think this is it. He's gonna whack and off us. I know he is. You know how King Shark is."

Klaus and Jerome do not immediately respond, and all of the men continue to look down on the ground, still feeling nervous, about what is going to happen now. Klaus doorbell rings.

"That's them right there. Come on guys, we're gonna see what he wants, and no matter what happens, we have to face the music guys. Stay positive, we don't know what he wants."

Dan and Jerome both shake their heads agreeing with Klaus. Directly following that Klaus opens up the door, and it's one of King Shark's guards, telling them to follow him. The men do, and they get into a van, driven by one of the Diamond Mafia guards. The van then starts to head directly to the destination, King Shark asked the driver, to report to, and arrive at.

Meanwhile, Detective Ross, who Klaus has associated with a couple times before, is in his office, drinking his coffee, looking at several different case files. Detective Ross, looks at all recent crime cases, in the Los Angeles area. When Detective Ross, comes across the story, related to the Platinum Aerospace building, in which the guys were all told to steal a hard drive out of, and it also resulted in the death of Paul, Detective Ross becomes very intrigued. The detective finds the incidentals, and the details relating to the case, very strange and unusual. He feels that there are many things that are not adding up, mor making sense. Detective Ross continues to read the police, and investigation report, that says the man was acting belligerent and drunk, and that's initially why the police were called. However, in the description of the drunk man, the security guard mentioned that he was a black-haired man, which fit the description more towards Dan, who was the actual individual, that the guard saw. Paul, who was the accosted victim, has salt and pepper, dirty blonde hair. The report says the drunk man was wearing a red shirt, which again, fits more to the guard talking about Dan. The day the men went to the Aerospace Building, Paul was wearing a green shirt. Upon noticing these discrepancies and errors, Detective Ross, shakes his head, and scrunches up his face in anger. Detective Ross gets up from his desk, and pulls out more documents, related to the case. The strangest piece of the report, which was puzzling Detective Ross greatly, was the fact, when Paul's blood alcohol level was checked, after he was shot by medical coroners, the blood test showed he had a point zero, blood alcohol level. Although virtually, Dan was sober, and wasn't drunk either, but it's the fact Detective Ross doesn't know, or is aware of the full details, surrounding the guys heist at the Aerospace building, it adds more confusion. If Paul wasn't drunk, why was did the security guard call the police, and say that there was a drunk man? Detective Ross then noticed that the reports mentions, the security camera feed was disabled, and reset.

Due to all of these revelations, Detective Ross is absolutely sure, that the way the incident was reported, with was initially the authorities assuming that Paul was a drunk man, that walked into the building, being a nuisance, was not true. Detective Ross has no idea what actually happened, but he knows, based on the faulty reporting, that is not what happened. Detective Ross then starts to worry if an innocent man was killed, and if there are other details, that need to be uncovered about this case. Detective Ross then pulls out his phone, and speaks.

"This is Ross, yeah, the Platinum Aerospace case. Yeah this is totally bullshit, and makes no sense. There is no way the guy that was killed, was the one the guard reported about. I'm getting an instant search warrant right now. Did coroners ever ID the suspect? Male Caucasian?"

Detective Ross continues to speak with the person on the other end of the phone, who is a fellow detective. The other detective, explains to Detective Ross, that the man was identified, and that fingerprints from DMV records, matched him to being Paul Surrey. Detective Ross, thanks the other detective, and he immediately begins to look up Paul's name through his database, and running a background check, to get further information. Detective Ross, then looks at Paul's driver's license photo, and notices that Paul looks familiar. Detective Ross cannot pin point, why Paul looks familiar to him. Detective Ross is certain, that he has met, or has seen Paul in person before. After going through Paul's criminal history, which aside from parking tickets, is relatively clean, Detective Ross then notices, that Paul was indirectly involved, with the situation with Ernest, and the police pursuit. As soon as Detective Ross notices this, he bangs his fist on his desk, and laughs at himself. Detective Ross then reads, that Paul, is associated with Dan, Ernest, Jerome, Bill, and above all Klaus. Detective Ross shakes his head, and pulls out his phone again and calls another detective. While still smiling and shaking his head, he speaks.

"Yeah this is Ross. You're not going to believe this. I think the Platinum situation, is connected to the gas truck pursuit a while back. Some of the same guys are involved. I'm gonna go check out the Aerospace building and investigate. I want to question those other guys now."

The detective on the other end understands, and Detective Ross disconnects the call. Although Detective Ross doesn't know the full details, he has a feeling that everything is connected, and it can't be simply coincidence, that this is happening. Detective Ross wants to speak with Klaus, and the rest of the guys, to at least get their side of the story. Detective Ross knows they are friends with each other, and they are close, so he hopes this will make the situation, become clearer. Detective Ross takes another sip of his coffee, and leans back on his chair, smiling to himself. Directly after that, Detective Ross grabs his keys, leaves his office, and starts to drive down to the Platinum Aerospace building, in which the guys did their heist at, the night before. Once inside the building, which Detective Ross was able to get a search warrant for, Detective Ross immediately directs himself to the camera control room, as he found it odd, that the cameras were disabled. He notices that based on how the security cameras are set, and after going through the history settings, someone did in fact mess with the cameras. Although the cameras were shut off, and reset, and the footage is lost, Detective Ross at least is satisfied, to know, that the security cameras, were tampered with. Whoever was in the building, didn't want to be seen. So Detective Ross knew that this was probably some type of criminal objective, and agenda. Detective Ross continues to investigate the building, and although he finds the room, where the guys found the hard drive, suspicious, as some drawers are open, from Klaus and Paul, being careless, and not fully closing them, Detective Ross, unfortunately has to keep the case cold. He was not able to come up with enough information, to get a solid basis on his investigation, and is slightly disappointed. However, Detective Ross, is happy that he was able to identify the man that was shot, and it was not the guy related to the initial report. Detective Ross is not sure if Paul was an innocent bystander, or up to no good. Detective Ross feels, this possibly confirms, that there were possibly multiple men at the scene. Detective Ross walks out of the building, puts his sunglasses on, and gets into his car. He drives back to the police station.

At this time, Klaus, and the rest of the guys, continue to stay in the van, which is heading to the destination, that the Diamond Mafia driver, is taking them to. Under much suspense, nervousness, and anxiety, the guys have no idea where they are going. With the only assumption is that King Shark wanted to meet them for brunch. Whether King Shark was telling the truth, or he has something else up his sleeve, the rest of the guys do not know and are unsure. Eventually, the guys start to slowly, but surely, give sighs of relief, once they notice, the driver is pulling up to a crowded IHOP restaurant. The guys then no longer feel scared, or on edge. King Shark, might have been truthful and honest, and he is treating the guys out to brunch. Klaus, Dan, and Jerome get out of the vehicle, and while they are standing beside the van, the driver speaks.

"King Shark is in the booth in the back. He wants you to sit him. Catch you guys later."

The driver then immediately drifts away from the scene, and Klaus, and the rest of the men, still stand outside the restaurant, puzzled. They then directly walk inside of the restaurant, which the fact it's Sunday, and during the weekend, the restaurant is quite crowded and packed. Although there are a lot of people inside, the guys quickly locate King Shark, sitting in the back of the restaurant. King Shark, is sitting with the heavy set African American guard, that the guys already met, whose name is Clark. King Shark waves his hand up in the air, and smiles at the guys, signaling them to sit with him. Klaus, Dan, and Jerome oblige, and start to walk over to the table, where King Shark is seated. The men all take a seat at the booth, with King Shark, and Clark, sitting on the other side. King Shark starts to read his menu, and speaks to the men.

"You guys can order whatever you like. This is my treat, alright. I hope you guys are hungry, because I am. Ha Ha. So, did you boys sleep well last night?"

Klaus starts to look around the restaurant, and Dan and Jerome, remain silent. Klaus continues to scope out everyone inside, and as he's still looking around, Klaus speaks.

"So, why did you call us here? Did we do something wrong, are we in trouble?"

Before King Shark can respond, the waitress arrives at the table, and puts carafe of coffee on the table, and several coffee mugs. King Shark thanks the waitress, and she walks away. King Shark then takes one of the coffee mugs, and pours himself a cup of coffee. He then reaches for the sugar packets, and cream container, and puts cream and sugar, into his coffee as well. King Shark takes a sip of his coffee, and looks at the menu. While looking at the menu, he speaks.

"No, you boys aren't in trouble, but I am. Not looking good for me. With the exception of you guys, I have idiots working for me. They can't do simple tasks and jobs right. I guess it's time to say, I talked it over with my assistant Clark here, you're promoted to 1st Class Tigers."

Upon hearing this news, Klaus continues to scope around the restaurant, and reluctantly, decides to pour himself a cup of coffee. Dan and Jerome follow suit, and start making themselves a cup of coffee as well. Klaus was slightly puzzled, and confused, that King Shark is having this conversation, out in the open in this restaurant. Being involved in the Diamond Mafia crime gang and group, is a private, serious matter, and Klaus starts to feel scared, talking about this type of stuff, at this current setting. Klaus then figures, that King Shark must be comfortable enough, and doesn't think that there are any spies, or rivals, or enemies in the building. Klaus was also shocked, that King Shark promoted them, and they have only been members of the group, for two days. Klaus, and the rest of the guys, have no idea what 1st Class Tigers rank means, but they know that it will come with great power, and great responsibility. At this time, the waitress arrives back at the table, to take the guys food order. King Shark, and Clark, then give their order to the waitress. Klaus, Dan, and Jerome, who are still feeling puzzled, are reluctant to give their order to the waitress. King Shark gives a cold stare to them, and starts to speak.

"Boys, you guys can order whatever you want. It's okay. I know you're hungry."

Klaus then looks down at the menu and shakes his head. Klaus gives the waitress his food order. Dan and Jerome, follow suit, and do the same. Following this, the waitress leaves the table. King Shark takes another sip of his coffee, and starts to speak softly to all the guys.

"1st class Tigers, basically means, you guys have my full protection, in addition to the fact, the other guys will have respect for you. You guys have a reputation now, and who knows. You guys keep this up, you guys could be Captains and Kingpins. Ha Ha. But boys, listen."

Klaus steadily looks around the restaurant, feeling nervous. King Shark then speaks.

"Hey, why are you looking around? You expecting someone? Stop looking around like that, I'm gonna kick you in the face if you don't. Don't make me regret being nice to you boys."

Dan then rubs Klaus on the shoulder, to comfort, and calm him down. King Shark then starts at the guys, takes a sip of his coffee, and laughs. King Shark then continues to speak.

"Alright, this Friday, so I'm gonna give you guys a few days to relax, kick back. But this Friday, there is a rival of mine. Real jerk, real asshole. I hate every aspect of him. He stole my Rolex, and I want you guys to break into his office and get it for me."

Klaus, although feeling nervous, is slightly agitated, that King Shark wants them to do, yet another task. Klaus is angry, because he, and the other guys know, there is no saying no, or refusing to do the task. The guys simply have to do it, or they will all be killed. King Shark takes another sip of his coffee, and hands a set of keys to Klaus. King Shark then continues speaking.

"This time it should be easier for you boys. Security should be lax. You guys look professional enough, so tell them you work in the building. You guys have the keys, I don't know where in his office the watch is, but I have faith in you boys. I need my watch back."

King Shark continues to sip his coffee, while the other guys listen to the next task, that he wishes for them to do. During this time, the waitress returns back to the table, and hands the guys their food orders. King Shark, and Clark, immediately begin eating. Klaus, Dan, and Jerome however, are slightly nervous, which is causing their appetite to be disturbed. King Shark notices, the guys are not touching their plates, and it causes him to feel agitated. King Shark continues to eat, and the guys still feel too nervous to eat. King Shark then speaks to them.

"If you guys don't eat, I'm gonna start fucking force feeding you. There are starving people in the world, and I'm giving you guys a free meal. You guys better fucking eat now."

Klaus, Dan, and Jerome, out of fear from King Shark's tone, start to immediately eat, King Shark then starts to laugh and smiles. All of the men carry on eating, and the table is awkwardly quiet for several minutes. King Shark then takes another sip of his coffee and speaks.

"Once he finds out I got his watch back, he's gonna think I did it. So I managed to find this copycat, replica, fake Rolex. Replace the watches, and he will never know. Ha Ha."

King Shark takes more bites of his food, and Klaus, Dan, and Jerome, nod their heads. The table is once again quiet for several minutes, with all of the men eating. The men are now fully understanding of the task. Although they have no choice, and the task is mandatory and required, the guys are comfortable with all the details. Klaus starts to feel slightly confident, and also starts to feel rebellious, that the guys, will achieve this task, without any problems at all. Klaus feels this task, will be easier, than the hard drive task. While Klaus is taking a bite of his food, he does however feel, there is a condition, catch, or caveat to this. Klaus feels that King Shark is not being completely honest. Klaus continues to eat his food, and speaks.

"So, that's it. You want us to steal a watch. There has to be a catch right. Isn't there?"

King Shark then forms an angry look on his face, and starts to pick up his fork. King Shark then thrusts the fork, onto Klaus left arm, slightly stabbing him. Klaus doesn't react to this at all, although King Shark, poking him with the fork, hurt him. King Shark then silently speaks.

"There is no fucking catch. The catch is, if you guys don't get that fucking watch, well, you already know what's going to happen. Say another word, and defy me again. I dare you."

Klaus doesn't react at all to King Shark, and neither do Dan or Jerome. Dan, once again, comforts Klaus by rubbing and massaging his back. Klaus feels that King Shark is not being completely true, and that the task seems far too easy, for there not to be a detail, that King Shark is leaving out. The actual truth, is that King Shark does not own the watch the men are trying to steal. King Shark wants to steal that watch, as it belongs to a rival gang leader. King Shark knows that if he can steal the watch, it would give him the satisfaction, the he stole from a rival gang and group. King Shark would also be able to sell the watch, and generate wealth to the Diamond Mafia group. What the guys also don't know, is the keys that King Shark handed the guys are obsolete. They are dud keys, which do not open the lock to the office. King Shark is aware of this, but wants to trick the guys into thinking the job will be easy, because they have a set of keys to the office. The keys will not work, and the guys will need to get inside the office, somehow, someway, other than using a key. In addition, King Shark lied, when he said that security was lax. It's not. The guys are going to have to find a way to sneak into the office, without being spotted, by security or by the security cameras, likewise, with the situation before, at the Platinum Aerospace Building. King Shark is one hundred percent sure the guys will not accomplish this task, and will fail, and get themselves into a dire situation, and result. Even if the guys are miraculously able to accomplish the task, King Shark, is going to continue to give the guys more difficult tasks, until they inevitably get caught by the police, in which King Shark will kill them, for being unsuccessful, they end up getting hurt, or worse, killed, in the process, either by the police, or through their own negligence. Or until they defy, and disobey his task requests, in which King Shark will kill the men, or not following his orders.

The men simply do not know this vital information, and the secrets and lies, that King Shark is withholding from them. The men regardless feel confident, because they still believe, and retain, that this task would be simple for them to accomplish, and they will succeed. Eventually, King Shark, and the rest of the men finish their meal. King Shark gets up from the table, and leaves out of the restaurant with Clark. Klaus, and other men, find it strange, that King Shark did not say any parting words. King Shark simply got up from the table, and walked out with Clark. Klaus, Dan, and Jerome, remain seated at the table. It was during this time, that King Shark, swindled, and bamboozled the men yet again. King Shark, who by his own admission, said that the was treating the guys out to eat, that's just not true. This is confirmed, when the waitress returns to the table, and hands Klaus, the check. Klaus then starts to shake his head and laughs, and Dan and Jerome laugh with Klaus as well. Klaus ends up taking his credit card out, and ends up paying for the entire meal. Although Klaus was laughing, it was mostly laughter, to hide the pain and frustration and anger. King Shark lied about treating them to the meal. Klaus can't believe King Shark pulled that stunt, and left them with the check to pay. After paying the check, and leaving the waitress a tip, Klaus, and the rest of the men, then start to walk out of the restaurant. Klaus, and the guys, wait in the parking lot, for the driver of the van to arrive. Five minutes, turn into fifteen minutes, turn into a half an hour, which turns into an hour. Because the men were instructed by King Shark, not to bring their phones, they couldn't contact ride share. At this time, Dan takes out his wallet, and hands Klaus and Jerome a dollar bill. Dan then speaks.

"This is some bullshit; I don't think they are picking us up. Let's just take the bus."

Klaus then looks down on the ground, and can't believe that they are being fooled with, once again. Klaus knows that King Shark didn't arrange for the driver to give them a ride back. It was now starting to make sense in Klaus mind, and Klaus then started to figure out, that King Shark was withholding information about the task they must do on Friday. Klaus sticks with the fact, he knows the task is far too easy, and it can't be that simple. If King Shark walked out on paying the check, and also didn't arrange a ride for the guys back, Klaus knew that King Shark is lying about the next task they must do. The worst part of it all, Klaus can't throw a tantrum, be upset, be defiant, or refuse King Shark's orders. As he, and the rest of the guys will be killed, if they don't obey King Shark. At this time, Klaus, Dan, and Jerome, start to walk to the appropriate bus stop, so they can get back to the house. Because he was a Bus Driver, Dan is able to find out the quickest bus the guys can take, to reach the house. Problem is, it's Sunday, and the bus schedule on Sunday, is haphazard. So the guys have to walk twenty blocks, to get to the right bus, and once they get on the right bus, they must walk twenty more blocks, off the closet bus stop, to Klaus residence. This is only because it's Sunday. If it were during the week, there would be a more convenient route they could take. Klaus thanks Dan for giving them money for the bus, and also the bus information. The guys then start trekking their way, to the bus stop. During the walk, Klaus is feeling really exhausted. Jerome notices this, and speaks.

"We're almost there Klaus. Dan is taking us to the nearest bus stop. You're doing good."

Klaus and Jerome smile at each other, and Klaus looks down the ground, and shakes his head. Eventually, the men make it to the bus stop. However, the bus is taking a while to get to the stop. The positive side, is the men are at the correct location. An hour later, the bus arrives at the bus stop, and the men prepare to get on the bus. The bus driver opens the door, and the bus driver, who is a short elderly Caucasian man with glasses. The bus driver squints his eyes, and takes his glasses off, to clean them. He instantly recognizes Dan. The bus driver then speaks.

"Dan, wow. I haven't seen you in a long time. How you been. How's life treating you?"

Dan then shakes the bus driver's hand, and hugs him. Dan shakes his head, and speaks.

"Oh damn, Tiberius, is that you? I'm doing great man. These are my roommates. Klaus, Jerome, this is Tiberius. He's an old coworker of mine. He's my first trainer too. Wow. Ha Ha."

Klaus and Jerome then shake the bus driver's hand. Dan and Tiberius, continue to speak for a few minutes, and touch base, and update each other. Dan then asks Tiberius, for a request.

"Hey man, listen. It's a long story, Ha Ha, but we're trying to get back home. My roommate, big guy over there, he's exhausted. Tiberius, I know it's not on the 130 Bus route, but can you drop us off at the Redondo Beach 8 bus stop. It's a closer walk for us. I appreciate it."

Tiberius then takes off his glasses, and cleans then with his shirt. He then starts to laugh, and pats Dan on the back. Tiberius closes the bus door, and starts driving. Tiberius then speaks.

"I can do better than that. For you Dan, I'll drop you guys off right in front of the house, it's okay. It's Sunday, nobody is gonna ride this damn bus today anyways. Okay boys. We're off. Sight tight, get comfortable, as it's going to be a long, and bumpy ride. Ha Ha."

Dan then shakes his head and laughs, and pats Tiberius on the back as well. Dan then takes a seat on the bus next to Klaus, with Jerome situated in the row in front of them. Tiberius continues to drive the bus, back to the house. During the bus ride, Dan takes a glance over at Klaus, who starts to shake his head and laughs. Dan puts on a slight smile, and speaks to him.

"What's wrong man? Wait, I know what you're thinking, I always happen to work my magic right? Ha Ha I do. That's why were great partners Klaus. You're nothing without me. Ha."

Klaus continues to have his vision pointing down. Klaus laughs, and responds to Dan.

"That's not what I'm thinking at all. I'm thinking your weird, and I can't believe you."

Dan shakes his head, and laughs in response to Klaus. Both of them continue to laugh, and Klaus and Dan fist bump each other. During the bus ride, Tiberius remains on the regular bus route, but is taking a slight detour, to drop the bus, directly at Klaus house. Although what Tiberius is doing is out of regulations, Tiberius plans to retire from the bus company in the summer, so even if they do dismiss and terminate him, which Tiberius doesn't think they will, he is willing to go against the rules, and offer a kind gesture to Dan, by going against the regulated bus route. During the bus trip, the guys start to look at several different parts of Los Angeles, and different buildings, and sights. The bus trip to the house, is rather long. An hour and a half ride in fact. Although during the ride, the men continue to converse with each other, and make light of the situation, and turning lemons, into lemonade over the matter. The guys continue to take the rather long bus trip home, trying to remain happy and calm with each other, despite the fact this is a rather strange event they are dealing with. Klaus also can't remember the last time he rode a city bus. It has been a while. Dan and Jerome however, are more used to city buses. As the men are getting closer to the house, Dan turns his vision towards Klaus, and asks him a question.

"So, what do you think is gonna happen with Paul. Are they gonna contact us or not? Are we gonna have a funeral for him? What's gonna happen with that, or do you even care?"

Klaus continues to look out the bus window, and whispers directly back to Dan.

"Don't talk to me about that shit. I have no idea what we're gonna do with Paul. I don't think Paul has any family. I'm not concerned. I do care but, ugh..., we'll talk later, okay?"

Dan nods his head, and looks away from Klaus. Jerome heard their conversation, but didn't offer any input, or respond back to them. Tiberius continues to drive back to house. Eventually, the bus does manage to arrive back at the house, and Tiberius starts to pull up to the house. Klaus informs Tiberius, as to which is the correct house, and Tiberius parks the bus, right in front of it. Klaus, Dan, and Jerome, then start to get off the bus. Klaus and Jerome, shake Tiberius hand, and Dan shakes Tiberius hand, thanks him for giving him, and the other guys a ride, and hugs him tightly. The men say goodbye to Tiberius, and he drives the bus away. Klaus, Dan, and Jerome, all stare at each other for a few seconds, and they all laugh. The men then all walk inside of the house, and Klaus immediately directs himself to the refrigerator. Klaus starts to open up the refrigerator door, and Dan and Jerome, report to the living room, and sit on the sofa. Dan turns the television on, and it is showing, "Star Trek: The Next Generation." Klaus starts to look through the refrigerator, and can hear Dan turn the television on, and starts to laugh. Klaus then decides to shout out to Dan and Jerome.

"Hey, you guys want a beer? There are three left in here. I have to go to the store, and buy more beer, I guess. Ha Ha. You dunderheads want a beer or not? Going once, going twice."

Dan and Jerome both agree to the beer, and Klaus shakes his head and laughs. Klaus then brings all three of the beers over to the living room, and hands Dan, and Jerome a beer. Klaus then sits down on his recliner, and starts to open his beer, drinking it. All three of the men remain in the living room, watching television. Dan, who has seen this episode before, starts to give funny commentary, to which Jerome is laughing at him. When the program goes on commercial break, Klaus at this time, once again pulls up his shirt sleeve, and looks at the Diamond Mafia tattoo, shaking his head. Klaus then takes several sips of his beer, and watches television. Things seem to be calm for right now. The guys had an eventful outing with King Shark. Even though he did not promise his end of the bargain, by paying for the check, and also, he left the guys stranded at the restaurant, the guys managed to still recover yet again, from this setback. All is currently well, or so it seems. The guys have no idea, that Detective Ross, is actually right outside Klaus residence, spying on him, and the other guys. Detective Ross saw the guys get off the city bus, and that didn't help his already tense suspicions about the guys. Detective Ross, starts to eat a cheeseburger, and listens to music in his car, while he continues to spy outside of the house. A half an hour passes, and Detective Ross, feels this is the perfect time, to speak to Klaus, and the rest of the guys. Detective Ross gets out of his car, and rings Klaus doorbell.

Upon hearing the doorbell ring, the guys stare at each other, and Dan then speaks.

"I'll go get it you guys."

Dan then starts to walk to the front door, and begins to open it. As he opens the door, Dan is shocked to see that it's Detective Ross. Dan and the detective stare at each other in silence for several minutes. The detective then starts to be nosy, and looks through the house. Dan then walks closer to Detective Ross, and closes the door behind him. Detective Ross then speaks.

"Hey, I remember you. You're Dan Mendoza correct? Hey listen Dan, is your friend Klaus home, it's really important I talk to you. I don't know if you guys know, but I think Klaus friend, Paul Surrey, he unfortunately was killed yesterday. I'm doing an investigation...."

At this time, Dan then remembers the rule King Shark gave the men, in regards to talking to the police. Dan knew that he, and the other guys could get into serious trouble, if King Shark new, they were giving information to the police. Dan quickly cuts the detective off and speaks.

"Oh, Detective Ross. Now is not a good time. Can we talk about this later please?"

Klaus, who is curious as to who is at the door, gets up from his recliner, and starts to walk to the front door. Klaus stands by the door, listening, and hears that it's Detective Ross. Even though Klaus wasn't worried that Dan would tell the detective any incriminating information, or any information that would get the guys in trouble, Klaus decides to walk out of the door, to speak with Detective Ross himself. Once Klaus is outside, he quickly closes the door behind him. Klaus and Detective Ross stare at each other for several seconds, and the detective speaks.

"Oh hey Klaus. Long time no see. Ha Ha. Klaus, your friend Paul, he was killed last night. We're doing an investigation, and have no idea how he passed away. The reports we initialed received are incorrect and make no sense. You don't mind if I come in and talk?"

Klaus then stares at Dan, and they both look at each other in silence. Klaus then starts to look around the neighborhood, and he scratches the back of his head. Klaus then responds.

"Oh no. Paul was killed. Oh lord. Well thank you detective for telling us that. We had no idea. We haven't seen Paul, we figured he was out with some friends. Detective, unfortunately I do mind if you come in. Unless you have a search warrant. So thank you detective, and yeah."

Klaus was unsure if he went about talking to the detective in the appropriate way. Detective Ross, was even more suspicious of the events, from the way Klaus was acting. Detective Ross then starts to look out to the distance. As he's doing that, he speaks to Dan.

"Um, Dan. If you don't mind me asking. What color shirt were you wearing yesterday?"

Dan then hesitates for a couple of seconds, staring at Klaus. Dan speaks to the detective.

"Oh gee. Isn't that funny, you can't remember stuff like that? Oh, it was a blue shirt."

Dan then started to slightly think ahead, knowing that if he said a red shirt, which Dan was actually wearing, it would be more suspicious. Detective Ross stares at Dan and nods his head. Detective Ross continues to look around the neighborhood, and then speaks to Klaus.

"Okay, blue shirt. Alright. Klaus, what were you doing last night? Tell me everything."

Klaus then starts to scratch the back of his head, and looks around. Klaus then speaks.

"Well, I was mostly here, with Dan, and Jerome. We were watching movies; we were eating some junk food. We had some beers, then we went to bed. Honestly detective, that's it."

Jerome, who is also curious, as to who is at the door, stands behind it, listening to everything. Klaus has an intuition, and feeling, that Jerome is behind him listening. Klaus is sure that Jerome would go along with their cover. Klaus then opens the front door, and starts to speak.

"Actually, you can ask Jerome. He will tell you the same thing. Isn't that right Jerome?"

Jerome then walks out, and stands in front of Klaus. At this time, Detective Ross starts to stare at Jerome deeply, and Klaus rests his hands on Jerome's shoulders. Detective Ross speaks.

"Hey Jerome, you remember me right. Detective Ross. Hey, now I want you to be honest, as it's against the law to lie to the police, okay? What were all of you doing last night?"

Jerome, without hesitation, and without looking away from the detective, speaks to him.

"Sir, Klaus, Dan, and myself, we were here at the house. Watching movies, playing video games. We were eating some tacos, and drinking. Then we all went to sleep. That's it. Honest."

Detective Ross then looks down on the ground, and shakes his head. The detective is sure that the men are lying, and he was hoping to get more information the case. However, because he didn't have any probable cause, or a search warrant, he did not have grounds to walk inside the house, and go through the guys belongings, to get more evidence, to see if the guys are up to no good. Detective Ross is trying hard not to leave this case cold, but at this time, he has to move onto other cases, as the evidence for this one, is not strong enough. Although he tried to get more evidence, and investigate more, the detective simply can't, and he's done all that he can do. Detective Ross, starts to probably think, Paul was some type of innocent bystander, and that got involved in a case of mistaken identity. Detective Ross believes the drunk man, probably was up to no good in the building, and Paul, was a hostage or innocent victim. Detective Ross slightly feels that maybe Paul and the drunk man were working together to rob the building, but Detective Ross, because Paul had no prior criminal history, believes this was an unfortunate case of Paul being at the wrong place, and the wrong time. Although Detective Ross doesn't know the purpose of Paul being at the building, he must simply move on. Detective Ross has no idea, that Paul, and the rest of the guys, are a part of the Diamond Mafia gang, and the true reason behind Paul's death, is that the men were trespassing, and trying to steal the hard drive. Detective Ross gives each of the guys a copy of his business card, and tells them to call him, if he has any information. Detective Ross then starts to walk towards his car, but then, he suddenly starts to remember something. Detective Ross walks back to the door, and speaks.

"Oh, I almost forgot. I don't know if you guys knew Paul had a younger brother, Porter. Well, he's listed as Paul's closest family member. They are having a funeral for him Thursday. Just thought that you guys should know, if you want to attend. Alright, good evening boys."

The men thank Detective Ross for giving them this information, and Detective Ross walks back to his car, and drives off. Klaus, Dan, and Jerome, then all stare at each other, and walk back into the house. Detective Ross, although he doesn't fully believe the men, seemed to have bought their alibi's well enough, and doesn't consider them prime people of interest in the case. Klaus thanks both Dan and Jerome for not blowing their cover. Once finding out that Paul has a funeral on Thursday, the guys now understand how busy the following week will be. They will have to attend Paul's funeral, and meet his brother for the first time; to which Klaus has no idea, why Paul didn't tell the guys he had a younger brother. Paul told the guys, that he didn't have any family at all, so this is rather strange and peculiar. Klaus, and the other guys, might find the reason for this, at the funeral. Not only that, on Friday, the guys will have to do their next task, that King Shark has given them, which is to break into the office building, to steal the Rolex watch. The guys, after successfully lying to Detective Ross, return back to the living room, and continue to watch their program, as if nothing happened. Another hour passes, of the guys keeping to themselves, watching television, when Klaus receives a phone call. Klaus picks up his phone, and notices that it is an unknown number. Klaus answers the phone anyways.

"Hello, good evening. This is Klaus. Is there something I can help you with?"

The person on the other end of the phone, doesn't respond right away. Klaus notices that the other end has a lot of interference. Although it's very audible, and muffled, Klaus hears what appears to be someone screaming in horror. This slightly agitated Klaus, but out of curiosity, he stays connected on the line. The person on the phone speaks.

"Yeah it's me. I wanted to let you guys know that, I'm so glad I can depend on you guys. It's hard for me to find trustworthy people, but I trust you boys. I'm not the person to fuck with, so yeah. Just calling to tell you boys goodnight, and we'll chat later. Go Tigers!"

The phone then hangs up, and Klaus sets his phone down, takes his glasses off, and rubs his eyes. Klaus didn't know why King Shark decided to call him, and also didn't know why the reception was so bad, and there was someone screaming. Klaus feels that he might have nightmares as a result of that call, and how strange it was. Dan and Jerome, are curious as to who Klaus was talking to on the phone, and Dan takes a sip of his beer, and speaks to Klaus.

"Who was that? You look really shook up. Everything alright with you man. You okay?"

Klaus then puts his glasses back on, and starts to smile, and shake his head. Klaus hesitates for several seconds, and remains quiet. Klaus then gets up from his recliner, and starts to stretch his body, and yawns. Klaus then shakes head, looks down on the ground, and speaks.

"Um yeah, that was King Shark, and like it sounded like he was in a car factory, or junkyard. Like it was hard to hear him. I also heard this guy screaming for his life. Wow. He just wanted to call and wish us goodnight. Ha Ha. So yeah. That was really random as hell."

Dan and Jerome, then start to instantly laugh, which causes Klaus to laugh as well. Klaus returns to sitting on his recliner, and the men return to watching television. As the night draws on, Dan decides to make the guys, Chicken Quesadillas, using leftover chicken in the refrigerator. Once Dan is finished making dinner, the guys all grab a plate, and return back to the living room. This time, the guys are watching the horror movie, "Joy Ride", with Paul Walker, and Steve Zahn. As the guys finish eating their dinner, they decide to all have a slice of the cake, that Emilio gave them. They guys have dessert, and dessert is finished, Jerome starts to wash the dishes. Klaus and Dan continue to remain in the living room, watching the movie. Jerome finishes the dishes, and returns back to the living room. When the movie is over, all of the men, walk out onto the balcony. Klaus takes out his pack of cigarettes, and gives Dan, and Jerome a cigarette. Klaus lights his cigarette, and starts to light it. Dan and Jerome light their cigarettes as well. The men all then start to enjoy their cigarettes out on the balcony, looking at the night sky.

Another day for the men has ended, and Klaus braces himself, as he knows things are not complete yet, and the antics and adventures, are soon to continue. Klaus continues to look outside his balcony, hearing the waves of the sea, crash against the shore, and also smelling the sea. Klaus takes more puffs of his cigarette, and gets up, and gives Dan a kiss on his cheek, and Jerome a kiss on his cheek. Both Dan and Jerome laugh at Klaus, and Klaus laughs as well. Klaus looks out to the distance, watching the beach, and shakes his head, and laughs.

CHAPTER 21:

CURTAIN CALL

Understand everything still, that the men have on their agenda, they try to conform their lives, around that. Things are most certainty, going to be different, but the guys understand their options. They can either be bothered by these changes, which in turn will allow them to be mentally blocked, further disrupting them from happiness and satisfaction. Or, they can simply do what they are doing now, which is accept these new changes and developments. From everything considered, the men have decided to accept the new details of their lives. The fact that if the men decide to go against everything, it could end up turning worse for them. The guys do have a choice, but in essence, they virtually do not. They must now live life, according to the consequences, and poor choices, that they have made. The men had much opportunity, to stop, and prevent themselves, from painting themselves into the corner that they have, and digging themselves, deeper into this hole. It is now at the point, where the men, are not going to be able, to rise back up. There is no opportunity for them to do so, and things are too far gone. The one thing that the men have, is each other. At least they are not experiencing all of this alone, and they have the social bond, and the men get along well. Their friendship between one another, remains tight, and that is probably the only reason why they are still strong, is due to the bond they have. The men are willing to take whatever setbacks they experience, in stride. Knowing that they at least have one another to turn to, and they can lean on each other, for moral support. The men are now involved with the Diamond Mafia group, and they must live double lives. They must put on a successful façade, of being law abiding citizens, but the fact of the matter is, they are not. They are members of a secret crime gang, and there is nothing they can do, to get out of it. This is the life that the men must live, and obey by, and that is the way it's going to be.

For now, remarkably, the men still have much on their plate, and a lot of things they have to cover. It may seem that things are shut down, and calm. That is further from the truth, and the exact opposite. The men are in a grave deal of trouble, and the unfortunate part is, they don't even know half of the trouble, they are actually in. So the fact the men are dealing with these issues, in addition, and on top of the fact, the men are being sabotaged, and tricked by King Shark, doesn't help any. King Shark, tasked the men, to do break into the office building, to steal a watch. The men believe that the task seems too good to be true, and in actuality, it is. King Shark lied, and did not give the full details of the heist, to them. He did this on purpose, as King Shark is not a man to be trusted, and he is a dangerous man. King Shark's man objective, is to keep giving the guys, more and more difficult tasks, until they eventually break. The guys on the other hand, start to get a false sense of comradery, and brotherhood with King Shark; thinking that they are scoring points with him. That is not true at all, and King Shark, things of the men, as very indispensable, and doesn't care at all about any of them. No matter what, whether the guys feel that the task is too simple, or not. They must do it, or they face the consequences, of King Shark killing them. The guys are going to have to break into the office, whether they want to or not. Despite the fact this is a dangerous task, it has to be done. This task is not up for discussion, and the men have to simply do it. Although King Shark, is giving the men several signs and clues, that he is not a man to be trusted. For example, King Shark promised the guys that he would take them out to eat, and it was going to be his treat. This was a lie, and King Shark walked out of the restaurant, leaving the guys with the check. In addition to that, King Shark did not give them a ride back to the house. The guys continue to be oblivious of King Shark's behavior, and still believe that he has the guys feelings in mind. He doesn't at all.

Aside from that, the men continue to keep things all together, and to keep things calm and collected. The guys, through the help of Dan, managed to make it back to the house, and during the bus trip back, they were able to socialize more with each other. Upon reaching the house, the men were shocked, when they found out that Detective Ross was at the door. The detective was doing a story, about the incident the men were involved in, at the Aerospace building. The same incident that ended up killing Paul. Detective Ross, still believes that this whole case, doesn't make a bit of sense, and he's trying to get more information. Detective Ross, was able to find out, that the guy who was killed, was Paul, and that Klaus, Dan, and Jerome, were also tied, and connected to Paul, as they were a part of the police pursuit situation and case as well. Detective Ross, still coming to dead ends, as far as solving the case, feels his only option, was to interview Klaus, and the other guys. Hoping that he could get the answers, that he's desperate to find. However, after talking with Klaus, Dan and Jerome, he realized, that the men all have their stories the same. Despite the fact that they are lying, and aren't being truthful to how all of the events happened, they had to manage to make sure that their lie was all the same, so that the Detective wasn't considering them as prime suspects, in the situation. The men knew if they were truthful, they would not only get in trouble by the police, but from King Shark as well. After the detective found out that the guys didn't give him any vital information, and all of their versions of the event, albeit they were fibbing, didn't contradict each other, Detective Ross had to leave, and at this time, put the case on hold. The detective continues to believe that possibly, Paul was a hostage, or an innocent bystander, who was at the wrong place at the wrong time. That is going to have to be enough for Detective Ross, as he will not know what actually happened, and that Klaus, and the rest of the men, were at that Aerospace building, trying to steal the hard drive. So Detective Ross, will have to deal with his own personal theory, of the case.

Now that the men have been able to lie to Detective Ross successfully, and he bought their versions of the night, things were back calm again. Or so the men thought, as it wasn't long before another peculiar event managed to happen. The guys were all watch television, feeling very happy and calm, when Klaus received a phone call. Upon picking up the phone, Klaus can hear a man screaming very loudly in the background, and the reception is also poor. It was King Shark calling Klaus, simply to tell him, and the rest of the men, good night. Klaus thought that this was rather strange, and odd, but instead of the guys being concerned over this, all that they could do is laugh. The men know what they have signed up for by now, so things such as that, shouldn't come as a surprise. Klaus hanged up the phone, and thought of that situation, as if it were nothing, and that it wasn't as severe and extreme, as it actually was. The men continue to go about the rest of their evening, despite that very chilling, and uncomfortable phone call from King Shark. Klaus, continues to reflect on how he got to this point, and where he went right, where we went wrong, and where he reached the point of no return. Klaus understands, that he went right, by living out his dream, and going what he did best, which was being radio host, and a very great one. His partnership with Stuart was amazing, and Klaus lived the life, he always wanted, without any complaints or issues. Stuart passed away, and the downward spiral begun. Klaus feels where he went wrong, was dealing with all of this. Originally trying to close himself off to the world, Klaus then started not to care. Klaus then began to take more risks, and started to take his life, as not as seriously anymore, and he simply didn't care about the risks, that he was putting himself, and others into. Klaus didn't see how any of his risks were going to lead to trouble, so therefore, nothing was going to stop, or prevent him from doing what he wanted.

The positive side of things, was Klaus was able to form a bond with the other guys, and it seems, the guys also had much faith, and trust in Klaus as well. So it was a mutual bond, that the guys had. It was due to this bond, that Klaus brought them on his show, as co-hosts as well. Which this decision turned out to he wrong, as Klaus lost his job, as a result of this. Not letting this bring him down either, Klaus kept on going, starting his own show. With the rest being history, fast forwarding to the present. Klaus feels he's constantly having to flashback all these events, as he wants to pinpoint, where exactly things went drastically wrong. Klaus then understands, that things went very south, when they started to lose, some of the guys in the group. First with Ernest, which was a total shock. Then with Bill, which was a very awful shock. Next with Paul, which was an extremely upsetting shock. The guys are now in the Diamond Mafia group, so things are looking extremely bad, and grim for all of them. However, this is the bed that the guys have all made, and they must lie down in it now. Without any complains or fussing, or any reluctance. The guys continue to go forward, knowing that their lives are at a delicate risk, and that they are all playing a dangerous, and unsafe game. It seems there is always something on the agenda between the men, starting with some closure the guys need. The men are all going to attend Paul's funeral, that is being held by his family. The guys recently were shocked to find out, that Paul, has a younger brother named Porter. The men, don't understand why Paul didn't tell them about his brother, and they hope by talking to his brother, they are able to find the reason why, they stopped talking to each other. There had to be a good reason, why Paul didn't tell the other guys, that he had a brother, so this is very perplexing to the men. The guys are set to attend Paul's funeral, and give Paul the proper closing, and send off that he needs. This is their time to remember Paul for the final time, by going to his funeral.

The day of Paul's funeral arrives, and the guys are all getting ready to attend. The funeral, is quite a drive, and distance away from where Klaus house is, and is located in Newport Beach, in Orange County, California, where Paul's younger brother Porter lives. Because the funeral is going to be a long distance, Klaus, and the rest of the guys, have to leave out of the house earlier, than expected, so that they are not late for the service. Klaus starts to put on his suit, and continues to get ready for Paul's funeral. This is something that he has done so much, that he lost count. Klaus has visited the funeral of his parents, the funeral of Stuart, the funeral of Ernest, the funeral of his Uncle Bill, and now, he's attending Paul's funeral. Klaus starts to feel, how strange it is, and depressing it is that he is going to all of these funerals, and Klaus starts to cry heavily. As Klaus continues to put on his suit, pitting his tie, and his suit jacket on, Klaus continues to feel upset, and sad, at how things currently are going. Klaus turns to look at Jerome, who is also getting ready for the funeral, putting a formal outfit on which consists of a suit and tie as well. Klaus and Jerome, finish getting ready for the funeral, and they walk out into the living room, and they notice Dan, who is already ready for the funeral, with his suit on, sitting at the living room couch, watching the morning news. Klaus then starts to speak to Dan.

"Oh great, you're already set to go. We will be leaving out in minute. I need to get a couple things, before we head out. Dan, could you hand me that card, that's on the table please."

Dan then nods his head, and reaches over the coffee table, to grab a sympathy card. Klaus then starts to sign it, and Dan and Jerome, sign it after that. Klaus then speaks to the men.

"I figured that his family would appreciate this. Nice kind gesture, as we were Paul's friends, and I'm sure his brother, and his family are upset. Jerome, go get those flowers please."

Jerome nods his head, and Jerome proceeds, to walk over to the kitchen area, and grabs the flower arrangement, that Klaus bought, which is situated on the kitchen counter. Jerome, then starts to rearrange the flowers that are in the vase. As he is doing that, he talks to the other guys.

"These are very lovely, and these flowers have a nice bright, beautiful color to them. Paul's family would like this very much. It's the least we can do."

Klaus and Dan nod their heads, and Jerome continues to hold the flowers, and Klaus hands Jerome the sympathy card as well. Dan then shuts the television off, and gets up from the sofa. Dan then starts to style his hair, and as he is doing that, speaks to the rest of the guys.

"So, are we about ready to go? Do you have everything you need now?"

Klaus then pulls out his phone, and starts to laugh to himself, and shakes his head. Klaus then starts to dial a number on his phone. As he's dialing the number, Klaus speaks to Dan.

"Not quite yet. Just to be on the safe side, I'm gonna call King Shark, and tell him that we are gonna go to Paul's funeral. I'm sure he is gonna say yes, even if he doesn't, oh well. If he ends up killing us, so be it. We're not gonna miss the funeral. Don't give a damn what he says."

Dan looks down on the ground, shake his head, and laughs. King Shark answers the phone, and Klaus asks him permission, to attend the funeral. King Shark says that it's fine. Klaus is relieved, and happy, that King shark allowed them to be present at the funeral. With King Shark's approval, the men then leave out of the house, and direct themselves, straight to Paul's funeral. As Klaus is driving on the highway, on his way to the funeral, the guys in the car, remain quiet, and they are fully aware, that today is a very, sensitive day. Funerals are not the most joyous of occasions, and they can be quite upsetting and depressing. Although it's bittersweet, as the men know, that attending this funeral, gives them the closure they need to give Paul, and respect, and memorialize, his death. Klaus continues to drive to the funeral, keeping all of his thoughts, and emotions to himself. Eventually, Klaus does manage to make it to the highway offramp, that he needs to exit out of. Klaus then starts to drive on the surface streets, leading up to the funeral. While he's doing that, for the first time, in the entire car trip, Dan turns his direction facing Klaus, and begins to talk to him.

"What do you think Paul's brother looks like? How many people do you think are going to be there? What do we tell his family? Do we say anything to them at all? What about..."

Klaus reaches a stoplight, and turns to look at Dan. Klaus then starts to give Dan a look of agitation, which in turn causes Dan who is giving Klaus eye contact, to stop talking. The stoplight then turns green, and Klaus continues to drive down the road. Dan looks forward and shakes his head, and Klaus remains driving. Klaus as he's driving, then starts to speak to Dan.

"Why are you asking me those questions? Man, I don't know. We're going to go, with the flow I guess. If someone asks a question, we already know what to reveal, and what not to reveal. I guess, try not to reveal that much attention to ourselves I suppose. We're gonna talk to his brother, give him the card and flowers, and give Paul his respects."

Klaus continues to drive closer to the funeral, and Dan simply nods his head. As Klaus steadily drives to the funeral, he takes note of the gloomy, overcast weather. This weather which gives off a marine layer, as they are in Newport Beach, a beach town and city, in Orange County, California. Klaus starts to drive, and turn through several streets, until he makes it to the cemetery, where the funeral will be held. Much to Klaus chagrin, and surprise, he notices something unpredictable, and something he was not expecting, or assuming. Klaus notices, that there is are only two people present at the service. Upon noticing that there aren't many people present, this makes Klaus feel slightly more comfortable, as he was afraid, that Paul would have this large group of relatives, in which Klaus wouldn't mind, although it would have caused slight anxiety for Klaus. On the other hand, it's bittersweet, as starts to feel concerned, that more of Paul's family, is not attending. Klaus was thinking, that more people were going to be there, and that Paul had this big family. It turns out, that was simply not true, and not the case. Dan and Jerome, notice how there isn't that many people present either, and feel shocked about this. Klaus continues to drive closer to the service location, and then starts to park his car. Klaus notices that both individuals at the funeral, start to look at him. Klaus then can see, that one man, who Klaus instantly realizes is Paul's brother, is a man with shoulder length curly hair, and is in a wheelchair, with glasses on, wearing a suit. The other man, is a short, handsome, Asian man, who is standing right next to Paul's brother. Klaus, turns his ignition off, and he, along with Dan and Jerome, get out of the car, and start to walk to the funeral service.

When Klaus approaches the man in the wheelchair, he extends his hand out to shake the man's hand. At this same time, Klaus then starts to softly speak to him.

"Hello, you must be Porter. My name is Klaus. These are my friends, Dan, and Jerome. We were all close with Paul, and friends of his. We came to give out respects. Nice to meet you."

Klaus, and the man in the wheelchair start to shake hands. The man, who has a very rough, yet gentle voice, starts to speak to Klaus, concurrently shaking his hand.

"As a matter of fact, I am Paulie's younger brother Porter. Believe it or not. Do you see the resemblance? This is my partner, Toshi, he's from Japan. Thank you very much for coming."

Klaus then shakes Toshi's hand as well. Dan, and Jerome, then shake both Porter's and Toshi's hand. All five of them, then remain silent, as Klaus turns his head, to look at Paul's coffin which is situated, in front of the service. Klaus then signals for Jerome, to walk over to the coffin, and put the flowers on top of it. As Jerome is going that, Klaus speaks to Porter.

"I figured you guys would like these. Paul was a great friend to us, and we miss him."

As Jerome is arranging the flowers on top of Paul's coffin, Porter then starts to speak.

"Oh, that's very kind of you. I appreciate that so much. I assume you must be one of Paulie's college buddies right? I know he had a lot of friends, and Paulie was very friendly."

Klaus then starts to shake the back of his head, and looks over to Paul's coffin. Jerome is still placing the flowers on top of it. While still staring over at Paul's coffin, Klaus then speaks.

"Um, no, I actually am not one of Paul's college friends. I actually only met him recently. I am, or, well, I was a radio host, and Paul was one of my fans, and I met him in real life, and the rest is history. Paul is very friendly, and he was very kind to us, and we miss him so much."

Porter nods his head, and looks over to Paul's coffin as well. Porter then speaks to Klaus.

"Ah, I see. Well, as you know, Paulie was an artist, as I am as well. We formed a bit of a rivalry, and I figured, with him being my older brother, he would side with me more. He was always there for me, as I was born with a spinal condition when I was born. So yeah."

Jerome at this time, walks back to the area the rest of the guys are in, and reaches into his jacket pocket, and hands Porter the sympathy card. As Jerome is doing that, he speaks to Porter.

"We're terribly sorry for you're the loss of your brother. This is from us. I'm sorry."

Porter accepts the card, and thanks all of the guys. Klaus then continues to look around the funeral service, and noticing how quaint, and quiet it is. Klaus begins to feel very emotional, and starts to think of all the happy times that he experienced with Paul. Klaus then starts to feel emotional over Paul's brother, and feels guilty, that they cannot tell him the truth surrounding Paul's death. Although Klaus, wants to show his empathy towards the situation, and is respectful, regardless of the information the he, and the other men are withholding. Klaus continues to stare at Paul's coffin, having a wave of sadness, and emotions. Klaus then starts to cry heavily, which in turn causes Porter to grab Klaus hand, comforting him. Porter then speaks.

"Paulie and I, we just figured it was best we went our separate ways. We still loved each other, and we promised to always help each other out. But I knew that the best decision was for us to do our own thing, and we did. I know Paulie didn't hate me, so it was okay by me."

Klaus nods his head, and takes out his handkerchief, wiping his tears. Due to Klaus feeling upset, Dan and Jerome, start to cry, and feel depressed as well. Klaus, and the rest of the men at this time, decide to sit down, next to Porter, and Toshi. Once the men are all seated, there is heavy silence for several minutes. The cemetery, has a lake in the center of it, and Klaus can hear the water of the lake, and also the duck's quacking in the water. Klaus is also able to hear the birds chirping in addition to that. Even though it is a gloomy, overcast day, the weather is still at a moderate temperature in climate. The men all continue to stay at this setting, quiet. Grieving over the loss of Paul, and being respectfully silent through all of this. As the events of the funeral continue, Porter then reaches into his pocket, and pulls out his phone. Porter then starts to scroll through his phone, and pulls out a picture, of himself and Paul. Porter then starts to show the phone to Klaus, and the other men. allowing him to see the picture as well. Klaus notices, that the picture is of Paul, resting his hands on Porter's shoulder, who is in his wheelchair. Klaus, can tell that the photo is relatively recent. Porter then starts to speak.

"This is the last photo that Paulie and I took. I'm gonna keep it always now. Paulie never liked to smile, I don't know why he didn't. But I know he was happy in this photo."

Porter then puts his phone back in his pocket, and starts to look forward, at Paul's coffin. The silence at the service, then starts to return. For several more minutes the guys remain quiet, although all of the men have several emotions of sadness during the service. Klaus then starts to cry heavily once again, and Klaus takes his glasses off, and starts to rub his eyes. Klaus looks down towards the ground and shakes his head. It was then, Klaus was feeling much guilt over Paul's death, and is very unhappy at this situation. Porter comforts Klaus, by massaging his back. Klaus then gets up from his seat, and starts to walk to his SUV, opening the back hatch. The other guys, look at Klaus, not sure as to what exactly he's doing, but don't think that anything unusual, and that Klaus is simply looking for something. Several seconds later, Klaus manages to find what he was looking for, and closes the back hatch of his SUV. Klaus then walks back to the service area, holding Paul's sketchpad in his hands. Klaus then hands it to Porter, and speaks.

"I want you to have this. This was Paul's sketchpad, and he was always drawing cartoons and animations, and stuff on it. I want you to have it. I wish I would have met you sooner, but I asked Paul if he had any siblings, and he told me no. So yeah. I would like for you to have this."

Porter then starts to open the sketchpad up, and looks through all the pictures, that Paul has drawn. Porter has a side smile on his face, and he shows the drawings Paul did, to Toshi. Once Porter has gone through all the sketches in the book, he closes it, and hands it back to Klaus. Porter then starts to rub Klaus on the arm, and speaks to him softly.

"This was very sweet, but no, you keep it. I have a bunch of Paulie's artwork at my house, that he did, so it's okay. I want you to have it, since you were a best friend of his, and you can have this as something to remember him by. Paulie was a very talented artist though. Ha."

Klaus then accepts that Porter wants for him to keep the sketchpad, and Klaus hands Paul's sketchpad, over to Jerome. The service yet again, returns to deep silence, and the guys all continue to give Paul his respects, and remember the memories that they have of him. At this time, Dan, and Jerome, walk up to Paul's coffin, and start to say their final words to him. Klaus watches them do this, and continues to feel upset. After Dan and Jerome, say their final words, Klaus then realizes, that he needs to give his final respects to Paul. Klaus then starts to prepare himself to say his final words to Paul. Klaus then starts to get up from his seat, and walks over to the front of the service, and stands in front of Paul's coffin. Klaus stands in front of it for several minutes, sobbing, and shaking his head. Klaus then starts to lean over Paul's coffin, and rubs his hands over it. Klaus then starts to kiss the top of Paul's coffin, and continues to cry. While he is rearranging the flowers on Paul's coffin, Klaus speaks.

"Paul, I'm sorry man. I'm truly sorry. I know you stuck with me, and you had your trust in me. I know you respected me greatly man, and I appreciate it. I want you to rest well man. We're gonna miss you, your brother is going to miss you. Goodbye Paul. Goodbye my friend."

Klaus then rearranges the flowers on the coffin once more, and then starts to return back to his seat, with the other guys. Klaus was happy that he managed to give Paul his final respects, and Klaus is confident, that Paul is going to rest easy, and this gives Klaus the confidence he needs. Although Klaus feels bouts of guilt, through the result of Paul's death, Klaus is sure, that Paul had great value towards Klaus, and thought of him as a true friend. As the funeral service continues, the men yet again, go back to their respectful silence, and sitting peacefully, with their vision directed forward at Paul's coffin. This continues for a half an hour, with the men remaining quiet. Eventually, Porter takes out his phone, and starts to speak to Klaus.

"I'm going to give you my phone number, and you can speak with me anytime you like. If you want to hang out sometime, I'd be willing to. I mean it, you can call me anytime you like."

Porter then starts to give Klaus his phone number, and likewise, Klaus does the same. Klaus then gets up from his seat, and starts to hug Porter tightly. They remaining hugging, for what seems like a minute, and Porter begins to softly speak to Klaus, giving him encouraging words. Klaus continues to cry and feel sad, as he is hugging Porter. Porter then starts to pat Klaus on the back, and kisses Klaus on the cheek. Klaus and Porter then stop hugging. Klaus then walks up to Toshi, and gives him a hug as well. Dan and Jerome, also hug Porter and Toshi, and say their goodbyes to them as well. At this time, Toshi then walks behind Porter, and starts to push his wheelchair. As Porter and Toshi are leaving out of the funeral, Porter speaks to the men.

"It was nice meeting you gentlemen. It's time for us to leave. I really appreciate you guys coming out here to Paulie's funeral. The rest of our family disowned us. It was nice that you guys are Paulie's friends. You boys are really lovely and special. You boys all take care."

Klaus, and the rest of the guys, nod their heads, as they watch Porter and Toshi, leave the funeral. Within minutes, Porter gets into the passenger side of the vehicle, which is adapted for his wheelchair to get inside of easily. Toshi then gets into the driver's side of the car. The both of them then quickly drive away from the funeral service. Klaus and the other men, watch as they both leave away from the scene. At this time, Klaus, Dan and Jerome, sit at the service, silently. They take glances over at Paul's coffin, and still feel emotional. The men remain here for about a half an hour longer still reminiscing about their happy memories with Paul. The guys then eventually decide to get up, and prepare to leave. Dan and Jerome, walk over to Paul's coffin one more time, kissing the top of it, and rearranging the flowers. Immediately following that, Klaus walks up to Paul's coffin one final time, and starts to move the flowers around, and kisses Paul's coffin. The guys have now completed giving Paul his proper send off, and start to walk away from the service. Klaus gets into his SUV, and Dan and Jerome, get into the vehicle as well. Klaus then starts to drive back to the house, still feeling very emotional, from the funeral service. By the time that Klaus, and the rest of the men get back to the house, it is now late in the afternoon. Klaus, directs himself to the kitchen, and opens up a top shelf in his kitchen, taking out a bottle of Smirnoff Vodka. Klaus then takes a shot glass from out of the cabinet, and starts to pour the vodka into the glass. Klaus takes several sips of the liquor, and shakes his head. Dan and Jerome, are sitting at the sofa, silently. The television is not on, and they are simply looking down at the ground feeling upset. Klaus takes yet another shot of the Vodka, while staring at both Dan and Jerome, on the living room sofa. Klaus then puts the bottle of Vodka back on the shelf, and puts his shot glass in the sink. Klaus then walks over to the living room, and takes a seat down on his recliner. Klaus then starts to relax back into the recliner, and closes his eyes. Dan at this time, then gets up from the sofa, and starts to speak to the other guys.

"Hey, I guess I'll start to make dinner. I'm gonna make some Spaghetti. The only thing in the refrigerator is ground beef. Like there isn't much left. I'll stretch it out to make something."

Klaus and Jerome, don't respond, and remain quiet. Dan laughs to himself, and shakes his head, and walks over to the kitchen, to make dinner. Once Dan is finished preparing the Spaghetti, he, along with Klaus and Jerome, all start to eat dinner. The guys all eat their meal in the living room, with the television strangely turned off. During this meal, the guys do not speak, or converse with each other. It then dawns on all of the men, that tomorrow, they are going to have to do the task that King Shark asked them to do. This is exactly why the men feel nervous, as they don't have a choice in taking on the task, and they are aware of how risky the task is. Klaus, also continues to feel, that King Shark lied, and the task isn't as simple and easy, as he explained it to be. The guys take this awkward time, to calmly eat, what could be their last dinner together. Although it was leftover ground beef, the Spaghetti that Dan has made, turned out to be very delicious, and the guys are all enjoying the meal greatly. Once the men are finished eating the Spaghetti, they all decide to have the cake Emilio gave them, for dessert. The men then start to eat the cake in the living room, with the television still turned off. When the guys all finish eating their dessert, Jerome then starts to wash all of the dishes. Klaus and Dan, remain in the living room, quiet, and not speaking to each other. The televisions steadily continues to stay off. Once Jerome is finished with the dishes, re turns to the living room sofa, and starts to lay down, and nap. Klaus and Dan watch Jerome fall asleep, and laugh to themselves. At this time, Klaus, who is still relaxing on his recliner, pulls out his phone, and starts to look at sports scores on it. While Klaus is scrolling through his phone, looking at sports scores, he speaks to Dan.

"Tomorrow is going to be intense; I just know it. But we don't have a choice do we? I can't believe we've gotten ourselves into this. I am sick and tired of being sick and tired. Damn."

Klaus then shakes his head, and puts his phone on the coffee table. Klaus then starts to get sleepy, and starts to rest his eyes, as he's leaning back in the recliner. Dan then speaks.

"Yeah, but what can we do? If we don't do it, we're screwed. If we do it, we're possibly screwed. So that's the deal, and that's the way it is. It's fucked up, but yeah. It's okay man."

Jerome is fast asleep, and continues to rest on the sofa. At this time, Klaus has immediately drifted off to sleep as well. Dan, who is unaware that Klaus is asleep, speaks to him.

"You know, thank you for all that you've done for us Klaus. I know we've had some rocky moments, and things were rough between us. You're my best friend man. I appreciate it."

When Dan doesn't hear Klaus respond to him, he looks over at Klaus, deep asleep on the recliner. Dan then shakes his head, and starts to laugh. Dan gets up from the sofa, and walks over to Jerome on the sofa. Dan runs his hands through Jerome's hair, and kisses him on the cheek. Dan then walks over to Klaus, and takes his glasses off, setting them on the coffee table. Dan then kisses Klaus on the forehead, and laughs. Dan then sits on the recliner next to Klaus, and likewise with the other guys, he leans back into the recliner, and quickly drifts off the sleep. Hours pass, and all the men remain in the living room, deep asleep. The following morning, Klaus awakens, and is slighted disorientated, when he notices that he, and the other guys were asleep the entire time. It is now Friday, and it is the day for them to do their next task. This is not up for discussion, and the guys must obey what King Shark tells them. This makes Klaus develop a nervous feeling in his stomach, that the guys have to follow King Shark's orders today. Klaus, while leaning back in his recliner, stares out his balcony window, noticing how good of a day it is today. The sun is shining bright, sky is blue, light clouds in the sky. The only issue, is that Klaus, and the other guys, must go, and break into the office building, in order to get the watch. Klaus then looks down on the ground, and shakes his head. Klaus gets up from the recliner, and walks over to the kitchen area. Klaus, wants to make himself some coffee, but is not able to, as the guys no longer have any more coffee grounds. Klaus instead makes himself a glass of Orange Juice, as that's the only thing left in the refrigerator. Klaus starts to take sips of his juice, and continues to feel nervous. Minutes later, both Dan and Jerome wake up. They also go into the kitchen, and have a glass of Orange Juice. The men are far too nervous to eat breakfast, so they don't. Before long, Klaus receives a phone call. He already knows that it is most likely King Shark. Klaus reluctantly picks up his phone, and notices it's from an unknown caller, further confirming that it is in fact King Shark calling. Klaus picks up the phone and speaks.

"Hello, good morning. This is Klaus. Is there something that I can help you with?"

King Shark on the other end of the phone, doesn't directly talk, but does respond back.

"Oh cut all that bullshit. You knew it was me calling. Listen, you guys have to start heading to that office now. I was gonna let you guys head out later, as I thought he was off today, but he's having an office meeting later, so you guys are gonna have to move right now."

Klaus starts to rub his hand over his forehead, and shakes his head. Klaus accepts this news, as King Shark immediately orders for them to report to the office, and relays other information that they need to know. Saying the van driver will give them a guide. Klaus then starts to tell Dan and Jerome, that they need to leave, and go to the office building now. Without any complaint, or argument, the guys all fully understand the current situation, although they are feeling very nervous and scared, and are full of doubt. The guys don't waste any time at all, not only because they can't afford to, but they want to hurry up, and get the task done, as quickly as possible. Not even within five minutes, if that, between his exchange with King Shark on the phone, Klaus, and the guys, start on with the task, of stealing the watch. Through the request of King Shark, the guys were asked, to leave their wallets, and phones at the house. The guys will be picked up soon, by one of King Shark's guard, in a van. The van driver will then drive them to the location of the office, where they must steal the watch. Half an hour later, the van driver arrives to Klaus residence. The men immediately, all get inside of the van, and it starts to head to the office building that the guys must steal the watch from. During the van ride, Klaus starts to look at the instructions that King Shark gave him and starts to shake his head. Klaus has not the slightest clue, or idea in the world, as to how the guys are going to do this task. The guys not only do not have their wallets, or access to any money, and they do not have their phones. Klaus is truly confused, and is of course second guessing everything, and is feeling nervous.

As the van gets closer to the office building, Klaus then starts to slowly, but surely, get his plan all sorted out. Likewise with the task they did before, Klaus wants to figure out some type of diversion, in order for them to sneak past the security, as even though King Shark said security was lax, Klaus didn't fully believe this one bit. Klaus, although he isn't sure how he's going to accomplish this quite yet, wants Jerome to act as food delivery person. This would act as an initial distraction for the front security guard. Meanwhile, as Jerome is distracting the guard, Klaus and Dan, will then walk to the camera control room, and disable the cameras. Once the cameras are disabled and reset, Klaus and Dan, will then direct themselves to the office, and unlock the office door, by using the keys that King Shark gave them. They will then enter the office, in order to steal the Rolex watch, and replace it with the fake replica, that King Shark gave them. With Jerome still distracting the guard, Klaus and Dan will escape out of the building. Klaus and Dan will then signal to Jerome, once they have gotten the watch. The men will then all escape and run away. Klaus knew that this was the only good plan, and that it at this point, Klaus wasn't confident at all that it was going to work, but the guys don't have any choice. They can at least try, and maybe they will be lucky enough to succeed, and actually pull it off. Gaining the assumed respect from King Shark, knowing they followed his orders. Before Klaus is able to continue to brainstorm his plan, and think of his thoughts, the van immediately, and unexpectantly, not only from the perspective of Klaus, but from the other guys as well, pulls up near the location of the office. This shocks the guys, as they were not expecting to arrive that fast. The office is located in Downtown LA, which for Friday afternoon, is quite busy, with people booming, and walking around the sidewalk. The driver cuts off the engine and speaks.

"Alright guys, this is where I have to drop you off. Here, take this. Press this when you guys have gotten the watch, and meet me back here, and I'll pick you guys up. Go Tigers!"

The van driver hands Klaus a GPS device, and Klaus accepts it. The driver also hands Klaus a packet of information, which Klaus accepts as well. Not even seconds after this, Klaus, and the other guys step out of the van. The van driver then immediately drives away from the area. Klaus, Dan and Jerome, all stare at each other, confused, and not able to speak, or gather their thoughts. At this time, Klaus continues to read the packet of information, related to their task, of stealing the watch. Dan and Jerome look at all the civilians walking around Downtown Los Angeles, and are quiet. Directly following this, Klaus then starts to talk to the guys.

"Guys, I have no idea, what in the fucking hell we're gonna do. I don't think this is gonna work, but remember, we all stuck together, and if King Shark kills us, we at least tried, right guys? Now listen, again, I'm not totally sure, but if we follow my plan, we might could do this."

Dan and Jerome, then focus their direction towards Klaus, as Klaus starts to tell them, the plan that he was able to quickly figure out. Klaus then starts to look in a trash can, located directly back the men. Klaus pulls out a bag, which has empty take out containers in it. Klaus hands the bag to Jerome, who doesn't question Klaus at all. Klaus then starts to speak.

"You're gonna be a delivery boy okay? You're gonna act as our main distraction and diversion. You can do this, don't worry. Walk in, and say that you need to deliver food to someone in the building, but you can't remember the office number. Explain that you're just gonna wait for them to walk down and accept it. Be creative, and use your imagination okay?"

Jerome, while still holding the back of food, nods his head, and agrees with Klaus. Following that, Klaus reaches into his pocket, and takes the packet of information out, and continues to read it again. Klaus shakes his head, and puts the papers back in his pocket. Klaus then starts to look around the area, and the civilians on the sidewalk. Klaus then speaks to Dan.

"You and me, well, we're going to improvise I guess. Again I don't know how we are going to be able to do this, but we have to pray. We're gonna go and head to the camera room first, disable the cameras, and then sneak up to the office, and switch the watches. Ugh. Damn."

Right after this, Dan nods his head, and Klaus then grabs Dan and Jerome, and starts to hug the both of them tightly. All three of the men then start to cry heavily, while still embracing their hug together. The men then start to believe, that they are not going to be able to do this, as this seems like a truly impossible task to complete. The guys all start to wonder if this is the end, and they are all going to be killed by King Shark, for not accomplishing this task. The guys do not know if this will be the last time they see each other. The men understand the risks involved, and this will be the hardest thing, the guys have encountered so far. Klaus kisses both Dan and Jerome on the forehead, and after that, the men all stop hugging, and immediately start to walk towards the entrance of the office building. Jerome, feeling extremely nervous and hesitant, walks ahead of both Klaus and Dan holding the bag of takeout food, ready to start his distraction, so that Klaus and Dan can sneak into the building. Several feet behind him, Klaus and Dan follow Jerome, but keep great distance, so they aren't drawing any suspicion with each other. Although it was only a couple minutes later, and it felt as though it was a couple hours later, Jerome does manage to make it to the front of the office building, and continues to hold the bag of takeout food, and Jerome takes a deep breath, and looks down on the ground, shaking his head. Jerome starts to gather all his thoughts, and how he's going to put on his act. Jerome looks strongly at the guard, who is a buff, bald Caucasian man. Jerome, without wasting anymore time, starts to walk inside the office building. Jerome and the guard make eye contact, and are silent with each other. Jerome then freezes under pressure, and cannot speak. After thirty seconds of this silence, the guard then starts to stare at Jerome, and speaks with him.

"Yes young man, is there something that you needed? How can I help you please?"

Jerome then starts to immediately doubt himself, and doesn't feel that he is going to do this. When Jerome looks out of the entrance of the building, and sees that Klaus and Dan are walking closer, Jerome walks to the other side of the lobby, and looks down on the ground. Jerome continues to hesitate, and doesn't know how to react, or stall the guard. Jerome continues to look confused, and frantically looks around, and walks around the lobby for several more seconds. This causes the guard to become slightly confused, and the guard continues to stare at Jerome. Klaus and Dan reach closer and closer to the entrance of the building, and Jerome then understands, that he must try his best, to not let the guard see Klaus and Dan, walk inside of the building. Jerome remains roaming around the lobby, and looking down on the grounds. While looking at the bag of food, Jerome then starts to speak to the guard.

"Oh hello. I am a delivery boy. I am here to drop off some food, but I don't know who it's for. They didn't give a name. I'm looking at the receipt, and yeah. Can you help me?"

The guard then gets up from his post, and starts to walk closer to Jerome. Luckily, while the guard is walking up to Jerome, Klaus and Dan, being patient, wait for the perfect time to them to sneak pass the lobby, and do so. The both of the men then, very rapidly, start to walk up the second floor of the building. In flash seconds, Klaus and Dan then walk into the camera control room, located on the second floor of the building. Klaus has another moment of luck, as he noticed the camera equipment is able to be hacked into, and uses the same technology, as the Aerospace building did. Dan shakes his head in amazement, as Klaus continues to disable the cameras, and reset them back to the time, the guys all entered the building. With the cameras now quickly disabled and reset, Klaus and Dan fist bump each other, and head to the office building, down the hall. Klaus pull out the keys that King Shark gave him, and starts to unlock the door quickly. However, Klaus is frustrated, when he realizes, that none of the keys fit. Klaus then starts to panic, and throws the keys down on the ground. Dan notices this, and speaks.

"Hey, hey. You have to fucking chill right now man. If you panic, we're not gonna be able to do this. Chill. It's fine. We'll think of something, we always do. Hope is not is not lost."

Klaus continues to lean his head against the wall, feeling hopeless. At this time, down at the lobby, Jerome continues to act out his distraction to the guard. The guard starts to look at the bag, and notices that there is no receipt on the bag. The guard looks at Jerome confused. Jerome understands that the guard figured out there isn't a receipt, and Jerome quickly responds back.

"Oh dear, I guess there isn't a receipt. I could have sworn there was one, when I picked it up at the restaurant. Tell you what, how about you let me stay down here, and I'm sure the person who ordered it, is going to come and accept it any minute now. I'm sure. Is that okay?"

The guard then nods his head at Jerome, and starts to walk away from him. Jerome watches at the guard walks back to his post.

When Jerome notices that the guard has a strange look on face, while looking down at his desk, Jerome is aware that the guard either noticed the cameras were disabled, or he is looking at Klaus and Dan walk about the building. Either way, Jerome knew that he had to continue to stall the guard. Jerome quickly calls the guard over.

"You know what, I think I found the receipt, it's at the bottom of the bag. Can you come and read it for me? I'm not allowed to touch any of the food in the bag. Company regulations."

The guard shakes his head, and gets up from his post. At this time, with the Klaus and Dan feeling that they are truly hopeless, and there is nothing at all they can do at this point. The men start to accept defeat, and Dan walks up to Klaus, and pats him on the back, and rubs the back of his shoulder. With Klaus having his hands covering his face, crying heavily, Dan starts to look across the room, and notices a side vestibule patio, leading to staircase, heading outside the building. There is a narrow gap, and space, between the staircase platform, and the room they have to go inside of. The room they have to get into, luckily has its window open, Dan immediately starts to act fast, and even though Klaus would be too big, Dan feels he's slender enough, to slither his way, into the window. Even though the top of the staircase is very high up on the second story, and if Dan falls, he could get seriously hurt, or worse, he is willing to take that risk. Dan weighs and understands all his options, and is fully aware as to what is at stake. Dan has a wide grin on his face, and kisses Klaus on the forehead, and speaks to him.

"This is our last hope. We don't have a key to get inside, so this is our only option man. I'm gonna try to stretch my body, and slide myself from the stairs, into that window. I think I'll be able to do it. At worst, I'll just fall, and crack my head open, but that's not gonna happen. I'll then swing into the window and I'll get in. This is it now. Wish me luck man."

Klaus simply shakes his head, and laughs, and Dan starts to open up the door, leading out the staircase. Acting very swiftly, Dan starts to stretch his legs, out from the top of the platform, and lays his body flat on the ground, as he tries to extend his legs out towards the window. Klaus watches Dan this entire time, and continues to laugh, and shake his head. Dan continues to position himself, trying to inch his way into the window. As Dan is doing this, back down at the lobby, the guard then walks over to Jerome, and the guard then starts to look inside the bag. Not only does the guard not see the receipt, that Jerome claimed was inside, but the guard also notices that all the food in the bag, is empty containers. The guard gives Jerome an angry look. Jerome then starts to gaze around the lobby, and immediately starts to speak to the guard.

"Oh damn, I don't know how this happened. I'm so sorry. Um, I'll wait for them to come down, and issue a refund. I guess someone thought this was funny, and this is some type of practical joke or prank. I'm terribly sorry. So I'll just wait here, and offer a refund to them."

The guard believes that something is up, and as he's walking back to his desk, he speaks.

"Uh huh. Really. Alright. You wait right there, don't you move. Don't go anywhere."

Jerome nods his head, and remains standing where he is. The guard notices that the cameras are still disabled, so therefore, he cannot see Dan trying to sneak outside, through the window. The guard then starts to call all the offices in the building, asking if they were expecting any food orders. While the guard is doing this, and not receiving any responses, as nobody else, except Klaus, Dan, and Jerome, are in the building, Dan continues to maneuver himself in the building. Dan who is very close from pulling his feet into the window, manages to slightly slip his feet, from the frame of the window, which causes Klaus to become alarmed, and starts to feel scared to look, as he doesn't think Dan can accomplish this. Dan recovers, and positions his legs, and feet, and stretches his body out. Within a few seconds, Dan crawls his way into the office building, and contorts his body into the window. Klaus simply can't believe this, and starts to shake his head, and chuckles to himself. Once Dan is inside the office, a second later, he opens the door, and allows Klaus in. Klaus and Dan then frantically start to find where the watch is. The office building is quite large, and King Shark, did not say the exact location, the watch would be located in. Klaus and Dan continue to frantically look for the watch, trying their best not to totally ransack the room, and add suspicion. Klaus and Dan hear the phone ring, which is the guard calling, but they ignore this, and don't answer. Klaus puts his hand over his forehead, and again feels hopeless. It was during this time when Klaus noticed that the office had a mini refrigerator in it. Klaus then opens up the refrigerator, and looks through the freezer, noticing a tv dinner box. Klaus opens the tv dinner box, and to his surprise, he finds the watch. Klaus has a wide smile on his face, and signals for Dan to come over. Klaus and Dan fist bump, and Klaus quickly replaces the watch, and puts the replica in the box. Both of the men then walk out.

Down at the lobby, the guard has called all the office buildings, and nobody responds. The guard then remembers, he doesn't recollect anyone walking through the front door, and is sure that nobody else is in the building. The guard then gets up, and walks over to talk to Jerome.

"Young man, I think you better leave. This was a cute prank, but I don't find it funny. Now get out of here, before I call the cops okay. I'm being very nice with you boy."

Jerome then starts to look around the lobby, unsure of what to do, and feels that he needs to stall the guard longer. At this same congruent time, Klaus and Dan report to the camera room, and enable the cameras back on, and put the cameras on a delay, so that the cameras, do not capture any of the men. Also at this same time, Jerome, who is down at the lobby, tries to stall the guard some more, and prepares to say something. However, suddenly, there is a loud glass shattering sound. The guard then turns his direction towards the sound and speaks.

"Hey, who the fuck is that. Whoever that is, you just made a big, big mistake. Hey!"

Jerome remains where he is, and watches as the guard walks further down the lobby where the glass shattered. The guard walks closer around the lobby, when something very shocking happens. All of a sudden, King Shark starts to walk closer into the lobby, and stares at the guard deeply. The guard then puts his hand over his gun, and shouts at King Shark.

"Sir, who the hell are you? Did you just bust my window? Sir you have to leave now."

King Shark, without saying anything, immediately shoots the guard in the head, killing him instantly. The guard falls down on the ground, and Jerome stands frozen, emotionless. During this, Klaus and Dan were running down the stairs, to the lobby, when the gunshot went off. Because King Shark used a silencer, they weren't able to hear it. Klaus and Dan arrive at the exact current time in the lobby, and notice the guard's dead body on the ground of the lobby, and Jerome standing on the other end, standing completely still, and scared. Klaus, Dan and Jerome, all remain motionless, as King Shark walks in the center of the lobby. King Shark puts his gun in his jacket pocket, and continues to walk around. King Shark then looks at Jerome, and laughs. King Shark immediately after, focuses his attention to Klaus and Dan, on the other side of the lobby. King Shark then walks up to Klaus, and speaks to him.

"Damn. What the fuck is with you guys? I thought I got you guys this time. Yeah, that's right, this was a setup. When I saw you guys sneak through the office, I knew you guys were gonna pull it off, and sure enough, you fucking did. GIVE ME THE FUCKING WATCH!"

Klaus immediately takes the watch out his pocket, and hands it to King Shark. King Shark then starts to dial his phone, and says code words to the person on the other end. King Shark hangs up the phone, and starts to look outside the entrance of the lobby. From the way the lobby is constructed, and obscured, no one walking outside, has any idea, as to what's happening. King Shark then pulls his gun from his suit jacket out again. King Shark kicks the guard down on the ground, and to make sure that he's dead, shoots him again in the head. Klaus, Dan and Jerome, continuing to watch, as King Shark continues to act violently and aggressively. King Shark then walks over to Jerome, and grabs him by his wrist. King Shark then speaks.

"You, get the fuck over here. Come on. Go and join your fucking buddies."

King Shark then drags Jerome over by where Klaus and Dan are in the lobby. Klaus then starts to hug Dan and Jerome tightly, and Klaus then starts to cry. Klaus then speaks.

"If you have any sense of manhood in your body. You would let us go right now. What more do you want from us? We did what you fucking asked us. Please. Have mercy. Please."

King Shark then starts to stare deeply at Klaus. King Shark then shoots several rounds into the floor, close to where Klaus, Dan, and Jerome are standing to scare them. King Shark then walks even closer to Klaus, and gets very close to his face. King Shark then whispers.

"Show mercy? Okay. I'm gonna give you one final test. You fail, you die. You pass, you're probably die anyways. So it's lose lose. You're fucking screwed, and you and your friends may die regardless. But, if you do pass, you're not gonna pass, who am I kidding. Find where our headquarters building is. Where you and your friends escaped. I'll give you a hint, all you have to do is remember where the van went that night. Meet me at headquarters tonight. You don't show up you die. If you show up, well, we will see. Bye gentleman. Ha Ha."

King Shark then walks out of the entrance of the lobby. Klaus continues to hug Dan, and Jerome tightly. All of the men, cry heavily. Klaus then shakes his head, and laughs.

CHAPTER 22:

THINK FAST

Things are continuing to be dramatic and intense, as the men have yet again, placed themselves, to the point of no return. The men were cornered, tricked, and swindled. Keeping in mind, the unfortunate part, is the men slightly saw this coming a mile away, and were prepared for things to flip, and twist. That is exactly what ended up happening, as the men who had some slight doubts about this, were eventually tricked, and fooled by King Shark. The entire plot, and setup, for the guys to join Diamond Mafia, was for them to gain a false sense of brotherhood, and security within the group, with King Shark eventually turning on them. King Shark originally wanted to keep his bond with the guys, but King Shark felt as though his reputation, didn't match that, and that he was being far too nice and kind. King Shark was probably, and possibly, jealous of what the men are able to accomplish. Despite the fact he was giving them impossible tasks to complete, the guys somehow managed to achieve victory with the tasks regardless, which caused King Shark to feel some type of envy, directed at the other guys. The watch stealing heist, was foiled from the very beginning. The guys for the most part, had no idea, that no matter what the outcome of the task was, whether they succeeded in the task or not, King Shark was going to kill them. King Shark knew that there wasn't any way, that the guys were going to finish the task, King Shark had no worries or doubts, that this was going to be the end for the guys. King Shark knew they would fail, either by not completing the task, in which King Shark would kill the men, as a consequence, and as a result of that. Or they would fail, because the guys would either be caught, or killed by the police, in which the guys would have to face the music with that. Or, another option, which is what ended up happening. King Shark, even if the guys were luckily enough to steal and replace the watch, King Shark would deal with them anyways.

The entire time, King Shark, was watching the guys outside the building, smiling to himself, knowing that the guys were going to fail miserably. King Shark, dealing with his own psychopathic issues, took delight, knowing that he tricked the guys into the task, and the guys had to follow his orders, no matter which way it is put. So even if the guys had any doubts, that this task was setup from the beginning, that didn't matter at all. The guys had to do the task anyways, or they were going to be killed by King Shark. While King Shark as outside the building, watching the whole ordeal, he was completely shocked when he found out that Dan was trying to sneak into the window. King Shark was also well aware, that the guys had no chance of breaking into the office, as the set of keys he gave them, would not unlock the door anyways, and the guys would either get caught, or end up not completing the task, either way, which would result in failure for the guys, and King Shark would kill them, regardless. Once King Shark found out that the guys, luckily found a way to get into the office, King Shark new that he had to do something about this right away. King Shark got out of his vehicle, and starting walking to the building. King Shark continues to be in disbelief, that the guys managed to find a method, to complete this very impossible task. Using a stone that was located out the window, King Shark, busted a back window of the building, which caught the attention of the guard. King Shark, had his full attention, and objective, into finally getting rid of the guys. Upon reaching the inside of the building, King Shark, quickly killed the guard. At this same current time, Klaus and Dan, were walking down the stairs of the building, and into the lobby. King Shark cornered all three of the men, and this was initially going to be it. King Shark was going to eliminate, Klaus, Dan, and Jerome, at this very moment. However, Klaus asked King Shark, to give him, and the other guys, mercy. King Shark decided to give into Klaus request, and is going to give the guys more time. Although it still wouldn't matter, as whether it's now or later, King Shark will strike.

King Shark, decides to give the men, one final task. This task, although sounds simple, is actually much more difficult, that it initially seems. All the men have to do, is find their way back to the factory warehouse, where the Diamond Mafia headquarters are. The same building, that Klaus, and the other men, were kidnapped, the night they did the story, on the Diamond Mafia mansion, stake out. Klaus, and the other men, using their own methods, and techniques to find this information out, must get to the headquarters building, before 7 p.m. If the men are not able to make it there in time, King Shark is going to kill them. If the guys manage to make it to the building in time, King Shark claims that he still might kill them anyways. So this is a very complicated, and puzzling situation, that the guys are encountering yet again. This is very intense, and the guys quickly all decide the choice they must make. The men understand, that this is the end for all of them, and they feel there is no turning back. The guys all believe, that finding where the headquarters building is, at least they can say they kept their dignity, and they are hoping there is a chance King Shark, might have sympathy for them, by completing yet another difficult and impossible task, by finding the headquarters building. If the guys do nothing, they are going to be killed by King Shark, and there are no doubts about that at all. However, if they are brave enough to take on the challenge, and accept, and attempt the task, there is a chance, things might work in their favor, although likely, they are going to be killed anyways. So the guys look at their options, and understand the choices that are at stake, and the men are all in agreement, to find, search, and locate where the headquarters building is, and confront King Shark. The guys of course, have no idea where this building is, and that's the whole entire point of the task. If King Shark knew this was going to be easy, he would have never brought this up. So King Shark is completely certain, the guys are going to fail this.

The guys continue to feel frozen, and are upset, that King Shark betrayed them, but they also understand that this is the nature of King Shark, and they should have been expecting for him to trick them, and give them false sense of security. Klaus was starting to regret not trusting his original feelings, of this task being a setup, as King Shark simply telling them to steal the watch seemed way too good to be true, Klaus knew that King Shark wasn't being truthful. There is however a strange paradox, that even if the guys were fully aware of this being a setup, the option of them refusing the task, and going to the police, was not available, and it was something that the guys simply couldn't do. Their only option, was to perform the task, whether it was impossible, and they were doomed to fail by King Shark regardless, or if the guys were assuming they were doing the task, to gain the respect of King Shark. Despite the fact, the men completed the task, King Shark was hoping that they wouldn't, and was disappointed over this fact. King Shark took matters into his own hands, and as the guys are not falling for King Shark's tricks. King Shark is going to dispose of them himself, and is also honest with his intentions, that the wants to eliminate the men, and eliminate them now. The guys simply and honestly, have one last chance to change things around, and confront King Shark. They have to make it to the headquarters building. Everything the guys have went through, is going to lead to this current, and present time. This will be a final countdown, and final showdown, between the guys, and King Shark. The guys must use their minds, to find where this building is. Even if King Shark kills them, which seems inevitable, and most likely, the guys know they completed the final task he set for them to do, and they also managed to find where the Diamond Mafia hideout, and secret headquarters are. The guys remain the lobby of the building, still unsure of what to do, and what their first step of this task, is going to be. Understanding that they must find the building.

As the guys continue to stand in the lobby, hugging each other King Shark has now been gone for about thirty seconds. The guys remain hugging each other, as they stare down at the guard's dead body. In this instance, Klaus, and the rest of the men understand, that if they don't leave out of the building soon, it will draw suspicion to them, and it will then shift to people thinking, that the guys killed the guard, when they didn't. In addition to this, the guys are also aware, that they don't have much time, and they must start their journey, into finding where the Diamond Mafia headquarters building is. For thirty more seconds, now being a minute, the guys still have not been able to move a muscle, or walk away from the location that they are currently in. Although it would seem like it is common sense for the guys to start getting a move on, they simply cannot act or move, and are still trying to process everything, that they just witness. The guys know that the instructions that King Shark gave them were concise and clear. Their only job, is to find where the headquarters building is, however, the guys at the moment, still feel emotional, and cannot move. Klaus and Dan, then realize, that the camera delay, is only set for five minutes, so if the guys don't leave out of the building soon, the cameras are going to be reset again, and Klaus, and the other guys will be seen on the surveillance cameras, incriminating them. Upon realizing this crucial fact, the guys then start to swiftly walk out of the building. Klaus, Dan, and Jerome, as they are leaving the building, try not to draw, any unneeded attention to themselves. Things are awkward for the first few seconds that the guys leave, but eventually, the guys snap out of their emotions, and soon put their minds together, and focus on what they need to do. The guys, who are all standing blocks away outside, from the building they were originally at, all stand on the sidewalk, continuing to get their thoughts situated, and looking at the other people, walking down the street. At this time, Jerome notices that he is still holding the bag of takeout food, and throws it away in a trashcan, directly adjacent to them. Directly following this, Klaus starts to look out to the distance, while he's doing that, he speaks.

"Do you guys know where the building was, because I don't. I do remember it was probably northwest of here. That's about it. I wasn't really paying attention to the route the van was taking, and I believe, the van even took two separate directions. Ugh. Any ideas?"

Dan and Jerome, likewise do the same thing that Klaus did, and the gaze their attention around the area, looking at the civilians, walking around the downtown area, minding their business. Dan then starts to look down on the ground, and shakes his head. Dan softly speaks.

"Man, if we knew, we would tell you. We don't know where the damn building is. We're trying to think. Although, I agree with you, and I do think it was probably somewhere in the valley, but I don't know exactly where. Damn. Can't think of anything right now. Sorry man."

Jerome then starts to look around the area, and has an idea. Jerome then speaks.

"I think you guys are right, and I do remember on our way to the building, we went down the 405. I'm like two hundred percent sure we did. Anyways, there is a library around the corner, how about we go use Google Maps or something, and we might get lucky, and find where it is."

Klaus and Dan then stare at each other for a few seconds, but they both agree with Jerome's plan and idea, and all of the men, then start to proceed to the library, located only a few minutes' walk, from where they are all currently at. The men also steadily, try not to draw attention to themselves, and blend in with everyone else. As the men are all directing themselves to the library, Klaus continues to try to think about all he can from that night, to get more clues, and information, to where the building is. Klaus at this time, then starts to remember, that there was a white colored mansion house, that was located directly next to the headquarters building, that had a lot of foliage in front of the property. Klaus doesn't know whether this new piece of information he just remembered would help, towards them locating the building, but he keeps it in mind for reference. The men very quickly locate the library, and walk up to the third floor, where all the computers, with internet access are located. Klaus and the other guys find an available computer, and Klaus starts to use Google Maps to find where the building is. As Klaus pulls up a map of Los Angeles on Google Maps, he starts to talk to the other guys.

"Okay, so we are down here in Downtown LA right. I think we all agree, that the building is somewhere up in this area. North of

Hollywood, but most likely, more west, and into the San Fernando Valley. But where exactly? Damn it, this is gonna be impossible. Shit."

Jerome then gets an index card, located on the table where the computers are, and grabs a pen. Jerome then starts to write down notes, of information that the guys already know, to narrow down the area, of where the headquarters building, might actually be. As Jerome is jotting down notes, Klaus continues to look through the map on the internet. Dan then tries to think deeply, if there is any information that he remembers, that could help the guys. For about ten minutes the guys are not able to have much luck, finding where the building is. Dan continues to think, Klaus remains searching on the computer. Jerome then speaks to the men.

"Alright you guys, we just have to think big, and just try out best to go over the route the van went. I wrote down all the clues we have, and we can do this. We have to stay positive, and put our minds together, and we are going to find the building. I just know we can. We can do it."

Klaus puts his hands over his face, shaking his head. Dan smiles to himself and speaks.

"Bloomfield Street, one of the streets a block away. I'm like 90 percent sure. Damn."

Jerome starts to write Bloomfield Street down on the index card, and Klaus immediately starts to search for Bloomfield Street, on Google Maps. As Klaus continues to search for the street, Dan tries to remember more information about the route the van took, from the headquarters building, to the Aerospace building. Klaus manages to find the direct length of Bloomfield Street, understanding that the entire street stretches from the entire San Fernando Valley, and it is one of the longest streets in this area of Los Angeles. Although the guys are helpful that Dan was able to think of this information, it doesn't help much. Also, Dan mentioned that Bloomfield is one of the side streets. It is not the direct street of the location of the headquarters. So the guys feel that this information isn't conclusive enough to their search. Yet, it does confirm the surrounding area the building is in, so Dan did manage to give somewhat vital information, related to the search. Klaus continues to go through the map. Jerome continues to think, and writes more notes on the index card. At this time, Jerome speaks to Klaus and Dan.

"Maybe it was a front, or a phony business or something. Like a disguise. I remember, the room we put the pallets together, there was a truck located right outside the window. I remember it now. The name, the logo, either it was called ThunderShock Liquidators, or LightningShock Liquidators or ThunderRain Liquidators. You guys remember that right?"

Jerome writes this information he just thought of down on the index card, and Klaus and Dan look at each other and smile. Klaus then runs his hands through Jerome's hair, and Dan kisses Jerome on the cheek. Klaus then starts to put ThunderShock Liquidators into Google. The business is legitimate, but it is located in Nebraska. Klaus then enters LightningShock Liquidators into Google. The business again shows up, but it is located in Florida. Klaus then tries to enter the last company name Jerome gave, which was ThunderRain Liquidators. This is the guys last hope, as the other company names, are not located in the Los Angeles area. This time, five locations show up in the San Fernando Valley region, with that company name. The guys all start to feel happy, that they are slowly, but surely, putting the pieces together, to find the location of the building. Klaus then starts to notice that all four ThunderRain Liquidators locations, are located in separate directions of each other. One is located North, one is located South, another is located East, and another is located West. By looking at the outside street view of the buildings, they all look identical, and any of the four, could be the building, the guys were at. Klaus then tries to remember the information that Dan gave, in which he said the building, was located near Bloomfield Street. That eliminates the East, and South locations, and Bloomfield Street, doesn't run in the directions of those locations, and Bloomfield Street, is located very close to the North, and West locations. The guys then start to hug and smile and laugh at each other, once they have now narrowed it down to two locations. They know that the Diamond Mafia headquarters, is either the North location, or the West location. Klaus then starts to remember the white mansion house that he saw outside of the building. This mansion house, incidentally, is where King Shark lives, as his residence, is right next to their fronted headquarters. Klaus then starts to look at the surrounding area of both locations, seeking a white mansion house. Klaus searches the North location first on Google Maps, and doesn't see a white mansion, which sightly disappoints and frustrates him. Dan and Jerome, try to console Klaus.

However, when Klaus searches the surrounding area of the West location, Klaus notices that directly next door to the West ThunderRain Liquidators location, is a white mansion house. Klaus then gets up from his chair, and starts to dance around the library. Dan then starts to do a victory dance with Klaus as well. Jerome laughs and smiles at Klaus and Dan, and Jerome starts to write the address down to the location, on the index card. Klaus and Dan continue to prance around the library, doing their victory dance. The men have managed to do, something that was impossible, and the guys had no chance at all succeeding in, which was finding the address to the Diamond Mafia headquarters. The guys managed to accomplish this, by using teamwork, and remembering little by little, information about that night. Klaus was able to remember the white house, situated next door. Dan was able to remember one of the streets, located nearby the building, and Jerome managed to remember the fronted name of a furniture company, that the Diamond Mafia uses, to not draw attention to their headquarters. Klaus and Dan then fist bump each other, and continue to feel amazed, that they managed to solve where the headquarters building was located. Now that the men have found out the address, to where the Diamond Mafia headquarters are, and where King Shark is, the men feel confident, and understand, that this is truly it. There is nothing else, and the men have reached the end of the line. The final confrontation with King Shark, is approaching now, and the guys no longer feel scared, and are willing to accept whatever chance, destiny, and fate, has in store for them. The men are understood over this matter, and the men will stick together, and end their journey together. Happy that they managed to at least complete their final impossible task, of finding the building.

At this time, Klaus, and the rest of the guys, then start to look up directions, as to how to reach the building. Klaus has his car back at his house at Redondo Beach, and there is an option for the guys to direct themselves back in the opposite direction to Redondo Beach, to get Klaus car. However, Dan feels the better idea, is for them to take public transportation. Dan, due to his prior knowledge of being a bus driver, knows a route the guys can take, which will lead them to the building. The guys are going to have to take the Los Angeles Metro, B Line Subway, to the North Hollywood station. After that, the guys must take two buses to reach the area of the Western location of the ThunderRain Liquidators building which is actually the Diamond Mafia building, located in Van Nuys. The guys then must take a slight half an hour walk, through a commercial area, to reach the building. Klaus and Jerome, accept Dan's directions, and trust him fully. The men then quickly exit of the library, still pleased and happy, they managed to do something, that was not scientifically able to be done, and the guys didn't have any slight of a chance of figuring out, which was the location of the Diamond Mafia building. The guys, although they feel slightly nervous as to how King Shark is going to react, and what he is going to do, no longer feel scared. The men all know, there is nothing else on the agenda, and they are the last on dock. Whatever happens from here, is the end, and the guys accept that. Their main sense of relief and satisfaction, was completing the last impossible task that King Shark gave them, which they managed to shockingly pass, and figure out. Nothing else is left on the shelf, and nothing else is in store. This is it, nothing else. Now, this is truly where they will end it.

Klaus, Dan, and Jerome, quickly get on the subway, on their way to the North Hollywood station. During the subway ride, Klaus starts to form an angry look on his face. Klaus no longer feels scared of King Shark, and neither to do the other guys. Klaus looks straight forward, while riding the subway, keeping the angry look on his face. Dan and Jerome, also have stoic looks on their faces, and feel determined, for their final showdown with King Shark. The North Hollywood station, is the final stop on the subway, so the guys remain on the subway, for quite some time. The men take advantage of the long subway trip, but preparing themselves, to deal with King Shark. The guys can't wait to see the look on King Shark's face, once he realizes, that they managed to locate where the building is. Klaus slightly smiles to himself. Relishing in the fact, that he is going to confront King Shark for the final time, and refuses to submit himself to him, and grovel in fear at King Shark. The guys continue to feel strong and determined. The guys have gone through so much in their journey, and it's bittersweet. The men, although they lost many in their group, stuck together. The men are accepting the fact, that King Shark will be angry, and this is going to be over for them. However, the men are glad that they had closure throughout their adventure, and they didn't leave any stones unturned. They outsmarted King Shark several times, and the guys are happy knowing that they are going out, and are being defeated by King Shark, because he was jealous of them, and because the guys outsmarted him, every time. They guys were always steps ahead of King Shark, and they were pleased with this.

Eventually, the subway arrives at the station, the guys must get off at. Klaus, Dan, and Jerome, then get off the subway, at North Hollywood station. The men then start to walk over to the first bus they must catch. The bus takes quite a while to arrive, about forty-five minutes. When the bus does reach the station, the guys all directly get on the bus. The bus ride is at a moderate length, but it's still a lengthy bus ride, for the men to still think about their thoughts. Although since they left the library, none of the men have said a single word to each other, they are not scared or anxious anymore, and they don't have any fear to King Shark anymore. The guys understand that King Shark might be physically more threatening to them, but the guys are mentally stronger than him. So therefore, the guys mentally adapt their minds, so they aren't scared of the situation. Klaus continues to stare out the window, still having the angry expression on his face. Anticipating the time, for him to finally approach King Shark. Dan and Jerome, still are confidant as well, and are ready to present themselves to King Shark. The bus continues moving forward, and the guys then arrive at the stop they need, to get on their second, and final bus. The guys get off the bus, and wait for the next bus, they must take. This bus remarkably doesn't take that long to arrive. Actually, the men only had to wait five minutes. The guys get on the bus, and it is another moderate bus trip, to their destination. The men continue to remain quiet with each other, understanding fully the situation that's going on. The men by this point, have begun to grasp, that they have reached the end of the road. It's no use being scared, if this is the end, and there is nothing else. The guys instead use a reverse psychology approach about the situation, and accept the fact, that they must be strong with this. They are all going to end this, and with King Shark's wrath together, and it's okay. They have all come to an understanding, that they won internally, and mentally, by beating King Shark; it allows the men to feel happy.

The bus arrives at the stop the men must get off at, and Klaus, Dan, and Jerome, all get off the bus. It is now 6 p.m. in the evening, so the men have made it before the time, King Shark asked them. It doesn't matter, as King Shark is adamant, that the guys are not going to be able to find the location, so the time limit, was redundant. However, the guys did technically follow the rules, and are arriving at the location, before time is up. The guys now have to walk through a commercial and industrial part of Van Nuys, to reach the Diamond Mafia fronted building, which is about a twenty-minute walk away. During their walk, the guys steadily remain quiet, like they have been for the past several hours, during their trip to the building. Klaus continues to look ahead, putting his body into beast mode. Dan and Jerome, follow directly next to Klaus, feeling strong as well. None of the guys are anxious, and they don't feel scared, as to what's going to happen next. They accept everything that will happen, at this final showdown. The men don't have time to make any regrets, as that's over with. The men can't change the past, and they will have to accept the consequences, and repercussions, resulting from everything that they have gone through. As the guys continue to walk, they come across Bloomfield street, as Dan remembered. The guys are definitely on the right track. Klaus, and the rest of the guys, have been walking for ten minutes, and Klaus starts to watch the evening Los Angeles sky. There are barely any clouds in the sky. The sky is clear and blue, and the climate and temperature is perfect. Klaus, and the other guys, feel comfortable, and if this is the last sight, and view, they all manage to see alive, they are happy for this, and it brings them much joy. The men, feeling this is their last moments together, so they want to make the most of it, and take as much as they can in. The guys continue to direct themselves to the building, with them now only being a couple of blocks away. The men carrying on walking, and before long, they are directly in front of the building, and they walk closer, and approach the building. The guys all notice the ThunderRain Liquidators truck, that's located in the back distance, behind the side gate of the building. When Klaus starts to see the white mansion, located directly next door, Klaus begins to form at slight smile. Dan and Jerome, also feel happy, knowing that this is for sure the correct building.

The guys start to reach the front gate of the building, and not even a second to waste, Klaus starts to push the intercom button. A few seconds later, a voice starts to speak.

"Foxtrot, Whiskey, Quebec. Foxtrot, Whiskey, Quebec. I like Strawberry Jam."

Klaus shakes his head and laughs, and presses the intercom button again. Klaus speaks.

"Don't give me that code military secret talk. Hey listen. Where the fuck is King Shark? I have something to say to this motherfucker. Tell him, Klaus and the boys are outside now. Ha."

Klaus then starts to laugh, and nods his head. Klaus looks over at Dan, who is laughing as well. Jerome, standing right next to them, is laughing too. Dan pushes the intercom and speaks.

"Yeah, you guys go get King Shark, right fucking now. We are waiting. We have a present to give him. The present is the shocked look on his fucking face, when he sees us. Ha."

The guys all continue to laugh, waiting outside the front gate. Things are for the moment quiet, and suspenseful. This remains, until when not even a few seconds later, guards creep up behind the guys, and the guys all have burlap sacks thrown over their heads. This time, the guys are not injected with a knockout agent. The guys don't fight back the guards, and don't resist. The men, still with the burlap sacks over their faces, are escorted to a back room, located inside the factory. Even though the men have burlap sacks over their heads, and cannot see anything, they can hear loud noises, from several machinery. The guys continue to be escorted in this area by the guards. Eventually, the guards sit all the guys down on chairs, and take their burlap sacks off. The guys then notice, three masked guards, pointing their guns at them. Klaus, Dan, and Jerome, don't feel scared, and instead smile at the guards, not showing any fear. Klaus then starts to look around the room, and realizes, that it seems to be a furniture, and reupholstery factory. This room is where sofas, chairs, bed frames, tables, desks, and other furniture is assembled. This room is also where furniture is painted, and also upholstered, repaired, and restored. Furniture is given cloth pattern, and also stuffed, sewn, and decoratively put together. There are also several heavy machines, used to cut, mold, and press the furniture. The entire room of the factory, is quite loud, as the machines continue to operate, and function. The guys all remain seated at this location, for several minutes, although they continue to feel secure and confident.

Eventually, after waiting about a half an hour, the man, that the guys were all hoping to see, arrives at the scene. King Shark, starts to walk into the area. As he's walking, King Shark intentionally, does not stare at the guys. King Shark takes a cigar from his suit jacket, and starts to take several puffs of his cigar. King Shark then, while sill intentionally not staring at the other guys, starts to walk around the furniture room, and turns on several more machines, and adjusts the settings of machines that are already on, so that they are moving faster, than they originally were. As a result of this, the noise in the room becomes louder. However, the guys still remain unphased by how King Shark is reacting, and do not feel an ounce of fear at him, anymore. King Shark finishes dealing with the machines in the room. King Shark then starts to walk back to the area, Klaus, and the other guys are at, and pulls out his gun from his suit jacket. King Shark then does something heinous, and starts to fatally shoot, two of the guards in the head, that just attacked Klaus, and the guys. King Shark then takes off the guard's masks, revealing that they are two Caucasian bearded men. One is bald, and the other has short black hair. King Shark then points his gun at the third guard, and shouts loudly at him.

"Take off your fucking mask, right now! TAKE OFF YOUR FUCKING MASK!"

The guard then quickly takes his mask off, and the guys can see, that the third guard, that King Shark didn't shoot, was Clark. King Shark then takes another puff of his cigar, and looks down on the ground, and shakes his head. King Shark then puts his cigar down on the table. King Shark then reaches for a pair of large industrial pliers, that are located on the table. King Shark grabs the pliers, and puts them in his pants pocket. King Shark then picks up his cigar, and takes another puff of it. King Shark then gets on his phone, and calls three additional guards. The guards all then arrive in the room, and King Shark asks each guard, to detain the guys. King Shark then takes another puff of his cigar, and turns to look at Clark. King Shark then speaks.

"Oh, I changed my mind. I don't need you after all. I'm done with you now. Bye Bye."

King Shark then starts to take his gun from his suit jacket, and starts to aim it at Clark. Feeling shocked, Clark then starts to aim his rifle at King Shark, and starts to speak to him.

"Hey, wait. What are you talking about? Damn it. You motherfucking bastard. Ugh..."

At this same exact moment, King Shark shoots Clark in the head, instantly killing him. The guys simply do not react to this at all, and silently watch how King Shark is acting, being fearless. Directly following this for the first time, King Shark turns to look at the guys, who are being detained by the masked guards King Shark called. King Shark then gives direct eye contact to Klaus. King Shark raises his eyebrows at Klaus, and Klaus returns a wide grin. Klaus speaks.

"Fuck you. Ha Ha."

King Shark then smiles back at Klaus, and not even a second later, King Shark launches himself up towards Klaus, and snatches him up from his chair. King Shark throws Klaus glasses off his head, and throws them on the ground, stomping on them after that. Klaus glasses are broken, with both the frames and lenses being crack. The guards continue to hold back, and detain, Dan and Jerome. King Shark then grabs Klaus over to the table he was standing at before. King Shark then kisses Klaus on the forehead, and starts to softly speak to him.

"You know, doughboy, I like you. I really like you. Because I like you so much, I'm gonna give you a makeover. I'm gonna have you looking like a work of art. Let's see. I want to start with these fingers. I don't think you'll need them, after I turn you into a statue. Ha Ha."

King Shark then takes the pliers from his pocket, and begins to squeeze Klaus left pinky finger with the pliers. With much brute force, King Shark rips Klaus pinky finger off his hand, and it falls on the ground. Initially in shock, Klaus soon reacts, screaming loudly, and starts to cry heavily. King Shark then starts to squeeze Klaus left middle finger with the pliers. Jerome sits and watches this, unable to react, feeling upset, being detained by the guard. Dan is also acting erratic, and tries to free himself from the guard, with no luck. King Shark then with much force, manages to rip Klaus middle finger, off his hand. Klaus continues to yelp, and scream in pain. At this time, King Shark drops the bloody pliers on the ground, and laughs, once he sees Klaus fingers on the ground. King Shark then takes off his suit jacket, and starts to speak.

"Whew, Damn. That was a lot harder than I thought it was. I'm gonna get to the other eight fingers in a minute don't worry. Ha Ha. Now. I don't know about you guys, but is it hot in here, or is it just me? Ha Ha. You guys are feeling hot now right? Well, you will be."

King Shark then starts to take a bottle of lighter fluid, and douses the machines in the room with it, and also pours some on the ground of the warehouse. The guards start to act shocked, as to what King Shark is doing. Dan and Jerome cannot react, as they are being detained by the guards. In this same instance, King Shark throws the lighter fluid bottle on the ground, and takes out his gun from his suit jacket. King Shark walks up to Klaus, and starts to wave the gun in his face. King Shark then laughs to himself, and then points the gun towards Klaus chest area, near his heart, and fires several rounds into Klaus chest. Klaus screams out in pain, and starts to fall to the ground, feeling weak. Jerome instantly starts to cry, and Dan, believing that King Shark has killed Klaus, uses his elbow to strike the guard holding him back, in his jaw, and Dan is free from the guard. Dan then not even within a second, grabs a pair of large scissors, located on the table next to King Shark and Klaus. Dan then strikes King Shark in the neck, hitting several arteries, causing King Shark to bleed strongly. King Shark instinctively follows this, by shooting Dan in the neck as well. As a result of the gunshots, the lighter fluid King Shark poured throughout the factory, causes a small fire to erupt, but the guys in the building, being distracted by King Shark and Dan, don't notice this at all. King Shark and Dan continue to tussle and fight, and they then both immediately fall to the ground, at the same time, feeling weak from being hit. King Shark and Dan, are bleeding heavily. Jerome, and the guards watch everything in shock. King Shark then starts to stare at Dan, and whispers out to him.

"I really like your hair man. Ha Ha. Well, I guess you boys got me. Fuck. Ha Ha."

Dan stares right back at King Shark, and silently responds back to him.

"We sure did, and I always thought your suits were nice man. Fuck off and die now. Ha."

King Shark then laughs, and closes his eyes. At this time, the room is silent for nearly ten seconds. One of the guards starts to take off his mask, and it's a bald Caucasian with a beard. The guard quickly walks up to King Shark, and checks his pulse. The guard notices that there is no pulse. The guard then tries to give CPR to King Shark, but it isn't working. King Shark is officially dead. Jerome stands behind watching, crying heavily, being detained by the guards. The guard then takes King Shark's suit jacket, and places it over his head. At this time, the same guard, checks Dan's pulse, and likewise with King Shark, there isn't one. The guard tries to gives Dan CPR, but it doesn't work. Dan dead as well. The guard then takes his jacket off, and places it over Dan. Jerome remains crying heavily, still being detained by the guard. The guard then walks over to where Klaus is. The guard instantly notices that Klaus is holding his chest with his right hand, and is still breathing, and moving. The guard then shouts out.

"Oh my god! FUCK. GUYS HE'S STILL BREATHING. GO GET DOC. HURRY!"

The other guards, who are both bald Caucasian men with bears as well, take off their masks. One of the guards run out of the room, and the other guard is detaining Jerome. Not even a minute later, an individual walks in the room, and Jerome is shocked to see who it is. Emilio starts to run behind the guard, and walks over to Klaus body. Emilio then approaches Klaus, and starts to shake his head and laughs. Jerome continues to feel shocked, that Emilio is a member of the Diamond Mafia group. Emilio then starts to speak to the guards.

"He's still breathing, but I don't know for long. If I don't operate on him now, he's probably gonna die in about half an hour. But I don't think it's gonna be worth it. He's losing blood from his fingers, which where are his fingers anyways. What did King Shark do to him?"

Jerome continues to feel shocked and confused, that Emilio works for Diamond Mafia, and refuses to believe that what is happening now, is actually happening. Emilio then leaves Klaus momentarily, and starts to check on both King Shark, and Dan. Emilio then speaks.

"Yeah, they are dead alright. Shit. Okay. I'm sorry, but I don't think I have enough time to help the other guy. He's gonna bleed out within the next few minutes or so, so it doesn't make any fucking difference. I also know him too. Long story, I'll tell you guys later. Damn it. Ugh."

Emilio then starts to walk out of the factory, but Jerome then starts to cry and scream out.

"Please, Emilio! Please! Have some kindness and love in your heart, and help him."

Emilio then stares down at the floor, and shakes his head. Emilio ignores Jerome's cry, and is walking out of the room. Emilio then stops himself, and looks across the room, puzzled.

"Hey, do you guys smell that? Is something burning. Oh Shit! We all have to move, that fire is about to explode and spread like any second now. Guys come on; we have to move now!"

As soon as Emilio warned the guys about the fire, it did indeed spread faster. The guard detaining Jerome, drops him to the ground, and Jerome walks over to where Klaus body, is and tries to get Klaus to stand up. Jerome kisses Klaus on the forehead, and whispers to him.

"DJ K. Oh god. Please get up. Hey, it's me Jerome. If you're still alive, please get up."

Klaus very weakly tries to get up, and one of the guards tries to drag Jerome away, but Jerome refuses. Klaus continues to stand himself up, as the fire spreads across the room. At this time Emilio walks over to where Klaus and Jerome are, and Emilio then softly speaks to Jerome.

"He's gonna die anyways, even if we do get him out of here, he's gonna bleed to death. There is nothing that I can do, I'm sorry. This building is gonna blow up any minute. Come on."

Jerome then starts to wrap his arms around Klaus neck, and screams out to Emilio.

"No, I'm not fucking going anywhere. If you want take him, I'm not leaving either. Please, have some heart man. Emilio please. At least try. Help me get him out of here. Please."

Emilio then throws his arms up in the air, and shakes his head. Emilio angrily shouts.

"Fuck it. Okay. Wow you're so stubborn and persistent, aren't you? I'll grab his right side, and you grab his left side. We have to hurry up and get out here, right now. Let's move."

Jerome and Emilio, then start to successfully get Klaus, who is still feeling very weak, unable to speak, and walk himself, up from the floor, and not even a few seconds after that, the fire grows, and spreads even larger and stronger. The men continue to run away from the building, and they all reach a van. One of the guards gets into the driver seat of the van, and the other guards get into the back of the van. Jerome and Emilio, get into the back of the Van as well, and they drag Klaus body, inside of the van in addition to that. The driver then starts the engine, and directs himself away from the building. Seconds after that, the entire Diamond Mafia headquarters, erupts in heavy fire, destroying the building heavily. If the men were five seconds slower, with leaving out of the building, they all would have most likely been perished in the fire. The driver continues to drive away from the scene, as Jerome and Emilio, watch the entire Diamond Mafia building crumble, and be destroyed. As the van continues to drive away, Klaus then starts to lay his head on Jerome's lap. Jerome then notices that Klaus face is turning a blue and purple color, and Jerome sobs heavily. Jerome then speaks softly to Emilio.

"Emilio please. You have to help him. Please. He's gonna die soon if you don't. Please."

Emilio looks down on the ground, and shakes his head. Emilio then responds to Jerome.

"I'm sorry, but there is nothing that I can do. Probably in another two minutes or so, he's going to die, so I'm really sorry, but he can't be helped. Don't know what else to say. I'm sorry."

Jerome then starts to massage Klaus head, as the driver of the van continues to speed away. The driver then starts to get on the highway, and continues to speed and proceed forward. At this time, Jerome continues to look down at Klaus, massaging his face. Klaus continues to remain motionless, and he loses much blood, and his body remains extremely weak. Emilio then turns to look at Klaus, and notices how lifeless his face looks. Emilio then takes his glasses off, and starts to cry Emilio then starts to rub his eyes, and starts to massage Klaus face. Emilio then put his hand over Klaus forehead. Emilio then starts to pray.

"Father Lord, please give this man the strength he needs. Father Lord, if this is the time you wish to take this man with you, we understand, but Father God, I ask if you could please give this man another chance. Spare his life. Father, Son, Holy Spirit, Jesus name, Amen."

Emilio then starts to kiss Klaus on the forehead. Directly following this prayer, Klaus then starts to cough, and screams out in pain. This causes Jerome to feel optimistic, and starts to smile. Emilio then notices that Klaus is still breathing, and coughing, and shouts to the driver.

"Hey Hunter. I really need your help right now. Do me a favor, and take me to my office okay. Please, get this fucking thing there as fast as you can. It's really important."

Emilio then starts to massage Klaus face, and Emilio smiles to himself. Emilio then turns his vision towards Jerome, and starts to hold Jerome's hand. Emilio then whispers to Jerome.

"It's not looking good. He's most likely still gonna die, but I think if we can get to my office fast enough, he's probably still gonna die, but if he's lucky enough, and damn, I hope he's lucky enough, he just might be able to make it. I can't make you any promises, but have hope."

Emilio then kisses Jerome on the forehead, and Jerome smiles back at him. The driver of the van continues to head to Emilio's office, as Klaus remains losing blood, and is very near death. It is very vital for the men to make it to Emilio's office in time, as if not, Klaus is most likely going to succumb to his current condition, and bleed to death. Jerome, and Emilio, remain keeping hope, that they will be able to save Klaus in time, and get him the medical assistance that he needs. Jerome is shocked, that Emilio has a medical degree, and is qualified and trained, to operate on people. Emilio has had to operate on other guys at Diamond Mafia in the past, which is why they gave him the nickname of Doc, as he is the one they consult, whenever they guys have any medical injuries, or issues. The van continues to drive down the highway, heading straight to Emilio's office. Within several minutes, the driver manages to quickly make it to Emilio's office, which is located in West Hollywood, quite a distance from Van Nuys, where the guys were previously at. Because the driver was speeding, and going fast, they managed to make it there in a short amount of time. The driver then parks the van, and the guards then start to take Klaus body out of the van. The guards, carry Klaus inside of Emilio's private doctor's office, and quickly set Klaus down on an exam table. Emilio then starts to shout to the guards.

"Um, hello? Don't just fucking stand there, I have a dying man here. IV's, morphine, my monitors, my tools. Don't act like you guys haven't been in here before. Come on guys. Ugh."

Emilio then starts to wash his hands, and one of the guards puts his surgical gown, surgical mask, goggles, and gloves on. Emilio then turns his direction to Jerome and speaks.

"Go outside, and wait buddy okay? He'll either make it, or he won't. It's okay."

Jerome nods his head, and the guards escort him out to the waiting lobby. At this time, one of the guards start to take Klaus shirt off, and Emilio then notices the Diamond Mafia tattoo on Klaus, the same exact one that he has, and the guards have as well. Emilio then slightly smiles under his mask, and smiles to himself. Jerome continues to wait outside in the lobby, with one of the guards running his hands through Jerome's hair, and patting him on the back. Jerome looks up at the guard, and smiles back to him. Back inside the exam room, Emilio, and with the help of the other guards, quickly start getting to work on Klaus. Emilio then puts an IV inside of Klaus arm, and starts to check Klaus vital signs, which are currently doing good. Emilio then starts to add disinfectant to Klaus left hand, which has missing severed fingers. Emilio then speaks.

"Okay, let's see what happens. Let's pray. Give me the scalpel please."

Emilio then starts to cut open Klaus chest area, to operate on him. Emilio then shakes his head, as he proceeds, to try to save Klaus life, and continues to operate on him.

CHAPTER 23:

RANDOM ACT OF KINDNESS

Now that the final showdown has been complete, things still haven't calmed or settled down. Not one bit entirely, and there is still much to reflect, and understand. Things all started, when the guys were giving the final task by King Shark. Once King Shark realized, the guys were going to pass the watch heist task, without any problems, King Shark at that point, became irate and envious, and wanted to finally put an end to the guys. However, King Shark knew how logically and intelligent the men were, and King Shark wanted to tease the guys longer. When the guys asked King Shark for mercy, he agreed to go along with this, on the condition that the men completed one final task. This final task, required the men to locate the, Diamond Mafia building. A building that they had no idea, where it was located. If the men were able to pass this task, King Shark would still kill them, but it would give a lot of morale points to the other guys if they are able to find exactly where this location is. The guys quickly set off for the task, which quite frankly, was not passable or beatable. The task, pure and simple was impossible to beat, and there was not a single chance in the world, the guys were going to find where the building is. However, the men still remained determined, and wanted to attempt to find the building anyways. The guys had nothing to lose. If they didn't show up to the building, King Shark was going to punish them anyways. So the guys wanted to at least find the building, for their own satisfaction, and gratitude. So with that all considered, the guys were determined, to find the location of the Diamond Mafia headquarters. The men directed their way to the library, with the only thing they had as a lead, was the fact Klaus, knew that there was a white mansion house, located next to the building, which the guys all knew was a factory of some sort. When the guys were in the library, Klaus, by using Google Maps, tried to put the puzzle together, little by little, mapping out the surrounding area of Los Angeles. The guys knew that the building was located in a specific region, so they began there. While the guys started to refresh their memory on the building, Dan remembered Bloomfield Street, for some reason. This piece of information that Dan was able to think of, was crucial, into helping the guys. Along with this piece of information, Jerome also remembered, that the building the guys were in, was a fronted business. Jerome then gave the name of a furniture company, that Diamond Mafia group, was using as a front, and it was also, another key piece of information that they needed, to find where the building was, and confront King Shark, one final time.

By using the information that Dan gave, and also using the information that Jerome game, Klaus then used the piece of information that he had, which was the house, that was located next to the building. Putting everything the guys managed to refresh their minds with, together, they managed to find exactly where the building was. After getting the address of the building, the guys left the library, and took the train, and the bus, to get to King Shark. Throughout the entire trip, Klaus and the guys knew, this was probably going to be, their last time together, and also their last time alive. The guys were not scared anymore, so the guys were happy that they managed to find the building, and they happy that things were going to end, on this positive note. The men were going to bow down gracefully with King Shark, and not be afraid of King Shark's actions. Once the guys arrived at the building, they were ready to see King Shark, and the guys were also expecting his wrath and anger, over the fact the guys completed yet another task, given by him. However, the guys were quickly ambushed, once they arrived at the building. Guards put bags over their heads, and the men did get their wish. The guys were all face to face with King Shark, and this was actually going to be it. Whatever King Shark was going to do, the guys were going to accept it, and deal with whatever results were. The men were taking to a furniture manufacturing room, where furniture is built, repaired, and upholstered. There were a lot of loud machines in the room, making the setting very thrilling. The guys had no idea what King Shark had up his sleeve, and what he had planned. The men knew that they were all going to be killed, and there was simply no use feeling scared over this situation. King Shark was going to do, what he was going to do, and there was nothing the guys can do about it.

King Shark unexpectantly killed his assistant Clark, shortly after he presented himself, to the other guys. This was a shock, and surprise, to everyone in the room. This was proof, that King Shark was about to do a series of morbid events. After killing Clark, King Shark continued to feel angry, and furious. King Shark decided to grab Klaus, and began torturing him. Things were happening very sudden and fast, King Shark was losing control, and being very psychotic. King Shark took ka pair of pliers, and began squeezing Klaus fingers from his left hand off. Klaus wailed in pian over this, and King Shark was acting extreme. Dan and Jerome, were detained by the guards, and couldn't react. Their only option was to watch, as King Shark, remained torturing Klaus. King Shark at this time, also managed to take a bottle of lighter fluid, and was dousing it around the room. King Shark's plan from the beginning, after killing the guys, was to burn their bodies, so there is no evidence by the police. King Shark didn't explain that this was his plan as he wanted the rest of the guys to be in suspense about it. King Shark carried on acting furious, when he shoots Klaus in the chest, presumably killing him. Even though Dan was being held back by the guard, seeing Klaus being shot in the chest by King Shark, gave Dan rage boost, and Dan managed to attack the guard, that was detaining him. Dan knew that he had to avenge Klaus, by going after King Shark. Once Dan was free from the guard, he picked up a pair of scissors, that was located on a table near King Shark, and started to violently stab him in the neck, repeatedly. King Shark in the same instance, shot Dan in the neck. Both Dan and King Shark, continue to fight and tussle with each other until they both landed on the ground, feeling weak from their blood loss. Shortly after this Dan and King Shark, both died. Dan managed to strike King Shark violently in the neck, which hit an artery. King Shark shot Dan in the neck, which also caused Dan to bleed profusely. Dan and King Shark lifeless bodies, remain on the floor for several seconds, as the rest of the people in the room watch.

Jerome is overthrown with emotions, and sadness, and was still being held back by the guard. At this time, one of the guards walks up to King Shark, and confirms that he is dead. The guard walks up to Dan as well, and he is also dead. When the guard walks up to Klaus, the guard notices that Klaus is still moving, although his breathing is weak. Klaus at this moment, is still alive. The guard calls for the other guard, to go and get the doctor, who the guys in Diamond Mafia, all call Doc. When the doctor arrives, Jerome is shocked to find out, that it is actually Emilio. The man that the guys all met previously, who was a friend of Bill. Jerome still cannot gather his thoughts well, and is shocked that Emilio is in the Diamond Mafia group. Emilio immediately starts to diagnose Klaus. Although Klaus is still alive, and breathing, Emilio notices that Klaus is losing far too much blood, and the chances of him being alive for much longer, are low. Because of this, Emilio, doesn't see the point in operating, or medically dealing with Klaus. Emilio feels that the best action, is not to move Klaus body, and leave him be. Emilio explains that Klaus will die regardless. If they do happen to get him out of the building, and get him help, he is going to pass away from the blood loss, despite all that. Not willing to accept this, Jerome pleads with Emilio, for him to at least try to save Klaus. However, Emilio doesn't budge or change his mind on the matter. Jerome feels very devasted and upset, that Emilio is not willing to help. As Emilio is walking away from the scene, he notices that the room is on fire, and tells everyone to evacuate out. The men in the room, then all start to panic over the fire, which is steadily growing, and will soon engulf the entire building, causing the building to explode, over the machines situated in the room. The guys all then start to evacuate, and exit out of the room.

At this time, Klaus body remains on the floor, and Klaus is very near death. Jerome remains on the floor next to Klaus, as the guards are trying to pull him away from the scene, as the building is on fire. Jerome is persistent on Emilio to help Klaus. Emilio explains to Jerome, his same sentiment, and that Klaus is going to die regardless. However, Emilio does manage to get Klaus out of the building, with the rest of the men. The guys then all successfully escape out of the Diamond Mafia building, with only a few seconds to spare, before the entire building, succumbs to the fire, and explodes. While the men are continuing to escape in the van away from the burning building, Klaus is still very weak, and near death. It was at this time, where Klaus was showing signs of still breathing, and Emilio realized, that there much be a chance, albeit very small, that Klaus could be worked on. Jerome continues to plead with Emilio, and Emilio starts to pray for Klaus health. Emilio instructs the Diamond Mafia guard, driving the van, to head to his medical office. They all reach the medical office, and Emilio immediately starts working to recover Klaus. Jerome is instructed by Emilio, to wait in the lobby outside. Emilio tells Jerome, that either Klaus can be saved, or he cannot be. Jerome understands this, but he is hoping that Emilio can help Klaus. All of these events, which have happened after watch heist, are extremely hectic, and heavy. Things are happening very fast, and things are very drastic. The guys were approached with King Shark one final time, and he was defeated. Dan managed to do the unthinkable, and was able to kill King Shark. Although Dan had to sacrifice himself, due to that. Klaus was also badly tortured by King Shark, and Klaus is clinging on, by a thread. Emilio is Klaus only remaining hope, for him to survive this entire situation. Jerome managed to escape with the other men, before the building exploded due to the flames. Things are really traumatic at this point, and there is no time to stop and think. Everything is emotional and very shocking to deal with. So many unanswered questions still linger, and everyone is still trying to process what exactly happened, back at the factory. King Shark, the Diamond Mafia boss was defeated. The Diamond Mafia headquarters is no more, and another shocking element of this all. Emilio is a member of the Diamond Mafia himself. Things continue to be shocking.

Emilio has been working on Klaus, in the exam room, for now an hour. Jerome, and the guards, wait outside in the lobby, as Emilio remains tending to Klaus wounds, and recovering him. Jerome looks down on the ground, feeling very depressed, hoping that Emilio can save Klaus. Minutes continue to drag on, and it has now been two hours, since Emilio started operating on Klaus. Jerome starts to worry, the longer that Klaus is in the exam room with Emilio. The only thing that Jerome can do at this time, is wait. Either Klaus will be saved, or he won't. Jerome deals with the outcome regardless. Another hour passes, and Jerome starts to look at the night sky outside, and is aware of how long Klaus has been in the exam room. Jerome then starts to take a nap, and lays his body across the chairs in the lobby. Jerome decides to drift off to sleep, in an effort to calm himself down, as he continues to wait, and be updated on Klaus condition. Jerome remains asleep for several minutes. Jerome continues to have hope, that Klaus is going to overcome this, and that Klaus is in great hands, with Emilio. As Jerome is resting in the lobby, he reflects more on all the events that happened. Today was yet another wild day. The guys left to do the watch heist, which was a setup from the beginning. After the watch heist, the guys then went on their journey, to locate the Diamond Mafia building. A task which was purely impossible, but the guys, using very little clues they had, were able to locate the building. Once the men were able to locate the building, they had their final encounter with King Shark. In this event strange events happened, one after the other. King Shark went on his rampage, in which he tortured Klaus greatly. Dan, thinking that Klaus was killed by King Shark, retaliates, by killing King Shark himself. King Shark ends up killing Dan, and both King Shark and Dan, both die during this. Klaus remains holding onto hope, although in very critical condition. The Diamond Mafia building, which is one fire, later explodes, with the men barely escaping. Jerome still can't see how all of this happened, in a short amount of time, but it did. Jerome is thankful that he managed to survive, and make it through this ordeal.

Eventually, Jerome is awakened, by a person, tapping him on the shoulder. Jerome while waking himself up, notices the person tapping on his shoulder is Emilio. Emilio then speaks.

"Hey, wake up, wake up. I wanted to let you know, that he's going to be okay. He's still very weak. However, he's going to be fine, and he's extremely lucky, I'll tell you that. Ha Ha."

Jerome then smiles, and starts to hug Emilio. As Jerome is hugging Emilio, he speaks.

"Oh god. Thank you so much for all of your help. I mean it. May I see him please?"

Emilio then nods his head, and asks Jerome to follow him. Emilio then directs Jerome, to a recovery room, located on the other end of the office building. Jerome continues to follow Emilio, when they approach the recovery room, Emilio opens the door, and Klaus is sleeping in a medical bed, hooked up to several machines. There is a Diamond Mafia guard sitting right next to Klaus, on a chair. Emilio taps the guard and the shoulder, and silently speaks to him.

"Hunter, it's okay. They aren't going to go anywhere. You can go. In fact, tell the other boys, that they can go home now. It's alright. I'll take care of everything. Thank you."

Emilio and the guard hug each other, and the guard then walks out of the room. The other Diamond Mafia guards, leave out of the building as well. Emilio, Klaus, and Jerome, remain the only people left in the building. Jerome asks permission by Emilio, if he can walk up to Klaus. Emilio agrees to this. Jerome then starts to walk up to Klaus in bed. Jerome starts to massage Klaus on the side of his face, and Jerome then kisses Klaus on the forehead. Emilio continues to watch as Jerome reunites with Klaus, and is comforting him, bedside. At this time, Emilio reaches for a stack of papers, that are located directly by Klaus. Emilio then starts to read the documents, and starts to write several things down. Emilio sets the papers down, and speaks.

"Alright. If King Shark aimed, like not even an inch from where he was shot, he would have died, almost instantaneously. So he is truly the luckiest man in the world. If he came into my office, probably five minutes sooner, he'd be a dead man as well. Lucky, lucky, lucky."

Jerome continues to conform and caress Klaus on the face. Emilio then starts to look at the machines that Klaus is hooked up to. Klaus vital signs, and readings are fine. While Jerome is continuing to comfort Klaus, Emilio then starts to explain more of Klaus condition, to Jerome.

"So I managed to remove the bullet out just fine. Fixed all of his heart arteries Stitched him up really good. Now, the next plan was his hand. King Shark ripped some of his fingers out. Damn. I don't have the severed fingers. I couldn't reattach them sadly. So he's unfortunately going to have only three fingers on his left hand, but I managed to seal the wounds up."

Jerome then picks up Klaus left hand, and notices that Emilio patched up Klaus open wounds, where King Shark, pulled Klaus fingers off. Jerome continues to comfort Klaus at this time, as Klaus continues to sleep. Emilio then excuses himself from the room, and is gone for several minutes. During this time, Jerome cries heavily, as he is staring at Klaus. Jerome is crying tears of joy, that Klaus is still here, and he is alive. Jerome is thankful that Emilio was able to save Klaus, although Klaus was on the near brink of death. Even though Klaus was shot in the chest, and near his heart, the bullet didn't strike a vital area, which is why Klaus didn't instantly die. In addition to that, Klaus was able to make it to Emilio's office just in time, before he died of the blood loss. Klaus was extremely lucky to have survived, everything considered. Jerome remains happy that Emilio managed to reconsider his decision to help save Klaus, after he originally felt that it wasn't worth the time to help him. Klaus managed to stick through it all. Klaus was very lucky to have been able to stay strong through all of that. Klaus is possibly also lucky, that it was Emilio, who by sheer coincidence, happened to be the doctor, for the Diamond Mafia group. Emilio, because he was Bill's Nephew, felt obligated to offer his help, and he didn't want to live with the guilt, that he was not able to help Klaus. Jerome remains caressing Klaus, and at this time, Emilio returns to the room with a white bag. Emilio then speaks.

"Okay, so he's going to need to take these pills. Some of them are pain killers, the other medications are antibiotics, that he's going to need. He's still sleeping right now, but when he wakes up, give him the meds. What else. Uh, make sure he eats a lot of fruits and vegetables."

Jerome nods his head, and continues to caress Klaus. Jerome then softly speaks to Emilio.

"Thank you, again. Really. This is like Christmas morning. Klaus is still here, and I don't know what else to say. I'm really thankful you helped him. Klaus, although he's not saying it now, Ha Ha, he's very thankful you helped him as well. Emilio, Thank you. God bless you."

Jerome and Emilio then hug tightly, as they are both hugging, Emilio then softly speaks.

"About the Diamond Mafia stuff, don't worry about it. Just lay for now. If the police ask you anything, don't say anything. Tell the police to call me, and the story is Klaus was in a car accident. Diamond Mafia for right now, is on hiatus, Unfortunately, there is nothing you guys can do to leave. However, we'll work something out, and we'll talk about it later. Okay?"

Emilio then kisses Jerome on the cheek, and Jerome nods his head. Emilio then takes another look at the monitors Klaus is hooked up to, and Klaus results on the screen are fine. Emilio then takes the stack of papers located next to Klaus. Emilio excuses himself, and leaves out of the room again, and Jerome continues to stand next to Klaus bed, caressing his face. Jerome then starts to look at the scar on Klaus chest, where he was shot, and where Emilio stitched him up. Jerome continues to be amazed, that Emilio was able to save Klaus life, and Klaus is still alive, despite everything that his body went through. Jerome remains thankful, for everything that Emilio was able to accomplish, giving Klaus his health back. In this same time, Emilio returns back into the room, and gives Jerome a copy of the papers. Jerome starts to read all the papers, and as he is doing that, Emilio speaks.

"This is a copy for you. So that we both have a copy. Basically what I managed to do, was legally say, that he was injured in a car wreck. It's very important, that you go along with this fib as well. So you can keep those documents in safe place. He's gonna be just fine."

Emilio then starts to run his hand over Klaus face, and pats him on the shoulder. Directly after this, Emilio looks down on the ground, and shakes his head. Emilio then speaks to Jerome.

"You know what, I didn't want to tell you earlier, but this is actually my home. You can stay here, if you like. I was hoping he would have woken up by now, but I guess not. He's either still out from the anesthesia, or he's just naturally tired and exhausted. Either way I guess."

Jerome nods his head, and remains comforting Klaus, caressing his hands through his face. Within an instant, Emilio then starts to unplug all the monitors. Emilio speaks to Jerome.

"He'll be okay. I don't think he's going to need to be monitored enough. He's a big tough guy, he'll be alright. He's just sleeping right now. So, you guys can hang out here, until he wakes up. So yeah. Whatever you guys do next, I guess is up to you guys. I guess, it's good night."

Emilio directly after this, then starts to walk himself out of the room. Jerome then speaks.

"Hey, wait a minute. If I could trouble you for something to eat please. Thank you."

Emilio then starts to laugh, and shakes his head. Emilio then walks out and speaks.

"There is a kitchen down the hall, and to the right. You can help yourself. Good night."

Jerome nods his head, and Emilio shuts the door behind him. Jerome then walks back over to Klaus, and comforts him for a bit. Jerome then allows Klaus to sleep, and doesn't bother him. Jerome then notices, that there is a television set in the room. Not wanting to disturb, or wake up Klaus, Jerome does not turn it on. Following this, Jerome takes another look at Klaus, and smiles to himself. Jerome then takes a blanket, that was by Klaus bed, and unfolds the blanket. Jerome then drapes Klaus with the blanket, and kisses Klaus on the forehead. Jerome then takes another blanket, and walks over to lounge chair, situated directly beside Klaus. Jerome then starts to feel slightly fatigued, and tired. After checking on Klaus, and noticing that he seems fine, Jerome then decided to get some rest. Jerome starts to relax on the lounge chair, and covers himself up with the blanket. Jerome closes his eyes, and immediately drifts off to sleep. Not even a couple hours later, Jerome is awakened, by the sounds of screaming. Jerome, not sure at first where the screaming is coming from, wakes up himself up, and notices that Klaus screaming out in pain. Jerome gets off the chair, and walks next to Klaus, speaking to him.

"Hey, what's wrong? Are you pain? Did you want me to give you something? Klaus, wait. I remember Emilio gave me some pain killers for you. I'll get you some water, wait."

Klaus continues to scream in pain, while Jerome walks to the kitchen, to get Klaus some water. Jerome manages to get the water, and walks back to the room. Jerome then puts the glass of water, on the side table of the room. Klaus continues to holler and scream in pain. Jerome then opens up the bag of medication Emilio gave him. Once Jerome locates the medicine that Klaus needs, Jerome takes two capsules out of the bottle. Jerome then starts to speak to Klaus.

"Here, take these. Emilio says that they will help with the pain. I got you some water."

Klaus then for the first time, opens his eyes, and starts to gaze around the room. With a confused, and puzzled look on his face, Klaus continues to look around. Klaus then screams out.

"What the hell? Where am I? Where are my glasses? Jerome, is that you? What is this?"

Jerome then shakes his head, and starts to laugh. Jerome then signals for Klaus to take the painkillers, and Klaus obliges, by swallowing the pills. Klaus then accepts the glass of water, and drinks it. Once Klaus has consumed the pills, Klaus continues to look around. Jerome speaks.

"Klaus, you asked like ten different questions, so I'll answer them. Ha Ha. King Shark broke your glasses. It's a long story. Dan is sadly dead, but he sacrificed himself for you, and killed King Shark. The Diamond Mafia building blew up. Emilio works for them, he saved you."

Klaus then starts to scratch the back of his head, and remains confused. It was now that Klaus started to put together, the facts he was able to remember. Klaus is aware that he, and the other guys, managed to locate the Diamond Mafia building. Klaus then remembers, that they were taken to this factory room, where King Shark confronted them. As Klaus continues to remember all the details, Klaus then remembers, that King Shark pulled some of his fingers off. Klaus then looks down at his left hand, and starts to see patched holes, where his fingers should be. Klaus then starts to cry upon looking at his hand. Jerome then walks over, and comforts him.

"It's okay. It's a long story, and you're really lucky to be alive. You're in Emilio's office, and this is also his house. I think Emilio is sleeping now, but when he wakes up tomorrow, we'll talk to him, and figure out what we're gonna do next. He told us not worry about anything."

Jerome then kisses Klaus on the forehead, while Klaus continues to cry heavily. Klaus is not able to remember anything else. Jerome explains to Klaus, more details of the event. How Klaus was shot in the chest by King Shark. As a result of that, Dan retaliated, by killing King Shark, in which Dan was accosted by King Shark as well. Things were happening very sudden, and it was a very traumatic scene. When King Shark shot Dan, it accidentally set off a fire, which quickly grew, all over the building. The guys were able to just narrowly escape from the building, right before it was about to explode. Jerome tries his best to continue to explain, everything that happened at the Diamond Mafia building. Klaus continues to feel confused, and can't believe how he managed to survive all of that. Klaus then starts to speak.

"So it's just us now huh? Damn. Jerome, I don't know how to thank you enough. I, well, we will talk more later, right now, I'm just really hungry. You don't have any food do you?"

Jerome then starts to laugh, and shakes his head. Jerome starts to walk out, and speaks.

"As a matter of fact Klaus, I do. Emilio said there's a kitchen down the hall. I'll be back."

Klaus starts to laugh, and shakes his head at Jerome. With Jerome now gone off to the kitchen, Klaus continues to look around the room. Although his vision is slightly shady, as he doesn't have his glasses on. Klaus continues to look at his left hand, which is missing fingers, and Klaus shakes his head, and puts his hand down. Klaus then starts to look at the scar on his chest, where King Shark shot him at. Emilio did a fantastic job of healing Klaus bullet wound, and stitching him up accordingly. Klaus again shakes his head at this, and is in slight disbelief. Klaus continues to look around the hospital room, and also can't believe, that Dan managed to kill King Shark, after King Shark shot him. Klaus is upset over Dan's death, but is thankful, that Dan was able to avenge what happened to him, by killing King Shark. Even though Klaus cannot remember ever detail as to what happened, he is starting to realize, what exactly happened. Klaus then understands, that it was because of the help and Jerome, and Emilio, that he is still here. Klaus feels very luckily, that he survived the entire event. Klaus is also pleased that he has Jerome has survived as well, and is with him. For the first time, Klaus starts to feel happy and proud. Klaus has a wide grin on his face, and he continues to shake his head. Klaus refuses to believe what happened, actually happened the way it did. Although he did manage to lose a few fingers, and he was also shot, Klaus is still here, and King Shark, is no more. Klaus remains in bed, still bringing himself back to Earth, and coming to his senses. Klaus remains in bed, still slightly confused, although now fully accepting the situation. While smiling to himself, Klaus, although his memory of everything is blocked, is now more aware. During this time, Jerome walks back into the room, with two microwave dinners. Jerome then speaks.

"Hmm, this is all that is in there. There is like rice, and beans and other stuff. But I have, let's see. Meatloaf with Mashed Potatoes and Broccoli, and I have another Meatloaf with Mashed Potatoes and Broccoli. Which one do you want? I'll take the other one. Ha Ha."

Klaus then starts to laugh, and shakes his head at Jerome. Klaus then responds to Jerome.

"Damn, that's a tough choice. Well, Meatloaf with Mashed Potatoes and Broccoli it is."

Klaus then starts to laugh, which causes Jerome to laugh as well. Jerome then walks out of the room, and to the kitchen, to heat up the microwave dinners. Klaus takes another sip of his water, and looks up at the ceiling shaking his head. Although the painkillers he took helped, Klaus still feels a great amount of pain, throughout his body. Klaus is hoping that if he gets some food into his system, that he will feel much better. Several minutes later, Jerome returns back to the room, with the Meatloaf dinners. Jerome also managed to make some wheat bread toast as well. Jerome sets one dinner on a tray, and puts it the tray on the side table. Jerome raises Klaus bed up, and puts the tray on Klaus lap. Klaus thanks Jerome, and Jerome then pulls the lounge chair up close to Klaus bed, and sits next to him. The both of the men then start to eat. Although it was a simple Meatloaf microwave dinner, the guys seem to be enjoying the food, very much. Initially, both Klaus and Jerome are quiet, while they are eating. This is the first time, that they are calm and collected, with each other. The both of them have several thoughts going through their mind, knowing that the guys went through so much, in just a very short amount of time. After eating, Klaus feels more refreshed, and he is still in pain, but is experiencing a less amount of pain, than he was feeling earlier. Klaus and Jerome occasionally would stare and smile at each other, but they were mainly quiet, and not discussing the events that just happened. Klaus and Jerome, then soon finish eating their food. Jerome then gets up, and throws their trash away in the hallway. Jerome then returns back into the room, and then speaks to Klaus.

"Oh dear. I forgot. Emilio said you have to take your antibiotic meds. Here, take these."

Klaus shakes his head, and has an angered look on his face. Jerome then gets the bottle of antibiotics, and takes two capsules out. Jerome then hands the medication to Klaus, who quickly swallows it. Klaus then takes a drink of his water, still with an angry look on his face. Klaus then shakes his head, and looks up at the ceiling. With his vision still looking up, Klaus speaks.

"Hey, do you know where my clothes are? I don't want to change, I know my clothes are all bloody and stuff, but I had a pack of cigarettes in my pocket. I really could use one now."

Jerome, who is putting Klaus medication back in the bag, quickly responds to Klaus.

"Oh, I don't think you should be smoking right now. I'll ask Emilio first later if you can."

Klaus then sits up in bed, and gives Jerome a cold stare. Feeling agitated Klaus responds.

"I don't fucking care, I asked where my clothes were. I don't need for you to act all Disney, and give me all that Public Service Announcement shit. Where are my fucking clothes?"

Jerome then starts to have a shocked look on his face. Jerome shakes his head and speaks.

"You know what, fuck this. Wow. You would have assumed that after all that, you would have learned something. Nope. You're still the same, and I can't believe this. Wow. Oh my god."

Jerome angrily walks out the room, and proceeds out, down the hallway. Klaus starts to feel guilty for the way he just acted, and didn't mean to hurt Jerome's feelings. Klaus shouts.

"Jerome, I'm sorry, okay. I didn't mean that, you know how I get. I'm just really cranky, like I had heart surgery, and like my fingers are gone. Give me a break. Jerome. Come back."

Jerome returns to the room, a few seconds later, with Klaus clothes. Klaus silently watches, as Jerome goes through the pants Klaus was wearing, to find the carton of cigarettes. Jerome is able to find the cigarettes, and sets the box of cigarettes down on the side table. Jerome then folds Klaus bloodied clothes up, and sets them aside. Jerome picks up the cigarettes, and with an angry look on his face, hands them to Klaus. Jerome then softly speaks to Klaus.

"Don't you ever, ever, talk to me like that again. Klaus, I'm here to help you, and I'll always be there for you. But if you're gonna act like that, you can forget it. Okay?"

Jerome then starts to walk away from Klaus, but Klaus, although feeling weak, manages to grab Jerome by the arm. Klaus and Jerome stare at each other for several seconds. Klaus then starts to smile at Jerome, and Jerome smiles back at Klaus. A few seconds later, Klaus speaks.

"I'm sorry. Hey, there is something I want to tell you. Come here for a second please."

Jerome then gets closer to Klaus. The both of them stare at each other, and Klaus passionately kisses Jerome, for several seconds. Klaus then runs his hands through Jerome's hair, and smiles. Jerome then walks back to the lounge chair, and takes a seat. Klaus then starts to take one of the cigarettes, and puts in his mouth. Klaus reaches for the cigarette lighter, and before he's able to light it, Jerome walks up from where he was seated, and snatches the lighter. Klaus, initially has a shocked look on his face. Jerome then grabs the carton of cigarettes and speaks.

"You must be tripping. If you want to smoke, all you had to do was tell me, you wanted to step out Klaus. Damn. You make things much harder than they need to be. Klaus, are you strong enough to get up? We can go outside and smoke, if that's what you want. Let's go."

Klaus then starts to shake his head, and laughs. Jerome then laughs back at Klaus. Directly following this, Klaus attempts to stand himself up, for the first time. Although he is having much difficulty at first, Jerome remains very patient with him, and understands that Klaus is feeling very weak, and is allowing for him to take his time. After about three minutes, Klaus remarkably is able to get himself out of bed, and starts to position himself, so he is standing up. Klaus, then while only wearing his surgical gown, walks out to the back patio with

Jerome, so that they both can smoke a cigarette. It is now very late into the night, creeping up past Midnight. Klaus and Jerome both notice how clear the night sky is, and how full the moon is as well. Klaus then starts to light his cigarette, and takes a puff of it. Jerome takes a cigarette from the carton as well, and smokes his cigarette. Klaus then puts his arm around Jerome, and they both sit at the back porch of Emilio's office, watching the late-night sky. Klaus is able to calm himself down during this time, although the timeline of all the events, is still foreign and strange to him. Klaus doesn't even know where he, and Jerome are going to go from here, but Klaus feels that he has plenty of time to think about all of that let. For now, Klaus is blessed that he survived, and he's still able to go on with his life. Klaus is very appreciative of his second chance, and is going to try to do better with his life, from this point forward. Klaus has a greater bond with Jerome, and is happy that Jerome is still by his side. Klaus feels upset that he lost Stuart, he feels upset that he lost Ernest, he feels upset that he lost his Uncle Bill, he feels upset that he lost Paul, and he's also upset that he lost Dan. However, Klaus is still glad that Jerome is still there, and it was because of Jerome, that Klaus is even still alive. Klaus continues to keep his arm around Jerome, embracing him. Klaus then kisses Jerome on the forehead, and they remain in this area.

The both of the men, don't want to leave, and they find this therapeutic. This is quite truly, the first time that things are being shut down, and things are relaxed. Klaus is fully aware of the madness that happened, and what led him to Emilio's office. Klaus still has much answered questions starting from the fact Emilio was a member of Diamond Mafia. That was the biggest, and most crucial mystery that Klaus was thinking. None of it was making much since, but Klaus wanted to eventually get to the bottom of everything, and hopefully, the thoughts that are plaguing his mind, and his unanswered questions, would finally be answered. Although for the moment, Klaus is still recovering himself, and is still in the initial shock stage, and he tries not to worry about all that, for now. Klaus is simply lucky to still be here, and he remains sticking by Jerome, on the back patio. This is a very peaceful time for them both.

Klaus and Jerome then leave from the patio, and walk back into the hospital room. Klaus positions himself back in bed, and Jerome then covers Klaus up with the blanket. Jerome kisses Klaus on the forehead, yet again. Jerome then directs himself to the side lounge chair, and covers himself up. Klaus watches as Jerome starts to fall asleep in the chair. Klaus then speaks.

"Hey, do you mind if I turn the television on. Maybe some TV would calm me down."

Jerome, although feeling tired, nods his head, and allows Klaus to watch TV. Klaus smiles and laughs to himself, and starts to turn the television set, in the room on. Klaus tries to keep the volume of the television down, in an effort, not to wake Jerome up. Because it is late at night, the only thing that is showing, is infomercials. Klaus gets tired of flipping through channels, and keeps the television on the infomercial, which is showcasing both a Montel Williams blender, and a George Foreman grill. At this point, Jerome is already fast asleep. Klaus continues to the infomercial on the television, although struggling to stay awake. Eventually, Klaus doses off to sleep, with the television still playing. Klaus was able to finally calm his mind, to adapt himself to sleep, and is continuing to recover, and refresh himself, back to who he was before. Klaus and Jerome continue to stay asleep, for several hours. The following morning, with it now being 10 a.m., Emilio walks into the hospital room, wearing a tracksuit. Emilio smiles to himself, when he notices that both Klaus, and Jerome are deep asleep. Emilio then walks over to the far side of the room, and starts to open up the curtains. Being that it is a bright sunny, clear Los Angeles day, the reflection of the sun, gleams into the room. This causes Klaus and Jerome to wake, as a result of the sunlight. Emilio continues to smile at Klaus and Jerome, as they are waking up. Emilio then walks up over to Klaus, and puts his arms around him. Klaus and Emilio then stare at each other for several seconds, and they both smile. Although they are not saying a single word, it seems their actions, are speaking louder than their words. Klaus is very thankful that Emilio managed to save his life. Emilio in return, is also happy, that he managed to do a good deed for Klaus. Emilio then starts to eventually speak to Klaus.

"If you have the time, I'll explain everything. I'm sure Jerome already explained what happened. But I'll fill you in. That way you can get a clearer picture. You guys don't have to worry about the King Shark situation. Don't tell the police anything, and please trust me."

Emilio then kisses Klaus on the cheek, and Emilio then starts to go over everything that happened yesterday. Jerome who is sitting on the lounge chair next to them, starts to smile to himself, and is happy for the help, that Emilio is giving them. Klaus continues to listen to Emilio relay all of the events, to which Klaus quickly accepts and understands. Once Klaus is fully updated on the situation, he then starts to cry. Although the crying is more tears of reflection. It is tears of growth. Klaus understands that this entire journey was rather hectic, and Klaus still believes that he has much unfinished business, to take care of. Emilio explains, that him being in Diamond Mafia, was purely coincidental. The fact Emilio was a friend of Bill's, and they have engaged with each other prior, was trivial, and incidental. Emilio explains that unfortunately, he cannot give the full details, as to how he joined the group, with Klaus and Jerome. Although, Emilio states, that now with the death of King Shark, Diamond Mafia group is going through a major development, and at this time, Emilio is not able to say, what will happen now. Emilio explains that King Shark is not the only Diamond Mafia boss, and that Emilio doesn't understand why King Shark decided to go rogue. Unfortunately, Klaus and Jerome, will indefinitely be indebted to the group. However, Emilio will try to make sure, that Klaus and Jerome, have protection, and that the Diamond Mafia group, will no longer pester or bother them. Emilio again reiterates, that Klaus and Jerome, cannot explain what happened to the police. The Diamond Mafia headquarters building was destroyed, and King Shark and Dan's bodies perished. Emilio says that they unfortunately have to stay out of the police's investigation, and remain quiet, to not further incriminate themselves. At this time, Emilio then rolls up his sleeve, and shows the same tattoo, that Klaus and Jerome have, conforming that he is indeed, a member of Diamond Mafia, likewise with the other guys. Emilio then kisses Klaus on the cheek, and speaks.

"You boys are going to be alright. As always, if you never need my help, I'm always here for you boys. Okay, if you're feeling better Klaus, you guys can go home now. Just make sure you take your medication if you feel any pain, alright. I'll chat with you guys later. Take care."

Emilio then starts to hug Klaus tightly, and kisses him again on the cheek. Emilio then walks over to Jerome, hugs Jerome tightly, and Emilio kisses Jerome on the cheek. Emilio then walks out of the room. Directly following this, Jerome hands Klaus the clothes he had on the day before. Even though his plaid shirt is very bloodied, Klaus doesn't care, and puts it on anyways. After Klaus is dressed, Klaus then gets out of bed, and he and Jerome then walk out of the hospital room. During this time, Emilio calls one of the Diamond Mafia guards, to give Klaus and Jerome, a ride back to the house. A guard pulls up in a van, to which Klaus and Jerome get inside of it. Once Klaus and Jerome make it back to the house, they both immediately direct themselves to the living room area, and Jerome sits on the sofa, and Klaus takes a seat on his recliner. They both remain in the living room, for several minutes, quiet. Both Klaus and Jerome think about what happened the day before, and how quiet the house is now. At one time, the entire group was together in this house, now it's only Klaus and Jerome left. At this time, Jerome gets up from the sofa, and starts to cuddle with Klaus on the recliner. Klaus starts to run his hands though Jerome's hair, while looking down at the ground. Klaus then turns his direction over to the balcony, noticing how the day is bright and sunny. Klaus continues to comfort Jerome, and at this time, Klaus again takes a look at his left hand, noticing the fingers that he's missing. Klaus remains feeling lucky, to have survived, and gotten past the ordeal with King Shark. Both Klaus and Jerome remain comforting each other, for several more minutes. Klaus then starts to feel hungry, and starts to walk over to the kitchen. Once Klaus realizes that there isn't any food in the refrigerator, he starts to laugh to himself. Klaus then shouts to Jerome.

"Hey, I'm hungry. I'm gonna order a pizza. Does that sound good to you? Ha Ha."

Jerome silently nods his head, and although Klaus was expecting for Jerome to give a verbal response, understands that Jerome agrees to his plan. Klaus then picks up phone, and starts to order a pizza. Klaus then tells Jerome that he is going to take a shower, and change. While Klaus is showering, Jerome turns on the television, and is watching episodes of "SpongeBob SquarePants.". Klaus gets out of the shower, and changes into a T-shirt, and shorts. Klaus returns back to the recliner, and relaxes. Klaus then starts to speak.

"Damn, I wish King Shark didn't break my glasses. Ha Ha."

Jerome, while looking at the television, laughs along with Klaus. Eventually, the pizza Klaus orders arrives at the house, and Klaus accepts it, and tips the delivery driver. Klaus takes the pizza, and a bottle of Coca Cola he ordered, and brings to the living room. Klaus and Jerome then start to eat their pizza. Jerome continues to watch cartoons, as Klaus takes bites of his pizza, starting outside his balcony window. While staring outside, Klaus shakes his head, and laughs.

CHAPTER 24:

BROADCAST

This adventure was rather strange, starting from the very beginning. Things seemed to shift, in different directions, becoming more and more intense, as time went along. This adventure was full of many events, lessons, trails and tribulations, and tests. This adventure started, with a very introverted man, named Klaus. Klaus was a person, that all his life, he felt different from others, and considered himself a recluse, that didn't like associating, or talking with other people. Klaus had to go through a lot during his upbringing. Starting with the fact, that he had deal with the loss of his parents at a young age. Klaus continued to feel reclusive, while growing up, and Klaus figured that his life would remain that way always. That was until, Klaus went to University, and he met his best friend Stuart. Things took a complete turn, and Klaus found someone, for the first time in his life, that he was comfortable talking to. Klaus and Stuart, naturally connected with each other, and became a strong partnership. Klaus never had anyone present themselves as a friend in his life, until Stuart came along. Klaus was very appreciative of this, and was lucky to have met Stuart. The friendship and relationship that Klaus had with Stuart was so strong, that they both had the same life passions, and desires. They both wanted to go into reporting media to others, in an entertaining fashion. Although they didn't know exactly, how they were going to achieve this plan and idea, this is what they wanted to go for. Everything considered, Klaus and Stuart, decided to start their own news show, highlighting the stories, that they felt were important, and that people should know. Klaus had to deal with the passing of Stuart. Klaus tried to keep Stuart's positive energy in mind, and Klaus wanted to make Stuart proud. However, Klaus was shaving much difficulty with this, and the doubt started to overthrow his body. Klaus couldn't do the show without Stuart. Just as when Klaus was going to shut the show down for good, and call it quits, he received a call from one of the listeners. This call happened to be from Dan. A person that Klaus would have a strong relationship with, for the entirely of the journey. Klaus spoke with Dan for quite some time, learning more about his life, and where he came from, and what his story was. Klaus was having such good rapport with Dan, that Klaus made him a co-host of the show.

Now with Klaus and Dan having their bond and friendship, Klaus went on to rebuild his life. Soon after this, Klaus came across a Janitor, that entered the wrong room in the studio by accident. Feeling intrigued by this Janitor, Klaus and Dan, both agreed to invite him onto the show, learning more about his back history, and forming a friendship with him. This Janitor, was Ernest. Klaus remained happy with his new life, with Dan and Ernest, and despite the fact, it was a huge development, and adjustment for Klaus, he managed to very quickly get used to how things were going, and none of it was strange or foreign anymore. It was simply the way it was. That was until Klaus was presented, with yet another event, which would shake the adventure, and the journey, very much. Klaus, now doing the radio show with Dan and Ernest, was shocked, when he saw a strange person standing outside his building one day. Klaus had no idea who this person was, and Klaus initially thought he was a High School student. Klaus later found out, that this person was his number fan, and he wasn't lying about that fact. This fan was Jerome, and Klaus judged him wrong, initially. Jerome is much older than he actuality looks, as a result of a growth disorder, and he is a gay black man as well, who has been through much adversity in his life. Jerome is autistic as well. Jerome does freelance writing and journalism. Although Klaus initially wasn't giving Jerome a chance, and finding Jerome annoying, Klaus for some reason, suddenly had a change of heart towards Jerome, after finding out that he is in fact, a knowledgeable fan of his, after Klaus quizzed him on trivia, related to his show. Klaus quickly allowed Jerome to join the team. Klaus later formed a neutralized romantic relationship with Jerome, which was hard to explain. Klaus was enjoying the company of Jerome, and Jerome enjoyed the company of Klaus. They later became a solid match with each other, and things were now improving greatly. In between this, Dan and Ernest, also were forming an interpersonal bond with each other too. Klaus allows Jerome to join the show as a co-host, to which Jerome was very happy.

Moving on, things remained stable, if only for a moment. Klaus was going to be introduced, to yet another key figure in his life. This person was going to be Paul. An artist, that likewise with Klaus, seems to be a reclusive to others in his life, and keeps to himself. Paul has many unpopular opinions, but he usually doesn't reveal them, and he comes in peace, usually. Klaus finds out, that Paul was the person who prank called his show several times, which caused Klaus to feel angry, and almost quit the show. Paul managed to do this, by luckily calling back to the show quick enough, and Klaus reconnecting Paul's number repeatedly. Even though Klaus was angry that Paul was the guy who was the prank caller, Klaus forgave Paul, and also gave him a second chance as well. Klaus started to find out more about Paul's life, and the things that he experienced, and went through. Although Paul lied and said he didn't have any family, that simply was not true, as Paul had a younger brother Porter, that although Paul loved his brother, he had a complicated relationship with him. Klaus found Paul so interesting, that he had no choice, but to allow him to join the team. It wasn't long, that Klaus would encounter, yet another giant milestone in his journey. This milestone however, was blood related, and it was different. This particular Milestone, would have Klaus reunite, with his estranged Uncle Bill.

Bill, was an army veteran, in which most of his life, was tied to the military. Although Bill had a military mindset, he was still a very kind hearted man, and treated everyone with respect. Bill was also very open minded, and didn't judge others at all. Bill is Klaus paternal Uncle, and the situations surrounding why Klaus became estranged from him, is very complex. However despite all of that, Klaus was very happy, to have come back into contact with Bill. The way it happened, was very uncanny as well. Bill happened to call Klaus show, in which Bill has been trying for years, to get through the lines. Klaus spoke with Bill, for a very long time, on air, and was in much disbelief, that he managed to speak to his Uncle. It was soon after that, in which Klaus was informed, that Bill was kicked out of his living facility, after he was being a nuisance to the staff. Understanding that he can't say no to his Uncle, Klaus allows Bill to move into his household. After Bill moves in, he forms a strong bond with Paul, and the both of them, remarkably becoming close with one another. Klaus is then made aware, that Bill has several health problems, that need to be taken care of. Klaus allows Bill to join the rest of the guys in the studio, to which Bill is happy for.

Very soon after this, Klaus is informed by his boss, Mr. Weston, that the new direction is he going with the show, is not allowed, or permitted. Mr. Weston fires Klaus, and instead of Klaus becoming angry or upset at this news, Klaus simply accepts it. Klaus eventually has a bright idea, that he should start his own independent news show, with himself, and the other guys, producing all of the content themselves. They would air their show live on the internet, and it would be a live and direct, remote show. The guys embarked on their first ever live news show, which was covering the teachers strike. Klaus was having a fantastic time doing his show, and was thankful and blessed, that he had the help of the other guys, to keep the show going smoothly. When the guys all completed their first show, they were very confident to do it again. Klaus only had to wait for the perfect opportunity for this to happen. So in the meantime, the guys did take a break from their show, and went on about their lives. Jerome finally managed to pass the driving test, and get his driver's license, with the help of Klaus. Dan and Ernest, have a fun night on the town together, by sneaking into a club, and bonding with each other. Paul and Bill continue to bond with each other, and enjoy playing chess. The guys were content with the way life was going, things were great. However, it was during this time, which Klaus became more aware of Bill's health, and his heart problems, which could lead him to a stroke, or heart attack. Bill didn't like visiting the doctor, and Klaus wanted to make his Uncle healthier. Due to this, Klaus decided to make it a habit, that he and Bill, would go on morning walks together, to improve Bill's health. Bill was in agreement with these walks, and was happy to spend time with Klaus as well.

The men all carried on with life, and things were again, stable and level. Although, the time for Klaus to spark another idea, soon arrived. Klaus was watching the news, and he noticed, that the police were staking out, a stolen gasoline truck. The low-speed pursuit, made Klaus very interested, and he knew he, and the other guys, had to report down there, to see it. Unfortunately, Ernest was run over by the suspect with the truck, and the suspect was later shot by police, as he was running from the scene. This devastated all of the men, Dan especially. They didn't go into this ordeal, thinking that one of the would get hurt. They also didn't go into this, thinking one of the would die. The guys did however move on, for Ernest's legacy. But Klaus did spring another idea into his head. Klaus, although the other men were hesitant on this idea, still wanted to carry on the show, and do the show for Ernest's honor. Klaus knew that the Mayor election was coming up, and this was going to be a very hot topic issue. This further sparked interest in the men, when they were divided on their own personal political stances. Klaus and Dan, supported one candidate. Paul and Bill, supported the other. Jerome, not wishing to get too involved in politics, was neutral, and wasn't voting. When Dan and Paul, began conflict with each other, Dan, who was very against the idea at first, changed his mind, and was totally interested in doing the election coverage. When the winner of the most votes for Mayor was announced, the candidate that Paul and Bill were supporting won. However, directly after this, Bill started to suffer from a really bad heart attack. The guys quickly went and got help for Bill, but he later passed away at the hospital. Klaus was very devastated and upset, and losing Bill was too much for him to handle.

Klaus then started to regret ever attending the election coverage in the first place. Although Klaus knew he tried to improve Bill's health, but it was time for him to go. Bill was given a ceremonious funeral, in which at this time, Klaus met Bill's old friend, Emilio, who works at the veteran's office. Emilio promised that he would always be there for Klaus and help him. The guys, were dealing with the death of Bill, and it was tough for them to move on at first, but they know that Bill was a very motivational and distinguished man, and he wouldn't want the guys to feel upset over his death. Bill would want the guys to be happy. The guys advance from this.

Not even a day after Bill's funeral, Klaus already has several ideas running through his mind. It all started, with a feeling that Klaus had, and the feeling he had throughout the entire journey. The feeling that was telling Klaus, and notifying Klaus, that something was about to happen, and it was going to be something drastic, and vital. Klaus was watching the news with the other guys, and noticed that there was a mansion house, in the Hollywood Hills, being on stake out. Although the news was being vague with the details, Klaus, from his prior research on conspiracy theories, and topics about true crime, and organized crime, knew that this house was featured in a past news story, related to the Diamond Mafia group. A crime gang and group, who is noted for their cases related to organized crime, and other criminal activity. Klaus wanted to get down to the scene immediately, and didn't care how unsafe this sounds. Dan was trying his best to persuade Klaus not to go down there, but Klaus didn't want to listen. The guys were split, as to going, or staying. Klaus decided to flip a coin to decide what the men are going to do. Dan lost the coin toss, and so Klaus and the other guys, quickly went down to the scene. The guys all started to turn on their equipment, and start doing their coverage of the event. Things at first were very boring and uneventful, however, when one of the suspects started to break out of the house, the action started, and the entire event shifted. Klaus and the guys continued to get more footage, now that the scene is livelier and more dramatic. Before long, Klaus, and the other guys are kidnapped, and injected with a knockout agent. The guys quickly find themselves in a strange building, which was the Diamond Mafia headquarters, with their hands bound and tied. The men come to their senses, and locate each other. With the help of Klaus and Paul's skills of untying knots, the men managed to get themselves untied, and start to find a way to escape out of the building. The men luckily find a way out, but are thwarted by guards, once they are outside.

It was then, the men first come into contact with King Shark. A very terrifying man, who is boss of the Diamond Mafia group. King Shark, originally having his intentions to kill the men, give the guys a second chance, and spare their lives. The only condition, is the men must all become members of the Diamond Mafia group. They must get tattooed as well. The guys must also pass a very difficult test, of retrieving a hard drive, from a secured building. If the men refuse any of this, they will be killed by King Shark. With the guys not having any choice at all, they quickly get started on the task. With Dan furthermore upset, that Klaus didn't listen to him, from the beginning. Klaus thinks of a solid plan to retrieve the hard drive, which the guys agree with. Things were going as planned, until Paul offered to disable the security alarms, as the guys were on their way out. Klaus allowed him to. The other guys who are now outside of the building, wait for Paul, who unfortunately was caught by the guard. Paul and the guard fight, and the police arrive, and Paul, and the guard, are both killed. Klaus and the rest of the men, are mortified as to what happened, but they had no time to react. Upon reaching back to King Shark, they give them the hard drive, and King Shark manages to leave the guys alone, for the moment. Telling them, that he will soon give them another task to complete. Klaus and the other guys know they can't report to the police about what happened, and must remain quiet. The death of Paul brought a large rift between Klaus and Dan. Klaus as well then kicked Dan and Jerome out of his house. But Klaus later apologized for acting this way, and everything was good with the guys at this point. The men were in acceptance, that they worked for Diamond Mafia, and there was nothing that they could do, to get themselves out of the mess, and situation they are in. The guys must accept whatever fate hands to them, and deal with the Diamond Mafia group. The guys continue to lay low, waiting for the next task that King Shark will ask of them to do, not aware that the task King Shark is giving them, are to set the guys up for failure. King Shark however is underestimating all of the guys, and not understanding their full potential.

The guys attend Paul's funeral, and they meet Paul's brother Porter for the first time. The men all give a proper farewell to Paul, and the guys carry on, knowing that they have to deal with the King Shark situation. King Shark did present the guys with another task. This time, to break into an office building in Downtown LA, and steal a watch, which King Shark claims is his. In actuality, the guys later found out, the watch is not King Shark's, and the entire plan was foiled. King Shark knew the guys were not going to pass the task. Even if they did happen to pass the task, he was going to kill them anyways. Despite the fact King Shark gave the guys the wrong set of keys, Dan managed to slither his way into the window, from outside the building and they were able to get inside, and switch the watch. Even though they did what King Shark asked, King Shark had the plan set up from the beginning, and was irate, and angry with the guys. King Shark kills the guard of the building, and was about to kill the other guys. However, King Shark decided to give the guys one final chance, and gives them a final task. To locate the building they were kidnapped at, and the building they were all tied up at, the night they did their last show. If the guys do not show up and locate the building, King Shark will kill them. If they do show up, King Shark was most likely going to kill them anyways. At this point, overthrown with anger, and the fact the guys knew they are mentally stronger than King Shark, they set off to find the building. Using their prior knowledge from what they remembered of that night, the guys locate the building, by using the internet at the library. The guys then set off to the building to confront King Shark, one final time. The men are aware that this could be the end for all of them, but they all wish to go down in honor together. When the guys encounter King Shark, the guards accost them, and cover their heads with bags. They are taken to a factory, where King Shark starts to act very erratically and unpredictable. The guys no longer feel scared of him.

King Shark, then kills his assistant Clark. King Shark then attacks Klaus, and starts ripping his fingers off. King Shark decides to get rid of Klaus for good, and shoots him in the chest, presumably killing him. Dan then starts to have a sudden energy of anger, and is able to free himself from the guard, and starts to attack King Shark, with a pair of scissors. Dan stabs King Shark violently in the neck, to which King Shark shoots Dan in the neck. Both Dan and King Shark faint at the same time from blood loss, and they both die. However, when one of the Diamond Mafia guards checks Klaus, he notices that Klaus is still breathing, and moving. The guard calls a man named Doc, who is actually shockingly Emilio. At this time, Emilio starts to look at Klaus, but feels that it's too late, and Klaus is going to die. Jerome asks Emilio to help Klaus anyways, but Emilio originally refuses. When King Shark shot Dan, it accidentally set off a fire, that King Shark didn't intend to start, until much later, when he killed all of the guys, and was going to burn their bodies to get rid of the evidence. Emilio notices that the building is on fire, and is going to explode any second. The guys in the building all start to evacuate, and escape into a van. Emilio relents his earlier decision, and helps drag Klaus out of the building. Just when the guys are escaping, the Diamond Mafia building explodes, and completely disintegrates. While in the van escaping from the scene, Jerome is persistent on saving Klaus, and continues to plead with Emilio to save him, to which Emilio still sticks with his convictions in that Klaus cannot be saved. Although, once Emilio notices that Klaus is still breathing, Emilio says a prayer for Klaus, and remembers the promise that he gave Klaus earlier, and that he would be there for him. instructs the driver to head to his office. The men immediately make it to the office, and Emilio starts to get to work on Klaus. Luckily, the area King Shark shot Klaus, was not located in a vital area, which if King Shark shot Klaus a few inches further, Klaus would have died instantly. If the guys did make it to Emilio's office a few minutes sooner, Klaus would have died from blood loss as well, despite that. So Klaus was extremely lucky to survive.

Emilio heals Klaus, and Jerome is very thankful. The entire event was stressful, and Klaus and Jerome, have survived it all. Although they had to lose Dan, who sacrificed himself, to save Klaus, by getting rid of King Shark. Klaus continued to recover in Emilio's office, still feeling terribly weak, from his injuries. Jerome remained at Klaus bed side, taking care of him, as he continues to recover, and bring himself back to reality. Klaus, later by speaking with Jerome and Emilio, is able to find out what exactly happened. Klaus still can't believe that he survived all of that, and he's still here. Although he had to deal with the pain of getting shot in the chest, and also losing some fingers, Klaus still feels lucky to still be here. Klaus and Emilio have a heartfelt moment, and Emilio still reminds Klaus, that if there is anything that he needs, he can always contact him, and he will be there for him. Now that Klaus has fully recovered, the next day, Klaus and Jerome leave Emilio's office, and they start to head home. When the men reach back at the house, it's rather awkward at first, because once upon a time, six guys were here, and now it's just two; Klaus and Jerome. Where do they go from here? What happens now? Being that there is no food in the refrigerator, Klaus orders a pizza for himself and Jerome. The eat the pizza, and although both Klaus and Jerome, understand how hectic this entire journey was, they simply don't want to talk about it now, and just be thankful they are still alive, and have gotten away from it. Emilio informs that although Klaus and Jerome will forever be in the Diamond Mafia group, Emilio makes sure that both of them will have indefinite protection, and that they won't be bothered anymore. King Shark is dead, but he was not the only boss of Diamond Mafia. Emilio says the other bosses will leave them alone. Emilio informs Klaus and Jerome, that they can't talk to the police, or tell them anything. They must keep affairs about the Diamond Mafia group extremely quiet, and they can say anything to the police, to incriminate themselves. Klaus and Jerome are fully aware of this, and understand this.

Now being at the present, and everything this journey included, Klaus and Jerome, remain unsure as to what their next plans are. Klaus informs Jerome, that the first thing that he wishes to do, is get his glasses fixed, that King Shark broke. The next morning, which is a Sunday, Klaus and Jerome both wake up, and it's a bright, sunny, clear day, with blue skies. Very light clouds in the sky, and it's lovely Los Angele weather. Klaus gets out of bed, and starts to stretch his body. Jerome is still in bed waking himself up. Klaus then speaks to Jerome.

"Hey, even though it's Sunday, my optometrist office is open. I need to ask them to make me a new pair of glasses. So can you drive me over there please?"

Jerome continues to wake himself up in bed, and stretches his body. Jerome then speaks.

"I don't know Klaus, I mean it's Sunday, can't you wait until tomorrow. I don't know... of course I'll drive you to the eye doctor. You have to see right? Ha Ha. Come on, let's go."

Klaus then shakes his head, and starts to laugh to himself. Not even minutes after this, Jerome gets into Klaus SUV, and Klaus sits in the passenger seat, as they both start to drive to the optometrist office, to get Klaus a new pair of glasses. Klaus continues to look out the window, noticing how quiet it is, that today is Sunday. There are not that many other cars in the road, and it's very peaceful and calm. Jerome arrives at the optometrist's office rather quickly, and they both get out of the vehicle. Klaus notices that the eye doctor doesn't open up until 11 a.m., and it's currently 10:45. Both of the men then then wait back in the car, until the eye doctor opens up. Klaus turns on the radio, and it is playing a "Grateful Dead" song. This was Klaus and Stuart's favorite band, and Klaus was happy that this particular song was playing on the radio, as both he and Stuart, liked this song. Jerome watches as Klaus sings along to all of the lyrics. Before long, it is time for the optometrist office to open. Klaus notices some of the optometrists walk into the building, and both Klaus and Jerome, once again get out of the vehicle, and walk to the building. Once they are in the building, Jerome takes a seat in the lobby, and Klaus walks up to the front desk of the office. Even though Klaus did not have an appointment, the optometrists, are fully aware of Klaus situation, and allow him to get his new glasses prescription, anyways. Klaus picks out a pair, that's identical to the pair he had before, and Klaus is also given, an updated eye exam, to go along with his new pair. Klaus then waits in the lobby with Jerome, until his glasses are ready. After an hour, Klaus glasses are finished, and he tries them on. After feeling satisfied with his glasses, Klaus leaves out of the building with Jerome. This time, Klaus decides to drive, as he has his vision back again.

Klaus then starts to head to the grocery store, as there isn't any food back at the house. On his way to the grocery store, Jerome who was staring out the window, notices something strange. There is a very pregnant dog, limping on the sidewalk. Jerome then screams out.

"Oh my god, Klaus. That dog, she's pregnant. She's a Shiba Inu too. Oh no. I bet her owners are worried about her. Klaus, we have to help her."

Klaus then immediately pulls the car over, and Klaus and Jerome then pick the dog up, and put her in the car. Jerome then holds the dog, and Klaus starts to drive. Klaus then speaks.

"Jerome, I don't know if any vets are open. I'm trying to think. I believe there is one on PCH, that's open on Sunday, it's worth a try. We have to get her to a vet though."

Jerome nods his head, and Jerome continues to hold the dog tightly. Klaus arrives at the vet office minutes later, and thankfully, the vet office is open. Klaus then grabs the dog, and he and Jerome then walk inside the vet office. Jerome then starts to speak to the vet technicians.

"We found a pregnant dog on the street. She's in a lot of pain. Please help her"

The vet technicians then take the dog out of Klaus hands, and Klaus and Jerome then sit at the lobby in the veterinarian's office. Klaus and Jerome continue to wait for several minutes, not knowing the condition of the dog. A couple hours pass, and the veterinarian, who is an attractive Hispanic woman, arrives in the lobby, and starts to speak with Klaus and Jerome.

"The dog is fine. She had five healthy puppies. It turns out the dog is microchipped. We contacted the owners, and we left them a voicemail and text message. Thank you for your help."

Klaus and Jerome then shake the veterinarian's hand. Following this, one of the vet technicians brings the puppies the dog had, out to the lobby, for them to see. The mother dog, is still recovering. Klaus and Jerome start to look at the puppies, who are very cute and beautiful. There are five puppies and the puppies are all male. Ten minutes after this, the dog owners arrive at the vet office. The owners are a couple, which is Caucasian man with short gray hair, although he's middle aged, and an African-American woman, with afro textured hair. The couple speak to the front desk, and they then direct themselves to Klaus and Jerome. The man then speaks.

"Oh god, thank you so much for brining Jameka to the vet. That's her name. When knew she was pregnant, but we don't know how she got out. We don't know how to thank you enough. I'm Josh, and this is my wife Lorraine. Tell you what, you can have one of the puppies."

Klaus and Jerome shake Josh and Lorraine's hand, and they also accept the offer of accepting one of the puppies. Even though Klaus has never owned a dog, he didn't want to reject the offer, of taking one of the puppies. Klaus and Jerome are happy that they managed to do a good deed, by taking the dog to the vet. Josh and Lorraine inform them, that they can get the puppy, in a few weeks, after the puppies have been weaned by the mother dog. Klaus gives the couple his information, and agrees to this plan. Klaus and Jerome then leave out of the vet's office, and then start to go where they where they were originally intending to visit, which was the supermarket. While at the supermarket, Klaus and Jerome continue to talk about how they rescued the dog, and how great of a feeling it was for them. Klaus and Jerome get all the groceries that they need, and they both return back to the house. While back at home, Klaus and Jerome, start to put the groceries into the refrigerator, Klaus hears that his doorbell is ringing, and Klaus is immediately puzzled, as to how is at the door. Klaus then speaks to Jerome.

"Hey Jerome, can you go and see who that is please? Thank you."

Jerome nods his head, and answers the door. To Jerome's surprise, he notices a familiar face. It is Hunter, the Diamond Mafia guard. Hunter, who is a Caucasian man with a beard, is wearing a white button up shirt, and black pants. Hunter then starts to speak to Jerome.

"Oh hey, um. You remember me right? Hey listen, can I talk to Klaus please."

Jerome nods his head, and walks into the kitchen, to get Klaus. Following this, Klaus walks to the front door, where he notices Hunter. Klaus, who has not seen Hunter before, as he had his mask on previously, was the driver of the van, when they were escaping the building. Klaus looks at Hunter with a confused look, and Hunter who was carrying a book, speaks.

"Hey, I don't know if you remember me. I think your friend does. I was the one that drove you guys out of the building when it was on fire. So in essence, I kinda saved you guys life. Ha Ha. Anyways. Klaus, I don't want to waste your time, but we went to school together."

Klaus then starts to shake his head and laughs. Hunter then opens up the book, which is a yearbook, and shows a younger picture of Klaus with hair, and also a younger picture of Hunter, with hair. Klaus then starts to laugh, and instinctively gives Hunter a hug. Klaus then starts to slightly remember Hunter from school, although they weren't friends, they were associates of one another. Klaus and Hunter both had hair at the time, and they are now both bald. Klaus invites Hunter in, Hunter and Klaus have a beer, and continue to talk with each other. Hunter shows Klaus his Diamond Mafia tattoo, over street racing, as Hunter likes to drive fast sports cars. Klaus then tells Hunter the entire story, from the beginning when he met Stuart, to now present day. Klaus and Hunter continue to bond, and Jerome respectfully listens to the both and them, and smiles. Klaus and Hunter speak for hours, and hours, Hunter has been at the house for such a long time, that Klaus asks and offers Hunter, to stay for dinner, which Hunter agrees. Klaus starts to cook a shrimp and scallop pasta from scratch. While Klaus is cooking, he continues to mingle, and chat with Hunter. Once Klaus is finished preparing dinner, Klaus, Jerome, and Hunter, all eat, and chat, and socialize some more. During their meal, Klaus explains to Hunter, that he's not currently working. Hunter then does a favor for Klaus.

"Hey, you know that AT&T is hiring for cable technicians? You told me you used to be a cable guy right? Go down there tomorrow, and apply. Tell them I sent you. Go for it. Ha Ha."

Klaus takes a sip of his beer, and smiles at Hunter. Klaus then nods his head. Klaus and Hunter continue talking for several more hours, and it seems that Klaus has made a friend in Hunter. Klaus asks if Hunter is married, to which Hunter responds that he's not. Hunter tells Klaus that he's bisexual, and doesn't find romantic relationships interest him. Hunter is Christian, and he actually just came from Church. At Church service, he felt obligated to reveal this information to Klaus, that they met before. With it being coincidence, they are both Diamond Mafia Members. Klaus and Hunter then walk out on the balcony, and have a cigarette with each other, and continue to converse with each other. Jerome remains in the living room, watching television. With it now being nighttime and quite late, Hunter says goodbye to Klaus, and they both give each other a wide hug. Hunter then hugs Jerome, and says goodbye to him as well. Klaus then walks Hunter to his car, and Hunter gives Klaus his phone number, and speaks.

"You can call me anytime Klaus. I don't care if it's two in the morning, or whatever. You want to go for a drink, go fishing, go to a Dodger or Laker game. I'm here. Peace."

Klaus and Hunter fist bump each other. Klaus then kisses Hunter on the cheek, and gives Hunter one final tight hug. Hunter then drives away. Klaus then looks down at the ground, laughs, and smiles to himself. Klaus was able to make another friend with Hunter, and was appreciative of this. Klaus walks back into the house, and notices that Jerome is at kitchen sink, doing the dishes. Klaus stares at Jerome, and smiles at him. Klaus then reaches for his medicine bag that Emilio gave him, and grabs the bottles of his antibiotics, and pain killers. Klaus swallows the pills, and drinks some water. Klaus sets his glass in the sink, and speaks to Jerome.

"You be a good boy, and make sure you do all those dishes. Okay? Ha Ha."

Klaus then kisses Jerome on the cheek, and runs his hands through Jerome's hair. Jerome simply smiles back at Klaus, and continues to do the dishes. Klaus returns to his recliner, and starts to relax in it. At this time, Klaus pulls out his laptop, and starts to update his resume, as he plans to go for a job interview the next day, at AT&T, to be a cable installer. Once Klaus finishes working on his resume, Jerome is finished with the dishes, and walks over to the living room. Feeling tired, and exhausted, Jerome starts to fall asleep on the sofa. Klaus who starts to drift to sleep as well, notices Jerome fast asleep on the sofa. Klaus smiles to himself, and quickly shuts the television in the living room off, and picks Jerome up, carrying him, behind his back. Klaus and Jerome then go into the bedroom, and quickly drift off the sleep. The following morning, Klaus wakes up bright and early, and starts to get ready for his job interview. Klaus puts on a suit and tie. Jerome who is in bed, watching Klaus get ready, starts to speak.

"Good luck DJ K. Oh, you know what, Hunter was saying a lot of motivational stuff yesterday, and while you guys were out on the balcony, I applied to the Apple Store. Ha Ha."

Klaus then starts to shake his head and laughs. Jerome explains to Klaus, that he has an interview at the Apple Store, to be an Apple technician and sales floor associate. Jerome says that his interview is not until noon, and that he's going to take the bus there. Klaus understands, and offers to pick Jerome up, after his interview, which Jerome accepts. Klaus then finishes getting ready for his interview, and kisses Jerome on the cheek. Klaus leaves out of the house, and drives down to the AT&T building for his interview. Klaus notices four other men in the lobby, and starts to feel worried, that he might not get the job. When it is time for Klaus to be interviewed, the man interviewing him, is a young and handsome, blonde hair clean cut man. Klaus hands the man his resume, and the interviewer is very impressed. After explaining the job description to Klaus, in which he is going to be doing cable installations at customers' homes, and also doing on site logistics and fiber optics work, Klaus accepts the job offer, and is hired. Klaus leaves out of the office, happy, and calls Hunter, to tell him the news, in which Hunter is happy for him. Jerome also manages to get hired during his interview, at the Apple Store. Jerome calls Klaus, letting him know he got the job, and Klaus is happy for Jerome. Klaus picks up Jerome, and the both go to the "Olive Garden" restaurant, to celebrate.

For the next few weeks, Klaus would report to work at AT&T, using the company provided van, whenever he had to do onsite cable installations. Jerome would work at the Apple Store, doing sales, and other troubleshooting work for customers. Occasionally, Klaus and Hunter would hang out quite a bit, and go to the bar together, and watch a sports game. Hunter would come over to the house as well, and eat dinner with Klaus and Jerome. Klaus and Hunter, have now become best friends. Things were going great, until Klaus remembered, what his intentions about doing the news show were going to be. It was a very quick and direct discussion with Jerome, that Klaus, with the help of Jerome would do very rare occasional internet blogs, and that would be it. Klaus doesn't feel he owes anybody any explanation, as to why he no longer wants to do this, and Klaus feels that maybe one day he will go back to that stuff, or maybe he won't. Jerome is understood on this, and respects Klaus decision over this, either way. For now, Klaus continues to work as a cable technician, and he's fine doing that. It was work that he did before, and so it comes very natural to him. Days continue to go by, and Klaus and Jerome, go about their lives as normal. Because the Diamond Mafia building was destroyed, Klaus and Jerome are not questioned about the situation, and the investigation is still on going. Klaus and Jerome are instructed not to talk to police about the incident regardless. So they have to keep everything related to the Diamond Mafia a secret, with Klaus new friendship with Hunter, and Klaus looking up to Emilio as a mentor figure, knowing he has Emilio's protection.

One Friday evening, Klaus was doing his ordinary work, and was installing cable for an elderly woman, who lived with her sister. The woman Klaus figured, was not that well versed on technology, and was asking Klaus a lot of questions. As Klaus continues to work, she speaks.

"Young man, are you sure I'm going to get the movie channels and premium networks?"

Klaus continues to install the woman's cable, and laughs. Klaus then responds to her.

"Yes ma'am, you're gonna get all that. I'm gonna hook you up honey, don't worry. Ha."

The woman then laughs and smiles back at Klaus. Once Klaus is finished installing the woman's' cable, the woman reaches out to hug Klaus, which Klaus felt was rather strange for customers to do. But Klaus agreed to go along with it. Klaus hugs the woman back, and says goodbye, and leaves her house. Klaus shift is over, and he starts to drive his service van, back to the building. At this time, while Klaus is still driving back to the AT&T building, Klaus receives a text message from Jerome, in which Jerome just clocked out from the Apple Store, informing him that the couple of the dog they rescued, said they can come and get the puppy now. Klaus starts to smile to himself, and tells Jerome that he's going to pick him up from work, and they are going to drive to the couple's house to get the dog. Klaus picks up Jerome, and Klaus immediately directs himself, to Josh and Lorraine's house. The couple invites Klaus and Jerome in, and the couple informs them, that some of their friends got attached to the puppies, and took interest, and all but one puppy, was adopted as a result of this. Lorraine hands the final puppy to Jerome, which Jerome stares at it, and starts to cry. Klaus starts to cry as well, noticing how cute the puppy looks. The puppy, which Jerome named Korbin, goes home with Klaus and Jerome, and Klaus is very pleased, to finally have a dog. When Klaus and Jerome arrive back at the house, Korbin the puppy, starts to run around the house, and gets himself situated and acquainted. Klaus then starts to laugh, and shakes his head. Klaus tells Jerome, that he's going to go get some dog food, and dog toys from the pet store, and that he will be right back. While Klaus is gone, Jerome continues to play with Korbin, and Jerome gets quickly attached to the dog. Klaus soon arrives back to the house, also with some Taco Bell takeout food. Klaus gives Korbin some dog food, and sets the toys out for Korbin to play with. Klaus and Jerome then start to eat their Taco Bell food. During this time, Klaus, who actually made a third stop at a jewelry store, takes the box from the jewelry store out his pocket, making sure that Jerome doesn't see it, and puts the box, on the side pocket of the recliner. Klaus stares at Jerome and laughs, and continues to eat his food. As the night goes on, Korbin eventually starts to take a nap. Jerome then eventually starts to get tired as well, and falls asleep on the sofa. Klaus, who is feeling tired himself as well, turns off the television in the living room, and picks Jerome up. Korbin wakes up as well, and follows Klaus and Jerome into the bedroom, to which Klaus starts to laugh. Korbin then starts to rest at the end of the bed. Klaus and Jerome then start to fall asleep. The next morning, Klaus wakes up early, and takes Korbin out for a walk. Klaus then returns back home, and notices that Jerome is still asleep. Klaus doesn't wake him, and Klaus lays down on the other end of the bed, resting his eyes. Later in the day, with it now being late in the afternoon, Klaus and Jerome are in the living room, watching television. Klaus then turns the television off. Jerome then starts to look at Klaus, and smiles at him. Klaus then speaks.

"Let's go hiking. Like, right now. Come on, it's not like we're going anything Let's go."

Jerome then laughs, and responds back to Klaus, in a very soft and friendly tone.

"You mean, right now? Um, I guess. Ha Ha. Alright. Let me get my hiking pack. Okay."

Jerome then walks off to get his hiking backpack, and Klaus then looks down on the ground, and smiles to himself. At this time, making sure Jerome doesn't see or notice, Klaus pulls out the box, located in the side recliner pocket. Klaus puts the box in his pocket, and smiles. Jerome then returns back to the living room, with his hiking backpack. Jerome then starts to pet Korbin, and Klaus pets him as well. Seconds after this, Klaus and Jerome leave out of the house, and then get inside Klaus SUV, and Klaus starts to drive out hiking. Before reaching the hiking trail, Klaus decides to make a stop at In N Out Burger, located a moderate distance away from the hiking trail, and gets food for himself and Jerome. Klaus then continues forward, to the hiking trail. Klaus takes glances over at Jerome during this trip, and Klaus starts to feel happy, that Jerome has no idea what Klaus has planned. Eventually, Klaus arrives at the hiking trail, and Klaus parks his car. Both Klaus and Jerome, then start to walk on the hiking trail. As with the previous times he has hiked, Klaus is feeling slightly tired, although he is still having a great time with Jerome. The men continue to go forward on the trail, and when they get to the halfway point, Jerome notices that Klaus is looking fatigued and exhausted. Jerome walks back down to Klaus to check on him, and Klaus tells him, that he's okay. Jerome walks ahead, and Klaus intentionally decides to stay behind, and smiles to himself. When the men reach a picnic area, Jerome sets his hiking pack down, and takes the food Klaus got, out of his bag as well. Jerome then looks around, and notices that Klaus is not nearby. Jerome then looks behind the trail, and when Klaus notices that Jerome sees him, Klaus intentionally falls back down the trail. Alarmed, Jerome starts to walk back down to Klaus. Jerome catches up to Klaus, and speaks.

"Oh my god. Klaus. I'm coming down there now. Klaus, Is everything okay?"

Jerome then picks up Klaus glasses that fell, and Jerome starts to massage Klaus face. Klaus then starts to laugh to himself, and as Jerome is comforting him, Klaus softly speaks.

"I'll be okay after this. Ha Ha."

Klaus then starts to kneel on one knee, and takes out the box in his pocket. Klaus opens up the box, and it's a Diamond ring. Jerome covers his face, and is shocked. Klaus then speaks.

"It's only us now. You know that right? I love you. Jerome, will you marry me?"

Jerome then gets on top of Klaus, and starts to wrestle with him. Jerome then speaks.

"Yes. DJ K. Klaus. I can't believe this. I love you too, and I will marry you."

Klaus then puts the ring on Jerome's finger, and Klaus and Jerome, passionately kiss, for nearly a minute. Then they both wrestle down on the ground. They remain doing this for several minutes, and they both eventually stop. Klaus and Jerome then sit down at the picnic bench, and start to eat their food. Klaus then while eating, looks out towards the distance, and smiles. Klaus continues to look at the sun at the hiking trail, and starts to bring Jerome closer to him. While having his arm around Jerome, Klaus starts to laugh, and shakes his head. Klaus then silently speaks to himself, as he is watching the view, out the distance, of the hiking trail.

"DJ K. is signing off. Ha Ha."

Klaus then kisses Jerome again, and continues to cuddle and snuggle with him. Klaus continues to watch the sun in the distance, and smiles to himself. The journey is now complete, and all loose ends have been tied. It was a rather complicated journey, but things are now completed. There were many several different twists and turns. New things to discover, new problems to solve, new obstacles to overcome, hurdles to jump across, lessons to be learned, and realizations to be understood. But everything is finished, and has concluded. In society, people go about their lives, at their own accord. What someone does, isn't anyone else's business, and why should it be? The only caveat, is when things are revealed to others. Whether that's through art, or information. That leaves much to be desired. If something is interesting enough, people are sure to tune in, and be drawn and immersed to it. Events are always happening in the world. Some of the events are good, some of these events are bad. One thing that is for certain, is that these events, are sure to give information to others. Whether it's the powers that be, and sources that are giving the information, or those consuming the information, none of that matters. The information will circulate regardless, and whatever the case may exactly be. It also doesn't matter if your opinion is agreed and desired by others, and unpopular; or if it's shunned, and disagreed over, and unpopular. The main thing, is getting that information out in the first place. Keeping in mind, that no publicity is bad publicity. The other thing to note, is becoming aware of how this information, is going to change or impact the world. That plays a major factor, when media is presented to others. Above all, when information and news is reported, it plays a global impact, and things are connected with each other. The story may change, new developments will probably be known, updates will be added, but the story will still be presented in the same way. What story will break out next? Only fate, destiny, and chance can answer that. What is one percent sure, absolutely certain, and definite, is that it is all going to be, Broadcast.

THE END

ABOUT THE AUTHOR

Brennen Tammons, was born in Los Angeles, California. He is an African American, gay writer. Having a unique imagination, allows him to explore diverse topics with his writing. He enjoys dancing, aerobic exercise, all types of music, (having a soft spot for jazz, soul, urban and electronic music), playing Nintendo games, and researching new topics and ideas.